First Edition Design Publishing

Beyond Murder

ISBN 978-1622873-39-5 PRINT
ISBN 978-1622873-40-1 HARDCOVER
ISBN 978-1622-873-38-8 EBOOK

LCCN 2013942879

July 2013

Published and Distributed by
First Edition Design Publishing, Inc.
P.O. Box 20217, Sarasota, FL 34276-3217
www.firsteditiondesignpublishing.com

Cover Design Deborah E Gordon

ACKNOWLEDGMENTS

There are many people who I wish to thank and if I inadvertently forget to mention them, I'm sorry.

Harvey, what can I say? You have always been my inspiration and without you the character of Stephen could never have come to life. To my girlfriend, Barbara, thank you for reading "Beyond Murder" and correcting the many spelling mistakes and the countless hours of your intent reading. You are truly patient and a blessing. Barbara's mother, dear Catherine, who I admired, was my inspiration for Mrs. Walsh.

To my many friends and cousins who encouraged me to not give up my dream, thank you. Cousins Wayne, Bruce, Beverly; (of a shalom), Barbara, Wendy and Jordan, my life as I grew up with you will always be in my heart and soul. How can one forget their routes; Dorchester and Quincy will always remain with me.

My parents and grandparents will always be remembered with love and fondness. Thank you for giving me life, direction and insight in the old world ways and the new world.

To my children and grandchildren, I hope that what I taught you will be lessons you'll never forget. "Treat others as you'd want them to treat you" should remain with you, always.

No story can ever be a story without my beloved animals. Simka, you'll always be the little queen and Boston, the black kitten who wormed his way into our lives and heart.

To my new friends Dave and Debbie from First Edition, thank you for your help and encouragement.

To my fans that enjoy reading the escapades of Suzanne, Nancy and their friends; thank you for your loyalty. Without you my creativity and imagination would be left inside my being without having a way to express my desires for a better world.

CHAPTER ONE

Free will is given to every human being. If we wish to incline ourselves toward goodness and righteousness, we are free to do so, and if we wish to incline ourselves toward evil, we are also free to do that. From Scripture (Genesis 3. 22) we learn that the human species, with its knowledge of good and evil, is unique among all earth's creatures. Of our own accord, by our own faculty of intelligence and understanding, we can distinguish between good and evil, doing as we choose. Nothing holds us back from making this choice between good and evil---the power is in our hands.

MAIMONIDES, 12TH CENTURY

BOSTON, MASSACHUSETTS. October 1993. 10:30 p. m.

The long, silver, barrel reflected off the bright light, shimmering, in the darkness. The gloved hand held the revolver deftly. With conviction, the man in the shadows pulled the trigger and smoke rose from the pistol. The abrupt intensity of the shot being fired propelled the beautiful woman against the brick wall. She gasped for breath as she tried to fight for air. The crimson blood now stained over her once white blouse. Sirens in the distance cautioned him to leave, but he had to be sure she was dead. Ignoring his instinct, he knelt down by the woman as she laid on the cold concrete. He lifted her limp arm and could feel a slight pulse. Standing over her, he let out a deep sigh and skillfully fired the remaining bullets into her head.

"If I can't have you no one will. I loved you," he cried desperately as he took her flaccid body and cradled it in his arms. Crying openly he knew he had to leave. He looked one last time at the woman he adored and cried, "I would have done anything for you. Why did you hurt me?" He started to run but the quiet, dark alleyway was ablaze with the headlights of the patrol cars. A policeman shouted for him to drop the gun. There was no place for him to run, it was too late. In a desperate attempt to scare the officer, he aimed the empty gun in his direction. The police officer didn't hesitate to shoot and with one loud final bullet the man fell to the ground.

All was quiet except for the soft sobs from the people in the audience. The theater lights were suddenly turned on, indicating the play was over. Suzanne sighed and caught her breath, as she expertly wiped the tears from her face.

The cast members came back on stage, one person, then two to three at a time. The clapping was steady. The leading actor appeared and the crowd roared, with most of the spectators rising to their feet. Madaline made her appearance and the audience was tumultuous. At the second curtain call the rest of the patrons stood, and Madaline was presented with two dozen red roses. Madaline threw kisses to everyone in attendance. With the fourth and final curtain call, which seemed to last five minutes, she gave a long, low bow to everyone and hurried back stage.

Suzanne and her party were among the pleased and elated audience that came to their feet and earnestly applauded. The critics were overjoyed as the new play, "Beyond Murder" was in its second week and was the best play of the season.

Back stage, with members of the cast, Suzanne and her group mingled easily with the crowd. Madaline spotted her dear friend and the people who had become the family members that she and her son, Kyle, had wanted and needed years ago.

Madaline warmly greeted her cherished friends. Affectionately hugging Suzanne she whispered, "Let's get out of here soon." With a fixed smile she continued to mingle amongst the small collection of the selected few people who felt privileged to be there. She waved to strangers who wanted recognition from this famous actress.

Making her way back to Suzanne she stopped, feigning exhaustion. Whispering in Suzanne's ear, "Come on, we'll go back to my suite, kick off our shoes and kibbitz. When you get there, call for room service. It won't take me long to get this gunk off my face and change into street clothes. We'll have our own party. How does that sound?"

Suzanne said, "Sounds great. I can hardly wait to catch up on what's been happening since we last talked."

Madaline was one of her best friends. Holding Madaline at arm's length Suzanne thought that she was beautiful as ever. With all her ups and downs in life, raising a child, practically by herself, the heartbreak of losing the love of her life, the divorces, and of course the natural progression of aging, it was a wonder she still looked radiant.

"I'll call the front desk to tell them you and your party will be arriving. Here's the key to my room."

"That's a good idea, I wouldn't like being thrown out nor have the police arrest us," Suzanne laughed as she hugged her friend good-by.

Madaline went back to the dressing room and got the peace and quiet she craved. She quickly and adeptly removed the heavy theatrical make-up and got up to change into her street clothes. As she headed for the closet to get her jeans and sweater she inadvertently saw a vase filled with a dozen black roses on the night table beside the couch. Madaline looked twice, not believing what she saw. A chill went through her body, she shuddered. 'Who could be so mean to send me these? If they think it's funny, it's not. 'From her extensive reading she knew that black roses represented death. As much as Madaline tried to think who would play this distasteful hoax, her mind went blank. She quickly threw the entire vase and flowers in the bathrooms basket and called for the back stage attendant to empty the entire contents of the waste basket in the dumpster. On her way out of the dressing room she took one last look where the black roses had been and a feeling of dread overcame her. She closed her eyes tightly, willing the sighting had not happened. The door closed behind her and goose bumps erupted over her entire body.

When going thru the lobby she asked the concierge if he could bring her a fresh batch of chocolate chip cookies. Nodding his head he answered, "Of course Madame. The pastry chef left for the evening but he made sure that the pastries you like were made and would meet with your satisfaction." He went to the kitchen and presented Madaline with a large plate of the warm, fresh, chocolate chip cookies. "I hope Ms. Madaline will be happy with these?"

"I always am, thank the chef for me," Madaline said.

By the time Madaline returned to her suite, she wanted to forget about the terrible incident that occurred. She tried to stop thinking about the flowers and how upset she was. Putting on a happy face she entered the room and tried getting into a party mood.

Madaline went to the tall, glass bar and put down the plate of cookies. She sat down and polished off her Reuben. "Suzanne; thanks for remembering to order my favorite sandwich. What can I get you from the bar?" Snapping her fingers Madaline sarcastically said, "Everybody, don't rush me at once."

"I normally would have my zinfandel, but I have to drive and you know if I have more than one I'll be in trouble. Suzanne went in back of the bar and poured herself a generous glass of White Zinfandel. She found that the slightly sweet drink went down her throat smoothly. Everyone was in a good mood. They laughed at the stories being told by everyone as they finished their own drinks. Madaline declared, as she polished off her own Compass Box Oak Cross blended malt Scotch whiskey, "Who would have thunk that nice Jewish girls, pardon me Mrs. Walsh, could tell such vulgar tales and drink this much booze?" Madaline took a bite from a warm, fresh, chocolate chip cookie. Before she realized, another two cookies were consumed, knowing that the fumes of them would enhance the senses of the velvety liquid going down her throat.

Suzanne exclaimed, "I have to admit it felt good to sit down and wait for the play to begin, Metamorphosis was busy today." Addressing everyone at the party she stated, "Who would have thought that when Peter, Nancy and I expanded the salon to include skin care, it would become such a well-known day spa, from Boston to other States in the Union and now worldwide."

Mrs. Walsh, Suzanne's mom, Dorothy, and her three daughters, Hope, Melanie and Taylor nodded their heads in agreement.

Raising her eyebrow Madaline started to say something but decided to leave it alone.

Knowing Madaline as well as she did, Suzanne caught that indecisive look that came across her face and automatically knew that something was on her mind. Thinking to herself she would have to talk to Madaline, if not tonight, very shortly.

"I can honestly say that I made the right decision to move into plays - - this fifth one is my first serious one."

Suzanne said, "In my opinion this is the best one yet. Don't get me wrong, all the other plays were wonderful as well, I've loved them all but this drama is different."

"I think you're used to seeing me in musical comedies."

"You're lucky that you're diversified and talented enough to be able to acclimate yourself to any type of acting," exclaimed a now sated Hope.

As Suzanne was enjoying the comfort of the soft, silky sofa, oblivious to all the noise and chattering around her, she looked at Madaline and felt that something was wrong, bothering her. She couldn't put her finger on what it was, but something was definitely not right, it wasn't her imagination. Instead, she put her head on the sofa's pillow and thought back to the first time she met Madaline Mason.

It was the first spring season that the Metamorphosis Salon was open. She had been fortunate that quite a few of Peter's and the other hairdresser's client's wanted facials. Still, she wanted her name to get out around town other than the customers from within the salon. Besides going to dermatologists located in downtown Boston, explaining how she could work along with them, she also went to owners of fur salons and other fine clothing establishments, offering her services to apply makeup to models when they presented fashion shows. She worked out a barter system with some of the owners and their managers in exchange for services. The business people loved Suzanne and soon her name started circulating around town that Suzanne, at the Metamorphosis Salon, was the best esthetician for facials and make up in the Boston proper area.

Madaline Mason, already a well-known movie star, was about to start a new aspect in her career. Her first romantic, comedy play was coming to Boston. The critics were leery and wanted to see for themselves how she could diversify her acting ability.

As much as they wanted to find fault with the play, they couldn't. The audience and critics adored her. She proved herself worthy of what makes a true star.

A couple of days before the production Madaline acquainted herself with the area and the theater. The other members of the production arrived early, but Madaline, being the professional she was, knew the play inside out, not needing the extra rehearsal time. Whenever she happened to travel in the Boston area she always stayed at the Ritz. She loved the view and would walk in the Boston Public Gardens, enjoying the aroma of the many fragrant flowers in bloom. She browsed and shopped in and around Newbury Street. Going into one of her favorite stores, she happened to mention that she would love to have a facial and massage, could they recommend someone? Suzanne's name was given to Madaline.

Suzanne was in awe when Madaline called for an appointment. She was one of her favorite movie stars, and was thrilled to be giving her idol a variety of services. Trying to act cool, calm and collected, she prepared her room, waiting for the famous actress to arrive.

Madaline made her dramatic entrance. Suzanne was to learn that she was always tardy. Casually seating herself on one of the French, Provincial chairs, lighting a cigarette from a gorgeous, white ivory, jeweled cigarette holder, under the "please no smoking" sign, she blew the gray vapor into the air. Madaline carelessly threw her olive green colored, suede, three quarter length coat, with a fox collar, beside her seat on the floor. She ignored the receptionists offer to hang her coat up in the closet. Suzanne extended her hand to Miss Mason, introducing herself as her esthetician, and took the garment from the carpet. She gave her a questionnaire to fill out, pertaining to her skin and the products she used. The receptionist was intimidated by this obviously aloof woman.

"Boy, this one is a real bitch. Did you see the way she ignored me and the no smoking sign? Good luck Suzanne, you'll need it."

"Cheryl, don't worry. I'll have her eating out of my hands by the end of the facial."

"I certainly hope so," the doubtful receptionists remarked.

She walked Madaline to her private room, handing her the clean, pink, terry cloth wrap. Taking the card she closed the door, waiting for her to undress and looked over the new client card.

Suzanne knocked gently on the door and entered the dimly lit room. The soft, yet, melodious, symphonic new age music, surrounded her, creating an atmosphere of peace, harmony and relaxation. When Suzanne removed the makeup from Madaline, she realized that she really didn't need to wear any. The woman was beautiful without any on. Her skin and features were flawless. Her blue eyes had a slight touch of violet, under naturally long, dark lashes. Her oval face had a slight, light, brown, beauty mark in the middle of her right cheek. When talking, her natural full lips accentuated her perfect, white teeth. Suzanne thought the woman was absolutely gorgeous. Suzanne evaluated her skin under the magnifying light. She explained the order of every procedure, its purpose and how it will benefit her skin.

Madaline liked Suzanne immediately. Suzanne didn't act intimidated by who she was or by her obvious lack of concern when reading the no smoking sign. Madaline sensed the two women were of the same age, their early to mid-twenties. Madaline had come a long way from the skinny, long legged girl who grew up on her grandparents and then her parent's farm in Fairfield, Iowa. She was now an accomplished actress who, through hard work, determination, and luck, was an independent woman who needed no one. She had just divorced her third husband and had no immediate desire to look for husband number four.

Madaline's son, Kyle, was eight years old and was back home in California. Now in his second year of school, Madaline didn't want to interrupt his schedule. In prior years Kyle would accompany his mother everywhere she went, bringing his nanny and tutor with them.

Madaline wanted to find out more about this young woman who was giving her one of the best facials she ever had. To Madaline's surprise, Suzanne would not let her talk, especially during the massage. Madaline liked Suzanne's direct approach, no nonsense attitude, yet could tell there was a kindness and gentleness about her, allowing her client to be pampered and cared for.

Usually Madaline didn't care about people who were not in the realm of show business. These were the people who she had a great deal in common. They knew what it was like to maintain grueling schedules when they were shooting a movie on location or at the studio. She appreciated the general public, who she needed for fans. They were better seen from a-far. There was something different about Suzanne, she didn't know what it was.

Coming out of the facial room, Madaline felt relaxed and refreshed. She was now ready to start rehearsals. In two days their Boston run would begin. She thanked Suzanne and made an appointment for other services. Once the grueling schedule of two performances a day began, for at least the next six weeks, she figured she would need all the relaxation she could get.

Even though she came across as being bitchy and arrogant, Suzanne liked Madaline. 'God knows what she had to do in order for her to be where she is today,' she contemplated, as she escorted the stately star to the front door. Suzanne was delighted that a famous actress such as Madaline wanted to get a massage and facial every day. Suzanne was honest and refused to give her a facial daily, explaining that having it done so often would do her more harm than good. She would do her make up while she was in the play and was happy to give her a daily massage.

Working with each other for six weeks, the two women found that they had a lot in common. When Madaline asked certain questions, that Suzanne thought was prying, she hesitated answering, but realized that Madaline was only being curious and wanted a friend to talk to. Repressing her fears and letting down her barrier, she told Madaline about her unhappy marriage; and subsequent divorce.

Suzanne was hesitant in telling her everything about Brian, but for some reason she found herself delving into the past, elaborating on the violence that she experienced. Soon the two women became fast friends.

Madaline loved Suzanne's product line and became a Metamorphosis' client. Years later, Madaline would make it her business to drop by for a friendly visit and treatment at Suzanne's Rodeo Drive Salon.

Madaline put on a different facade when seen by the general public. The aloof and conceited person she portrayed was an act. For Suzanne and a few of her intimate friends, a loving, warm, and caring person was behind the indifferent character that most people saw.

"You hew, Suzanne, are you there?" Snapping her fingers, "You seem a million miles away and your tea is ice cold. Let me pour you another cup."

"Thanks. I was remembering when we first met. You were such a brat!!! It seems like yesterday, but the years have flown by."

"The real name to describe me is a bitch." They both laughed.

"I can't begin to tell you how wonderful it is to see my extended family again. It's been too long since we've been together like this.

Madaline observed that Dorothy even though she was getting on in years, was still lovely looking. Mrs. Walsh, who was like a surrogate mother, raised Suzanne's three daughters when she was a young woman herself. She was now using a beautiful mahogany cane. She was stately and underneath the quiet facade, a devilish twinkle still gleamed in those Irish blue eyes.

Madaline was, by far, their mother's favorite celebrity. She never forgot a birthday, Chanukah card or present for her 'extended family.' She was fun to be with, and they truly loved her. She made them feel special. Once in a while, when her son, Kyle, was on school vacation, she would have him accompany her at the time she visited Suzanne and her family. Since he was an only child they took him under their wings and made him their adopted brother. Suzanne considered him like the son she didn't have.

Before leaving Suzanne took Madaline aside. "I might be out of place saying this, but I know you, and something isn't right. You can put on a great act but you can't fool me. I'm going to call you tomorrow and during one of your breaks from rehearsal, even if I have to cancel a client, you and I are going to talk. I'm not taking no for an answer."

"I can't fool you, can I?" Madaline acknowledged. "Okay, I'll call you at the beginning of the day and tell you what time we can meet. I'm sure it's nothing to worry about, but you're right, I have to tell someone, or I'll go crazy. I'll see you tomorrow." 'I knew something was wrong from the look I saw on her face when she entered the room,' Suzanne said to herself. Madaline was thankful and hugged her friend goodbye.

Suzanne couldn't wait to get home. She enjoyed being with her family and one of her best friends but she wanted to get undressed, snuggle into her comfortable bed with Simka, her beautiful Maine Coon cat, purring beside her.

Before Suzanne went to sleep she gazed out the window, looking at the bright stars illuminating the clear sky, smiling, she asked herself, 'where did all these years go? It seems like only yesterday that Mrs. Walsh was a vibrant woman, taking charge of the household and my young family.' She remembered that when she had to work nights, Mrs. Walsh would put the girls to sleep, cuddling and softly singing the many Irish ballads and lullabies, enabling them to go into the arms of Morpheus. The phones shrill ring brought Suzanne out of her reverie.

As soon as Suzanne heard Stephen's voice she immediately awoke." Hi honey. I hope you aren't sleeping?"

"No, we got home a while ago from seeing Madaline's new play, 'Beyond Murder.' As usual, she was great, along with the play."

In his typically low, sexy voice Stephen expressed his thoughts." I've been thinking of you all night. I miss your soft, warm body next to mine. When are you coming here so I can hold you in my arms and make my dreams come true?"

"Stephen, I miss you too. I thought you'd be coming here in a few weeks. I have to admit that I was going to arrive in Texas within this week. Unfortunately, some crazy things might be happening so my original plan may have to be abandoned."

He tried not to show his disappointment. "To be honest with you I thought that it was automatic that you'd be visiting me; we probably got our signals crossed."

"Oh Stephen, you have no idea how much I want to get away and be with you, but I can't give you a definite answer. I know you're coming into the Boston area partly for business but we'll figure a way to be with each other, won't we?"

"Of course we will. I hope that when I get there you'll have time for me. Remember I love you and as Sunny told Cher, "Love Will Keep Us Together." Suzanne laughed at his remark and told him the same.

Unfortunately, Stephen didn't feel as jubilant as Suzanne. Frustrated, he sighed and thought to himself, 'I hope you finish whatever is so important.'

Suzanne sensed his displeasure and hoped that she would be with him shortly. While lying in bed, waiting for sleep to take over, she had a hard time getting comfortable. Stephen and her as youngsters came to mind. He was her first boyfriend and she his first love. Recollections of their times at the beach, proms, and dancing to American Bandstand, and at the Totem Pole were cherished memories. Their friends labeled them the perfect couple and most likely to get married. The guilt would never go away as she remembered breaking up with him for a nonsensical reason. If all had happened as they planned when they were teenagers, she was sure that their marriage would have lasted. Meeting in Bermuda brought a smile to her pouting lips. 'Shit happens and then you sometimes have to live with your decisions.' She turned onto her other side, her mind still troubled, sleep eluded her.

Besides being happy to hear from Stephen, she knew that her getting away was impossible. 'In a few weeks when he comes to town, we'll be with each other and our relationship won't be as strained as it is now. I hope that Madaline is all right. I'm not prepared to hear about anything bad.' Suzanne tossed and turned, slightly moving Simka.

DALLAS, TEXAS

Stephen gently returned the receiver into the cradle. He felt alone and hurt. It had been a while since he and Suzanne had seen each other. Talking on the telephone didn't give Stephen the same satisfaction as he wanted. 'Being with the person you love, holding them, being able to see her face, her expressions, as we talk and laugh at different events and happenings, are so important,' he thought as he pulled the covers over his lean and well-muscled body. All he wanted was to experience the same closeness that they shared whenever they were together. 'How long has it been?' he asked himself, as he tried remembering the last time he held her in his arms. He wondered if she still shared the same feelings for him as he obviously did for her.

He invited her many times to come to Texas or go away on vacations together. He wanted to go back to Bermuda once more and experience the craving and passion that had enveloped them when they met again, by chance, on the beautiful island. He still had the same feelings and emotions for Suzanne as when they started seeing each other after all those years of separation. Feelings of doubt crept into his mind. 'I'm as busy as she is and I'd make time to be with her,' he thought as he turned on his side, looking at the picture of the two of them together on the sands of Tobacco Bay on his night table. 'Is she mad at me? Did I do or say something that pissed her off?'

A small voice, he tried eliminating from his mind, crept into his subliminal thoughts. 'You know what Suzanne is disappointed about. She's mad that you're still a married man and won't make our relationship legal. Suzanne realized years ago that I have a hard time getting rid of or saying goodbye to anything or anyone. It's a compulsive behavior that I should have seen a psychiatrist about years ago. Hey, if I did, I wouldn't have missed her like I did and when I saw her I would have thought twice about going back to my one and only love. She's sick of being thought of as my girlfriend. It's been too long to keep making excuses on why you don't marry her and finally divorce Lou Anne. Even though people think of us as a married couple when they first meet us, in Suzanne's mind she is resentful that this isn't the case. How many times has she told me that she wanted me to get divorced? Even though it's been awhile since she last mentioned the idea, I know it's still on her mind.'

Kicking the covers off himself, he got out of bed and headed to the living room. He poured a shot of tequila and sat down on the beige, leather sofa. Putting on the CD player he put his head against the sofa and while listening to some of his favorite Muddy Water's soul music, images of Suzanne filled his mind. He drained the glass and poured another shot as, once again, pictures of Suzanne and Lou Anne floated in front of him. This time a sinister and laughing Lou Anne appeared. His two beautiful boys, oh how he missed them, were crying and pleading for their mother to drive slower. Her haunting chortle stayed in his mind.

'Does Suzanne think that I don't want to marry her? for God's sake, I'd marry her in a minute if, in my mind, I'd be able to live with myself after I divorce Lou Anne. How can I abandon her, even though I know, in my heart, that Suzanne's the only woman that I ever loved, still love, and will forever love in my heart and soul. How can Lou Anne take care of herself and get the proper care if I'm not around to oversee her caretakers? If she were an independent woman, not a paraplegic, and could make a life for herself, I'd wed Suzanne in a second. Thankfully she stopped drinking after the car accident. Not one night goes by that I don't visualize my twin boys crying out to me before the crash. Even if she were an alcoholic, how could she start drinking first thing in the morning? Didn't she realize she had a responsibility to her sons to drive safely?'

'I've tried to overcome my compulsive behavior. Doesn't Suzanne know this? If only life can change and I can, once again, do as I really want to do. I often wonder why God allows people like Lou Anne that has no quality of life, to go on, and why many young and wonderful people leave us to cry alone in despair. I wish life could start over again. I'm sure that Suzanne feels that way also. To be young and live out your life with the one that you truly love, raise a beautiful family and live happily ever after. Boy what a corny thought. How many times does that really happen? According to the divorce statistics, not many,' he laughed out loud. Quickly and with a feeling of discouragement he threw the empty glass against the unlit fireplace. 'I'll clean the mess in the morning,' he thought to himself as he headed back to his bedroom, hoping that Morpheus would soon take over.

STONEY BROOK

Suzanne got up earlier than usual and went into the family room. She sat on the sofa looking lovingly at the pictures on the mantle, above the green marble fireplace. The picture of her and Stephen as youngsters and the formal portrait of the two of them in front of the white, grand piano were reminders of the devotion and love that they shared. Tears welled up in her eyes as thoughts of the unfulfilled portions of their lives, that could never be recaptured, re-occurred. The many years of separation from one another never left her. She also wanted to be with him, having him caress her and make passionate love that only he could do. She had many pending issues that had to be concluded and yet, she wanted to abandon all unsettled projects, leave matters of contention behind her and run into Stephen's open arms.

While driving to work she remembered the horror she endured while being married to Brian. The nightmares kept reoccurring and haunted her. She would run away from him, knowing that if and when he caught her, the beatings would take place. Each time these nightmares happened, with different types of abuse resurfacing, invading her peaceful sleep; they seemed so real.

As much as she wanted to abandon her obligations to family, friends and work and say to hell with it all, she knew in her heart it wasn't possible. Without realizing what was about to happen, the unforeseeable future was unclear. Many issues emerged that would make Suzanne's and Stephen's encounter unachievable.

CHAPTER TWO

The next morning Suzanne was in the kitchen sipping her morning cup of tea. The telephones' ring interrupted the rare, tranquility that she was experiencing.

"Suzanne, I'm glad I got you before you left for the day," Nancy spoke anxiously.

"Did something happen to the salon?" Suzanne asked her business partner. "You sound upset. What's wrong?"

"I got a call from the prison authorities. Peter tried to kill himself last evening."

Immediately grabbing the kitchen chair, Suzanne held on to it for stability. "Is he all-right, where is he now?"

"He's at Emerson Hospital. They found him before it was too late. Suzanne, will you come with me? I need you."

"Of course, you know that I'm always there for you."

She slowly ascended the stairs to the second floor of her home. She knew she had to shower and dress before Nancy came, but felt too weak to do anything at that moment.

Peter and Nancy had started out on Newbury Street, in Boston years ago, owning a well-known and profitable hair salon. Nancy, who was independently wealthy, had financed the business. Suzanne was an artist at the time of their meeting and was introduced to them by Peter's younger brother, Allen. Suzanne and Allen had shared an art exhibit and showing at Justin Ferris's art gallery located on fashionable Newbury Street. It seemed incredible to Suzanne that from that one meeting a budding friendship and business partnership evolved. To this day Suzanne shook her head in amazement everytime she thought of the years that the business has been successful and expanded to many cities throughout the States and now in Europe as well.

Peter was one of the best known stylists in the Boston area and because of his feelings of inadequacy, got involved with drugs. Consequently matters got out of control. As a result of Suzanne's crazy lifestyle with Brian and then Suzanne's involvement working with the FBI, Peter ultimately got caught in the middle of the entire messy situation and as a result, wound up serving time in prison.

She looked out the window at the bright sunshine and wondered how such unhappiness could occur when everything outside looked beautiful. She loved the fall season, it was her favorite. She enjoyed seeing the sunlight embracing the different colors of the leaves before they fell off the trees. Suzanne loved painting the leaves, both on the trees and scattered throughout the ground, with the different shades of reds, yellows, burnt umber and the many colors making up the fall seasons beauty. She could picture them being trampled on by the various small critters in the woods.

Suzanne forced herself into the shower. The hot, pulsating water felt as if it were knives thrusting through her skin. In a way, she liked the self-imposed pain. She wanted to transfer Peter's misery and anguish to herself.

Toweling herself off, she suddenly remembered the appointment that she had with Madaline. Suzanne called her and luckily Madaline answered the phone.

"Thank God you haven't left for the theater." Suzanne went on to explain what happened to Peter and how she and Nancy had to see him.

"I'm not going to put off our conversation. I'll make sure that we get together sometime tomorrow or the next day. Tell me it's not about you or Kyle's health."

After being assured that was not the case, Suzanne felt better. "I'll make sure to call you first thing tomorrow morning and we'll make plans to get together. I love you, and I'm sure everything will be all-right."

Nancy beeped her horn and waited for Suzanne to come out from the house. They drove in silence to the hospital. Nancy reached for Suzanne's hand and patted it gently. Words were not necessary.

The guard outside the hospital room, his long legs resting on a spare metal chair, reading a Sports Illustrated, stopped the two women at the entrance. Nancy, anticipating such action, received permission from the proper authorities and showed the patrolman her letter of admittance.

Peter appeared to be sleeping as the two women approached the bed. He surprised them by abruptly opening his eyes. An amused but pleased smirk crossed his face.

"Hey, what's the matter with you? You scared the day-lights out of us," Nancy chastised her ex-husband.

Peter didn't say a word. A look of remorse appeared on his face. Trying to break the low spirited atmosphere that hovered about, Suzanne effortlessly discussed various matters that occurred at the Spa. "Peter, everyone at the spa misses your wonderful personality. Of course there's no hair stylist that can compare to your work. Your clients can't wait for you to return."

Gazing into space, Peter was apathetic. "Come on, do you honestly think I want to be seen around there. If and when I get out of this hell hole, I'll want to start a new life. I certainly screwed up the first half, maybe if I learned from my mistakes, and I think I have, the second period of my existence will be better."

"Cut the crap," Nancy finally chimed in. "Peter, if I've learned anything in life, it's that no one ever changes. If a person was nasty and a brat when they were little, they'll grow up being offensive and obnoxious. Someone who was polite, a good and admirable kid, they'll become a nice adult. Sometimes situations occur that might change the way they behave, but for the most part, everyone has their same character traits and temperament. So don't tell me you've changed. Sure, you made mistakes, we all have, but hopefully you can now recognize wrong from right."

"Don't eliminate all your friends and people who love you." Suzanne interrupted, "We won't let you out of our lives."

Finally looking directly at the two women in his life who meant so much to him, he expressed sorrow. "Look Nancy, I feel bad that you and Suzanne are upset. I don't know what came over me, a brain fart!" Peter exclaimed as he tried to laugh.

Nancy and Suzanne each took hold of his hand, the white bandages on his wrists, a reminder of what he had done to himself.

The psyche nurse came into the room. "Okay, I think Peter needs his rest now."

"I'll be back tomorrow," Nancy announced as she kissed him gently on the forehead.

"He didn't look as bad as I thought he would," Suzanne said as they left the lot of the Emerson Hospital.

"Does Alan know what happened? He should be informed, he is his only sibling. What about his parents? I'd better call them. I know they'll blame me. They hold me responsible for everything bad that's happened, from his getting involved in drugs to the divorce," Nancy uttered.

She didn't say much as they headed back to Stoney Brook. Nancy's mind was overflowing with thoughts of Peter. So many hopes and dreams were left unfulfilled. It didn't seem fair, she concluded, as she reflected days gone by.

'When we were first married, life seemed wonderful...nothing would ever come between us. Sure, we came from different worlds but our love for one another would overcome any obstacle that might occur.'

The sudden, unfortunate accident that took her parents' lives left her financially independent and rich. Although sad, she was lucky, that her parents were both doctors and independently wealthy. They were able to help others who were less fortunate in suppressed countries. Money was no object.... The terrible accident occurred when her parents had flown to Portugal for a medical conference where her father was a guest speaker. After the conference they were to take a private plane to Africa to another symposium. They never made it. The small, single engine plane crashed in the Ahaggar Mountains in Algeria. The only thing lacking was love and affection that her parents were incapable of showing. All she ever wanted was to be held, cuddled and feel adored. Parents usually give this kind of love to their children, in her case, an only child. She finally felt this kind of devotion when she unexpectedly met Peter, who she thought, was the man of her dreams. After they married, Nancy was busy finding the house they envisioned, fancy yet warm enough to call 'their home.' She wanted to fill the house with children, that she could bestow up them the warmth and love that parents give to their offspring. Nancy would turn her imagination into reality.

Peter wanted to open a hair salon of his own. Nancy didn't see anything unusual or a problem taking place if she provided the financing for Peter's dream. She would give him the world if she could. She appreciated all the love, thoughtfulness and adoration that he offered her. After exhausting many locations, the site they chose was located on the exclusive Newbury Street in Boston.

They both loved being near the water and decided to purchase a mansion, overlooking the ocean north of Boston. It was overwhelming but appealing for Nancy to furnish both the salon and the new home simultaneously. She was on cloud nine. Ever since she could remember, something always occurred that would ruin her state of enthusiasm. Peter kept busy establishing his reputation and clientele. There was little time for him to enjoy their beautiful home. Nancy ignored the subtle changes in her husband and although she tried helping him at the salon, felt disheartened. After all, how much shopping could she do? Being an only child Nancy couldn't wait to fulfill her motherly instincts. Her own mother, not the demonstrative sort that she would have loved to have, made her want to love and care for a child of her own. The final blow came when Peter changed his mind and wouldn't hear about having children. Adoption wasn't an option he would pursue. Disheartened, Nancy didn't know what to do. Suzanne was like the sister she never had. Looking over at her best friend while she confidently drove back to Stoney Brook, Nancy was grateful that she had someone she could confide in.

"You're awfully quiet, are you okay?" Suzanne asked.

Nancy assured her, "I'm fine, a little melancholy after seeing Peter in such a bad state."

Suzanne patted her hand. Words were not necessary.

Driving back to Ipswich Nancy shut off the radio's constant droning. Nancy enjoyed singing along with the music of the 50's and 60's but today it seemed tumultuous. She turned on the classical station and at once felt peaceful. Different thoughts kept distracting her ability to pay attention to the heavy traffic on Rte. 128 and I95. Here she was a healthy, vibrant, young woman who was trying to get on with her new life. She wasn't the one who asked that her life be turned upside down. It didn't seem fair that everything that she cared for or wanted never materialized.

Nancy thought, 'I didn't hate the world or become a recluse or a bitter person after I lost my parents unexpectedly. I think I became a, what would Suzanne call me, oh yea, a mench. I'm a responsible adult who loves life and the people who mean so much to me. Then why do I feel so alone and depressed? I know I have every right to feel the way I do, but jeez, can't life start turning around? Money isn't everything. People who are in debt or can never seem to make ends meet would certainly differ in their views. As long as I have my health and have a meaningful relationship, what else is there to want? I would appreciate a great man who has the same values as I do. I wouldn't mind him being tall, dark, handsome and great in bed. I didn't think that, did I? You bet your sweet ass I did.' Nancy laughed out loud.

Nancy picked up the mail and tossed the many unsolicited catalogs into the trash. She sat down on the bench in the kitchen, overlooking the constant changing water. She loved watching the foamy waves as they hit the shore.

Once in bed Nancy pulled the soft, downy comforter up to her neck and tried to sleep. Every noise imaginable kept her awake. Tossing and turning, kicking the second sheet from under the mattress, she tucked it underneath her feet, she felt as if she were in a soft cocoon and fell fast asleep.

When Nancy woke up the next morning she was determined to start life anew. 'I have so much to be thankful for, Suzanne and her family are like my own. It's not that I'm some old and unattractive woman. I'm still young. I'll just have to make up my mind to start getting out and become more social. After all, no one is knocking my door down to ask me out for a date. That's what I'll do, I'll make it my business to get back into the dating scene. I won't tell Suzanne, or anyone else for that matter, because they'll constantly be asking me questions about who I'm seeing.'

Alan, Peter's brother, couldn't get comfortable. As he sat on the brown leather sofa he put on the television, hoping that watching anything, however trivial, would keep him occupied. Dozing, as often happens while viewing the senseless shows, the sleep he needed didn't occur. He went into the kitchen and made another pot of coffee. Pouring himself a large cup he automatically reached for the chocolate chip cookies in the canister. 'This is ridiculous,' he thought to himself, 'if I keep drinking caffeine I'll never settle down.' He read the Sunday paper for the second time and mentally checked off the newest movies that he'd like Bill and himself to see. Alan wasn't used to Bill, his lover and best friend, being away for this length of time. He missed him. He picked up his cell phone and called Bill. They chatted for a while and Bill asked, "By the way, how's your brother doing? The last time I spoke to you, you sounded upset and couldn't get into what the problem was."

"That's probably the reason why I'm so restless tonight. Peter is having an awful time." Lighting up a cigarette he continued. "I got a call from his doctor from jail and was told that Peter tried committing suicide. Can you believe that? The stupid bastard! He sure messed up his life. He's still young and he's so talented. My parents almost died when they got the news. They flew up from Florida to be with him and lend him support. He never could do anything wrong. 'The Prophetic Son.' I on the other hand could stand on my hands, spit quarters out of my mouth, and at the same time recite the almanac and still they'd say, 'isn't that nice, but look what your brother has done.' Can you believe that shit? I'm sorry to sound so insensitive about the situation, I'm really not. I'll do anything I can to help Peter. I only hope that he wants to help himself." Changing the subject Alan asked, "So when will you be coming home?"

"The way you sound I should be flying out tonight. The business that I came out here for is almost done; I'll probably be home in another week. I miss seeing you and can't wait till I see your beautiful self again. Call me anytime and keep the faith. Things will get better and Peter will take care of Peter, like he always does. Your parents are another story. God forbid anyone should find out what their son tried to do to himself. They must be beside themselves with worry, hurt, and anger. I bet they're blaming Nancy for this happening to him," Bill exclaimed. "You know them so well. Have a great nights rest. I love you."

Before going to sleep Allen lit another cigarette and slowly blew smoke rings in the air. He shook his head in bewilderment.

He went back into the study and put the television on again. Resisting the urge for more coffee and cookies, he instead put his feet up on the brown leather couch. Putting a comforter over his slim body, he tried watching Jay Leno. He changed the channel to an old movie station. He hoped that the movie would be boring so he could fall asleep with no disturbing dreams.

The movie he decided to watch took place in an old museum with lots of castles surrounding a quaint European village. Allen suddenly remembered his conversation with Justin a few days ago. He was well aware of the increasing amount of robberies taking place throughout the United States and Europe. He remembered reading articles from the art journals. The increasing occurrences of pilferage plaguing the various museums and private sectors were becoming astonishing. He'd spoken to some friends who lived in France, Scotland and England and listened to the gossip running rampant among their friends. He supposed that Justin was right and this new interest in old art was becoming difficult to contain. 'I hope they catch the bastards real soon before more valuable art work is stolen. I remember reading how the Nazis confiscated many pieces of valuable art and to this day some are still missing.' While still watching the film he fell asleep.

CHAPTER THREE

The maddening Monday morning commute into Boston was to be expected as Suzanne pulled into the parking lot on Newbury Street. She didn't mind coming into work early, she enjoyed the peace and quiet of the salon until the clients started to arrive at 9 a. m.

She was grateful that her receptionist put today's lunch date with Justin Ferris into her appointment book. She poured herself a cup of hot tea waiting for the warmth of the liquid to slowly travel down to the cavity of her chest.

The morning hours rapidly flew by and Suzanne was looking forward to seeing Justin again. When Justin called to remind her of their lunch she told him, "I'll be leaving in about twenty minutes, after I'm finished with my client." Suzanne told him that she made plans with Madaline to meet her back at Madaline's suite after their lunch date. Suzanne thought to herself that whatever was troubling Madaline wasn't some sort of catastrophe.

Suzanne felt a tinge of nostalgia thinking back of how and when she met him. It seemed ages ago when he arranged to meet with her after he saw some of her paintings. His prestigious gallery was where she and Alan had their combined first art showing. Since that presentation they remained close. She felt fortunate to have Justin as a good friend.

Justin was seated when Suzanne spotted him at the corner booth at the Sweet Pepper, a casual restaurant down the street from her spa. Always a gentleman, Justin stood as Suzanne walked over to the table. He bent down, indiscreetly, allowing her to kiss him on both cheeks. She stood on her tip toes, for Justin, over 6' 5", was a picture of towering strength. "Before we begin, don't forget to say hi to Madaline. Is everything okay with her and Kyle?" a concerned Justin asked. "Yes, after our lunch we'll get together."

Suzanne squirmed herself in the booth in order to get comfortable. She took his hands into hers. She couldn't help but notice the difference in their hand size. She remembered her Papa Jack, who was also a large, big-boned man. When she was a little girl, Papa would pat and smooth her long blonde hair, bringing back bitter, sweet memories. She used to love putting her head on his large belly, while curled up next to him on the sofa, when they watched some of his favorite television shows. To this day, his laughter would always come to mind when she saw re-runs of the Red Fox show.

"I'm glad you called, it's been too long since we've lunched together." She straightened the silverware in front of her. "I don't have to ask how you are, you look great," Suzanne pronounced.

"I'm fine, as always a little too fine," as he patted his considerable large stomach. He had a special manner that exhibited an unquestionable pomp grandeur, which made most people feel intimidated. When Suzanne first met him she also felt overawe. When she got to know him, he was like a big teddy bear. Catching up on their personal affairs and events, Justin leaned over the table and presented Suzanne with a check.

"What's this for?" Suzanne asked.

"A couple of months ago someone bought one of your paintings, and last week two more paintings sold. I wanted to wait and surprise you with this extra money."

"Thank you, what a pleasant surprise. You could have mailed the check with a note inside."

"And give up an opportunity to see and talk to you, never."

With apprehension, he asked if she was still seeing Stephen. He was somewhat disappointed, yet cynical, when she answered yes. Although Justin liked Stephen, he'd get upset every time he thought about their relationship. 'It wasn't fair that Suzanne was in love with a married man. She deserves a real partner, one that can give all of him-self to her.' Thinking of all the heartache that she endured when she was married to Brian also made him agitated.

"Justin, you seem in another world. It's a beautiful day, we finally have a chance to sit down and enjoy each other's company, what's wrong?"

Justin waved his hands, "nothing my dear."

"Don't lie. We've been friends too long, you know I can read you like a book."

Smiling, he shook his head and waited until the waiter finished clearing off their dishes from the table.

With a knowing glance Suzanne teased him. "Come on, we don't keep things from one another."

"I only want the best for you…for you to be happy, that's all." Changing the subject Justin suggested, "Let's indulge in some opulent dessert."

"Are you trying to tempt me with these delicious sweets?" If you are, it won't work." Smiling at her dear friend, who she regarded as a faithful and true confidant, she gently stroked his hand. "I know you're only thinking of my happiness, for that I love you. Don't worry, frankly I'm fine."

Justin bit into his hot brownie Sunday, smothered with chocolate sauce, topped with vanilla ice cream and whipped cream. A cherry had to be placed on the top or he wouldn't feel the Sunday was complete. After finishing his dessert he patted his stomach and guiltlessly gave a wicked smile and said to Suzanne, "I can't help it, I enjoy eating. It's one of life's small pleasures."

"Hey, it's fine with me, you can take pleasure in anything you want." Suzanne smiled, continuing to sip more tea.

While drinking the hot liquid, thoughts of Stephen brought a slight smile to Suzanne. It was over two years since she had met and again fallen in love with this man who had been her first and only love. Thoughts of their years of separation, how they missed out on having a normal life, with children of their own, often kept her awake at night. Tears would fall onto her cheeks as these sorrowful reflections continuously haunted her. Of course it mattered that he was still a married man. 'After all,' Suzanne thought, 'I'm a moral person who would never deliberately hurt another human being.' The difficulties couldn't be swept under the carpet much longer. But for now she was dining with Justin and wouldn't let these problems interfere with the day.

"I'm sorry Justin; I forgot to tell you what happened this weekend. Nancy called and I feel that she needs my support. It really got me flustered." Suzanne filled in the disturbing details of what transpired between Peter and Nancy.

Justin sighed, his large chest expanding. Vapor could be seen as he slowly exhaled. "Is there anything that I can do for Nancy, - - - Peter as well? I love them both. Even today I can't believe the awful mess that happened, it ruined Peter's life. I only hope that Peter will come to his senses and rid himself of these self-imposed demons. Peter is still young, has a brilliant career ahead of him. And Nancy, what can I say about that dear girl? She's such a love. Alan keeps me abreast of Peter's situation. He's been a tremendous help in the business."

As he downed his espresso, "By the way, have you heard from Lawrence lately?"

"I'm glad that you brought Lawrence into the conversation. No, I haven't. Justin, you and I know that he might have a bit of a crush on me. Not that there's anything wrong with that."

"Well, my dear girl, you are fair game to any unmarried man. You're not married and do I see an engagement ring on your hand? No! So, what's a nice man, who has everything to give you, waiting for? Obviously he's infatuated with you and there's nothing wrong with the two of you going out on a casual date, is there?"

"Justin, I'm surprised at you. You know that I'm committed to Stephen. I love him and I couldn't give Lawrence any false hope that we might have something together. I think that Larry is a great guy; basically a wonderful father. I have all the respect in the world for him, especially when it comes to business."

"Didn't you go out with him the last time he was in town?"

"Yes, but I didn't consider that a date. We doubled with my old friend Beverly and her husband Louis. If you remember, Louis introduced Larry and me. We went to the Bay Tower Room and because Louis is one of his trusted accountants, we discussed his many business ventures and ways that I can improve mine."

Trying to change the subject, Suzanne asked Justin, "What have you've been up to and do you have new protégés?"

Beckoning the waiter, Suzanne asked for refills.

"I don't come across many young and talented artists like Alan and you." Taking a deep sigh, "If only I could," he said out loud. "Thankfully Alan still paints and I must say he's getting better with age. His interpretations are magnificent. If he continues the way he's going I'll probably make him a partner. After all, I am getting older and I don't have any children or siblings who would be interested in keeping the gallery going."

They then discussed the dramatic art theft that recently took place at the Elizabeth Gardner Museum.

"I've my own theory on who stole the precious items and why the magnificent pieces were taken."

Whispering, so no one could hear, Suzanne asked, "Tell me this theory of yours?"

"Well of course you know that the paintings were extremely valuable. I believe it's the work of a complete irresponsible, nonprofessional who ordered these few pictures to be appropriated for his private art collection. He may even want to keep them awhile, hide them, and then make them available to the underground market. More money than you can imagine can be made if sold to the 'right people.' Anyone in the art field would know and realize you never cut into a picture. It totally destroys the value of the painting. There have been quite a few art thefts happening throughout our country as well as abroad. It's just a hunch, a speculation, but it's all I have to go on. Another theory I have is that someone from the New England area, who has always been looked into by the police, might be responsible. No one can prove his involvement but from what I've heard, he might be the culprit. He's taken other art pieces and antiques. The police can't prove his guilt."

Contemplating on what Justin said made sense to Suzanne. "Have you gone to the authorities with what you just told me?" Suzanne asked as she finished her third cup of tea.

"No. Without something substantial to back up my ideas, it's purely conjectural."

"Before we say good bye it crossed my mind that I received a letter from one of my friends in Paris. She told me about all the art thefts and robberies that were happening. It seems friends of hers from all over Europe have expressed concern about the burglaries that have been taking place. A lot of European families that had money at one time are not as rich as they'd like people to think they are. They were left family heirlooms, valuable paintings and many objects that are worth a lot of money. They don't have the extra capital to pay for insurance. These families are sitting ducks for these crooks that thrive off people in their state of existence." Shaking her head Suzanne then told Justin about her friend, Renée's cousin, who lives in England and had his entire fortune stolen from his castle when he was on holiday with a few friends. His friends paid his way. Only his very best pals are aware of his financial problems.

Suzanne got up first and kissed him on both cheeks. "Let's see each other on a more regular basis when I'm home."

She walked back to see Madaline in her suite. Riding up the elevator Suzanne couldn't wait to talk to her friend. Madaline opened the door and practically pulled Suzanne into the living room. Suzanne instructed Madaline to "Sit down and calm your-self." Sitting on the couch Suzanne took hold of her hand. "Just sit for a moment. Take a deep breath, inhale, exhale, that's a girl; keep doing it for a few minutes." When Madaline seemed a little less agitated, Suzanne asked, "Okay, what happened to make you so upset?"

"I honestly don't know how to begin. You know that the show is doing great and the audience loves me. When I got back to my dressing room after seeing you, I inadvertently saw something out of the corner of my eye. There, sitting atop one of the end tables was a vase filled with a dozen black roses, we both know that is a symbol of death."

"Suzanne, I couldn't help it, I lost my cool. I asked one of the maintenance men to dispose of them. I mean, who would do such a cruel thing like that?" She asked her friend. Suzanne could see why Madaline was visibly shaking.

"Are you sure that someone didn't put them in your dressing room by mistake? Maybe they were intended to go to another person. It happens all the time."

"I don't think that's the case. I have lots of friends but I've also made a lot of enemies along the way. I've been wracking my brain trying to think who it could be."

"Was there a card enclosed with the flowers? Was there a box with the florist's name on it?"

"To be honest with you, I was so upset that I didn't look for those things. I just wanted them out of my room."

"I can understand," Suzanne agreed with her friend. "Do you think that last nights garbage could still be in back of the theater? Sometimes the dump trucks don't come every day." Not waiting for her friend to reply, she told Madaline that they should go and see if they're still there. "If they are, we'll examine the trash dumpsters. It's an outward chance, but a possibility, we might be in luck, that they might not have been emptied yet."

"I'll put on some old clothes if we're going to go through those disgusting containers." Madaline announced. "Quick, let's change, that's in case they're still full."

"Can I borrow some 'schloompy' (dirty) clothes? What I do for you!," Suzanne said as she was handed worn, jogging pants with an old tee shirt. "How come you travel with these types of schmatter's?(rags) I thought you'd have maybe one bad outfit, but two, it's incredible. They changed into the attire.

"I hope nobody recognizes me!" Madaline exclaimed as she tried hiding her face with large, dark, black sunglasses, to keep her anonymous. She descended the elevator, walked through the lobby with Suzanne by her side.

"I hope the stench will come out once we go through the trash. Obviously these clothes will have to be thrown out." Suzanne said as she looked throughout the lobby, hoping no one she knew would notice her either.

They got to the back of the theater and started rummaging through the garbage. Madaline, who was taller than Suzanne, suddenly fell into one of the cans and started screaming. Suzanne was laughing so hard she thought her sides would burst. "Stop that screaming you maniac; be careful a rat doesn't bite you," she again laughed hysterically.

"It's okay for you to laugh, you're not the one that fell into this God awful filthy rubbish," Madaline said as she spit out some wilted lettuce.

"Just shut up and start digging. If we don't find it in this barrel there are three more that we have to look through. Besides, you're already reeking, so it won't matter if you climb into the other ones." Madaline gave her a look that if looks could kill, Suzanne would be dead. "Okay. Okay, I'll be a good friend and go into one of the containers and start looking."

At the end of their mission they found the entire contents of the vase and flowers. "Of course it had to be in the last dumpster," Madaline said aloud. "I feel like one of the detectives you see on TV. I hope we can be as successful as they are when the programs over," Suzanne said as she tried wiping some grime off her hands.

Looking at the dirt on each other's face, arms, hands, and clothes, they couldn't help but giggle as they saw soggy lettuce, saran wrap and odd pieces they couldn't make out, clinging to their clothing and skin.

Madaline said, "my entire body feels like I have the heebiejeebies."

"I feel dirty, gross, like creepy crawlers are over my entire body;" Suzanne exclaimed, as she wiggled around hoping to dislodge some of the dirty items off of her clothes and exposed body parts. "Let's bring the things we found and go to the room," Suzanne suggested.

They headed up to Madaline's suite with the paraphernalia in hand. Two couples emerged from the fourth floor and looked at each other with distain. They examined the two vagabonds, who they thought didn't belong at such a prestigious hotel. As they got off at the eighth floor they overheard the women complain how awful the stench was. "How could the Ritz let such riffraff into the hotel?" Madaline and Suzanne acted as if there was nothing wrong and looked straight ahead.

When the elevator doors closed the two friends looked at each and went into a fit of laughter. "Before we forget," Madaline told Suzanne, "We'll have to put these clothes in a plastic bag." I'll take the garbage bag to the incinerator when we're finished. I wouldn't give that assignment to the housekeeper." Shrugging her shoulders Madaline said, "Whatever."

Entering the beautiful suite they hurried to the sofa. Putting her hand up she shouted, "Wait, don't you dare sit on that beautiful couch. The odor will never, ever, go away, no matter how much maintenance tries to clean it. I'm taking these grungy clothes off, take a shower, change and then I'll be in a better mood to thoroughly go through the vase of flowers and the box that it was delivered in," Suzanne adamantly declared.

"After you're through with the shower, I'll do the same." Madaline took off all her garments in the middle of the large room and waited for Suzanne to finish cleaning up.

Changed and finally clean, both women sat down. They sifted through the evidence. They opened the envelope that was attached to the flowers and took out the card. The only thing that was on it was a picture of a skull and bones.

"Let's go to the florist shop that the flowers came from. It's not too late if we hurry." Suzanne looked at Madaline and shooed her out the door.

"That's great. Someone wants' to either hurt or kill me. That's just wonderful."

"Don't jump to conclusions," stated Suzanne. "We'll get to the bottom of this, one way or the other. At this time in the day we'd be better off walking than to take my car and stay in traffic that's heading out of Boston." They quickly walked to the Florist Shop, which was down the street. The sales person was very nice and did remember the person who bought them. "He specifically wanted them sent to the theater. Unfortunately, the man paid in cash so I don't have a credit card with a name on it. It's unusual for black roses to be here in the first place. Somehow the owner bought them with our regular order. Maybe it's the fall and Halloween will be here shortly. I mentioned that to the gentleman as he handed me the cash."

"Can you describe the man?" Suzanne asked. "Like his height, weight, coloring of his skin and hair. Is there anything unusual that you can remember about him?"

"The color of his eyes would be helpful," Madaline interrupted.

Scratching his bald head he tried to concentrate. "I'm sorry ladies. Maybe if I think a-while I'll be able to help you."

Handing him one of her cards, Suzanne told him to call her any time if he remembered anything.

"That's just peachy," Madaline said to Suzanne as they left the establishment and headed back to the hotel. "What can we do now?" asked a concerned Madaline. "I really don't know," said Suzanne. "Maybe if you write down some of the people that you think REALY HATE YOU, we'll get a better feel for the situation."

"Their names can fill a book," a remorseful Madaline admitted." It can't be that bad," replied Suzanne. "Let's go back to the hotel and start."

'When you're in my kind of business, you have dealings with all types of individuals. Personalities differ, there's a lot of jealousy, it's not so hard."

"I'm glad I'm not in 'the arts' if I had this many people disliking or envious of me. In my business, people are grateful and enjoy their experience at my many spas. If I have to let one of the estheticians or stylists go, they can sometimes get nasty and vindictive. Come to think of it, I'd be afraid to put down the people who don't like me," Suzanne admitted.

"It's getting late. Do you want to stay over? Your salon is down the street and you won't have to fight the morning commute."

"Thanks, Madaline, but it isn't that late and I have a lot of catching up to do with the financials and truthfully, I like sleeping in my own bed."

She walked to where the car was parked, handed the man her ticket and was on her way home.

As Suzanne lay in bed, she couldn't help thinking about Madaline's predicament. Reflecting, she hoped that they'd be able to narrow the list down and find out who did this to her friend. Simka jumped up on her bed and cuddled close to Suzanne. She scratched her cat in back of the ears. The purring put Suzanne to sleep.

When Suzanne got to the office the receptionist told her that Hope called." She told me that whenever you get a chance to call her."

As she dialed Hope's cell number she said a silent prayer hoping all was well. So much was happening that she didn't know if she could take any more bad news.

Before dialing, she couldn't help thinking about her daughters. Hope was a typical first child, if there really was such a thing. Of Suzanne's children, Hope looked more like her than the others. Hope had Suzanne's fair complexion and large, dark brown eyes. Her natural light blond hair had waves throughout. She inherited Mama Pessa's two large dimples. She also had an infectious smile. She was an inch taller than her mothers', five feet four inches. When Hope and her mother were together, Hope would get mad when strangers thought that they were sisters. When younger, Hope and she were very close but through the years, because of conflicts with each other, Hope and Suzanne's relationship fell apart. Suzanne hoped that someday their relationship would return to the way it used to be.

Suzanne remembered, when the girls were growing up, repeating her thoughts to the girls as they matured. "Become independent and make your dreams come true, rely on yourself and make your visions become reality." Suzanne hoped that her way of thinking was an inspiration that all of her daughters took to heart.

Melanie, Suzanne's second daughter, was the complete opposite of her older sister. She had a God given daintiness. As much as she looked like her father she was definitely a romantic like Suzanne. This self-willed young lady turned out to be an independent delightful young woman who Suzanne was very proud of. She truly abided by Suzanne's motto: "Do unto others as you'd want them to do unto you."

Taylor, the youngest of her daughters was the wild one. She was the only girl on the block to ride a moped when they were the 'in' thing to do. She was a tomboy but truly refreshing. Her oval face had not one flaw on her natural golden complexion. A slight cleft adorned her chin. She was a high spirited, dynamic, individual, who made everyone that was lucky to be in her presence, happy. After looking at the profits Suzanne realized that Taylor was the best salesperson of them all.

Suzanne dialed Hope's cell phone. Her daughter's voice brought Suzanne out of her pensive thoughts.

"Thanks honey, it was a nice time, wasn't it? Yesterday I had lunch with Justin and from there I visited Madaline. I took most of the afternoon and evening off. "

"That's strange. We just saw Madaline the evening before, how come you saw her again last night?" Hope inquired.

"There's nothing strange about it. It isn't often that we can get together and we felt we didn't have enough alone time. You know how it is with us women." Suzanne would never tell anyone about Madaline's predicament. 'Well, maybe I can confide in Nancy if Madaline says it's okay.'

"How is Justin? It seems ages since I've seen him."

"Justin is well and as always, has great stories to tell." After some light conversation Suzanne mentioned she had to get back to work.

"Mom, wait a second, I have to speak to you about an important matter." Hope didn't know how to begin, but plunged ahead.

"Spencer and I have been seeing each other for over a year now. I think I'm in love, really in love. I'm convinced that Spencer is going to ask me to marry him." With a squeal of excitement in her voice she continued. "I'm so happy, I hope you like him. Do you?"

She liked Spencer since their first meeting, but.... Suzanne wanted to end their conversation before she said something that would make them have another fight. "Of course I like him. He seems to be a nice young man. He's always been very courteous and friendly." With that said, she begged off the phone. Sitting in her chair thoughts she didn't want to think about and say aloud materialized.

Spencer was brought up with a vast amount of wealth. He was taught all the social graces. She could never picture him as a young boy playing stick ball or field hockey on the street as she did as a youngster. Her girls attended public schools. Spencer went to private schools, a prestigious collage, country clubs and learned tennis and golf as a youngster. Did he realize that people like Suzanne or Hope weren't allowed at his country club? That's why the Jewish people flocked to the Catskills to be amongst their own kind. In and around the Boston area or other States as well, a Jewish person would not be admitted to Country Clubs – golf clubs, even for socialization, because we weren't 'their kind of people.' 'We were forced to build our own country clubs for golf and socialization in the predominately Jewish areas.' She remembered going to the Blue Hills Country Club in Canton and the Sydney Hills Country club in Newton; where Jewish people were predominant.

Both sides of his family came from old money. They never knew what it was like to struggle and want for material things. If he makes her happy, she'd better keep her mouth shut, or else everything could backfire. She prayed to God that she'd be able to do so. Being one not to keep her feelings at bay, she had to learn to be quiet and not tell her daughter how she really felt.

"Tell me, do you like his parents?"

"His parents seem nice. I don't get to see them much, they're always busy. They travel quite a bit now that his father retired."

Suzanne thought or surmised how differently she grew up from them. She was brought up in the city, a three story tenement building to be exact. In her neighborhood mostly Jewish people lived and interacted with each other. Everyone congregated or shopped on Blue Hill Avenue in Dorchester or in Mattapan. All the specialty stores were owned by Jewish people and unless you went into Boston Proper itself or into Filene's Basement, one wouldn't think of shopping elsewhere. During the Jewish Holidays, all of Boston's schools closed, young adults would go to Franklin Field, sit on the stone wall and socialize with each other. That was the "thing" to do!!!

Suzanne wondered if Spencer's parents had any inkling of what it was to be brought up in a Jewish community where the outside world looked upon you as a different species. People's attitudes changed throughout the years but even if you were born and brought up in another part of the country like New York or Philadelphia, one Jewish person could usually tell another Jewish person apart from a different nationality.

Suzanne didn't want to get into a serious conversation with Hope as to their religious differences. She felt there would be time enough, if and when, he asked her to marry him. Hanging up the receiver one final thought entered her mind. 'I wonder what his parents think of their only son marrying a Jewish girl. Especially from parents that were divorced? Did they consider Hope and her family from the other side of the tracks? Of course it's not like I'm poor, but, they might consider us nouveau riche. We're not the Vanderbilt's and our family didn't graduate from Harvard.' With a deep sigh, Suzanne closed her eyes for a second to gain her composure. Taking a deep breath she attempted to free herself from agitation and anxiety. She walked out of her office and quietly closed the door behind her. Taking the clients card from the holder she was ready to enter the zone she loved, into the world she enjoyed, leaving all negative thoughts behind her and make the people who trusted her to look and feel better about themselves. Suzanne walked into the darkened room, a smile on her face.

CHAPTER FOUR

Justin's words kept repeating themselves as she resumed her work. She couldn't get the theft of the Gardner Museum off her mind. Suzanne remembered when Nancy took her to Paris for the first time. Sitting in the living room of Nancy's friend's large apartment, she remembered admiring the many unique and unusual paintings that adorned Madam Reneé Roubiliac's home. She later found out that they were originals that were painted by some of the world renowned masters, when they were still struggling artists. Trying to get Justin's words off her mind, Suzanne was grateful for a full schedule.

After a lengthy, busy day Suzanne couldn't wait to get home. By the time Suzanne reached her driveway she was tired but relieved. Mrs. Walsh had a pot of hot tea waiting for her, Simka waited patiently by the door, wanting to be recognized and patted. The two women recapitulated the day's events. Going up the stairs Simka ran ahead, waiting for her to reach the landing. Suzanne snuggled under the sheets and comforter, Simka, as always, rested her head on the same pillow as Suzanne's. She had a hard time falling asleep, the moons bright glow cast it's light into her bedroom. Thoughts of Brian reemerged. It brought back such painful memories. Suzanne remembered all too well the anxiety, nauseous feelings she experienced when Brian would arrive home in the early morning hours, 'working' ... his excuse. She would never forget the churning of her stomach, the racing of her aching heart whenever they fought. His domineering, Jekyll, Hyde personality forever made her feel inadequate and not a total woman. The tears she shed wishing she had married Stephen instead, realizing all too late that she married for the wrong reasons. She had run away from her heart and into the arms of an older man who would never take the place of her first love. She married on the rebound and was sure she was punished for this unthinkable act.

Nancy asked Suzanne if they could meet for dinner. Suzanne arrived at Max Steins in Lexington first. She ordered a White Zinfandel. There were many thoughts that Suzanne wanted to sort out. At the same time, she wanted to avoid thinking of them. She tried to concentrate on the music to clear her mind. But the stark reality of her relationship with Stephen, Hope's soon to be engagement, Peter and Nancy's problems, leading to their ultimate separation and divorce, now Madaline's dilemma, caused her great concern.

Waiting for Nancy she munched on the nuts provided. The foremost problem, she figured out, was how to help Madaline and find out who was scaring her and what that person would ultimately do. She could relate to Madaline's reaction. She remembered when she was stalked by an unknown person. It turned out to be Brian. Until she found out who the culprit was, she couldn't get a good night sleep. The entire episode drove her crazy. There had to be some way to find out who's after Madaline. She was thinking back about Madaline's upbringing and her ultimate success. Could it be someone from her past or in the theater? She couldn't rule any possibilities out.

Suzanne saw the top of Nancy's red hair as she ascended the staircase and waved. Suzanne put her pad and pen away.

"What a surprise to find you seated at a table. I'm overwhelmed that you're actually drinking before I arrived," Nancy said as she sat down, motioning for service from the bar maid as she hustled about the room.

Over dinner the friends had a gab fest. They articulated their frustrations and grievances about their life, family and work. The drinks that they had, enabled them to let all the anger they felt be known. "We'll order strong coffee. Do you think that we were able to solve the problems of the world and our own problems at the same time?" Suzanne asked as she got her wallet out to pay her portion of the bill.

Nancy didn't mind the long drive home. She decided to put on her favorite radio station and listened to the music of the '50's and '60's. Singing along with The Drifters 'Up on the Roof' and so many other songs of that great era made the trip easier.

Nancy elected to wear a nice comfortable and warm pair of pajamas. She roamed around her large, lonely house. 'Even when Peter and I were married he worked so many long hours it seemed as if I lived here by myself anyway.' These thoughts made her sorrowful, as she poured Dewar's Scotch over ice cubes in a short glass. She again filled her glass. During her many years of traveling, she was exposed to some of the most expensive and rare wines from all over the world. She had to admit, although very good, she still preferred her scotch.

She put on the stereo, sat down on the new flowered blue and yellow shantung sofa, put her head back against the high backed pillow and let herself drift off and think about times gone by. It seemed like only yesterday, but couldn't believe that she wasn't that same young girl, cavorting with her friends and enjoying life to its fullest.

Mrs. Walsh was waiting by the door. "Well it's about time that you got home. You have work tomorrow and I know that you'll be cranky. Let me get you some coffee and you'll feel better."

"You know me too well, but another cup of coffee will kill me. I feel like a teenager whose parents wait for their child to get home. But please, a cup of tea is all that I want. I forced myself to have a few cups of coffee at the restaurant and that's enough for me."

The morning came and as predicted, Suzanne's mood was not as pleasant as usual. Simka was purring and rubbing against her leg. She bent down and patted her fluffy, beautiful Maine Coon. "Okay, okay, I won't be late tonight, I promise," she said to both Mrs. Walsh and Simka. After gulping down her juice, tea and a Finagle Bagel she was ready for another day of pampering her clientele.

Crossing the walkway she heard a faint cry. Suzanne didn't see anything and proceeded to get into her car. Again she heard a slight meow and got out of the auto. Walking toward the front door was an emaciated black kitten. She knelt down and patted it. She noticed that its ear had been chewed, and saw at least four broken teeth, all in all, it looked pretty beat up. The kitten kept rubbing against her legs, purring, meowing and wanting to be petted.

Shooing the kitten away Suzanne couldn't get it to leave her alone. She almost tripped on him more than once. "Come on sweaty, I have to get to work. Go home, go home now."

Mrs. Walsh, hearing the commotion, opened the front door.

"I can't get this little munchkin to leave me alone," declared an impatient Suzanne.

Putting her head down, an embarrassed Mrs. Walsh proceeded to explain, "I forgot to tell you that he's been around here for more than a week. "Defensively she said, "I have to admit I did give him some water and food, though I didn't bring him into the house, because I thought he'd never leave. Simka is the Queen around here you know."

"I know that!" An irritable Suzanne responded. Ignoring Suzanne, Mrs. Walsh continued.

"He's been sleeping on one of the patio chairs at night because he's very smart. He knows that the skunks, possums and who knows what other critters come to the patio foraging for food and look into the sliding glass window. I've watched him and he's so smart, Suzanne, he doesn't move a muscle, for fear of being detected."

"Oh great, just what we need right now. You know that I'm a sucker for animals, especially cats. My mother hated them and every time I brought a kitten home she'd give it away. Remember when Tayler brought home Simka as a birthday present for Hope? Who do you think Simka attached her-self to? Yup me! I do love her. Being a Maine Coon cat she has that beautiful full fur and thick fluffy tail. Her face is absolutely gorgeous."

"Meanwhile, what are we going to do about the little black munchkin?" asked a concerned Mrs. Walsh. Suzanne expressed amusement, shaking her head as she opened the car door. "The question is what are YOU going to do with this poor, undernourished, sweet kitten? After all, this is your predicament," Suzanne said as she drove away.

"Well, maybe we might try to see if they'll acclimate," Mrs. Walsh proclaimed.

Stopping at the end of the driveway she yelled to Mrs. Walsh, "I don't think that's a good idea for now. He looks pretty beat up and who knows what bacteria the poor thing might have. I'll call the vet from work and make an appointment for him before we bring the cat into the house."

After the vet gave the kitten all its shots, pulled four teeth and had a prescription waiting for Suzanne to get rid of the "bugs" that were in his intestines, the veterinarian gave the go ahead to take him home. 'It cost me over four hundred dollars to get this kitten fixed up. I hope Mrs. Walsh likes him as much tomorrow as she did when she first saw him.'

The next day Suzanne got to work and was grateful that her first client had cancelled. Nancy called and they made arrangements for a business meeting for later in the week. Meanwhile her plans to see Stephen were once again put on hold.

Suzanne stayed later than usual at Metamorphosis, making sure that Madaline would be back in her suite.

Suzanne called to tell her she'd be right over. Knowing Madaline as she did, she didn't want to frighten her when she knocked at the door.

Taking her friends hand she directed Madaline to the sofa. "I've been thinking all day about your plight and I think I know how to narrow the list down."

"We know that whoever went to the flower shop was a man. He must live around this area, otherwise he could have wired the shipment to the theater. We have to find out who lives in and around the Boston area that could possibly have a motive or close to someone, who he might be working for or has a connection to that person who hates you."

"You can really make a person feel loved," Madaline chortled, as she got some papers, and pens out. On the beautiful sofa Madaline crossed her legs, Indian style. Madaline looked very serious as she started writing. Meanwhile Suzanne was looking over the list as her friend was busy writing. As far as Suzanne could calculate there seemed to be about 15 or 20 people listed that seemed like good contenders.

"Of these people, who do you honestly feel would hate you enough to try and kill you? I'm not trying to scare you more than you are, but this is a serious matter. Do you think we should call the police and let them handle this situation?"

"If I thought that the person was bent on killing me, I think I'd already be dead. Whoever is doing this, I'm sure this incident won't be the last. I'll try to narrow the list down and see if anything else happens."

Suzanne asked, "Do you really think another event will happen? As a matter of fact, the more I think about it, you're right. You know, it might not be a bad idea if we can find out from one of my friends, Tim or Kevin, from the FBI, a good private detective to hire and watch your back. What do you think of the idea?"

"You know for a nice Jewish mensch, (a decent human being) there might be something to what you said. Yes, I'd love for you to call one of them or heck, both, for that matter, and get names of some good private investigators, or as the TV calls them, PI's."

"Okay, let's get serious. First thing tomorrow morning I'll make the call to my friends in the FBI. I'm sure those guys will have someone that will be able to help us," Suzanne assured Madaline. "Be sure to double lock your door and don't answer it for anyone. Even if they say they're from housekeeping. Call down to the desk to make sure. Remember, this isn't a concern to be taken lightly. I'm going home now. I'll call you first thing in the morning after I speak to either Tim or Kevin."

"Thanks for all your help Suzanne," said Madaline. "I don't think I'd be able to handle this situation by myself. Be careful driving." Suzanne hugged her friend goodbye and hurried to her car.

True to her word, as soon as she woke up, she called Tim and Kevin at their office in Boston. She was connected to Tim. She explained what had happened to Madaline and needed a good P. I. to help them.

The phone was quiet for a couple of moments; Suzanne thought they had been disconnected. In the background she could hear paper's rustling. Tim picked up the receiver. "Sorry to keep you waiting, I had to make sure that Paul Winston is still around. You're in luck. I'll get in touch with him, give him your number and I'm sure you'll be hearing from him shortly. By the way he's a retired FBI agent and he's good."

Suzanne walked into her office when her cell phone rang. Sure enough it was Paul Winston. "Tim gave me a short version of your predicament and I'll be glad to speak with the two of you. Pick a day and time that's good. I'll tell you if it works for me."

After giving Suzanne his office address they made a time to meet. Suzanne was impressed that his offices were on State Street in Boston. Madaline was to meet her at the spa and from there they'd walk to number One State Street. A secretary was not there to greet them so they sat down in the waiting area and read a few magazines, hoping to see Mr. Winston or his assistant. Accessing his office they found it to be sparsely furnished. A very masculine décor showed in the worn, brown, leather, sofa and chair, with a beat up looking coffee table in front of it. "I have to admit it's a bit meager with only a computer, telephone, and some file cabinets on the side. Needless to say, that even though he has his office at a prestigious location, it's rather scantily put together. He must own one of the smaller agencies," Madaline articulated.

Suzanne thought, 'don't let first impressions fool us.' Finally Mr. Winston opened his own door and greeted the two women and asked them in. Apologizing for his secretary's absence he gave, what seemed a lame excuse, and got right down to business.

Paul extended his hand and introduced himself to the two women. They in turn did the same. Walking to his chair in back of his desk he quickly glanced at the two lovely ladies, thinking to himself that they were both beautiful in different ways.

"Tim filled me in on most of the details. I'd like Ms. Mason to tell me, in your own words, what happened. If I agree to take on the case I want you to be aware that this isn't going to be cheap. I get a retainer up front and also charge by the hour and any expenses I may find necessary to use. It can get costly," Mr. Winston pronounced.

"Don't worry about the finances Mr. Winston," Madaline assured him.

Looking a little embarrassed Paul asked Madaline, "Are you the Madaline Mason, the actress and stage star? When Tim told me some of the details, he didn't mention any names, only telling me that two of his friends needed help. When you introduced yourselves, I couldn't help but wonder." Suzanne had never seen Madaline blush and was surprised at her reaction.

When Suzanne and Madaline left his office they didn't say much to each other. Finally they sat down in Suzanne's workplace. "I don't believe what we're doing. He seems like a nice guy but his desk was worse than his secretaries or receptionists. His work table looks like he got it out of a Salvation Army store. The finish is so worn that I can't tell what type of wood it was and the carpet is down to the bare threads. I certainly hope he's as good as Tim says he is, because my first impression wasn't very good," Madaline exclaimed. She made herself comfortable on a beautiful, blue, French Provincial chair in front of Suzanne's lavish and nicely appointed French, dark wood, with burl accent, desk.

"You can't go by first impressions, Madaline. He did come highly recommended by Tim and I trust Tim's judgment. Let's hear his plan first and then we can decide if we want him or get another name from Tim."

"Okay, I'll be patient, but I pray he's good," Madaline told Suzanne.

When Madaline went back to the theater to perform her nightly production she was surprised to find Paul waiting for her when the play was finished. "Let's go back to my dressing room, if you don't mind Mr. Winston."

"Sure, I just got here because I didn't want to make a spectacle of myself. I want to be as inconspicuous as possible."

He sat down on the sofa and Madaline sat opposite him on the overstuffed chair. "I'm taking the assumption that I'm hired. If so, we should go over a contract that I brought and explain how I work and get paid. I'll ask you some questions that we didn't go over in my office. Then according to what you tell me I'll clarify and give you my plan of action that I'd like to take." After listening to Madaline explain what happened and was scared that someone was either stalking her or trying to do her harm, Paul sat quietly for a while.

"You do have something to worry about. It doesn't make sense, but in these types of situations, not many things add up. I'd like a list of people who you think might want to do harm to you and I want an extensive list. I expect the list within the next day. The faster we get going the sooner we'll find this person or people who are responsible."

"Once I get the list from you I'll make some calls to cops I know. The internet is quite a way to communicate with some of my informants and hopefully, I'll be able to narrow the list down to a few people. If I have to, I might have to travel to various parts of the States and I'll be mindful of my personal expenses. Meanwhile if any incident occurs I'm giving you my personal cell number. I always have it on me so I'll answer it night or day. We're not sure what this bozo is trying to do. It might have been this one episode or he may want to do bodily harm to you. Let's hope Murder isn't on his or her agenda."

Can I ask you a silly question?"

"Sure, go ahead, I've been asked everything imaginable." Madaline was intrigued by this man who was once an FBI agent. She found him to be an attractive man if you liked the tall, well built, large hazel eyes and wavy, dark hair that was beginning to recede. She thought that he must work out at a gym constantly because his physique was quite impressive. Madaline could actually visualize his muscular body underneath his suit.

"Mr. Winston, do you carry a gun or firearm?" He chuckled but didn't want this beautiful woman to think he was laughing about her question. "Yes, I do. Most people in my profession have a license to carry, especially interstate and outside the States."

"Have you had to use it on occasion?"

"Let's put it this way, I try not to if I can help it. Sometimes it can't be avoided. Please don't ask if I've killed anyone because I won't answer. I'll always have your back covered. Don't be nervous. I try to be as inconspicuous as possible. 'It's easy for you to say,' Madaline thought. With that said she dismissed him, telling him she had to change. "Nice seeing you again Miss Mason."

While changing into her stage clothes she thought to herself, 'well he didn't wait to find out if I wanted him to act on my behalf and never asked me to sign a contract. I guess he's that sure of himself.' With a chortle she went into the curtained area and put on her first costume of the evening.

He sat in his supped up Viper for a while contemplating his next move. He realized that he left without her signed signature and with a shrug he left and went back to his Lexington house where he put his Viper next to his old police issued nondescript Chrysler that had a special engine that could outrun most cars, including his Viper. He remembered when his chief gave him the car as a present when he was accepted into the FBI.

They met at Joe Teccis' and went over plans for another expansion.

Suzanne asked Nancy, "What are you going to do once Peter gets out of jail?"

"There's not much that I can do. We're divorced and there's no going back. I hope that he learned his lesson and won't get caught up in the drug scene again. We had our good times but now its time for me to move on." Raising her hand for silence, Nancy continued. "I've been thinking of dating but before you say anything let me have my say. I didn't want to tell you or anyone about my decision to put myself back into the meat market, as people call it. I'm scared because there are so many issues that go along with the dating scene."

"There are real jerks, kooks and losers out there. I won't go into a bar to pick up some nice looking guy, who'll do who knows what. He could be another Jack the Ripper or Ted Bundy. A lot of people are putting adds in the paper, but again, how would I screen them? I also hear that the Internet has some sites for people to meet. I'm all mixed up. The best thing for me is to be fixed up through someone that I know, yet all my friends are married and so are their friends. I don't want to think about it for now, but I had to tell you what's on my mind. Now let's forget about it and get on with this dinner meeting."

Suzanne interrupted, "Nancy, what are your feelings if Peter wants to come back to the salon. In my estimation, he's the best hair stylist in Boston."

"Truthfully, I don't really care. He might, but I don't think he will. For the good of the company, I hope that he does return. If I'm to take him at his word while he was in the hospital, he's not thinking of returning back to the spa. Only time will tell," Nancy said out loud.

"I'm glad that you told me your feelings about dating. It hurts that you didn't talk about this dating thing when it first entered your mind. We're like sisters. I can't believe that it took you this long to tell me your thoughts about looking for a guy. It's an important decision."

"I don't know Suzanne. I didn't want to make a big deal about meeting anyone, that's all." Squeezing Nancy's hands that were resting on the table Suzanne looked at her. "I promise that I won't bug you about this situation. Feel free to talk to me when you have any concerns or things that you need to talk about. You know I'll always be here for you. By the way, a few people I know have found some very nice men through the dating services on the internet." Putting up her hand, Suzanne said, "That's the last you'll hear about this subject from me, I promise." Nancy gave her a look as if to say, 'ya, I believe that as if you'd want to sell me the Brooklyn Bridge. '

In between their courses they finalized their plans about their Japanese expansion. "I'm concerned about our ability to oversee an operation that's so far away," an anxious Nancy verbalized. "We keep going over the same issues and we'd better get a solid hold on this situation if we're going to take on this market. Maybe if we think about it one of us will have a solution. Do you have any people or a special person that you know, who's in this profession that's of Japanese heritage?"

"I'll try to put my thinking cap on and maybe I can think of someone," Suzanne said.

"Now, let's get back to you and your family. What's happening?"

"There are things and then there are things. Do you want me to give you the short, peaceful version or the long, unabridged version on what life's all about? There are a lot of things going on."

"Hope thinks she's in love." She then told Nancy about Hope and Spencer. Sometimes if you say uncomplimentary remarks about their intended, they might go back and tell that person what you said. Then the other person will always remember those remarks and a good relationship will be hard to maintain if you even get to have a relationship at all. On the other hand, if you keep your thoughts to yourself, and the rapport doesn't turn out to be the best, you kick yourself for not speaking up. You're damned if you do, damned if you don't. Kids think that they know best. When they become older, are parents themselves, they realize what parenting is all about."

"We now have a new addition to our family as well. Mrs. Walsh found a young kitten and he's living with us. I had to take him to the Veterinarian because I wanted to get him checked out. To make a long story short, they extracted four teeth and had his front paws declawed. From being out in the field, for such a long time, he developed some sort of bacterial infection from eating rodents and now has to be on special medicine until this bacteria clears up. Apparently he did belong to someone because he was neutered, but that person or family either abandoned or lost him. As far as I'm concerned he'll become a house cat and never go out. He is rather cute and can't get enough patting or love. He's all black, no white whatsoever on him. His eyes are even black. We've decided to call him Boston."

Suzanne continued telling Nancy about other aspects in her life and what happened when she saw Justin. I haven't heard from Alan for a while. I hope all is well between him and Bill. I have a feeling that they're doing fine. I'll have to call him and make plans for all of us to get together, maybe when you get home from Japan."

"Maybe I shouldn't have asked you what's taking place in your life. I have a headache just hearing you talk about all the things that are going on with you and your family," Nancy admitted, grabbing the bill out of Suzanne's hand." Come on, we'll continue this conversation when I return from Japan," Nancy said as she paid their bill.

As the two friends were leaving the restaurant, Suzanne looked at Nancy and blurted, "You could put your name into one of those dating services or go on line and punch in plenty of fish."

"See, I knew I shouldn't have told you what's on my mind. Now you'll be bugging me all the time," Nancy chided.

CHAPTER FIVE

Yoshy got in his seat on the airplane; it felt good to sit down. All he wanted was to be left alone and catch up on some reading material. He knew that once back in San Diego, he would be inundated with work, having to attend the many meetings that was expected of him. "Good morning Mr. Makino. It's good seeing you again," the pretty flight attendant asked, "Is there anything I can get you?"

"Thank you, I'm fine, I'm all set for now." Buckling the seat belt he closed his eyes, waiting for the roar of the engines and the take-off to begin.

Yoshirhiro, or Yoshy, as his intimate friends and colleagues called him, couldn't wait to get back to the States. He was thrilled to be going back to San Diego. Although he enjoyed seeing his family, he loved his work and all the challenges put before him. Yoshy knew that Toshiko, his dutiful wife for many years, enjoyed cooking for him while he was home. 'Another reason for going back to the States,' he thought to himself. 'If I keep eating all the food that Toshiko prepares and expects me to eat, and unfortunately I enjoy everything she puts before me, I'd waddle like a duck.' He visualized himself walking down the hallway of his office building, quacking.

Kazuhiko, his only child and son was getting older and acquiring a life of his own. Yoshy knew that one day Kazuhiko would take over for him and become president of the large corporation that Yoshy had conceived and built. It was one of the largest electronics manufacturing companies in the world. Once again Yoshy tried concentrating on the folder before him.

"Excuse me," a beautiful young lady verbalized as she tried to take her seat beside Yoshy. He got up from his aisle seat and let her get to the assigned window location. Adjusting herself, she looked out the window and took a deep breath, then slowly exhaled. She was grateful that she was able to make the plane on time and was glad to be going back home to the States.

'When I finally get back to Massachusetts I'm glad I'm taking a cab home. Maybe I'll stay over for a few days to acclimate from the trip. Who am I kidding,' she thought,' with all that's happened in my life in the past few years, my nerves are shot to hell. I really have to take hold of myself. I might start taking yoga classes again to get my energy level where it's supposed to be. The yoga used to relax and calm me. My nerves are frayed since my divorce, expanding our business, and now I find myself vulnerable to any single man. Who the hell wants one. They're all nuts, they want sex right away and I don't need the hassle of what everyone calls 'the meat market. '

Extending her hand, "my name is Nancy, Nancy Trembly, we do have a rather long flight ahead of us." Smiling, Yoshy welcomed the pretty, nicely shaped, young red headed woman seated beside him and grasped her hand. 'At least this one's a looker. Last time I had a fat, obnoxious man who breathed so heavy I thought I'd go out of my mind,' He thought to himself. He produced a card as a way of introducing himself to his traveling companion. 'After all we'll be seated next to each other for an extended period of time.'

Nancy dropped his card into her purse and tried to be friendly. "This was my first trip to Japan. Everyone that I've talked to told me it's a beautiful country, but seeing it for myself made me appreciate it. Friends who've traveled to Japan found the people to be very courteous. Acquaintances also told me the masses of people would be overwhelming. Once I got used to the crowds, I ignored the confused state that I found myself in."

"I live in a small town in Massachusetts called Ipswich. It takes a bit of getting used to once you've lived in a large metropolis and then move to a suburb. I love it because my home is right by the ocean and I've learned to enjoy the peace and quiet, except when the seagulls start squawking." She noticed that all he did was nod his head in agreement. She thought he probably didn't understand a word she was saying. Nancy laughed quietly to herself. She admonished herself for rambling on. Thinking it was nerves, she turned away from, she couldn't remember his name, and picked up a magazine and tried reading it.

Yoshy was happy that the woman next to him finally stopped talking. He was getting a headache listening to her prattling on and on. He settled into his seat and picked up the magazine he was previously reading.

About an hour and a half into the flight he found himself clearing his throat as he started conversing with Nancy. "For myself, I've always lived in the city. I do have a place on a lovely island that I occasionally visit when I prefer time alone." Being curious he asked, "What made you visit Japan and are you traveling alone?" Thinking to himself he realized that he should have reserved the entire row in first class. 'One never knows who'll be sitting beside you.' Nancy quickly answered him thinking, 'he speaks English. '

Nancy courteously answered his question. "I usually travel with my business partner, Suzanne, but this time I wanted to attend to this assignment by myself. You see I'm part owner of a very large chain of skin care salons and spas. We're thinking of expanding and feel Japan would be the next logical location for our venture."

"I hope your dealings were successful."

"Yes, thank you for your concern. I think with careful planning and making right decisions we hope to have a salon in at least one major city in your Country. Do you travel to the States often?"

"Hai. I travel back and forth a lot. I've come to feel that San Diego is like my second home. I am the president of a very large computer company with many offices around the world."

"I hope I'm not boring you with my chattering."

Yoshy, a man who insisted on his privacy and liked his solitude; felt obligated to be cordial to the beautiful, red headed woman called Nancy, seated next to him. "No, I enjoy hearing what you think of our Country. But now I must rest. He closed his eyes for a while and thought to himself that he should be used to the flight by now. After napping for a while, he opened his literature.

Nancy tried to get comfortable but to no avail. She hated being sedentary and seated for long periods of time with nothing important to do. Attempting to deviate from her uncomfortable position, she picked up the novel that she purchased at the airport. She always enjoyed reading James Patterson and his Alex Cross novels. Putting her seat in a reclining position she tried focusing on it, after a while realized she couldn't concentrate. She closed the paperback and shut her eyes.

Love and gratitude were the feelings she had whenever she thought about Suzanne. Suzanne replaced the loneliness she had growing up without siblings or parents. Although Peter was then her husband, Suzanne and her clan were ultimately the people who replaced the family she desperately wanted and needed. Frowning, she thought of Peter who should have been her best friend and partner in life. Instead she resented his inability to provide the emotional support she needed.

She couldn't put aside the resentment she felt towards Peter. 'I should have left and divorced him when he first told me he changed his mind about having a child.'

Nancy remembered when Suzanne became an integral part of the salon. Eventually through hard work and diligence Peter's and Suzanne's dreams became reality. The new part of the business, skin and makeup, caught on and the two entities melded well together. They added other services to their operation and it became a one stop shopping place. It kept Peter focused and busy. People from outlining areas and the Boston Proper couldn't wait to get an appointment at the "exclusive Metamorphosis Salon." 'Peters' reputation became synonymous with the great hair stylists throughout the country. Sometimes people had to wait weeks or months for an appointment with the 'fabulous Peter'. Suzanne's reputation was growing as well.

She had faith that he would learn from his mistakes and acquire an ability to love someone other than himself. 'Maybe that's what he needs,' she thought as she lost herself in slumber.

The turbulent weather began. The streak of lightning illuminated the cabin, frightening many of the passengers. The fasten seat belt sign came back on. The screams, from the fellow travelers awakened those who lay in the arms of Morpheus. Frenzied, Nancy grabbed Yoshy's arm, throwing his briefcase that was on his lap, to the floor.

"Oh, I'm soo sorry. I guess I panicked, I feel so foolish. Let me help you pick up the papers that have fallen out of your beautiful case."

"We can't do that until we get out of this turbulence. Just stay calm and wait it out," Yoshy instructed a stunned Nancy, as he saw her body visibly quivering.

The "Fasten Your Seat Belt" sign disappeared as well as the turbulence. 'This plane can't land fast enough,' Nancy thought as she tried to present a composed posture.

"Daijōbu desu, Goshimpai naku," (it's okay, no need to worry.) Yoshy tried calming Nancy while retrieving his scattered material. The stewardess quickly presented herself and offered them refreshments. "A hot cup of tea will calm your nerves," professed Yoshy as he put his work away. Yoshy sipped his sake while Nancy enjoyed her green tea. The hot liquid seemed to calm her emotional stress.

"I can't help but notice your beautiful leather brief-case. The leather is so soft and it seems to have many compartments. Would it be rude of me to ask where you got it? I'm usually not this forward, but it's a handsome piece."

Thinking to himself that he found most American's to be brash, obnoxious, and forward, admittedly not all of them. He couldn't let his true feelings come out. "I believe I bought this particular case somewhere in the States. I know the name of the store will come to me if I think of it for a while." Placing his index finger to his temple, closing his eyes, he let his mind relax. Yoshy tried to remember where in California he bought the sturdy brown leather case. "Hai, it was in a leather store on Rodeo Drive, in Beverly Hills, California.... I think the name of the place is Bally's, but I'm not absolutely sure. I am honored by your compliment."

"I can't thank you enough for remembering the name of the store. We do have a Beverly Hills location. The next time there, I'll go by the specialty shop."

Nancy realized that when they opened a Metamorphosis Salon in Japan she'd have to get used to the long flight, become accustomed to the Japanese people and their traditional etiquette. She closed her eyes and hoped sleep would again come to her.

Yoshy tried concentrating on his work but found it hard to pay attention to the words before him. His thoughts were a million miles away. He couldn't wait to get back to San Diego and find out if his latest project had been accomplished and his newest acquisition was where it was supposed to be. He could feel the tingling sensation in his loins as his penis enlarged by the mere thought of his latest art pieces. If this particular work, that he had admired for such a long time, was finally to be his, and his alone, to treasure, to adore with little regard for anyone who got in his way, he had to make sure that nothing would encumber his plan.

It had been many years that Yoshy became obsessive about valuable works of art and artifacts that were unusual. Thinking back, he couldn't remember the exact experience that made him appreciate the finer material objects. All he thought about was how he could acquire these priceless pieces. Of course his business was the main stream of his life that afforded him the necessary means for his fixation.

Nancy couldn't focus on the paperwork before her. Although she had more money than she'd ever need or use, her stomach was in knots. The preconceived notion that she and Suzanne would invest so much of their money into a spa in a country where the cost of living was astronomical, was inconceivable, if it were not laughable.

Nancy shook her head in bewilderment as she thought of Suzanne. She knew that the woman had no fears. She appreciated that any normal business woman wouldn't rely on gut feelings to open businesses. That was not the case when it came to Suzanne. Nancy had to admit that, so far, Suzanne's opinions and thoughts were right on the money.

Knowing that they would be landing shortly she let out a deep breath. Suzanne suddenly came to mind. Although she approved of her judgment in business, she felt that Suzanne was out of the realm in reality. Respecting her as an astute business woman, and very well admired in the industry, she thought that when it came to Stephen, Suzanne didn't think with her head, just her heart.

'She doesn't get the full picture,' Nancy thought. 'I couldn't go through the heartache that Suzanne does, enduring the knowledge that he's still a married man. The excuses he gives Suzanne makes me angry. Everyone that knows and loves Suzanne thinks that he should divorce his wife and marry, supposedly, his one and only love. I couldn't have people think of me as a "kept" woman. Of course people who don't know the entire story of their love, previous relationship and their undying adoration for each other could never understand.' On another level she also wished that Suzanne would give Lawrence a chance. 'Maybe she'll come to her senses and realize what a gem he is.' Nancy thought as she heard the plane's engines slowing down.

The airplane ride was tiring for all the passengers as they approached the runway after the long and confined flight. As the plane made its landing both Yoshy and Nancy were glad to be on solid ground. Each smiling as their individual thoughts and plans for the next project would become reality. Yoshy extended his hand and at the same time bowed slightly to his traveling companion for the last twelve hours. "Here is another one of my business cards. Please feel free to call me the next time you are in Japan. If I'm there I will be glad to show you around and answer any questions you might have. I'd love to show you the real Japan, not the tourist version. It was very nice talking to you."

Nancy also bowed, imitating the bow she received from Mr. Makino. Keeping her arms straight she let her palms slide down her thighs while lowering her torso. "Thank you very much for your card. I have my business cards somewhere in my purse." After riffling through her disorganized purse she came up with the business cards that all her friends advised her to have made. Nancy was glad that she paid attention to the people who had visited Japan and complied with this society where most Japanese people presented and expected businesses cards in return. She handed him her card and wished him a pleasant stay in San Diego.

The limo driver patiently waited for Mr. Makino to approach. With a quick gait he moved around the car and, after bowing, opened the door for his employer. As soon as Yoshy settled himself into the comfort of his limousine he dialed the telephone. He hoped the person he was calling was home. He hated talking to an answering machine that, all too often, people used for screening calls. To his amazement Mr. Jones answered. "Mr. Jones, Mr. Makino. Is my package waiting for me to pick up?"

"Well, no sir. It'll be ready in a few weeks. Some unexpected business forced me to postpone our little operation. I assure you that I'll have the package ready by then." Anticipating anger, Curtis continued, "There's more to this job than you can imagine. A lot of preparation has to be done to ensure nothing gets in my way. I'm sure it will be well worth the wait."

"Very well, I don't want any more excuses or delays. Do you understand?"

"Yes sir. Keep your eyes on the newspapers and the T. V. in the next few weeks. I'm sure you'll find some news that you'll find interesting. See you soon Mr. Makino."

'That man is the most frustrating person I've come across,' thought Curtis. 'If it weren't for all the money I receive from every one of the fine pieces I deliver to him, I'd tell him to go fuck him-self. I hate groveling. I shouldn't have to make excuses but I have to keep my temper and do my job efficiently and hope that no one gets hurt in the process.'

Curtis Jones paced his small bedroom and the feeling of claustrophobia was engulfing him. The plans of the huge mansion lay strewn around the bed and floor. The papers with the elaborate security system and it's intricate detail was covering the top of the plain maple desk situated on the outside wall. He had been studying the details of the floor plan and the exact location of the paintings that he had to steal. He thought of the people he worked for in Europe and realized that they were far more cordial. Their politeness was gained through their upbringing, he was sure of it. There were thieves in Europe and over the world that didn't have scruples, but at least he knew where he stood with them. Mr. Makino made Curtis nervous. He wasn't sure how he would deal with an imperfect job. Those beady eyes concerned him. He didn't trust him worth a dime. There was something sinister about that short, hot shot that didn't sit right with Curtis. He'd heard of the oriental gangs and how they deal with people who cross them. He realized that he'd have to pay better attention and make sure that everything went according to plan, Curtis contemplated as he, once more, went over every detail necessary for this robbery.

Curtis missed Kyle. As he looked around the cluttered apartment he grew irritated. He hated disorder. Once the theft was completed he would be able to clean up the mess and resume seeing Kyle. He found it difficult lying to Kyle about him having to take certain art courses that were mandatory in order for him to continue with his next degree. He knew it was necessary, because he couldn't let Kyle, his lover, know what his extra-curricular activity and hobby was. As far as he was concerned the heist couldn't come fast enough.

Suzanne wanted to hear from Nancy. It seemed like eternity since Nancy had gone to Japan to forge ahead with the plans for their newest investment. Suzanne kept calling Nancy's house and hung up the telephone when the answering machine, once again, came on.

'What is taking her so long to get home from the airport?' Suzanne asked herself. 'She should be home within an hour of departure. I hope nothing went wrong with the connection and she's okay.' While she was waiting for Nancy's arrival she decided to finish the wash and tidy up a bit. Simka followed her everywhere and kept rubbing against her legs. Her bushy tail was up, waiting for Suzanne to scratch the back of her ears. The purring began and Suzanne stopped what she was doing, put her bin of folded clothes on the floor, and sat on the first carpeted step and kept rubbing this small, beautiful Maine Coon cat, who thought she was a human. The repeated motion put Suzanne at ease. Within minutes, Boston turned the corner and pushed his way in front of Simka to make sure that he was also patted. Simka hissed and walked away, leaving Suzanne rubbing Boston as he rolled onto his back and let Suzanne scratch his stomach. "You are an impossible munchkin," she laughed as she got up from the step. His purring continued as she finished her chores.

She remembered when Mrs. Walsh, straight from Ireland, helped raise her children and would do everything pertaining to the house, leaving no task undone, allowing Suzanne to finish school. Now that Catherine was older and had bad arthritis Suzanne insisted on doing the cleaning and laundry. People who didn't know her well asked why she kept Mrs. Walsh. "After all, the children are grown and out of the house. She's an older woman who can't keep up with the responsibilities of the household." 'Didn't people ever hear of loyalty? There is no one like Mrs. Walsh,' Suzanne thought. 'She's like a surgate mother to me and grandmother to the girls. As far as I'm concerned she'll be with us as long as the good Lord sees fit to keep her. '

With one hand deftly holding her clean laundry, her chin on top of the clothing to assure them from not falling, the other hand grasping the railing, she expertly climbed the staircase. Suzanne got into her nightgown and put on her old, soft, and comfortable slippers. "Don't look at me that way. I'm not climbing into bed with you right now so just hold your horses." She resisted the temptation to climb into bed, get under the satiny comforter, cuddle with Simka and Boston and forget all the troubles of the world and whatever crazy thoughts about work and family that would invade her mind. Instead she once again headed downstairs.

Suzanne looked over her upcoming calendar and leaving no stone unturned, tried to rearrange her schedule for the next few weeks. She still wanted to go to Texas and surprise Stephen with a visit. She knew how happy he would be with an impromptu meeting. She missed Stephen and knew that he was getting impatient with her. He didn't understand how frustrated she was that she was unable to shift other people in her place. It seemed everyone had excuses and couldn't help her out. 'What if I were sick and couldn't work, then people would be sure to make the necessary changes. Well, I'll have to wait until Stephen comes here in a few more weeks,' a disappointed Suzanne thought.

Mrs. Walsh came downstairs and joined Suzanne at the kitchen table. "Okay, what's on your mind? What's bothering you? Spit it out." Suzanne told her she was worried about her father and how he seemed to be tired all the time.

"Well, I'm sure you realize that your parents are getting older, as I am. These things happen. If you feel that your father should be seen by a doctor or specialist, and it will relieve your mind, then talk to your parents and see what's going on. What else are you worried about?"

"Spencer will probably ask Hope to marry him. Having had a bad relationship and ultimately divorce, one becomes very sensitive to this subject. Marriage is hard enough, these days, without the added burdens of religious and cultural differences. His parents might be polite to Hope, for they're well educated, come from old money and are polished. I on the other hand, might appear to be miss sophisticate, but I'm a city kid and I don't mind swearing when I feel like it. I'm well rounded and know the score. But I'd bet my bottom dollar that they won't be happy having Hope for a daughter-in-law. They'll think of her as a social climber, and being raised Jewish is another problem. In their circle that's really frowned upon."

"Suzanne, are you voicing your concerns and transferring your feelings to theirs? It seems to me that you're prejudging them without any substantial justification. You might be pleasantly surprised. You're going to drive yourself crazy with all of your worrying."

ANDERLECHT BELGIUM

Lawrence sat behind his massive, cherry wood desk at his corporate headquarters in Belgium. The children were safely back at their particular private schools. While he missed them when they were gone, he needed this respite to gain back the energy that was drained from him so effectively when they were home. He was luckier than most parents raising children singularly, in the fact that his parents, staff and nannies were always there to help. Hubert, Hendrik and Carolyn were growing up nicely, though not entirely without the typical teenage rebellion and incidents. When profoundly troubled he often talked to his dear, deceased wife, Elizabeth, of the frustrations that resulted from various occurrences. Laughing to himself, she never had answers to his difficult situations but it still felt good to get them off his chest.

It was many years since Elizabeth died unexpectedly. He still missed her. Although many of his friends and colleagues tried to fix him up with an "appropriate woman," he didn't want any part of the dating scene. Through the years he had an occasional date and when deemed necessary, escorted a lovely woman to one of the more important social events. He was considered one of the most eligible, desirable bachelors of the century, handsome, rich, intelligent and witty. Many flirtatious women made excuses to gain his attention, but all failed. The only woman who aroused any type of stimulation was Suzanne. He was fascinated by her and stirred emotions in him that he hadn't felt in years.

He leaned back in his chair, put his feet up on his large, beautifully appointed desk and closed his eyes. Images of Suzanne penetrated his thoughts. It was two years ago when he first met Suzanne, thanks to Louis. Since then every time he saw or thought of her, feelings he hadn't had in years stirred inside his heart and soul. There were barriers that had to be broken but he realized that only his desire and determination would prevail. Suzanne had self-imposed these limitations on their relationship and although frustration sometimes cast an obstruction, he knew that his fortitude and dauntless perseverance would ultimately win her over.

In another month he would be back in the States for business and would get in touch with her. He'd promised Suzanne that the next time he was in Boston they'd take off for a week or so and she would show him all the sights of the region, realizing that one week would not be enough.

A smile crossed his face as he envisioned her by his side driving thru the various towns, cities and States close by.

Suzanne was having a restless night's sleep. The hot toddy didn't help her. She tossed from one side to the other, waiting for slumber to embrace her when the telephones' ring interrupted her thoughts.

"Suzanne, is that you? It's me Lawrence. I know you don't get to bed till very late so I thought I'd take a chance and find you up. How are you and what's going on?"

"Oh my gosh, Suzanne exclaimed, I don't believe it. I think of you often and yes, I wasn't asleep so I'll forgive you for calling at this hour. Larry, it's so nice hearing your voice. I'm fine and the family is well. There is so much going on that

I don't know if there are enough hours for me to even start relating all the things that are happening."

Lawrence detested the nickname "Larry" but for some reason didn't mind, and even liked it, when Suzanne referred to him other than to his given name.

"Well, I'm coming to the States in four weeks and was hoping that we'll be able to see each other. I was thinking that if you could take a couple of days off you would accompany me to parts of New England that I haven't seen. Friends of mine recommended that I see Maine and Vermont."

"What a lovely idea. Maine is one of my favorite states and there are many delightful and fun places to see. I love Ogunquit and the Marginal Way. It's breathtaking to walk along the path and see the beautiful ocean right there. To see the surf crashing against the large rocks is magnificent and if you love fresh fish then the restaurants are great. Then we can continue up the coast to Wells, Kennybunk and Kennybunkport. I love going into the small shops and browsing."

"If you truly fall in love with Maine, on our next journey there, we could eat at The White Barn. I think we should put it in both our calendars. We'll go there around Christmas time. The restaurant is beautiful around the holidays. The owner is a European gentleman and you'd enjoy the food, I especially like the way it's presented, typically European. It reminds me of some of the great European restaurants that I've been to."

"That sound's wonderful Suzanne. Put it in your calendar and I'll make sure I'll put the date into mine."

Suzanne continued, "We could also go to the White Mountains in New Hampshire. The grandeur of the mountains is spectacular and they also have large lakes hidden at the base of these mountains. Maybe you've heard of the Mount Washington Hotel? It's a grand old, beautiful hotel. When you see the red roof you know you've arrived."

Larry said. "I've heard about the ghost that roams around the hotel. You know there are many stories of haunted castles throughout Europe. Someday I'll have to take and show you some of the beautiful areas of the country that you've only heard of but never seen. Of course we'll have to stay at some of the more notable ones that are said to be haunted. Separate bedrooms if you're wondering," Lawrence laughed out loud.

"If I'm around at the time of your visit then I'll look forward to showing you the area. How long will you be in the States?" Suzanne asked, trying to change the subject.

"At least a month," Lawrence responded as he grinned from ear to ear. 'Maybe longer if I have anything to say about it. I might actually make you fall in love with me.'

"Call me either at my office or at home when you're in Boston and I'll have a better idea of my schedule." 'What am I saying? I can't make any commitment when so much is happening all around me. I couldn't make an obligation to Stephen, how can I tell Larry I'll go away with him. I must be going crazy. When he calls me at the time he's in Boston, I'll have to make my excuse then.' Suzanne put down the phone and looked at the ceiling, feelings of guilt overwhelmed her.

Suzanne lay in bed after the call and found it more difficult to fall asleep. Larry's admiration for her, she knew, deep within her heart, couldn't be ignored much longer. Feelings of remorse and frustration besieged her when she wanted to go away and leave all her cares and worries behind. 'How can I make time decisions when this stupid incident with Madaline has to be dealt with?' Suzanne closed her eyes and realized it was useless. Thoughts of Larry and Stephen kept running through her mind. The more elusive Stephen was becoming the more Larry appealed to her.

Thoughts of Lawrence, or Larry as she liked to call him, kept resurfacing. Was she being silly by not taking his intentions seriously? She'd known him for many years and had nothing but respect and admiration for this wonderful gentleman. He was a decent man with integrity that she found it hard not to find him interesting and irresistibly manly. She couldn't forget well-built and handsome as well. She knew in her heart that she could never become serious with him because she really loved Stephen. But, then thoughts of all his excuses for not divorcing his so called, wife, came to mind. She found herself getting angry.

CHAPTER SIX

Suzanne thought of their sleeping arrangements and although he was desirable, and a handsome man, there was no way that she would sleep with him. They would have to get separate rooms. All of a sudden she started getting hot flashes and threw the covers off her. 'This is ridiculous, a grown woman thinking about having a fling and I'm not even married. I'm single and rightly so, I can go with whomever I please.' She knew this was bravado but still in the recesses of her mind a little voice kept repeating the names Stephen and Lawrence and their faces kept swirling around in her head. She picked up a novel on her night-side table and started reading. Within ten minutes she was asleep.

He couldn't help but feel elated each time he spoke to Suzanne. She was vibrant, beautiful and a great conversationalist. She made him happy just by listening to the way her voice exuded excitement.

Gathering important papers to take home with him, he put an ascot around his neck, buttoned the dark wool coat and walked to the automobile. A smile appeared on his face as he thought of Suzanne. He was a patient man and knew that anything good was worth waiting for. He couldn't put off returning to the States to be near her once again.

Suzanne was in her office when Madaline called. "I don't know if Paul Winston has called you but I think he's tracking every person I know or who I've been in contact with throughout my life. It might prove to be embarrassing. I got a call from my third husband's mother, for God Sakes. I didn't know what to say when she lit into me about someone noising around about her "wonderful Barry." I wanted to gag. I could have told her some real good stories about her "wonderful Barry" but I didn't want to get into a pissing contest. I can't sleep at night, thinking about all the people who hate me. Why would anyone want to hurt me, or for that matter, kill me? Don't you dare get smart assed with me, just let me vent."

On the way home from work her mind went into overload. 'I know she has a lot of enemies, but God, everyone has people that hate them.' Her cell phone rang and she barely answered before it went into message. "Suzanne, pick up the dam phone, I have to tell you what happened. I was on stage after everyone was finished with rehearsal. I was just taking my time and all of a sudden Paul runs onto the stage and pushes me, like five feet. He knocked me on my ass and I was shaking like a leaf. All of a sudden the steel beam comes crashing down where I was standing a minute ago. He runs up the stairs but he couldn't find anyone. The main stagehand came out and he was flabbergasted."

"There was no reason for that beam to crash. I mean it's supposed to be secured. Can you imagine if everyone was on stage and that landed on someone? They'd be dead. I'm still shaking. Paul said it definitely was tampered with. The police were called to investigate. They took all kinds of prints, but Paul said they wouldn't find any, because whoever messed around with it apparently knew what they were doing, making sure that no prints would be found. Paul saw to it that the incident wouldn't get reported to the news media. That's all we'd need. I didn't even see Paul in the theater. He's like an invisible person."

Suzanne dialed Madaline back. "First of all, thank God you're okay. I'm glad that the police are involved. Maybe they can be of help."

"I hope so, but it's unlikely. I'm putting my bet on Paul."

"Oh! It's Paul now. We're getting a little chummy are we?"

"Knock it off, Suzanne, I'm just saying he's awfully nice and I feel safe with him around. That's all."

By the time Suzanne was on Rt. 3 her headache was unbearable. She couldn't wait to force dinner down and go to sleep.

The quiet and darkness of the house contributed to her restlessness. The normal noises that one would ignore during the light of day magnified itself with every sound. They generated from the clanging furnace, natural creaking floorboards, and settling of the house. Simka and Boston were on either side of her, softly snoring. With all these issues turbulently swirling within her, she fell into an unsettled sleep.

Madaline was exhausted, especially after yesterday's fiasco. She didn't feel safe anywhere she went. She imagined noises. Besides, the grueling schedule of performing twice daily, seven days a week, was taking its toll on her. Even though she managed to go to the Metamorphosis Salon for her daily relaxation massage, she realized she needed more rest. In between acting in the play, always reading parts for new scripts that continually came to her from her manager and agent, shopping and talking to her many friends from all over the world got tiring. Trying to contact Kyle, who never seemed to be home, was getting her angry and worried. 'Where the hell could he be? He never seems to be home.' She tried hooking up with either Suzanne or Nancy but their schedules always conflicted. She was thankful that she knew that Paul was no more than seconds away from her.

When she finally heard from Kyle he seemed tired and a bit distant. Attempting to seek answers to issues that he seemed to avoid talking about, she risked calling her daughter-in-law, Carol Williams. Carol was one of the top models for the Ford Modeling Agency. She found that Carol was out of the country shooting for the winter issue of Glamour magazine. Carol was then heading to Israel for a private showing. She had an empty feeling whenever she thought about her son and Carol's marriage. She loved her daughter-in-law and couldn't love her any more than if she were her own. Seeing a lot of her friends having grandchildren made Madaline envious. She would love having grandkids of her own and doubted that wish would be fulfilled in the immediate future. Being pessimistic with all that was happening to her, Madaline thoughts ran wild. 'Kids now a days postpone starting a family thinking there's plenty of time. Little do they realize just how fast time passes. They want to save money, establish themselves professionally and get all traveling out of their system so then they can devote time for their family, if and when they decide to start one. The longer they wait and if they are in their mid-forties to start a family, people don't realize that they won't have the same patience and stamina that they'd have for children if they had them earlier in their lives. '

Madaline felt alone and wanted to express her feelings and emotions to someone that she could bitch to and let out her frustrations. Racking her brain to find a friend that wasn't away or too busy with their own issues and businesses she scanned her private telephone directory. As she was about to pick up the receiver and call Alan, someone knocked on her suite door. Absentmindedly, she opened the door without asking who was there. Paul came barging in and reamed her a new asshole. Pointing his finger at her he yelled, "Didn't I tell you to never, ever, answer this door? If someone tells you they're from the hotel, call the front desk. Didn't I, Didn't I," he yelled. He moved fast and suddenly she found herself thrown onto the sofa.

She tried calming herself but all she could do was cry. Her entire body was shaking and tears were flowing from her eyes. She felt awful. Paul saw how frightened she was. He realized and felt bad that he came down so hard on her. He tried calming her, sitting next to her, he put his arm around her shoulder. 'God she's beautiful' he thought as he tried soothing her. The sobs continued and suddenly she looked up and saw this muscular man, rough, ruddy skin, a beautiful cleft chin, salt and pepper wavy hair and all she saw was a hero. She didn't know how it happened. Suddenly he was kissing her tears away.

She loved the way he felt. His lips were soft, and supple. Before she realized, she brought her arms around his neck and kissed his neck, then their lips met. It had been years since Madaline felt exhilaration like this. The kiss seemed to last forever. He gently rubbed her back and slightly lifted her sweater so he could feel the taught, firm, smooth skin from her shoulders to her waist. He definitely wanted more but reigned himself in. 'Stop this, it's not ethical. I can't do this to her. Even though she's beautiful, as a matter of fact, dam right gorgeous, I can't compromise us like this. For God sakes, she's my client."

He pulled away, gently pulling down the back of her sweater and slowly parted his lips from hers. "I'm sorry Madaline, really, truly am sorry. I didn't mean to come down so hard on you. I've been worried and want to look after you. I'm sorry I made you cry. I want to apologize for breaking my own rule. We have a professional relationship which I can't compromise. I hope you can forgive me." He put his hands on his face and his elbows on his knees. He kept shaking his head.

Madaline was shocked. It'd been years since she felt this type of magnetism. 'He pulled away,' she thought. 'Geez, I must really be losing my touch. How could he just stop in the middle of our kissing?' Straightening herself up, she wiped her tears and acted as if nothing happened. "It's an accident for God sake, get a grip. I apologize that I made you mad and I promise it won't happen again. As far as us kissing, we got carried away, that's all. Can I get you a drink or something?" Madaline asked, trying not to show how upset and disappointed she was. "By the way, why did you come over unexpectedly?"

"No apparent reason, I wanted to check up on you, that's all. I'll take a rain check on that drink, thanks, Madaline, I better go. Again, I'm sorry. Just be careful and don't open the door unless you know who's on the other side. Okay?"

"I promise, as God is my witness, an incident like that will never happen again. Though I'm keeping you at your word, the drink will be here waiting for you."

"I'll definitely take a rain check when we get to the bottom of this episode. Till then, I'll be watching your back without you realizing it. Act normal and we'll find out who the culprit is."

He closed the door and took the elevator down to the lobby and all the while kept wanting to kick himself for letting his feelings show.

Madaline put her back to the door and closed her eyes. 'Boy, that was some kiss! I hope he solves my case quickly. I'd love to get to know Paul on a more personal level.' She went back to the sofa, clutched the loose pillow and held it to her chest. She closed her eyes and tried to remember when a man kissed her last. 'It must have been uneventful if I can't remember when or who the hell it was.' After resting for a while she got up and dressed for this evenings performance.

'I'm running late.' Madaline thought. 'I'll have to call Alan when I have time to talk to him. Maybe I'll call him after the play. '

Knowing Alan as she did, she knew that it was never too late to call him. Alan picked up the phone, answering on the second ring. "My God, what a pleasant surprise. How are you doing? I went to see Beyond Murder two weeks ago with some of my friends and we still haven't stopped talking about it. Girl, you are great!!"

"Why didn't you let me know that you were in the audience? I would have had you and your friends back stage and then go out for a bite to eat. I'm always famished after a show."

"I didn't think that you'd want to be bothered, especially during a week day. Anyways, some of my friends are obnoxious, if you know what I mean. I don't think they'd have appreciated you're going out of your way to be with them. Anyway, it's moot. I'd have wanted you all to myself."

"You say such flattering things. Now that I'm in Boston we'll have to get together. Tell me, how is your brother doing? Suzanne told me what happened. Is he doing better? What have you been up to?"

"First of all, what can I say? He fucked his life up royally. Only he can rectify what he became and the way he conducts his affairs. I don't blame Nancy for wanting to go on with her life. She's too young, beautiful and vivacious to want to be pitied. I'd go after her myself if she were a different gender. Only kidding. I don't know if Peter will go back to his profession. That's the only work that he does well and if he doesn't get over what happened and knows what he wants from life, then I think he'll be screwed and never find an answer."

My parents will completely forget what transpired, blocking it from their minds and never talk or think about the incident again. They'll make up an excuse in their minds. But that is always how it's been with my parents and Peter The Great. He never could do anything wrong. I, on the other hand, could never do anything right. Even today, with my paintings selling for thousands and my name mentioned in many periodicals and magazines, they have never once said how proud they are of me or my work. Go figure it out. They didn't even know that I was gay until a few years ago."

"As far as my work, it's going great. Justin asked me to become a partner and we'll be opening galleries in major cities throughout the States and eventually we'll go on to Europe. But that's not in the immediate future for now. Hey, let's try to make a date when Nancy, Suzanne, Justin and I can get free. We'll make an effort. Knowing that it has to be after the performance, we'll keep it in the Boston area. Thanks for calling and I'll get back to you real soon."

Madeline never tired of Alan's descriptive escapades. "Well, I'd better let you go. I have to get up early. Now make sure that you get a day and time for all of us to get together. By the way Bill is also invited."

"I know that silly." Alan hung up the phone and went into the den to sit next to his love, Bill.

Alan always enjoyed talking to Madaline. She was one of his favorite people. He was thankful that Suzanne introduced them and the rest was history. He wondered how Kyle was doing. 'That boy, a man now, is so talented. His photographs are featured in all of the hottest magazines.' Sometimes Alan wondered if there wasn't a little something about him that he was hiding.

'Kyle seems a lot like me before I came out. But no, he's happily married or seems to be. Though, in the circle that Kyles in,' Alan thought, 'it's not unusual for a guy to be married and live a double life.' Alan knew a lot of gay and transvestites that had wives and families, thinking to himself that an arrangement like that would be hard to take. He imagined the transsexual's children telling their friends that they have two mothers. That freaked him out. He was happy that Bill and he had found each other and we're partners for life.

Madaline found herself wound up and couldn't relax. She poured herbal bath salts into the steaming tub and waited patiently for the bath water to fill to the desired level. Sitting in the tub, enjoying the peace and tranquility, she took a sip of the chardonnay and rested her head on the white, foam pillow that was in back of her head. It was good hearing Alan's voice again. He was a lovely young man. She couldn't understand how parents would show such unbiased favoritism amongst siblings. Thankfully she had Kyle. She had wanted other children, heaving a big sigh, but accepting that it wasn't in the cards. Taking another sip of wine, she wanted to get a buzz so she wouldn't have to think of the shame that she was hiding. She felt sorry for herself and every year on a certain date she'd go to her room, wherever she was, and cry herself to sleep. For years Madaline fought the evil thoughts that continually plagued her. She was ashamed and embarrassed by what happened that God awful day. It wasn't her or her parent's fault she kept telling herself. They just didn't believe her for whatever reason.

To this day, she couldn't understand the way she was treated by parents who, she thought, were so wonderful. Even after all this time she couldn't forget the hurt, embarrassment and shame she felt. 'If only I didn't spend so much time doing my chores or taking care of my horse. I didn't understand why Trigger started neighing and rearing up his front legs. Before I knew what was happening, a cold, calloused hand went over my mouth and a knife was put to the side of my throat. He dragged me into the barn, pushed me down on the hay pile, pulled down my pants, ripped my shirt, and raped me. I couldn't see his face because of the scarf he was wearing. I remember trying to fight him off, punching and kicking as much as I could. He just laughed and kept saying, "I love a tough little cowgirl like you. Keep fighting me. I get longer and harder every time you try to hurt me."

"I was so innocent and young that I didn't know what he meant by those words. I figured it mustn't be good, I was exhausted, tired and scared shitless. My knees and entire body was shaking, I don't know how he pried them apart. I eventually gave up the struggle. Then I remember feeling pain. I'd never felt anything like it. After he was done with me, he pushed me to the side. I was shivering all over. I quickly got up and jumped on his back as he was walking away. I was happy that I was able to grab his red and blue handkerchief. With one swift motion I pulled it down off of his face. I couldn't believe who had done this terrible and dishonorable thing to me. He was my father's best friend. He'd give me and my sibling's rides into town. He was always at our house. We considered him kin. I remember spitting in his face and all he did was laugh. I can still smell the alcohol on his breath. I wanted to throw up. I ran as fast as I could to my house and took 2 steps at a time to the second floor where the bedrooms were. I threw myself across the bed and couldn't stop crying and quivering. I filled the tub with scalding hot water and kept scrubbing myself with a rough wash cloth until I bled and the water became red. I wanted to die.'

All her life she imagined herself falling in love, having a nice wedding, honeymoon and living happily ever after. Of course she would have 4 children, 2 boys and 2 girls. She had already picked out their names.

'God has a way of punishing you if you do something against his wishes' she thought, as she again drained her glass and poured another glass of wine. She often asked herself why she couldn't get pregnant after having Kyle. 'I'll never know. After all I went through, going to countless doctors, they couldn't figure it out. I guess it wasn't meant to be. I'm lucky that I at least have one wonderful son. Someday, someday, I might have the nerve to find my other child '

Assuming that I was lucky enough to have had other children, I could never pit one against the other like the Tremblays do and never choose favorites. They are so lucky to have such a wonderful son like Alan. They should thank their lucky stars. Not that I'm prejudice or anything like that but I'm thankful that Kyle is such a great young man, handsome, smart, intelligent, and has a nice wife, what else could I ask for? Weeell, maybe a grandchild or two, but who's counting.' Emptying her glass she quickly refilled it and waited for the buzz to hit her. 'To have this quiet time is just what I need,' she thought, as she emptied some of the now tepid water from the tub and replenished it with more hot water. Thinking again of Alan and Peter's situation she couldn't help but wonder if Kyle had come to her as an adolescent or young man and told her that he was gay, what her reaction would be. 'Yes, I know that I'd be disappointed but I would still love him. After all, half of the actors and friends of mine are gay. '

Draining her umteenth glass of wine she quickly climbed out of the tub and wrapped the luxurious, heavy cotton bathrobe around herself, avoiding any kind of cool that might cause her to get chilled and ultimately become sick.

Madaline was wobbly as she tried walking to the luxurious bed. She got under the soft downy comforter and thanked God that Kyle was well, healthy and a "normal" young man. She picked up a new script that was sent to her. As she lay in bed, trying to read the words, they were indiscernible. She could feel herself dozing just before she dropped the manuscript and fell into slumber.

Justin walked from his Newbury Street office and gallery to Commonwealth Ave., where his condo was located. The air was brisk and invigorating. Watching the college students carrying backpacks and conversing with one another, reminded him of his college days studying in the States and abroad. He patted the tail wagging, golden retriever that he saw daily, being walked by a stunning young lady. He took a goody out of his pocket to give to the dog. Justin climbed the brick steps to the large building that he purchased years ago. He was lucky when two apartments became available on the first and second floor at the same time. With the help of an experienced and imaginative architect and contractor he was able to make a two story condo that was massive. Opening the beautiful walnut and glass door he piled the mail onto his Louis the 4th secretariat table and allowed himself to sit down and relax on his soft, overstuffed, brown leather sofa. Justin couldn't imagine himself in a home that had delicate and nonfunctional furniture to sit on. He propped his large feet atop the coffee table that he specifically had made for the room.

Sighing, Justin thought, 'after all, I do have a rather large frame. I like and appreciate the eclectic look. The fragile and unusual pieces of art, furniture and statues that I have scattered about makes me feel good when people admire them. Though it isn't often that I entertain here.' He would record the episodes from the chefs from all the new television shows and watch them at his leisure. Justin loved to experiment with different dishes and enjoyed going to the market to purchase the unusual delicacies that helped make up these uncommon feasts.

Justin liked to entertain large crowds and usually did this at his gallery. They could walk around, mingle and enjoy the new pieces of art that he acquired. For these people he hired the best caterer in the area. He enjoyed preparing his favorite dishes for guests in his luxurious dwelling for a few of his intimate friends.

He kicked off his size 16 shoes and wiggled his toes, he picked up the latest art journals. He became engrossed, especially interested in the newsletters from Culture Without Context and other books from the Illicit Antiques Research Centre. These manuscripts had reports and articles of archeology to preserve the world's cultural heritage. What he found interesting was there had been an unusually high rate of thefts from some of the castles and museums throughout Europe, which he already knew about. Some of the Earls and Counts of these castles he knew intimately. All of these pieces that were listed were so valuable that the estimated insurance pricing would be difficult to pay.

As he read these articles it peaked his interest even more. Thoughts of someone invading his home and privacy was unimaginable. 'I would be heartbroken if even one of my possessions was stolen. How violated I would feel if someone broke into my house and took the beautiful pieces of art that I adore.' Many of these Counts and Barons, although highly regarded, didn't have the wealth people thought they did. They still put on airs and if they hadn't inherited their luxurious castles and mansions they wouldn't be living as they were. They told him, confidentially, that it was hard for them to pay taxes, servants, and to keep up pretenses.

He also read and heard from curators around the world that these crimes amounted to between $4.5 and $8 billion dollars a year. Profits from art sales directly fund European organized crime. These scumbags serve as main suppliers to the worldwide trade of weapons, arms and drugs. Other thefts from museums, such as Degas, Cezanne, Van Gogh, Monet and Picasso are sold or bartered on a closed black market for an equivalent value of goods or services.

Justin remembered 2 individuals who were finally captured and paid their dues. Claiming he had dementia, it didn't stop Robert Mararosian from stealing seven paintings from Michael Bakurin. Michael couldn't have loved the return of Cezanne's painting, Bouilloireet Fruits. He eventually auctioned the painting at Sotheby's and received $29.3 million for it. Another sick individual built a secret gallery for his private collection of stolen art. No one would consider Stephane Breitwieser, who worked as a waiter and lived with his mother at the time, an art thief. When he was finally caught trying to steal a Bugle from a museum in Lucerne, Switzerland, he admitted stealing 239 artworks and other exhibits together valued at $2.4 billion dollars. For all of his escapades and the hurt rendered to many individuals who either had these pieces in their homes or donated them to museums, he received 26 months in prison. He was such a devoted connoisseur he was able to recall the smallest detail of every piece he stole.

Justin put down the articles and wondered around his palatial home admiring his paintings and objects that he methodically picked. 'I already spoke to many of my friends and told them my theory about the Gardner Museums art theft. But now I'm really going to pursue my gut feeling and try to find out who this culprit or group is. I'll first try going to the police and if nothing happens there, then I'll contact the FBI, and Interpol, which runs the sole international data base, and Scotland Yard. I also know of 2 national agencies as well, TREIMA in France and Italy's LEONARDO. I don't need anyone to help me, I can do it myself. I'll keep my eyes and ears open to hearsay, not arousing anyone's attention.' Being the kind of person he was, he had to find a way, no matter what it took, to help catch these conniving and dangerous thieves. 'It has its advantages to be a well-respected connoisseur of art and admired in the art community here and abroad.'

Pouring himself a Merlot he took out the steak that he had marinating in the refrigerator, and put it onto the counter top. He knew it was late to eat but he really didn't care. If he went to bed hungry he'd never fall asleep. A pre-made salad was taken out of the refrigerator. Going to the stove and examining the green beans, guaranteeing they were done to perfection, they had to be crunchy, he drained them and sprinkled almonds on top. He didn't mind eating alone, he was used to it. It gave him time to contemplate many decisions and then read the paper, even though most of the stories were unhappy ones. On his second glass of Merlot the phone interrupted his enjoyable meal.

"Oh Alan, it's you," exclaimed Justin. "Then I don't mind the interruption, even though my steak is made to perfection and is scrumptious. it melts in my mouth and the green beans are perfect, and will get cold, and my home made salad dressing is delightful. Other than that, how can I help you?"

"I'll call you back, better yet, you call me when you're through with your dinner. Since Bill is away for business, I find myself eating take out. I'm so sick and tired of Burger King and Chinese that if I see another double burger or lo mien I'll run."

"That's all right my dear young man. I'm half teasing you. After all, with all the weight I've gained I should be eating half portions. What can I do for you?"

"Well, you know how you want to make me a partner. I want to know when the papers will be drawn up?"

"I was thinking that when Bill comes home from this latest business trip, he and I can take an excursion throughout Europe where I'll do some preliminary work. Do some unofficial scouting of places we might want to locate our galleries."

"My dear Alan, there would be nothing more that I'd enjoy than to see you and Bill take pleasure in seeing the many splendid sights of Europe. But now I need you here in the states. There are many things going on that I need your help with. I have to spend some time in Europe myself, but that's down the road a bit. For now, put a hold on the thought and we'll talk about your idea at our leisure. Now my steak awaits me. Oh dear, I forgot to take the bread out of the oven. I'm as bad as Suzanne I'm afraid. She's always forgetting something or another when entertaining."

CHAPTER SEVEN

Besides Yoshy anticipating the new paintings he would be getting from Mr. Jones, he couldn't wait to see Robin. He felt Robin was the best thing that ever happened to him. It was incredible how they met, fell in love and eventually became lovers. He bought her the brick mansion they cohabited in, whenever he was in San Diego.

The light of his private line flashed, interrupting his thoughts. He quickly answered it. He hoped it was Mr. Jones but knew better, it was too early. Mr. Jones had informed Yoshy that the job would take another couple of weeks. He wondered who was calling him? Not many people knew his private number.

"Hi honey, I thought you told me you'd be back about this time. For some strange reason I found myself dialing your number."

"You can understand how surprised I was when you answered. When did you get back?"

"I landed last evening but I didn't want to disturb you so I stayed in my office, catching up on work that I missed. I'm, glad you called. When I come home tonight we'll go out for dinner, okay with you?"

"Sure, tell me what time you want me to be ready and I'll be waiting for you with open arms."

"Let's say around seven thirty. I'll have my driver let me off at the house and from there we'll walk to any restaurant you'd like. I know we don't live far from any of your favorite places. Make the reservation. All I ask is that they put us at a secluded table." The weather hadn't dropped as much as he had anticipated. He wished that he'd dressed in a cooler shirt and pants as he left his office.

She clicked off the television when she heard the key unlocking the front door. She put her arms around Yoshy and kissed him passionately. All logical thoughts left him as he slid his hands under her bright, yellow, cotton sweater and felt her smooth skin as he returned her kiss. Letting her go, he held her at arm's length, smiling as he admired her flawless, pale complexion, framed by her long blond hair. Her blue eyes sparkled and her cheerful smile revealed her naturally white, perfect, straight, teeth while her cheeks emphasized two large dimples.

"It's good to hold you once again in my arms. You'll never know how I've missed you. Come, you won't need a sweater. We'll talk on our way to the restaurant." The warm night air made the walk perfect. Yasuhito, his limo driver didn't have to be told what to do. He followed the hand holding couple discreetly, a block away, making sure that his boss would not be bothered by any undesirable characters.

The waiter knew them and ushered the lovely looking couple to their usual table. "Thank you, Tony, for accommodating us on such short notice."

"Always a pleasure to be of service to you Mr. Makino."

"Yoshy, I'm glad you're back. It's been too long since your last visit." With a mischievous twinkle in her eyes, she said, "I'll show you my appreciation when we go home after our meal."

Whenever he was in the States he tried forgetting about his family, friends, and acquaintances. The old saying, when in Rome due as the Roman's do, was a motto that Yoshy adhered to. Although he liked his traditional Japanese food, and his saké he tried acclimating to the American style cooking.

Yoshy wanted to forget all business matters and concentrate on being with Robin. His eyes sparkled. He had a hard time containing his emotions, looking over her voluptuous body and focusing on her gorgeous breasts. "I feel like a large piece of roast beef and I know you love veal, Osso Bucco, or the rack of lamb that they prepare so well. Let's drink, and eat to our hearts content," commented Yoshy. They toasted each other. "I'll call for my driver to pick us up when we're through. I don't want to waste any time." With a grin he told Robin, "We'll manage to think of something to do afterwards."

Yoshy leaned back with his chair, closed his eyes, feeling full after consuming the entire dinner. "Yoshy, are you okay?"

"Yes, yes, my beautiful butterfly. I should be used to the time difference, but every time I come to the States, I need a few days to catch up. I usually get jet lag, but this occasion was ridiculous, that red head sitting beside me wouldn't be quiet and I couldn't get a minute's peace or sleep. Don't worry my pet. I'm not that tired to disappoint either of us."

"Oh Yoshy, you're so sweet. It's been many years, yet it feels as if it were yesterday, that we've been together." She continued, "I mean getting the beautiful house and providing all the furniture and everything that I need to make this our home." Reaching over the table she held his hand. "I'll always be devoted to you." She kissed the back of his soft, but manly hands. "You're so generous and handsome as well. I'll forever love, care and always be true to you."

"No more work for my sweetheart. You are only to enjoy yourself and be there for me whenever I come home to the States."

Yoshy got his key out and opened the door. While going directly into the master suite, he started taking his clothes off and saw Robin doing the same, leaving a trail of clothes behind. They went directly into the shower and washed each other, getting aroused while they washed the other person. He loved the way Robins' hands, so soft and nimble, worked the soap into a glorious lather and washed his entire body. He loved the way her fingers lingered around his nipples and pulled at them ever so lightly. She then followed his torso down to his groin, making his manhood stand erect, while her fingers lingered and caressed him. After he climaxed she washed him again. He in turn, repeated the method, feeling her large, uplifted breasts, washing them and pulling her nipples till she cried in frustration. He sucked her nipples while his soapy hands found her sensual spot and couldn't stop touching her until he felt her quiver and knew, once she moaned, he had made her happy.

They then dried each other off and went directly under the soft covers of their comfortable bed. Yoshy couldn't get enough of her. After a few minutes of re-cooperation time he once again couldn't contain himself. His hands automatically caressed her body, lingering at her erotic areas and realized how hot Robin was becoming.

After both were sated they cuddled and fell into slumber. The next morning he felt relaxed and ready for a full day's work. After consuming a delicious breakfast that Robin prepared, he knew that his driver/bodyguard, Yasuhito, would be patiently waiting for him outside the house. Smiling, he said to himself, 'I don't have to go back to Japan for Shinjuku or the Ginza. I have my personal Kabuki-cho, Ginza, especially icbi-ryu with me here in America.' Yoshy put his head on the soft leather headrest of the limo, thinking how life couldn't be better.

Arriving at his spacious office he sat back in his black leather chair, once again thinking of Mr. Curtis Jones. 'I hope Mr. Jones will complete this latest task efficiently. There's no reason to imagine otherwise. In the past, Mr. Jones always accomplished his assignments with speed and unquestioned expertise. It's been a year,' Yoshy thought to himself, 'Usually Mr. Jones doesn't take this long to complete a task I ask him to do.' Yoshy appreciated that this particular job was more involved than the others had been. It was now coming to fruition and he knew he had to curtail his excitement. He forced himself to get back to the immediate business at hand.

Curtis went to work at the art gallery as usual, his stomach in knots. This would be the last evening of his charade. He couldn't wait to get rid of his awful disguise. He'd make sure to burn the clothes he wore for this janitorial job in another part of town. He hated wearing the stupid beard and mustache. It always made his skin itch. As much as he complained about the disgusting blond wig, while looking in the mirror, he thought that the color did something for his complexion. 'Maybe someday I'll dye my hair blond and put darker lowlights in it. Kyle will flip out when he sees how it changes my looks.'

'It will be worth everything I've gone through if all goes according to my plan. I'll obtain Gainsborough's Blue Boy and Sir Thomas Lawrence's Pinky for Mr. Makino. At the same time I might be able to take a painting that I've admired for years. I've always loved George Romney's, The Clavering Children. If I take a large, burlap bag, I might be able to pick up that Silver-Gilt Standing Cup and Cover from London and at the same time I might just throw in the pair of Silver Candelabras that Thomas Heming made in London. Wouldn't it be a hoot to entertain and be able to have these Candelabras in the middle of the table?'

Composing himself he walked into the main gallery. He started to re-arrange some of the paintings on the wall, making room for new acquisitions that he recently unpacked. He saw one of his regular customers come through the front door with a new designer, raising an eyebrow he thought to himself, 'maybe she has a new lover.'

The two of them made him show all the new pieces since the last time she was in. After spending over an hour and ½ with them, they walked out with an Italo-Flemish (c. 1600), bronze statue.

At noon he checked his large tool kit which he used as his lunch box that camouflaged his implements. His fellow janitorial workers kidded him unmercifully on how many sandwiches he could get into the box and were amazed that his weight didn't fluctuate. He was able to squeeze the burlap bag into his tool kit. Making sure all his equipment was there, he double checked his plastic baggy containing the capsules of Seconal. He was sure he only needed one capsule to do the job on Al who was an older man and slightly built. Lou had a few extra pounds and was big boned. After contemplating awhile, he decided to put one and a half capsules into Al's coffee and two full ones into Lou's drink.

Curtis tried to contain his nervousness by finding miscellaneous duties he had put off. Occasionally he looked behind, thinking he heard an odd noise. Berating himself for acting irrational, he finished his chores and started another task to occupy his time until the gallery closed for the evening. After all the employees left, he checked the building one last time and gathered all his belongings that he had to take. As a gift to himself he decided to get dressed into his disguise in the comfort of the ladies lounge rather than being cramped in his car. 'What the hell,' he thought to himself, 'thank God this will be the last time I have to put this stupid outfit on. No one's around, I might as well make use of the spacious rest room '

The reflection of the stranger looking back in the mirror made Curtis laugh aloud. 'Shit, no one would know it's me. Dam, I'm good.' He said theatrically as he shut off the bathroom overhead light and headed for the alarm system to close the gallery for the evening. As he drove off, he thought, 'I'm soo good, I scare myself. Maybe I should audition for Kyle's mom, acting is a hell of a lot easier than being a thief, if I'm lucky to become famous, the money would be comparable.' He peeled out of the narrow driveway to do his last crime, if he had his say in the matter!!!

He drove to Dependable Cleaners. A small foreign compact cut him off as he was making a left turn. Honking his horn, he shouted 'imbecile' at the stupid bitch who almost made him get into an accident. His whole plan would have gone awry as he drew in a deep breath and straightened the wheel of his car. Calming himself down he arrived at the cleaning job whistling, knowing that this was his last evening of washing, waxing floors, polishing furniture, emptying trash cans and cleaning hoppers. 'This job is for Plebeians,' Curtis thought as he sighed. He readied himself for the tasks ahead.

"Hey Lou, you're awful quiet tonight, how come, you feelin okay?" Curtis muttered as he looked out the passenger's side window of the Dependable Cleaners Van.

"Nay, I'm feelin a little unda tha weatha tonight, that's all. Stop at Dunky's for a hot cup of java and some donuts. Want your regular? My treat tonight cause I promised Al I'd spring for the snacks since he's celebratin his new grandkid."

Curtis said, "Oh yeh, I almost forgot. In that case get a whole dozen, assorted, make sure there's plenty of chocolate ones."

"Fuck you, you'll eat what I git and like it," Lou said as he got out of the van. Curtis hated the name Charley every time they spoke to him.

"Al says he'll meet us at tha Huntington Museum cause he took tha otha van tonight. He went to tha hospital to see the new grandkid. I hope he appreciates thees donuts," Lou was licking his lips in anticipation.

A bunch of teenage girls were walking down the street, fooling around and talking to each other. Curtis (Charley) berated Lou, "If you turn your neck any further, you'll get a kink and won't be able to turn it around the right way." Laughing, Charley said, "You'll look like one of them gals from, what's that movie with Cher, the blonde cutie and Jack Nicklis or Nickelson or whatever."

"Ya, ya" pointing his finger at Charley, " ya mean Witches of Eastwick?"

"That's it, that's it. Why do you always have to look at them biiig tit gals walkin down the street?" asked Curtis.

"If I didn't look, I wouldn't be normal, man. Ya don't see me looking at no faggots that swish down tha street and can't wait for a guy to pick em up," cackled Lou. "Leave me alone and let me look. The missis, she says slong as you look and don't touch, you'll be okay. She says if she eva finds me screwin around she'll cut my balls off. I'll sound like one of dem suprano singers." He started coughing as his laughing became more intense.

Curtis, aka Charley, tried to contain his chuckling as he thought to himself, 'if you only knew.'

Curtis and Lou finished cleaning the rest rooms and started walking up the main staircase to the second floor when Curtis realized he'd better get rid of Lou and Al shortly so he could start his operation. Making sure they would be put out for a long time he made certain to put the right amount of Seconal into the right person's coffee.

"Come on Lou, move your ass. Al is probably waitin for us and wonderin where the hell his coffee is."

Curt hoped the sweet tasting donuts would hide the bitter taste of the seconal in their coffee or he'd be in deep shit.

"Cheer's Al, let's hope you'll be havin more and more grankids to spoil in your old age. Next time we can celbrate with a beer and hope I win the lottery so's I don't have to work cleanin up after other people's shit," Lou thought out loud.

The two men went about their regular duties and all the while Curtis kept his eyes open for any signs of tiredness befalling either man. Curtis felt the nerve racking state he was in, the last half hour drained his energy. Mumbling to himself he thought back to the other thefts and realized that they were a piece of cake compared to the preparation he had to do for this job. He knew that the first few pieces were easy, but he still had to take his time and make sure that everything was done properly. Another thought came to mind, as he waited for his co-workers to show signs of fatigue. 'The guys who did the Gardner Museum heist must have had time issues. They didn't take nearly as many paintings that I would have. '

He remembered all the hard work and many times he traveled to the Huntington Museum, getting the feel of this massive gallery, gardens and property. Curtis admired the beautiful mansion and loved to walk through the Botanical Gardens, the flowers, and cactus gardens that surrounded the property. The colorful annuals and young redwood trees set off the lines to the entrance of the Pavilion. He found peace and serenity whenever there.

Curtis made sure he would wear a different disguise so the guards wouldn't recognize him and become suspicious. There was a lot of preparation that had to be done and the details were insurmountable. Mr. Makino had no idea what he had to go through. The alarm system was not as intricate as he thought it would have been. He scrutinized the entire mansion and found out the company that installed the system. One of his connections happened to work for the security company and he found a way to get the detailed plans of the museum. He then set forth in obtaining the security plan layout. Until he knew the complete wiring he wouldn't be a happy camper. He analyzed the scheme until he knew it by heart.

Curtis kept glancing at his partners for any signs of tiredness. He nonchalantly wandered into the room where he saw Al yawning and rubbing his eyes. Lou's pace seemed to be slowing down as well, his feet were now shuffling. Just a few more minutes, he speculated, as he grasped the handle of his tool kit for good luck. He knew he had about three hours to finish his undertaking and be far away from the Huntington Museum before the police would be notified that the separate alarm system was not going off as scheduled. He didn't care about the cameras because of his disguise and with the phony name and social security number he had given to his employer, he had all the confidence in the world he could never be traced. He was sure that he covered all the bases.

He saw Al slumped on the floor in the corner near the fireplace. Curtis knelt down and felt his pulse, it seemed to be a little slow but he seemed okay. He then found Lou sprawled out, comatose, in the middle of the hallway leading to the staircase. His adrenalin kicked in and he was no longer tired. Curtis wasn't sure how long he needed to do the job properly. Looking back at his other capers, to be on the safe side, he allotted himself ample time to remove the pieces properly, for he didn't want to extract the pictures in the same way that the thieves who did the Gardner Museum job. He stood in front of Thomas Gainsborough's Blue Boy for a minute or two and admired the workmanship and realized that the form reminded him of Gainsborough's friend Van Dyke, who Gainsborough admired and befriended.

Instead of cutting into this priceless treasure he lifted the picture, out from its place on the wall and removed the picture from the frame. Ensuring the original painting beneath would not be compromised he put on a light coat of polymer medium that contained no odor and let that dry for a few minutes. He started mixing his designers gouache opaque water colors quickly and began with bold strokes for his latest abstract design. Satisfied that not one bit of the original painting could be seen through his "new" original piece of art, he then quickly moved to Sir Thomas Lawrence's Pinky and repeated the procedure. This time he decided to try a different design for his abstract composition and, thought, 'I could sell my own pictures for a small fortune. God I'm good.' He deftly carried the two valuable paintings and his tool kit with him as he buoyantly leaped over Lou, who was an obvious obstacle blocking the stairway. For a moment he looked over the many valuable paintings and as he did he couldn't help admire the George Romney's portrait of The Clavering Children, painted in 1777. He contemplated on removing it for himself and then he spontaneously lifted this magnificent piece from the wall and also brought it with him. He knew that he didn't have to prepare this painting the same way as the other two. The two art pieces he got for Mr. Makino were going out of the country and it was vital that these two well know master pieces wouldn't be detected.

He was aware that he'd always keep The Clavering Children's painting for himself and never part with it. He walked out of the museum with the paintings under his arms. He planned to put them into the van, then he would transfer everything into his personal car which he had hidden elsewhere. He quickly walked back to the museum to retrieve the other valuable pieces he wanted for himself. He thought, 'If I can take this piece, why not take something that I've always admired and if times get rough, which I doubt, I can always sell them to the highest bidder.' Grabbing his burlap sack, he swiftly put the Silver Gilt Standing Cup and Cover into his bag, layed some plastic bubble wrap around it and then deftly put the pair of Silver Candelabras by Thomas Heming into the bag as well.

He flew down the stairs, leaving other portraits and many first edition and valuable works from E. Dwight Church, Robert Hoe (including the Gutenberg Bible) to be admired by the public. He tried but couldn't leave Ellesmere manuscript of Chaucer's Canterbury Tales. As he was leaving the library he couldn't help but notice the first edition of Shakespeare's collected plays. They contained 36 plays, twenty of them printed for the first time. These were early editions of Shakespeare. They were unsurpassed by any other gallery. After carefully putting the plays neatly in his box, assuring their safety, he spotted, on his way out of the library John James Audubon, The Birds Of America. The four volumes contained illustrations of 1,065 birds. 'The great size of the folios and the scientific accuracy of the images make a powerful impression,' he thought, as he grabbed those as well.

He put the box against the wall, where he could easily grab it on his way out. Taking the steps, two at a time, he flew back to where the other masterpiece paintings were standing against the wall and retrieved them. Curtis altogether made four trips to the van. On his last trip he picked up the box that contained the Silver Gilt Standing Cup that was underneath the pair of Thomas Heming's Silver Candelabras, making sure that the bubble wrap was secure. When he finished his last delivery into the van he went back to make sure that Al and Lou were still out cold, but physically okay. He blew kisses towards the cameras and then gave the finger as he made his way out the door.

Once outside the security camera's range, he removed his wig, beard and mustache in the van. Curtis then headed back to the rented car, that he had parked a few blocks away in the early part of the day. He was thankful that he was in good shape to run back and forth as quickly as he did. He had to wipe down both the rented car and van, the last thing he needed was finger prints left behind. 'I can't wait to abandon this Enterprise piece of shit. It's definitely not of my caliber,' he thought, as he transferred all his goods into his Jaguar which was parked a few blocks from The Dependable Cleaners.

Using his cell phone, he rang Mr. Makino's personal number. He let the phone ring a few times and when the answering machine clicked on he told Mr. Makino his new purchases were ready for him to pick up at the Studio tomorrow morning.

When Curtis had settled down and his heart stopped beating rapidly, he took a deep breath and tried to relax. He couldn't contain the excitement that he felt thinking that besides getting the money promised him by Mr. Makino he also was able to fulfill his dream and, on impulse, took the rare original first early editions of William Shakespeare's collected plays. 'I've always loved reading Geoffrey Chaucer's, The Canterbury Tales, it's so elaborately decorated and I love the beautiful manuscript.' He was extremely excited about acquiring the one masterpeice that he always admired. 'Imagine, besides getting The Clavering Children I'm finally able to own the rare standing cup and put it on one of my pedestals. When I have an intimate dinner party, I can't wait for peoples' reaction when I light beautiful, white, tall, tapered candles into MY silver candelabras. People are so stupid. Thankfully none of my friends are into the art world and the ones that are will never recognize these beautiful pieces as the valuable works that were stolen from the Huntington Museum.' He was flying high and felt better than any speed or drug that he'd ever taken.

Lying on his bed, he was finally able to relax. All the elaborate material that was strewn over his apartment was put away. He hated the mess he had to live with while the plans were being investigated. Curtis couldn't leave one detail out or he knew he'd be screwed. He picked up his phone, not caring or realizing the time of night.

"Hi, this is Curtis, I'm finished with my classes so anytime you want to come over, I'm ready, willing and able," he throatily mouthed over the phone after Kyle answered the telephone on the second ring. Curtis quickly put the pieces that were his, way back in his closet knowing that after Kyle left in the morning he'd find a small pod; assuring climate control, rent it, until he could display the pieces in a new, larger apartment or condo. Thinking about his new acquisitions he decided to leave the Clavering Children out, to admire it and take pleasure in knowing that one day it would hang over his mantle in a larger dwelling. He was sure that Kyle would think it was a reproduction.

CHAPTER EIGHT

When Al and Lou awoke in a stupor they didn't know what happened. They couldn't find Charley and were worried that something awful took place. "We'd betta get outa here and tell the boss what come about. He'll probably have a conniption. I hope we don't lose this account. It's one of the easia ones. Come on let's get the hell outa here and call the cleaning company. I don't like the feelin I'm havin."

"Lou, don't you think we should get in touch with the museum and tell the head guys what happened?"

"I don know. Let's scram and the boss will tell us what to do," Lou pushed Al out of the building.

The security people were milling about doing their everyday chores. Suddenly one of the men looked at a wall and noticed something was different. "Gary, can you come here a minute?"

"Sure, what's wrong?" "This doesn't look right. I know this place like the back of my hand and I swear that something's missing."

Gary called the head of security." Hey Colby, Gary, I think you'd better come over to the main gallery a.s.a.p." Not asking any questions, Colby Lewis left his morning coffee on the table, rushed through the long hall and taking two steps at a time on the main staircase entered one of the British Galleries, which housed about 20 paintings of splendid portraits. They were, as far as the security service thought, the finest full-length British portraits to be found anywhere.

"What's going on Buddy?"

"Get into the middle of the room and tell me what you think?"

"Oh my God, Oh my God, three of the paintings are missing. How could that happen? Our alarm system is one of the finest in the world. We would have been notified if someone were to break in. Did you ask administration if they might have loaned the portraits to some other museum?"

"I didn't even think about it. I was so panic-stricken I didn't consider anything else except the missing paintings," a now embarrassed Gary admitted, putting his head down.

"Before we panic, let's go to the administration building and find out if there is truly a BIG PROBLEM."

The three security guards ran down to the administration office and knocked loudly on the curator's glass door.

"Come in, come in. I know that knock by heart now. What can I do for you gentlemen?" asked Donald Munroe.

Gary and his partner, Irving, let Colby do the talking. After explaining what they saw, or didn't see, the curator's face became pale as a ghost. "I received a message from the cleaning company this morning and was about to dial their number when you knocked. I think I'll hold off my return phone call. Gentlemen, I think this is a matter for the police at this point." His hands shook as he dialed the number for the authorities nearest them and afterwards they'd call the alarm company.

One of the street patrol cars got to the Museum within 4 minutes. Going into the gallery, patrolman Cohen called for backup. Although the museum was cooled with air conditioning, sweat was pouring off the staff of the Huntington Museum.

Within the next 15 minutes Detective Aaron Templeton and Detective Bruce Klein arrived on the scene. They spoke to all the parties involved and wrote up a report. "Before I finish the details, I want you gentlemen to go over every inch of this museum and find out if anything else has been stolen. It could be other paintings or small ornate items that you could easily overlook," Detective Klein ordered. It took about another five hours for the security guards and the curator to identify the other articles that were taken.

Donald Munroe was pacing back and forth. "This is the first time since I've been working here that we've had to shut down the museum. I can't believe this is happening," he said aloud to anyone who was paying attention to his prattle.

Detective Klein told the administrators of the museum, "I'll finish writing out a full statement, bring it to headquarters and get on this robbery a. s. a. p. We'll have to get our men on the street to find out if this was a local job or professionals who knew exactly what they wanted. If they're known thugs or anyone we've busted before it won't be too hard to track them down. We have a lot of undercover agents on the streets and very little gets by them. Don't worry. We'll get to the bottom of this." Nodding his head to the guards, security, curator, and the other officers, Bruce headed downtown to his precinct. In the car Bruce Klein told his partner his true feeling. "I hope this will be a clean and simple bust but I have a gut sensation we're going to need help from the upper echelons."

"What do you mean by that?" Aaron asked his partner. "All I'm saying is if we can't deliver the goods, and it looks like a complicated case, we'll have to get in touch with Quantico and let the FBI and Interpol get involved."

"Geez, and here I thought we'd be able to nab these crooks in no time at all." Bruce told Aaron about the notorious gangs in America and Europe that specialize in robberies of this sort. "I hope this isn't one of them."

With his entire body trembling Donald Monroe spoke to all concerned. "I have all the confidence that this matter will be solved soon. I'd better call the alarm company and the insurance company and notifying them of the grand theft. I don't understand why the alarms didn't go off?"

Pacing back and forth Mr. Munroe was worried how he would inform the board of directors about their predicament, the robbery and their course of action.

The evening before Yoshy was to pick up his paintings he was excited and couldn't sit still, for even a minute. "Yoshy honey, I've never seen you so uptight. Patting the seat next to her, Robin persuaded Yoshy to sit down. When seated she got up and stood in back of the couch and started giving him a relaxing massage. "Close your eyes and let yourself relax," coaxed Robin.

"Oh, Oh, that feels soo good, keep it up, oh yeah, oh oh" said Yoshy, as Robins fingers deftly found his tense muscles and massaged them. Her fingers and thumbs pressed hard against his shoulders and upper back, then lessened a bit when she massaged his neck then gently went to his scalp and the sides of his head never taking her fingers off of his skin. After a good half an hour of constant pampering she let go and let him relax. "Do you feel more at ease than you did before I performed my magic fingers on you?" A smile came on Yoshy's face and he nodded. "Thank you, I guess I needed that pampering."

"Are you staying the night?"

"I wish I could, but I have a very important meeting tomorrow and I have to prepare for it tonight. I'll probably stay at the office to have all the material I need at my disposal. I'm not sure how long I'll be in town this time. I'll let you know."

"I'll wait to hear from you." Yoshy kissed her tenderly on her protruded lips.

Curtis opened the door when he heard Yoshy knock. Beckoning him in, Curtis could see the attitude that Mr. Makino was having as soon as Yoshy stepped into the living room. Yoshy was happy that his pieces were finally here. He tried to contain his anger. "I will see you at the gallery later today. I can't tell you how pleased I am with your latest piece of work. Though, I'm upset it had to take so long. In the future I don't want to wait a whole year, do you understand?"

Curtis didn't want to raise his voice but found it hard not to. He knew that Kyle was in the other room, most likely showering. He wanted to be as discreet as possible. "Wait a second. in the first place you wanted this plan to go without a hitch. in order for me to be a professional I had to be cautious and make sure that the authorities would't think anything unusual about your new acquisitions, especially if they are to be flown on a commercial airline. I don't like to do things half assed. I won't tolerate violence of any kind and I had to make sure I didn't get caught. Because if I get arrested, you can bet that I won't be going to jail alone."

"After our little transfer later today, I was going to tell you that this is the last job I'll be doing for you. so instead of later, I'm telling you now that I'm thru, kaput! It's been nice working for you and I hope that you're pleased with the outcome." Putting his hand out to shake Yoshy's, expecting a returned handshake, he couldn't understand Mr. Makino's reaction and underlying fury. Though, if Curtis looked closer, or he was more observant, he would have detected the enraged look that came over the man who had paid him for many of his "toys" and all the undeclared money that he had hidden in his Swiss and overseas accounts. Ignoring his lack of ungracious behavior, he overlooked his rudeness and pulled his hand away. "Well, it's been a pleasure doing business with you, anyway."

Disregarding what he heard Curtis telling him, he continued. "I don't understand. Why are you calling it quits? I thought we have a good working relationship?"

"Lower your voice will you," Curtis whispered as he turned around to see if Kyle was within earshot of their conversation. "When I first started, I did it for extra money. My job will never allow me to afford the many luxuries that I want. At the beginning the thrill was exciting and I wanted to prove to myself that I could get away with it. Now that I've invested my extra money wisely and with todays' money, I'll be able to open my own gallery. Then I'll be too busy to play these games that you seem to enjoy." Leading him to the door Curtis squeezed Yoshy's arm and said, "Have a nice day and I'll see you at the gallery later."

Kyle was in the shower, the hot water beating on his lean body. He vigorously soaped himself and put the hand held shower head on vibration as the water rinsed off the sudsy residue. He watched the suds twirl down the drain. The excess water dripped on the white towel on the floor as he dried himself off. He thought it unusual when he heard Curtis' voice raised and expressing his displeasure with an unexpected guest. Not one to be intrusive he couldn't help but hear the angry voices in the next room. He put on the white, heavy, terry cloth bathrobe and unobserved, went quietly into the bedroom, leaving the door ajar. He observed the medium built, tall Japanese gentleman pointing his finger at Curtis.

Once Kyle saw the Japanese gentleman leave, he quickly walked back into the shower area, pretending to still be drying off. "Oh hi, sleepyhead. I let myself in and let you sleep. I thought I'd take a shower before we had breakfast."

Curtis quickly showered, hoping the hot water would wash away the rage he was experiencing and the perspiration that he had running down his body. He hated confrontations. 'Didn't Yoshy know better than to come to my apartment? In a way it's better that I told him off and we had this argument here instead of causing a scene at the gallery later today.'

Once out of the shower he motioned for Kyle to join him on the bed. "Let's have breakfast later, I have something on my mind that we'll both enjoy eating," as he patted the mattress. Kyle slid into bed next to Curtis. God, it felt good to have Kyle lying next to him once again. He slid his leg on top of Kyle's and gently rubbed his chest. His hungry mouth found Kyle's as he nibbled his lips, thrusting his tongue into Kyle's warm, moist opening. Kyle responded excitedly as the two lovers fondled each other with frenzied desire.

Afterwards, Kyle rolled over and looked into his lovers eyes. "I'm glad Carol is away on assignment. It's been awhile since we've been together. I'm glad your classes are over. Luckily I have some of my clothes here," he said as he could feel himself getting aroused once more. Curtis started to stimulate and make love to Kyle again. After the two men lay beside each other, their bodies spent, Kyle wondered if he should mention or question Curtis about the man he saw in Curtis's living room. Pondering, Kyle decided not to interrupt their mood with silly questions. If Curtis wanted to tell him something in confidence that was fine with him. If he didn't want to discuss what happened that was also okay. Kyle lay in Curtis's arms feeling loved, protected and satisfied.

Curtis didn't want the morning to end but knew that he had to get to work. It didn't matter that he'd be a little late. First things first. He knew of a storage facility and wanted to get rid of the pieces until he was ready to display them. Curtis realized he'd be late but it didn't matter as long he was able to attend to the business at hand. It would be worth a little shouting from the gallery's owner once he exchanged the merchandise for his long awaited money.

Yoshy was angry as he lifted the receiver off the telephone while he was being chauffeured back to his office. Dialing the scarcely used number he spoke with annoyance to the voice who answered the ringing. "I want a job done within the next week and I don't want any foul ups. I need someone eliminated without any messy scene. I want it done fast and clean. Can it be accomplished, my friend?"

Takashi was used to unexpected phone calls in the middle of the day or night. Since he was a young boy and gave his life to his gang leader he was not surprised at any requested service. It had been awhile since he had heard from Mr. Makino. Knowing him as he did, he knew he'd better call his oyabun, (underworld leader, often referred to as the father, head of The Yakuza) and tell him of the latest job that was asked of him.

Nobuaki was looking forward to a peaceful, uninterrupted day when the shrill ring of the telephone intruded his anticipated seclusion and escape from every day annoying circumstances. Takashi told him of their old friends request and waited patiently for his leader's response.

"Hai, hai, okaē, okaē, nanjidesuka? (yes, yes, okay, okay, what time is it?) Watashihoshil dekiru suguni mo akiraka zutsu."

"Watasi hoshil dekiru suguni mo akiraika zutsu." (I need a minute to clear headache) "This morning get in touch with Hirohito and tell him to come by my office at 3:00 o'clock. Meanwhile I will contact Yoshy and find out the details that will be important in executing his request. Tell Hiro to talk to no one about our impending meeting. Thank you for calling."

Hiro, as his friends called him, was busy preparing for his daily routine when Takashi phoned to tell him of his meeting with Nobuaki. Hiro didn't question the unexpected demand. His duty was to obey his leader and not complain. Driving through the congested streets, he dodged a couple of tourists who didn't pay attention or were unaware of the California laws on jay walking. He beeped his horn scaring the pale white ghosts who dare stride in front of his path. 'That will teach them.' He laughed as he continued driving till he reached his destination. He parked his car on the hill and walked up the street, nodding to the few people he recognized before he reached Nobuaki's elegant, hand carved, wooden, front door.

He was let in by Mitsuko, a beautiful, young woman whom Nobuaki rescued from one of their love club operations. Mitsuko bowed deeply, lowering her head as she put her hands together, almost touching her nose. Hiro let himself into Nobuaki's office on the second floor and waited patiently for his leader to enter. Hiro let his eyes wander around the well-appointed room admiring the ornate wood mouldings encompassing the large office. A picture of Nobuaki's family was displayed in a gold frame on his massive cherry desk.

Nobuaki entered the room. "Ohayo gozaimas Nobuaki san," as he bowed in front of his leader. Nobuaki bowed to Hiro and directed him to sit down. "I just got off the telephone with our good friend Makino san and we have a very important job that has to be done," Nobuaki commanded. "One of his business acquaintances has to be eliminated and it has to be done quickly and efficiently. I will get a picture of this person and have it delivered to you as soon as possible. I will leave the way it is to be carried out to you. Whatever way you decide, I don't have to tell you, but, make sure you don't leave any evidence and it is to be concluded within the next week. Do you have any questions?"

"No, just get the picture to me and his address, both at home and his business. You can leave the rest up to me; I promise there will be no blunders."

Hirohito, absently let his thumb play with his right pinky finger and felt the rough stubble that was left of the severed top of the smallest digit. 'No,' he thought to himself, 'I don't want any more severed fingers. There will be no bungling this time,' he reflected as he headed out of Nobuaki's office and down the winding staircase.

Kyle couldn't wait to finish his last session of the shoot. It had been a long, tedious, hot day, especially under the many lights. On occasion, he worked with some nice girls who didn't let their ego's go to their head. He detested working with the Divas. He conceded that most of the models were super bitches, afraid of the time when the all telling camera lens would show their age or flaws. He commanded and received a considerable amount of money plus national recognition, Kyle didn't let that go to his head. Lauren, one of the models, sexily walked up to Kyle. Looking directly into Kyle's violet blue eyes, hoping he would respond to her suggestive movements, she asked, "Good shoot today, wasn't it?" Not waiting for an answer she forged ahead, "Let me help you put away your lights and equipment, maybe we can go out for a few drinks."

"Thanks Lauren, but why don't you go with the others, it's going to take me awhile to finish cleaning up. Besides, I've already made plans for this evening."

Kyle raced up the stairs two at a time, anticipating the wonderful evening that lay ahead with Curtis. The living room of his apartment was dark as he unlocked the front door. Throwing his brief case on the brown tweed chair, he quickly poured himself a drink at the bar. He had to unwind from the grueling day he had. At last carefree and at ease, he put his feet on the coffee table, sipping his gimlet, waited patiently until he and Curtis would get together. With a smile, his thoughts brought him back to the other evening.

On his 2nd Gimlet, his wife, Carol came to mind. It seemed like a hundred years, he thought, but in reality only a few, since he and Carol were together and celebrated their first anniversary. 'How stupid, fearful and weak I was not to admit to myself or the people I love, that I never had the feelings that I should have for her. I do care for Carol, but sexual feelings for her, or for that matter, anyone of the opposite sex, isn't there. How happy Carol seemed on our first anniversary when we toasted to married life. Thankfully, our jobs are so that we're away from each other most of the time, traveling.'

He knew that his mother loved Carol like the daughter she never had. 'How can I disappoint her and the people I love with this revelation?' He resented the fact that Carol expected him to be home with her when she wasn't traveling and away on location. He found it more difficult to keep living this double life and lie. Laying his head back on the comfortable, white sofa's pillow, he knew of no way to get out of his current situation, unless he came out of the closet and told the truth. Closing his eyes he thought again of Curtis and wished he could be open about their love for one another and to hell with what others think.

It took Takashi fifteen minutes to arrive at Hiro's doorstep. Greeting each other with bows, Hiro warmly welcomed his old friend and colleague into his meager apartment.

"Well I see life is treating you kindly," Hiro teased Takashi, as he patted his friend's now quite evident paunch protruding over his stomach.

"Too much sitting around doing the office work for Nobuaki," Takashi admitted. "I'd rather be out in the streets, or doing a job for you. Nobuaki says I make a better office worker than enforcer. I dare not disobey Nobuaki, but at times I miss the excitement of our work."

Hiro agreed, "Yes, I know what you mean. I also would go stir crazy sitting around doing mundane office work and not being out like you used to, an enforcer doing what you know best."

"It's easier on the nerves, but the different assignments used to keep me fit and on my toes. Well, I'd better be going." He handed Hiro the paper work. "Give me a call if you need any help or have questions." Takashi bowed as he left Hiro's apartment.

After Takashi left, Hiro sat on the plain sofa starring at the young man's photo before him. He always made copies of all the photos and assignments. 'You never know if I might need them in the future.' He wondered what this poor bastard did to deserve such a short lived life. His instructions were only to make sure the job was done fast and clean. Once in a while Hiro liked the messy torturing type of assignments but didn't balk when he was instructed otherwise.

When all the reports were ingrained into his mind, Hiro quickly put on his holster and gun and started out the door. He wanted to trail Mr. Curtis Jones for a few days to make sure he didn't vary his pattern of day to day living. If he was to do the job efficiently and accurately he couldn't afford to deal with any diversions.

He wandered into the Walkander Gallery admiring the unusual artifacts and paintings. He spotted Mr. Jones as he left one part of the gallery and entered, what Hiro assumed to be, his office. It took only a few days for Hiro to acquire a pattern of life style that Mr. Jones lived. He observed another nice looking gentleman living with Mr. Jones and wasn't sure if he was his roommate or guest visiting for a while. Without being conspicuous he made a few inquiries about this other young man and found some unanswerable questions. 'Just what relationship did this other man have with Curtis Jones?' No one seemed to know.

Takashi and Nobuaki didn't want any screw ups so the only way to do the job quickly and without anyone else getting in the way would be to kill him either on the way to his work or coming home. Time was running out and he didn't want to anger Nobuaki. No, he decided, 'I won't have time to do it in the street and make it look like a robbery. I'll have to wait until this other guy is out of the apartment, then I can make it look like a foiled attempted robbery. 'Yes,' Hiro decided, 'I will do it in his apartment.'

Curtis decided to make himself and Kyle fresh brewed hazelnut coffee. As the coffee beans grinded in the Minalta, Curtis listened intently to the local news and weather forecast as it blared from the television in the living room. He waited with anticipation for any news about the recent theft. He was disappointed that nothing was mentioned. He didn't understand why the theft wasn't reported.

Lately there had been more rain than usual and he was curious if today's cloudiness would dissipate allowing him to use his convertible. Curtis began preparing their morning breakfast. He could hear Kyle whistling in the shower and a smile appeared as he envisioned Kyle toweling himself dry. Kyle spoke loud enough for Curtis to hear: "Last night was wonderful. It'll be good if Carol's assignments are back to back," Kyle said as he emerged from the bedroom. "By the way, did I tell you that my Uncle, he's really not my uncle, but he's very close to the family, might be coming out from Boston. His name is Justin and you'll love him."

"That's nice," a nonchalant Curtis replied. Not really caring if he ever met Kyle's supposed "uncle." 'Maybe he'll take us out to dinner and foot the Bill,' he thought as he hurriedly straightened up the apartment. "By the way, when do you think that lovely Carol will be coming back?"

"I don't know. I'm sure she'll call me and let me know." Kyle sat down on the kitchen chair as Curtis theatrically placed before him the steaming hot plate of pancakes and bacon. "Here kind sir, eat to your heart's content," a melodramatic Curtis declared. "I'm supposed to pick Carol up from her assignment in a couple of weeks. After I hear from her I'll let you know."

"We usually spend some quiet time at home but sometimes she likes to spend her first night eating at Ciro's and then go dancing next door at the Side Bar. Can you believe that? Always looking to be photographed and talked about in the tabloids. You'd think she'd be exhausted from the long plane trip and those grueling hours of modeling. Oh well, my mom always said Carol has great showmanship."

CHAPTER NINE

Hiro remembered Takashi's remorse of not performing anything worthwhile except staying in the office doing routine office work. The more Hiro thought of Takashi's unhappiness he took it upon himself to let Takashi do the task that Nobuaki asked him to do. 'Nobuaki only wants this person executed and as long as the job is done right, he won't mind. He left it to my discretion to have this Curtis Jones killed. He didn't say I was the person to do the job. I hope Nobuaki doesn't get upset if he finds out that I asked Takashi to do my work. Takashi better not screw up. '

Takashi was waiting patiently in his car. He was surprised and happy that Hiro called him at the last minute to take over the assignment that he wanted for himself. He went to Hiro's apartment and got all the information necessary to carry out the task. Takashi didn't want to let Hiro down. 'Maybe', he thought to himself, 'if I prove myself and do a fabulous job of eliminating this Curtis Jones, Nobuaki will get me away from doing his paper work and I'll be able to work the field again.' 'He situated the automobile at the top of the hill enabling him clear vision of the apartment complex where Curtis lived.

He saw Kyle emerge from the building first. Making sure Kyle didn't return, he impassively sang along with the music on the radio until he saw that the coast was clear. He put on plastic booties on top of his shoes, so some forensic freak wouldn't find any shoe prints. He then put on gloves ensuring his prints weren't visible on anything he touched. The knock on Curtis' door was persistent. Thinking it was Kyle coming back for something he forgot he wondered why he didn't use his key. Curtis yelled from the bathroom, "hold your horses, I'm coming." He quickly put on his pants. "Did you forget your key?" Curtis asked as he opened the door, expecting to see Kyle standing before him. He was stunned that Kyle wasn't the person knocking.

The barrel of the gun felt cold against his wet stomach.

"Who the hell are you, what do you want? Get that God dam gun away from me. You must have the wrong apartment, man. Now leave." Curtis tried pushing the door and put his foot in the doorway, trying to prevent this man that looked like a sumo wrestler, from entering. Coming out of the shower Curtis realized it was futile since he was barefoot. Takashi's menacing smile gave Curtis a terrible feeling in his gut besides scaring the shit out of him. He realized that the cold gun remained on his stomach. Takashi had his foot blocking Curtis from shutting the entrance. Curtis was no match for this giant of a man. Takashi shoved Curtis back into the room and closed the door while he knocked Curtis temporarily off balance. Enjoying a man that tried to fight back, Takashi hit him with the blunt end of his silenced revolver. Curtis' lip split open, the blood started spouting uncontrollably. He then hit him in the solar plexus, knocking the wind out of him, Curtis doubled over with pain. Takashi again cuffed Curtis hard across his face with the handle of the gun, above his eye. For good measure he hit Curtis' nose with the blunt end of the gun and Takashi heard Curtis' nose break.

Curtis tried yelling something at Takashi, but was incoherent. The words were not coming out as Curtis wanted them to. "Shut up pretty boy. Don't ask any questions and do as I say. Get yourself into your bedroom now, fast. Take off your pants and lie down on the bed. Now! Move it. "Curtis dare not question this lunatic. Curtis was terrified. He didn't know what to do. He could feel the bile rising. He wanted to throw up, yet dared not show his fear. He knew that his nose was broken, he couldn't breathe. Blood was pouring from the cut above his eye and he was sure that the skin was split wide open. Curtis figured that if he co-operated with this slimy yellow bastard he might get off with only this terrible beating. Curtis didn't understand why this was happening, thinking that this jerk was going to rob him. 'Maybe it's gay bashing, who knows but I don't think so.'

'Maybe I can reason with this nut case,' he thought as he tried to gain his composure. Every time he tried raising his head the throbbing was making everything spin, he fought hard not to lose consciousness. He couldn't get the cobwebs out of his head. He told Takashi, "Take anything you want. I won't go to the police. Don't hurt me," Kyle's words came out like gibberish. Takashi felt sorry for this man, only for an instant, until the pulsating of the nob on his pinky reminded him not to screw up.

Curtis realized he would not be able to dissuade this man who obviously had only one purpose on his mind. Racing against the clock, his adrenalin, working at its max, he forced his body to get out of the bed, ignoring the multiple pains, he swiftly bolted towards the door. Takashi turned him around as he slammed the bedroom door shut. Curtis then scratched and was trying to get the bedside lamp to hit, as hard as he could, this maniac. Takashi knocked the lamp out of Curtis' hand. Curtis realized he was no match for this obviously powerful, well-built killer. Takashi was suddenly taken aback when Curtis quickly shot his arm into Takashi's throat. Startled, coughing for a few seconds, he wrestled this slender man against the bed frame. Curtis once more pushed himself up and tried kneeing this powerhouse in the groin. When he realized that it didn't work he again tried clawing his face and bite his unused fore arm as hard as possible but obviously, was no match for him. 'He looks and acts like a nut case,' Curtis thought as he tried wrestling the gun away from Takashi, but he would not release the weapon from his dominant grip. Takashi's trigger finger automatically, like an ingrained habit, pulled back, discharging the bullet that ripped thru Curtis's stomach.

While the blood oozed out, spilling onto the bed linens and rug, Kyle realized that only one man would deliver such an evil order. As the excruciating pain was racking his body all he could think of was, 'Fuck you Mr. Makino.' He knew he didn't have much longer, for the pain was worsening. He tried to get up, grabbing onto the arm of a chair. He needed to fight back, but the pain was getting the best of him. He wanted to render this asshole as much pain as he was feeling. Curtis, running as best he could, the pain worsening, tried to knock this big thug down and get the gun from him. He knew he didn't stand a chance, but he still had to try. Takashi fought him off and pushed him down onto the bed. Curtis was weakening. He couldn't catch his breath as he saw himself bleed out. He wanted to sleep but tried valiantly to squelch the thought. The look of surprise was apparent on his face as he turned paler and succumbed to the obvious bullet that was taking his life. His life's plans and goals were seeping away. The two last things he remembered were that he was too young to die. Kyle's beautiful face hovered above his as the world turned black.

For good measure Takashi put a bullet through Curtis's heart. As many times as Takashi killed someone in cold blood, the sight of his victim, lying there helplessly, waiting for some release, still made him ill. Takashi knew that, his victim was dead. 'I guess I got carried away. Oh well, at least I know this one won't be able to testify against me. He's dead as a door nail!'

The apartment was in disarray from their fighting. The bed, walls and other areas in the bedroom looked like accented designs were splattered with red and brown paint, along with various surfaces throughout the two rooms and hallway. The carpet, especially in the bedroom, was soaking wet with the red blood that was draining from Curtis's entire body. Takashi wanted the authorities to think that the killer was looking for some cash or other belongings. He opened the draws, scattering the clothing and other articles from the bureau, chest and tables. Takashi found Curtis's wallet and removed what little money he found. He took the credit cards from their compartments and lifted the set of keys that were laying in front of the fallen dresser. He would give the keys to someone in the organization, knowing that the car would disappear, never to be found. He was glad that he used the silencer, ensuring quiet. He quickly grabbed the computer and brought it to his car. He then went back, making sure the coast was clear and dismantled the large flat screen television to insure the intrusion look like a robbery that went bad. Takashi felt his back tighten as he carried the t. v. and put it into the back seat of his automobile. I'd better get in better shape if I go out on assignments again. '

Takashi again went back to Curtis' apartment making sure none of the neighbors heard the commotion. Most of the people who lived in the apartment complex, he thought, had already left for work. Before he went to the door one last time, a beautiful painting he hadn't noticed caught his attention. Takashi grabbed it as he looked out the crack of the entrance, making sure no one would see him emerge from the apartment. He closed the door, after wiping clean the knob and anything he thought he may have touched. He quickly ran down the stairs, The Clavering Children oil picture held tightly between his beefy hands. Getting back into his car, he lowered the radio, not wanting to attract attention. He sped off, nervously feeling his nub once more.

Nobuaki was sitting at his desk when he heard the knock on his door. "Sit down, sit down my friend. Do you have good news to tell me?" Hirokito smiled and told Nobuaki that the deed was done. He then recanted all of the gory details that his friend told him. Nobuaki, an intuitive man, although pleased with the end result had an eerie feeling. "Tell me Hiro, do you have something you want to tell me? I want honesty nothing less." Hiro was beside himself with worry. He didn't know how Nobuaki would react if he revealed that Takashi was the actual killer. Finally, Hiro told him why he asked Takashi to do the job he was supposed to do. Nobuaki was angry that his orders were not obeyed. He felt betrayed. "Hiro, you know how I feel about someone going against my instructions. As far as I can see there's no excuse."

"Nobuaki, you didn't mention that this job was to be performed by me. You told me that you wanted the job done, and done right. I thought you didn't care, as long as the guy got killed and it was done efficiently. I'm sorry if I misunderstood your orders. I'm truly sorry." He bowed his head in contrition. "I can't apologize enough, my loyal leader. You know that I wouldn't do anything to upset you," a contrite Hiro said. "I thought that you were loyal. You lied to me. I want you and Takashi in this room tomorrow. You bring dishonor to our family. Yes, I'm happy that the man was executed but it doesn't take away the shame I'm feeling. Bring whatever you have to for restitution for going against the Yakuza. You know that you've made a grave mistake. Yabizume must be done," he told his captain.

Suddenly a smile emerged on Nobuaki's face. He got up and slapped Hiro on the back. "You are still my best Captain and after this talk I'm sure this type of disobedience will never happen again. You can go now. This is going to be the second time Yabizume must be performed. Takashi will be dealt with in the same manner." He dismissed Hiro. "Go, go, I must call Yoshy and tell him that the deed that he wanted is done."

Yoshy was at his desk, trying desperately not to be impatient. He put his papers in front of him and looked at the P & L of his corporation. While he was concentrating on his executive decisions the phone interrupted his train of thought.

A big smile crossed Yoshy's face when he heard his old friend, Nobuaki's voice. As he heard the good news, he expelled a sigh of relief. "I can't thank you enough, my colleague and whatever you want will be yours."

"That's not necessary. But if I need assistance with certain matters, I won't hesitate to call on you. Take care, my good friend, now you can sleep in peace."

Leaving work was both relief and at the same time sadness. He knew that Robin would not be happy with him leaving so quickly. He loved the tranquility that Robin afforded him whenever he came home. He'd miss their love making and casual talk while sitting around watching the old cowboy movies on TV. He learned to love the old movies since he was a youngster. Sitting down next to her, holding hands, he was reluctant to tell her about his impending departure.

"I can't thank you enough for all the pleasures that you have given me. Who would think that I, Mr. Yoshirhiro Makino, head of a large corporation, could sit down and watch old cowboy movies with the woman that I love sitting next to me. You taught me patience, sincerity and how to love someone, not expecting anything in return. You give me such happiness that words can never describe how I feel about you. But unfortunately, I do have some bad news that you must hear and understand. I have to return to Japan as soon as possible for a very important meeting. Before I see my beautiful butterfly pouting, I promise that I'll be returning within a few weeks if not sooner."

"Yoshy, I can't bear it when you're away. I miss you so much." Sadness was visibly displayed on her face. "Do you think that one day you'll take me to Japan and see all of the wonderful sights? I'd love to see your main headquarters and meet all of your colleagues." A naïve Robin asked.

"There are many things that you bring up. I don't know which one to answer first." Lifting one eyebrow he looked at Robin directly, "maybe someday Japan will be in your future."

"I'll be home before you know it. Don't forget that I once brought you to my beautiful hide away and you loved it there. We'll go there again, soon, I promise."

Yoshy was excited about bringing home his latest two paintings and couldn't wait to display them along with his other acquisitions. Of course when he arrived home he'd have to see Michiko, his devoted wife and son Kazuhiko. He heard Kazuhiko was doing well at the university and couldn't wait to take him into his business.

Yoshy would have to find a way to get to the Island of Bepo and deposit his fine works of art without rousing suspicion on why he was leaving to go off to another island. He was lucky that Michiko never questioned him and was always agreeable to whatever he wanted to do. 'She is a beautiful woman,' he thought to himself, 'but there's no one like Robin,' he reminded himself as a big smile crossed his face. He called the airlines to make reservations to return to his homeland.

Carol was still upset and angry at Kyle for not staying home with her on the first evening of her return from Cyprus. 'Yes,' she admitted, 'he hadn't expected her home that evening, but still....... . She wanted to surprise him.' She didn't understand why she didn't come before his stupid friends. When he returned from work a couple of days later she kept jibbing him. "I hope that you had a great night out with your friends," Carol sarcastically said. Usually she'd make him a coffee and some breakfast, but today she made coffee for herself. 'To hell with him,' she thought. She sat down reading the paper, ignoring him as best she could. "Do you have anything you'd like to say to me? I'm sorry is good for starters, which I think I deserve."

Taking a line from a famous movie he declared, "Frankly, my dear, I don't give a dam."

"Well if that's the attitude your going to have, you can just go to hell. Sleep in the guest room for as long as you want. Until I get an apology from you, you and I won't be together, and you know what that means."

Deep inside Kyle was thrilled. He didn't have to put on any pretenses and he was sure that before long this silly, childlike, behavior of hers will be gone and she'll sneak into his bed and try to make amends.

"By the way, my agency called and they want me to do a shoot in Cyprus and Israel again. With the way things are here, I might as well take the assignment. I thought that I'd take at least a month off so that we'd be able to spend some time together and have fun. I guess that won't be happening. I might as well start packing and see you whenever I get back. The Greek men are gorgeous and find me irresistible. Maybe this time I won't say no to them. Put that in your pipe and smoke it. As far as I'm concerned you're history."

Tears were welling up in her eyes. Carol had to sit down for she was afraid that she would fall apart and start babbling like a fool. She wanted to act strong and uncaring, but she really loved Kyle. From the day she first saw him she fell in love with this legend. Besides being tall and handsome those violet eyes were mesmerizing. She later found out that as handsome as he was, he was also a gentleman and courteous. She never had to worry about his trying to rape her or get her into bed like those other leaches. He took their courtship nice and slow. Sometimes she thought, a little too slow, but what the heck, if they were to get married than they'd never stop screwing.

Feeling sorry for the way things turned out the other evening and since then, Kyle put his arms around his loving wife. He saw how disturbed she was and the feeling of guilt crept over him. "Carol, I'm truly sorry for the way things turned out this week. It could have been avoided if I knew that you were coming home sooner than expected. I would have looked like a fool to these guys. You know how that is, it's a guy thing." He got a tissue and wiped her eyes, mascara running down her beautiful high cheek bones. Let's try to forget it and start fresh, like you just arrived today. Okay?"

Still sobbing and out of breath she nodded her head and put her head on his wide shoulders. "I'm sorry too for the way that I overreacted. It just surprised me that you wouldn't be thrilled to see me earlier than expected. We both acted like children." They kissed and then proceeded to their bedroom." I have to tell you that it's too late for me to break my newest assignment. I'll be leaving within the next two days," a contrite Carol told Kyle.

The next morning Kyle woke up early and prepared breakfast for the two of them. He was ashamed and felt that he had betrayed Curtis. But what was he supposed to do? 'After all she's still my wife and I do have feelings for her,' he chided himself. He knew that he couldn't see Curtis for a while until Carol went on another assignment, which he found out wouldn't be long. When he got to his studio he called Curtis' apartment expecting for him to pick up the telephone.

'That's funny,' he thought to himself. 'He must have gone to the gallery early.

He called the gallery at 11:00 a. m., knowing that by this time everyone would be there. When the person who picked up the phone told him that Curtis hadn't shown up this morning, Kyle thought that was odd. 'Oh well, everyone has one of those days. I guess I'll wait until he calls me. Maybe he's in one of his hissy fits because Carol came home and he knows that I'm with her.'

Kyle went about his business taking various shots of many models. Some young girls and some not so young, who tried looking 10 years younger than their age. They wore skimpy bathing suits and revealing dresses that he'd be ashamed to be seen in. He had to admit that their skin was beautiful and unblemished. Makeup went on them like silk. Other models were the seniors and he adored working with them. They let you do anything to them. They were happy getting the work. They had to hide their age spots and wrinkles. He made sure that he wouldn't let the camera reveal their true age. The male models were next, granted they were good looking, he could sense their arrogance and self-absorption. Some of them tried making passes at Kyle as well, but he only had eyes for Curtis. 'Anyway, how do they know I'm NOT straight?'

"Aunt Suzanne, how nice of you to call."

"I hope I'm not disturbing you."

"You could never disturb me. What's up?"

"Well I was thinking of you and haven't heard from you in a while and thought I'd pick up the phone and call. I saw your mother's play in Boston. We try to see each other quite a bit when we have the time. Do you get a chance to call her?"

"Is this a friendly call or are you chiding me for not speaking to her as often as I should?"

"A little of both," said Suzanne. "Seriously, I spoke to Madaline the other day and she's worried that she hadn't heard from you in a while. I know boys are different than girls but there's no excuse for not picking up the phone and touching base. She's concerned about you and loves you very much. I know, I know, I'm a meddlesome old bitch, humor me."

"You're right Aunt Suzanne, I'll call her late this evening after the production is through and she's back at the hotel. I realize there's a 3 hour difference. By the way, Carol is home from her shoot and I know that mother will love hearing from her as well. Thanks for the remind and make sure to send my love to all the girls, Mrs. Walsh and your folks. Thanks again and I love you."

He sat on the sofa happily reminiscing. He thought of Aunt Suzanne and her entire family, who he felt was his. He couldn't remember when he first met them but knew that he was very young. They took him in like a member of the clan and always were there for him, through thick and thin. Even though he lived in California, they would fly down to see him during their vacation. All of them had a blast cruising around the Hollywood Hills and the many beaches up and down the coast. They tried surfing and he could remember that Hope and Taylor were naturals on the surf board. Melanie was too hesitant and had a hard time staying on the board. Melanie was more reserved of the three girls and he thought the most stunning. The girls were all gorgeous in his eyes and each beautiful in their own way.

Whenever he found himself on the east coast, he would call them up. They would put their plans on hold and always make time for him. Sometimes he would long for those days. Life seemed so simple then. He didn't have the responsibilities that he was now faced with. He certainly wasn't in this predicament that he found himself in. If he could go back to his younger years. 'I wish I could confide in the girls. I know they'd understand the quandary that I'm having. They'd help me get through it. Aunt Suzanne would especially be great. One of her best friends, Alan, came out a while ago and that didn't stop their relationship.'

Another day went by and Suzanne still hadn't heard from Nancy. Nancy was becoming a regular traveler to Japan and enjoyed going back to this incredible place. Nancy's job was to negotiate the business dealings with the realtors and find some estheticians who would be willing to work for an American company. After one of her many trips Nancy was due back. All of a sudden it dawned on her to try Nancy's cell phone. She speed dialed the number that Hope programed in for her. She let Nancy's cell phone ring and was expecting her message to come on when Nancy answered.

"I don't believe I finally got a hold of you. I've been worried sick. Where the hell have you been?"

"I'm sorry. I should have called you. I didn't have a direct flight so when we landed in San Diego I decided to stay here for a couple of days, like I did the first time I flew to Japan. The weather is great. I'm doing some shopping and enjoying myself."

"I'm glad that you're having such a wonderful time. Here I am worried sick about you and you don't have a care in the world. What's wrong with you? No, don't answer that. I forgot, you're the typical only child that only thinks about herself."

"That's not fair! That's a low blow, even for you Suzanne. I really have so much on my mind that I forgot about the time or what day it is. Anyway, you're also an only child, so don't you dare say anything negative about only children. As you always told me; you weren't spoiled, just loved."

Suzanne said, "I've been dying to talk to you about Japan and how it went. I know, I know, we spoke to each other often while you were there, but it's not the same. There are many things that we have to talk about. When will you be getting home?"

"I'm really not sure. Let me have a few more days to myself and then I'll get back and we'll discuss everything that has to be done. Don't forget the time difference has screwed my system up and with all the personal things going on I felt that I needed some time for myself. Can you understand that?"

Taking a deep breath and letting herself calm down, Suzanne assured Nancy that she understood exactly what she was going through. "Enjoy yourself."

'I wish that I could take a few days off for myself,' Suzanne thought as she closed her cell phone. 'I wish I was with her,'

Suzanne thought about all the things that were on her mind and got frustrated thinking about them. Sooner or later she had to talk to Hope and couldn't keep postponing the inevitable. Hope was her first born and even if they clashed on many issues, she loved her with all her heart. Hope and Suzanne had gone through a lot of heartache and issues in years gone by, more so than the younger girls. Hope and she had received the brunt of Brian's tirades and she knew that without the counseling that she made sure Hope received, she would never have gotten over the trauma that Brian inflicted upon her.

The issue with Stephen was still unresolved. What should she do about the situation with him? How much longer could he wait for her to finally take some time off from the salons and see him? Why couldn't they have a normal life like other people? She laughed to herself, 'am I crazy, we're not like other people, especially since he's not divorced. '

With all that said and done she put a wet, cold washcloth on her forehead, went into the music room and put on her favorite CD's, put her head back and listened to the music.

SAN DIEGO

Nancy felt guilty about her unexpected excursion but realized that if she didn't do this for herself she wouldn't be able to function properly. She plopped down on the cover of her bed in the hotel room and closed her eyes. She didn't want to think about anything negative and Peter's situation would fall into that category. She had to take stock of her life and find new beginnings. That didn't mean that she'd give up the Metamorphosis Salons, no, she had to add a new dimension. Personally she felt unfulfilled. 'How long has it been since I felt in love?' she asked herself.

'I think I have to take the bull by the horns and just go for it.' A queasy feeling came over her, trying to ignore the nervousness. She thought of ways to change her life style and still maintain being the same person that she was.

CHAPTER TEN

"Get out of here! Do you understand that when I say I don't want to be disturbed, what that means? Now get out of my dressing room and don't come back until I say it's okay with me." 'That stupid little bitch,' Madaline thought to herself, as she laid down on the old, ragged and worn, but comfortable sofa. She rested her head on the soft pillow that she brought with her everywhere she traveled. She raised her limbs, extending her long, shapely legs to the edge of the dull, grayish, sofa that was at one time a beautiful shade of blue, and closed her eyes. She was sick and tired of stupid people who didn't follow directions or pay attention to details. She realized she had scared Betty, who was the understudy, but the hell with her. When she saw the look of fear on Betty's face, the way she scurried out of the room, Madaline laughed out loud. She loved being a diva. She enjoyed creating the image of an impossible person to get close to. She learned years ago, never to trust or become close to most people. Unfortunately, through pain, suffering, and getting hurt by people she thought were friends, she had to be this way. She often asked herself who she could count on to bare her sole? Madaline had many secrets to unburden and only a few people she'd feel free to do so. That was one of the reasons she put a protective shield around herself and her personal life.

Madaline closed her eyes. She tried to unwind and relax from her grueling schedule but thoughts, she attempted to keep at bay, kept reoccurring. With everyday situations that come up, she now had to worry about this lunatic that was stalking her and most likely, try to kill her. 'Wonderful,' she thought, as she wiped her sweaty forehead with a tissue. 'I don't think these sweats are from my hot flashes either.' She suddenly found herself laughing out loud and hoped no one was listening. Yes, she was an actress and a personality that people loved and enjoyed. She was very young when she embarked on her career and had been eager to please the press and her adoring public. She wanted to be herself and let people know the kind of person she really was, and become ingratiated by all. With all her charm she tried to captivate her audiences, always being on display. The reality set in when a few, so called, reporters and columnists, printed unfavorable stories and untruths that almost damaged her budding career. Thinking back to the articles brought back some painful memories.

Her first movie had been a smashing success putting her in the limelight. An old, worn out, columnists, who still carried quite a bit of clout, took an instant disliking to Madaline. 'Personally, I think she must have been jealous.' The writer thought of her as a young, beautiful, but untalented upstart who would only stay in show business for a few years and snatch a wealthy, old, rich executive producer or director and ride on his laurels, to become a trophy wife. She circulated a rumor around Hollywood that Madaline had been in jail for robbery and some preposterous fable that told of her becoming a lesbian while incarcerated. Other stories started traveling around town about her life style. Even though she had this one hit, another would be out of the question if people believed the sordid tales spread about town. Whenever she found herself at one of the famous restaurants or shopping about town, the public and those in the profession started avoiding her like the plague. She saw the whispers behind cupped fingers and could only imagine what they were saying about her. She didn't know how to deal with all this adverse publicity but was determined that she would put a stop to these untruths and rumors. Thoughts of that time in her life gave her chills, as if ice cubes were thrown down her back. Goosebumps made the hair on her arms stand up and she covered herself with a throw.

FAIRFIELD, IOWA

Madaline only knew about the small, friendly town that she was born, schooled and raised in. Until she was a young teenager she loved her parents, siblings and all the friendly neighbors that were part of her life. The large farm that she was brought up in was comforting. Being the eldest child, it was expected of her to get up early and do the many chores that had to be done before going off to school. She loved going to the chicken house. Picking out the warm eggs, that the hens just laid in their cages, she put them in the basket that she carried every day for the family's breakfast. This was her favorite meal. When her brothers and sisters finished the various chores appointed to them, they would all sit at their assigned places along the long, pine, wooden bench that matched the kitchen table. She loved the way her mother made the fresh eggs. They would be served with the season's well-preserved, crisp, bacon, that they had curing safely in the storage facility that was in the large holding barn.

She could still imagine smelling the wonderful aroma of the warm bread, baking in the oven to slice for toast with their hearty meal. Of course homemade jam was heaped high in a bowl in the center of the eating area to be put on the toast. For pastimes during the slow season, the farmers, including her father, would race their fastest horse and wager on the animal that came in first. Her father, in her opinion, had the best quarter horse in the entire county. Jeannie was by far, the finest quarter horse in and around the province. Each farmer used their fastest racer. He never told her mother about these wages between the neighboring men. He knew that his wife would disapprove of betting their hard earned money. On one of the occasions, her father's Jeannie, beat out every horse that was racing against her. Instead of money, he agreed to get a new foal from one of the farmer's best stallion quarter horses' in the area. He was familiar, which was essential, with the up line and breeding that this foal came from. He knew that this little one, when matured, could even beat Jeannie.

When her father brought the beautiful, chestnut colt to the stall, it was love at first sight for Madaline. She made sure to get up early so that after she finished her chores, she had time to groom and talk to him as if he were human. In any event, she named him Trigger, after one of her favorite cowboys', Roy Rogers' personal horse. After school and homework done, she again had to check on and feed the animals. Eventually this chore would get passed down to the next sibling. Her mother was a hard, but nurturing and loving woman who expected her offspring to excel in school. She, herself, never finished high school. She self-taught herself. Ma, as most relatives called her, wanted her children to attend college and have a profession other than farming. She put away all and any extra money, that no one new about, and hid it.

Her family was the first in the area to own a television set. Instead of sitting down with friends and family, watching the new, small screen, Philco television, she would take the portable, General Electric, salmon and cream radio out to the barn. While listening to the new rock 'n roll music, dance to the various singers, and at the same time she'd groom and play with trigger. She tried teaching Trigger tricks that she saw Roy Rogers' do with his steadfast companion. When he was all set, she broke him in so that he could get used to having a saddle on his back. He would then be ready for Madaline to ride him in the pen. Eventually, her goal was to jaunt with him around the property and nearby valleys in the area. Most of the terrain was flat, so in the beginning it was easy riding.

After a hard workout she would then wash Trigger down and groom him. Once in a while, after that chore was done, she allowed herself time to sit down with family and friends to watch the various T. V. programs. She laughed to herself remembering all the old performers and their comedy shows. Madaline loved seeing them all. Whenever she watched I love Lucy, Starring Lucille Ball, or a rerun of the popular show, she thought of her old friend, Ann. Ann eventually went on to become a great comedian, who made people all over the world laugh. Without the friendship she had with Ann, she didn't think she would have become the successful personality that she now was. She would get close to the television during the Ed Sullivan Show and sigh when Eddy Fisher, wearing his army uniform would sing. She thought he was singing to her alone.

Her siblings loved the many talk and game shows. When she got a little older she would watch many of the sitcoms and laugh at the comedians on Rowan and Martin's Laugh In. As a teenager, all the friends and neighbors, along with her siblings were mesmerized by The Dick Clark Show (American Bandstand) and dance to the "hot records" of the time. Over the years she felt fortunate to have met some of these fine writers who became famous on their own when she went into the field of theater and movies. Unfortunately many of these wonderful actors and actresses, who later became her friends, have since passed on.

As she was lying down she thought, 'it's sad that the youth of today would look at most acting professionals with scorn, thinking that they were old by the time they were in your early40's or 50's. Youngster today lacked imagination. Children are taught computers at a very young age, while attending grade school. Granted, their world is quite different than ours was at the same given time. Once in a while these computer children do have imagination and creativity, especially in the artistic world. Could you imagine; the movies or television of today could never be what they are without these ingenious people. Hello, Star Wars and other animated shows. 'Sighing, she thought, 'what happened to interaction of the family? Madaline remembered sitting down as a unit eating their dinner together and discussing what happened during the day and current events.

Taking another deep breath, she closed her eyes and thought, 'although there are some people who are extremely talented and imaginative, Steven Spielberg, Jim Carey and a slew of others that are insurmountable to imagine. The way they can perceive ideas and because of the computer age, many people can make imaginary figures come to life. That kind of talent is great but still, I'd rather see real people instead of animated creatures that become heroes to the youth.

As she laid down, a compress on her forehead, she laughed to herself, thinking that the kids of today probably never heard of these great, talented people. 'They would be bored stiff watching the classics.'

Madaline could still remember that awful day when her life was destroyed. She thought that her existence was just great and she didn't have a care in the world. She loved her entire family and the neighbors were always there to help in any given situation. It was a great community to grow up in - - or so she thought.

After that awful afternoon that Uncle Harry raped and shamed her she didn't know what to do. Did she go to her parents who she thought would comfort and help her with the trauma, self-hatred and dread she was feeling? That evening after scrubbing her skin raw she finally went downstairs to help her mother with the supper. Thankfully it wasn't her turn to do the dishes. She couldn't look at anyone and was extremely quiet.

"What's wrong with you girl?' her dad asked. "You don't look so good. Are you ailing?"

"Why don't you go upstairs and go to sleep early. I'll bring you a hot cup of tea and that will cure what ale's ya," her mother generously offered.

Madaline quietly went upstairs and cried herself to sleep. When her mother came to her room with the tea, she gently shook Madaline, and waiting for her to wake, she held her in her arms and asked what's wrong. Madaline couldn't even mention what had happened; she was traumatized and embarrassed. She just wanted IT to go away. She remained quiet for a few more days and gradually tried to forget what was done to her. Whenever 'Uncle Harry' came over to play cards with her father and their other friends, she couldn't look at him and immediately went upstairs. He'd wink at her when she walked by. She turned her face trying not to look at him. Repulsion and shame overtook her.

Madaline went about her chores as usual and always watched for anything unusual that didn't sound right. She still rode Trigger and talked to him as if he could understand everything she said. Sometimes she really thought he knew what she was saying. One evening Uncle Harry was at their house and he caught her by her arm before she had a chance to run up the stairs.

"What's wrong with you girl? You never seem to be like your old self." In front of her parents and their friends he blatantly put his finger on his cheek, he declared, "Come here and give Uncle Harry a kiss on my cheek."

She was stunned. How could he do this to her knowing what happened in the barn? She wanted to spit at him but thought better of it since everyone was in the parlor. She gave him a peck and took the stairs two at a time.

"I honestly don't know what's got into that girl. She used to be so outgoing and cheerful, and now she's quiet and withdrawn. I hope she gets better and kicks what's ailing her," her concerned mother spoke out loud for everyone to hear.

One day she was upstairs doing her homework when she looked at the calendar on her bureau. She asked herself, 'Shouldn't she have gotten her menstrual period by now?" She let a few more days go by and then she really got concerned. She noticed that her breasts were hurting and her stomach looked a little distended. Madaline then remembered the nauseous feeling she was getting after each meal. She had heard about fast and bad girls getting pregnant. This couldn't be happening to her. She wasn't like those other girls. She was Madaline and she couldn't conceive anything like that occurring. She didn't know what to do. She wanted to die or run away. Where would she go?

Finally when the house was quiet and her mother was by herself did she dare approach her. "Ma, I have something to ask and tell you and I want you to listen and try to come up with a solution," a very solemn Madaline declared.

Her mother, now concerned, especially since Madaline had been acting strange and not like herself, wiped her hands on the dishtowel and sat on the sofa with her daughter. 'Was she sick and had to be taken to Dr. Mathews? She asked herself. 'What if it's serious and she has to go to the hospital?' All these concerns entered her mother's mind before Madaline told her the story.

"I don't know where to begin." She started sobbing and tried telling what happened to her that awful afternoon. Her body was shivering and she couldn't catch her breath.

"I was in the barn, taking care of Trigger, as I usually do after school. The haystack was to the right of me. Trigger was tied on either side with rope, because I was going to wash and groom him. All of a sudden, a hand reached out to me from behind. I tried turning around but he put a knife to my neck." As she tried relating the story, her sobbing was pitiful; she had a hard time catching her breath.

"Go on girl."

"From where I was standing, he reeked from booze. Madaline then told her mother the awful happening. I shake all over when I think of it."

"He raped me ma, he raped me. After he lay on top of me I tried getting him off me. As he was walking away I pulled his red scarf down. He then started slapping me and warned me not to say a word to anybody. I scratched his face with what little nails I have. He just kept laughing and said no one will believe me." Trying to catch her breath she then blurted out, it was Uncle Harry, Uncle Harry, the man everyone adores. I hate him for what he did to me. I always wanted to be a virgin on my wedding night. He's ruined my entire life."

'He wasn't a real uncle, but so close to my dad, they were like brothers. He was always at the house. My dad and he went to school together since the first grade." "Are you sure it was Uncle Harry?" Her mother asked her. Madaline couldn't believe her ears.

"What happened to the wonderful mother who I thought would be understanding and stand by me, no matter what?" Madaline yelled and was mortified by her mother's reaction. 'Her ma's response was certainly not what she expected.' Her mother was crying along with her eldest daughter.

"You go upstairs now and I'll be telling your father about this. He'll figure something out." Her mother asked, "Are you sneaking off and seeing that Billy Martin from down a ways?"

Billy Martin was her friend. They grew up together and confided each other's hopes, wishes and future plans. Besides her family Billy was her best friend. How could her Ma think such awful thoughts about Billy?

"I can't believe that Uncle Harry could do such an awful thing, especially to kin folk," was her father's reply. Her mother went into the kitchen and sat by the fireplace, balling like a baby.

Madaline was sure that she was pregnant and didn't know what to do. She should have had her period 2 weeks ago. 'How could my mother think such an awful thing about me? I hope pa has some sensibility and beats the crap out of Uncle Harry.'

That evening, when everyone else was in bed, asleep, she heard her parents talking and then their footsteps on the stairs. She was scared to death. She didn't know what they would say. Their faces were grim and her mother looked like she'd been crying. Sitting on her bed her parents tried talking calmly to her. "Now Madaline, we know you're a good girl. Things like this happen all the time; though we never expected this to come about to you. You know we love you with all our hearts but we're a God Fearing family and can't have this shame put on us. We're go'n to Billy Martin's parents and explain the situation to them. I'm sure they'll understand, you and Billy will quietly get married. We're sure he's a nice young man and own up to his obligation."

Madaline couldn't believe what she was hearing. "What about that bastard that raped your daughter? Don't you believe me?" She heard herself shouting. "He came from behind, defiled me and do you understand the word RAPE?"

"Don't talk to me that way, young lady, Shouted her mother."

"What's happened to the parents that I love so much, who I thought trusted and believed in me? What are you going to say to that scum Uncle Harry? Just let him in the house as usual and maybe he'll do the same thing to Cindy, when she gets a little older!!" Now almost screaming hysterically, "Billy and I are just friends. He'd never do a thing like that to me. I've always obeyed you and would never violate your trust in me. Please," she begged, "don't go over to the Martins," begged Madaline. "Can't you see that that bastard 'Uncle Harry' isn't the nice guy you think he is? I don't believe that you'd believe that he's so God fearing when, for Gods' sake, he's the biggest asshole in the world."

"Young lady, don't you dare use the Lord's name in vain. I can't believe you'd make up a story like this. I've known Harry since we were youngin's, he's like a brother to me," shouted her father. "No, I don't believe you!" Meanwhile, her mother was wringing her hands, crying and rocking back and forth on the edge of Madaline's bed.

Madaline was crying hysterically now and wouldn't let either of her parents touch her. "I'm ashamed to call you my parents."

"You don't mean what you're sayin. You know we love you. If you don't want to marry Billy, which we think you should, then we have no other option. We want you to go to Aunt Mabel's house in South Dakota. You'll stay there till the baby comes. We'll tell people that we put you to boarding school for a while, cause you're so smart."

"Do you think that people around here are going to fall for that lie? If you do this to me, then, I swear to God, I'll never forgive you for the rest of my life, I swear it."

"You don't know what your sayin, honey. As soon as this terrible ordeal is over, well, everything'll go back to normal, you'll see," as her mother shed tears.

"We'll pack your bags for you and we'll call Aunt Mabel right now. Aunt Mabel will be expecting ya. The baby will be put up for adoption to some couple who can't have kids of their own. They'll take the poor little thing in and give it a good home. We'll make sure that they're good people and believe in God. God be with you child and everything will be all right," her father told her as he tried putting his arm around her. Madaline slouched down on her bed, flinging her dad's arm away.

"He should be tried and put in jail." Madaline screamed at her mother and father as she jumped out of her bed and ran down the stairs. Yelling behind her, "it's not an ordeal. It's my life and the life of my baby!"

She ran out the front door, hearing it shut behind her. She ran into Trigger's stall. She put her arms around his long neck, talking and crying to him at the same time.

It was the worst 9 months that Madaline ever went through. She had the baby on her aunt's bed with a mid-wife helping. They took the baby immediately away. "Can't I at least have a chance to hold my baby?" A tearful Madaline asked. "Is it a boy or a girl, can you tell me that?"

"The baby's healthy and will be fine with its adoptive parents. They'll be able to provide a good home for it and love the poor thing. Now you get some rest, it's been a long, hard labor. You've been through a terrible ordeal."

'There's that word again, ordeal. If someone ever so much as says that word, I'll spit it their face.' She was left alone wanting to hold this child that she had carried for nine months. She couldn't believe that they wouldn't let them hold 'her' baby. 'I've carried this child in my body. It isn't fair that I can't cuddle it and at least know if it's a boy or a girl. How cruel can they be?' She screamed at her aunt and the midwife. "I deserve the right to at least see it, even though my baby was conceived in a wrong way."

She knew that she would love this little baby with all her heart and soul. She'd be a good mother, she'd go home and raise this child, on her own, if she had to, she thought to herself. Trying to catch her breath she couldn't feel more alone in her entire life. She cried herself to sleep.

Her aunt kept Madaline for another month, wanting to make sure that her niece was ready to travel and have a better frame of mind. Madaline went home after 'her confinement.' The incident was never mentioned again by either her parents or siblings. From that time forth she hated her parents and didn't trust anybody every again.

One evening, a few months after her daughter came home, when everyone was asleep, her mother crept into her bedroom. Taking Madaline by the hand, she led her downstairs where they could be alone and not have anyone hear what her mother was going to say to her eldest daughter.

"I spoke to Billy Martin. I know that what you told your father and me was the truth. I never told your father that I spoke to Billy. He'd kill me if he knew I went behind his back. I've been saving money for years, so that you, and your brothers and sisters would have money for college. Swear to me you won't tell a soul. You have to swear." At first Madaline couldn't look into her mother's eyes. She shook her head and tried ignoring her. Realizing how her eldest daughter was feeling, she too felt the pain that Madaline was going through. She took Madaline's hand and pushed an envelope in her daughter's palm.

Madaline started crying. She let her mother hold her in her arms. The heart wrenching sobs wouldn't stop. "I'm sorry that things turned out the way they did honey. I never wanted for you to be hurt. Go away, someplace far, and start a new life for yourself. I don't want to see you go, but I know what's best for you. You'll never be able to hold your head up high, knowin that everyone will be talkin about you. You have too much pride, I know that. I can understand if you hate me and your daddy, but please try to understand where we're comin from. The only thing I'm gona ask from you is to let me know where you are, and if you're doing well. Promise me that."

Madaline was both hurt and surprised at what her mother had done for her. She knew it took a lot for her mom to admit what she did and realized that she was wrong. 'I can't believe she gave me all her savings so I can start a new life. Even though I want to hate her, I know I can't. I realize my father is an ignorant man. I'll never forgive him, never! My poor brothers and sisters will always stay in Fairfield for the rest of their lives, unless a miracle happens. It made me happy that when he saw me, after all the time that I was away, he neighed and wouldn't stop neighing until I patted him and rode him across the meadow like we used to do.'

When Madaline climbed the steps to her bedroom, she had many misgivings. She lay in bed, just thinking and thinking. 'I'll never forget my baby's birthday and somehow I'll find my child and make contact.'

'I know I'll miss everyone that I grew up with but somehow I'll survive.' With hatred in her heart she knew that whatever it takes she'd get even with 'Uncle Harry'. 'No matter what it costs or how long it takes, he'll regret the day he ever laid a hand on me.'

CHAPTER ELEVEN

On the way to the train station, she walked past the Martins' house. She saw Billy planting seeds into the ground for new crops come spring time. She stopped and was watching Billy do his chores when he spotted her. He motioned for her to come over. Reluctantly, she started walking and then found herself running, with all her might to his side and into his arms. Before she said a word the tears were pouring down her face. Billy took her in his arms and held her tightly. "Now, now, stop crying and shivering commanded Billy. I know what happened. Your mom came by and talked to me and the family. Tell me who did this to you and I swear, as God is my witness, I'll kill the bastard!"

"It was that no good, Uncle Harry. Can you believe it? Every time I think about what happened I want to kill him myself." Her body was trembling and she couldn't stop shivering. Wrenching free from his protective arms she looked into his eyes and said, "Promise me, Billy, that you won't lay a hand on that scumbag. He's not worth your going to jail, no matter what that Bastard did to me. You've got to promise. I'll get him no matter what it takes. Believe me; he's dead as a door nail. I swear on my Grammy's grave he'll wish he weren't alive when I get through with him. Madaline kissed her best friend on his cheek, hugged him with all her might, finally letting him go. She straightened herself up and with dignity started walking down the path, letting the tears fall freely down her cheeks, out to the road to start a new life.

HOLLYWOOD CALIFORNIA

When Madaline decided to leave Fairfield, Iowa and go to Hollywood, where she always dreamed of going, she was scared to death. She wanted to take her chances to become one of the few, out of many, who make it big in the 'city of sin.' Madaline read all the latest books about the stars and how they got discovered. She wanted to become a star! Madeline didn't know a sole or have any clue as where to live. By chance, fate or a predetermined course of events, made possible by the Lord up above, she got off the bus after the long, tedious, and bumpy ride from Iowa to California. The bus ride was grueling and the many pit stops that it made, took a lot out of Madaline and all the people who were going to destinations unknown.

It was a hot summer's day, one that weakens a person if they subject themselves to the environment for a long period of time. The blazing sun, with its roasting heat, diffusing it's feverish and scorching fire, beat upon Madaline as she walked through the streets of this large and unfamiliar city. With the money that her mother gave her, and the little money she had managed to save, working at the local diner, after returning from her Aunt Mabel's and her grueling experience, she knew that she had to be frugal. First thing on her list was to find a place to live, that wasn't expensive. The bus fair took some money, but not as much as if she traveled by train. 'Sure, it took more time, but what the heck; all I have on my hands right now is time.' Madaline knew she had to be prudent and spend her money wisely, willing to take any type of job available. She debated whether to stop at a drug store and grab a quick soda to quench her thirst. After reasoning that the few cents would not break her bank, she went into the pharmacy. She deliberated, for only a moment, and lifted herself onto one of the red, vinyl, round seats at the counter in front of the window and sat down.

"Excuse me, are you saving this seat for anyone? If not, do you mind if I sit down and rest my tired, aching feet?" The young red head told her it wasn't being saved. Madaline ordered a vanilla frappe. Lifting the suitcase, she put it beside her, resting it on top of the unoccupied seat on the other side of her. Extending her hand to the girl sitting next to her, "my name is Madaline" and introduced herself to the beautiful young lady.

"Hi, my name is Ann Browning. Boy it's hot out today. Are you from around here? Seeing the suitcase, I guess I shouldn't ask such a silly question."

"That's okay," Madaline laughed.

An embarrassed Ann replied, "I'm sorry, I guess I wasn't thinking."

"I just got into town a few hours ago and the heat just got me. I come from a small town in Iowa, called Fairfield, and I should be used to the heat. I guess I'm a bit nervous, not knowing anyone in town or for that matter, if I'll be able to find a place to stay for the night. Do you live in L. A.?"

"Yes, I'm not originally from these parts. I used to live in Madison, Wisconsin and came to California a few years back. I haven't met anyone, so far that originally came from this area, though I don't regret making the move. What made you decide to come here? Is it for a vacation or are you out to find fame and fortune like so many of us?," she asked with an amusing smile.

"I guess I'm one of the hopefuls who want to become a movie star. I've never seen a place like this before. Of course I've seen pictures...but gee, to actually be here is something I can't put into words. I can't describe the feeling I got when I put my feet on the ground and made it to the place that I've been dreaming of for years. I wanted to kneel down and kiss the pavement when I finally got to my destination. I know it's a stupid thing for me to think, but gee wilikers, it's so different from Fairfield. Can you understand what I mean?"

"Yes I can. I was in your shoes a few years ago. Not Dorothy's shoes from the Wizard of Oz." Ann laughed a laugh that was contagious. "Say, if you really don't know anyone, and if you think I'm not some weirdo, I live in a beautiful old home that rents out rooms to people in your situation. As it happens, one of the rooms became available a few days ago and if you want, I can bring you there and you can take a look at it. You're under no obligation. It's not too far from downtown. We can grab a bus and then you can make up your mind."

"That sounds wonderful." Madaline really didn't want to spend the money for, yet, another bus. She couldn't stand the thought of getting onto one again. "Gee, I'm glad I decided to come in from the hot sun and get something to drink. I probably would have never met you. You're like my guardian angel. I can't thank you enough."

"Don't say that just yet. You don't know me. You'd have met someone else, but I'm not sure they'd be the type of person you'd really want to associate with. There are a lot of weird people here. They'd die for some nice, pretty girl who they'd think is fresh meat, if you get my point."

Madaline pretended to understand what Ann was referring to. She nodded her head, making believe she appreciated the advice.

The bus ride didn't take long, and left them off a few blocks from Ann's rooming house. Glancing out the side of her eye, Madaline couldn't help but admire this tall, attractive red head that walked briskly. Ann talked enthusiastically with animated gestures about this unusual town. She made Madaline laugh and at the same time feel welcome and at home.

Rounding the corner Madaline viewed the large grey Victorian residence, built in about the late eighteen hundreds. She observed the name on the corner of the street was Kellum Ave. It was situated just outside L. A. Madaline noticed that the white ginger bread trim lent a fairytale look to what could be conceived as an ominous old manor. Taking in all the sights, trying not to be conspicuous, she saw a beautiful formal garden with a Greek revival miniature temple and a Buddha situated in the back of the lot. Some magnificent stained windows, in odd shaped forms, were located in the front and sides of the large house. 'If a person was lucky enough to get a room with one of those windows, they could stare out and view the world in a completely different perspective,' Madaline thought as she trudged along, trying to keep up with Ann.

The large suitcase was becoming heavy, and as she mounted the wide front stairs, Madaline said a silent prayer that they arrived and everything would work out in her favor. An oval glass windowed front door, with two sidelights, lent light and airiness to the large foyer once they were inside.

"Mrs. McCallum, are you around?" Ann yelled out, waiting for a reply from the owner of the house.

Coming out from the back, she walked through the dining room, wiping her hands on a worn, yellowed dishtowel. Walking with a shuffled gait, an older, motherly type woman came towards them.

"Now what's all the shouting about?"

"Mrs. McCallum, I'd like you to meet Madaline Mason." Anne said as she had her fingers crossed in back of her. I thought if you haven't rented the room that Tony vacated, that you'd rent it to my friend here."

With a discerning eye, Mrs. McCallum looked Madaline over, from head to toe. "Well, the Queen of England just called and asked if I might be able to rent a room to one of her cousins, but I refused. What makes you think I'd take in a young girl like this? She's probably a run away. My luck, I'd be picked up for aiding and abetting a minor." Drawling out her next word she continued, "B U T maybe I could be persuaded to find it in my heart to rent out the room, if I want to. Tell me young lady, and I mean young lady, how come you're away from where you come from? You don't look old enough to be out on your own." Squinting her eyes she asked, "You didn't run away from home did you and have your folks and a bunch of people worrying or the police looking for you?"

Madaline found herself scared of this older, profound mistress of the boarding house.

"Oh no mam, not at all, I assure you I have my folks blessing and love."

"Well, if you can pay the rent on time, we rent it by the week, and if you obey my rules, we'll get along fine. I don't allow any hanky-panky goings on in my boarding house. There are to be no boys allowed upstairs in your room and no cooking in there either. We have a dining room where I expect you to take your meals. I provide a nice hearty breakfast and every evening a good dinner is served at six o'clock -- promptly. That's all included in your rent. If you miss a meal, that's your problem. I don't want you meandering into the house, late in the evening, disturbing the other guests. Even though you're paying rent, I keep a curfew and expect it to be obeyed." Changing the expression on her face, she continued. "No one can take my motherly instincts away from me yet." Looking directly into Madaline's eyes she asked, "If you want to look at the room, Ann can show you where it is," She softly said.

"Yes, I would like to, very much," a delighted Madaline answered.

The room was on the second floor, a large corner room, with one of the windows that she had admired, looking out at the street. A large, double, canopy bed was situated in an alcove with two unusual sconces, with lights, mounted on the wall on either side of the bed. A dark, mahogany, double dresser with another lamp, a beautiful, Dresden female figurine dressed in a burgundy evening dress, made up the only other furniture in this nice size room. "It's so quaint. I love it. Ann, I can't thank you enough. I'm so lucky I met you." She walked towards Ann and gave her a hug. "You have no idea what a feeling of relief I have knowing that I have a nice, homey, clean place I can call my own."

In the back of Madaline's mind she berated herself. 'Here I am accepting a room and I don't even know the week's rent. I hope I don't go through my money faster than I thought I would. '

"Don't thank me quite so fast. Mrs. McCallum is nice, but she can be a royal pain in the ass. Believe me, she'll drive you crazy if you get too close to her. Do your own thing and you'll get along fine. Her breakfasts are great, but her evening meals are something else to be desired. I guess not too many people can screw up bacon and eggs."

As they descended the spiral staircase Madaline couldn't help but be grateful and said a silent prayer to God for sending Ann into her life.

Madaline found Mrs. McCallum in the kitchen and told her she liked the room but wanted to know how much the rent would be. "To tell you the truth, I don't have a set price. Each room is different and if you're lucky enough to get a larger room, than I have to ask for more money. You looked at Toni's old room, which is larger than most of my rooms." Looking Madaline over again she tried figuring this young, beautiful girl out, but reserved her judgment till she got to know her better. "Let's say about $20 a week." Madaline figured out the amount by the month and her mouth dropped. "I'd really like to take the room," looking down at the floor Madaline spoke again. "I'll be honest with you, as much as I'd like the room, that's a little steep for my budget. I came out here with a certain amount of money. I'm sorry but $20 a week would eat up my budget sooner than I anticipated."

Mrs. McCallum wiped her hands on the half apron she was wearing and put her hand to her chin pondering Madaline's remark. Looking the young girl over she thought for a moment, and then told Madaline that she could pay $15 a week until Madaline found work. Madaline looked down at the floor. Shuffling her thin soled shoes she made Mrs. McCallum an offer of $12.50. "I wish I could pay you more and I promise that as soon as I get a job I'll make up the difference. If you let me, I'll be glad to do some chores around the house. I can clean the bathrooms and wash the floors if need be."

Madaline looked with hope and expectation at this motherly type person who tried to act stern. Looking directly at Madaline and for a few minutes not a word was said. Finally Mrs. McCallum smiled and told her where the cleaning materials were kept and she'd have to do the chores two to three times a week, depending on the weather. Madaline jumped for joy and hugged this chubby, older woman that she met not even an hour ago. They'd discuss the rent when Madaline's situation changed. "You have a deal Mrs. McCallum. I assure you, I'm a respectable girl and as soon as I get a regular job I won't mind paying the extra money." With a nod of her head Mrs. McCallum stood a moment then turned around and headed back into the kitchen.

Ann was working at MGM for a few years and was considered a pretty good bit actress. She loved comedy and was just catching the eye of one of the directors at the studio. When Ann first met Madaline she just finished filming her first large part in a sizeable budgeted movie and was waiting with baited breath for the film to be released.

It was one of those grueling weeks for Ann. She still had her part-time accounting job and couldn't wait to give it up and be able to act in the movie industry full time. The movie had finally come out and Ann was trying to act nonchalant.

"For such a good actress, you're doing a terrible job," Madaline told her friend.

"What do you mean by that?"

"You're driving me and everybody else who lives here crazy by reading the papers. You keep pacing the floor and pretty soon you'll wear a spot in the rug. You're smoking up a storm and I bet your finger nails are all chewed up."

"You think you're so smart, don't you? One day you'll be in my shoes and then I hope I'm around to see how you'll act. Madaline, this critic's review will either make or break me. I admit I'm nervous, you'd be to if your career was riding on this."

"Hey, I didn't mean to poke fun of you. What can we do to get your mind off this situation? Want to take a walk or go bowling?"

"Bowling, I haven't done that in years. Thanks, but I don't think I'll be good company tonight. The next twenty four hours can't go by fast enough for me. I'll be okay. Thanks for caring. By the way, with all my self-absorption, how did you make out at the studio? I told Mac that you'd be coming over."

"Well, by the time I got out of the diner, it was pretty late. I'm thinking of looking elsewhere for a waitressing job. I need something in the evenings so I can be available to go to the studio during the day." Ann nodded her head in approval.

Madaline couldn't wait to finish her shift at the diner and buy the evening paper. There were quite a few people standing at the bus stop, most of whom Madaline had seen every evening since taking the bus to and from work daily. That didn't deter Madaline from squeezing to the front of the line, assuring her a seat. She ignored the rude remarks or dirty looks given by the other commuters when she sat down on one of the few available seats. 'Let everyone get pissed off, I don't care. My feet are killing me. They probably don't have the grueling schedule that I have. It seems all I do is walk back and forth, bringing the orders to the right customers. Hey, as long as I smile and don't screw up their orders I'm bound to get good tips.'

Picking up a left over paper she found the review she was looking for. The movie got so, so, reviews but the one favorable remark was about the delightful long, legged, beautiful, red head who stole the whole show. It went on to say that she made the movie worth seeing and one should not miss it. The columnist went on to say that they were sure Miss Ann Browning would be seen in more movies in the future. Madaline let out a delightful yell and a big yes, then self-consciously refolded the newspaper and slumped in her seat.

Once off the bus she ran all the way to the rooming house, and quickly yelled for Ann. Ann came running down the spiral staircase. They both grabbed each other and were jumping up and down with joy. Mrs. McCallum came through the swinging kitchen door, reached the hallway in record time and asked, "What's all the commotion about? All this yelling nearly scared the living day lights out of me."

"Didn't Ann tell you or show you the review of her new movie?"

"No, you know I don't have time to read the papers. Just keeping this large house spic and span and getting the food prepared for my borders is enough for a body and doesn't give me much spare time. What have I missed this time? She chimed in before Madaline could tell her the good news.

"Did I tell you that some very important actors and actresses lived here before they made it big?" "It looks like you probably will be having another famous actress living here. Ann's performance was one of the most favorable comments made about the movie in this evenings review. Come on Ann, let's go out for the evening to celebrate; my treat," an exuberant Madaline exclaimed.

As Mrs. McCallum made her way back into the kitchen, Ann whispered, "Not having to eat her meal is going to be celebration enough for me." Laughing they changed and went downtown for Chinese Food.

One day Ann came hurrying home from the movie lot. "Thank God you didn't leave for your job this evening. I'm invited to a large party off Mulholland Drive. Some big shot writer is throwing this huge party and they invited me and said I can invite a friend. Call in sick this evening and come."

"I'd love to, but I don't have anything to wear that would be appropriate."

"Don't be silly. We're built similar. Let's see what I have in my closet that you can wear. Sometimes I get cast offs from a few of the high budgeted films. Beggars can't be choosers." She laughed as she pulled Madaline up the winding staircase.

After trying on various outfits and rejecting them all, Ann went to the very end of her closet and pulled out a plain but stylish persimmon cotton dress. "All we have to do is dress it up with some unusual jewelry. Let me see how it looks on you."

"Isn't it a bit tight and revealing on top?"

"Are you kidding? You look great in it. Most women would give anything to have your figure. You'll have every male's head turning. I hope Rod is home tonight. I'll ask him to drive us or see if I can borrow his car. You know there aren't any buses that go to the posh neighborhoods, if you get the drift."

Ann fastened an unusual white choker around Madeline's neck and gave her the matching earrings and bracelet to put on. "Would you be my roommate if and when we can afford to move?"

After promising Rod practically everything she had except her first born, Ann found herself driving Madaline through L. A. and Beverly Hills and onto the roads in Rod's bright blue Chevy Impala convertible. They drove through the hills by Laurel Canyon Blvd. and Coldwater Canyon Drive, leading to Mulholland Drive.

"I can't believe the spectacular view from up here. I remember when you brought me to The Griffith Observatory and Planetarium on one of my first nights in L. A. I think I told you that I knew of the observatory since I watched James Dean in 'Rebel without a Cause'. I was thrilled that I was standing in the same spot that James might have stood," a jubilant Madaline exclaimed. "I thought that view was breathtaking, but driving through these mountains is just as magnificent. It's a bit frightening, especially when we don't really know where we're going."

"Hey, speak for yourself. Even though I usually don't travel these roads, I know how to read maps and I'll get us to our destination in no time." A confident Ann replied.

"You know Ann, California is so very different from Fairfield. There aren't any mountains and the land is very flat. You can travel for hours at a time and all you see are flat fields with corn growing, or in the winter, the fields are barren. California is different and beautiful."

"This is the first time that you mentioned your home. How come you never speak about your family or your life as a kid? I've told you everything about me. Don't you miss your folks and friends?"

"Don't look at me; just keep your eyes on these winding roads. No, I guess I don't miss them. Someday I'll have a long chat with you and tell you about my, 'supposedly wonderful family.' For now I don't want to get into it and ruin this potentially good evening. I feel like a little girl looking out from behind a partially closed door into a grown-up party. I don't want anything to spoil my anticipation for what I hope will be a great night." Giggling, Madaline said, "I feel like Alice in Wonderland."

After two disappointing and frustrated attempts to find the house that the party was at, they unexpectedly came across the large home, hidden and concealed by massive trees and shrubs.

"Are you sure this is the right house?"

"Look at all the cars lined up the street and driveway. There's only one way to find out, come on."

Walking up the dirt road they were in awe of all the newest model cars and limousines, many with chauffeurs, waiting for their owners to re-appear. The cars lined up appeared to be a quarter mile down the narrow, windy, road. They were greeted by a maid who took their sweaters and directed them to the rest of the party, which was by now, in full swing. The house was massive, quite deceptive from the outside. A band was playing by the patio, to the side of the large in ground swimming pool.

"I can't believe all the people here. Is that who I think it is?" Madaline asked as she discreetly pointed to George Hamilton. "He's more handsome in person, if that's possible."

They took drinks offered to them by a waiter passing by and walked through the patio area, observing the many guests, overhearing their conversations, trying not to betray that they were eavesdropping.

Ann finally saw the host and bringing Madaline with her, introduced her to him and a few of his guests that were with him. Robert Wagner stopped Ann as she and Madaline were wandering about. "I saw the picture and read the reviews of your movie, kid. Great job! I bet Meyer will sign you up for a long contract. Just make sure you get a good agent and let him help you with the negotiations."

A beautiful young woman came to his side, entwining her arm through his. "Natalie, I'd like you to meet Ann Browning and her friend, excuse me, but I didn't catch your name."

Extending her hand, "Madaline, Madaline Mason, it's a pleasure Miss Wood."

"Bob told me about the movie and your acting. Ann, I'm sure we'll be seeing more of you." Natalie verbalized.

"Thank you for the compliment, I hope so."

Madaline never saw so many stars gathered at one place and was in awe. Ann's enthusiasm was contagious, as Madaline found herself in the midst of these famous people, some that she had looked up to and idolized from afar. Others she surmised were producers, directors and writers, who were not recognized as easily, but who were the backbone of the industry.

The extra outside spotlights and candles were not necessary, for the sky was ablaze with light from the moonlight and shining stars. Ann and Madaline circulated about, admiring the beautiful grounds and conversing with the other guests.

Brad Thomas disliked most parties. This one was no exception. The only reason he found himself here was he promised his current wife, Sheila, that he would take her out more often. While she was having a great time, talking with her friends, he found himself wandering about, oblivious to the other guests, just passing the time until Sheila wanted to go home. He sat on one of the ledges, amongst the brambles, smoking his pipe and thinking of his next movie. He was tired. He just finished filming a huge epic, one that had taken him over three years to complete. All he wanted to do was relax for a while. He was one of the most revered and sought after directors in the field, and knew that he would be asked to direct another large production soon.

It was the type of business that one couldn't get away from for any length of time. Otherwise rumors would start to circulate that you wanted to retire. Either you weren't interested or if your next movie were to bomb, you were washed up. No, he couldn't take that chance. He had to make all his money and fame while he still had it in him and was young enough to take the grueling work and opportunities. Brad needed to make lots of money to keep up with all the alimonies he had to pay out each month. As long as he kept directing and was successful, he'd have no problem delivering his obligations.

Puffing his Meerschaum intensely, he couldn't help but stare at the beautiful young woman who was wandering below, oblivious of his watchful eye. He had seen many gorgeous and well-endowed females throughout his career, but there was something different about this tall and strikingly exquisite girl that he had not seen in many years. He had to find out who she was and acquaint himself with her.

Walking down from the ledge Brad spotted the host. He caught up to Mike. Brad professed, “I haven't had more fun at a party like this in a long time.” Brad patted him on his back. Mike was appreciative of Brad's comment and thanked him for coming. I'm glad you made it. You must be beat and glad the movie is over. Do you have any idea when it will be released?”

“No, it's up to the editors and production staff now.”

“Say Mike, who is that beautiful young girl over there?"

"Do you mean the young lady that's with Ann Browning?"

"Yes."

"I don't remember her name, but let's go over and I'll introduce you."

"Don't turn around, but the most gorgeous hunk of man I've seen is heading this way with Mike. I bet he wants to meet me. I think he's the director, Brad Thomas. Maybe he wants me for a new film he'll be making."

"Ann I hope so, but I think all this champagne is going to your head."

Fluffing her hair with her hand she pretended to be startled when Mike came over and made the introductions. Practically ignoring Ann, Brad started conversing with Madaline, who was completely surprised by the unwarranted attention. Disregarding everyone else, Brad proceeded to talk to Madaline. After a while, the desire to have Madaline to himself, without the vigilant, scrutinizing eyes of the other guests, seized him. "If you'll excuse me, I'd like to take Madaline and show her some of the spectacular views from up above." Suddenly he took her by her arm and guided her through the crowd. He led her towards the path, headed for the hills, away from the rest of the people. Madaline looked back for Ann and saw her. Madaline just put her shoulders to her head and made a face as if to say, what the hell am I doing with this man? Ann had a look of dismay on her face.

"Don't be afraid, I won't harm you." Brad said to Madaline as she started to protest his impromptu action. His laughter was infectious as she objected to his rash behavior. "I promise not to bite." Unexpectedly they came to a clearing, the flat rocks creating a perfect seat. "Isn't this a wonderful view?" Brad asked Madaline, “have you ever seen such a perfect night?"

"It seems most nights are beautiful in California. When I first came out here, Ann took me to the Griffith Observatory and I had never heard of it except when I saw Rebel Without a Cause. That's also beautiful."

"I gather you aren't from around these parts. You have a freshness about you that I haven't seen in years. I hope you don't lose it with time."

He looked into her eyes that were like sparkling amethysts. He listened intently as she spoke of her past. His deep profound interest invited and enticed her to speak openly about her dreams and hopes of the future. There were circumstances and situations from the past that Madaline purposely avoided talking about. It was no one's business, she thought, as she successfully turned the subject away from herself and with an impassioned glance, looked deeply into his dark brown eyes.

"Enough about me, I'm getting bored listening to myself prattle on. From what Ann briefly told me, you're a director. As you can tell, I'm not up on who's who in Hollywood. What have you directed? Maybe I've seen a few of your movies."

Brad laughed to himself. Madaline was so naïve she really didn't know who he was or how famous a director she was talking to. Either that or she was the best darn actress he'd come across in a while. He named off a few of his latest movies and saw Madaline's look of surprise. "Now I remember hearing your name," Madaline exclaimed. I can't believe that I'm talking to you. I mean your name is synonymous with greatness. I'm honored."

CHAPTER TWELVE

Brad felt himself blush, not many people could bring on that reaction, he thought, as he lit his pipe once again.

At first Madaline was nervous when such a handsome and forceful man coerced and dramatically transported her to this remote area, devoid of other guests. As she gazed into his warm, large eyes and open face, all at once she felt at ease and was unafraid. He was a tall man, with broad shoulders, and still well built for an older gentleman, Madaline surmised he was in his late thirties or early forties. Once again, he looked deeply into her eyes, as if penetrating her very soul.

"If you don't mind my saying so, you are absolutely gorgeous. When I gaze into your eyes, it's like sinking into the depths of the sea. You are a remarkable young woman, from what I've seen so far."

Turning her face away from him, she didn't want him to see the bright red rush that suddenly enveloped and veiled her. "Not to be rude, but I bet you tell a lot of women what you just told me and flatter them to no end."

With proficiency, he tenderly guided her face back. "I know you're going to find this hard to believe, but I make it a practice never to discuss or reveal what I'm thinking. It's quite unusual for me to do so. If you'll allow yourself to trust me, I would like to see you again. I'd like you to take a screen test and if I think you have potential, I'll help you break into the business. Now, I'm not promising that if your test is terrible that I'd be able to do the impossible, but if I like what I see on the screen, then I can work with you and we can go from there."

"I don't know what to say, except thank you. I find this unbelievable." I hope you're not of those casting directors that has a couch in his dressing room and with a little coaxing, get the new upstart into his, 'so called bed'."

Brad laughed and laughed. 'This young woman was so naïve; she actually came out and spoke what she was thinking.'

"I can assure you, I'm not that type of director."

Brad continued, "This is the type of business I'm in. Making people's dreams and fantasies come true." Seeing her as a delicate and fragile flower, he gently took her soft hands into his, caressing her long fingers, and with his soft, tenuous lips, tenderly kissed them slowly and sensuous. Madaline felt a physical excitement she never thought possible. Looking into his warm, dark eyes, she wanted him to continue, moving his moist lips to parts she only dreamed of. No, she thought, this is wrong. I don't know this man from Adam. She removed her hands from his gentle grip and resisting her desires, she deftly rose.

"I have to get back to my friend, she must be worried sick. I hope you're a man of your word and mean what you say, Mr. Thomas, and arrange for a screen test. I would be very grateful."

Taking her hand, he guided her down the path. I never say anything I don't mean. You'll be hearing from me soon."

As they got to the edge of the grounds he turned her around to face him.

"I truly enjoyed talking to you Madaline. I know we'll be seeing more of each other. You're like a breath of fresh air amongst this stale and musty atmosphere, and Madaline, please call me Brad."

Driving back from the party, Ann couldn't ask enough questions. "Ann, I love you to death, but I really don't want to continue this stupid conversation. Yes, I think he's handsome and no, I didn't make a date with him. For God sakes, Ann, I saw the wedding band on his finger. If I should work with him, it will only be a professional relationship."

"What do you mean by working with him? Did he offer you a part in his next movie?"

"No, he said that he'll see what he can do to get me a screen test."

"Oh my God, Oh my God, when Brad Thomas says he'll try to get you a screen test, you'll be in like Flynn. I'm telling you if you test well you'll be like gold. I saw the way he looked at you and I know when a man has the hots for a girl."

"Stop looking at me and watch these winding roads. You're talking ridiculous. I'm really tired, and all this foolish assumption is just stupid and controversial. I'm not getting my hopes up. I learned a long time ago, to only rely on myself. You can't count on people, even the ones you think you can. Besides, I don't know if I've had enough acting lessons to give a good screen test," confessed Madaline.

"I think we'd better make sure that you fit in more classes, at least until he gives you a call," suggested Ann, as she deftly maneuvered around the windy roads.

The bed felt good as Madaline rested, waiting for Morpheus to take over. The moonlight showed brightly, illuminating the mediocre size room through the flimsy, white, starched curtains. She closed her eyes, hoping the darkness would bring about sleep. As much as she tried, sleep eluded her. Brads handsome face kept appearing before her. She didn't want to get her hopes up, too many times she had been disappointed. 'No', she thought, 'if it's meant to be, it'll be!'

The next week Madaline accepted his invitation to go to the beach. The beautiful ocean, its waves swelling, breaking before them, was a magnificent sight. The whitecaps surging, then curling and rolling it's now slow force towards the blanket that Brad and Madaline were laying on. Brad, with his laughing eyes and warm smile, finished putting the lotion on Madaline's torso. His firm hands caressing her shoulders, down the small of her back, rolling her over, he gently proceeding to her chest, abdomen and down her long and well-shaped legs, stopping at just the right spots, till she tingled with anticipation. His kiss was warm and sensuous as his lips now moved in the same direction as where his hands had been. Madaline could feel the moistness between her legs and wanted his lips and hands to continue their search and uncover her most hidden desires and secrets. The hot sweat woke her as she heard herself moaning aloud. She stayed in bed for a while, not wanting to forget his face or the realistic orgasm she thought she experienced when she had the sensual dream.

Yawning, Brad headed up to his bedroom with Sheila trailing behind. 'God she can talk and talk. I can't stand to hear her voice anymore.' It took him two weeks after their marriage to realize he had made a mistake. Sheila was his third wife, and he had hoped his last. He found out, all too late, what a shrew she really was. Her beautiful and voluptuous body didn't make up for the emptiness between her head or her rash and materialistic behavior. He quickly got under the comforter. He put the pillow over his head, hoping to drown out the incessant chatter. All he wanted was to get some sleep. It had been a long and lonely five years of marriage. Sheila was only interested in social status and was the most materialistic, unspiritual, greedy person he had known. She loved the idea of shopping along Rodeo Drive and frequented the most expensive stores, charging anything she wanted. The idea of her being Mrs. Bradford Thomas was a giant victorious conquest that she made sure everyone knew.

Closing his eyes, he tried thinking about his next film and all the work that lay before him. Suddenly Madaline's face appeared. Those beautiful blue, with specks of violet, eyes bore down on him. He reached out, touching her large, firm breasts, heaving up and down, rhythmic to her breathing. Her mouth opened slightly, his tongue slowly moistening her large full lips. He could hear her moan of fulfillment as his hands caressed the rest of her perfect body. The poking was relentless, as Sheila's fingers kept poking at his body. He did not want his dream to end. He woke up startled, an erection quite evident.

"I thought you'd like to rid yourself of your giant hard on. The way you were groaning made me think you'd like to take advantage of whatever you were thinking of; hopefully doing some very kinky things to me. How about it Brad?"

"Dam it Sheila, is that all you have on your mind. I'm tired and I wasn't dreaming about what you think I was. Just let me go to sleep." He turned his back to her, pretending to sleep.

"You know Brad, you're boring. All you think about is work. Lucky for you I find other things to do with my time, otherwise I'd already be tired of you."

'She doesn't have to tell me what occupies her time. Shopping, shopping and more shopping is all she thinks about. She calls me a bore. She has nothing between her ears. The only thing going for her is her pretty face.' Yawning, he willed himself to sleep, hoping he'd have only good dreams, if any at all, that he would remember.

Madaline went about her usual routine the following days. She didn't take what Brad had said to her seriously. She thought, 'he must have had too much to drink or he is one of those guys that is full of empty promises. He probably thought I'm the type of girl who worships men that have power in the industry or would go to bed with him for a contract. Well, he'll find out I'm not that type of girl. If I would be lucky enough to become an actress, I'll do it on my own merits and not have to sleep with a man to get the big break.' Even though she was pessimistic about Brad's promise of a screen test, Madaline signed up for the extra acting classes that Ann suggested.

Madaline was working as a file clerk during the day and trying to get in the extra acting classes while waitressing at a local hamburger joint at night. Her boss was good about her taking time off during the day to go to the studios for any possible work. Ann was working on getting a few bit parts for Madaline. She had to learn to bide her time.

Ann came running into the restaurant. "Madaline, there was a message for you at the house. I couldn't wait until you got home to tell you. You have an appointment for a screen test in three days."

"Hey lady, cut the bull. Are you gonna put my order in or what?" The large, heavy set man, smoking a thick stinky cigar yelled out.

Holding back her temper, Madaline put on a phony smile to the customer and told him to hold his horses. "I'll put it right in." Grabbing Ann she dragged her into the kitchen. She was jumping for joy and couldn't stop hugging her best friend.

"Thank you so much. I knew you'd be able to do something for me."

"Hey, wait a sec. As much as I wish it'd been me that got the test for you, it wasn't. When you get home tonight, we'll go over what you should do. Thank God you've been going to the extra acting classes with me."

"Ann, go back to what you said a few minutes ago. It wasn't you that got me the screen test. Do you think it was Brad Thomas that arranged it for me?"

"I don't know. But, at this point who cares as long as you show them how good of an actress you are." Madaline went to the boarding house that evening and was grateful that she had her supper at the diner. She couldn't endure another one of Mrs. McCallum's repulsive dinners.

Meanwhile, Ann landed another large role in a comedy. It seemed she had caught the eye of some producers and they wanted to make her another Carol Lombard. Ann met Madaline at the gate of the studio. "I'll walk you to the sound stage where you're supposed to be and I'll wait for you when you're through. They might call me away and I'll be at my sound stage. I know you'll do well. Do your best and you'll be fine." She hugged her friend and opened the door.

Mike Reardon introduced himself to Madaline once again and gave her the script that she was to read. "I'll let you study it for a while, and then in about an hour, I want to see you here. You can have a seat in the back or you can go to the cafeteria if you want to."

"Thank you, I'll take a seat in back and read it over." When the hour was over Madaline was nervous as hell when she walked onto the empty stage. The cameras were ahead and she tried to ignore them and forced herself not to be nervous, telling herself to read the script as she interpreted the part to be.

Brad saw the takes of the test and liked what he saw. He couldn't believe that with her beautiful looks she also had talent. Everyone in the screening room agreed with Brad's assumption. He didn't know how he was going to do it, but he was determined that Madaline Mason, an unknown, would be the star in his next film.

A loud knock on Madaline's door startled her and she abruptly sat up. She shook her head so that the bad thoughts in her dreams would go away.

"A half an hour till show time Ms. Mason," the stage manager yelled.

She had to freshen her makeup and touch up the wig that was on her head. She got up slowly and, then remembering how late it was, quickly changed into costume. Taking a deep breath she knew she was ready to perform to another packed house and make her audience happy once again.

After the last curtain call Madaline went directly to her room and changed into comfortable clothes. After all the adoring fans left the back stage and landing; the regular patrons had long departed from the theater, she let herself out of the rear stage door. Walking across the street to the safety of her hotel room she couldn't wait to get into her bed clothes and get under the warm covers. She was tired from her grueling schedule and wanted to get a restful, good night's sleep.

The phone's incessant ringing woke her. 'Who could be calling at this hour of the night?' She picked up the phone on the night table beside the bed and thought to herself, 'this better be a mighty important call', as she groggily picked up the receiver.

"Hi mom, an ashamed Kyle said to his mother. I know it's late but with the time difference and all I thought I'd wait till the show was over and you were in your hotel room."

Not minding that he woke her up from a deep sleep, she was glad to hear her son's voice. "It's so good hearing from you." Giving him a little jib she said, "I thought that your fingers were broken and you couldn't use the phone to dial."

"I'm truly sorry that I've been negligent in calling you. I've been busy with work and by the time I think of calling you, with the time difference and all, I don't bother. Like tonight, for instance, I know you've had a long day and you always put such effort into your performance, that I felt guilty calling."

"Don't ever feel that way. You know no matter what time it is or where I am, I always want to hear from you. After all, who else do I have? You're the light of my life. So tell me, how's Carol doing? Is she home from her latest assignment and how long will she be home this time?"

"She came home a few days ago and I really don't know how long her leisure time will last. Her next assignment will be in Cypress."

"It would be great if you could accompany her on her next job. After all it's been awhile since the two of you have taken a vacation. You've been married for over a year now and I wouldn't mind becoming a grandmother."

"Now mother, Carol and I have discussed this subject many times in the past, and we're both not ready to make a commitment that would impact our lives at this time."

"I hope you don't think that I'm being meddlesome, I'm not you know, but I have to say what's on my mind," Madaline admitted.

"I understand. Carol is rated one of the top models and it wouldn't be the right time for her to take a leave of absence. She wants to maintain her figure for as long as she can and, to be honest with you, I don't blame her." Kyle confessed.

"Let's get on a different subject. How is work going and what have you been up to? A curious Madaline asked. "I've heard through the grapevine that your pictures will be on some very elite magazines. I'm so proud of you."

"I wanted to tell you before you hear it from the grapevine, National Geographic got in touch with me and wants to set up a meeting. It would be entirely different than the type of work that I'm doing, but I think it might be an interesting assignment. Carol's away half the time and you know how I love animals. I heard they want me to travel to Africa and catch some of the wild animals in their natural habitat."

"That's a wonderful idea. You'll have to tell me what happens. Who knows, you might call me from some remote area of the world. Seriously though, I really think that this type of assignment will just add more to your already great portfolio. It will give me an excuse to travel to some exotic place. You know how I love to go to different places and get the flavor of that particular culture. It will be even better to be able to say, 'that's my son who's doing the photography', "an excited Madaline exclaimed.

Laughing at his mother's enthusiasm, Kyle got ready to say good night. "Well I better go now and let you get your beauty rest. After all, everyone expects to see you beautiful and vivacious when you appear on the stage."

"Thanks for calling and next time don't wait so long to call me. Send love and kisses to Carol. You know I love you and I need to hear your voice more often."

Throwing kisses over the phone she reluctantly hung up.

Kyle put down the telephone receiver and sat on the comfortable striped round chair. 'How am I going to tell my mother, Carol, and all the people I love, how I really feel? Do I have to live this lie forever? Will Curtis wait for me to, as they say, come out of the closet? Maybe I should give Alan a call one of these days and discuss my dilemma with him. He'll be understanding and probably give me good advice. It's too late to call this evening. I'll make the phone call in the very near future.' Meanwhile, Kyle was getting upset that he hadn't heard from Curtis is a few days. He'd wait a while longer and then go to the apartment. He had to find out what was wrong. It wasn't like him not to get in touch with him.

After the phone call from Kyle, Madaline had a hard time falling back to sleep. She appreciated Kyle's call but couldn't put her finger on the way she felt. Was it agitation, or merely a mother's intuition that Kyle had more on his mind? 'Now I'm glad that I have only one child. I can't imagine how Suzanne has to deal with 3 different personalities at the same time. '

'No wonder the poor dear is in a frenzy most of the time. Of course she doesn't let on how she really feels, but being intuitive, I know all the pressures that she's under. She's told me a lot of her story but there are certain details that she keeps hidden within her heart. I can relate to that. I'm sure she has had some very hurtful circumstances that happened that she's kept to herself. I hope that someday she'll be able to let her emotions come to the surface. I'm sure she'll feel better, like I'm the expert on keeping things to myself. I hope one day we'll both be able to unburden our souls and use it as a catharsis to purge all the negativity that's hidden within us.' She put the spare pillow under her head and fell back to sleep.

CHAPTER THIRTEEN

When the maid knocked on the door to her suite in the hotel, Madaline realized she had overslept. "Come back later" she instructed the young Jamaican cleaning girl. She padded her way to the bathroom, put on the shower and let the water get as hot as she could stand it. She let the spray, like little needles, go over her entire body, enjoying the sensation. She found the pulsating water invigorating and would dissipate the stupor she was in.

Toweling herself dry and getting into comfortable clothes, she leisurely went downstairs to the coffee shop for breakfast. She enjoyed sitting by herself and indulged in a muffin with a large cup of hazelnut coffee. She was thankful that a guest at the hotel didn't come over and asked her for an autograph.

She knew she had to keep in good shape, in order to continue the grueling schedule. "I have to keep busy otherwise I'll start thinking about everything that has happened in my life. Unfortunately some bad things I'd like to forget never really leave my thoughts.' She took the last bite of the blueberry muffin washing it down with her flavored coffee, which was now lukewarm. She found herself, halfheartedly leafing through the Boston Globe. One of the reasons she didn't like reading the Globe was that she felt the articles were slanted far to the left. Although many people in the entertainment field were liberals she was one of the few that were an independent, leaning towards the right side of the government, more conservative.

With a sigh, 'I'd better get to the theater and start another rehearsal, otherwise the rest of the cast will think that I'm acting like a diva. I do like acting snobbish and aloof' she thought to herself. 'When they know that I'm working my hardest in either a play or on a movie set, I get more co-operation from the fellow actors, cast members, and crew. Collectively, we're all necessary and important people that make a movie successful. After all, I and all the other members of the set want to get the best possible work from everyone. Sometimes when we're doing a movie from a book, the author can be a pain in the ass if he sees that his original manuscript is being changed and it doesn't resemble the initial published work.'

On the way to the theater she picked up a Herald Newspaper. Once there, she sat down on a cold metal folding chair, put her feet on another metal chair and opened the pages. She was waiting for the other cast members to come to work; realizing that she had arrived early. The reason she liked reading the Herald was that it was a smaller paper and easier to handle. She liked the articles better, besides having a better arts section. Even though she didn't have time to indulge in the smaller clubs that featured some of the older jazz singers, R & B, and even Rock 'n Roll artists, plus others like The Persuasions, which in her mind was one of the best a cappella groups that she heard sing; she appreciated that they were being kept busy. 'Someday, I'll have to make time to bring Suzanne, Nancy, and maybe Beverly with me to either Sculler's at the Charles Hotel or to The House of Blues. I might as well take advantage of this great city', she thought to herself. 'I'll have the understudy, what's her name, oh yes, Betty, who by now knows my part very well, to act during the second performance, and then the three or four of us can let our hair down and enjoy these small, intimate treasures.'

Madaline wondered where Paul was for the past few days. Even though he called her on a regular basis she missed the feeling of safety having him around. Paul had to go out of State for a while, trying to confirm leads that might help them find who was after Madaline. He assured her he would be back by tomorrow evening. She hoped nothing bad would happen to her in the meantime. Rehearsal for the play was to begin in a half an hour. She had nothing but time on her hands as she finished reading. The director bellowed and the cast came on the stage.

"The rehearsal won't take long kids, by now we know the play backwards and forwards. We'll go through it once and then you can do what you want for the rest of the day. I'll see you back here about 1 hour before the curtain goes up. Have a good one."

Madaline took a diversion and went into Metamorphosis, hoping that Suzanne might be there and possibly got a cancellation. It wasn't often when she had this extra time on her hands. Sure enough, they were able to squeeze her in for a facial and massage.

When Suzanne came out of her room she saw Madaline standing in front of the appointment desk, Suzanne was delighted. Seeing Madaline, she gave her a big hug. "My schedule is grueling. But, I'll be able to take a little break just before you come into my room. We might be able to grab a quick lunch. Now I don't want us chattering through the facial, she chastised her friend. I want you to lie down and relax, enjoy the pampering that I'm going to give you. Don't say a word. I know what you're going through and I want to see you relax," commanded Suzanne. "Yes sir" she saluted, as they walked out of the salon, arm in arm, to enjoy some food.

"Why don't we get together later this evening after the play and do something. Maybe we can go to the late show at Sculler's," suggested Madaline.

"It might take a while for me to take my costume and makeup off. If you don't mind waiting, it'll be worth it. We'll eat something there. See you later. "Pick me up when you finish work. I'll be waiting for you. Call me and I'll tell you where we'll meet. "Suzanne assured Madaline that she had paper work to catch up on and that will keep her busy until they met.

The wind was picking up as Suzanne was taking Madaline back to where she was staying. Suzanne's was driving when her cell phone began to ring. "That's odd. No one calls me this late at night. Once in a while Stephen does. I hope everything is all right."

"Answer the phone already," Madaline ordered.

Covering the mouth piece Suzanne whispered to Madaline that her mother was calling. Suzanne was quiet for a while and listened to what her mom had to say. She tried conveying what was going on to Madaline but her mother was talking so fast that she had a hard time understanding and hearing her at the same time. She had to have been on the telephone for at least a ½ an hour when she finally said goodbye and promised to call tomorrow, as she closed the cellphone.

"Don't leave me in suspense. What happened?" Asked Madaline.

"My mother normally wouldn't call me this late, but she couldn't sleep. She was upset, I had a hard time trying to gather all the information and make sense out of the whole thing. As they've gotten older my parents hate the winters in New England."

"Yes, yes, I know all that. Now get to the meat of the matter, don't get flustered and go off on another subject like you sometimes do." Throwing her hands in the air Madaline was exasperated. Now tell me, what's going on with your folks?" an impatient Madaline asked.

Suzanne related what her mother told her. "It boils down to my dad sometimes gets confused, especially when driving. To make a long story short, he finally got home, after some confusion and my mother insists she will always drive with him and become 'THE NAVIGATOR'."

While driving Suzanne seemed very quiet. "What's wrong? Madaline asked. Is something other than your folks situation bothering you?"

"I'm thinking this is just the start of it. My parents aren't spring chickens at this point in their lives and it's only a matter of time before something bad will happen to either one of them. Besides, being an only child is really a burden. I'm lucky that I have my daughters to help me. They're very close to my parents. "My dad was the only positive male influence they had. He was always good to them and had a personality completely different and opposite than Brian's. Thank God."

"Well, let me tell you something. I've heard from a lot of my, so called friends, who are really acquaintances, that have a lot of children, or come from a large family; it means nothing. Have you ever heard the saying, 'one mother can raise 10 kids but 10 kids can't take care of one mother.' It's all about how people are raised and how close they are to their parents. I'm not saying that will happen in your family. I've been around your tribe practically forever, and knowing them as I do, they'll come thru for you. So don't worry, take one day at a time."

"Thanks Madaline. It means a lot hearing you have confidence in me and my family. But it's still frightening to realize that they're getting up there in age and many things can happen the older they become."

"I hope that your parents stay healthy for quite a while and that they can enjoy their retirement. They've been married for many years and do everything, from what you tell me, even go shopping together. I'm afraid that when one of them passes away it won't be long before the other one goes."

"You know Madaline, the progression of life stinks. Everyone gets old and then you die."

"Gee, what a great attitude. Remind me to tell you some really great stories. I hope you laugh instead of cry. But if you laugh, which I doubt, I hope you piss in your pants from laughter, which by the way, I understand happens when a person get older.

Madaline hugged Suzanne and the two friends were in their own thoughts.

"Tell me Madaline, you never seem to talk about your family back home in Iowa. How come?"

"We're almost at the hotel and I'll tell you all about it when we have more time, okay." Madaline knew that she'd tried to avoid that subject as long as she could.

The bed felt nice, warm and comfy. After another grueling day and evening, Madaline enjoyed the peace and quiet of her inner sanctum. Of course the city's police or ambulance sirens could always be heard, but like certain noises, you ignore them and block them from your mind. She hoped that if she dreamed tonight, it will be a good one. With that thought in mind she drifted into oblivion. That was not to be the case.

The labor pains were awful and she just wanted the baby to get out. She kept feeling the contractions and they were God awful. Her aunt and the midwife kept giving her cold compresses on her forehead and her aunt kept telling Madaline to squeeze her hand as hard as she could. "Bear down honey, keep pushing and bear down, the midwife encouraged. Nothing would take away the pain. The suffering finally ended and she heard the baby cry. She wanted to hold it but was told she couldn't. Her aunt said that if she held the baby, it would be worse for her because she would want to keep the poor little darling.

"You know we have to put the baby up for adoption, don't you. If you hold it you'd never want to let it out of your arms. All I can tell you is that the little one looks healthy. Can you hear the pair of lungs? One of these days you'll thank me."

Then another pain of abandonment took over. 'What did I do that was so awful that I'm being punished like this?' She kept asking herself. Then she was back home in Fairfield amongst all her siblings and parents. They acted as if everything was normal and nothing had happened. How can this be, she was bewildered. She often wondered if her sisters and brothers knew the truth, but was afraid to bring up the subject. She immediately ran to Trigger. She couldn't get over how big he was. He'd grown so much in the time that she was away. He gave her the loudest neigh she ever heard. His tail was swishing and he knew that she had brought carrots and some apples for him to nibble on. She couldn't wait to ride him, take off and never return. She hated the sight of everyone around her, even when the friendly neighbors came over to say hi.

Sweat was pouring from her head and she found it trickling down her neck as she realized her hair was now damp. Madaline quickly sat up in bed, realizing that the recurring dream wouldn't go away.

She felt herself drifting back to sleep and other dreams interrupted her from sleeping soundly.

Brad was captivated by Madaline. A few close associates, aware of his fascination with Madaline, warned him to be careful and watchful for a very jealous Sheila.

"There are a lot of rumors flying around this town." Now I'm not saying that they're true, but as one of your best friends, make sure Sheila doesn't get suspicious."

"Mike, as much as I'd like there to be, there's nothing going on between Madaline and me. She's just a kid. A gorgeous and beautiful one, but none the less, she's a professional. You'd swear she'd been brought up in the industry."

"Well, just be forewarned. Sheila mentioned something about getting even with Madaline to my wife. You know how jealous woman can get."

It didn't take Sheila long to be vindictive. The faces of Sheila, Betsy St. Germain, the gossip columnist, and other malicious and spiteful friends of Sheila whirled around in Madaline's dream. Madaline suddenly sat up, her body quivering. She got out of bed and remembering where she hid her package of cigarettes; went to it immediately. She lit one up sitting down on the sofa. She didn't want to think of all the nasty details that happened that made her vengeful but shaking her head, she tried getting these thoughts out of her mind. She looked at the bright red ash at the end of her cigarette and cursed herself for breaking her will power to give the nasty habit up.

She smiled thinking that she was the one that got the last laugh. With all the lie's told about her; she made it a priority and decided to get even with Sheila. Little did she realize that the outcome would make her the happiest person she ever thought possible. She owed her friend, Ann, big time for telling her the gossip that was running rampant throughout the studio. After many years of Brad trying to get divorced from a nasty Sheila, Brad and Madaline walked down the aisle to face a happy and wonderful marriage that lasted many years, unfortunately not as many as Madaline would have liked. She'd never forget the fantastic marriage they had.

Lighting up another cigarette Madaline couldn't help think of how she devised a plan to say 'to hell with everyone, this time I'm doing it my way and no one can stop me from giving pay back, and pay backs a bitch. '

Vengeance was not an easy matter for Madaline. Usually a forgiving and trusting person Madaline was out for blood. Hours would go by and she found herself lying on her bed, different ideas running through her head as various situations re-enacted in her mind. It was only then that she knew what her recourse would be.

She often saw Brad throughout the day when she went to the studio. Making sure their paths crossed, she was very friendly the next time they met. He offered her a ride home as always, expecting to be rebuffed. He couldn't believe it when she gladly accepted. With a twinkle in her eyes, she blatantly displayed all of her womanly charms. It didn't take a great deal of acting to flirt with Brad. From the first time she saw him she thought he was attractive and sexy. Being raised to respect matrimony, she wouldn't think of ever going out with a married man. Thanks to Sheila, her attitude changed. If Sheila wanted to play hard ball, then she would also play dirty. Sure enough, Brad went for the bait. On the drive home he asked her for dinner that evening.

"Isn't it a coincidence, but my plans fell through just a short time ago?"

"How would you like to keep me company this evening? Sheila has some function she has to go to and I hate to eat alone."

They drove through the hills and came upon a remote, yet an unusual restaurant. Jumping out of his convertible he quickly came to her side and opened the door.

"Once in a while I come up here. The food is good and people mind their own business, if you know what I mean."

They sat by a window overlooking the beautiful view of the city below. "I'm glad your plans changed. When I've asked you before you've been nice but sort of standoffish. What made you decide to accept my invitation?"

"Let's say I was hungry."

Reaching across the table she took his hand into hers. "I don't know if I ever really thanked you properly for the break you gave me. I do appreciate it. I realize if it wasn't for you and your directing skill, I honestly don't think I would've come out looking so good."

"You're not giving yourself enough credit. You're a very talented actress." He loved looking into her eyes. I haven't come across a person like you in many years."

"And what do you mean by that?" Her large blue eyes gleaming mischievously.

God how he wanted her, he thought, as he watched her from the other side of the table. "All I mean is that you are a very sincere young woman. When you've lived here as long as I have you'll remember what I said. Most of the people I meet usually aren't genuine. There's always an angle or if they're nice to you there has to be something in it for them. I sensed something different about you. I hope my instincts are right." Picking up the menu, he tried concentrating on the items. "The crab legs are delicious. Have you made up your mind on what to order?"

For the first time in years Madaline allowed herself to feel alive and happy. She enjoyed Brad's company and didn't want to see the evening end. She tried erasing the fact that she was out with a married man. She really didn't want to be vindictive but she realized that going out for dinner wasn't really going to hurt anyone. She tried convincing herself of this thought as he escorted her out of the establishment.

The night air felt invigorating as the wind's breeze whisked past her face, fanning her hair wildly about, as they drove the convertible down the winding roads.

"I've had a wonderful time Brad. Thanks for the terrific meal and of course your company."

They came to the front of her house. He parked the car by the curb. He turned to her and ran his fingers thru her tousled hair.

"I don't have to tell you what a good time I had, do I? I'd like to see you again. Before you say no I want you to listen to what I have to say. I know you're a decent young woman and know my marital status. Would you believe it if I told you I don't love my wife. You think it's a line that most men say when they want affairs. You have to believe me Madaline, I want to leave Sheila as soon as possible." He gently held Madaline by her shoulders, bringing her closer to him.

"I've wanted to be with you from the first time I saw you at the party. You can't doubt my sincerity. You're always on my mind. I think about you day and night. Madaline, tell me you'll see me again, soon." Teasing Brad she said, "We'll see each other at the studio. We always manage to pass one another during the day."

CHAPTER FOURTEEN

He couldn't resist those luscious full lips any longer. He slowly took her chin and lifted her head to meet his. He moved his mouth closer and finally kissed her long and tenderly, nibbling her soft, sensuous lips.

Madaline couldn't contain her feelings any longer. She loved the way his lips felt on hers and without any acting, she lovingly kissed him back. After what seemed hours, in reality only minutes, Madaline pulled away. Guilt overcame her. "We have to stop this Brad. Not here."

"When can we be with each other again? Say you'll see me tomorrow evening."

"I'm a working girl Brad, remember. I still have to work as a waitress in the evenings."

"Not for long if I have anything to say about it. You're going to be so busy with acting jobs that you'll be giving up your waitressing by next week. Guaranteed. Have I ever told you that I love the name Madaline?"

It didn't take long for Brad to make good on his promises. He wanted to possess and cherish her more than anything in the world. His infatuation turned to love and he wasn't going to let anything stand in his way, especially his cunning and insincere wife.

Madaline was becoming an accomplished actress thanks to Brad's direction and guidance. Before long people forgot or didn't care about the rumors that almost destroyed Madeline and her career. As soon as one movie was finished, another script would be waiting for her approval.

After fishing her latest movie and hearing and seeing the rave revues of Madaline's acting ability; unselfishly, Brad was overjoyed. He surprised Madaline with a trip to Hawaii and wouldn't hear any objections to their unexpected vacation. It was a sabbatical for both of them, one that they would never forget.

Walking along the beach, holding hands, their footprints trailing behind in the outgoing tide, they were joyous and in love.

Tears were freely flowing down her cheeks as Madaline reflected back and thought about what their first beautiful home would look like. She wanted it to be made mostly of glass, overlooking the ever changing ocean. It didn't' take long for her dreams to come true. From most rooms in their home they could hear the waves crashing on the rocks below. They shared every aspect of their lives, talking incessantly about their dreams and future together. Every moment they had a chance, they would make love in front of the fireplace and listen to the soft music playing in the background. They would often steel away, go down the steps to the sand, in the still of the night, to the beach below their home and in each other's arms they again would make love. They lived in a world of their own. Words could not describe the satisfaction she derived to finally have contentment in her life with a man that she loved and adored. She knew he felt the same way about her.

Madaline realized she couldn't go back to sleep and after consuming a half a pack of Salem Light 100's threw the rest of the package in the wastebasket. She went into the shower to get ready to go to work.

Once at the theater she took her time getting into costume. It seemed that the other actors were hurrying about and it was nice, for a change, not to rush. The afternoon show was great and she allowed herself to relax and catch up on the sleep she didn't have the evening before. She fell fast asleep on the beloved, bluish, grey sofa.

It seemed hours had gone by when she felt herself slowly awakening from her long nap. A loud knocking interrupted her thoughts.

Most of the janitorial staff and back stage hands were fearful of Madaline's reputation and temper. Nonetheless, one brave sole was picked to interrupt 'the queen' as everyone called her behind her back. "Sorry to break into your leisure time, Ms. Mason, but your son Kyle is on the phone and I think it's pretty urgent."

After last night's fiasco, with her mother's phone call, Suzanne called the girls using the conference call on the telephone, informing them of the situation. "Unfortunately, I think this is going to be the first of many things happening to my parents, and your grandparents. I hope not, but I bet there are situations that my mother hasn't told me about."

"Now mom, have faith. Think positive and we'll get through anything," Melanie said.

"I try to be an upbeat person, smile all the time and make an effort to help people in need. I AM a positive person. Sometimes things happen that are inevitable and out of our control. I realize that my parents are getting along in years and I know that they'll be needing my help more and more." An unhappy Suzanne told Melanie and the other two girls.

"Now mom, get those thoughts out of your head. You're only as old as you feel, and nana and papa have a great life down in Florida. They have lots of friends and go out all the time. I think you're worrying for nothing."

"I hope that you're right. Well, I have to get off the phone and get ready for work. Have a good day and I'll speak to you soon. I love you."

"I love you too Mom, have a good day and stop worrying," Commanded Melanie. The other children followed her lead and told her to keep smiling and that they loved her as well.

While Suzanne was driving to work her cell phone rang. With trepidation she answered it. Thankfully it was Nancy telling her that she would be catching the next flight and be home by this evening. Suzanne was both happy and relieved. She couldn't wait to find out what happened in Japan, once again. It was important to find out what Nancy's final decision would be. She visited all the islands and seen them for herself, now was the time to discuss all the aspects of their ultimate decision.

Nancy thought the flight back from Japan was a lot better than the last flight from there. She remembered the turbulence and was thankful there was none this time. The stewardess came down the aisle asking what they would like for a drink. After downing her coffee, Nancy tried to relax and let her mind wonder. She kept thinking about being single once again and the feelings she was having.

A shiver went through her body as she thought of her new life. She tried being optimistic and re-assured herself that she would be the same person she always was. 'Though it'll be different in many ways.'

She asked herself how to go about getting back into the dating scene? She tried concentrating on this month's Newsweekly publication. She was reading the same stories she had seen on the various television news stations. Fox and CNN were her favorites. She put down Newsweek and opted for Vogue. Seeing the beautiful models all acting happy and not an ounce of fat on them, made her feel self-conscious. 'It's not normal', she thought, as she looked around the cabin of the airplane and viewed the women. These are normal women who aren't afraid of carrying an extra 10 to 20 pounds. So they don't all wear make-up, so what. Though I don't think I'm an average woman. After all, I own a Day Spa, and admittedly, sometimes take advantage of the services provided there. I have more money than I know what to do with, when looking in the mirror I see an attractive, not overweight, woman who wears makeup, has pretty hair, most of the time, and-----I'm as unhappy as hell.' She wanted to cry and let all of her feelings and frustrations out.

'I'll hook up on one of those singles dating services and lists that I hear about on the web. I'll be cautious and won't give them my address or nothing personal until I meet them. It can only be for a lunchtime date, I've heard that some of the guys are weird. One of my friends told me about Plenty of Fish. What a crazy name. Oh well, I guess there are plenty of fish in the sea. Time will tell," Nancy thought as she buckled her belt for landing.

Nancy collected the baggage from the turnstile and finally found her car. On the way home she turned on the CD player and listened to her favorite artists. She rounded the bend and could hear the waves of the ocean splattering on the shore and rocks. High tide must be in she thought to herself as she climbed up to her front door.

'God, it feels good to be home. There really isn't anything like home.' She put her mail aside and plopped down on her comfy sofa. She only wanted comfortable furniture that she could sink into. Peter didn't like animals and she seriously was thinking of getting a cat. 'Suzanne seems to adore her Simka and Boston and loves cuddling with them. Maybe if I get a little kitten and nurture it, I'll have something that loves me, unconditional love. It will greet me when I come home. Tomorrow I'll go on the internet and look up the different breeds of cats. I'm sure that I'll find one that will be compatible with me and the house.' With those thoughts she brought her luggage upstairs and not bothering to unpack, got into her pajamas and fell fast asleep.

Suzanne couldn't wait to talk to Nancy. She knew not to disturb her this evening realizing that she'd be exhausted from the difference in travel time. Still she was on pins and needles just imagining what news Nancy had to tell her.

Suzanne was still perplexed about her parent's situation and the way her love life was turning out. Stephen and her just couldn't seem to get together long enough to really have a meaningful relationship. And then there was Lawrence. Thinking that he's such a sweat man, she knew that he liked her in ways that flattered a woman. She didn't want to lead him on until she resolved her state of affairs with Stephen.

Suzanne, who normally didn't drink, took a large beer mug and poured Malibu Caribbean Rum, pineapple juice, blue curacao with not much ice into the glass and took a large swallow. 'Maybe that's what I need. I feel like getting drunk and tying one on, as I hear many of my acquaintances say. It'll be good for me. Yup, I'll take this glass up to bed with me, fall fast asleep and not have a care in the world.' Before falling into unconsciousness she thought she remembered saying to herself, 'I'd better not get used to this. '

It was hard for Suzanne to get up the next morning. She felt groggy. She wasn't used to drinking like she did last evening. After taking a shower she hoped her head would be a lot clearer. She thought to herself that she was lucky she didn't drink a bottle of wine because that was supposed to be a worse hangover, or so a few of the girls at the shops told her.

Suzanne got to work and was looking at her schedule when Nancy called her. Looking at her appointment book, Suzanne thought that 3 O'clock would be good for them to meet. She would be on pins and needles until she heard everything that Nancy had to say.

When Nancy arrived they decided they needed a quiet place that they could talk without being disturbed. "Let's drive to my house," suggested Nancy. We can call out for Chinese food."

"Sounds good to me. Besides we'll beat the evening commute." Suzanne was excited as she followed Nancy back to Ipswich. She couldn't wait to find out what Nancy's thoughts were and if they should forge ahead with their plans.

As they sat crossed leg on the carpet, gluttonously eating the pork ribs, egg rolls, vegetable lo mein, chicken fried rice, chicken with peanuts, beef wanton in oyster sauce and of course scallion pancakes, that Nancy had picked up at the local Chinese restaurant, they both tried talking at once.

"First of all, I'm glad to see that you're eating with regular utensils rather than the chop sticks that the restaurant supplies. The carpet would be a mess," Nancy laughed. "As many times that I ate in Japanese restaurants, I still can't master the use of chop sticks. I must be a real klutz."

Shaking her head Suzanne said, "That's not true, personally I can't use them. Whenever Stephen and I dine out at a Japanese or Chinese restaurant, Stephen uses those sticks like he was brought up with them. Some people just get it and some don't. If that's the case I guess I'm a klutz too."

Trying to get up Nancy exclaimed, "I can't breathe. I ate too much."

"I'm so full I think I'm going to burst, in a couple of hours we'll be hungry again." Suzanne helped Nancy up off the floor. She admired Nancy's taste as she looked at her gold with specks of red marble countertops. Cabinets were molded cherry wood and the newest appliances. "I love the way you redecorated your house and the kitchen area is beyond gorgeous. The double ovens must be a God send, especially when you entertain. I would die for a kitchen like this someday."

"Unfortunately I don't entertain or have many guests over like you do. Maybe someday when my life gets back to normal, I'll have use for this kitchen, but for now I just walk by and admire it." A remorseful Nancy acknowledged.

"You definitely will. I'm sure of that. Now let's get down to business.

Sitting in the large living room Nancy related her latest events in Japan. "First of all, the flight over was uneventful but very long. I had to walk around the isles often so my legs wouldn't cramp. Thankfully I slept most of the way. Like last time, the airport is large. It took me forever to collect my luggage from the turnstile. The Japanese airline was wonderful and the stewardesses couldn't do enough for you." Taking a deep breath, Nancy continued. "The real estate agents were very helpful and I visited a lot of Japanese spas. The estheticians and massage therapists asked a lot of questions about the way we do things in America. They didn't feel threatened by our opening a spa in Tokeo. I don't know if that's good or bad. I couldn't get a true feeling because they always had a smile and were very gracious. I still don't truly understand them. While in Tokeo I tried calling a very nice Japanese gentleman that I met on my first visit. He was very gracious and I have a card of his in my pocketbook somewhere. He said that I should call him the next time I visited Japan and he would show me around. Unfortunately, he was out of town again. He's the president of a large computer company and travels to and from Japan and The United States often."

"That sounds great, but I'm a little hesitant about the way the other spas weren't worried about us becoming competitors. If this were the States, people would probably throw daggers at us."

Suzanne laughed. "Seriously, we'll have to do a lot more investigating about the various areas. I'll have to analyze the amount of people that take advantage of spa services and if they'd be amendable to foreigners owning a spa, and how the idea of having an American and European style facial would make them feel. Of course we'd be using our traditional French products as well as our own."

"From what I gathered and saw," Nancy continued, "There seems to be other nationalities that have opened spas in the major cities like Tokeo. It doesn't seem to be a problem. There are so many people, overpopulated I would say, that there must be an abundance of people with money that like being pampered. Don't forget, the Japanese people like anything American, except our automobiles," Nancy jokingly said. "Seriously." Suzanne confidently told Nancy, "I think if we do a consisive market analysis, and meet with the right people, my idea might be valid. Do you realize that I'm acting like a true business woman and doing and thinking about opening the salon the way other businesses make their decisions?"

"Suzanne, I'm proud at the way your mind is working. Yes, very proud."

"I want you to know how appreciative I am for what you've done for the company."

"Thanks Suzanne." She walked over to her friend and hugged her. She was a lot taller than Suzanne, and kissed the top of her head. When I was younger, away at the various boarding schools, I thought nothing of flying to another country with a few of my friends. If you have to travel for the business you'll get used to it," Nancy predicted.

"You're right. Of course I traveled to Bermuda a couple of times. I was always worried about money, I was lucky that I had any time for myself, let alone time to travel. All I was used to was Boston proper, Quincy, and some of Massachusetts. When I started traveling into New Hampshire, Maine, Rhode Island, Texas, and eventually South Carolina, which is still my first love, I was like a kid eating her first piece of candy. So thanks again and next time, hopefully soon, both of us will go there together."

Giving Nancy a hug, she thanked her for the food and the good company. "I'm glad we got a lot of business done this evening".

"I'll speak to you tomorrow and we'll make up a schedule for the salons." On her way home she chided herself for not staying over Nancy's. She had to admit she was getting sleepy at the wheel. 'I think I ate too much. When I over eat I always get tired. The next time this happens, I'll sleep over.'

Tears fell from Suzanne's eyes thinking of her younger days. Her father was the first man she loved. He was so good and she thought he was the most handsome man in the world. Even nicer looking than Gene Autry or The Cisco Kid. God, she hoped that he and her mom would stay healthy for a long time. Years ago, he had melanoma that Susanne detected while they were sunning in the back yard. It was stage 4 and no one really knew how serious that was. One of her clients was a nurse and got her an appointment for him to see a renowned specialist. After all sorts of tests, to see if it had spread to other organs, they removed it and told him that it hadn't metastasized. She was too young to remember that when he was a younger man he had to have his prostate biopsied and even though he had a high count the doctor told him it was fine.

Suzanne realized that she was in a depressed state of mind and admonished herself for it. 'No more bad thoughts,' she reprimanded herself. She was almost home now, just a few more exits and she'd go to bed, cuddle with Simka and Boston, who would run down the stairs to greet her. Cuddling with the two cats she, once again, hoped that her parents would live a full, fun and long life.

Suzanne was grateful that her first client was at 11:00 a.m. She was able to sleep a little later, it felt good to stay in bed for a while and not have to fight the morning traffic. While resting she couldn't stop thinking about the information that Nancy obtained from this last visit. She wasn't looking forward to flying all the way to Japan and being on a plane for such a long time. She still hated flying with a passion, never getting over the fear. She didn't mind traveling by car to her various spas but when she had to go to the ones that were far away, she'd literally have nightmares for weeks before the flight. 'Somehow I'm going to suck up my panic of flying and get over it. I don't know how, but somehow I'll manage, I hope,' Suzanne thought to herself.

CHAPTER FIFTEEN

SAN DIEGO, CALIFORNIA

Rich Colangelo walked over to his friend and ex-partner, who was sitting at the desk, gathering information, taking phone calls and booking people. Colangelo waited patiently till Tom had finished his boring work load.

Tom Curran was working the desk, looking at the clock, waiting till his shift ended at 7:00. He promised his wife that he definitely would be home tonight to eat with the family. Tom had requested working the desk after being a homicide detective for over 25 years. His wife was getting tired of all the overtime and late night calls. Helen felt she and the kids were neglected and came last in his life. She thought that all he lived for was his job. She went as far as going to a lawyer to start divorce proceedings. After Helen told Tom about what she did, he re-accessed his life's work. He had been in the homicide division for years and with his partner, Rich Colangelo for over 20. Colangelo felt awful when Tom asked to be assigned to the desk. Rich felt lost without Tom, as if an appendage had been severed from his body. Rich understood the circumstances that made Tom do what he did. He also knew that Tom loved his line of work and the feelings that made him want to give back to the community. Since he was a young boy, he often told Rich, 'all I ever wanted to be was a policeman. I didn't ever want to become anything else. '

"Hey, don't look at me that way, an unhappy Tom uttered. I know, I know," as he took a deep breath. What was I supposed to do? I really love Helen and the kids. I could tell she wasn't threatening this time. It was either the family or the job. I had no other choice, you understand, don't you?"

Rich nodded his head. "Unfortunately, I do. I took the job! Maybe because I really wasn't in love with Holly. We were lucky that no kids were involved. It would have been a bitch if there were. You and Helen have been with each other for years and the kids are great. You'll be ready for retirement soon. I think you made the right choice. You had no option. Maybe someday I'll find the right girl, if she comes along, and I might have to make the same decision that you had to make. I hope not. I'm getting used to the bachelor life style, if you know what I mean?"

Tom answered the call that came in at exactly 6:50. A person was arriving home from work and as she was going up the stairs an awful smell was emanating from an apartment on the first floor. She asked for a policeman to come over and see what was causing the odor.

He saw Rich at his desk, writing out the constant reports that went along with the job. "Hey, Colangelo just got a call from someone complaining of a terrible odor in one of the apartments in her building. Handing him the piece of paper, "I think you'd better get over there and see what's going on."

"What do they think we are, pest control?" Rich saw the look that his old partner gave him. "Okay, okay, I'm going, call me Rich the exterminator."

'In as much as I like my new partner, Stu Tower, I miss the big, heavy lug that's usually beside me. After all, we were together longer that most married couples. ' He thought as he pulled out of his designated parking spot in his blue Mercury.

It took a short time for Rich to get across town. Most of the commuters were home by now. Taking the brick steps, 2 at a time, he opened the heavy wooden door. Once inside, he pushed the buzzer of the person calling in the complaint. "Miss Silver, San Diego police. Want to come down and show me which apartment you think the stench is in." Rich could tell where the smell was coming from. On the stairwell Rich noted that she had to be in her late eighty's. Using a cane to descend the stairs her fragile body made it difficult to proceed quickly. Rich tried not to show his impatience. It seemed hours, but in reality, it took a good ten minutes for Miss Silver to get to the bottom of the staircase. Upon observing further, he noticed that the glasses she wore were like the bottom of a thick coke bottle. He started asking some information and she immediately stopped him, bending up her right arm. "Hold your horses, young man. I can't hear a word you're saying until I turn up my hearing aids." 'Great,' He thought. "Now I'm ready."

"For starters, when was the first time you noticed the odor?" Putting her hands on her chin, Rich could tell she was in deep thought. "I guess it was when I came home from the grocery store this evening. That's why I called the police."

"I just have a few more questions to ask and then you can go back upstairs. Miss Silver, do you have a janitor or maintenance man that might have a master set of keys?"

"Young man, you don't have to yell. I can hear you fine, now that my aids are turned up." He wrote the information down and thanked the senior citizen for all of her help.

Being a homicide cop for years he didn't have to guess what was behind the door. He knocked cautiously. It didn't surprise him that no one answered. Going down to the basement he found the janitor's small apartment. Explaining the situation and showing him his badge and I. D., Rich had no trouble having the custodian open the dwelling.

"Thanks for your help. I think you'd better stay in the vestibule." Rich slowly opened the door. Cautiously, looking about, his Glock securely in his hand, he saw the disheveled and messy living room. Blood was all around, the carpet still damp. He didn't think that anyone who might have caused this disarray was still here, but he couldn't be sure. Rich guardedly walked down the hallway looking in the bathroom and the small kitchen which he noticed was immaculate. He slowly opened the bedroom door and saw the body splayed on the bed. Again, blood was everywhere. He almost gagged seeing the decayed body. After all these years, he still couldn't stand the stink of death. The metallic smell surrounded him. He knew not to touch anything. Calling the precinct he asked them to get in touch with the Medical Examiner. With the crime rate as high as it was he realized that it would take a while for the ME to arrive. Rich put on booties and gloves that he always carried with him. The apartment had to be secured, otherwise the different people, coming and going, could contaminate the scene. He didn't want any of the cops disturbing any evidence that may help them in the future. He corded off the area in and out of the apartment. Rich stuck a piece of gum in his mouth and waited patiently outside until the M. E. got there.

Molly Weiner had been the chief Medical Examiner for over 15 years and was well respected by everyone in the profession. By the time Molly disembarked her van, the police had secured the building and Rich made sure that none of the other officers disrupted the scene. "Thanks for protecting the evidence."

She put on the plastic booties over her shoes and plastic gloves on her hands. She dusted for prints on all the door handles, scraped under the fingernails of the dead man to see if there might be some DNA evidence, and then got down on her hands and knees to scrape the fibers of the carpet for any other data. She then examined and dusted any and all areas and surfaces that the killer might have left some finger prints or proof of identity. All the bullets had made a clean exit and they were able to recover the shell casings. Molly determined that Curtis Jones had been dead for at least 3 days. As many years Molly had been a medical examiner, the smell of death still made her sick to her stomach. This evening was not an exception. The odor was horrendous. Many of the policemen had to put handkerchiefs over their noses and excused themselves while they vomited on the street. The maggots made their discovery and started to claim their prize.

Rich took Molly aside hoping that she'd be able to tell him more details. "Rich you know as well as I do that the longer a body is found after the death, the harder it is for us to get a reliable read. Even though this is a clean environment, it still didn't stop the maggots from eating their prey and the natural decomposition of the body. Once we have him on the table we'll be thorough and be able to tell you more information. I did notice that there's someone's skin under his finger nails. From what I can tell, he put up one hell of a fight. We'll be able to get DNA from the skin that we find and see if this killer has a record. It'll make the job a lot easier."

"Thanks Molly, do you have any idea when we'll get the report from the lab?"

"I have a few more bodies to clean up in the morning. I'll do you a favor and get to this guy first thing in the afternoon. As far as the DNA goes, it depends how far backed up the lab is. Don't hold your breath waiting."

As soon as the dispatchers radioed in the crime scene, the news people were out there with their microphones on and cameras with glaring flash bulbs going off. These despicable objects were shoved in the faces of the detectives and ME. The media was hungry for any information to tell their viewers. Rich often wondered how the media found out so fast. Like vultures, eyeing the prey, they couldn't wait until all the gory details were told. Rich always found them offensive.

Molly was a pro and could handle the media. They didn't even know that they were being duped.

Rich then called his new partner, Stu, and told him about the situation. "I guess you'd better get over here, even though I tried saving you the trip. I'll wait and then we'll see what we can come up with. Most of the tenants, I presume, are home by now. I'll get some of the patrol men to knock on the doors. Maybe one of the tenants heard a commotion a few days ago."

After Molly took all the necessary vials and scrapings that could help with her part of the investigation she then allowed Rich, with the other detectives to feel free to do what they had to do. The body was placed in a body bag, tagged and put in the ambulance. With sirens blasting, the vehicle was driven to the hospital by the attendants who rushed to take the cadaver into the catacombs of the hospitals' holding refrigerator in the morgue until Molly was ready to work on Mr. Jones. Stu turned to Rich and sarcastically asked, "Ever wonder why those guys drive the ambulance so fast and have the lights blazing and sirens on loud as can be? After all, the guy isn't in a hurry. He's already met his maker." Rich laughed and replied, "Maybe the driver has a hot date tonight, doesn't want to be late."

They went through all Mr. Jones draws and closets and found some clothing that apparently didn't belong to the murdered victim because of the difference in clothes and shoes sizes. Rich Colangelo found papers and pictures of a man that obviously shared his apartment. "I wonder who this mysterious other is? Why hasn't the man been here in three days? What kind of relationship did they have?" Rich wanted these questions answered, "I hope we find out soon," Rich told Stu.

"We'll take these pictures and see if we can get a make on this guy. If he's ever been taken into custody or arrested there's sure to be a file on him. Luckily we live in a day and age where the computer comes in handy."

"Ain't that the truth," agreed Stu. Rich and Stu noted that the TV was missing along with the computer. "Hey Rich, looks like everything's been taken out of his wallet and I don't see his car keys." Rich listened intently and at the same time was making his own assumption of things that might have been removed. "While we're here, we might as well go through his draws and anything that can be moved, and see if we find anything that will tell us more about this guy."

"Sounds good to me, when we're through let's go out for a bite to eat, I'm starved."

"Stu, I knew there was a reason why they made us partners."

Rich and Stu looked in and underneath the draws. Nothing was found. They both removed the bloody mattress and was about to lift the box spring when Rich spotted a small cut in it. "Stu, come over here. I've got a pocket knife and I'm going to make this hole larger. Any objections?"

"None. Let's see what he might have in there. Maybe some money rolled up, hey?"

"You never know until we try." After digging and getting some of the stuffing out they finally saw the small key that was hidden. "Well, well, looky here," Rich said. "I wonder what this little goody is to? Could be anything from a safe to a lock of some sort." Stu asked, "How the hell are we going to find out what it opens?" Rich answered, "I don't know but it looks like quite an assignment."

"Even though he's nice enough, we'll soon find out if Stu has enough experience," he muttered to Tom when he saw him back at the precinct the next day. They kept an officer at the apartment to make sure that no one disturbs the crime scene. I hope that the person sharing the flat with Mr. Jones will show up. Stu stayed with me and we found this little surprise hidden in the box spring. Do you think you can keep it in holding? But before you do, I'd like to take it to a locksmith and have a copy made. Any objections?"

"I didn't hear a word you said, I'm getting old."

Mr. Weintraub was upset that Curtis hadn't come to work and, he also, hadn't been able to reach him.

Kyle was beside himself with worry. After the fourth day he couldn't wait any longer and went to the apartment that he sometimes shared with Curtis.

Kyle was visibly upset when he saw the yellow tape in front of the door. Kyle opened the door with his key and saw a policeman in the apartment. He saw the chalk outline of a body and hoped it wasn't what he thought it was. The officer noticed how upset this young man was and asked him his name and the reason for his visit.

The officer had Kyle sit down and immediately called the lead detectives on the case. "I have a man here, who I think you'll be very interested in talking to.

"We'll be right over. Come on Stu, I think we have a break in the case."

When Rich and Stu got to the apartment they saw an obviously upset young man sitting nervously in a hard, high back chair, biting his nails. Whispering to his partner Rich said, "I guess this is the mystery man we've been waiting for."

Rich introduced himself and Stu to Kyle. Putting one foot on top of the coffee table, an aggressive, threatening Rich looked directly into Kyle's' eyes. "Before we start talking, what's your name and how do you know the deceased?"

Kyle could feel his perspiration beginning to flow from under his arms. The back of his neck felt clammy and his hands were visibly shaking as he tried to get the pack of cigarettes out of his shirt pocket.

"Hey Kyle, I know this is a traumatic scene, but buddy, we've got to get some questions answered. Need a light?"

Kyle conscientiously nodded. By now he was visibly upset. Taking a deep drag from his Marlboro lights, his hand was trembling. "I can't believe that you're talking about Curtis. I don't think he had an enemy in the world. He was a great guy and everyone liked him. You're sure it was Curtis you found?"

"We went through his draws, found, what we think, was an extra wallet and saw his picture on a few documents. So yes, it's definitely him. How were you and Curtis related? Or should I ask, how do you know the man we found?"

Kyle had so many thoughts going through his mind. 'Do I tell him we were good friends or how do I play this out? I can't let him know that we were lovers. My God, if anyone, especially Carol or my mom finds out the truth, I think I'll die. I know my mom will be upset but when she calms down, she'll be able to accept it. Lots of her friends are either gay or switch hitters. Carol's the one who'll freak out. She'll be mortified.' "I've known Curtis for years. I first got to know him from being a patron at one of the galleries he used to work at. We then started talking and found out that we had a lot in common. Since then we've become good friends."

Rich turned his back to Kyle and lifting his eyebrow, looked at Stu as if to say, do you believe this guy? "Kyle, a few of the neighbors in the building told us that a young man, they didn't know his name, frequently came over and sometimes visited the night or stayed over for a few days or so. Now Kyle, could you, by any chance, be that young man?"

'Those fucking, old, farts," he said aloud. "Don't they have anything else going on in their lives? I bet that old lady from upstairs and some other old coots watch Curtis's door to see who visited him," a furious Kyle verbalized. "Maybe they always noticed his guests, and just maybe, saw who actually came in and callously killed Curtis." Rich explained. "When my wife goes out of town on working assignments, I would occasionally stay over. I don't like being alone. By the way, my wife is Carol Williams, the famous model. Have you heard of her?"

"No kidding," Stu interjected. "I've seen her on some magazine covers and such. I don't mean Penthouse or Hustler, but some of them nicer ones."

"Sorry, but I don't know the name. Maybe if I saw a picture, I'd recognize her," Rich proclaimed." As I was saying, you are probably the young man that they saw. Do you know anyone else that Mr. Jones was friendly with or close enough to that they would also be nightly guests?"

"I don't know what you're trying to say? There are people that I know from his work place but I don't know many of his other personal friends." Kyle was fidgeting in his seat, feeling uncomfortable. "I don't keep tabs on Curtis or who his other acquaintances are. Maybe those so called 'busy bodies' that kept such a close eye on Curtis's apartment, could tell you more about his visitors," an agitated Kyle replied.

Rich knew by the way Kyle was answering and acting that he was keeping something from Stu and himself.

"Mr. Mason, or should I call you Kyle, you seem to be really shaken up. I realize you were his friend and all, but I have a hunch that you know more than you're telling us." Kyle took another cigarette from the pack and Rich again lit it for a bewildered Kyle.

"Listen, I don't know what you're implying, but I had nothing to do with this situation. Before, when you asked me if I knew anyone that might have reason or disliked Curtis, there was an incident about a week or so ago that just came to mind."

"Really," Stu interjected. How come you just thought to tell us now?"

"I, I, don't know?" "Because he doesn't, I mean didn't, really have any enemies, that I know of, that is, I almost forgot about that particular incident."

"Why don't you tell us what happened?" Rich requested.

"It was one of the nights that Carol was away. Curtis asked me if I wanted to stay over, knowing that I hated being by myself. It was in the morning and I had just finished showering. I couldn't help but hear loud voices and obviously a confrontation was taking place."

"Why did you think that Curtis was agitated? Do you remember seeing this unknown man before?" Rich asked Kyle, in a derogatory way, why he thought that the two men were mad at each other. "Obviously because both their voices were elevated," Kyle answered in a snide remark. "I really didn't get a good look at the guy, I'm sure it was a man, maybe an oriental guy, I did notice that he had some sort of accent. If I think about it, I might be able to figure out what kind of inflection he may have projected."

With a nod of his head, Rich and Stu went to a corner and softly talked. "I wonder where Kyle slept since I see only one bedroom and one bed. Maybe the couch opens up, but if so, did he make it before he showered or was it out? I don't want to make rash assumptions, but it certainly looks suspicious to me," Stu said.

The longer they spoke, the more nervous Kyle became. He tried listening to what they were saying, but the more he tried to unobtrusively stretch his neck, the further frustrated he became.

Rich and Stu came back to where Kyle was sitting. Getting in his face, Rich told him, "Personally I think you're lying, but who am I to make that call. Isn't it funny that all of a sudden you remembered that particular day? You think he's oriental but not sure what he looks like or what kind of accent he has. I find that a little hard to believe." Rich accused Kyle while Stu stood there with a morose look on his face.

"Kyle, do you think that if we bring you to headquarters you'd be able to help the police artist and get a description of the man?"

"Sure, but like I said before, I didn't get a good look of him."

Rich and Stu went into another room. Rich remarked that Kyle seems either drugged or out of it. "It might be he's traumatized by it all," Stu said, sticking up for the young man who was obviously nervous and upset. When they got back from their conference they were surprised by Kyle's new attitude.

"You know guys, I'm thinking that I better just shut up and if you have any more questions you want to ask me, I believe a lawyer should be present. What do you think of that?" a now sardonic Kyle answered.

"Well, you know Mr. Mason, I think that's a good idea. I think we'll take you to the precinct and confine you to your own special room. Not that we're arresting you or anything but I hope you'll still be co-operative."

"Sure, I'll do anything you want me to do but I still want to get in touch with my lawyer."

In the back seat, Kyle almost wet his pants. 'I can't believe these idiots think that I killed Curtis. What a bunch of horse shit. Is this what the legal system is all about? Trying to pin a crime on an innocent person?'

"You okay back there?" asked a concerned Rich.

"I'm just great. Never felt better in my life." Kyle sarcastically replied.

"I might have put the cuffs on you a little too tight. When we get to the precinct I'll release them, okay?" Stu told Kyle.

Once at headquarters they left Kyle in a private room. "Let him stay here for a bit and let him ponder. Meanwhile we'll look and see if we have a file on him and find out all we can about this Kyle Mason. If he calls a lawyer then we'll read him his Miranda rights and bring him to Tom to collect his things. We won't formally charge him but it'll scare the hell out of him. Let his mouth piece do all the talking when and if he's summoned," Rich told Stu. "I wish that the lab would hurry up with the results from that DNA sample. Once we do, we can swab this character and see if it matches. I think Molly has some hair fibers that were found in the apartment as well. Let's see if some of them are Kyle's."

"Don't forget Rich, he did stay over Curtis' apartment and it's only natural that his hairs would be there."

"No shit, Dick Tracy, but we have a long way to go before this case is closed. Before his piece comes, we'll bring him to Tom and it'll scare the hell out of him being finger printed and all," Rich smugly informed Stu.

"Once your lawyer shows up we'll leave the two of you alone to talk. Meanwhile we'll put you in a private room, since you're Madaline Mason's son. I don't think you'll try to escape. Be a good boy now and we'll get to the bottom of this crime."

"How did you find out that I'm Madaline's son?"

"A little birdie told me."

Rich marched Kyle in front of Tom and had Kyle give Tom all of his personal belongings. Tom wrote down everything that was placed before him. "I have to finger print you, so if you'll come with me I'll make it fast. Oh ya, I'm not as good at taking pictures as you are, so bear with me. Tom explained what he was doing to this young upstart. "You'll get everything back when you get out of our 'house of hospitality'."

"Gee, Thanks." Kyle remarked

After Colangelo finished all the prep work he walked over to Tom Curran's desk. "What a pain in the ass this one's going to be. I think we've got our man, but then who knows? I wish that you and I were still a team. I like Stu and all, but gee, he's not you."

A sullen Tom proclaimed. "What if you call me up; you can use my cell number, and if you need a little help, I'd be more than happy to oblige in the investigation."

"Thanks, I certainly won't be invited to Helen's Thanksgiving dinner if she finds out that you'll be helping me. For that matter, Christmas also, and then I'd never get any presents from you and your family. As a matter of fact, thinking about it, the only presents I get are from you and Helen. Boy, that's pretty pathetic."

Tom looked crushed. "I didn't mean to make you upset. Forget this conversation ever took place."

All of a sudden Rich started laughing. "If you don't tell anybody, neither will I." Rich put his pinkie finger over the desk and Tom curled his pinkie around Rich's.

"I promise I won't tell a soul. Do you think I want Helen to find out? I'd be out of the house and thrown on my butt before you say 'Jack rabbit'.

"I knew you couldn't get through a year without my help. Yup, not even 6 months," putting his thumbs on pretend suspenders, and a smile from ear to ear, a proud Tom proclaimed. Thinking for a second, the crease in-between his eyebrows deepened as a concerned tom asked, "you promise to keep this between you and me? I don't want Stu to find out about our little arrangement. Are you okay with that?" a concerned Tom asked.

"It'll have to be that way. I'll keep you informed of all that's going on and you can do some reconnaissance for me. With all your contacts we'll figure this murder out, just wait and see." Rich slapped Tom on the back as he walked to his desk.

Rich called Molly's office to find out if she worked on Curtis yet. "What do you think, that he's the only body I have on my agenda? I have at least 5 other people to take care of before your Mr. Jones is on my examining table."

Rich asked demurely, "What if I bribe you with taking you out for a nice dinner by the waterfront?"

"Are you trying to induce me. That's against the rules you know. But, we might accidently meet, let's say tomorrow, in front of The Blue Fish. But I don't think Mike would like that. He might be quiet and secure in our relationship, but I don't think he'd be happy if I were to go out with another man." Laughing, she explained, "We've been married for over 10 years and even though it seems I'm always at work, Mike helps out with the housework, especially with the 2 boys. It's a bitch when they get to an age when, it seems all you do is drive them to their various practices, games and lessons."

"I got divorced before any kids came. I hear it from all the guys on the force, and know what you're talking about. I really want to wrap up this case as fast as possible."

"Ya, ya, Just me clowning around. I know that you and Mike make a great team. But seriously, I'll buy you a cup of coffee and your favorite donut if you can speed up the procedure on this Curtis Jones. This Kyle Mason that's being held, will be let out shortly, because we don't have enough proof against him, yet. I'm quite sure he's our guy, but I want to be absolutely sure. If he's brought to trial the DA will be up our asses if we don't have enough evidence to convict him. You and I know what a bitch she can be if he's found innocent and someone else committed the murder. Her time will be up soon and she'll be running for re-election. She wants as many convictions as she can get."

"Okay, okay, make sure it's an apple filled donut and you might want to throw in a plain honey dipped one, if you really want to bribe me." Molly Laughed. "Seriously, I'll see what I can do."

Meanwhile Kyle was going crazy. He'd made the phone call to his mother and was waiting to hear from a lawyer she contacted to act on his behalf. He could hear a couple of drunks in the cell down the hall. 'Boy they're loud. I hope they fall asleep real fast.' While he was giving the heavy set policeman his possessions he saw some women of the night waiting to be booked. He wondered how long it would take for their Johns to bail them out. 'How depressing. I hope that Carol stays out of the country and doesn't get wind of what's happened. Knowing how gossip has no boundaries, I'm sure she'll find out soon. Those bastards don't know how to shut their mouths or for that matter, the media can't help being who they are. The entire world will find out in a matter of hours, if I'm correct. Shit, I hope they find the real killer so my name will be cleared. '

CHAPTER SIXTEEN

Instead of heading directly into Boston from her Newport, Rhode Island salon, Suzanne decided to go home.

Suzanne enjoyed the bright sunshine coming through the spacious plant window in the kitchen. Taking down one plant at a time, she admired the fullness of her hot pink Cyclamen, its flowers in full bloom. She watered it gently, letting the excess water drain from the bottom. Everyone who came into her home extolled on the beauty of her plants, especially her favorite flowering cyclamen. It was odd, she thought, how it flowered almost continuously, only stopping twice a year. Memories of her beloved grandfather, Jake, came to mind as she gently wiped the excess water from the dish. Everyone praised his garden and house plants. His friends and relatives said he had a 'green thumb' and often sent him their sick plants to be healed.

Returning the plant back to its rightful place on the shelf she couldn't help but think back, when she was a little girl, how good she felt every time she visited her grandparents' home. It was a very small bungalow in Quincy, the locals called it Quincy Point, but it was like a palace to her. Coming from the city as she did, she remembered the feelings of peace and contentment that would come over her as she held her papa's hand and walking together through his garden, admiring the many flowers and fresh vegetables, co-existing within the area of his cultivated, modest, yet beautiful garden.

The noiseless atmosphere was eerie. Mrs. Walsh, her trusted and dear housekeeper, was out doing errands. Although Suzanne disliked being alone for long periods of time she sometimes welcomed the peace and quiet, especially when important matters weighed heavily on her mind. She gazed into the now lukewarm, orange, brownish tea, reflecting back to her childhood. It was never quiet in her old neighborhood in Dorchester. Growing up as an only child one would think it lonely, but Suzanne was never by herself in the small, clean apartment. Her parents and grandparents never left her home alone, in no way using the services of a babysitter. Relatives always came over without having an invitation extended to them. 'My neighborhood itself was clamorous. There was always someone yelling in the street, either to their friends, neighbors, or screaming instructions to their children. No wonder I have a hard time being by myself,' she thought, as she tried enjoying the solitude.

Suzanne knew she shouldn't feel guilty about sitting down in the middle of a work week, the never ending sin of misbehaving or the weakness of giving into her own wants and feelings, just because she felt like it. She found a pad and paper and started writing a special shopping list for the upcoming Passover holidays. The five pound box of matzo was the first on the list. Knowing that at least half would be left over, she still left it, thinking old habits never die. She knew the girls in the Boston salon couldn't wait until she brought the remaining boxes in, sharing the crackers, as they called the matzo, savoring the taste, especially if she brought left over chopped liver or haroses to be spread on top. Many of the girls liked it plain or a pat of butter spread evenly with maybe some strawberry jam generously distributed on top of the butter. Writing down the rest of the food needed for the Passover meal (Sedar) and subsequent week, she examined the list, scanning it, thinking of any items she might have omitted.

Considering the different Jewish holidays, other than Roshashana, the New Year, and Yum Kippur, The Day Of Atonement, Passover was her next favorite Jewish holiday. She looked forward to another Sader meal, realizing this year would be different than others. This year Hope asked her mother if Spenser could join them. 'This will certainly be an unusual experience for Mr. Spenser Bradley' she thought, as she recalled her youth and a warmth swept over her as she closed her eyes, trying to visualize past holidays spent with her parents, grandparents, aunts, uncles and cousins.

Now that her grandparents were gone, traditions seemed different. No longer would the hustle and bustle of preparing her grandparents' house, her aunts helping her grandmother examine the home from attic to basement, ridding the house of any sign of leavened bread or any food containing yeast, or other types of food not considered right for the Passover week, (chomets). All of it was removed and sent in cardboard boxes to their Christian neighbors to eat and enjoy. For one week, matzo (unleavened bread) and the various pancakes, puddings and rolls, made of unleavened ingredients replaced all the bread products to be served. Dishes and silverware were replaced with the Passover sets, different ones for dairy or meat. Her paternal grandparents were Orthodox, and they had four sets of dishes and silverware. Many years had passed since her grandparents were on this earth. Still, she felt their presence in many ways, a feeling, a thought, if not physically, their spirit was always with her. They inspired and taught her the meaning of life, family and love. The stories they told amongst their children and relatives were as real to Suzanne as if she were living them herself.

The very core of this celebration is about food. The family banquet, held on the first and second evenings of Passover, was an elaborate ritual

Thinking back to the various foods, her grandmother would turn over in her grave if she knew that Suzanne bought gefilte fish already made in the jar. Both her grandmothers taught Suzanne how to buy for and prepare the tasty fish recipe, and God forbid she should use any shortcuts. 'Oh how times have changed,' she thought as she sat at the table re-examining her extensive list. 'I had better make time to go shopping or all the food will be sold out before I have a chance to finish preparing for the Sedar,' she scolded herself as she heard Mrs. Walsh enter. I can't forget the apples, nuts, honey, cinnamon and Jewish wine to make chorosis. I still prefer making my own rather than buying the ready-made. Oh yes, I have to call the butcher to save me two shank bones.'

"What a pleasant surprise finding you home in the middle of the day. I hope nothing's wrong."

"You've lived with me so long you're starting to sound like a Jewish mother. I decided to finish the rest of my work at home and then I got sidetracked thinking about the upcoming Passover holiday. We will be having a guest this year. Hope asked if we'd mind having Spencer join us. Since custom dictates guests be invited to our family table, or anyone away from home, for that matter, I couldn't very well say no, now could I?" From what Hope has intimidated, I have a feeling he'll become part of our family."

"Do I detect something in your voice that you have misgivings?" asked Mrs. Walsh.

"I don't know, I may have my doubts and there's an uncertainty deep down that I can't place my finger on. Give me time, though, and I'll form an opinion soon enough."

The loud ringing of the telephone brought each woman out of her reflective thoughts on the previous Passover holidays.

"Don't get up Mrs. Walsh, I'll get it."

At first Suzanne thought it was a prank telephone call, for the voice on the other end of the line was an outcry and very hard to understand. Just as she was about to hang up she realized that the caller was uttering her name.

Madaline tried gaining her composure as she spoke to her friend, attempting to quell the nauseating feeling she felt rising, like a bitter bile, through her system.

"Suzanne, do you think you can come over to my hotel now? I think I'm falling apart. Right now I'm at the Colonial, but I'm heading directly to the Ritz."

"I'm home so don't worry if I'm not right there. Before I leave, are you okay? Did someone try to do you harm again?"

"Yes then no to the second question, just get here as soon as possible," a hysterical Madaline pleaded.

Knowing Madaline for many years, she understood her friend better than most people. There were few reasons or things that would upset Madaline and she hoped that her son, Kyle, was all right and was not the reason for the emotional call. She prayed nothing like a serious accident had happened.

Suzanne knocked on the door and Madaline, eyes red and swollen, beckoned her in. Suzanne closed the door and enfolding her friend in her arms, slowly stroking her hair, like a mother does when comforting a child, in a low, melodious voice, reassuring her everything would be all right. Suzanne hadn't realized how small and petite Madaline was. She could feel her bony frame through her clothes. Leading her to the beautiful French Provincial sofa, she gently put Madaline on it. Sitting on and in the midst of the pastel yellow tones, Suzanne felt as if she were in a lemon grove, the soft furniture providing a calming effect.

"You stay right here, I'm going to make you a stiff drink, your usual scotch. I'll be right back."

Walking over to the glass and marble bar she deftly poured a substantial amount of the amber liquid into the cut crystal tumbler. With an affirmative tone, unlike the Suzanne Madaline was used to, instructed her friend to take a large swallow.

"Now I want you to take a deep breath, tell me, calmly, what has happened? Is it about Kyle? Without becoming hysterical, we'll see what we can do."

"I really don't know much more than I did an hour or so ago when Kyle called me from police headquarters, and informed me that he'd been arrested for suspicion of murdering his friend, Curtis Jones. He wants me to get him the best lawyer and, quote, unquote, get me the hell out of here. He told me that he was innocent and they've arrested him on all circumstantial evidence. I've called my lawyer and I'm waiting for him to return my call."

"All I could think of was thank God Kyle hadn't been in an accident and that physically he's all right. Besides my lawyer, I didn't know who I could turn to and confide my thoughts to, so I automatically called you. I hope you don't mind."

Madaline's energy and high adrenaline seemed to have dissipated all at once. Drying away tears that were streaming down her face, with the same tissue she blew her nose in, the shivering started again.

"Don't be silly. If you can't call your best friend, especially in a situation like this, than what are best friends for? We can't do anything until your lawyer calls you back and goes and speaks to Kyle."

"His secretary told me that Nathan Kirsch, my lawyer's name, was in court and as soon as he returned to the office he'll call."

"I know that my understudy can execute the play this evening. I don't know if I should cancel my performances for the entire week and have the understudy play my part. I want to get to my son as soon as possible. Part of me wants to rush to his side and help him and the professional side tells me the show must go on. Suzanne I don't know what to do. What would you do if you were in my place?"

"Oh no you don't. Don't put me in this awkward predicament. I can't make up your mind for you. As soon as the press finds out you're leaving for the West Coast for a personal reason, the papers are going to find out why and have a field day. I'm sure that even as we speak the media has found out about Kyle's arrest and it will make the headlines and news stations by tomorrow, if not on tonight's news. You and I know the reporters are brutal and they'll have a field day with this situation. Is your lawyer good enough to handle a possible murder case, if it goes to trial?"

"Nathan is a fine lawyer and he has helped me through many tough predicaments, but I don't think, in all honesty, he can handle this type of case. He'll get me the best lawyer for this type of situation, I'm sure."

The encumbrance and annoying slow movement of the clocks hands added to the tense emotions of the two women sitting with their individual thoughts waiting for the important call. The hours were slowly passing, Madaline was on her third drink and as she stirred the ice cubes within the glass, the sound of the square ice reminded her of the wind chimes hanging from her deck back home. Life seemed easier years ago, or so she thought, when Kyle was still a youngster, happy, without a care in the world, frolicking and running along the sandy beach, their house overlooking the magnificent blue waters of the pacific.

Madaline wondered if Kyle's life might have turned out differently if he had been raised in a more stable environment. It wasn't her fault, she kept telling herself, that the men that she allowed into her life were complete assholes and life didn't turn out the way she had hoped or dreamed it might. Madaline was sure her life would have been like a fairy tale, her, Brad and Kyle living happily ever after, like a queen with her king and little prince. If only Brad had not died the tragic, sudden way he did. He was too young to have suffered a fatal heart attack and leave his budding family. Tears fell from her eyes as she remembered his head on her lap, cradling him, waiting for the ambulance to come. She kept calling out his name but he didn't respond. It happened suddenly, one moment they were laughing in the living room and the next thing Madaline remembers seeing Brad falling to the floor, as if in slow motion. But life doesn't always continue the way we hope or wish, she sighed as Brad's face passed before her.

Madaline remembered when she and Kyle would be down at the beach and build sand castles and collect many shells to bring home to show his father. He was so innocent, loving and a happy child. He was caring, loved animals and would never kill an ant or spider. He'd rather walk over the poor insect rather than squish it. "Mommy, this is the best castle we ever made. Can we keep it?"

"I'm sorry honey, but when the tide comes in our beautiful castle will go away. But I have my camera underneath my robe on the blanket. What if I take a picture with you beside the castle with your toy soldiers lined up to protect the kingdom?"

Getting up off of the sofa Madaline went to her bedroom. She took that picture everywhere she traveled, King Kyle and his castle. She looked at the photo and shook her head in bewilderment.

Kyle was the love of her life, with the exception of Brad. Despite the unusual circumstances of her childhood, she never thought it possible or capable to find it in her heart to love two people as she loved Brad and Kyle.

Madaline remembered as if it were yesterday. All her friends gathered around her and tried to make life worth living, she wanted to die. She realized that Brad wouldn't want her to go just yet, for she had Kyle to take care of, nurture and raise him to become a wonderful young man that they both could be proud of. Madaline found herself becoming more depressed every day. She couldn't function without the anxiety and antidepressant medicines that the doctors prescribed for her. If she didn't have them as a crutch, she would have gone off the deep end. Knowing that she had Kyle to care for was a big help. He didn't understand why his daddy wasn't there anymore. Madaline tried her best to soothe him and make him understand what happened but realized that he was just a little child and couldn't comprehend what unexpectedly occurred

While all of this turmoil was going on Kyle was put into a private school. Nannies were hired to care for her young child, when he was home for the holidays from the undisclosed institutes. It took many years to function without the help of drugs. It turned out that she was one of the lucky ones that didn't have to go into detox. Madaline finally accepted the inevitable and tried to make a life for herself without her knight in shining armor.

The shrill ringing of the telephone obstructed the imagery visions of Kyle playing with his castle and her hypnotic state. A pleasant voiced woman, Madaline presumed a secretary, asked, "Miss Mason, please, this is the office of attorney Miles Freeman."

"Speaking."

"Wait one moment."

"Miss Mason, Miles Freeman." His voice was deep and powerful. She could tell from his spoken word that he was intellectual, yet thoughtful. She envisioned him a man of large proportion, one that has no problem taking command of any given situation. "I got off the telephone with Nathan Kirsh, a very good friend and colleague. From what Nathan tells me, you and your son are in need of my services."

Madaline explained that she needed him. From what she learned from Kyle, which was little, he had been arrested for suspicion of murder. A friend of her son's, Curtis Jones, had been found murdered and after some investigating the police came to the conclusion that Kyle committed the murder. "I personally don't think that the evidence they have is conclusive, but that's my opinion," stated Madaline.

"Mr. Freeman, I'm sure you hear this a dozen times a day, I'm telling you my son is innocent. Kyle doesn't have a mean bone in his body. I know of your reputation and I want you to get my son out of jail and clear his name. I don't care what it takes."

"I'm going over to where the police are holding Kyle, and after I speak to him I'll know a few more details and a better idea of what we're dealing with. I'll keep you informed and will get back to you when I have more information. Hopefully, I'll be able to get Kyle released on bail and then we'll go from there."

"I presume that you're taking on my son's case. If so, I can't thank you enough."

"Don't thank me quite yet Miss Mason. Thank me when he's out of jail and they drop this charge."

"Have you decided if you're going out to the coast or will you stay here and finish the play?"

"I think I'll stay here and try to keep busy. I'll keep abreast of the situation by telephone. If Kyle wants me out there, I'll go. I would drive him crazy with worry if I were nearby. Right now the show must go on and I'll help Kyle every way that I can.

By the time Suzanne left the Ritz it was after the heavy commuter traffic. She couldn't contain all the thoughts going through her mind. She realized that it had been awhile since she'd last seen Kyle. Kids get older, go on their own and you only hear what's happening with them when they want you to know what's going on in their lives. As much as Madaline had extolled about her only and handsome son there was obviously more than either Madaline knew or she wanted to reveal.

She agreed with Madaline, and believed with all her heart, that Kyle was not capable of committing a homicide. But on the other hand anyone or mostly anyone, if driven to insanity, could commit such a crime. Suzanne remembered many times that if she had a method to kill Brian she probably would have.

Thinking back to her horrible existence brought tears to her eyes. Years ago abuse was not talked about openly like it is now. She was afraid that if she were to leave Brian that she'd be unable to support the children on her own. No, she thought, she had to tolerate all the abuse and when the time was right, she'd end the degradation she had to endure. A blast from a horn got Suzanne out of her reverie.

Life was good now. She and her loved ones had their health, the business was prospering and she was in love with Stephen. What else could she ask for? She knew that there was always something happening that made life chaotic, a needle to burst one's bubble.

Mrs. Walsh greeted Suzanne with concern. "Tell me everything and don't leave anything out. Come sit down on the sofa. Would you like something to drink?"

After filling in the details that Suzanne could report to Mrs. Walsh, she had to succumb to her wearied body and mind.

The phone's reverberating noise woke Suzanne from a deep sleep she desperately needed.

"Mom, I just heard on the nightly news that Kyle has been arrested. What's going on?"

All of her girls sounded alike on the telephone. Suzanne found herself concentrating to discern which of her children woke her from her much needed Morpheus.

"Hope, I'll tell you all about it after I take a shower in the morning. Are you working in Boston today? Good. We'll be able to find out more from Madaline very shortly. I'll fill you and the girls in on all the details when Madaline calls me."

CHAPTER SEVENTEEN

Nancy realized she had to fly back to Japan to finalize the exact location where their spa would be situated. It took her longer than she or Suzanne had anticipated, therefore Nancy became very frustrated. When she was in Japan she called Mr. Yoshirhiro. Nancy was told that he was again, in San Diego on business. Disappointed, she had to rely on local real estate agents, that she found difficult to understand, to help in her endeavor to find a good location for their, soon to be, establishment. After many phone calls back and forth with Suzanne they decided to have faith on what the agent advised. They were going to set the spa in a very fashionable area of Tokyo.

After another grueling flight back to the States, she couldn't wait to get back home and relax.

While Nancy made her way up the coast, on the way to her house, or as most people called it, "The Castle", she appreciated the undisturbed tranquility. She sought the peacefulness of the area after her long journey. It had been a hectic trip, one that she was glad to see end. Upon entering her noiseless home Nancy deposited her few pieces of luggage in the large marble foyer. 'It's been a long and exhausting trip to the far east, as always,' she thought, as she made her way into the den. Ignoring the need to unpack and sort her clothing, she seated herself on the comfortable, pale, yellow, chintz sofa in the den. Her head automatically fell back onto the high back sofa. Nancy kicked off her shoes and put her tired feet on the creamy, yellowish, red trimmed, wooden coffee table in front of her. Since the first time she had visited the different islands that are located off the east coast of Asia, she realized how much she missed America. After viewing the archipelago and inspecting each island and the likelihood of locating one of the spas in that particular Island, she found herself having endless conference calls with Suzanne.

The darkness and solitude felt good and soon she could feel herself being taken over by the unanxious and contented feelings she had hoped for.

She awoke chilled after the relevant hours of sleep she had needed. 'I was so tired, I didn't even make it upstairs to my bedroom', she laughed to herself. Nancy walked barefoot into the kitchen and automatically grinded the Ethiopian coffee beans in her Melitta bean grinder and waited for the fresh coffee to finish perking. The hearty aroma filled the house as Nancy sat at her kitchen table sipping the hot liquid. She looked out the window and observed a few sandpipers scurrying along the sand towards the green brush and shrubs near the water's edge. As she was looking at the beautiful ocean the phones ringing brought Nancy out of her tranquil state.

An enthusiastic Suzanne asked, "Hi, I hope you had a good flight?"

"Yes, I got in last evening and am sitting down enjoying my first cup of good coffee in about two weeks. Thank God for small favors. When will we be able to get together? A lot of business decisions have to be discussed. We have to be in agreement."

"How about tomorrow evening? By the way a lot has happened since the last time we spoke. My head is spinning with all the problems that have come about.

Before you get nervous, the problems that I'm talking about has nothing to do with the business so don't worry."

"It's going to kill me not to know, I'll wait until tomorrow night. See you then and be careful driving home from work;" ordered Nancy.

Redialing, Nancy waited until Suzanne picked up. "It's me again. What time do you want me at your house?"

Suzanne said. "I'll meet you at my house, say around eight. I think I have a late patient so eight o'clock will work out better for me. I'll ask Mrs. Walsh to make something special for us."

"That's fine. But please, no sushi, "begged Nancy. Suzanne laughed as they said goodbye once again.

'At last peace and tranquility,' Nancy thought to herself, as she opened the windows to let the fresh air in. She enjoyed the smell of the ocean. It reminded her of being stranded on an isolated island with water surrounding the secluded retreat. Nancy hated being cooped up in a hotel room, even though she had to admit, the suite she stayed in was sizeable. Nancy slowly unpacked her toiletries and clothing. She expended an hour of her time putting away the unused clothes into their designated draws and her walk in closet, a separate pile of clothes to be washed. She automatically put the television on to curb the stillness in the house. Going through the pile of mail in front of her, she tossed unwanted circulars away and put the pile of bills to one side. She thought she heard Madeline's name mentioned along with Kyle's. She walked across the room to raise the volume. The TV anchor man was saying that Kyle Mason, son of famous actress, Madaline Mason, was being held in jail for suspicion of Murder. She then heard the name Curtis Jones was the murdered victim, who they suspect was a dear friend of Kyle's. Nancy was shocked and had to sit down. Trying not to get hyper or spontaneous she refrained from calling Suzanne immediately. 'This is what Suzanne was talking about. 'She wanted to tell me in person rather than having me hear it from another source,'

When Nancy arrived at Suzanne's home, Mrs. Walsh greeted her. "Suzanne will be right down. Come, wait in the den while I finish making dinner," she told Nancy.

Suzanne came down the staircase, Simka and Boston trailing behind her. With a sincere hug she sat next to Nancy. "Let's sit at the dining room table and not talk about anything important, like the shop or the matter I discussed over the phone. Mrs. Walsh prepared a fantastic brisket for us to enjoy, just the way you like it."

After complimenting Mrs. Walsh on her excellent dinner they asked if they could help with the cleanup. "No, no, I know the two of you have a lot to discuss since your trip abroad. Mrs. Walsh shooed them upstairs into Suzanne's office for privacy. The two friends and partners adjourned to discuss the issues that lay before them. Nancy recounted the events and happenings with their soon to be Japan salon.

Nancy cleared her throat and admitted that she unexpectedly heard the news about Madaline and Kyle while watching the television. "It's in all the media and I hope that Madaline and Kyle can get out of this mess and cope with the adverse publicity."

Suzanne was relieved that Nancy knew about Madaline's sorrow and didn't have to deliver the dire predicament that their friends were in. "As you can imagine, poor Madaline is beside herself with grief. Madaline is still here in Boston finishing her engagement and I'm telling you, the woman is incredible. Even though the newspapers are having a field day about the arrest, Madaline's performances are still wonderful. I think, between you and I, I'm going to fly down to California. While rearranging my schedule will be difficult, I'll do some investigating on my own. You've know Kyle as long as I have and I doubt he could be involved in murder. What do you think about my going there and trying to find out about this 'so called' murder investigation?"

"Well first of all, I agree with you about Kyle. Secondly, if you think you're going to go down to California by yourself you're out of your mind. I thought we were a team. Both in Metamorphosis and everything else in life, especially helping out an old friend."

"I didn't want to impose on you, especially since you must be exhausted from your trip."

"Well, this does come at an inopportune time, but we'll manage to do everything we have to and still try to solve this terrible crime. Anyone who knows this young man would never be able to accuse him of killing anyone. I remember him as being very sensitive about ones feelings. No, he could never be guilty of committing this murder that they say he has." They called the airlines and booked a flight out within the next week.

When Nancy arrived back home from Suzanne's house, completely satiated from Mrs. Walsh's dinner, she finished the last of the unpacking. She picked up her bills and filed them in order of their dates. Finished with the unavoidable chores, Nancy climbed the winding staircase to her massive bedroom suite. Alone with no one to hold or cuddle, she lay in the dark, waiting for Morpheus to take over. She thought about many past experiences in her life, with Peter, her parents, Suzanne and lastly, Madeline. She still became embittered when thoughts of Peter occurred. 'How could he have demolished such a wonderful life and career she thought,' as she cuddled the pillow beside her. Berating herself she thought, 'I was such a fool to not have seen the signs of despair and his frenzied, erratic pattern of behavior. All I ever wanted was someone to adore, who loved me in return and raise a family of my own. I need children to give my love, affection and devotion to, something that I was deprived of.' She often talked aloud to God and nights like these Nancy often expressed her inner most thoughts and desires. 'Dear God, the clock is ticking faster, will I ever be granted the happiness I want? I have so much tenderness and compassion, every day that goes by I feel so alone. Please God, hear my prayers and help me overcome my bitterness and disappointment. I have so much to give.' Her subconscious prevented her from obtaining the sleep that she needed.

Bringing back to mind her conversation with Suzanne she turned over and with her hands under her head, eyes wide open, that she desperately wanted to close, kept going over the dilemma Madeline and Kyle were facing. 'Yes,' she thought, before the flow of darkness took her into slumber, 'we'll try to help our friends through this ordeal.'

Suzanne woke from a restless sleep. 'It's futile to lay here with all these disturbing thoughts running through my mind.' She threw off the covers as she pulled herself up and sat on the edge of the bed. She hurriedly dressed. While waiting for the water to boil for a quick cup of tea, she compiled a list of obligations that had to be taken care of before she could journey to the sunny coast of California. Suzanne wrote a note informing Mrs. Walsh that she left for work early.

Suzanne phoned her daughter Taylor, assuming she was still at home. "Hi honey, sorry to call so early but I need you and possibly Hope to help me out. Nancy and I are going to California for a while on some unexpected business and I hope that between the two of you, you'll be able to fill in for me for a few weeks. I'm looking at the schedule and you're supposed to be at our Rodeo Drive salon and I'm supposed to be at our Dallas one. If one of you girls replace me, the clients won't be as upset if they find out that it's one of my daughters that's taking over for me."

"Let me wake up a bit before you start delegating instructions to me mother, I'm still half asleep. Now what's this business about the two of you going to California?"

"Looking over the schedule it looks like you're supposed to be in our California salon for the next couple of weeks and if you can change places with me for a few weeks I'd appreciate it."

"But WHY are you and Nancy going to California so suddenly?"

"It's somewhat personal if you don't mind."

A sleepy Taylor asked, "Does it have anything to do with the terrible mess Kyle is in?" "It might, but I rather not go into it now. I hope this doesn't foul up your plans but I really need this favor from you."

Rubbing her eyes Taylor kicked off her covers and slowly emerged from the bed, the telephone receiver deftly held to her ear. "Mom, if I can help in any way, you know I will. I'll make a few phone calls and rearrange my schedule. But you owe me one..."

"You are a doll honey. I want to see you before I go away again. I miss seeing you and the other girls now that you're all living on your own. Would you call up your sisters for me and see if we all can get together for dinner before we go off in different directions?"

"Mom," a husky voiced Taylor declared, "you're so funny. You still would like to have us around all the time, wouldn't you?"

"Well, of course, even though I travel most of the time, with running the business and taking care of all the demands I have, sometimes I wish life were a little simpler. I used to agonize whenever you or your sisters where out late. I could never get to sleep until I knew you were home safe and sound. What I don't know can't hurt me."

Before hanging up Suzanne had to end the phone conversation by saying, "Don't get me wrong, I still worry about you. Do you think I raised you all these years and let you fly the coop without you girls constantly on my mind? I appeared angry when you came in later than your curfew, but I was grateful that you were safe and sound. I feel I've lost control of you. You know what a control freak I am." Her daughter laughed out loud, "Yes mother, we all know what a control freak you are."

"What are you going to do about Stephen?" winked Mrs. Walsh.

"Stephen," Suzanne said aloud. Jumping up from her chair at the table she ran to the phone. "Oh my God, I thought we would be seeing each other this coming week when I worked at my Dallas salon. I have to call him and tell him of my change in plans. Nancy and I are going to California and while we're there we'll see Kyle and try to sort out the mess he's in." While she dialed Stephen's number she had to put down the receiver because of Mrs. Walsh's' ranting.

Pointing a finger Mrs. Walsh admonishingly warned Suzanne, "Well, you and Nancy better be careful. I don't like the two of you playing detectives again. You never know what you two might find out and why go looking for trouble. Didn't the two of you learn a lesson from your last episode?"

"Don't worry. We'll be careful and I'm sure it won't be as complicated or get involved with sinister characters like the last time."

"Famous last words missy, don't worry. You never know what life has in store and sometimes events and people are more complicated than you think they are," Mrs. Walsh chided.

Trying to change the subject Suzanne brought up her and Nancy's ideas for their latest venture; their Japanese salon. "I can't tell you how excited I am. I know this will be our largest and best spa yet. Everyone there loves anything American. It will cost a small fortune, but I know we'll make it back in no time."

Mrs. Walsh knew what Suzanne was up to. She let her warning of danger glide.

"There are a few pitfalls that we'll have to iron out. Living so far away is going to be difficult. It's not like we'll be able to hop on a plane and be at our next salon in a matter of a few hours. You realize that we really won't have the same control over our estheticians and other personnel there that we have at our other establishments. We'll have to get someone who is very efficient as a manager. I was thinking maybe if Nancy and I find someone that we like and proves herself dependable and good we could make her a deal of some sort. Maybe part owner of that spa. That way she'll have more of an incentive to be honest and try her best. What do you think?" asked Suzanne.

"I think that's a great idea," Mrs. Walsh agreed.

"I'll put an ad in the Tokyo paper and meanwhile I'll put some feelers out from some of my contemporaries if they know of a good Japanese esthetician either in Japan or here in the States that will be willing to re-locate. She'll have to know and speak fluent Japanese."

The phones ringing interrupted their conversation and thoughts.

Nancy started talking immediately after Suzanne picked up her cell. "I've been thinking about something else, and I don't want any interruptions please, until I finish." Suzanne cut in on her friend, "Excuse me, but don't you even acknowledge the person who answers the phone. What if you dialed the wrong number?"

"Don't be silly," chided Nancy, I have your number programed into my cell. Your number is dialed automatically." Nancy spoke as she took a deep breath and continued. Suzanne sat down shaking her head at Mrs. Walsh and let Nancy talk. "Wouldn't it be wonderful if we bought a small Lear Jet, say one that held fifteen passengers or so with a lounge area and sleeping compartment. That way we'll have transportation available at any time. Just think about it before you dismiss my idea as preposterous. Of course we would have to hire our own pilot and crew. I have expendable money, and why not use it to our advantage. You know it makes sense. It will save us a lot of aggravation and we'll be able to get business done while we're flying and also some needed rest. Besides, we won't have to depend on anyone else's schedule."

As much as Suzanne wanted to find fault with Nancy's idea she couldn't." All right we'll look into it as soon as we get back from California and get this mess straightened out." Suzanne shook her head as she put down the phone. '

Suzanne lifted the receiver of the telephone and then hung it up. She didn't want to make this call. She dreaded phoning Stephen with this latest intrusion, denying them the joy of being with each other. 'What excuse can I possibly tell him without actually acknowledging the fact that I'm electing to make the trip to California but not to Texas, where we could be with each other. I know he'll be mad as hell at me and rightly so,' she thought. She finally picked up the receiver and dialed his number. Counting the rings, she held her breath hoping he wouldn't answer. On the fifth ring Stephen cheerfully answered.

"Hi. I'm glad I got you in. How are you? You seem awfully happy."

"Actually, I saw your number on caller ID. I was hoping to hear from you and it was you calling; my prayers have been answered. I wanted to speak to you in the worst way."

"So why didn't you lift your phone and dial my number? It's not like I'm out on the town having a grand old time. I would have loved you calling me. Since when do we have to stand on formalities and wait for the other person to call?" An irritated tone to her usual pleasant voice emerged as Suzanne was trying to hold back her annoyance and didn't want an argument to ensue. Stephen, oblivious to her perturbation, filled her in on matters that have been going on and what he had in mind for them to do when she arrived. He then finally asked the question that Suzanne was dreading.

"First of all what time can I pick you up at the airport? Or wait a second. Will you be renting a car so that you can have your own transportation?" Not taking a breath he continued, "Will you be able to take more time off and come down here for a bit before your obligations at the salon have to be met? That way we'll be able to spend more time together," Stephen asked and explained with what seemed pleading in his voice.

As much as she wanted to say yes, for she missed him as much as he missed her, the inevitable questions had to be answered. She wanted to avoid the answer she had to give him. Knowing the disappointing news had to be given, she went forth.

'I can't tell him the real reason for this trip to California. Last time that Nancy and I played 'Suzie The Slueth' he made me promise him that I would never get involved with anything dangerous again. I can't tell him, even though I'll be breaking my word. If we have to contact the police that are in charge of the case, we will. Hell, if they don't satisfy us with whatever information they have, Nancy and I might have to get in touch with Tim and Kevin. They might believe us and introduce us to some agents located in California. '

She really was disappointed, but knew, under any circumstance, she couldn't alter her plans. Trying to sound remorseful, and in a way she was, she made up an excuse that she hoped he'd believe. 'Remember what your mother always told you, a liar and cheat always get caught.' Trying to clear her head there was silence on the other end of the phone. "Hello, hello Stephen, are you still there?"

"Of course I am. As much as I'd like to hang up on you, I won't. What do you want me to say? I'm deliriously happy? I won't give you the satisfaction of getting mad at me and turning the decision you made around and blame me for the anger I'm feeling at this moment. I'm sorry that some of the choices you've made throughout your lifetime have been poor ones. This is just another one of your wrong decisions. I can't change your mind, for I know by now that once you make it up, no one can alter it. Yes, I'm upset and furious about you're going to California rather than being with me. Suzanne, I don't know what makes you tick. I hope that I'll get over being mad and that whatever you do out there, you'll have a great time."

'Oh sure, Nancy and I will have a ball. If he knew what we're up to I honestly think he'd kill us.' As much as Suzanne wanted to tell Stephen the truth about her abrupt change of plans, she knew she couldn't. The last time she and Nancy got into trouble and helped Mrs. Pearlman out of her family's dilemma, Stephen was pissed. Suzanne honestly felt that what she was going to do would never put her in harm's way and vulnerable to imminent danger. She knew in her heart that she had to try to help Madaline. 'After all, they are family, and Nancy and Madaline would do the same for me.' She then asked herself; 'do I feel that Stephen is like family or do I have more misgivings about our relationship than I realized?'

"I know you're not going to believe me, but there are circumstances that have happened that make my decision necessary. I really can't talk about it, I'd rather be with you. Don't you think that I want to be in your arms and have you hold me and do all the things that make us both happy? Don't answer. Just listen and have no doubt when I say I love you. I'll make this up to you one way or another, I promise."

"By the way, I saw the news last week and it's still on all the stations about Madaline's son, Kyle. What's going on?" Stephen asked. "I know this has nothing to do with your decision, but maybe you can give me the low down on what's happening." "It's nothing, really. A misunderstanding and everyone is getting into the act. Madaline assured me that everything is under control," Suzanne lied.

"Now getting back to our situation, Suzanne, you're a grown woman and no matter what I say, you'll justify your actions. So I'll go about my business, stay out of trouble and come back safe and sound. You know that I love you too. If I have to, I'd wait for eternity to see you again. I can't wait to kiss you and be with you, by for now, I love you." A disgruntled Stephen handled his disappointment as best he could.

Suzanne heard the inevitable click and with tears streaming down her face pulled the covers snuggly around her torso. It had been a few months since they had last been with each other and she realized how very much she missed him. She tried putting her desire and cravings to the wayside but her body ached to feel the nearness of his muscular body and his manhood inside her. Feelings of frustration oppressed her before slumber took over.

CHAPTER EIGHTEEN

Stephen sat at his desk, taking deep breathes to calm himself. Frustration and anger was apparent as he made his way to the brown leather sofa on the opposite side of his study. He didn't know how to react to Suzanne's obvious lack of concern about their relationship. He thought that she loved him with all her heart and then she turns around and does something like this that dispels all the actions of the past. He shook his head to rid himself of these unpleasant ideas. His hands were literally tied because he knew there was nothing he could do or say that would dissuade her plan. He loved her more than life itself and only hoped that they would be with each other soon.

Going into his living room, he poured himself a Wild Turkey and hoped that Lawrence had nothing to do with their predicament. Even though Susanne assured him that she and Lawrence were only friends, he was jealous, and try as he might, he couldn't get that thought out of his mind. After 2 more drinks, his frustration got the best of him. He threw the glass, with all his might, across the room, hitting the fireplace. Books and the fire side set went toppling to the floor. 'I'll clean the mess tomorrow morning,' he told himself as he slowly walked to the second floor and couldn't wait till he felt the comfortable bed under his tired body.

"Mom, I'm glad I caught you. I spoke to Taylor and she told me about your plans. What's up?"

"Just some unexpected business that Nancy and I have to take care of. Do you think you can help us out on such short notice?" Hope wavered, "Sure, you know we will. But I was hoping to have you alone for a while. I think Spencer and I will be getting engaged shortly and there's something serious I have to discuss with you."

With uncertainty Suzanne questioned Hope further. "It sounds serious. Is everything all right? You're not pregnant?"

"Mother, in this day and age I don't think you have to worry about me expecting. No, I just want to talk about something that's been on my mind for a while now and I want to chat. It can wait until you get back from the west coast."

"Are you sure? Because I can change my schedule in the next few days and spend some time alone with you," a concerned Suzanne answered.

"No that's all right. I'll come by the house with Melanie and Taylor tomorrow, and after they leave we'll be able to talk without being interrupted.

"Mom, please don't mention our conversation in front of the other girls. What I have to say is private and only you can know, for now. Okay?"

"Sure," a disturbed Suzanne said as she hung up the telephone.

Suzanne tried not to show her anxiety when her daughters joined her for dinner the next evening. For once she had to possess self-discipline.

"Mom you didn't hear one word I said," an irritated Melanie exclaimed.

"I'm sorry. My mind seems to be a million miles away. Please excuse my inattention and I promise it won't happen again." Suzanne tried to concentrate on the conversation and made a concerted effort to join the lively discussion.

"Do you know how long you'll be in California?" asked Taylor. "No, but I hope not more than a month."

"A month. Don't you think that's a long time to be away? I mean, we're so dependent on you and Nancy at this point. Not that we're not good, but all the girls and young men that work for you will be a little nervous not having either of you around for that length of time."

"Let me say this. Say for instance, and it's only an inevitable concern, but what if something did happen to either Nancy or me. Either one of us aren't old, but God forbid, anything beyond our power can happen. I hope that we live to a ripe old age and still be kicking butt. After all, I have a long life to live, enough to see grandchildren and spoil them. You know I had to work very hard, when your father and I divorced, that I couldn't be the kind of mother that I wanted to be. I didn't have the privilege to stay home and play with you as you got older; I couldn't give you rides to your games or even attend them. I worked hard to make sure that you had everything that you wanted. I was so ashamed to be the first person in the neighborhood, or for that matter in our family, to get divorced. I can't work as I do forever and this will give you an opportunity to use your managerial skills. Don't you think that you girls can manage our business and do it with pride and keep Metamorphosis salons?"

"We have discussed that possibility amongst ourselves," Melanie replied.

"What's all the secrecy and why can't you tell us why you're going?" inquired Hope.

"What is this? An interrogation? I think I'm old enough that I don't have to account to you children for my every move. All of a sudden I feel as if I'm at an inquisition. This is supposed to be a nice, peaceful dinner before I leave. I wanted to thank all of you for pitching in and helping me out so that I can get away. So why do I feel guilty?"

"It's just that you're always here or at one of the salons. Yes, maybe we are a little spoiled. It's just so out of character for you."

"Are you all right and not hiding something awful from us," interrupted a concerned Taylor.

"I'll give you odds that all of you were on a conference call till the wee hours of the night discussing this dinner and the conversation that will be taking place. I can assure you nothing's wrong with my health. You know I could never keep anything like that from you. Nancy and I have to settle a business matter that has come up."

"It just seems odd. But we promise not to pry into your business or challenge your judgment," assured Taylor. "We'll tell you where you can reach us," assured Suzanne.

As the girls were leaving Suzanne tactfully asked Hope to stay a while longer.

"Honey, I want you to tell me what's on your mind. You said it can wait until I return, but I won't be able to give full attention to my business until I know what you have to say."

"Mom, I don't want to get into this until we can spend awhile together. My thoughts might upset you."

Patting the sofa's pillow, Suzanne motioned for her daughter. "Hope, sit down on the sofa next to me and let's talk. You know you can tell me anything."

Reluctantly Hope began telling Suzanne her feelings. She was nervous and couldn't sit still. "Spenser and I are talking about getting married soon. Before we do, I've done a lot of soul searching and," half mumbling without looking Suzanne in the eyes blurted out, "I want to change my religion." Putting her hand up before Suzanne could get a word in, she continued. "I don't want you to be hurt."

"You don't want me to be hurt? Let me tell you, I and your grandparents will be hurt."

Suzanne felt her heart palpitating but tried to ignore the cold shivers going through her body. 'Don't lose it, keep a cool head and get control of yourself,' Suzanne closed her eyes and kept repeating what she was thinking.

"You should be proud that you're Jewish and you simply cannot abandon the religion of your birth and ancestors. Wiping away some strands of hair that had fallen into her face Suzanne continued her barrage. Did Spencer ask you to turn to his faith?"

"No mom, Spencer has nothing to do with this. When I told him I was thinking of converting to his faith he also asked me questions. I got to thinking that if and when Spencer and I do marry, I want to bring my children up in a house that has one religion."

"I see, Suzanne said sarcastically. Why don't you ask Spencer if he'd change to Judaism? You think that's a good reason to give up your religion and faith? To me that's a sorry excuse. If you were to marry a Jewish fellow we wouldn't be having this conversation."

"No I guess not. But I'm not marrying a 'nice Jewish young man.' Spencer is the man I want to spend the rest of my life with and bear his children. It will make life a lot easier if the whole family has one religion. I was confused when we were little. I knew we were Jewish, though we celebrated Chanukah, we also celebrated Christmas and Easter with dad's whole family? I would be petrified that the kids at Sunday school and at the Temple would ever find out about us having a Christmas tree or going over to Nana Morse's house for our Easter ham dinner."

"Now you wait one second, we celebrated the Jewish holidays religiously and only celebrated Christmas and Easter for Santa and the Easter Bunny. I admit I was a youngster myself when I got married and started a family. When your father begged me to have a Christmas tree, like he used to have as a child, I went along with his request. I was too young and stupid to realize that I was giving you kids mixed messages. I tried to instill in all of you religious guidance, awareness and a sense of tradition and pride."

"My God, Hope, my grandparents would be turning in their graves if they thought that one of their great grandchildren would break away from their religion. We have such a wonderful heritage. Did you learn anything in religious school or the sermons that the Rabbi told the Congregation during the Holidays? The terrible oppression and pogroms that people went through is incomprehensible. People of different religions than ours would come barreling into our serene villages, drunk, mostly on horseback, with swords in hand and annihilate our entire people along with our businesses and homes. They would rape woman and children and kill, by the masses, because of our religious beliefs.

Our people survived slavery and holocausts that exterminated us by the millions."

"The Jewish people were and still are brilliant people. If you think about it, many were bankers, owned mines, entrepreneurs, and even poor farmers made sure that there children were schooled. Even though Mama Pessa had a hard time writing the English language, she spoke several European languages. I remember her sitting down at our kitchen table practicing how to write her name in English. We are a proud people and you never forget it. You should be proud of your heritage. Besides, once you're born to a mother who is Jewish, you're always considered Jewish. I bet you never knew that?"

"Before you so readily convert, if I were you, I'd think more about the decision you make." Suzanne sat on the sofa with tears in her eyes, trying not to completely break down in front of Hope. So many memories of her own childhood came flooding back. Growing up she remembered all the stories told to her of the valiant people who wanted a better life for themselves and their children. Thinking how brave the parents were when they sent one or two of their children off to a different land, having a relative sponsor these little ones, not knowing if they'd ever live to see them again. Suzanne doubted if she could penetrate her thoughts to Hope. Suzanne thought to herself, 'Someday if she does change her religion I know that she'll live to regret it.'

"Mom I'm going to tell you something that I've never told a soul. I was always embarrassed when there were so few Jewish kids at school and the other kids would tease the kids who had obvious Jewish names. They weren't like the other kids at school. They were studious and just acted a little different. I always had two sets of friends and God forbid, I didn't want to be made fun of and persecuted like many of my Jewish schoolmates. You do remember that most of my girlfriends were Christians. As a matter of fact when Ash Wednesday would come and all the kids went to church to get their ashes, I'd take some cigarette ashes and put it on my forehead, so I wouldn't feel out of place. I know, I know, you're going to say that's pathetic."

"My sentiments exactly. I didn't realize it was so difficult growing up in a community that we were a minority. I thought it would be good to raise kids amongst all kinds of religions and nationalities. I didn't want to have you brought up so closed minded as not to see how the other side lives. Now after all this maybe I was wrong. When I was a youngster growing up, Jewish children were the majority, the school system closed down for the Jewish holidays.

"Maybe, when I first married, I should have moved and lived in a community where there were many Jewish kids, like Newton or Brookline. Like the saying goes, 'would have, should have.' I'm truly sorry that you were embarrassed to be proud of your heritage. I'm looking at you and I don't really know who you are any more. All I can say is shame on you for feeling that way and not coming to me and telling me how you felt. Someday I hope that God will forgive you. I'm not happy about your decision, but I'll keep my mouth shut. I'll tell you now. It will kill your grandparents."

Trying to ignore her mother's speech, Hope continued, "I will always be proud of being Jewish, if I do change, it isn't because I'm disillusioned with the Jewish religion. I'm doing it for the sake of my future family."

"I'm telling you it will break your grandparent's heart not to see a first grandson have a bris." Suzanne told Hope.

If you're changing your religion just for the sake of your children then I think you're changing for the wrong reason. To me, your family, the Jewish community here, and most of all in your heart, you'll never be anything else." Tears were now welling in both Suzanne's and Hope's eyes.

Grabbing her mother and hugging her, Hope didn't want to let go." Mom, I know this is hurting you and I'm sorry. Spencer wants me to tell you that it's not his idea. He doesn't care if I change my religion or not."

Wiping away the tears that were flowing readily down her face she pulled herself up and tried to get composure. "So are you and Spencer officially engaged?"

"I think he's taking me to the jewelers building next week and we'll plan to get married by the end of next fall."

"If you still feel you want to convert, I want you to know that I will abide by your wishes. I won't be happy about it but you are a grown woman and I always will love you." Most Jewish families sit and mourn if one of their children converts. They have a Shiva, as if that child is dead. I won't do that, but right now my heart feels empty."

"You know mom, I don't want you to blame yourself. You did a great job bringing us up, especially after the divorce and all. You instilled in us a great sense of values and religious beliefs. Best of all, I have great traditions that I will carry on to my children. They will always know that I was and still consider myself Jewish. I will educate them about my first religion and instruct them how to appreciate my culture, to enjoy the great ethnic foods that you and my grandmothers tried to teach me to make."

'Sure,' Suzanne thought, 'they'll never have the appreciation of our holidays and foods. Oh well, it's their loss. Maybe they'll join our family when the Holidays come and their children will partake in the rituals. One can only hope. '

Suzanne realized it was late. There was little else to say. Walking Hope to the door they kissed and holding her daughter a little longer than necessary she said goodnight. After Hope left, Suzanne stood against the inside door and let her tears flow, the sobbing wouldn't stop.

Lying in bed Suzanne tossed and turned. She knew that once Hope made up her mind nothing could dissuade her. It would be difficult for her and her parents to see Hope married in a church without the ritual of the groom breaking the glass. She remembered the Kazatsky, the Russian dance, as one man after another would get in the middle of the people dancing around him. These men in the center went down like the Russian dancers you've seen in costume, squatting down on their heels and crossing their arms, would kick out their leg, one at a time. Another gentleman would continue this great dance until everyone was exhausted. Suzanne wondered if the Jewish guests at the wedding would perform the traditional Horah dance and in a large circle dance around the bride and groom. She laughed envisioning the expressions and reactions on Spencer's parents and relatives faces; seeing these dances performed by the Jewish guests and relatives at the wedding. Suzanne turned over on her side and with a deep sigh fell into a fast and weary sleep.

Nancy aroused Suzanne at 7:30 A. M. Her cheerful voice aggravated Suzanne. "Someone got up on the wrong side of the bed this morning, what's wrong?"

"You know me too well. I just had a bad night and I don't want to discuss it."

"I won't bug you, but I hope you'll tell me about last night's dinner with the girls. I'm sure everyone had a great time."

"I'd rather not talk about it. Okay, yes, it had to do with a conversation I had with Hope after everyone left. I was given some upsetting news. It's not health related so don't worry about that. Seriously, I really don't want any further discussion about last evening. I want to suppress the last part of the evening. Please! When I feel that I can resolve what problem I might have in my mind, then I'll unburden my emotions to you. Until then, don't even bring anything up. Okay?"

Suzanne headed for the bathroom. She looked in the mirror and was sick at the sight of the woman looking back at her. The bags under her eyes were awful. 'Dam kids, there's always an unknown situation that knocks the socks off of you. '

Nancy told Suzanne the schedule that she'd like to see them achieve when they were in California. "First of all we're going there on a mission. I think it's sweet of you to try to get some nice vacation time in, but no, no. I appreciate what you're trying to do, but I want to get this matter done and finished with. This isn't a game. So thanks, but no thanks." 'Then I'll attend to the matter at hand concerning Miss Hope,' Suzanne thought as she hurriedly dressed for today's work.

Nancy put down the receiver and shook her head. 'I understand Suzanne's position, I realize we have an insurmountable task, but I'm not worried. We'll do our own investigation and get Kyle cleared of that awful murder and in the process, we'll, hopefully, find the guilty party.'

SAN DIEGO, CALIFORNIA

"Suzanne, you seem distracted. Are you all right?" a concerned Nancy asked.

"Sure, I have a lot on my mind that's all. Nothing that I can't handle."

"Are you sure you want to make this trip to California?"

"It's one hell of a time to ask as we're seated on the plane waiting for it to take off."

Nancy tried suppressing a smirk on her face as the sign for the passengers to fasten their seat belts came on.

"Honestly, I'm fine. I hope Stephen can make time in his schedule to meet us there, even if it will only be for a couple of days."

Suzanne hoped the flight wouldn't be as bad as she expected it to be. Usually she would take a Lorazepam an hour or so before take-off. This time she felt she could handle her nervousness without having to take medication to numb her and take away her anxieties. She always feared flying, and this time was no different than any other. Suzanne acknowledged that maybe she didn't care what happened in light of her situation. 'I better get hold of myself or I'm liable to get committed to McLane Hospital in Waltham. I have to keep my feelings to myself and at bay. God, there's so much on my mind. Besides Madeline's first problem this terrible calamity with Kyle is added to the mix. Between Stephen, Lawrence and Hope I sometimes feel over-whelmed, crazy. I know in my mind that these complex situations will turn out fine, and resolve themselves. Especially as a Jew, it is said that our life is only lent to us. Only God can give and take a life. Many times I've felt overwhelmed and depressed, but then, with time and prayer, everything will get resolved. I have to believe that God will intervene or some other miracle will come about.' With these thoughts Suzanne picked up a magazine and started reading.

"This is a great take off. Don't you agree?" Nancy asked. She didn't realize how morose Suzanne was feeling.

"Sure it's been great." Suzanne had to hide her foreboding emotions. 'Get these thoughts out of your mind, girl, just relax and have a positive attitude. We have a lot to do in California and we have to find a way to absolve Kyle. '

Turning to Nancy, Suzanne expressed her opinion of how they should begin their quest to find the real killer or killers and get Kyle released from this accusation. "I really don't know where to start. I guess the best thing we can do is visit Kyle's lawyer, talk to Kyle and go from there. After that we'll play it by ear.

Nancy interjected. "I think the first thing we should do is settle us into our hotel and go from there."

A perturbed Susanne asked. "I thought Madaline offered us the use of her home. Didn't I mention that to you before you made reservations for the airline?"

"Gee, I guess I completely forgot about it. At the time I had a lot on my mind. I just came back from my Japan trip, and then you hit me with what happened to Madaline and Kyle. Besides, Kyle is in San Diego and Madaline's house is in Laguna Beach. I think we should stay in San Diego. The commute would be a bitch if we had to take it every day. I'm sorry," a contrite Nancy tried to explain.

"That's all right. I understand what you're saying. We'll go to the hotel and then we'll play it by ear, okay?" Susanne tried to apologize to Nancy. "I understand how easily that happened. We both have a lot on our plates. Knowing how you like to travel, I bet you reserved us a room at the Four Seasons."

Shaking her head in agreement, "Yup, you know me like a book."

Out of the blue Nancy proclaimed, "Since I've been without a man that I care for, it's been a couple of years now, it seems like forever. I miss the companionship that I'd be sharing with a special person. And let's not kid each other. I miss the intimacy that normally goes along with it. Of course, the last few years between Peter and me wasn't something that I'd brag about. I hardly ever knew about intimacy."

"Are you talking about passion and desire, you hot blooded red head?"

"She whispered in Suzanne's ear, I'm talking good, old fashioned, sex, okay?"

"Are you a little horny dear?" Nancy turned red and tried to ignore Suzanne's last question. Nancy attempted to change the subject, knowing all too well that if they kept talking about dating Suzanne wouldn't stop the barrage of questions.

She had to get Suzanne's mind on something else. She berated herself for bringing up the topic.

Nancy informed Suzanne, "While we're out in California I've made arrangements to go to an airplane factory and see what kind of plane we'll need that will suit our needs. Try to kill two birds with one stone as the saying goes."

"Great, you know how much I love to fly and now you're thinking of owning your own plane. I have to be sick in the head letting you talk me into this venture." Nancy told Suzanne that she should remember that this airplane would be hers as well. "It will belong to the Metamorphosis Salons. At least we'll have control over maintenance and keep the airplane in great shape. Suzanne, as you taught me, gay cukin!!" They both laughed.

Taking the magazine from the nylon pocket in front of her, she tried to read, but couldn't pay attention. She turned to Nancy. "Seriously though, in this day and age I realize how difficult it must be for a single person to enjoy having a sexual relationship. There are so many diseases, not that there weren't years ago, but they hid it under the rug. The topic is talked about more. It's frightening. When you have sex now it's not just your partner you're having a relationship with but the other people who they've had sex with. Not that I'm married, but I'm lucky to have just one partner. Even if we don't get to see one another very often, but when we do, we have a great time." Suzanne winked at her partner and best friend. The plane started descending. The fluffy clouds overhead were now a thing of the past as they headed towards the runway.

CHAPTER NINETEEN

"They entered the lobby. It was very plush and beautifully decorated. "Watch your footing" a motherly Suzanne warned Nancy. These tile floors are very slippery, especially with your high heels."

"I'm used to wearing them everywhere, don't worry," Nancy tried alleviating Suzanne's fear. After signing in they took the elevator to the 9th floor and had no trouble finding their room. "It's beautiful," declared Suzanne. Look at this spacious mirrored closet. Come look at the bathroom. I've never seen one as large as this one in any hotel that I've stayed in. It's almost as large as the one you had remodeled in your house in Ipswich."

"Just be careful when you open the refrigerator," warned Nancy. "You might get thirsty or want some goodies during the night. Don't you dare take any from that money machine, the cost is exorbitant. I learned my lesson the first time I was in a hotel room and I'd never seen one before. We'll buy some refreshments and bring them upstairs and it won't cost us as much. Okay with you?"

"Sure, you're the maven when it comes to hotel suites. I mean, I'm just a plain old Dorchester girl with no knowledge of any refinement."

"Cut the shit, girlfriend. Since you've been hanging around Justin and me, as they say, You've come a long way baby!" They both dropped on their beds and couldn't stop giggling. "Listen to us, we're acting like two teenage girls," Suzanne said.

They both spontaneously got under the covers and fell into a deep sleep. Feeling refreshed after her needed nap, Suzanne took a long, hot shower, attempting to be as quiet as possible, not to wake Nancy from her required rest.

Madaline finished her second show, ran to her hotel room and dialed her friends. "I hope I didn't disturb either of you but I wanted to make sure that you got there safely."

"I saw the itinerary you left. How come you're not staying at my house?" Giving Nancy a dirty look she assured Madaline when they finished their business they'd take advantage of her hospitality. "We'll be here for just awhile till some of our business is attended to and we assure you, we'll be privileged to stay at your beautiful home. We'll be sure to call you on a regular basis and update you if anything changes. I know you must be tired after the show and also we'll let you go and again, don't worry honey, everything will turn out fine."

Suzanne sat on her bed, notebook and pencil in hand, and said to Nancy, "Okay, let's write down a plan on who we should see first. We'll try to make appointments for tomorrow morning."

"Sounds good to me," as she dictated a list for Suzanne to follow. She then got up from her bed and went into the shower, "I'll be ready within an hour. Let's take a walk and eat dinner at a nice restaurant. Okay with you?"

Before they left Boston, Suzanne managed to pry the name of the lawyer that was handling Kyle's case from Madaline when she went back to the dressing room of the theater.

Suzanne spoke to Mr. Freeman's secretary and she was nice enough to squeeze the two women in 'Mr. Freeman's busy schedule.' Suzanne and Nancy would meet the 'famous attorney' the day after their arrival.

Miles Freeman's office was as impressive as the dramatic looking gentleman that greeted the two women from Boston. What surprised Suzanne most was the casual, yet well groomed gentleman sitting across from them. From hearing his voice over the telephone she expected to see a younger and robust gentleman. The polished man seated, with his legs crossed, had to be at least sixty seven years old. Although he was of a greater age than Suzanne had anticipated, she observed a lean, willowy, yet muscular, distinguished man. She realized that nothing went unnoticed through his piercing, large, hazel eyes. His eloquent mannerism dramatically emphasized his forceful voice that was heard throughout the large room. 'No wonder he's such a powerful and dominant figure in the legal arena,' Suzanne thought to herself as his charismatic personality unfolded when he spoke.

After shaking hands Suzanne got down to the nature of their visit. Miles, as he bid the two women to call him, thanked them for making this special trip, but was surprised that they would interrupt their busy schedule to think that they could help." After all, we do have the best private investigators working on the case. I personally oversee Calvin, who has a fine reputation and staff. He has helped me in many a case, and I might add, he usually comes through for me." Both Suzanne and Nancy thought he was being a bit patronizing but ignored his condescending manner.

Disregarding his obvious irreverence Suzanne asked Miles some questions that she and Nancy thought relevant to the matter in hand. Trying not to show her annoyance with his obvious manner of disrespect, he reluctantly answered their inquiries. Suzanne and Nancy thanked him for his time. "Well that's one arrogant son of a bitch," Nancy stated as they emerged from the elevator.

"I think we're going to work on this case alone, without any help from that jerk. Or, for that matter, ask his 'private investigator,' Calvin, any questions that we might have."

"I have to agree with you, he is a real pompous asshole. I know he has a callous reputation but I think he let it go to his head. We'll do just fine without him," Suzanne stated.

Next they made arrangements to visit Kyle at his apartment. The women were happy that Carol was still on assignment. "I have a feeling there's a lot more to the story than Kyle is telling. I've known him for many years and sometimes if someone has a secret, they're more willing to tell an old reliable friend than even their closest relatives."

"You mean like Madaline or Carol don't you? What are you getting at Suzanne?" asked Nancy.

"For some time now, since hearing Madaline talk about the case, something doesn't add up. I have a gut feeling and I really don't want to say anything else about it until I gently nudge Kyle into admitting what I think it might be."

"Okay, I'll let you get it out of him without my asking you anymore questions. I'm aware you've been disturbed about this issue for a while and I'm not going to add to your qualms."

"Thanks," we'll visit with Kyle." Suzanne glided the rented Jaguar into the visitor's space at his luxurious town house.

Kyle looked fatigued and pale when he opened the door. Kissing both women he held onto his "aunt Suzanne" a little longer than normal. "You look great" he pronounced to both women as he led them to the sofa. "What brings both of you out here. It's a bit unusual isn't it?"

"We usually don't travel together if that's what you're getting at. But we are opening a new spa in Japan and there's still a lot of negotiating that has to be done," a scrutinizing Suzanne explained.

"We had to stop in California and we decided to stay over a few extra days and lend you some mothering and support while Madaline's still in Boston," Nancy explained.

"Mother mentioned about your new adventure and she also stated that she's flying down here before her New York engagement. I told her it's unnecessary, but she wouldn't hear of it."

"Personally from a mother's point of view I can understand her wanting to see you and hold you close to her. After all, you're all she has. If she can't be supportive and see for herself how you're holding up during this frightful and confounding situation, than what else can she do?" Suzanne explained.

Sitting on the comfortable tan leather sofa, holding the iced coffee Kyle served them. Suzanne looked around the beautiful room. Pictures of his famous mother adorned the walls along with his father. Suzanne and her family, Nancy and Peter with an assortment of acclaimed shots of the models he photographed that appeared on the covers of some of the best and well known magazines around the world, also were displayed. Suzanne thought it surprising that she saw only one picture on the wall of Kyle and Carol together. Telling herself that more pictures of the happy couple are probably in their bedroom.

After pre-arranging with Suzanne that she'd leave for a while, Nancy excused herself and told them she'd be back after she went downtown to 'window shop.'

Sipping a second glass of iced coffee Suzanne remarked, "Your apartment is beautiful. I didn't expect otherwise. Tell me Kyle, how are you really doing? Save the bullshit for other people. This is Suzanne, your 'adopted aunt' you're talking to. I want to know more than Madaline has told me about this so called acquaintance and the professional relationship you had with him."

Rich was still hungry when he got off the phone with Molly. Thinking of Molly, he had to admit that she was one of the best medical examiners he knew and worked with. He respected her immensely. He walked to his refrigerator and all he could find was ketchup, pickles, a half-gallon of curdled milk, and some green hot dogs. While throwing out the spoiled food he called his buddy and new partner, Stu and asked him if he had eaten dinner yet. "I'm glad that you're a bachelor like me and don't have a set schedule. After all our hard work, I think we deserve a night to ourselves. I'll pick you up in my mustang at the station's parking lot and leave the Crown Vic there." Stu told Rich that he felt grimy and need of a shower. "How about we meet at the Blue fish in 45 minutes? I've got to clean up my act and make myself presentable for my date. Be on time, I hate my dates to be late." Stu chuckled to himself as he got into the shower.

Rich loved his Mustang, so far his favorite car. The sucker had such power; it could get to 60 or 80 MPR within a couple of seconds. It was worth the special engine that was designed just for it, Rich thought to himself. Stu was waiting for him at a table when he walked into the dim- lit restaurant.

"I'm glad you asked me to come. Even though I'm exhausted, I didn't feel like having a beer and left over pizza. Doesn't it suck to eat alone every night?" Stu asked a surprised Rich.

"Stu, I thought you liked being and living alone? It got around the rumor mill that you were content being a seasoned bachelor?" Stu was serious when he exclaimed, "It's nice not having anyone to bitch to you about nothing and then trying to boss you around like they have you by the balls." Rich was surprised at his partner's feelings but acknowledged his own view on the subject. "Seriously, I know how it feels. Thankfully I got out of that kind of relationship. I like doing what I want to do, when I want to do it. Not having to ask anyone for their approval or permission of what you can or cannot do." Changing the subject, Rich asked, "Have you looked at the menu yet? I think I know it by heart. I eat here at least twice a week. I hate my cooking, if you know what I mean?" Rich stated, "Since you're my date for the evening, the nights on me." Holding his hand up towards Stu he stated, "But please, don't be extravagant, or this will be the last time I ask you out."

Stu smiled as Rich ordered 2 Bud lights. How come you don't have to use the car assigned to you by our lovely State?"

"I guess I'm one of the privileged ones. Seriously, most of the time I use the Vic, but when I feel I need a little more power, I jump into my Mustang. You realize I'm the senior detective here and besides, the Captain gave me his blessing. Now let's order."

Suzanne and Nancy left the hotel and took a left. "I hope there's a good restaurant that's close by," a hungry Nancy declared. "I'm so starved that I'd go for a McDonalds or Burger King. But around this area I think we'll find something halfway decent."

"Hey, that restaurant across the street looks inviting. Let's go and see what they have for a menu," suggested Suzanne. She was famished as Nancy and couldn't wait until they were seated.

Stu was finishing his salad when the two women were seated three tables in front of them. He couldn't take his eyes off the two beautiful women. Rich noticed his friend's inattention and commented. "Am I that boring that you can't answer my question?"

"Sorry man, what was it you were saying?" apologized Stu.

"It must be very interesting for you to keep staring. What's so important, or do you see an actress who you've always had the hots for?"

"No, no, two woman sat down a couple of tables from ours, and man, they are quite the lookers."

"I'm sure you're so horny that anything other than an orangutan is beautiful to you about now. There are so many great looking women around these parts that you're exaggerating, besides being delusional. Here comes our main course. Enjoy!"

Rich excused himself and headed for the men's room. He couldn't help but notice the two women that Stu was talking about. The red head was gorgeous, with those large, green eyes, and the long, silky, red hair. He had to stop himself from going over to them and introduce himself, but knew better not to. 'I must admit, I have a partner with good taste. They are something else. They blow the stars out the window,' Rich thought as he past their table. Sitting back at the booth Rich acknowledged that the two woman certainly looked classy. They could be in the movie industry, but I doubt it."

"How do you know that they're not?" Stu asked.

"For one thing, they don't act obnoxious. Another thing, they're not looking all over the restaurant, gazing around for people to recognize them, and they're not wearing sun glasses. They seem too classy, that's all," replied Rich.

"No wonder you're senior detective. I wouldn't have made those observations. I'd better start hanging around you more and learn some things that I haven't picked up on. If Tom was as good as you, no wonder you miss him. The two of you must have made quite a team."

Trying not to appear smug, Rich replied, "Ya, I guess we did make a great pair. In a while you and I'll be the team and the guys will be envious of us, just wait and see. Listen and watch, that's all I ask of you. Hey, who knows, maybe you'll teach this old dog some new tricks. Looking over the dessert menu, Rich related to Stu that "Molly promised me that she'd make this homicide top priority. She's already examined Curtis Jones and is waiting for the lab reports as we speak. Her word is good. Of course, I had to bribe her with coffee and donuts, but who gives a shit. Besides, I like shooting the shit with her while she's doing her job. In my opinion, she's one of the best."

On their way out Rich couldn't help but look back and admire the two women who were having their coffee and teas. 'I'd better not make it so obvious that I'm looking at the red head. Oh well, there's plenty of fish in the sea,'

BOSTON, MASSACHUSETTS

Madaline couldn't wait till this performance was over. She wanted to tell Paul that she had the feeling that someone was watching her all day. As a matter of fact, the more she thought about it, she sensed the presence of a person following her for more than a week. Madaline knew that Paul was somewhere close by. She hoped her feelings were wrong, but wanted Paul to be aware of her perception.

She kept making excuses that it was probably a reporter after an exclusive about Kyle's plight.

After changing into her street clothes, she wanted him to walk her to her hotel room. Paul made sure to take their time and meander the few blocks to her hotel. He felt the desire to be with Madaline as long as possible, without her being cognizant of his feelings for her. He instead made easy conversation and hoped she wouldn't get the vibes of how he really felt. They were at the corner of Tremont and Boylston Street waiting for the light to change. They stepped off the curb once the little orange man appeared on the light. Suddenly, a car came careening around the corner and deliberately tried mowing Madaline down. Paul pushed her back on the sidewalk. She fell and could tell that her ankle was either broken or she had a very bad sprain. Her hands were bleeding from the scrapes she got when she sprawled onto the cement walkway. Madaline couldn't stop shaking as Paul picked her up. She cried in pain as he held her skillfully, putting his arm gently around her waist. "You'd better put the arm that doesn't hurt as much around my neck. We'll grab a cab and get you to the nearest hospital and get that ankle x-rayed. I'll call the police from the emergency room and then try to figure out who would intentionally do this to you."

In between sobs Madaline asked Paul, "Do you really think that it was intentional?" Paul asked, "By any chance did you happen to see what make and color the car was?" "Everything happened so fast that I think I can remember, but I'm trying to visualize the license number or a partial one." Paul explained the necessity of trying to remember the number as they got into the cab.

Madaline asked Paul while the doctor examined her, "What do you think?" I sense its awful funny that the car came barreling around the corner just as we were crossing the street. Lucky for you I have great reflexes. Otherwise we might not even be heading for the emergency room, but the morgue instead."

"Thanks for the encouraging words." Before the cab dropped them off at Mass General Hospital, as Madaline was hobbling out of the back seat, holding on to Paul she then told him her sense that someone had been following her for about a week or so.

"You're just telling me now? I can't believe you wouldn't have mentioned it to me. That's what you're paying me for Madaline. Do you think this is fun and games, because, lady it's not. This is a serious situation and the sooner we can find out who's trying to kill you, the less chance that you'll be harmed." He looked at her scornfully and shook his head in disbelief.

After the x-rays were taken they found out that Madaline was lucky and had a bad sprained ankle. The doctor informed her that sometimes a break is better because a bad sprain can be more painful than an actual break. As Paul was helping Madaline into her hotel room it was difficult for her to learn how to manage using crutches. Paul, I can't thank you enough for what you did. I mean you risked your life to save mine. I'll never forget that."

"Hey, it's my job to protect you. That's why you're paying me the big bucks," he smiled as they sat on the comfortable sofa. Paul got up and filled an empty glass with water and handed Madaline the pill that the doctor gave her. "Make sure that you take these as prescribed." All Madaline wanted to do was lie on her bed, relax and go to sleep. She didn't want to sound rude so she listened to what Paul had to say. "Now we have to hunker down and find this maniac that's behind all this nonsense. This isn't the time, because the pills you're taking for the pain will make you loopy. Tomorrow I'll come by and no excuses or baloney, we'll make out a list. I want to know everything that's happened in your life, even before you became an actress. Understand? You know, thinking about it, I'm going to sleep on the sofa tonight. Can't take a chance that the maniac might come back, knowing that you'll probably be on pain meds, try to get into the room. Do you want me to help you into bed?" He didn't want to seem pushy. "I promise to be quiet and not disturb you, once you're settled in, okay?"

Madaline had mixed emotions. On one hand she liked the idea of Paul staying in the room, making sure she'd be protected. On the other hand, if she weren't so bloody groggy, she'd love for him to hold her in his powerful arms and make love to her the way she imagined that he would. He certainly wouldn't be sleeping on the sofa if she had anything to say about it. Once he got her in bed, Paul pulled down the covers, he found two spare pillows in the closet and put her sprained leg up on them to elevate and eliminate any unnecessary swelling. It didn't take long for Madaline to fall fast asleep.

Paul had a hard time getting comfortable. The sofa, although pretty, was not meant for a large framed man to use as a bed. Luckily there was an extra blanket in the closet and he used it to cover himself. His thoughts kept going back to Madaline and how much he was getting to care for her. She was nothing like her reputation perceived her to be. 'After this episode is over, I'm going to have a hard time staying away from her,' he admitted to himself. Not having much room, the sofa was exceptionally narrow, he punched the pillow to relieve the tension but still wasn't able to get comfortable.

For breakfast they called for room service. "I'd better call my director and tell him what happened. Lucky Betty, who's my understudy, knows my part well. It could be a good break for her." Paul raised his eyebrow when she mentioned how 'Betty' would benefit by Madaline's accident.

After breakfast Madaline called Suzanne and Nancy and told them what had happened. Suzanne and Nancy couldn't believe how lucky their friend was that Paul had been there to avoid, what could have been, a terrible tragedy.

CHAPTER TWENTY

SAN DIEGO

Madaline begged her and Nancy not to say a word about her awful mishap. "I don't want Kyle to worry needlessly. He has enough on his plate that he has to deal with. Even if we call it an accident, he'll worry about me needlessly, and only add to his worries. I hope that Kyle doesn't find out about this latest event. Thankfully, there were no reporters at the hospital last night, so the hit and run will go unreported, please God. We couldn't file a complaint with the police because we were unable to see a license plate. Everything happened so fast we couldn't identify or give a great description of the car, only that it was black or a dark color. I'm grateful that a sprained ankle is the only thing that happened to me."

"I realize it's early for you to find out what actually happened out in California, but keep me posted. I guess I'll be down and out for a couple of weeks before I can perform again. Maybe the rest will do me good. I was thinking that while I'm out for these few weeks that I should visit Kyle, but thought better of it because then I'd have to tell him what's happening. Of course I can lie but he'd see the expression on my face and he knows me like a book. So on that note, I guess I'll stay put and do as the doctor and Paul orders. Be careful and I hope that the business you're doing will be successful."

Madaline, knowing her friends all too well, knew the real reason they went to San Diego. They could bullshit her from now till doomsday, but in her heart she surmised that there wasn't any business to settle and they had no reason in hell to fly to California, except to see Kyle and try to help him. Shaking her head she couldn't help but smile, realizing that Suzanne and Nancy were the two best people and friends in her life. Hopefully they should also know that she would, intern, do anything for them. Madaline knew that Suzanne told her that in their spare time they would visit with Kyle and make it seem as if Kyle was the last matter on their agenda. 'Yes, I believe that like I have a hole in my head.' Madaline thought as she adjusted herself on the bed to get more comfortable.

Suzanne and Nancy left Kyle's apartment after Suzanne was unable to get him to confirm what she thought his relationship was with Curtis Jones. She wanted him to feel comfortable and confident that what he told her would strictly be held in confidence.

Trying not to think of Madaline's predicament, and adhering to her wishes, Suzanne forged ahead, the next day going back to Kyle's living quarters. Once they sat for a while and she filled him in on what was going on in her life and her true feelings on what was happening with Hope, she thought he'd be able to shed his burden with his aunt. After sitting down with coffee and teas they went into the living area where she knew she wouldn't relent until he told her the truth, or what she assumed to be the truth.

"What is the real relationship you had with Curtis Jones?" Suzanne looked directly into Kyle's eyes, not letting him avert hers.

Suzanne could see the alarmed and on edge manner by which Kyle squirmed in his chair as he tried to hide his agitation. Kyle asked Suzanne as he tried to make light of the situation, "What is this an inquisition? Come on Aunt Suzanne, this is me, Kyle, you're talking to."

"Don't try putting the ball back in my court young man. I know you didn't kill him so let's get that perfectly clear. I've known you practically all your life and you wouldn't hurt a fly. That's not what I'm getting at. I want you to tell me the truth about your relationship with Curtis. How long did you know him and for God Sakes, don't bullshit me. Why would you have some of your personal belongings and clothes at his apartment if you were only business acquaintances?"

"It was easier for me to use his apartment when I had to stay in the city than to go clear across town."

"Kyle do you think people are stupid? I'm not. The police will put two and two together and find a motive, which they already think they have. You probably could tell your mother that story and because she loves you unconditionally, she believes whatever you tell her. Why wouldn't you use your studio that's in the city?" Looking directly into his eyes Suzanne saw the frightened look of the child she once knew. Not taking her eyes off him she continued questioning him.

He avoided her eyes and suddenly got up. "Can I get you another cup of tea or anything else?"

"I don't feel like having anything at this time, thank you. You can't avoid me any longer Kyle." Patting the sofa with her hand, "Please, sit down and be honest with me. I'm not the kind of person who'll think you're awful, if you tell me the truth, that's all I'm asking of you. I'm not judgmental or your enemy."

"I feel as if I'm back at police headquarters."

"The only difference is I'm looking out for you Kyle. I'm not looking to pin a murder on you. I love you and your mother. I have to know the truth and somehow Nancy and I will try to help you."

"That's what mother hired Mr. Freeman for."

"Oh I met with Mr. Miles Freeman. Quite an impressive gentleman. But he doesn't have a heart Kyle. He would represent you whether you were guilty or not. As long as he's being paid, and I can imagine how much. He'll try to get you off one way or another. The difference is Nancy and I will try to find out who really killed Curtis. I think that's what you'd want, isn't it?"

"You have to believe me when I tell you I didn't kill Curtis. But won't it be hard for you and Nancy to find out who the murderer really is? I don't think that the two of you are capable of doing this kind of work. Not that I'm demeaning you, but this isn't the type of work that you do! I only wish that you can help, but it will take a miracle to save my ass."

"Let's say that I'm a miracle worker. Nancy and I, in our spare time, like to solve crimes."

A funny expression was on Kyle's face as if to say what the hell are you talking about. Kyle asked Suzanne, "since when?"

"Let's say Nancy and I have many hidden talents no one else is privy to. Seriously Kyle, I don't want anyone else knowing about our talk and what will become 'our research.' I know Mr. Freeman has a private investigator that he uses but just humor two women and let us help you."

Shaking his head in disbelief he began. "I don't know how to start, but here goes. Carol is a wonderful woman and we have a very good relationship. I know she's absolutely gorgeous. I mean that's how we met. I was working with her on one of her photo shoots, and I couldn't get over how beautiful she is. One thing led to another and before I knew it, after a whirlwind romance, we got married on the spur of the moment. Now don't get me wrong, I love Carol, more than I've ever loved another woman, excluding mother and obviously you and your girls."

"I always knew, deep in my heart, that I found guys attractive. I tried quelling my excitability and titillating feelings about other guys. I know in this day and age everyone is coming out of the closet, but I still didn't want such a thing be known to anyone else. Even though mother is liberal and a lot of our friends are gay, I still couldn't hurt Carol. It's not that I don't enjoy myself sexually with her, I do, but I find myself faking how much I enjoy having sex with her. But Curtis and I have," shaking his head, "had a type of relationship that I never thought possible." He tried holding his emotions at bay, as he was obviously flustered. Tears fell from his eyes.

Suzanne stayed still, waiting for him to continue. She had all she could do to quell her motherly instincts and put her arms around him. Holding herself back she nodded her head for him to continue.

"He was exciting and handsome. I felt I could be myself whenever I was with him. Do you know what it's like living a lie every day?" Holding his hand up he continued. "Don't answer just yet. I'll tell you. It's hell. I would have loved being able to walk down the street with Curtis holding my hand or being able to caress him any dam time I felt like it, rather than stifling my automatic responsiveness. I hungered for him like a famished child, craving for his love and affection. I thought I had it all. On the outside everyone thought I was the privileged child of a famous actress who is rich and would do anything for me. On the other hand I have a beautiful and sought after wife, who adorns so many magazines, I can't count them all. She's a great model who people crave to work with. I, on the other hand, am a talented and a respected, professional photographer. I have woman begging to have affairs with me. Little do these girls know, before I met Curtis, that I'd rather be boffing the guy models than these cupie dolls parading in front of me baring it all."

Suzanne heaved a sigh of relief and leaned over to this young man, who she loved like a son, and not holding back her emotions, cradled him in her arms. "I still love you Kyle and I know your true friends and mother won't feel anything less of you. Carol is a different story. Besides her anger she's going to feel betrayed and embarrassed, emotionally and professionally. You can't blame her for these feelings. Some feel angry that their husbands cheated on them for another woman, maybe richer or younger than themselves. Others, on the other hand, would rather have their husband leave them for another gender."

"It's totally uncontrollable to know how a person will take this kind of information. You can be sure that she'll say awful things about you, and you have to be prepared for it. Getting to the request you asked of me, you know that what you've told me will never go beyond this room. I'd like to take Nancy in my confidence, if it's all right with you? If Nancy and I feel we have to confide in

Justin, only because of his knowledge of the art world, I hope you'll leave it to our discretion to ask for his help."

"I know you're thinking of me and sure, just Nancy and maybe Justin, can know my hidden secret. I do trust what you promised me. Until I get enough courage to tell mother and Carol I know you'll keep your word." Getting up off the sofa, Suzanne turned her back to Kyle and took a deep breath. Closing her eyes, she suddenly turned around and faced him. "Kyle, life is so unfair at times. You wonder why things happen, and then you have to let it go and say to yourself, it's meant to be. Shit happens, and then you die."

"Getting back to the question you asked me about living a lie, yes, I know firsthand what that's about. For years, when I was married to Brian, I lived in a world all by myself. I lived a lie. What he did to me and Hope will never be forgotten. I was so ashamed of being an abused wife and then when he started physically hurting Hope I wanted to kill him. I honestly thought of murder, but then I realized that if I did kill him, what would become of my daughters. It was an awful dilemma to be in."

"Everyone thought that we had a perfect marriage and a wonderful family life. What a crock of shit. Talk about dysfunctional. I never knew what a dysfunctional family was until years later. I was an adult when I found out what that means and how many folks live with this burden and never tell a soul."

"I think a lot of families have some abnormal behaviors and are unwilling to discuss it with others for fear of what people will think of them or the consequences that may follow," Suzanne explained.

"No one will ever know about your being gay and your sexual preference, not until you're ready to come out of the closet. Now I would like you to make me a stiff drink." Gazing out the window Suzanne spotted Nancy and motioned her to come in.

Nancy and Suzanne didn't leave Kyle's apartment for several hours. The silence in the car was strange on the way back to The Four Seasons. Once the car was put away the two women decided to change and then take a walk around the hotel. The two woman were quiet and as much as they looked at the displays in the windows and once in a while, went into the fashionable stores and boutiques to browse at some of the trendy merchandise on display, they're hearts weren't in it.

With only the sound of strangers wondering amongst them, cash registers ringing, and sales people talking to customers, the two friends were lost in their individual train of thought.

Nancy's thoughts were of Kyle's apprehension and consideration for his loved ones. When the news finally hit the papers and tabloids she knew that his wife's embarrassment and humiliation will be indescribable. It was bad enough that Carol had to go through the trial but then when this part of his life was revealed, she would be forever remorseful. His mother is used to all kinds of publicity, and a real trooper. She'll somehow recover and get through all the bad press. Nancy didn't know how to help him alleviate his perplexing situation.

Nancy remembered, all too well, the hurt and mental pain she suffered when the distressing acknowledgment came out in the press and television about Peter and his involvement with gangsters, money laundering, his addiction and dealing with illegal substances. To this day she still has a hard time thinking about Peter and how he ruined his life and their union as a couple.

Suzanne's thoughts were of Madeline and her reaction to the overall state of Kyle's' affair. She hoped her friend, whose outward demeanor was hard as nails, would not crumble under this unusual and unsettling, severe enigma. They decided to have lunch on a terrace at one of the restaurants they passed days ago. The sun's rays illuminated the water with the many boats bobbing in the inlet.

Suzanne was methodically making a list, in her mind, of what she and Nancy had to do in the next few days. First they had to find out all they could about Curtis Jones. His personal life style and his work. Not knowing how long it would take them, she then thought of who else they could get to help them.

Even though they enjoyed looking throughout the stores, they were bored. "Let's go back to our room and bounce some ideas off one another," Suzanne suggested. "It might prove useful." Nancy agreed as Suzanne automatically started to cross the street. "Hey lady, watch where you're going, do you want to get hit?" The driver automatically beeped his horn and putting his head out the window of his car again yelled at Suzanne. "Don't you know we have strict jay walking laws in our great state?"

Suzanne was shook up as she carefully maneuvered to the other side of the street. Nancy caught up to her and just shook her head. "You must really have your head up your ass with that stupid stunt. What the hell were you thinking?" Nancy declared.

A look of contrition came on Suzanne's face. "I'm sorry. I didn't even realize what happened. I automatically tried getting to the other side of the street, without thinking of anything else. We do it all the time in Boston."

"I know we do, but guess what, we're not in Boston. You'd better get your head back on your shoulders and start thinking straight. We can't afford for either one of us to be a scatter brain. I know you've got a lot happening in your personal life, but so do I."

Once back in their room Suzanne suggested, "Let's write up a plan of action that we both agree on and then go out for dinner. We'll work off the notes when we come back and try to go to never, never land. Maybe we'll think of things to add to the list. When we wake up in the morning, we'll decide on which one of these to prioritize." Coming back to the suite, full from the great meal that they consumed, Suzanne and Nancy got into comfortable night clothes. As soon as Suzanne's head hit the pillow, she was fast asleep.

As Nancy lay in bed she couldn't fall asleep as easily as Suzanne. She kept thinking of Kyle's situation and how they possibly can undo the bad publicity and consequences that will certainly happen once the press comes out with his involvement with Curtis Jones. 'I don't even know where to start.' Nancy began making a mental list in her mind. One thing after another kept intertwining and became a jumble of confusion as she struggled to fight Morpheus.

Suzanne got up well rested and gently shook Nancy. I 'm going into the shower now. When I come out of the shower, hop in, then we'll look the list over during breakfast."

"I'll meet you down in the restaurant if you don't get your tushy going."

"I'm trying to take my time with my make-up, but how can I improve on perfection?" Suzanne said as she teased Nancy.

After ordering a large breakfast the two friends were able to relax while enjoying their coffee and tea. "Why don't you get the paper and pen out and check off the ideas you have and I'll, in turn, tell you my thoughts," Suzanne suggested as she started to look over and add more details and ideas on the piece of paper. After a few suggestions she couldn't think of anything else to write down.

Nancy started out quickly, jotting down the ideas that were on her mind as well. Suddenly the two partners looked at each other.

Putting down their cups, Suzanne blurted out, "it seems both of us are avoiding the inevitable"

"And what do you mean by that?" Nancy asked.

"Well, we don't have too much to go on. Do you realize that for the last 10 minutes we've been quiet as church mice and haven't talked to each other about what's on our secretarial pads. This sullen silence is driving me crazy," Suzanne blurted out. "I know what you're thinking about, but talk to me, so we both can be on the same page."

"I'm sorry I gave you the impression of not wanting to talk this out with you Suzanne, but so many thoughts are going through my mind. I'm sick to my stomach worrying about poor Madaline and Kyle. I was thinking how we can find out about Curtis Jones. I mean we have to find everything out about him. From his private life to his business relationships. We know he pissed someone off enough to kill him."

"You're absolutely right. I doubt it was a robbery from what Kyle told us. I'm considering calling Justin and ask him to come down and lend us a hand. He knows so much about the art world. He would be invaluable."

"I wonder if Kyle will be upset with us if we tell Justin the truth about him?" Blurted Nancy. "No, I already asked Kyle if we could confide in Justin. He told me he had no problem with that. Then he'll have the entire picture and will be able to help us."

"I doubt that Kyle's being gay will upset Justin, after all, his partner, my brother in law, Alan, has a significant other," Nancy said.

Suzanne was excited. "Just think Nancy, if Justin can change his plans, like we had to, or wants to, do you know what his help will do for us?" Thinking out loud, Nancy confirmed Suzanne's idea, "I'm sure he will."

Suzanne squeezed Nancy's hand in excitement. Signing the bill to their room, Suzanne declared, "Let's call him right now."

"Suzanne, there's a three hour difference in time. The poor man is probably still sleeping."

"Okay, okay, I almost forgot. Let's go upstairs anyway. We'll sit around, watch TV, then I'll set the alarm and make sure that I call him when he's at work. If he should agree to come out here, he'll have to re-arrange his schedule as well, so, yes, work will be the best place to call him."

The ear-piercing pitch of the alarm startled them both. She then remembered the reason why she set the alarm. Dialing Justin's telephone number she hoped she caught him at a slow time. The phone rang several times. Just when Suzanne was about to hang up and tell Nancy that they missed him, Justin picked up the receiver.

"Suzanne what a nice surprise. I thought I heard from the grapevine that you and Nancy were in California. It must have been a fast trip if you're home so soon."

"As a matter of fact, we're still out on the west coast. I'm going to ask you a very big favor and think about what I'm going to ask you before you give me an answer, okay?"

"Suzanne, you know I'd do anything for you and Nancy. Especially when it involves Madaline and Kyle, how can I say no? Of course I'll come. You can tell me all about the details and what's happening when you pick me up at the airport. Let me make arrangements for the flight, and get Alan to take over my obligations here. I promise I won't tell him a thing about what we're about to do. You don't want me to tell him, do you?" questioned Justin.

"You've got that right. The less people that know what we're up to the better," admitted Suzanne. "Call us once your arrangements are made. Love you and see you soon."

Suzanne hung up the receiver. With a loud YES she put her elbows back and her thumbs up. "Yes, Yes, he said he'd help us. I'm happy and know that everything will turn out right." With a more serious look and a huge sigh, she announced to Nancy, "I'm glad that's attended to. While we're waiting for Justin's call, why don't we go downtown and visit with the lead detective on the case. He seems to think that Kyle is the guilty party and I want to find out why. Who knows, maybe we can persuade him that he's wrong and he might be able to help us out. What do you think?"

"I thank God for the invention of the cell phone. Let's go!" Nancy got up from her chair and started for the door.

Rich got into the office a little later than usual. Tom was sitting behind the front desk gulping his third cup of coffee. "Rough night, I see," Tom jokingly said to Rich as he saw his x-partner coming through the door.

"Yah, there was a robbery at a convenience store and we found the poor Vic slumped behind the counter. A shotgun got him between the eyes. The poor guy didn't have a chance. From what we calculated the robbers didn't get much. We waited till the MI came and declared him officially dead. Then we had to go to his house and tell the guy's wife what happened. They're from some foreign country and it was hard trying to get what happened across. After she realized what we were saying it was beyond belief the time we had consoling her. I'm surprised half the city didn't hear the wailing. I can understand the poor woman and I hope she has relatives in this country that will help her in this difficult time."

"Did you get any film from the store?" Tom asked. "Yes, surprisingly, the film is pretty clear, not grainy like they usually are. We got a couple of shots of three guys in hooded sweatshirts but amazingly we were able to catch a glimpse of two of the guy's faces. With our sources out amongst the gangs I won't be surprised if we can get an arrest within a day or two."

"Well, if that's the case, that's one for the good guys," Tom said as he high fived his ex-partner.

"For what it's worth, got a few new murders last night and taking it upon myself, went to the Captain and asked him if I could give them to another detective. Hope you're not mad, but I thought you'd like to concentrate on this Kyle Mason case."

"As a matter of fact, thanks. Stu and I will be working the poor Asian guy's murder and the Curtis murder simultaneously. We've done more than two cases at a time but I'm glad some other detectives will be able to divide up the rest of them."

"Christ, the Curtis case is the same as any other as far as I'm concerned." Slamming his fist on Tom's desk, "I don't care if Kyle's mother is the fucking Queen of England. I'll treat it as any other murder. As far as the store clerk, we'll find the prick that killed the poor innocent bastard. His wife's whole world has been destroyed and I don't know if they had little kids."

CHAPTER TWENTY ONE

Flo, Captain Morgan's secretary, came out of her office. "Rich, the Captain wants you in his office."

"Okay, tell him I'll be right there." Rich looked at Tom and shrugged. "I wonder what's this about? I'll find out soon enough, I guess." Rich looked around for Stu but he was nowhere in sight. He went into the Captains office.

Captain Morgan motioned for Rich to shut the door. Rich thought to himself how much The Captain was respected amongst his peers and the community. "Captain, you asked me to come and see you?"

"Thanks for coming in. I don't know if you're aware that Tom asked me if I could give some new cases to other detectives. I thought it over and I told him to go with it. It's not that I think you can't handle another case, but I feel I want you to concentrate on this Jones murder. By the way I heard about the store clerk as well. As far as the Jones murder, right now we really don't have a lot to go on. If this case against Mason doesn't go right, the DA will ream our asses. Nothing can go wrong. You're one of a few guys, who I can depend upon, that will make sure that we have all the significant and unquestionable evidence that we need to do it right. I don't want you to be distracted by anything else that might spoil our case against him. Okay?" Coughing slightly, "I'm hearing around town that we might give 'special treatment' to Mr. Mason, because his mother is so well known. They don't realize that by her being famous might be a hindrance rather than helpful.

"I'll make sure all the info is up to date and nothing goes wrong with our case against Mason. I was going to go over to where Jones works and ask around about what he was like and if they knew any other friends, acquaintances, or business relationships he might have had. Even though it might seem insignificant to them, it might help us to double check these leads. Hey, you never know what shows up."

Rich went back to his desk, gathering up all the material he thought necessary for the case. He was looking for Stu and getting mad that he was nowhere in sight. I better call Molly soon and find out if the medical reports have come back from the lab. If anyone can find anything out of kilter, she can.

Just as he was about to call Stu and then Molly on his cell, he spotted the two women that were in the restaurant last evening. He tried not to be conspicuous and after they talked to Tom, he saw them heading for his desk. Rich pretended to be reading some papers. It didn't take them long to be in front of him, waiting for an acknowledgment of their presence.

Suzanne cleared her throat, trying to gain his attention. Rich looked up and put down the papers. "Hi, can I help you?"

"As a matter of fact, we hope so." Putting out her hand, "I'm Suzanne Morse and my partner, Nancy Tremblay. I can see by the name plate on your desk that you're Detective Colangelo." Extending his hand he shook the two women's and said, "I assume you met Detective Curran."

"Yes, he was nice enough to direct us to you, is it possible we can find somewhere quiet where we can talk?"

Rich couldn't believe that the gorgeous red head, that he had admired, was standing before him. He had a hard time keeping his eyes from gawking, like a fool, at this beautiful woman. Clearing his throat, trying to stay focused, he motioned for them to follow him down the hallway. "This isn't the best room, or the Taj Mahal, but for now, this'll have to do."

He didn't know if he should hold out the chairs for them, and decided not to. He took the seat at the head of the table and motioned for them to be seated. "Now, what's this about?"

Suzanne, folding her hands in front of her, took a deep breath and told Rich what they were there for. "Before you argue with us, let me explain our relationship with Kyle and his mother.

As Suzanne starting to talk, Stu walked into the room. "Sorry I'm late, I had to go over the ME's office and get some information that I thought you'd want to know about."

"That's okay. Let me introduce you to Suzanne Morse and Nancy Tremblay. This is Stu Tower, my partner;" he laughed and winked at Stu as he motioned him to have a seat. "I'll get to you very shortly Stu, but right now these two young women were just explaining the reason why they're here."

Nancy kept looking, trying not to be obvious, at the handsome Detective Colangelo. He looked familiar, but couldn't place where she might have seen him. Nancy let Suzanne do most of the talking and when she felt it necessary, she would then approach them with her input. She tried to conceal her eyes gazing at Detective Colangelo. She was afraid her throat might constrict. She felt nervous and intimidated by this handsome Detective. Without realizing it, her stomach felt like a million butterflies were inside her.

Rich tried concentrating on what Suzanne was saying, but found it difficult not to look and admire Miss Tremblay. 'I heard Ms. Morse introduce themselves as Ms. I don't see a wedding ring on either ladies; nor are they wearing an engagement ring on their hands. Seems interesting. Now Colangelo, keep focused on what Ms. Morse is saying.' He listened intently and even though they had some good points that seemed valid, he'd have to see what the final outcome will be when Molly finishes her work or if she told Stu anything interesting pertaining to the case.

"I think it's a wonderful gesture that you two good friends of Ms. Mason would try to help in this very publicized case. Another point that you should ask yourselves is if you might be more of a hindrance than helpful."

"I don't mean to be disrespectful, but it takes more than a couple of women who, although full of sincere efforts, will handicap us and our team of professional detectives. It's taken many years of diligent training, which I doubt you have in this type of situation, to be of any help." Rich begrudgingly asserted.

Suzanne wasn't happy with his attitude. She debated telling him about how they were involved with the crime in Boston. She even wondered if she should call Tim Cassidy and Kevin Halloran from the Boston division of the FBI. She really didn't want to pull any trump card at this time, or get the FBI involved. If it got to the point where they wouldn't let them co-operate, then she'd have no choice than to involve her two friends that Nancy and her had become close to. The silence was evident that the two factions were at a standstill.

"I'm baffled by your attitude, detective. I would think that you'd want all the help you can get. For your information, we're not novices to the world of crime. Without going into all the details, believe me when we say that we can be of help to you," Suzanne declared.

Covering his mouth with his hands, trying to contain his smile, because of his skepticism, he struggled not to show his amusement. "I can't thank you enough for your concern, but we have everything under control. I'll call you if we come up with anything other than what you already know. I thank you again, and hopefully, you won't impair our efforts. I'll have Stu show you ladies out. On second thought, here are our cards with both our numbers. If you find anything of importance don't hesitate to call, day or night. We'll do the same if possible." Looking directly at Nancy, he again reiterated the importance of calling either of them if they found anything out. 'Maybe I should ask for their cards. Having Nancy's number won't be a bad idea. What am I thinking? Yah, she's gorgeous as hell, but there are a lot of beautiful women out there. But it seems that she's a lot different than the type of woman I'd be attracted to.' Trying to think of reasons why being interested in her would be impossible, he listed, in his head, logically, the reasons to keep at arm's length with Ms. Nancy Tremblay.

Once out on the street, Suzanne turned to Nancy. "I think he's as arrogant as that Miles Freeman. It's apparent that both gentlemen, if you can call them that, are full of themselves. What's with these California professionals who think their shit doesn't stink. Anyway, we'll show them a thing of two."

"Suzanne, we have many obstacles to overcome, I know we can do it. We have to be diligent and do our own investigation. Once Justin arrives, I'm sure he'll help us immensely. Especially in the art world. It's apparent that's where we start. Even though the detectives will be interrogating the people at his gallery, we'll be there and question them as well. As women, we might be more insightful and get more out of them. Any detail that his fellow workers, at first, might not of thought of will be helpful. Then we have Justin who'll be invaluable. Of course we don't have the privileged information that the ME will be giving them. But knowing how devious and innovated we can be might be to our advantage. Let's start at his apartment. I'm sure there must be something that they overlooked," Nancy stated.

Walking for a while to retrieve their rented car, Suzanne looked over to Nancy and realized that her partner was quiet. "Nancy I haven't heard a word from you for at least ½ hour. Usually you're so talkative I can't get a word in. What's on your mind?

"I can't get that detective out of my mind. I know I've seen him somewhere, but I can't place it. It's driving me crazy."

Suzanne had to keep her eyes on the road while driving to Cutis' apartment. "I have to admit, he's handsome if you like the tall, dark, lean ones. I haven't seen you so contemplative in a long time. It's nice to see you like this, but be careful, he's our nemesis."

"I don't want to dwell on him. But, I find his large, dark eyes intriguing. Those lashes are to die for. It's not fair that a man should get those kinds of eyelashes. His mouth is full and the little I saw of his smile, his teeth are a brilliant white. Also, his dark complexion makes him a little mysterious."

"Girl, you sound smitten. Just do me a favor, concentrate on our assignment and afterwards do what you want. I'm trying to put off all my problems, and believe me, it's killing me."

Suzanne went around the block two times before a parking space, near his apartment became available. "I don't see any yellow tape or police cars around," pronounced Suzanne. "They probably took off all the tape when the police finished getting all the "supposed evidence" they needed. It's been a while since they discovered his body. Let's see if Kyle's key still fits," Nancy exclaimed, as they walked up the steps to his apartment.

In front of the building Nancy declared, "At least the building isn't wealthy enough to have a valet outside and that we need permission to enter."

"Maybe if they did, Curtis wouldn't be in the morgue, awaiting the outcome of the Medical Examiner's results," Suzanne answered.

Looking into her purse Suzanne pulled out a credit card and some other instruments that Mel, from the FBI training squad had given her. "I don't believe that you had the insight to bring these implements with you. Do you still remember how to use them and why are you pulling them out?" A concerned Nancy asked.

"Are you kidding? You're best friend happens to be a National Honor Society alumnus. I never forget anything. And as a girl scout our motto was and still is, 'always be prepared.' Remember that if you, someday, decide to oppose me. Besides Kyle's key doesn't work. They must have changed the lock.

"I'm really upset that you would think that I would do anything to hurt you." Nancy said.

Suzanne shoved Nancy lightly, "I'm only kidding, lighten up and let's get going. Look out for any passersby or anything that might look suspicious. We have to work fast".

"The next people who rent the apartment won't know what happened in their new residence until they hear about the murder from one of the tenants," Suzanne declared as she opened the door.

They found the mailbox still locked. "You can find out a lot about a person from the mail he receives. I don't think it'll be hard to open. Lucky for the killer that Curtis lived on the first floor. Do me a favor and let me know if you hear anything in the building. There might be a neighbor that is suspicious. I'll open the box with these instruments and then be right back. Thank God that the crime occurred a while now that the police are finished watching the place."

Suzanne let out a sigh as she opened the door with his mail in hand. "Quick, close the door. I hope you brought the large flashlight I gave you."

"I might not have been a girl scout, but I did remember to bring it plus a second one for you," Nancy smugly answered.

"We can't have any light on under the door. Anyone that passes this apartment knows that no one lives here anymore. We'll look at the mail later but

I'm sure there's nothing here that's important," Suzanne surmised. Nancy said, "I see that the computer was either stolen or the police took it. And there doesn't seem to be a television in the apartment. That's odd."

Trying to be quiet, the two women looked over the living room and then went into the master bedroom. "If he had something to hide it wouldn't be out in the open. Let's use our brains, think hard, and visualize where you'd put something that you wouldn't want anyone to find. Since the computer is gone we don't have much of a choice."

"Do you think he'd be stupid enough to hide any material under the wall to wall carpeting or in one of his desk draws?" Nancy asked.

'The police probably looked there, but it wouldn't hurt to go there again."

"I'd think that would be too obvious. Do you think he might have a hidden space in his wall that wouldn't be noticeable, like under a painting or maybe somewhere in the bathroom?" Thinking to herself, she said to Nancy, no, the walls and bathroom are also too apparent.

"What do you think we'll find, if we're lucky enough to find a hiding place?" asked Nancy.

"I really don't know. If he had a secret life for instance, he wouldn't put the material into the computer. He'd be smart enough to know that now a day's people can hack into them easily enough. No, we're looking for papers, like receipts or notes that he didn't want anyone else to find."

"You mean like Kyle, don't you? I understand your point of view and you have a good approach. I mean, if Kyle was his lover and stayed over a lot, he couldn't let him see any evidence of another lifestyle," confirmed Nancy.

The two women were on their hands and knees, crawling like infants, looking at all the walls and under the carpeting and the wooden floors that were exposed. They inspected every room from top to bottom. "We're looking for new plaster or something like new paint or floor boards that can be opened from another source," whispered Suzanne.

Nancy got Suzanne's attention. "Let's have a look in the master and spare bedrooms and closets. That's where I would hide something that I didn't want to be found." Again they crawled on their hands and knees, from the bedrooms to the closets, their hands and eyes guiding them. Suddenly Suzanne's cell phone rang. "Oh shit, I forgot to turn off this stupid thing. I could have at least put it on silence," whispered Suzanne. "I hope no-one heard the ring." Cursing at herself Suzanne shut it off. She announced to Nancy, "I'll get the message later when we're out of here."

"Suzanne!, put the extra flashlight over here," directed Nancy. "This plaster, way in back of the wall, doesn't look the same color as the rest of the closet. It seems brighter and I don't know, just different."

"Some of his long raincoats had that part of the wall hidden. They probably looked into the pockets of all his suits and coats, but weren't that diligent when examining the entire closet. That's the difference between men and women. I personally feel we're more cunning. Did you bring that knife that you bought at that specialty store on Newton Street, in Boston with you? We might be able to pick the plaster away with it," declared an excited Suzanne.."

"There doesn't seem to have a line or crack in it so, obviously, there shouldn't be a special object in there," Suzanne skeptically told her friend.

"Don't forget, he was an artist and if he wanted to, he could conceal or cover up a wall, for instance, without being detected."

Suzanne told Nancy, "Maybe he hid material in the actual wall, in between the studs. Let's get to the other closets. He might have been eccentric to have multiple hiding places, in the apartment or safe deposit boxes hidden between the floor boards as well as in between the wall studs."

"You know, Suzanne, the police must have realized that he might have some safe deposit boxes or some other post office mailboxes. They had to have already figured that out. They're not stupid. I'm sure that when the police took his computer and hard drive they're having their experts see if anything of importance is in it. If I were the police that's the first thing that I'd take out of here. If the boxes do exist the numbers might have been in the computer."

"Or," interrupted Suzanne, "Maybe the thief took the computer and the police are bluffing and don't have anything substantial to go on except gut feeling or bluffing. If they're faking, Kyle can't be a suspect for much longer. They could have found a key or keys that they unexpectedly got under his desk or who knows where. They must have gone over this place with a fine tooth comb. But I hope there weren't any women on Detective Colangelo's team. We're oh so more cunning," a smug Nancy whispered.

"How on earth can we find out?"

"I guess we'll have to put our brain power to working overtime and maybe we'll go over the same places that the police have." "I don't care if we do, as long as we can get the same information. Meanwhile, let's get something to break open the wall that you think looks suspicious. I wish we had a pick ax, but this sharp knife will have to do," whispered Suzanne. "Nancy, that's why it's important for us to find physical evidence in case they can't confirm info from his hard drive."

"I hope he was a gourmet cook and has some good sharp knives. In a way it's better to use a sharp carving implement, the kind one would use as a blade to carve a body with." Nancy turned around, making a menacing face and a noise, lifting up her hand as if to plunge a sharp tool, pretending to be Jason and use it on Suzanne.

Suzanne jumped and squelched a scream. "You idiot, stop that, you almost scared me half to death."

Nancy composed herself. "It definitely won't make as much noise as a hand ax. I only hope that the neighbor who lives next door comes home late. If they hear anything unusual, you can be assured the authorities will be called and we'll be dead meat."

"Not being prejudiced, but don't, you know what I'm trying to say, they like to cook more than the average guy. If so, he definitely will have better cutlery than the typical bachelor."

Getting herself off her knees, Suzanne started opening the draws. Shaking her head she reprimanded Nancy. "I can't believe what I heard you say. You are truly awful and prejudice."

After opening six draws they came across the cutlery draw. "See I told you," blurted Nancy. With a triumphant smile she retrieved several sharp knives and some very razor-edged ones and started for the closet. "I'll start on this closet and Suzanne, you go to the other ones. Make sure you don't make too much noise and don't miss a thing."

Shaking her head in dismay, Suzanne followed with the rest of the pointed knives and followed her dear friend's instructions.

"I still like the idea of your Swiss Knife. It might take longer, but it will be quieter. Let's make as little noise as possible," instructed Suzanne. 'We can't have anyone hearing us and call the police."

"Da, you think so," Nancy sarcastically said.

Suzanne went to the other closets and met Nancy when there were two more left to investigate. "I'll stay with you Nancy, I couldn't find a thing in the others. Maybe if we work together the process will go by faster."

Susanne was delighted when she could see the studs. "We just have a little more to do and I think we've hit pay dirt. I hope he has papers in here that will give us insight into what he was all about."

The two women started digging rapidly, until they had a clear view of the studs and the envelops in between them. Nancy commented, "He was a clever one, wasn't he?"

Suzanne declared, "Yes he was. You'd know it would be in the last closet. Our luck."

"Don't complain Suzanne, at least we got what we came for."

With a look of satisfaction and pleased with herself, she nodded to Nancy to work fast. Suzanne hurriedly put all the envelopes that she could get her hands on into the large bank bag. I knew it, I knew it, that bastard was a clever son of a bitch. Let's grab all these papers and go over them at the hotel" suggested Suzanne.

"Now we have to be careful that no one sees us leaving with documents. Put all of your envelopes and any stray papers into the large bag that I brought. I'm sure that all of the paperwork will fit into it. The only thing that I'm worried about is leaving our finger prints all over the place. We'd better try to hide the hole with some sort of undershirt of something and then put the longer items in the back of the closet. I suggest we wash the knives thoroughly, put them away and try to leave the apartment as clean as possible. We'll wipe all the draws, handles and anything that we've touched. Is there anything else you can think of that might incriminate us?" Suzanne dictated, as she speedily put the rest of her packets and large pieces into the bag. "I wonder what interesting material they found on his computer. That's if they actually have it." Suzanne asked as she opened the door for Nancy.

Nancy thought for a second and told Suzanne to get the undershirt that they put into the hole and take it with them. "We can't possibly rid our prints off of the shirt. "Who cares if they find the hole now, it's empty. Besides, all the plaster is a mess and we can't possibly get rid of it. The police probably won't come back for more evidence, but if they do they'll definitely find our hand prints and foots prints all over the place." Nancy was proud of her smart thinking and smugly smiled at Suzanne.

They left as soon as they thought everything was back to normal. "The hell with the closet," Nancy said as she and Suzanne carefully proceeded out the door, making sure that no one saw them leaving the apartment.

Stu couldn't wait until Rich got through speaking with the Captain. As soon as he walked out the door, Stu was all over him. "I'm so excited I almost came in my pants," he laughed, as he dragged Rich over to his desk. Remember I told you I went to see the M. E., well there's a lot more coming out. First of all, the trace evidence came back. Along with the carpet fibers they found some interesting items. I don't know how they could do it, but they were able to tell the different shoe sizes that were in the apartment, from God knows how long. The M. E. will confirm that under Curtis's fingernails, he must have fought like a lion, she found some DNA that might be useful."

CHAPTER TWENTY TWO

Rich couldn't believe that Stu had taken the initiative to go to the M. E. office before he had a chance to speak with Molly. He had to give credit where credit was due. "So tell me, what did they find out that was different or that can help us fry that little prick, Mason?"

"You might not like it, but we have to get a DNA sample of Kyle a.s.a.p."

Rich was glad that Stu was excited but at the same time he was upset. He couldn't understand the animosity he was feeling. 'I should have been the one getting in touch with and talking to Molly. He really went over me, but I can't show how angry I really am. If I did, it might stop his initiative for future assignments.' "That's great. I was about to contact Molly myself this afternoon, but I see you beat me to it. I'll call her soon and we'll meet for lunch, if she can spare the time."

Deliberately, he made sure Stu knew that he wasn't invited to this meeting. Going by Tom's desk on his way out he gave him the thumbs up and whispering to his old partner, "I'll be in touch with you soon."

Getting into his Mustang, he headed to the Medical Examiner's office and from there they would go to a small café. Heading to the hospital Rich put a jazz station on and tried to relax. The police radio kept making noises in the background, disturbing the music Rich was trying to listen to. He purposely controlled his breathing, trying to put himself at ease. Nancy's face kept appearing before him. 'Why can't I get her out of my mind?' He would have loved to sit down with her in a dimly lit room, glasses of wine on the table and talk and talk. He wanted to know all about her.

He was lucky to find a parking space near the hospital. He didn't want to park illegally in any doctors spot. Rich didn't have to worry about getting a ticket because he had the authority to park anywhere he wanted, as long as he was on official business. He knew that Molly wouldn't be long and then they would head out to the café, which was down the street.

Taking the elevator to the basement he got off. Immediately the smell of corpses and all the medicinal odors repelled him. 'I don't know how she can stand these putrid, dank, foul smelling and medicinal substances. Just breathing them in all day would make me sick. I guess she's gotten used to them by now.' Opening the double doors he saw Molly finishing up her latest victim. She started putting away her apparatus when she saw Rich come into her domain. She had her assistant finish the tedious work that had to be done and waved to Rich. Putting up her pointer finger, as to say I'll be but a moment, she started removing the surgical hat, paper boots, gloves, and cover all. She went into the other room, put all the clothes in the covered trash bin and washed up. She then put on her regular garments. She greeted Rich warmly as she joined him at the doorway.

"I've had a very busy morning, all sorts of accidents, murders, and if you can think of any other type of victims, I had them as well. I had to finish in order to get ready for their family to make arrangement for funerals. Besides I had to get evidence for the police and the D. A.'s office. Who would think that in this small community so many kinds of deaths would occur? Of course with the Navy here and all, you'd expect something, but this is ridiculous. Let's forget about it all and enjoy our lunch, no matter how brief it may be."

Rich made sure they were seated in the most secluded table that was available.

"Now tell me what's this about. Not that I don't like meeting with you, but with my schedule, and your work load, this must be important."

Teasing Molly, Rich took her hand and announced, "I want you to know that if anything happens with your marriage, I'll be disappointed if you don't give me a chance to let me keep company with you."

"Cut the crap and tell me what's this about." The waiter came to their table and took their orders. "Now what can I do for you this time?"

"I'm hurt. Do you think this is all about business?" Rich pouted like a young boy being reprimanded by his mother. Taking a sip of seltzer water, he got down to the real reason for their meeting.

"You have, by now, heard that I'm officially the chief detective on the Jones case. It was great that Stu visited you and tried prying information from you that might be pertinent to our case. I really do appreciate the effort, but I would like any information to come directly to me. He hasn't worked with me long, shit he just made detective a couple of months ago. I feel he has to earn the respect of all the guys at the station, especially mine. Now, what can you tell me that you know. From there we'll figure out what we have to do at our end."

"First of all, Stu thought he was doing you a favor by being able to pass on any information that I gave him. Knowing how you are, don't take that offensively, I only gave him as little information as possible, without him getting suspicious. I could get in a lot of trouble if this conversation gets out."

"I know, and I thank you for understanding. Really, I do. Please relate anything you find that might help us clear up this case."

"It seems that he fought like hell with the person who killed him. We were able to get samples from the skin that was under his nails and from what we deducted, he wasn't Caucasian. It seems his ethnic group type is Asian. Now a days, with such an influx of different geographical divisions, it's going to be difficult to obtain the exact heritage of this individual. You know I'll do everything in my power to get it nailed down."

"I guess that means we have to let Kyle Mason off the suspect list. I thought for sure he did it. He and Curtis had a relationship that was secretive and, let's not kid ourselves, the husband, lover or close relation usually is the murderer. Now, it seems, we have to start all over again."

"I'm sorry to differ with your opinion but the facts are the facts. I guess you'd better start looking for more information about Curtis Jones that will help you clean up this case. By the way, we did manage to find some different shoe sizes that recently visited his apartment. We now have certain devices that can find this sort of thing, if the place of the murder has carpeting. I will tell you that the sizes vary. The prominent shoe size was that of Curtis and Kyle's. But there were a few that where noticeably quite different. They were a man's shoe, but much smaller. We can only guess, right now on the exact size, but we'll come close enough. Even if he was wearing boots, we could tell what size his shoe was by the indentations on the carpet."

"With this evidence it does appear that we are looking for a smaller than average shoe size but I don't think it was a child's shoe. We'll keep looking into it. Oh, another thing, the bullets that killed him were not from a gun that is easily available in the States. Although we know that now- a- days, anyone can obtain any gun available through the black market. I hope we get the bastard that did this. I don't care what his preferred gender was. He didn't deserve to die that way. By the way, tomorrow I'll make time to examine Mr. Hakeem, the store clerk that was blown away between his eyes. He's a mess, but not as bad as Mr. Jones."

"Let's get this straight, going back to the Jones case. Are you saying that it's a definite that Kyle isn't the murderer? I'd love to keep him a little longer and try my hardest to find something to pin on him. Hey, maybe he and this Asian guy conspired and both of them killed him." Molly looked across the table at Rich and laughed. "If what you mentioned wasn't so funny I'd have you committed. Seriously, you might have a point and I can't rule your theory out. So if you want to keep Kyle sitting around, waiting and worrying, all you have to do is find the Asian man that Curtis was acquainted with."

"Getting back to the store murder, the men working for me found a few casings around the back of the counter and that should help determine what kind of gun was used. I haven't forgotten about the poor guy and I'll do my damdest to find his killer or killers."

"With the info you told me it looks like I have to start from zero or try to find a way to implement Kyle with who killed this Curtis Jones. Oh well, what else would I expect. Although I have to admit in my heart I wanted to get a conviction on Kyle Mason. It might be prejudice but maybe it's because he's rich and has a knock out for a wife. You never heard me say this, did you?"

Kissing Rich on the cheek, "Thanks for lunch. You know if I find anything else you'll be the first to know. For your information I didn't hear a word you said and we didn't eat together. Seriously, I've got to get back. I'm back loaded as it is. If I don't get my butt into gear, I'll be behind and never catch up. Hope to see you soon under better circumstances."

Keeping the door open for Molly he turned his head, looking at her. By the way, I think I'll still get Kyle's DNA, you never know."

Rich went back into the restaurant and sat in his seat for a while longer. He asked the waiter for another DASANI and took his time drinking it down. 'I wish this was a beer, but I don't want to go back to the precinct halfcocked. This really puts us in a bind. I'll have to use my sources in the black market and see what Stu and I can find out. Looking into his seltzer water, he again thought of the two women who visited him at the station. 'I guess they know their friend. I really should apologize to them. I wonder how I can reach them?'

As Rich was getting into his car he thought to himself for a while before turning on the engine. 'I won't be so quick to let him go as a suspect, not yet that is. Suzanne and Nancy got into their comfortable jogging suits and sitting Indian style on Suzanne's bed, started going through the paper's, invoices, notes, and personal articles that they thought would be imperative to the case. "Wait, we haven't looked at these five large envelopes," Suzanne told Nancy. While looking over the materials Suzanne put her head up and said, "Oh my God, look at these papers. It looks like they're the floor plans of the Huntington Museum. If I'm not mistaken it was robbed a few days ago, or within this last month. Here, here, look at these. It looks like strategic plans for the alarm system. I can't believe what I'm seeing. Nancy, come here and look at these papers."

Nancy told Suzanne, "I also found something of interest. It seems he has receipts for check stubs from a cleaning company. It seems to be the type of company that cleans offices and such."

Holding her hand out she asked, "Can I see them please." Suzanne looked them over and told Nancy that they were going to visit this company and then head to the Huntington Museum and look around. "Between the two places, something of interest might come about."

"We'll need Justin for his expertise in the art world, and I'm sure he'll be a great help. I hope he comes here soon, besides being nice to see him, I can't wait to find out what he'll come up with," Suzanne voiced. She unfolded her legs, stretched and put the complete set of plans on the floor and on their beds.

"I'd better see who called while we were in Curtis' closet. I forgot all about it. Stephen called," she announced to Nancy. "What am I going to tell him? If I tell him we're on vacation, he'll get pissed that I took a vacation over seeing him. What can I say? I know he'll get mad if I tell him the truth. He knew what happened the last time we played 'Suzie the Sleuth' and I promised him that would never happen again."

"Go on the offensive. You can do it. Tell him we came down here on business. Maybe that our Beverly Hills salon is having some discrepancy with the books. We have to get to the bottom of it or it's a matter of great importance or who knows, we might have to close down the salon if we don't find out who's stealing some products and altering the books. Tell him it doesn't seem to be the manager. We are worried that the manager took a long time to get to us. It seems she tried figuring it out by herself but couldn't. I think he'd fall for that explanation. We are on business, even though it doesn't pertain to the salon. What he doesn't know won't hurt him. Maybe, I don't know how long this is going to take. Perhaps, you can make arrangements to go to Texas after this is all done. Conceivably he can come here for a short visit, if he doesn't catch on."

Looking at Nancy, "I'm in a real dilemma. I'm afraid I won't be able to answer his questions or have the right response." "Girl you are deceptive and you're made up explanations make sense." "Let's hope he believes my story."

"Just go with your gut feeling when you start talking. Field the questions and then come back with a perfect alibi. You can get yourself out of anything, as long as you give him a plausible excuse. I like my story. You should use it," a confident Nancy asserted herself.

Suzanne took a deep breath and looked to Nancy for support. Dialing the number, she crossed her fingers. "Hi, I just retrieved my messages and called you immediately. What's going on?"

"I called you at home and Mrs. Walsh told me that you had some business in California. I thought you'd be calling me and we'd make arrangements to see one another. How long will you be there for? Do you think that we might be able to hook up after your business is through?"

Suzanne sighed with relief." I'd love to see you as soon as this business arrangement is in order. The trouble is I'm not sure on how long it will take. Hopefully it won't take more than a few weeks." Suzanne then went on to explain the story that Nancy told her to tell him. She hoped that the story was viable.

"A few weeks. Suzanne it's been months since we've actually seen each other. If it's not any trouble I have a couple of days off and it would be nothing to fly over and be with you. Are you amenable to that? I can call you at the end of the week and see how you're coming along with your business dealings and then I can book a flight. It might be only a few days or a week, depending on how my work load is. I really hope that it can be for a week. I can't wait till I hold you once more in my arms and we can share our thoughts, take care of our desires, and just be there for each other. Does that sound good to you?"

"That sounds great. Can you actually leave for that length of time? Not that I don't want to see you. It will be wonderful to finally get together in person and able to be with one another. I love you." Winking at Nancy, "Right now Nancy is down in the lobby waiting for me to meet her for our reservations. I wish we could talk longer, but I'll call you by the end of the week and we'll work something out." Kissing him over the phone she hung up, mad at herself for not able to tell him the truth.

"You did a great job, I'm proud of you. If everything goes according to plan we should be able to wrap this all up by the end of the week. Hopefully it won't take longer, but let's play it by ear and see what happens. "She went to Suzanne and gave her a hug.

"Okay, let's get going. We'll arrange all the papers by categories and order of dates. Then we'll get the different names of the individuals who are on the slips and try to figure what the meanings to these papers are. Does that sound all right with you?"

In the middle of their work, Suzanne blurted out, "I feel like such a liar and cheat. I can't help feeling the way I do." She murmured to Nancy.

"Why don't you call Stephen back and make definite arrangements for a date that you can get together. I'm sure our work can wait for a week. Even if he's here, you don't have to be with him 24/7. Meanwhile I can try to figure out some of the files and relate what I find to you. I think that's the best plan we have. We don't have any other options, my friend."

"I feel so guilty. You really wouldn't mind if I were to be with Stephen for a couple of days of the week?"

"I'm sure by that time Jason will be here and the two of us can do some investigating."

Rich was racking his brains on how to find and get in touch with Ms. Nancy Tremblay. Hitting the side of his head with his palm he suddenly realized that they signed in with his x-partner and friend Tom Curran. He went over to Tom's desk, sat on the edge and started some light conversation. Rich started chit chatting, bringing up mundane occurrences. He then told Tom what Molly came up with and now, supposedly, the case against Kyle looked dismal. "I still think Mason has something to do with it, but for now it looks like we're going to have to start from scratch. By the way, do you happen to have the address and cell numbers for those two women who came the other day? They're friends of Kyle's and I'd like to discuss the Curtis Jones case with them."

"As a matter of fact, I do. Let me get my log book for that date. As soon as I get my glasses on I'll be able to see. Isn't life a bitch? I'm still vain enough to try to seem a little younger than I really am." Rich chuckled. Tom took his glasses out of his right side shirt pocket, jokingly giving Rich a dirty look." Wait til you get to be my age and see how you'll like it. Not that I'm old, mind you, but it's just that my eyes need a little help." They both laughed. "Here it is." He wrote down the present address of the hotel they were staying at and respectively they're individual cell numbers. "Thanks, buddy, I owe you one."

"If I were to collect all the IOU's that I have on you, I'd never have to work another day of my life. So tell me more about what Molly found that has everyone thinking that Kyle might be innocent?"

"Rich filled Tom in with Molly's findings. "We're going to have to look for another avenue or motive. I'll definitely need your help when the time comes. It's going to be hard work, not so cut and dried like we thought."

"You know I'll be there for you and the department. I'm not dead yet. All these years working homicide helped me with contacts that can fill an entire book. Tell me when and I'll be ready."

"Thanks pal. I'll let you know as soon as something viable comes my way. Maybe when we put all the pieces of the puzzle together, we'll need your connections and knowledge. You know you're one of the men that I respect and will listen to anything you come up with."

Walking out the door he got into his mustang and decided to drop by the Four Seasons and see if Nancy and Suzanne were still there.

He walked into the posh hotel. Pulling out his ID, he introduced himself to the desk clerk and then the manager. With reluctance, the manager called their room to notify them of their visitor.

"Thanks for the info, I appreciate." Getting on the elevator he nodded to the guests he was sharing the beautiful glass and etched walled elevator with till he got to the 7th Floor. He knocked on the door. It was graciously opened by Nancy. He stood there for an instant and couldn't help but appreciate how beautiful she looked, even in work clothes. They obviously weren't dressed for a luncheon or anything fancy.

She stood in the doorway, admiring the brawny man before her. Her legs felt like rubber as she escorted him into the living room. "How is it that we have the honor of your presence? The last time we spoke it seemed that you and your department had everything under control." Nancy asked sarcastically. Nancy was glad that she and Suzanne put away all the critical papers a few hours ago. 'Otherwise I wouldn't have been able to ask Detective Colangelo into our temporary abode, she thought to herself.

"I'm here to inform you that we might have another person other than Mr. Mason as a suspect. Without going into detail, I know that you and your friend would like to know this."

"How ungracious of me. Please, I forget your name." 'I've memorized his name by heart but he doesn't have to know.' "Please have a seat. I'll call Suzanne out of the other room and we can both hear what you have to say. Walking towards the closed bedroom door, with her back to him, she turned her head and said, "By the way, we're more than friends," as she gently knocked on the bedroom door.

'Here it comes. I knew it was too good to be true, of course, their lovers.' All he could see was her entire body, with that beautiful butt, facing him. 'What a shame I can't get a piece of that great ass.'

Turning around to look at Detective Colangelo she suppressed the laughter within her. 'I'm glad that I might have confused him. The way he looks at my body, especially my butt, it's as if he wants to devour me.' Suzanne finished what she was doing and they both made an appearance in front of Detective Colangelo. Nancy didn't want him to think that she was anything except heterosexual, in case, she thought, he might be single and available.

Nancy explained they were visiting San Diego for two different reasons. "We are business partners and own exclusive spas in the States and Abroad; one is located in Beverly Hills. Although I'm sure this information has nothing to do with the case."

Suzanne acknowledged Detective Colangelo. "Detective, what do we owe this pleasure? It seemed that the last time we spoke you couldn't get rid of us fast enough," Suzanne spoke honestly.

With egg on his face, he apologized for his abrupt conversation that they had at headquarters. "I'm here to tell you, like I told Nancy, that we've found evidence that might get Kyle off the hook, as they say."

Suzanne thought, 'it's Nancy now.'

With a smug expression she continued to berate him. "We told you that we've known Kyle for many years, and although he's our friend, we knew that he was innocent. By the way, we've been doing some work with the Boston FBI and we're not novices when it comes to crime." Suzanne had no qualms of giving him the business and to let him know that they were right about Kyle.

'Oh boy, Suzanne's really pushing it.' Nancy thought as she cleared her throat. "Would you like something to drink Detective? We can have it brought up in a few minutes. 'I hope he doesn't think we really work on a regular basis with the FBI. The way Suzanne makes it sound, it's as if we do.'

"As a matter of fact, if you don't mind, and it's not any trouble, some coffee would be nice."

While waiting for room service to come Rich gave them a run down on what had transpired since their last encounter. "Even though we found some different incriminating evidence that might make us take a different look at Mr. Mason, it doesn't entirely eliminate our first opinion that he has something to do with the crime. But it does give us some other options."

"Detective Colangelo, we've also obtained information that I think you and your department might find interesting. Without going into detail, I think this acquired knowledge might very well help us catch the real culprit."

Rich questioned the two friends. "Did I hear what I thought I heard? You're still thinking of going ahead and looking into this case on your own?"

"It's a free world, for now that is," Suzanne answered curtly.

"Well mam, if you're not an official officer, you could get in trouble by the authorities, especially if you hinder our investigation. I wouldn't want you or your partner getting into a situation that would put you in a dangerous position or peril," a perplexed Detective Colangelo answered.

Pouring coffee for two of them, Suzanne declined and opted for a pot of hot water instead. She put her tea bag into the empty cup, letting the tea bag steep and as a war of wills wouldn't blink while looking at the detective. After a while Detective Colangelo dropped his eyes and gave in to Suzanne, who he thought was one ballsy lady. Too headstrong for his likes but a woman that he could respect.

As they drank their personal drinks, they seemed to be at a stalemate.

Nancy couldn't help looking at Rich with her large green eyes and Suzanne almost threw up as she thought she saw Nancy batting her lashes at him.

"Let's put the facts on the table, shall we Detective. We have information that you would find rather interesting. On the other hand, you might have acquired facts that might help us. Why can't we work together on this? If you don't want to because you and your department think we'll get hurt and cause the department embarrassment I assure you that if you make a few phone calls to Tim Cassidy and Kevin Halloran of the Boston FBI, it will affirm our obvious skill in the department of justice."

Tipping his head in agreement, he continued. "Well Ms. Morse, I might just do that. Thank you for your hospitality and I'll be getting back to both of you shortly."

"With that, he abruptly got up and walked himself to the door. I'll be speaking to you shortly, I'm sure." He slowly closed the door.

"Suzanne why did you act so pompous?" an irritated Nancy asked.

"He doesn't think we're capable of handling this situation. Yes, I wanted to show off a bit and I'm glad I did."

"Suzanne, you and I know that we're clever and can do this job. Especially when Justin arrives. In a way, maybe that will give him an excuse to get back to us."

"Wait a second, okay. You didn't tell me that you're interested in him. Are you? Never mind, by the goofy look on your face, I can tell that you are."

"You are infatuated with him, aren't you? I'll admit he's good looking and his build under that suit is gorgeous, or so I can imagine. He must work out all the time. It's obvious that the two of you have a mutual attraction. You can feel the heat scorching the room just sitting between the two of you."

Nancy looked embarrassed as she got off the sofa and started writing some script on the note paper that was on the large cherry wood desk.

Suzanne didn't know what to do. She got up from the sofa and started pacing the floor. After a while she announced to Nancy. "I'm going to call and speak to either Kevin or Tim and let them know what I did. Yes, I know, I know, they'll probably get pissed thinking that I represented myself as a person who works along with them on a regular basis. Honestly, I was bullshit that he had the audacity to think we wouldn't be able to handle any of this investigation."

After what seemed hours, Kevin finally called Suzanne back. Closing her cell phone, she addressed Nancy. "Okay, he was upset that I misrepresented our association with the FBI. When I finally got through telling him about our mission and what I thought of Rich Colangelo and Miles Freeman, who by the way, are like two pees in a pod, they are pompous assholes, as far as I'm concerned, he couldn't stop laughing. He wished us luck and told me to call him anytime and he would try to help us if he and Tim could. By the way, he was going to stick up for us and confirm that we've helped him and his partner out on more than one occasion if the detective should call him for a reference."

Nancy kept shaking her head in amazement. "Do you really believe that we helped him on more than one case?"

"As a matter of fact, yes. Do I have to remind you that by finding Brian and his co-partners guilty of fraud, money laundering, drug conspiracy and a few more charges that are too numerous to mention," waving her hand in the air, Suzanne looked towards Nancy for acknowledgment, "A lot of various hoodlums got what was coming to them." Nancy hated to admit that Suzanne had a valid point. "Yes I do."

"Let's get dressed and go down to the lounge. I feel like a good stiff drink and then we can get something to eat later," Nancy declared as she went into the bedroom to change.

The two women sat at the bar, talking about what should be done next.

"After dinner let's call Justin and find out what his plans are and when we can expect him," Suzanne declared. She got off the stool and brought her drink to the table that the attendant said was ready.

CHAPTER TWENTY THREE

Suzanne was in a sound and peaceful sleep when the alarm's ringing woke her. Slowly putting her legs on the side of the bed she gradually lifted herself up. Stretching, she observed Nancy still in deep slumber. She took a hot shower, not wanting to disturb her until she was ready. 'Let the dear sleep as long as possible,' she thought to herself. 'She's going to need all the rest she can get. We have so many papers and files to go through, it'll probably take hours and hours of intense reading to piece the puzzle together. '

Suzanne gently nudged Nancy, trying to wake her. A smile was on Nancy's face and Suzanne hoped that she didn't interrupt a nice dream.

Stretching her arms she opened one eye and saw Suzanne smiling down at her. "Wake up sleepy head. I let you sleep for as long as possible. Take a shower and get refreshed. We'll go down for breakfast and spend the rest of the day going over the paperwork that we found in Curtis's hiding spots. Does that sound good to you?"

Slowly getting up, she put the shower water on hot and stayed there for about 15 minutes. Toweling herself dry, she yelled to Suzanne, "I'll be ready in a few. I won't bother putting on makeup. After all, we'll be staying here, working our asses off."

"Not literally," Suzanne answered, "I have a small enough one as it is, thank you, I wouldn't want it any less."

"I don't know about you," Nancy announced, "I'm famished".

Sitting down at a table in the hotels café, enjoying their tea and coffee, they looked at each other and didn't know what to say. Suddenly, Suzanne proclaimed, "Justin will be coming here shortly. I can't wait to see him and get his input on the situation."

"If I remember correctly, he told us that his flight will be arriving tonight at about 10.00 pm at LAX. We'll pick him up, let him get settled in his room and then go over the details that we found on the plans and security system of the Huntington. We'll also tell him about the gallery Curtis worked for. I think we'll be able to handle the cleaning company. I'm sure he'll want to eat something before we take him to the hotel. You know how the airlines are. They don't even give you a sandwich. You're lucky to get coffee, tea, or any type of soft drink without having to pay for it. If I remember, he did mention that he was flying first class, so that won't be any trouble about him being famished," continued Nancy.

"We might as well stop for some sort of snack to quell our hunger in the middle of the night. I'm sure he'll be exhausted after the long flight. We'll have to fill him in on some of the details and then let the poor baby sleep. Just in case he only wants a nap we can then tell him more if he wakes up rearing to go. And we'll have the snacks to sustain us till the morning," pronounced Suzanne, as she poured another cup of tea.

"Maybe after a couple of days of brainstorming I'll have a better idea when I can make arrangements to meet with Stephen. I promise I won't take more than five days. Hell, I might be able to get away for a few hours or so, like you suggested, so I won't be out of the mix. I don't want to miss a thing. Of course, I'll be calling in to find out what's going on. I don't want to arouse suspicion, so I'll try to call whenever I can get free".

"Suzanne, you sound as if this get together will be a chore. I really hope you don't feel that way. If you do, Stephen will be able to tell and then you'll have new issues to contend with."

"I know, I know. I really can't wait to see him and get together, but it's not the best timing, you know? I wish he could wait for another month, at least, until we can be sure that the case is closed. Then I think, what if it takes more than a month, poo,poo, then he'll really get pissed and we'll be more estranged from one another. Dam if you do and Dam if you don't. It seems that when we talk over the phone there's a hidden agitation from both of us. You want to know a secret Nancy?"

"I know you're dying to tell me, so go ahead."

"Sometimes I wish I never met up with Stephen for the second time in our lives. There are so many complicated issues that plague us. It would seem easier not having to think of the agenda's and complications that could happen and then the knowing that after all these years of loving one another, I know we'll never be able to make our union legal. I shouldn't be thinking these thoughts, but dam it, I do. I resent his feeling responsible for what happened but does he really think of me or does he think of his feelings first? Sometimes if I think about our situation a feeling of relief comes to the surface if I think we were to break up."

Nancy was shocked at Suzanne's revelation and sipped another cup of coffee. "Suzanne you really don't mean what you just said, do you? The two of you love each other and I don't think you'd be happy being apart."

Looking into her cup of tea she took another scone. Suzanne contemplated her response. "These feelings didn't happen overnight." She found the raspberry jelly and put it onto the delicious cranberry scone. I've been thinking what various people have said, especially my dear friends. I think they're right. Sometimes I do think he's selfish and thinks only of himself, in his mind he thinks he's taking care of Lou Ellen and doesn't want to do her any more harm than she's already been through. I realize I sound callous but it gets frustrating, you know. If we ever break up I'll miss him terribly, but I realize that life has to go on. I want security. I certainly don't need financial protection but the assurance that I'm his wife and he only cares about me. It must sound rather selfish on my part, but he can't let go of the past. On the other hand, he doesn't want to think of the future. He pretends that nothing is wrong and I should be happy the way our relationship is going. It's getting harder and harder for me to keep going this way. It may seem selfish on my part but I feel he's the selfish one and only thinks of himself."

"Wow, you're blowing my mind. I thought I'd never hear these words coming from you. You must be pretty mad at him and it's been building up for some time. I can't tell you what to do, but I want you to think seriously and realize the consequences that will happen if you act on these feelings."

"Thanks for hearing me out Nancy. I'll do a lot of thinking before I take any action. But there comes a time that I can't take it anymore. Let's change the subject and concentrate on what we came here for."

Nancy shook her head and tried getting back to reality.

"I know what you're saying, but try taking it a day at a time. As soon as Justin arrives, some sort of plan will take place. By then we'll have more information to give him. Once we have an outline of what has to be done, I'm sure you'll be able to go with a knowledge that we'll be fine."

"I will take it a day at a time. Understand, I'd have to call him before his intentional flight. I don't want any more aggravation in my life. I know it could be worse, but with all the things that are happening all at once it gets overwhelming," Suzanne admitted. "Don't look now, but I think I see that Rich Colangelo in the lobby. Don't turn around and look, it will be conspicuous. I wonder what he wants?"

"It probably isn't him. If you haven't noticed, there are many handsome men around. He's just one of a few," Nancy announced as she slowly turned.

Suzanne was adamant, "I'm telling you, it's him. Let's take our time with breakfast and see if he goes away. He's asking the desk clerk something."

Suzanne expounded, "It might have to do with the case. Why would he come here if it wasn't?"

"Maybe he's checking to see if we're in our rooms."

"If he is, he'll find out we're not," Suzanne proclaimed.

"I suppose you're right." Deep down, Nancy hoped that it wasn't all about the murder. She left her feelings at bay and pretended that she had nothing on her mind than the case they were trying to solve.

Suzanne saw Detective Colangelo heading towards their table. "Shit," she proclaimed to Nancy, "It seems he found us." Suzanne observed the way he strutted. 'Boy is this man full of himself.' With a phony smile she acknowledged him and asked him to join them.

"Thanks." Rich explained, "The gentleman at the desk saw you go into the dining room for breakfast and was nice enough to inform me."

"What do we owe the pleasure of your company?" Suzanne curiously asked.

"It looks like you haven't received your meal yet, do you mind if I order some coffee and join you for breakfast, I'm famished."

"Just the baskets of breads have come. You're right, our breakfast is still coming. Feel free to order," Nancy suggested.

'What a nerve,' Suzanne thought as she took a piece of banana nut bread out of the basket and slathered it with butter. The breads reminded her of the Thanksgiving meals that her family and Beverly's family shared on that special holiday. Different breads and pecan rolls were on the table for anyone to take along with the Turkey and fixings to be enjoyed by all.

After finishing his first cup of coffee he got to the real reason for his visit. Looking at both women Rich proceeded, "I hope I'm not invading your privacy. I took your advice and called Tim Cassidy of Boston's FBI. I mean you said it was okay to confirm what you told me." He looked at Suzanne as he spoke. Trying to be inconspicuous, he tried avoiding Nancy's presence and directed his conversation to Suzanne.

"That's all right detective. I said you should contact him if you had any misgivings of our ability to help solve this murder investigation. Isn't that right

Nancy?" 'I hope he doesn't avoid looking at Nancy this entire meal.' "Tell us what Tim told you about Nancy and myself."

"First of all, I want to apologize for my doubting the two of you. You have to understand that what you told me is highly unusual for lay people to do and be part of a full-fledged investigation." Looking at both Nancy and Suzanne he addressed the women. 'I hope I don't make it obvious that I like Nancy when I speak to her. If my neck gets red, I'll be so embarrassed.' "I still would like for the two of you to not be directly involved in our investigation. I realize that you have quite a bit invested in this search for the person who is responsible for the murder. Why don't you nice ladies be thankful that Kyle isn't going to be prosecuted, just yet, and go about your regular business?" Looking at the two women he continued his speech. "I realize that you have gone to a lot of trouble to help us. The department cannot thank you enough. Our division would still like it if you would tell us what you found out that can help us find the right person. It's not that we don't appreciate your help but that's our job."

"Wait a second. The problem is the comment you made about Kyle not being prosecuted, just yet." "I hope that you're not still thinking of him as a suspect," Suzanne pronounced. Feeling embarrassed he pretended and ignored her outburst. He continued, clearing his throat, "The police and I realize that you've done a lot of work in helping the investigation. Is this information that you came about pertains to Mr. Jones? If so, can you tell us about it? I admit we might have overlooked some important facts that we're unaware of." The waitress finished cleaning up their plates and left another pot of coffee for Nancy and Rich. She ignored Suzanne and Suzanne had to finally ask her for another pot of hot water for tea. An annoyed Suzanne thought to herself, 'talk about discrimination, why do coffee drinkers always get asked from the wait staff if they want more coffee, but tea drinkers have to practically beg for another cup of tea.'

"Getting back to your question Detective Colangelo. I know that you think that we might have obtained information that could help you in the investigation of your case to apprehend the real criminal or criminals." Finishing the omelet in front of her Suzanne contemplated her next sentence. "What makes you think we have any information? Even if we do, with the way your department and precinct talked to us, if we did find something, I don't know if we'd share our findings with you. I realize your unit could get a court order for such information, but I assure you, that wouldn't be wise. When and if we might find something that would help, we probably will be glad to assist you. Unfortunately, we haven't found anything yet. You see, even though we have some substantial information, there's a lot more that has to be done, on our part that is, before we come to you with all of our findings." Holding up her hands Suzanne continued, "We seem to think that when you took Mr. Jones' computer, you also obtained information from his hard drive, that would co-ordinate with some of our data. I'm not asking you for that knowledge, am I?"

"First of all we were unable to get his computer. The thief must have taken it with some of the other belongings of his. That's not to say that we don't have any evidence."

Nancy felt embarrassed for the way Suzanne was talking down to Detective Colangelo. She realized the situation that he put them in, but really, did she have to go this far? She wondered, as she stole a look at Rich Colangelo and his gorgeous profile, if he would concede. Suzanne continued the onslaught. "I'm almost positive that we'll be finding information that will astound you, but this information is in the process of being had. I do thank you for your concession of us being real in the field of law but without your full co-operation it will be very difficult for us to divulge our information. I hope that you can understand our side of the story," Suzanne once again told him.

"I think that if I go back to my captain and tell him about our conversation, he might want to bring the two of you in and we'll take it from there. This isn't a threat of any kind, you have to understand. Under the circumstance, my hands are tied. My captain is a great and conscientious man and I don't think he'll give you a hard time as long as we can work together and evaluate all the data between us."

"That's sounds reasonable," a determined Nancy intervened. Looking at Suzanne, leaving her no other choice, isn't that right?"

Suzanne cleared her throat, for lack of a better response. "I think a meeting would be beneficial for all parties. Yes, by all means, talk to your captain and call us when you have a specific time and date. Now if you'll excuse us, my partner and I have a lot of work ahead of us. Thank you for joining us for breakfast and we'll be waiting for your call."

When the two women returned to the suite Nancy couldn't contain her anger. "Suzanne how could you have been so cold and rude? I've never seen you like that, he's only trying to get on with this investigation. I'm sure that they must have some important facts that will also help us."

"Nancy sit down, please. I hope you realize, that at this point, I bet we've got more information than the entire precinct and department that Detective Colangelo is working out of. The valuable information we found is probably more than Mr. Jones put into his computer. Granted, he told us that they didn't have the computer. If that's true, then all of The Huntington Museum's layout, the entire security system for the museum, as well as the other facts that we saw will definitely be of importance to them. And, when I told him we didn't have anything yet to report, that wasn't a lie. We haven't gone through all the papers. I think they need our help more than we need theirs."

"Sure they could drag us into court, but I honestly don't think they will. Maybe in his accounting records, if they've gone to local banks, he could have imputed the data and bank information and I'll give them that. Don't forget, we have the knowledge of all the oversea bank accounts that Curtis had. That will be very difficult for them to obtain, unless they get help from the FBI or Interpole and even if they do, I don't know if the oversea banks would give them that confidential information. The laws are changing all the time. But we also have that info and the real hard copies. Let's continue our work and wait for them to contact us. So far they don't know how valuable Justin is, he's our ace in the hole," Suzanne told Nancy.

The plane taxied to the tarmac and the passengers disembarked to the concourse. It wasn't hard to spot Justin as he entered the terminal, towering over the other passengers, he strode briskly towards the two women. With opened arms he encompassed his friends, embracing them affectionately.

"I've worked out a plan and I can't wait to begin our escapade. I feel like Mickey Spalane. I doubt if you girls heard of him."

"Now wait a darn minute," Suzanne exclaimed, "I do remember hearing about him."

"I'll tell you all about the plan on our way to Madeline's house. I presume I'm staying there with the two of you."

"Justin, I apologize for not mentioning that we're not staying at Madaline's. Instead, our temporary home is the Four Seasons in San Diego. We hope you're not disappointed with our decision?" Nancy asked Justin.

"Not at all. Although I'd love to see her house and how she decorated it. Maybe we'll be able to go there after this mission is accomplished."

"We wouldn't have it any other way," Suzanne responded as she loaded his suitcases into the trunk of the rented car. With undisguised appreciation and gratitude Suzanne enlightened Justin on more information since their last conversation.

"We've kept in touch with Kyle. Although he's frightened and at the same time resentful and impatient with the judicial system, he's starting to remember some pieces of information that might come in handy. There are more than a few incidents, that at the time, didn't seem important. He thinks looking back at them now, might prove beneficial to us in getting the real culprits. It might be purely coincidental, but on more than one occasion Kyle remembers hearing Curtis talking to a Japanese businessman who was very interested in having him acquire some paintings for his individual collection."

"Don't forget to mention the one time he overheard a heated argument between Curtis and an unknown individual at Curtis's apartment," an inspired Nancy interjected.

Waving her hand, trying to concentrate on getting out of the airport, Suzanne said, "I think we forgot to tell you that they now think that Kyle might be innocent or that he did it with another person. No matter what the outcome is, we came all this way I would like to find out who the murderer is that almost ruined Kyle's life."

"How did they come to that conclusion," asked Justin.

Nancy answered, "I think Rich Colangelo, who happens to be the head detective on this case, mentioned something about the Medical Examiner finding some pertinent information that wouldn't give the DA a solid case against Kyle."

"But he didn't say what that information was?" Justin asked. "No, but knowing the judicial system they won't go to trial unless they're sure they'll win. They have to have rock solid evidence," Suzanne informed Justin.

Suzanne honked her horn at a motorist who cut in front of her as she tried to emerge into another lane. An agitated Suzanne commented, "One thing I've learned is that very few people use their horns in California as we do back east." Making sure that she could move easily into another lane Suzanne continued her discussion. Glancing into the mirror, Suzanne made sure Justin noticed her wink. Pretending to be upset she continued. "Before I was so rudely interrupted, I was about to mention that piece of information."

"Does Kyle have any idea who the gentleman was that had the heated exchange with Mr. Jones?"

"Unfortunately he doesn't." Suzanne said as she exited off the freeway.

HEADING HOME TO DENYENCHOFU, JAPAN

Before departing for the airport Yoshy sat quietly on his white linen sofa gently stroking his crystal glass mug filled with his favorite beer. He knew that he'd have it the next time he came back to the States. Closing his eyes he tried to relax and forget the incident that lately caused him so much worry and aggravation. 'I'm glad that I asked Nobuaki that favor. Maybe now I won't be as upset as I was before the task was performed.'

Yoshy couldn't wait to return to Beppo where the hot springs and minerals made him feel healthy and robust. Obviously the mental strain of the downward trend in the commercial enterprise of his business was becoming an incessant concern.

Toshiko, Yoshy's wife considered herself honored that she had such a wonderful, devoted husband and father. Toshiko considered her main task in life was taking care of her home and have everything skillfully prepared when Yoshy returned back from his business obligations overseas. The one remaining responsibility was that Kazuhiko, their son, study hard enough to pass the tough entrance exam to one of the country's best universities. Yoshy realized that Kazuhiko had to excel so that when he graduated from the top university that he could take his son into his company with great pride and honor. 'After all' he thought to himself, 'I have worked hard and what a high reward for Kazuhiko to follow in my footsteps.'

Robin couldn't understand Yoshy's concern for his son's results of the latest exam and constantly badgered her lover to stay in California to be with her. He wanted to see an end to her constant harassing. Yoshy left Robin in tears at their departure. He wished Robin would be more understanding like his dutiful and submissive wife, Toshiko. He liked it when he entered the airplane. He loved being doted on and he could relax and think of nothing but enjoying the beer or sake served him. Yoshy wanted to head home and after finding out the results of his sons exams and talking to Kazuhiko in person, head for his cabin, away from the crowds and pressures of his business. All he wanted to do was sit by himself and admire his latest acquisitions. He loved all his works of art with an ardent passion. Most of his art collection had been acquired through reputable art dealers and although it cost him a small fortune he gladly paid their exorbitant asking price. Once in a while he would lapse in a pain of guilt when he thought of the few art pieces he had to acquire by other means. 'In reality I guess they're more than a few.'

He felt himself drifting into a much needed sleep. It didn't bother him that he deprives other people from admiring and enjoying these pieces of art, which he selfishly thought of as his own. Knowing that these particular masterpieces would never be for sale he didn't care how he acquired them. 'They are mine, all mine, and no one can tell me not to view, handle or admire them. When I want to see them I will.' Yoshy fell into a deep slumber, a sinful smirk visibly affixed to his face. The images of the various priceless paintings and object d'art vividly appeared, advancing, then suddenly seized by an unknown foe and taken away. He awoke in a cold sweat, visibly shaken by his bad dream.

"Is there anything I can get you Mr. Makino?" a concerned attendant asked when she walked past and saw how upset her passenger looked.

*"Lie, Lie, goshimpai naku. Daijobu desu, Yoshy firmly declared as he straightened himself in the comfortable seat and pretended to occupy himself with work. (*No, no, No need to worry, it's o. k. /I'm o. k.)

The continuous pulsating migraine was just starting to ease as Yoshy arrived at his house in the suburbs of Denyenchofu. An unusual exuberant Toshiko greeted her husband as he entered the small two story house. Yoshy was not used to seeing his wife in such an obvious state of amiability. Attending to her husband's wishes, a perpetually obedient Toshiko waited for Yoshy to approach and embrace her after their absence from one another. She had so much to tell him that she couldn't contain her excitement for one moment more. After Yoshy was comfortable and with a glass of sake in his hand. Toshiko waited for her husband to request her presence next to him. Yoshy tried to contain his confused amusement at his wife's obvious joyous state but couldn't restrain himself. "Tell me, what has you in this happy mood?"

"It's Kazuhiko. We received the results of the entrance exams. Our son has passed with, how they say in United States, flying colors." She stifled a joyful laugh, in back of the hands that were concealing her mouth. Not one to show outward affection, Yoshy embraced Toshiko and kissed her lovingly on the cheek. Forgetting himself momentarily he lovingly enfolded his petite, beautiful, wife in his arms and kissed her passionately.

Toshiko lies beside her husband, encompassed by his muscular arms. She listened for Yoshy's steady breathing. She timidly looked up assuming to see a sleeping, satisfied husband. Instead she encountered Yoshy looking down at her beautiful face, an admiring grin upon his face. He stroked her hair lovingly, impulsively kissing the top of her head.

Enjoying his dinner of Yakitori* *(chunks of chicken basted in a sweet soy sauce and grilled over a charcoal fire on thin skewers), tempura and rice, Yoshy and Toshiko talked in great detail of their sons accomplishment and their expectations for his future. After Yoshy took the oshibori that his wife handed him to wipe his hands and face, he thanked her for the delicious meal she prepared for him. "As much as I want to remain here for a few days I can only stay over the night. I must depart tomorrow morning." Yoshy avoided looking directly into Toshiko's eyes, lest she observe the deceit that only a master such as he uttered. "I have pressing business that has to be done and I have to attend to it as soon as possible. I'm not sure when I'll be home next but tell Kazuhiko how proud I am that he passed his exams. No, No, better yet I will leave a note for my smart son and express to him my feelings. I thought for sure that Kazuhiko would be home to have a heart to heart talk with him but I forgot that he's at University."

Toshiko prepared Yoshy's bath and readied herself for bed. As she lay in bed waiting for his body to lay next to her, different emotions passed through her as thoughts of her beloved Yoshihiro spread forth, resembling a wild brush fire out of control. She wanted to believe every word he told her but deep down she knew that there was a secret side to her husband that no one was privy to. For years she overlooked and ignored her discernment and had the capacity to fool herself in wanting to believe every word he told her. But as she matured and learned that her intuition and judgment was keen, she cleverly avoided any confrontation. 'After all,' she thought, 'Yoshy is a good provider and a fine husband and father. Yes, he does have weaknesses, but I try to overlook them. I will be here for him when he decides to come home next.' A complacent smile appeared on her face as she lost herself in slumber.

Toshiko remembered the day Yoshy came home from one of his business trips and announced that they were going to tear down their old home and make it more Westernized. At first she was distraught at the idea. For years that was all she knew. Some of their friends had already became more Westernized, but Toshiko was reluctant to give up the old traditional ways. As much as she wanted to stay and observe the ancestral tendency she found herself giving in to her husband's demands and become more modernized. Her husband had the last say.

She couldn't stop her husband's desire to change and become like his contemporaries, who adhered to the Western cultures. Toshiko found herself sleeping on a bed instead of the traditional mat. She still maintained some soji's around the house, reminding her of the old Japanese ways. As long as she could still have some old traditions amongst the modern décor, she could cope with his demands. 'I have to remember that I am subservient to my husband, as I was brought up to be by my beloved parents. Although I have conflicting emotions, I can't let my reading material of the new Japan take over the way I was brought up. I have to maintain my docile personality in front of Yoshy.'

Yoshy couldn't wait to return to his house in Beppu. It took a little more than two hours from the time Yoshy departed from the Haneda Airport in Tokyo to arrive at his beautiful mini style palace situated on a hill with a panoramic view of the city and the ocean. Yoshy quickly undressed and put on his yukata as he readied himself to relax and soak in his very own hot spring bath. He closed his eyes and enjoyed the quiet and solitude that this isolated refuge enabled him to luxuriate in. He found an unusual gratification that he couldn't explain, even to himself, as he wondered why he didn't want to share this hidden retreat with anyone, except on occasion, Robin.

Later that evening he sat on the sofa admiring the various objects that only he was privy to. Yoshy rose and walked over to the collection of original della Robbias and 16th century Italian bronzes. He lovingly touched the ancient bronze Chinese vase of the Shang Dynasty and the bronze eagle that adorned a gold embroidered battle flag of one of Napoleon's regiments that were situated on a gilt console table. Yoshy saw the reflections, by the ornate gold leaf Venetian style mirror, of the 18th century European porcelains and the large bronze figures of Old Age and Youth and a mask of Dionysus, all by Allard, sitting atop a carved marble mantelpiece with elaborate gilt over mantle.

Seated on a settee of 16th century Venice's Palazzo Cornaro, Yoshy sipped his nightcap, appreciating the numerous works of art that he had acquired. He loved them all, recognizing the value of each. 'Yes,' he thought, a quick shiver going through his body, as he reconciled his justification of dispatching larceny and murder.

'The robberies were worth the expense,' he reflected as he became engrossed in the beautiful paintings hanging on the walls. From the Isabella Stewart Gardner Museum, the Concert, Rembrandt's Storm on the Sea of Galilee, A Lady and Gentleman, Chez Tortoni, and his most recent acquisitions from the Huntington Museum, Gainsborough's The Blue Boy, Sir Thomas Lawrence's Pinkie, Sir Joshua Reynolds, The Young Fortune Teller and George Romney's The Clavering Children. He couldn't rationalize the stupidity of why those ignorant fools carved into his beloved paintings when he received them from the people who stole the precious art from the Gardner Museum. He now wished that he had engaged Curtis for that robbery, for when he took the painting home with him on the plane, his heart was in his mouth, hoping the paintings wouldn't be found amongst his belongings. 'I guess I travel frequently enough that the inspectors ignore my luggage whenever I travel back and forth to Japan. '

He normally would have used Mr. Jones to perform this deed but unfortunately he was unavailable to do the heist. He relied on some men, who obviously didn't know much about art.' I should have waited for Mr. Jones to perform the theft,' He often told himself. 'I'm glad that most of my paintings were stolen by Curtis Jones, who, a lover of art himself, appreciated the collection of paintings and sculpture and carefully executed the thefts.' Yoshy would miss Mr. Jones and his well-planned robberies from the series of country house break-ins, belonging to stately homes in England and France to the numerous museums and galleries around the world. 'What a surprise when Nobuaki gave me the painting of the Clavering Children. I'm sure that Curtis had taken this picture as a keepsake for himself. Nobuaki must have gotten this piece of art from the man that killed Curtis. I don't know how it wound up with Nobuaki, but it was very nice for him to give it to me. I know he's cognizant for my love of art. That was a nice gesture on his part. I'll have to send him a great present as appreciation for all the work he accomplished,' Yoshy thought as he sat there admiring his collection.

CHAPTER TWENTY FOUR

CALIFORNIA

Justin left Kyle's apartment after spending many hours talking to him and inquiring about his late friend Curtis Jones. Pondering the many answers to his questions that Kyle disclosed, he was not satisfied with what he heard. Justin knew that he'd have to find the answers out for himself.

Parking the rented car on the street he walked leisurely to the gallery that Curtis Jones had worked, taking time to admire the window displays of the department and specialty stores lining the prestigious neighborhood. It reminded him of Newbury Street and the area surrounding it. As much as he thought of himself as a progressive person, one who enjoyed fresh and modern ideas, looking at the latest fashions actually repulsed him. He didn't understand how anyone in their right mind could wear the clothing presented and be pleased with what they saw looking at the reflection of themselves in the mirror. He asked himself, 'whatever happened to the word beautiful and femininity.' Most of the clothes he saw were bisexual and could be worn by either sex. The new design of shoes, with their ornate laces, sparkling and gaudy embellishments of gold, silver and stones were despicable in his eyes. He honestly didn't know how the young girls of today could wear the high heels that were part of these shoes. 'If I had children and they didn't have my artistic ability, I would advise them to become podiatrists. They would make a fortune when these young ladies become older and have foot problems from wearing these foolish looking footwear. I wonder how much money these designers make? They have so little fabric covering the actual shoe that the profit margin must be huge.'

When traveling throughout Europe he made sure that he would be visiting France for the annual fashion shows. Remembering all his many dear friends, who set trends in the industry. 'God, Edith Head would be mortified. Carmen Marc Vevlo, Ralph Lauren, Giorgio Armani, Givenchy, Yves Saint Laurent and of course Hardy Ames, the British Queens favorite designer, would never think of designing clothes as these. They designed classic, refined and never daring attire; once in a while he had to concede that some plunging necklines and unusual hems were worn by many actresses that these beloved people designed clothes for.'

'Nowadays, one didn't know if a girl or boy were passing you on the street.' Of course he recognized the woman when he attended many of the social events he had to attend. The fabric of today's clothes was beautiful, as they were back in the days of movies and older fashions. But did they have to show their almost full bosom with the fabric down to their navel? He realized that the young models and actresses were proud of their bodies but by baring it all, it left little to the imagination. The older designers were progressive but Justin knew that some of them would be turning over in their graves if they saw what the designers were putting forth today. 'Oh well, to each their own,' Justin thought to himself, as he passed the establishments walking to the gallery.

Justin walked into the Weintraub Gallery and introduced himself to the owner. 'Occasionally one sometimes has to dispense with the truth and be a bit deceitful,' he told himself as he invented a plausible fabrication that brought him into the prestigious gallery.

"I've heard a great deal about you and your gallery," an excited Mr. Weintraub exclaimed." How can I assist you?"

"Thank you for the compliment. A friend of mine from Sotheby's told me you have a few paintings that you just acquired and I was interested in them for one of my patrons. There are quite a few artistic riches that many an obscure gallery has hanging on it's walls that would be surprising to many, wouldn't you say?" Justin accurately proclaimed.

Stammering for a second Mr. Weintraub's mind wandered, trying to think which one of his paintings would be worth an astonishing value.

"I would like to take my time roaming about your large display rooms, during that time I will note which pieces I might be interested in. When I'm through maybe we can go out for lunch and discuss some subjects that I am sure will be beneficial for both of us."

Counting his unscheduled, impending millions, Mr. Weintraub waited with anticipation. He gleefully rubbed his hands together, a large smile on his face, as he went into his private room in the back of the gallery.

The bar with the bright, bold colors adorning the walls was packed with assorted humanity as the luncheon crowd enjoyed the flavorful array of culinary delights. After a half an hour wait the two gentlemen were escorted to their table where Mr. Weintraub proceeded to inquire about Justin's findings. Diverting the inevitable questions, Justin avoided the show of curiosity, and adeptly, using his knowledge, switched to becoming the credible questioner.

"So tell me Mr. Weintraub, how long have you been in business and what credentials do you have. How long has this gallery been opened and what sort of gross income do you generate?" Half listening to his reply, Justin sat back in his chair, slowly sipping his dry martini. Assessing the slim, middle aged man seated across the table, Justin pretended interest, noting that this man, who thought highly of himself, lacked substance. Justin observed that Mr. Weintraub, like other self-centered, egotistical people whom he met, was very superficial. Laughing to himself he thought that Suzanne would have a field day with this gentleman who had a perpetual tan.

"By the way, a while ago, I heard about an employee of yours who, I believe, was your assistant, and he met with an untimely passing. What happened?" an inquiring Justin asked.

Quickly downing his Manhattan, Art Weintraub, his hands visibly shaking, didn't want to dredge up painful memories. Although he could never forget Curtis, his untimely and fatal demise was a continual perplexing issue. He could feel the sweat excreting from the pores of his skin. Hoping his new Armani shirt wouldn't show visible signs of nervous perspiration, he expertly loosened his matching tie, trusting the air-conditioning would cool him down. Feigning indifference he replied, "I've been in the art field for approximately twenty years and have owned my own gallery for the last fifteen. As you know from owning your own gallery there are many hidden costs that the public is unaware of. I figure after the first five years I started to make a decent profit."

The waiter came over and after ordering their meal another round of drinks were brought over. "Curtis Jones is a subject that is still painful for me to discuss. I had such high hopes and aspirations for the young man. I was going to make him a partner and we were to open another gallery. I have varied interests and although I love the gallery, at my age I feel I've worked hard for many years. I want to enjoy life to the fullest. Considering my outside interests, I left Curtis in charge of the daily operation of the gallery. I valued his education and knowledge in the art field."

Taking a deep breath as if talking to himself, he muttered, "what a waste of such a young life." Shaking his head he proclaimed, "I hope they prosecute the bastard responsible for his murder and he should never be let out of prison. Not being selfish, but since Curtis is no longer the manager I find myself having to work more hours. I anticipate that I can find a replacement for him. It'll be hard for me to get as caring an individual who put many hours taking care of my gallery."

Clearing his throat Justin continued probing and finally brought the conversation back to the original reason for their luncheon. "I noticed a few paintings that, how shall I say it tactfully, are beautiful, but I wonder how you acquired them. I have a thorough list of paintings that were stolen from a good many mansions in Scotland, France and England. Now I could buy them from you without you being a bit suspicious and make a huge profit. But once you get to know me I have a reputation to uphold and am an honest man. I would never act in such a rogue fashion. I say let's work together and find out how you acquired these paintings and go from there. What do you say, Art?"

Art Weintraub was completely taken by surprise and was both grateful and indebted for Justin's honesty. He tried to quell the nauseous feeling emitting from within. "I honestly don't know what you're talking about." Justin saw that he was telling the truth. "For the last few years Curtis purchased most of the paintings. He always had invoices, not that I had any desire or felt a need to question them. I guess that's not being a good business man, but I trusted Curtis and left everything up to him." Looking Justin directly in the eyes he continued, "I feel like a potz, a shlemeil." Art Weintraub ordered another drink and downed it in two gulps. "Can you imagine, I'm supposed to be such an entrepreneur, people look up to me. Boy, have I been made a fool of. I can't believe this is happening to me."

"It's easy for me to tell you not to worry. But believe me when I tell you that I believe you didn't know what was occurring. We'll try to figure out what ensued and get to the bottom of this horrific scene." Finishing their meal the two men quickly started on their journey of rectitude.

"Tell me more about Mr. Jones. Did he have certain clients that he attended to. Take your time and think hard. Maybe regular patrons only would go to Mr. Jones. I'm in no rush so don't think time is of the essence."

"Thanks." Ordering another drink, Mr. Weintraub concentrated on Justin's suggestion. His frown became more apparent as he jotted notes on a piece of paper that he delicately extracted from his suits' breast pocket. Back at the gallery I have an extensive list of the customers that Curtis would acquire art pieces for. I'll be glad to make a copy of them and you can look it over. Come to think about it, there's one gentleman that comes to mind. I saw him talking to Curtis for a while in the back of the gallery. That was not the first time I'd seen him in my establishment talking to Curtis. He was an oriental gentleman. I think maybe of Japanese descent. Of course, there are many other designers who," shaking his head as in disbelief, "Were always consulting with Curtis. But there was something unusual about that gentleman, that I sensed, didn't seem Kosher, if you know what I mean."

"If you can do me a favor, when you get back to the gallery, it would help immensely to look up, in your records the pieces of art he acquired and his name and address, as with the other people you can think of. "I would surely appreciate it."

Leaving the restaurant, Mr. Weintraub shook Justin's hand and assured him that he would get on the mission as soon as possible.

"We'll get to the bottom of this and put this horrific ordeal to rest, once and for all," assured Justin as he made his way to the rented car. Justin noticed Mr. Weintraub walking a bit unsteady. He hoped all the drinks that Mr. Weintraub consumed wouldn't affect his driving, going back to his place of business.

Suzanne had a hard time concentrating on the business at hand. Her mind was going in many directions. Thoughts of her immediate family kept re-entering her mind as she worked on her client. The girls were being patient but after this prolonged visit to the California salon her daughters where becoming resentful at her obvious absence. Hope wanted and needed Suzanne's input on her upcoming wedding. Suzanne tried suppressing her numerous thoughts and emotions after Hope disclosed her intentions of converting her religion to that of Spencer's. 'Keep your emotions at bay,' she cautioned herself, as she felt her muscles tensing and thus bearing down a little too hard on her clients shoulders when she remembered Hope's words.

After finishing for the day Suzanne sat at her desk in the office of the Beverly Hills Salon. She remembered once before when she experienced overwhelming emotions that continuously disrupted her state of mind. Thoughts of Rabbi Mann came to her. Years ago his wisdom and guidance insurmountably helped her come to terms with certain painful situations that caused mental distress. Before Suzanne was born her father's family had turned to this holy man, and teacher for inspiration and direction in their lives. She was named Brina Shima, after her father's mother, in Rabbi Mann's small synagogue (place of worship) and remembered the many stories her father, Morris, recounted of his and his brothers' boyhood growing up in an orthodox household. Putting away her client's cards she decided that she needed to talk to this wise old man who she respected.

The rabbi's wife (affectionately called the rebbetzin) answered the phone. Rebecca Mann was a beautiful woman. Not being a person that would receive admiring glances for her outward beauty, but when one was in her presence, they were captivated by her inward virtue and beauty. Her labored breathing concerned Suzanne." Are you all right? You seem out of breath." When she laughed her large belly jounced and her entire body was set in motion. "Nothing that losing seventy five pounds wouldn't cure. I was preparing the meal for the Rabbi and was in the kitchen. She knew Suzanne well, having lived in the community for many years and present, along with her husband, at whatever events the Pollack family planned. "It's so good to hear from you, Suzanneala. I hope you and your family are well?"

"Yes, we are. The girls are all grown up and living on their own. I try to see my parents as often as I can, especially since they're getting up there in age. How are you, and your family?"

"We're all well, and have 10 grandchildren, Ken a hora.

"Would Rabbi Mann be home, and if so, could I please speak to him?"

"You just missed him by ten minutes. He went to see one of his congregants in the hospital. You remember Sam the Junk Man, well he had an operation and the Rabbi went to visit. He should be home within the hour."

"Thank you, rebbetzin. Tell the Rabbi that I'll try to call him back in the next few days if I have a chance. Nothing to worry about, I just wanted to talk to him. Would it be inconvenient if I leave my cell number with you? Rabbi can call me back at his convenience."

"Of course my dear. I'll leave the message with my husband."

Suzanne felt completely despondent. Usually, not a moody person, feelings of melancholy emerged. She wished that the Rabbi had been home so she could discuss her feelings and know that whatever her thoughts, he would not be judgmental.

Suzanne returned to the hotel and was grateful that Nancy and Justin were still out. She sat on the yellow and blue chintz sofa in the living room area and admired the matching drapes. Appreciating the solitude she shut the overhead lights; picking up one of the pretty decorative pillows, placed it behind her head. Closing her eyes, she let herself drift, imagining she was riding on a sailboat among the waves, moving with the motion, her mind reflecting back while looking at the sun's rays on the water. 'It's too bad I never learned to swim. I've been on so many motor and sail boats that I should have tried harder to learn. What a shame that after my parents gave me so many different lessons and still I was afraid to let go and just swim.' Suzanne fell into a deep, well needed sleep.

Chattering by the front entrance disturbed her reverie. Slowly arising from the comfortable sofa, the door opened and she saw her two friends enter.

Suzanne's cell phone rang and she immediately answered it. "Oh hi Rabbi, I'm so glad that you called." She walked into the bedroom and quietly closed the door.

Her two friends looked at each other and just shrugged.

When Suzanne and Rabbi Mann dispersed with congeniality, Suzanne told him what was bothering her. Her thoughts on her troubled mental torment were causing her anguish that she didn't want to have. The man of wisdom took a while to answer. He had to find the right words to help Suzanne, who he knew since she was an infant.

"Suzanne, let me begin by saying that you are a fine woman, a good, abiding Jewish Madala, who I've known for many years. You've had your ups and downs like all of us experience. You brought your daughters up with respect, love, and a kindness that most people couldn't have done under your obligations and duress. Let me tell you some stories and then you tell me what you learn from these Rabbis from long ago. Suzanne listened intently to his words of wisdom and sat there mesmerized. To make a long story short let me say this last piece of knowledge. It doesn't matter that Hope changes her religion. She doesn't realize that once born through a Jewish mother, that child will always, in Gods heart, always be considered a Jew. She knows, deep down, that no matter what church she attends, she'll still feel the yiddishkite that she grew up with. She'll teach her children, without realizing it, about the Jewish religion and customs that she grew up with. Remember, her children will be considered Jewish. I even think that although she baptizes her offspring, knowing Hope as I do, she'll still ask you and her grandparents to take the baby to the temple to give it a Hebrew name. Suzanne, don't be tormented by her decision. Remember what I've told you. Keep it in your mind and heart that you and I know the truth as does God."

"Rabbi, I can't thank you enough for your talk and wisdom," Suzanne emotionally verbalized. "I told Hope about her always being Jewish and in Gods eyes it wouldn't change. At least I remembered that much," Suzanne gave a halfhearted laugh. "One thing that I was sure of was that I'd never disown my child for changing her faith. I feel sorry for those people who see life as black or white. There's always grey, at least I think that way. My feelings are as long as she believes in God and is a good person and treats people with respect, that's all that matters to me. I feel much better and know, even if I don't tell Hope that I spoke to you, the truth. I'm definitely not distressed as I've been since finding out what she intends to do. I can't thank you enough. I can't wait to see and thank you in person. May you and your family have a long and healthy life." With that said, she walked out of the bedroom, a look of peace and contentment showed on her face.

Justin walked over to Suzanne and gently taking her by the arm escorted her to one of the sea pink and dawn blue striped chairs next to the beautiful fireplace in the suite. "I have just what the doctor ordered. Knowing that you don't enjoy indulging in a nice glass of hard liquid refreshment, a cup of hot tea is on the way. And yes, I know that the tea bag goes into the cup before I pour the hot water into it."

"Suzanne we have so much to tell you, but before we do, I must say I haven't seen you look this happy and content since your talk with the Rabbi. I won't ask you what transpired, it's your business, but whatever was spoken, it certainly did the trick."

"Thanks Justin."

"Yes, it's a personal matter and I appreciate your consideration. Maybe someday I'll divulge to you and Nancy our conversation, but for now thanks."

Nancy, sitting opposite Suzanne, couldn't contain the excitement building up within her. "Justin and I went to see Kyle and afterwards went to Curtis' apartment. Kyle again gave us his extra key but apparently the police, or maybe the owner of the apartment building, changed the locks, we couldn't get in. You weren't with us so we weren't able to use your expertise in getting into places we shouldn't be going. Meanwhile Justin had the best idea of all. If all the clues go in this direction we've struck gold. Justin has very strong suspicions that Curtis was involved in a very large international stolen art ring."

"You've got to be kidding," Suzanne uttered as she put her finished tea cup down on the top of the glass table next to her chair.

"If you don't mind, I'd like to finish the story and explain my position," Justin vocalized, as he rose from the comfortable sofa and began his tale. Suzanne was mesmerized as he strolled back and forth in front of the fireplace and continued his eloquent speech. "In the United States the only police departments that have officers who specialize in art theft are in New York and Los Angeles. Because we are already in California, today Nancy and I went to their department. Unfortunately, when I told them about Kyle's friend and the unidentified Japanese gentleman who seemed very interested and agitated about some art dealings they had together, the detectives gave little heed to my suggestion that this man might have something to do with the murder.

They did seem interested in the painting I saw at Art Weintraub's Gallery. I told them after I get the information from the other authorities I would get back to them. They were very receptive and thanked me for all this work that, they felt, was unnecessary but happy that I did it. They're looking forward to my getting in touch with the agencies that deal with international art theft. They told me that they sometimes work with some of those agencies as well and are looking forward to bring about the evidence that will convict the true criminal. They can't wait till I get back to them."

"I then got in touch with a dear friend of mine, Cindy, who has an investigative agency that specializes in art theft and investigates international thefts, be it large museums, individual homes, mansions or palaces. She was employed by the Smithsonian Institution and Interpol, the International Police Network, in its Washington office before she started her own agency about 12 years ago. With her help I think we'll ultimately be able to help Kyle. I realize that he's innocent, but the suspicion of some people will never leave until the right person is prosecuted. She agreed that the Japanese gentleman seems a viable suspect."

"Did you know that according to Interpol figures, 6,200 art objects were stolen in 1985. In the first eight months of 1988 more than 9,000 art thefts were reported. Auction houses have access to the foundation's art theft archives, which list more than 32,000 stolen works. But because it is a $1 billion a year industry, and increasing every year, as art prices have soared, the growing cost of insuring these pieces has become exorbitant. Premiums are at an all-time high. On the average, most museums pay one-half percent per month per million of valuation. That means if a museum has one or more pieces worth $100 million, the annual premium is $600,000. Most museums can't afford this. That's why individuals who have valuable art treasures that have been passed down from generation to generation can't afford to insure their beloved pieces."

"It seems that Mr. Curtis had a very lucrative business going on besides working as a curator and also being a manager of Mr. Weintraub's art gallery." Justin stopped pacing and taking in a deep breath shook his head. "I seem to be convoluting the issues. Let me conclude by telling you that this problem is very complex. There are many pieces to the puzzle that have to be put together. With Cindy's help we may be able to find the real murderer."

"I don't know about the two of you but I'm exhausted just hearing your eloquent presentation. There is so much to learn about the sinister, rich collectors who arrange thefts of priceless works or are willing to purchase such objects that my head is spinning. Let's take a break and while we're eating dinner you can tell us more about this world of art thievery," Suzanne suggested.

BOSTON MASSACHUSETTS

Madaline was restless after a week of confinement. Paul was worse than any doctor. He made sure that she limited her walking and put bounds on how long she could stand up and walk. The doctors told her to take it easy and use constraint in the use of her foot. She was to use crutches at all times until she was seen in another two weeks. 'This is ridiculous,' Madaline thought as she watched the boring television shows from her bed. 'I feel that Paul has me in prison. I can't go anywhere without him being there to help me. One good thing about being laid up like this is I get to speak to Kyle often and for once, I'm getting rest like I never had before. Beside the fact that Paul isn't hard to look at. I can't wait till I'm completely better and maybe I can make a move on him. Oh, listen to me. I should be ashamed of myself. He's the investigator that's paid to take care of me and make sure I'm not in harm's way. '

A loud knock on her hotel room door took her out of her meditative state. It took her awhile to get out of the bed and when she picked up her crutch and finally made it to the door. She made sure to ask who it was. Satisfied that it was Paul she gladly let him in.

Not saying hello, he hurried to the sofa and told her to join him. Madaline had seen him focused before, but the distraught look on his face scared her. "I've been thinking and nothing makes sense. We've gone over your list at least a dozen times and something's missing. It doesn't add up." Looking deep into her beautiful, violet eyes he took her gently by her shoulders. "Madaline, I know you think you've told me everything about yourself and the people you have contact with, but there has to be something you're not telling me."

"Think real hard because the next time an accident might happen, it could be fatal. I don't want to scare you but it's serious. I've been lucky with most of my cases and I can gladly say that the people I worked for came out of their situations with not a scar. I admire and like you too much not to get to the bottom of this." Trying not to laugh, he put his hand over his mouth. "After all, I wouldn't want your case to discredit my reputation as being a top notch PI. I don't know if you realize how serious this person is and wants to either cause you bodily harm or even see you dead."

Madaline sat there with her mouth open. She was at a loss for words. At once she seemed exposed and wanted to unlock the buried secret in her heart and soul. As close as she was to her old friend Anne, Suzanne and Nancy, she felt she could never unburden her heart to them or anyone. She sat there startled. She didn't know where to begin. Madaline could feel the brim of her eyes spewing with salted tears.

Whenever a role called for tears she always thought of her first born. The ultimate giving her loved one away, not knowing whether it was a girl or boy, not being able to love that child, even if it was conceived in a bad way, made her heart break. She often wondered who had adopted her baby, where it was being raised and if the child was ultimately happy. What did this child, who was now a grown up, look like and have any characteristics of her? What color eyes, complexion, hair, how tall and what kind of built did this person have? She wanted the baby to have grown up happy and become successful. She often hoped it was a girl and looked like her. All of these unanswered questions were like knives sticking into her very soul. How could she, after all these years, unburden her torment to this man, really a stranger to her, begin to tell her story.

Paul saw Madaline's tears and knew that he hit a home run. The tears he saw falling from her eyes onto her cheeks were genuine. He moved closer to her. She was in mental pain. He knew from experience that when someone kept secrets hidden, it was awful to finally unburden those hidden, hush-hush, clouded mysteries. He wanted to shield this woman, who he had grown to admire, and if he admitted, fallen in love. Paul saw her torment and emotional distress. With all his wishing, he hoped she would reveal her secret. He could see her anxiety and sorrow and suddenly pulled her closer and held her in his arms. He patted her hair then went lower and rubbed her back with long strokes. He cradled Madaline in his arms like a parent consoling his child.

His soft whispers of encouragement made Madaline feel stronger. Her sobs started subsiding and he held her at arm's length, wiping her tears with his hands. "Hey, it's not as bad as you think. Just relax and try to take deep breaths. You're all right. Unburden your soul and have trust in me," an encouraging Paul coaxed. He could feel her tension relax a bit.

Madaline felt ill. After all these years of keeping her one secret to only herself, she now felt obligated to tell, of all people, Paul, this hidden, veiled, personal matter.

CHAPTER TWENTY FIVE

Justin finished telling Nancy and Suzanne about other aspects in solving thefts through print and it was truly a fascinating subject. If what Justin said was true, with Cindy's help, Suzanne was sure that they would find Curtis Jones' killer. "Edward Murrey, the managing editor of Trace, a glossy international magazine, also a friend of Cindy's, will try to lend a hand to recognize some of the stolen antiques. Especially with other reputable art dealers and friends who are appraisers, belonging to Appraisers Association of America, are bound to come up with some answers," Justin explained to his two friends.

Suzanne, Nancy and Justin were positive that these people would be of assistance in getting to the bottom of the crime. Justin went on to clarify that because the Appraisers Association of America addresses stolen art in its code of ethics, the Art Loss Register, established a few years ago at the International Foundation for Art Research, with the support of a number of concerned companies, including major auction houses, most always knew when artifacts were stolen and then tried to be sold on the open market. Suzanne was leaving this part of the investigation to the experts in their field. The auction houses are major users of the system and refuse to handle stolen art. With everyone's help Suzanne was sure that they would catch the people responsible and see that the authorities would deal with these crooks.

Meanwhile, Suzanne and Nancy went through the various papers that they found from Curtis's hiding place. There was a multitude of papers that had to be sorted out. On a separate part of the floor, they put piles of papers from various banks, both in America and foreign countries, and in the off shore banks that had sizeable amounts of money in the accounts. They also found names of stolen art pieces with pictures and on the opposite side of the ledger, names of the museums from all over the world, private collections and the names of European estates they thought might correspond to the theft of these valuable items.

In another two ledgers they were fortunate to find the names of the people whose homes that these various art objects and pictures were taken from. It was unconscionable the money that Curtis received when exchanging these pieces to the people who ordered these abducted works. The two women tried matching the various pieces with their new owners. They then sorted the piles from The United States and foreign countries. It was unimaginable to read the amount of paintings that were stolen from the many museums throughout America and abroad. "Nancy, look at these castles and large establishments, from various countries, that had some serious, well known paintings stolen."

"Oh my God, I remember visiting some of these buildings, with a few of the girls that I went to private school with. We were impressed and in awe by these paintings. We stayed for hours examining the various colors, pigmentations and the different size brushes used by these famous artists. We were amazed that the palate knives used to facilitate making objects, like a simple seed from a lemon, for instance, it's amazing. These artists were such talented people. Some of the girls were in the art program and hoped to become interior decorators, graphic artists and a few of the real serious girls, who always excelled and never got less then A's, wanted to eventually become curators of famous museums and galleries. I think it's awful the way these villains take advantage of people whose ancestors were once wealthy aristocrats, noblemen, counts, duchesses, and so forth, who inherited these properties from their relatives. These people usually don't have the money for the enormous insurance policies that are required for these priceless pieces," exclaimed Nancy.

"Are you finally done with your opinions?" A frustrated Suzanne pointed out. "There is so much to do. It looks like we'll be here for hours to sort out all this work. We have to continue with this project and when we're through, I know that we'll feel we've done all the necessary steps and go to the police with our information."

"I'm sorry if I droned on about the plight of these people. I'll just keep it to myself and I agree, let's get to work," an apologetic Nancy replied.

Both women, again, got on the carpeted floor and spread the rest of the papers in front of them. They sorted the information as to financial holdings and establishments in the various countries and the dates when the money was deposited. They hoped that they'd be able to match the deposits with when the various artifacts were stolen. They expected that Curtis had written the names of the people that appropriated them. "We certainly have a lot of work ahead of us."

"I agree Suzanne. I know this room is huge but with all these files I hope we'll have enough room to spread them all out."

"Never mind that, I want to be able to walk. I've been sitting with my legs on my tush that when I finally get up my lower extremities will be asleep and have muscle cramps. Yes, I know, be careful and walk around the various piles of paper when I have to use the bathroom. Now where did I put my reading glasses? Have you seen them?" asked a concerned Suzanne.

"I swear, if your head wasn't attached to your beautiful body, you'd have lost it long ago."

"My mother used to tell me that all the time. Half the time I can't find my keys and when I do, they were right where I should have easily found them. Oh well, we all can't be as perfect as you," declared a witty Suzanne as she cuffed Nancy on the back of her thick red hair. She touched her own hair and found her glasses sitting on top of her head. Suzanne shook her head as she got up to get a glass of water.

Suzanne made a decisive effort not to let her personal agendas hinder what was in front of her. In 2½ hours they found themselves with only a fourth of the material filed and sorted. "I don't know about you," exclaimed Nancy but besides my butt, my back is killing me."

"Hey, you're a lot younger than I am. Do you hear me grumbling?"

"Weeeell, aren't you the woman who was complaining about muscle cramps?" Suzanne then told Nancy, "I know you so well that I can see the pain on your face when your body is aching."

"Let's take a little break and get some lunch. I really want to go to a restaurant, I can't stand looking at this room any longer," declared Nancy.

"I'll go along with that." Helping each other up, they walked back and forth to get the feelings back in their legs. Looking like the Hunchbacks of Notre Dame, they tried straightening their sore backs. After half an hour Suzanne started feeling human again. "Let's primp a bit to look presentable in the public's eye."

"I don't know why we're worrying about how people see us, I could care less. Besides, I don't know them and I don't want to start," A snobbish Nancy replied.

"I don't believe I'm hearing this. You are the most down to earth person I know," stated Suzanne.

"By now, shouldn't you know when I'm jiving you?"

After stuffing themselves with a light but fulfilling lunch they went back to their grueling effort to finish the job at hand.

The following day Suzanne had to work at her Beverly Hills Salon and was looking forward to the break from filing and sorting out the numerous documents. Thoughts of her immediate family kept re-entering as she worked on her client. Her daughters where patient but after this prolonged visit to her California salon they were becoming resentful at her obvious absence. The last time she spoke to the girls she could hear their questions, without being said, as to why she was in California for such a long time. Hope wanted and needed Suzanne's input for her upcoming wedding

Forcing to withdraw from herself and put a different perspective on her current family situation she tried to look at the matter as an outsider. How would she react and what advice would she give if one of her clients told her that her daughter was converting. 'Was it fair to Hope for Suzanne to resent her oldest daughter's decision?' She asked herself. What little she saw of Spencer she liked. Chastising herself, Suzanne effectively finished her client and prepared herself mentally to finish the day's work. Her being away from home, and from the other locations, in order to fulfill her obligation to her good friend was putting an undue burden and strain on her daughters and employees. The only solution to this dilemma was for her and Nancy to solve this case as soon as possible so they could get on with their own lives.

Nancy came into the salon at the end of the day. Mentally and physically exhausted, Suzanne slumped into one of the comfortable waiting room chairs.

"Do we have plans for this evening? The design for the jet is finished and the engineer would like us to meet with him this evening."

"That was rather fast. I didn't realize he would have the plans ready this soon. Sure I guess so. I better call Robert Redford and break our dinner date. I'm wondering what's your hurry to finish this plane business. I mean we have so much more work to do on this art business that I don't understand how you can bring the airplane into the equation," Suzanne verbalized.

"Don't be a wise ass. Are we getting a little nervous thinking about flying in our own plane?" Nancy chortled.

"You know Nancy, nobody likes you. You are a mean and nasty person." Nancy walked over to Suzanne and hugged her dear friend." Come on, I'll treat you to dinner."

Oblivious to Suzanne's apprehension, Nancy went on to explain how she finally chose the manufacturer and make of their new aircraft. "Do you realize how many privately owned jets are out there?" Waving her hand in the air she continued. "I could have bought a great used jet but decided if we're going to get a plane then we'll get a new one. That way we can custom design the interior and decide on the cabin length and height to our own specifications." Nancy continued. "We also have to make sure of the fuel capacity and be able to fly many miles before we have to refuel. That's going to be imperative when we make jaunts too far away countries. Of course the cock pit is very important as well. I can see in your eyes that you really don't care." Suzanne felt embarrassed about her obvious inattention. "I'm sorry Nancy, please continue."

"Well, there are a lot of manufacturers and I had a lot of research to do before I made up my mind." While waiting for their table Suzanne got serious. "Nancy, I know that once you get something in your mind, you won't let it go until it's finished. I appreciate your concern about my fear of flying and really, even if I don't say it enough, thank you for all you've done. I know it's not been easy and I honestly don't know if I would have had the patience to do all the exploration necessary for this assignment. So thanks. The little I know about corporate jets is that they're extremely expensive. I'm talking mega millions."

"Suzanne, I've never really told you the amount of money that I have. You don't ask so I keep quiet about my finances. I can assure you that by buying this air transportation, yes it will cut into my money by hundreds of thousands, if not a million or so, but let me assure you, it won't break my bank. Why do you think that when you announce that you'd like to open a new spa I don't blink an eye?" Putting her hand on top of Suzanne's, Nancy continued. "Honey, we both have certain qualities that the other person doesn't have. That doesn't make one person better than the other. You are creative, have imagination plus great ideas and thankfully, I can help you fulfill your dreams. If I didn't have confidence in you and your abilities, believe me, I wouldn't be here. Don't you worry about the cost and enjoy going along for the ride." Laughing out loud Nancy announced, "I'm so funny. Not to embarrass you, but did you get my quip?"

"As a matter of fact I did." Suzanne tried to suppress her laugh but had a hard time doing so. Trying to change the subject, "what time do we have to meet this man?"

"I want to stop you before we head out," Nancy held onto Suzanne's arm. "Just because I was lucky to have inherited mega millions I'm also a great business woman. Do you think I'd invest in the spas if they weren't extremely lucrative and I feel my investments have paid off?"

Not another word was spoken. Suzanne smiled when the waiter came over with their meals.

"We have plenty of time. Let's enjoy our dinner. When we're through I'll call the manufacturer's rep. I want your input about certain interior designs and I know you'll become excited once you see the artistic arrangement on paper. Till then relax, eat to your heart's content. The cockpit is important and realistically, the two of us should take flying lessons in case, God forbid, pooh, pooh, anything should happen to the pilot. I know about some of the instruments and auto pilot, but it would be to our benefit to really know how to fly this airplane."

"I don't believe what I'm hearing. First she gets me to try to conquer my fear of flying. By the way I think I'm doing pretty good, even if I say so myself. Now I'm told that in order to have our own plane we should take lessons and learn to fly it in case of an emergency. I really think you're going insane. Who do you think I am? Sky King's wife? Do you really think I'm going to go along with your asinine idea?" a perturbed Suzanne asked her friend. Looking across the table at Nancy, Suzanne realized that she was serious. "Okay, okay, I'll think about what you're saying. I'll take it under advisement. Before I do go along with this crazy notion, and I'm not saying yes for sure, you'll probably have to hog tie me and put me on a lot of drugs." Suzanne was nervous and intimidated.

Nancy could see perspiration on Suzanne's forehead. Suzanne suggested that they change the subject. "At least till our meeting with this representative, if that's okay with you? We can't get away from our main objective. You think that I'm bad with my A. D. D.? Let me tell you Missy, you're almost as bad as I am. You have a dozen ideas going through that pretty head of yours," declared Suzanne. "All at one time."

"Sure, sure, I'll give you time to digest what I've suggested. But one last thing, you'll find out that I'm right, a conciliatory Nancy announced."

Over cocktails the two women discussed the situation they found themselves involved with. "I hope Justin comes through for us and can help us prove Kyle is completely innocent of any wrong doing." A concerned Suzanne pronounced as the waiter brought out their desserts. "I realize that technically they really don't consider him a suspect at this time. But you never know what might come about. I really want, and hope that you also feel the same way; to find the rightful killer of Curtis Jones. If the police don't, people will always believe, in the back of their minds, that Kyle was the person who killed his lover."

"Knowing Justin, I'm sure he has everything under control," Nancy acknowledged. "By the way, where is Justin this evening?" Finishing her shrimp scampi she was ready to eat half of the dessert she ordered. Suzanne informed Nancy that Justin was meeting with a New York art attorney and general counsel for the AAA who happens to be in California for his nephew's Bar Mitzvah."

Trying to change her dear friends thoughts she continued, "Meanwhile if the engineer has done his job and we like his plans, I don't see what's to stop us from owning and flying our own plane within the month. That'll be exciting!"

"I'm so thrilled. Can't you see me jumping in the isles for joy," Suzanne sarcastically replied. "I'm sure it's going to take more than a month to finish this assignment. I'd be afraid to fly in the thing if they need that short a time to get all the kinks out of it. Let's hope that after a month they come back and with sincere apologies, tell us it'll take a little longer than they had anticipated," Suzanne retorted. "By the way, we were still talking about the art project. Let's not change the subject thank you."

Nancy enjoyed teasing her best friend but couldn't help taking pleasure in the hope and knowledge that Suzanne will eventually overcome her emotional insecurity of flying. "Suzanne stop being a pessimist. You're the person who's the optimist. You always see the glass half full. Once we own our means of transportation, you'll see how nice it'll be. We'll make sure that the maintenance will always be up to par and then it will be in our complete control. I'm sure once you know where everything is supposed to be and every bolt, wire and tire has been inspected, it will put you at ease. I don't know if you realize that we get our own hanger and imagine, no security lines or delays. There's a special lounge for people like us, with waitresses to accommodate our food preference. They also indulge your every whim. That's reasonable requests, that is."

"Oh darn, I thought they might put a Genie in a bottle and get Stephen to get divorced and ask me to marry him."

"Suzanne, you are truly crazy."

With Suzanne's one eyebrow lifting," are you sure it's only food that they want to assist us with?"

"Suzanne Morse, your mind is in the gutter," Nancy frowned as she gently slapped her partner's hand. "Let's toast to having control of situations," Suzanne asserted as she lifted her glass of rosé. Looking up, she said a silent prayer, (Dear God, I hope we're making the right decision and everything will go as planned). 'I think I'll be saying the serenity prayer all the time we're in the air,' Suzanne thought to herself as she tried adjusting to the idea that Nancy proposed. "After the meeting let's get back to the hotel and try to finish the current assignment."

SAN DIEGO, CALIFORNIA

Yoshy was once again seated behind his desk at his California offices trying to assess the latest cutbacks of his enormous organization. His secretary interrupted his train of thought. "Excuse me Mr. Makino, a Mr. Nobuaki for you on line one. He said it was important."

"Ohayo gozaimas (good morning)I hope I'm not interrupting."

"It's all right. What can I do for you, my trusted friend? I was hoping we could get together for dinner within the next few days. A matter has been brought to my attention that I think you should be made aware of." Not a man to waste time Yoshy arranged to meet with his old friend and leader (The oyabun – the leader of a particular Yakuza organization) of the Yakuza (One of the many Japanese crime organizations, they are located throughout Japan and the United States --- like the mafia) at the Polo Lounge the following evening.

The unexpected rain storm caught most people by surprise as they dashed for cover. Yoshy was no exception. He ran from his limousine to the entrance of the Beverly Hills Hotel hoping the down-pour didn't ruin his expensive silk suit. Flapping his suit coat he walked quickly to the men's room blotting his coat and suit jacket with the towels provided. Concentrating on this procedure he didn't notice the rather large gentleman emerging from the stall and standing in front of the wash basin. Yoshy felt better as the excess moisture seemed to be evaporating from his outer garments. He once again walked to the lobby and looked into the lounge to see if his friend had already been seated. Unable to spot him he seated himself on one of the comfortable sofas provided in the vestibule and waited patiently for his friend to appear.

Suzanne, Nancy and Justin were seated at one of the booths waiting to place their order when Justin noticed an old acquaintance at one of the tables across the room. Excusing himself he left the two women telling them to order him a scotch on the rocks. "Nancy, I hope Justin will be able to tell us something viable, anything will be better than nothing. It'll be interesting to hear what he has to say about his talk with Mr. Weintraub" an anxious Suzanne proclaimed. "I'm getting rather frustrated with our inability to process all the information we have and will be getting. I'd like to get this assignment done."

"Not to mention that you might be eager to return home to your family. By the way, when is Stephen coming to California to see you?" Suzanne waved her hand as if avoiding the discussion. "You know me all to well," Suzanne replied with a twinkle in her eyes. Trying to avoid the subject matter, she announced that she saw Justin talking to his friends.

"After a while Justin returned to their table. While waiting for their round of drinks, Justin told them about his friend who he unexpectedly saw. "As a matter of fact William is quite well known in the art community and he might be able to help me sort out some of the questions that are bothering me about Mr. Curtis Jones and his extra-curricular activities. I have a rather impressive list of art objects that I found in Mr. Weintraub's gallery that might have been stolen from estates in Europe. Besides giving the list to Cindy and Edward Murrey, I just gave a list of them to William and he'll get back to me in a few days. I think there is more to this Curtis Jones than meets the eye," Justin declared. "I hope we can sort this out for all our sakes."

"Speaking for myself, and I'm sure Nancy, I can't tell you how much we appreciate all that you're doing. Did you mention to your friend William about the files we found and the various bank accounts from around the world? We also were able to find where Dependable Cleansers is located and we'll be paying them a visit within a day or two. We'll talk to the people who he worked with and get some input there. Also there were a few numbers on his phone bill that came up occasionally. Some telephone numbers couldn't be traced because of some sort of barrier that was a private number or something like that. Besides the obvious banks and people who we found bought some of the stolen goods, the name of a chemical company and the company that designed the security system for the art museum was on the list as well, Suzanne exclaimed. I'm sure that he knew someone at the security company that gave him the plans. We'll try to find the traitor once we speak to the owner of the company."

Suzanne and I are doing extensive research but I think we have to go to the detective who's in charge of this case. With all the information we've obtained I think we're in a position to negotiate the information that they've got along with theirs. What's your opinion Justin?"

With all the help of the people that I know in the art world, I'm sure some of the questions we have will be answered shortly. That doesn't stop us from trying to collaborate with the people in charge of this crime. Yes Nancy, I think it's a great idea. The sooner the better as far as I'm concerned," Justin agreed.

"Changing the subject I think we were lucky we were able to secure a suite that consists of two bedrooms with two king size beds in each one of the rooms. As far as the weather, the Californians want us to believe that they have perfect weather all the time. This downpour we're experiencing today is an example. They must have their share of foul weather once in a while," Nancy exclaimed as she sipped her wine. Nancy recounted her and Suzanne's meeting with the engineer designing their different toy, as she liked to describe their new means of transportation to Justin. "By the way Justin, I want you to know that this airplane will be at your disposal anytime you might want or have need for it. The cabin length is 26 ft. by 7ft. 5" in height. You might have to bend a little while walking, but there are two spacious living areas that enhance productivity and it will accommodate each person's needs. There'll be a lot of open space and the cabin is spacious. The oval windows will provide abundant sunshine and we have 100 per percent fresh air from our filtration system. I figure that with all our international traveling, this plane will meet our needs. We can relax and have a pleasurable flight while doing any work that has to be done."

"Suzanne you seem a bit quiet. Are you all right?" A concerned Justin asked.

"It's a bit overwhelming for me to imagine all of this. I'm a poor girl from Dorcherster and it freaks me out thinking that I'll be having my own plane. My friends back home wouldn't believe how I've prospered. She remembered how people told her of mama Pollack's ability to see into the future. She wondered if she somehow inherited her ability to have prophecies, good and bad. She remembered that mama Pollack told one of her great grandson's to play the lottery and, sure enough, he won a million dollars that evening. Nancy snapped her fingers in front of Suzanne's face. "Suzanne, you look like you're a million miles away, are you okay?" Suzanne came out of her reverie and just chuckled to herself when Nancy mentioned the 'million' miles away. "Sure, I just got caught up with the past and got emotional thinking of my grandmother Pollack."

"Thank you Nancy. If I ever find myself in a bind, I'll certainly take you up on your generous offer. Looking over to Suzanne, Justin proclaimed to Nancy. "I see our friend is rather quiet" Justin teased, as the waitress brought his dessert of a mile high, crushed Oreo, ice cream pie over with their coffees and tea. "Are you sure neither of you would like to share this delightful, tantalizing confection?"

"Just looking at it I can see myself gaining five pounds," Suzanne grimaced as she sipped her regular Salada tea." And I don't think you're funny, even one iota, ridiculing me on my phobia about airplanes. Everyone has fears or concerns about something in their lives. Most people don't admit they're mortal or relay the fright they have to others. Who'd want to be ridiculed by their trusted friends," she acrimoniously lectured as she looked from one friend to the other. "Come on," coaxed Suzanne, "Let me hear, just one of your fears, each of you. Ha, I knew it, you're afraid to be vulnerable if anyone knows about them," Suzanne smugly smiled as she finished her tea. "If looks could kill we would be dead" teased Nancy. Justin exaggerated a wounded heart.

As they were leaving, Nancy noticed a gentleman seated on the couch in the lobby. Not wanting to be obtrusive, Nancy couldn't help looking at him and thought she knew him from somewhere but couldn't remember from where.

Yoshy looked up and saw the attractive red headed woman looking his way.

She looked vaguely familiar. He spotted Nobuaki heading his way and rose to greet him. At once Nancy remembered the nice gentleman who she spent many hours seated next to on the plane when she was flying home from Japan. Not wanting to be rude and interrupt his obvious meeting she hesitated going over to him. However, even though she sent him a note of thanks, she wanted to thank him personally for the beautiful briefcase he sent to her office after she inquired about his well-made one. "Excuse me, I'll be right back," she explained to her friends as she walked over to see Yoshy once again.

Nobuaki was the first to notice the elegantly attired woman approaching. Stopping their conversation, they waited for the uninvited woman to intrude. Extending her hand, she once again introduced herself to Yoshy and thanked him for the briefcase that she now used regularly. Yoshy introduced his friend to Nancy. Nobuaki bowed stiffly and couldn't wait until Nancy left. He hated interruptions when he had serious matters on his mind.

In the background the soft music contributed to the placid atmosphere of the hotel. It seemed apparent to Yoshy that Nobuaki had something of importance to discuss but was taking his time, enjoying the relaxing mood of the restaurant. "Well I'd better get back to my friends. Again, thank you for the lovely briefcase. Turning to Nobuaki she bowed, "It was very nice meeting you." Nancy put her hand out to shake the other gentleman's hand, but instead he bowed as she remembered most Japanese people do.

Dismissing the interruption, once the waiter brought their drinks, Nobuaki became serious. "My friend, how long have we known one another? Twenty five years would you say? In all these years have I not been a good and loyal friend?"

"Yes, of course you know how highly I regard our friendship. What is this meeting about? I feel you are obviously troubled. I hope I'm not the cause of your worries. What can I do to help? After all, you always help me in my time of need."

"I heard some rumors that disturbed me greatly. These terrible accusations put my organization in great danger. It seems word is out on the street that one of my men had a key part in the death of one Curtis Jones. As far as I know only you, Hirokito, one other of my trustee captains and myself were the only people privy of this information. I don't want the Yakuza blamed for any crime in the white man's world." He whispered, "What the pale faces don't know won't hurt them. Seriously, I have to get to the bottom of this report and squelch it. Do you have any idea how this rumor started?"

"Yoshy told Nobuaki that "I also heard some gossip about the murder. I honestly don't know how it started. Are you sure that Hiro actually committed the crime? I once heard that he often calls upon his good friend Takashi to do some of his dirty work. I understand that at the time of the killing, Takashi took one of the dead man's paintings abruptly, for a job well done. I believe that is the painting that he bestowed to you and you generously gave it to me. Is that not true? But getting back to our conversation, now this is just hear say and might not be factual. I know how much you use, rely and trust Hirokito."

"I swear on my only child's life I don't know anything about what you're now telling me." Obviously distraught, his small eyes squinted as he let Nobuaki's words penetrate his thoughts. "How can this be? As you said only the four of us know of this. I can assure you I haven't told a soul. Why would I? That would seal my fate and establish me as the major source of the crime. I know you wouldn't, but what about Hirokito or Takashi? Are you sure one of them didn't let something slip." Nobuaki defended his loyal and trustworthy soldiers. "Hirokito has been with me and the Yakuza for many years, as Takashi. They know the penalty for disobedience and the consequences if he should let any of our dealings be known. One way or another, someone will pay dearly for this indiscretion. I might bring Takashi over to my house and ask him some pertinent questions. I'll get to the bottom of this, if it's the last thing I do." Yoshy had a hard time finishing his meal because of the lump that suddenly appeared in his throat as he heard the menacing threat of his friend.

Heading back to their hotel Justin once again explained his plans to his two trusted friends. "I'll make sure we resolve this terrible situation in record time. After all, although I have all the confidence in the world leaving Alan in charge of both galleries, I'll feel better when I'm back making all the decisions." Looking in the rear view mirror, waiting to see his response, Suzanne amusingly expressed her thought. "Are we a little paranoid about losing control of your galleries?" A stern look, eyebrows coming together got the response she was waiting for. "That's not fair, you know I have all the confidence in the world in Alan's decision making. I admit it's hard to let go after many years being the only person making judgmental calls. I guess it comes with the territory." Justin shook his head and announced, "Age does seem a factor according to what other people think. The younger generation doesn't seem to have the respect for the older person's ideas and experiences. They'll never realize the wisdom we've retained throughout the years. Those people soon find out that time doesn't stand still and that someday all of them find themselves in the same position."

Back in the hotel room the three friends had one last cordial before retiring for the evening. "By the way Justin," Suzanne proclaimed, that was a very good observation you made about middle aged people and the younger generation. I might add that what goes around comes around and life is full of surprises." Raising the remaining glass of Ameretto, Suzanne lifted her glass. "I'll drink to that." They clicked their glasses and were ready to end another day.

Lying down, trying to lose herself in slumber, Suzanne found herself unable to do so. The stillness, usually comforting and peaceful, had the reverse affect. The darkness enveloped her, like an albatross, suffocating with each breath she tried to take. Struggling to gain her composure, she attempted to gain control of the various situations that incessantly pushed Morpheus out of reach. Her heart ached for Madaline and Kyle's dilemma. For everyone's sake she had to get to the bottom of this terrible injustice. Although people saw two beautiful, rich, and well known celebrities in their own right, Kyle and Madeline's' life would be ruined if Suzanne, Nancy and Justin didn't find the real killer or killers and end this horrible nightmare that her two dear friends found themselves in. In the back of people's mind their questions would never be answered unless the real murderer was found. 'This time I have to admit that Nancy is right about going to the authorities and working together. I hope they want to.'

At the same time, her own perplexing situation kept reappearing, haunting her like the ghosts of her deceased ancestors. She could see her dear departed grandparents turning in their graves at the thought of one of their great-grandchildren turning her back on the customs and religion of their heritage. Suzanne knew she couldn't keep putting off the inevitable. She had to tell her parents about Hope's decision to convert. It was one thing to tell Hope that she wouldn't give her a hard time about changing religion, but deep down Suzanne was heartsick. Although Suzanne didn't feel herself an orthodox or religious zealot, she felt spiritually, and morally God fearing. She believed in honesty, keeping the Ten Commandments and treating others as she would want them to treat her. Knowing that her forebears went through persecution just because they were born Jewish, her own great grandparents and great aunts and many cousins were persecuted and later killed because they were Jews, only made Suzanne feel worse.

Anguished and mournful, Suzanne couldn't help but think, 'my own flesh and blood could denounce what the Talmud teaches us to live by and no longer worship with us and share the Jewish Holidays and customs truly is making me sick. I know I shouldn't feel this way, but, God, what can I do? I know I'm a good person, I have faith in Your beliefs and yes I'm proud that I'm of the Jewish faith. Yet deep in my heart I'm mournful. I can't lie to you and say I don't care because I do care. I know Hope will be baptised and taught about another religion and she'll teach her children to believe in a Christian God. God forgive me, but I can't disown her. I won't go to her baptism, yet if and when she has children do you think I'll then give in and attend theirs? I don't know those answers, yet I'll keep praying for your guidance and when the time comes, only then, I'll know what I'm to do.' Suzanne was sobbing quietly, thinking about her heritage and feeling sorry for herself that she wouldn't have one of Hope's children or grandchildren be named after herself when she died. (for in the Jewish religion when someone dies a child is named after them, only then will they have immortality of the soul.)' And what is to happen annually on the anniversary of my death. No one will light a candle and recite a prayer in my honor.'

(*From the book: What is a Jew? by Rabbi Morris N. Kertzer 4th edition. What is the Torah? Torah is our way of life, "All the vastness and variety of the Jewish tradition." It is synonymous with learning, wisdom, love of God. Without it, life has neither meaning nor value. More narrowly, the Torah is the most revered and sacred object of Jewish ritual the beautiful, hand-written scroll of the Five Books of Moses (the Bible from Genesis to Deuteronomy) which is housed in the Ark of the Synagogue. The Torah scroll is made of parchment, wrapped around two wooden poles or rollers. What is the Talmud? (Consists of sixty-three books of legal, ethical and historical writings of the ancient rabbis. It was edited in the year 499 c. e. in the religious academies of Babylonia, where most Jews of that period lived. The Talmud is a compendium of law and lore, and has been for centuries the major textbook of Jewish schools.)

After tossing and turning for what seemed hours, sleep finally took over. She found herself dreaming of herself, as a youth, living back in Dorchester and enjoying her days living with her parents, grandparents, aunts, uncles, all of her cousins and life as a youngster amongst her peers. She could never forget her involvement in the Hect House and the many summers walking the length of Nantasket beach and finally exhausted, laying down on her and her friends blanket on the sand at Kenburma Street. Those were the days when you wouldn't think of going out with anyone other than someone of your own faith. 'How times have changed,' she thought, as she slowly emerged from her dream. Thoughts of her Christian friends in Quincy made her feel a little better. 'They and their families were wonderful people and had great values. They believed in God. Most people are good and it doesn't matter what religion they are, if you're good you're good.' With a smile on her face, as the rays of the sun shone through the curtains, Suzanne gradually awakened. "Good morning," Suzanne cheerfully acknowledged as her two friends were finishing their breakfast.

"We thought we'd let you sleep in this morning, after all, it's not often Justin and I have a chance to talk about you."

"Very funny," Suzanne retorted trying to act angry. Ignoring Suzanne, Nancy remarked, "isn't it nice to see the sun once again." Justin agreed. "After all, California is known for its sunshine. Now, what's on the agenda for today?" a curious Suzanne asked.

"Well, I'm heading downtown with William to visit Mr. Weintraub's gallery." Justin told Suzanne and Nancy as he poured Suzanne her tea. "I don't know about the two of you, but I'm getting frustrated," Nancy declared. "It seems we're just spinning our wheels and going nowhere."

Suzanne poured another cup of tea and said, "I have a gut feeling something is going to break. It's like a sixth sense." "We still have to go and see Detective Colangelo and give him all the information we gathered. I'm sure he and the people working the case will find our efforts useful and speed up the process. After all, we are the ones that found that stack of papers and ledgers. You'd call it shit luck. I hope with all our effort they'll be able to assimilate the papers and make some sense from the information we gathered," announced a pleased Nancy.

"Come on Suzanne, admit when you're defeated. There's nothing wrong with being human and giving up. Let the authorities do their thing. I'm sure they'll find the real murderer soon," Nancy half-heartedly spoke what was on her mind. "That's what I really believe and at this point, until I'm told differently, I don't feel our work has been in vain. We know that the informant from the alarm company got him the plans and that was how Curtis Jones was able to get into the Huntington Museum and we now know that he was part of the cleaning crew that came in after the museum closed. He was a shrewd one, he made everything work to his advantage," Nancy proclaimed.

Adamantly defending her position Suzanne announced, "I'm staying here for a while longer. If you want to go back home than I think you should. I really appreciate what you've done and you're right about not getting very far in our investigation. And, Metamorphosis does need one of us at headquarters. Please, Nancy, don't feel you have to stay on my account. I promise that I'll just stay here a while longer and wait for Justin to finish his part. I also can't forget that Stephen will be here within a day or two."

"If you really won't get mad, I'd like to get home; even for a few days. I'll probably come back if I get bored, which will probably happen. Will you call me every day, even if nothing new develops?"

"Sure I will. Let me call the airlines and get you an airline ticket for home."

CHAPTER TWENTY SIX

"You won't need to. Last evening I got a phone call and saw the final plans for our jet. I wanted to surprise you, but my plot has been diverted. The two of you were sound asleep. I didn't want to disturb you so I met him at the hotel's lounge. I took it upon myself to accept the designs he made. I'm really excited being the first person using our new means of transportation. Can you believe it, our plane is finished and I'll be the first to use it, and I know how much that kills you," Nancy declared as she walked over to Suzanne and gave her a gentle squeeze on the way to her room to pack.

"Nancy, you were the person who persuaded us to make it happen. It's only fitting that you be the one to first use it. But what about the flying lessons we need to take in order to own the plane?"

"I worked it out with the company and when I get home I'll start the lessons. When you get home you'll also take them. To make you feel more secure, I'll be flying with you, alongside the instructor."

"It better be good, cause I'll never find a partner as whacky as you." Suzanne got up and ruffled Nancy's red hair and hugged her tightly. "Seriously, I know all will go well and you'll call us once you're home. Listen, I'm talking to you like I'd talk to my kids. Shoot me now or forever hold your piece. Besides, it's like a hop, skip, and jump from California to Boston. It's not an international flight where you'd have more hours in the air."

On the ride to the airport Suzanne broached the subject of Nancy's recent divorce from Peter. Getting up the nerve Suzanne took a deep breath and asked Nancy if she thought about dating yet. "You know you're still young and I'd hate to see you waste the few remaining good years you have left. How about me setting you up with one of Stephen's bachelor friends or eligible men? You can only mourn for so long and then you have to get on with your life."

"You know Suzanne, I hope you're only teasing. I'm still young. There are more important things in life than having to worry about a man." Gently punching her friend's arm Nancy changed the subject. "Seriously, I'll be speaking to you every day for an update. When the time is right you'll be the first to know when I'm ready to jump into the dating scene. Meanwhile the pilot will fly back here and when you're ready he'll pick you up and get you home soon. I'm sure Hope needs you to help with her wedding plans."

As Nancy was climbing the stairs to board the plane she looked back and yelled so Suzanne could hear her,' remember, there are plenty of fish in the sea!' She then vanished into the luxurious cabin. Poking her head out of the cabin one more time she yelled to Suzanne and Justin, "I might just come back sooner than you think if the two of you don't get your act together and solve this stupid mystery. Don't forget to call Detective Colangelo and set up a meeting, a.s.a.p., and start working together. I'm sure all the pieces of the puzzle will fill in before you know it."

About one hour after they left Nancy off at the airport, there was a knock on their door. Suzanne and Justin looked at each other and wondered if the other had ordered anything from room service. Suzanne arose and asked who was there. "It's me Nancy, would you please let me in." With a look of confusion on her face, she looked over to Justin and shook her head.

"What brings you back so quickly? We heard you tell us you might surprise us by flying back, but this is ridiculous. Did something go wrong with the plane? Not that I'm glad to see you," Suzanne verbalized as she hugged Nancy. Jokingly Justin asked Nancy, "Did you find out that the airplane wasn't really ready yet?"

"You wish it. No, I got to thinking about what I'd really like to do and don't you dare laugh at me, when I tell you what's on my mind."

"Go ahead. Justin and I promise not to ask any questions or laugh at your remarks."

"You got me thinking about my current situation of being single once again and if you say a word until I finish my story, honesty, I'll never forgive either of you."

"I was seated in the rich, leather, swivel chair and picked up one of the updated magazines that was supplied. While reading some article that didn't mean much, Rich Colangelo's face suddenly appeared before me. The pilots were making their plans for takeoff and talking to the tower. I don't know what came over me but I stopped them from engaging the engines and told them that I changed my mind. Thanking them I told them to take a few days off and we'll call them when we're ready to depart. Now that's taking my heart over sensibility. You must think I'm crazy." Putting her palm up she stopped her two friends from speaking. "Before you utter one word, I think there might be an attraction between us. He hasn't said anything to encourage me, but I feel something when he looks at me. I haven't been able to get him off my mind and leaving would be a coward's way out. I'll give it until we finish the job that we came out here to do and if nothing comes out of it the way I hope it does, then," shaking her head she declared, "what the hell, I tried my best."

Suzanne and Justin looked at each other and shook their heads. Justin got off the chair and went over to Nancy. Enveloping her in his massive arms he held her. He kissed her forehead and then holding her away from him he spoke. "With all that you've gone through these past years, you'd be disappointed with yourself if you didn't listen to your heart and tried to see if there's a chemistry between the two of you. All I can say and I'm sure that Suzanne would agree with me, go for it girl!"

Sighing, she smiled deeply. "Thanks for not saying or thinking I'm crazy. You're not verbalizing that I'm a bit of a mashugana means a lot to me. Thanks for your support."

"All is fair in love and war," declared Suzanne as she sat down.

"With most of our papers sorted out and the information we accumulated, I think it's time that we get in touch with detective Colangelo and collaborate. Tomorrow seems as good a time as any other," Suzanne told her friends.

"That's a great idea and I don't know why I didn't think of it. I'll call him tomorrow morning and make a time for all of us to meet. After all, how would it look if I went alone," Nancy winked at Suzanne and Justin.

Yoshy had a hard time concentrating on business. He couldn't understand how the Yakuza's name became associated with the murder of Curtis Jones. He kept going over and over in his mind about the various people who could have breached this confidential information.

"Excuse me, Mr. Makino, Robin Sinclair on line 2." "Yoshy, darlin. When are we gonna get together. I miss you. It's been so long. Are you still mad at your little darlin?" Relaxing just a bit, Yoshy was glad for this intrusion. "Of course I miss you. How about this evening, unless you have plans?"

"I'd break anything for you, you know that."

"Good, I'll see you about 7:15. How about a quiet evening, just the two of us?"

"Sounds good to me."

On the way to Robin's Yoshy could feel his excitement as he remembered how Robin felt in his arms. It seemed an eternity since he had made love of any kind. Instructing his driver to pick him up in the morning Yoshy let himself in. Soft music played background music as a drink was waiting for him on the table in the hall. A loving note and instructions were beside the liquid refreshment. Removing his clothes he lowered himself into the hot bubble bath that was waiting for him. Closing his eyes, enjoying the tension release from his muscles, he was greatly surprised when a naked Robin came in and knelt beside the tub with wash cloth in hand.

The soft cloth felt good as the circular motion started at his shoulders and crept downward with increased pressure. She gently lifted his arms and massaged his skin with the cleansing gel on her hands as she let her hands replace the cloth. Finger by finger, taking her time, deliberately and tenderly with changing motion, then emerging her soft hands onto his legs, repeating the same, waiting for the suggestive procedure to take full effect. His organ was now hard as she repeated the movements. She continued her seduction. He pulled her into the bathwater, holding her at arm's length above him. Her large breasts swaying and touched his chest. His excitement was more than he could have imagined as he lowered her onto his inviting throbbing instrument. "You confident little kitten. You knew to take off your clothes and wash me suggestively. The vixen I wanted emerged and surmised what would happen once my response was yielding to your seduction. "You foxy lady!" Yoshy laughed as he lifted her off him and they both emerged from the now lukewarm water.

Her warm body felt good as he lay beside her. He heard her rhythmic breathing and looked down onto her beautiful, guileless face. Unfortunately, he remembered, what had occurred. Without realizing that he mentioned names and Robin was aware of his friendship with Nobuaki, and Nobuaki's association, he concluded he must have bragged about his art acquisitions and how his friend helped him out of a complicated situation, after one of their love making sessions. Although Robin was naive, her immaturity, in all probability, led her to disclose this important information. He felt violated that she would tell someone his personal business dealings. He could feel his anger mounting and knew he somehow had to suppress it. "Here I'm thinking it's Robin who's responsible for this breach and it might not be her. How can I be sure, he asked himself? His mind was racing. Somehow he had to get to the truth or Nobuaki would go after no one else but yours truly. He hoped with all his heart Robin didn't betray him. He was confident she wouldn't, then he fell into a deep sleep.

Taking two steps at a time Justin knocked loudly on the bedroom door to Suzanne's sanctum. Out of breath, Justin rushed in, not realizing that she was trying to go to sleep. "Well, all is not lost," boasted Justin as he recounted the events of his long day. "Remember I said I was going to the Weintraub Gallery, with William? We then decided to visit the man in charge of the museum."

"Yes," replied Suzanne, slowly emerging from a sleep instilled daze. "I found out that one of the men from the cleaning crew is missing. It seems that the other two cleaning men were drugged. Apparently, to me at least, he was the man who stole the paintings. He seems to have vanished into thin air. This janitor used someone else's social security number and the police can't produce him because that poor bastard died two years ago. According to his description this man must have done his homework and is or was a cleaver person. Anyway, when I went back to the Weintraub gallery and asked the owner if anyone he might of known or saw ever visited there, I then gave the description from what the owner of Dependable Cleaners told me. At first he couldn't think of a person. After a few minutes something might have jarred his memory. He told me that he saw a person such as I described coming out of his gallery one evening when he had to go back to the store unexpectedly. He thought that the gallery was closed. Thinking it was strange, the following morning he asked Curtis who the man was. Curtis dismissed Mr. Weintraub's question with a joke saying he must have been seeing things. Now I'm not any Sherlock Holmes, but it seems to me that there is a lot more to this Curtis Jones than meets the eye."

"Unfortunately, because of his demise, we can't get the answers from him, and because of his death, poor Kyle has had his whole life turned upside down. Now I know this is far-fetched, but hear me out, what if Curtis Jones and this cleaning man was one in the same?" Completely awake Suzanne sat upright and gave Justin her full attention. "Go on, I'm with you all the way." "By the way, Nancy and I had a similar discussion and wondered how the thief was able to get into the Museum with such ease. It makes sense," she said as she rubbed her eyes waiting for his next conjecture. "I'm saying this because Nancy and I went to the cleaning company. In some of the papers we found we had pay stubs in a different person's name other than Curtis.' It collaborates our theory. Suzanne agreed with Justin, "It makes sense that once Curtis died they couldn't find the cleaning man because they were one in the same." "You know Justin this is so bizarre that it could be true. I'll go to Kyle's house later today and find out from Kyle more information about Curtis, even the smallest detail. Why don't you try to find any background and family information about Mr. Jones and then we'll compare our notes." Suzanne was so excited she had a hard time falling back to sleep after Justin left her room. 'Maybe that's why the police can't seem to get anywhere with this case. Most people are logical and by God, maybe we needed a little bit of creative imagination and gut intuition with some luck to clear this case,' she thought as she turned over and tried having Morpheus take over.

Suzanne awoke early. Many thoughts emerged as she sat down and made herself a cup of tea. Before she put a list of the cleaning people who cleaned the

Huntington, she remembered one of the papers she and Nancy found. They knew it had something to do with the museum. She thought it was the floor plan and another paper showed how the security system was laid out. She called out to Nancy and the two women remembered these papers and it was one of the items that they were bringing to Detective Colangelo.

"Let me bring the papers to Rich," Nancy announced. With a gleam in Suzanne's eyes, she agreed. As soon as Suzanne let herself into the suite she sat on the sofa and patted the seat for Nancy to sit next to her. "Before going into the spa, let me tell you what's transpired since I left you at the hotel. I decided to also go to the cleaning office and interrogated, listen to me, I sound like a police woman, the two guys who worked with this Cyle. The description fits Curtis to a tea. Well, almost. This Cyle had blond hair and wore a beard and mustache. If you ask me, not too imaginative. Being an artist himself he could have found other ways to make sure he wouldn't be recognized. Remember that movie with Eddy Murphy about the Nutty Professor. Now that was makeup and his makeup people changed his build as well. If he had done a good job I honestly don't think that anyone would have been able to guess it was him, even with his disguises. Anyway, there are a lot of ways he could have disposed of his cover up. I think I'll check some of the car rental agencies and see what might come about. I'm telling you, Nancy, this keeps getting better and better all the time."

After filling her friend in with all the details, Nancy asked if she would mind going with her next month to their new Japan Spa. "I'd love to, only if Kyle's case looks as if its going to go our way."

"Suzanne, don't give me that bullshit. You'd think of anything not to fly that distance especially in your own plane. I know you all too well. And don't make excuses about Hope's wedding. A few problems have come up at the Spa and only you and I can fix them. Give me your word that you'll come with me. Besides, we can make a mini vacation out of this, I know you've been under a lot of stress between Kyle and Hope. This will help you unwind." After promising Nancy she would make the trip did her friend end their conversation? "By the way, I found out that many of the Islands that comprise Japan has hot springs, when you're there you submerge yourself in them. They're supposed to give you medicinal and spiritual effects like you've never experienced before. Personally, I can't wait to try it."

'You make it sound very attractive. I might even enjoy the relaxation once we figure out the problem you seem to think we have over there. But, and this is a big but, we have to have all the evidence to make sure this puzzle is solved. That's the only way I'll be able to go with a clear conscience." After thinking Suzanne's ultimatum over Nancy nodded her head in agreement. "You win. I only hope we can clear this dilemma quickly.

Suzanne found the ride to Kyle's luxurious apartment depressing. Talking to Kyle at his spacious apartment still felt empty without Carol's presence. "Don't worry, you'll be out and about, working and leading a normal life." assured Suzanne as she touched his fingers. "That's laughable" a scornful Kyle replied. "I don't think I'll ever be able to lead what you call a normal life again." I'll pretend I didn't hear that. I want to find out as much as I can about Curtis. Don't dismiss anything. I know this is painful but believe me, I think Justin, Nancy and I will find a way to get all suspicions and accusations away from people thinking that you're not innocent. I assure you that the three of us will find the person who killed Curtis."

She then turned on her tape recorder. Kyle looked at the recorder with suspicion. "I see that look. I promise you that no one will get their hands on the information you're telling me. I'd die before letting anyone know about this confidential conversation. Except Nancy and Justin of course." Suzanne started asking and listening all about their relationship and the little known facts about Curtis Jones. "Don't forget to give me some pictures of Curtis. I think it's necessary that we have them to go by."

After leaving Kyle's place Nancy was waiting for Suzanne to emerge from his apartment, ready to drive back to the hotel." I want you and I to go over more of the documents that we found hidden at Curtis's apartment." 'With all this international banking and off shore laundering it seems like yesterday when we dealt with a similar situation with the entire drug cartel and money laundering scheme,' Suzanne thought to herself.

Mitsuko was cleaning Nobuaki's spacious apartment. Obedient as always her heart missed a beat as she answered the door and let in Hirokito. Not daring to look directly into his eyes, she quietly led him into her master's private quarters. Nobuaki motioned for Hirohito to sit as he finished his conversation. "My loyal follower, I have some disturbing news that does not sit well with me. Maybe we can clear up this matter and get to the bottom of our troubles."

"What is it Nobuaki? I've never seen you so upset. Let me help you."

"It seems the white world has found out that we're responsible for Mr. Curtis Jones' death. Now I have to find out how this information got to them. Do you have any idea?" a perplexed Nobuaki asked. Dumbfounded, Hirokito shook his head in dismay. "I swear by my life and that of my loved ones, no one knows of my involvement in this matter. As far as I'm concerned only you, Yoshihiro, Takashi and I knew. How can such a thing happen?"

"I don't know, that's why I summoned you here. We'll find out who leaked this betrayal, that person will know the consequence."

Hirokito was sick to his stomach. He had used Takashi many times and there was never a screw-up. The man was sharp as a tack and reliable. In the past, Hiro could always depend on him to do anything asked of him and do it right. Feeling the digit of his pinkie finger he was sure that another digit would be removed. He didn't want another yabizume to happen if his oyabun found information incriminating any of his family, especially the people he trusted. He had to call Takashi or better yet, go and find out what might have gone wrong.

Hiro parked his car. With trepidation he knocked on Takashi's door. After a few minutes Takashi opened his wooden entrance. "Come in, come in, what brings my friend to this part of town? Can I get you some tea or maybe something stronger? "Motioning for his friend to sit down he smiled as if he hadn't a care in the world.

Hiro, trying to be gracious, shook his head no and wanted to get to the reason of his visit. He took the liberty of sitting on an oversized chair and looked into his friend's eyes. "I saw Nobuaki and he wasn't pleased by a rumor that he heard. It has to do with the murder of Mr. Curtis Jones. Somehow the word is out that the murder was committed by the Yakuza. Not good." Crossing his legs he kept staring at Takashi, making Takashi nervous. "What's on your mind, my dear friend?"

"I received a call and went to our oyabun's house. He's very disappointed in what he hears. I am ultimately his Saiko-komon. (the next in authority) You my friend, my brother, Waka gashira, as you know. The word is out on the streets that the person who killed the pale ghost also took a painting. Is this true?"

Suddenly Takashi's stomach was in knots. He wanted to vomit. He felt like a caged animal ready to be executed. "Hiro, you've known me all your life. You're like a brother to me. I don't know why the Yakuza is being blamed for this killing. Honestly, I don't. Yes, I took a painting from the apartment. Maybe I shouldn't have, no I should have known better to do such an act. I didn't mean anything by it. It was a keepsake for me. Can you understand? I then felt guilty and remember I gave it to you. You in turn gave it to Nobuaki and he was very appreciative of your gesture."

"Yes, I remember, I wanted him to think that I was the person doing the job asked of me. That's why I gave him the picture."

Hiro clicked his tongue, shaking his head. Nobuaki is very disappointed in the way this incident is turning out. Ultimately, I'm the one who should have gone through with my consignment. I'm his Saiko-Komon. I thought you would be able to do the murder without any screw-ups. Now we both will pay for my stupidity in asking you to do what was my assignment. Nobuaki will see both of us as soon as possible. By the way, have you told anyone about this job?"

"No, I swear on my devotion to the Yakuza. I never mentioned a word to anyone."

"Then how did this incident become common knowledge on the streets, huh?"

"I don't know. Wait a second, one of my friends visited me and saw the picture sitting up against my wall. He admired it and made a comment about it. I guess I told him that I got it from a pale ghost and he started laughing. He put two and two together and must have told some other friends. I swear, on my mother's life, it was an accident. I'm not sure if he's the person responsible for the rumor. In my opinion he is a stupid person who wouldn't have put the two incidents together. No, come to think of it, it couldn't have been him."

"Well, we are both going to pay a high price for your stupidity. Come with me, we have to present our severed digit, wrapped in a towel to our Oyabun. We'll ask him to forgive us and swear nothing like this will ever happen again."

Takashi was shaking all over. "This has never happened to me before. I'm scared."

"Unfortunately, this will be my second act of forgiveness. This will teach me not to ask anyone for help. I'll do my own job from now on. Come, let's get this over with. The quicker the better. I hope you have some very sharp knives."

Justin, Nancy and Suzanne spent the entire evening going over Kyle's taped conversation. Justin asked for Suzanne to reverse the tape a bit. "Go back to the part when Kyle was coming out of the shower and he heard the stranger talking to Curtis. Did Kyle say he sounded foreign or had an accent?" Nancy interrupted, "I also think Kyle said something about opening the door just a crack and he saw the man. If I'm not mistaken, go back to that part Justin, that Kyle thought he was of oriental heritage. Not an ordinary man but a man of distinction and well dressed."

"Well that narrows it down to about a couple of million people we can look for," Justin sarcastically announced. "Not that I'm putting pressure on us, but we'd better do some fast and conclusive investigating. I promised Nancy that I'd go to Japan with her in the next month. We can't forget that there are a lot of spa's that need our input and help. Let's outline some sort of plan and get going."

"Justin, do you remember what Kyle told us how the oriental man was dressed? Before I went to Japan, on my first trip with Nancy, I looked up on the net all sorts of material I could get my hands on about Japanese customs. I remember reading about a large and different organization, made up of various gangs from Japan. Let me think..... Oh yes, they were called The Yakuza. It's an all man's society. It's like the mafia in America. It seems that The Yakuza has branched into Japan's government and also has organizations here in the States. Now I'm not saying that The Yakuza is responsible for the killing, but somehow they might be linked. What do you think?" asked Suzanne.

"Let's get in touch with Rich and find out more about this organization," Justin suggested.

It seemed the days flew by as Justin and Suzanne questioned people that knew or had dealings with the elusive Curtis Jones. Again they went to the professional cleaning company that hired him to work at the Huntington Museum. "Da," Suzanne muttered, if we had gone to the Huntington Museum first they could have told us the name of the cleaning company that they dealt with. I feel like an idiot." Suzanne berated herself in front of Justin. "Well dear, all of us aren't perfect like me." Justin smiled as he expertly filed his nails against his shirt top. Suzanne and Justin booked it over to the cleaning establishment and got the two men who they wanted to speak to. They questioned the gentlemen who were victimized by the thief who stole the paintings. All in all Justin and Suzanne had a pretty good idea and knowledge of one Curtis Jones. When Suzanne showed the two co-workers Curtis' picture they couldn't positively identify him. On a second picture that Suzanne found she drew the blond hair, mustache and beard. Al and Lou thought that this was the man they knew as their fellow work mate. Nancy, meanwhile was doing her own investigating.

When the three friends converged Nancy suggested, "I think it's time for us to get together with detective Colangelo. The department has resources available to them that they can use. They have fantastic artists and imaging processes that we could never get a hold of." Suzanne said, "We could if we called our friends from the Boston FBI, but I really don't want to impose on them. I know they'd be willing to help us, but let's try to co-operate with the San Diego police department and see what we come up with."

Nancy arranged a meeting for the next day.

Suzanne looked at Justin and wanted to cry. "How can I not get to the bottom of this? Nancy and I will have to postpone our trip to Japan for a while until we go over all the papers we found in Curtis's closet and get the numbers and places where he had accounts. From there we'll try to coincide the dates of some thefts from Europe or here in the States and try to piece this puzzle together. We still have a few more days left. Let's get to business," Suzanne explained to her two friends. "I bet when we go to headquarters and meet with Detective Colangelo and his team, between the two factions something will come out of this information."

"By the way, detective Colangelo has some positive feedback from the police artists and they're going to show the pictures to the gentlemen that worked along with Curtis. I have a good feeling about this. Detective Colangelo showed me the various sketches and were able to get different versions because of Kyle's many pictures. This Curtis loved to pose and especially for someone as famous a photographer as Kyle. I guess they could have gone to the morgue but it was easier for the artists to use these pictures. Personally, I don't know how a Medical Examiner and their assistants can stand to go down there day after day."

"Not to be redundant, but I already did that with the cleaning people. We went there together, remember?"

"I must have forgotten when I spoke to Rich. Anyway, he told me that the M.E. has gathered more information and it seems everything is coming together. The only thing that they haven't been able to do is to find the weapon that actually killed him. He thinks that some of his informants on the streets, might be able to find out certain information that people would be reluctant to give the police. "Nancy informed her two comrades. "Luckily some police men, and Rich is one of them, has a good relationship with these characters. It seems that this community of defeated people, most of them down and out are homeless, want to befriend the cops. It seems that they're targets for characters that pick on them, steal what little they have, sometimes killing them, just for the fun of it. These people that prey on the destitute are scum who I'm sure will go to hell," Nancy declared as she had to walk away, ashamed that her friends should see the tears coming from her eyes.

BOSTON, MASSACHUSETTS

Madaline didn't know where to begin. She trusted Paul and wanted to unburden all the unpleasant and hurtful incidents and experiences that happened to her throughout her life time. She saw Paul waiting patiently.... waiting for her to begin. "I know this isn't going to be easy for you, but you have to trust me. What is said will only be between us, I swear. But, these life's happenings have to be discussed. Maybe we'll be able to sort them out and finally get to the bottom of who wants to hurt you."

Trying not to look directly at Paul, she put her finger in her mouth. "I don't know where to begin."

"Honey, start at the very beginning and go on." She took a deep breath and started telling him about her childhood, parents, siblings, and friends. Taking another deep breath, her entire insides quivering, she had a difficult time relating the horrible incident that changed her life forever. "His name was 'Uncle Harry.' He wasn't our real uncle, but all of us kids called him that. He was my daddy's oldest and best friend and was always at our house helping my dad out doing chores and mending fences and things like that. Sometimes he would drive us kids places when my parents were busy and they sort of relied on him to help us out. I don't remember him having a job or anything; maybe I tried suppressing that information."

While relating the betrayal and horrible event that happened, tears freely flowed from Madaline's eyes. She tried wiping them with Kleenex but no matter how she tried taking control of her emotions, she couldn't. Madaline was visibly shaking. Paul understood her discomfort but urged her on. "Can you believe that my beloved parents didn't believe me. How could they have thought that I was the type of girl that played around and got caught? I have never forgiven them and I don't know if I'll ever be able to." She told Paul all about her Aunt's house and how she couldn't hold the baby and didn't know if it was a boy or girl. Taking another deep breath she continued. "When I finally came back home everyone made believe that my having this baby never happened."

"Life went back to normal and they pretended that all was fine. Everyone but me. I was never the same again. My mom was the only person that had empathy and gave me her meager savings to leave and find a new beginning. I was scared to death. I was still a youngster and I was left alone, not knowing what I wanted to do or where to go. I remember reading those magazines about movie stars and that's how I went to Hollywood. That's the only time in my life that I found happiness. Of course there are always people who are jealous and try making it difficult for a new person to get into the business." Taking another deep breath she calmed down a bit and offered Paul some lunch and refreshments to be brought up to the room. "After we eat I'll continue with my life story. I hope it will help you get to the bottom of this horrible nightmare."

Paul relaxed a bit and assured her that by her relating everything to him it would help. "There are a lot of possibilities that I'll be investigating."

Madaline had a hard time swallowing her lunch, trying to keep it down was a chore. She knew that by cleansing her heart and soul it would be a beginning to the end. Pushing himself from the table after enjoying his corned beef on rye sandwich he finished his coffee and pronounced, "Are you ready to continue?"

With paper and pen in hand he continued writing down the imperative notes that, hopefully, would help him with his investigation.

It was easier for Madaline to relate the happenings in Hollywood and her involvement with Brad and her continued success in the business. She actually laughed when relating the times she had with Anne Browning and Mrs. McCalum. "Anne, besides Brad, were the two people I could rely on while living in the city of sin." She then told him about 'dear Sheila' and the gossip columnist who tried ruining her reputation. All of this was written down by Paul. "You have to realize that in my type of business people are two faced. Nice to your face but behind your back ready to put the knife to you. I was lucky that Suzanne and Nancy became the type of friends that I can rely on. There are other people in my profession that I can call friends but they're few and far between."

Paul wanted all the names of the people involved in her entire life and where she thought they might be living.

"The only person I don't know that you'll be able to find is my child. By now an adult."

"I'm going to get in contact with your aunt and the midwife."

"I don't know if they're still alive. I certainly hope so. They thought they were being helpful to me and the family."

"I can't even imagine the emotions you had to go through. God, it must have been awful."

"I'll never forget those months for the rest of my life."

Paul took Madaline in his arms, trying not to let his feelings show. "I can't thank you enough for finally being honest. With this information I believe we'll get down to this business shortly."

"Paul, Suzanne and Nancy have no idea about my life before I came to Hollywood. Even Kyle doesn't know. He remembers Brad and some of my so called husbands after Brad. Those were the biggest mistakes in my life. I guess I was looking to fill the void that Brad left. But I can honestly say that he was the love of my life. I don't think I'll ever be able to replace that feeling. I would appreciate that what was said today won't go any further than this room. I don't want Kyle, Suzanne or Nancy knowing about any of this. As a matter of fact, one of my oldest friends in Hollywood, Ann Browning, doesn't have a clue of my life before I came to Hollywood. I mentioned that I was raised on a farm and had a few siblings. She tried prying more information from me, but I wouldn't tell a soul. I was so ashamed of what my life had been like before I came to the 'city of sin'."

Getting up from his chair and holding Madaline at arm's length he assured her that whatever was said in confidence would never be told to anyone; that her secret was safe with him. Looking directly into her eyes, that he thought were the most beautiful he'd ever seen, he vowed, "We'll get to the bottom of this and afterwards, when this nightmare is behind us, we'll go out and celebrate." On his way out the door he hoped that Madaline would change her mind and let him, if not replace Brad, become part of a new life and a happy beginning for them both.

CHAPTER TWENTY SEVEN

As promised, Paul arrived early at the hotel, ready to work. With more pens and papers in hand, he confidently knocked on Madaline's door. Paul sat at the table waiting for Madaline to finish dressing.

"Paul, my stomach is growling, would you mind if we go downstairs and have some coffee and maybe, if you feel up to it, we might look at the breakfast menu. I realize that we have a lot of work ahead of us. If we begin with a hearty breakfast I know that I'll have a better attitude and I'll be able to remember events a lot better. As it is, this will be a grueling enterprise. We should do everything in our power to help us proceed in the best possible way."

"That's very thoughtful Madaline, but if it's all right with you, I'd rather have coffee and breakfast brought up. I don't think we can waste any time at this point."

"Okay, whatever you say. I guess you're right, let's sit down and get started. I know that what I tell you will seem repetitious," Madaline pouted as she called for room service.

"I took a massive amount of notes and think that maybe something else, that you could have forgotten, might come to mind. Now this might not be true, but I'd rather be cautious than do things half baked. Before we start I'd like you to be able to timeline the people and incidents that were in your life and we can then fill in any blanks that you might have forgotten. Does that sound okay with you?"

"Exactly how far back do you want me to go?" Madaline was showing her nervousness by twirling her hair and trying not to look directly at Paul's eyes.

"Let's start with your parents, their ages, where they were born and then go on to you and your siblings. The children you went to school with and every neighbor in town."

"Isn't that going very far back? I don't mean to misjudge your ability, I know you've been doing this type of work for many years, but I think that's a little far-fetched."

"Why don't you humor me and do as I ask. It might seem trivial, but I assure you, when least expected, something or someone might come to mind that could possibly be your nemesis."

"Well, okay, you're the boss." Madaline had to think about her parents and siblings for quite a while to get the time line right. She tried to remember who the children were that had been her classmates. "This is the first time in years that I've thought of these kids, who by now are grownups. Lucky for you I came from a very small community, the grades were held in the same large room. It sounds like 'Little House on the Prairie' but believe me when I tell you it wasn't like that."

"What do you mean by that," Paul asked. "Well, in a way, if I remember that particular television show, most of the people were nice, except the rich girl with the blond curls. She was really jealous and a bitch."

"Did you get along with all of your classmates or were there one or two that gave you any type of trouble.

"Most of the kids were great. The teacher knew all of us since we started school from the first grade on. On occasion there were two girls who were jealous of me and my large family. They didn't beat me up or anything like that, but they did mean and hurtful things like stealing my homework, making up stories about me and my family. We tried ignoring them most of the time. You see, growing up in a small town such as ours, nothing is ever private. Some kids were mean and nasty but for the most part nothing bad happened. Now a days what they did was absolutely bullying but because they were girls, they didn't think about it in that sort of way."

"By any chance would you remember their names and it'll be up to me to find out what happened to them since then."

Smiling at Paul, Madaline told him that they were probably still in the area, married and raising children. "By now they must have some grandchildren and are helping raise them as well. Don't forget some people are hypocrites, even though they've probably changed their ways and go to church every week. I'm sure that they forgot what happened."

Ignoring Madaline's remark he told her to continue. "Besides my family my best friend and confident was Billy Martin. He lived down a ways and their farm was next to ours. Billy was an only child so he enjoyed coming to our house and blended right in."

"Wasn't he the young man that your parents thought got you pregnant?" Paul asked.

"Yes, and it was stupid. When we were younger, like most kids, we'd talk about someday getting married and having children of our own. We were youngsters. As we matured we'd laugh about our thoughts and still remained friends. When I landed in LA I would write him and tell him what was happening and he was my confidant. He always responded and we kept our friendship for years. After a while as our lives got busy and more complicated the letters became less frequent and eventually we went our separate ways. I never forgot the way my parents acted when they found out about the terrible accident and since then I haven't had the same relationship with my family. As a matter of fact, I never got in touch with any of them again. Once in a while I'd call my mother and let her know that I was fine and tell her on more than one occasion that without her money I would never have been able to make it through those first grueling years."

"Madaline, do you know what happened to Billy after you stopped corresponding? Did he ever get married and does he still live in the same area?"

"It's been many years since I thought of him, I honestly don't know. But if you think that Billy might be the culprit, I think you're off base. He was a great friend through my entire life and I honestly don't think he'd ever want to see any harm come to me."

"I'll take your intuition into consideration, but I still have to follow through with him. I hope you understand where I'm coming from."

"I do, I hope this situation resolves quickly. I don't want to make any more enemies than I have."

With a frown Paul asked, "Do you really have many people that dislike you? If so, I know it will be grueling but I'd like you to take your time and write their names down and the reason for them disliking you."

"If you're serious, the list will take forever. In this business everyone is envious and tries to stab you in the back. There might be some people who have more grudges than others. I'll admit that, but I think these are petty and don't amount to anything."

"Leave that up to me to discern what kind of grudges they have. If any of them really hate you enough to do something that would hurt you and maybe want to see you dead, injured, or permanently disfigured for life, I have to know."

"Now you really have me worried. Between my movies and stage work there are many people that this particular list would fill an entire book. Honestly, I'm a nice, kind, and considerate person and try to be as pleasant as possible to all the people that I work with. I have to admit that I'm a perfectionist and sometimes make people's lives miserable when things don't work out the way I want them to. It's not that I'm a diva, like a have a reputation to be, but when I say jump, I expect people to ask how high." At that remark Madaline had to laugh.

"Remind me never to get on your bad side," Paul chuckled. ."I know this particular assignment will be difficult to do, but I really want you to go all the way back to the beginning of your career and go from there. Try to remember all the movies you've been in and then go into the plays. Who knows, this could be the list that will probably be the most valuable. I want you to list everyone, from designers, make-up artists, hairdressers, other actors who played with you and even stand ins."

"Do you want me to include stage hands, which will be very difficult to name? The actresses, the stand-ins, who know the entire play will be a breeze compared to some of the other people you want me to list. These stand-ins wait on pins and needles hoping that something happens to me so that they might get discovered. I mean it. They can't wait to become famous from the wonderful performance that they give."

"That's exactly what I'm getting at."

"Okay, now let's go backtrack a bit to your youth and think of the other farmers in the area. I also want you to give me the name of your aunt and that mid-wife who helped deliver your baby. I know it's going to be a painful memory, but a very important one. We have to find that baby, who is by now a grown up person and how they feel about adoption and how they grew up. By that I mean what kind of parents did they have, what kind of life they lived, how they were treated by their adopted parents and I'll try to find out everything I can about them. I'll contact agencies to lawyers who provide private adoptions."

Madaline was exhausted and truly wanted this nightmare to end. "I know I'm famished. You must be equally tired and hungry. The breakfast we had just didn't do it for me. Would it be possible to stop for a while and get out of here and go out to a restaurant? Not a fancy one, just somewhere that has descent food."

"I thought you'd never ask. My hand feels like I'll get carpal tunnel any moment. Let's leave for about two hours and then come back and continue. We should re-coop by then and see how much farther we can go. I know you have to get back for your evening performance and I'll take it under consideration to make sure that you get some rest before you have to go on."

`"Thanks for the consideration," Madaline remarked sarcastically, as they left the suite to fulfill the desire for food that would eradicate the hunger that they were experiencing. They accomplished to satisfy the ravenous feeling that was interrupting their train of thought and again started from her marriages, people who were hurt by them, gossip columnists, and then he went to Uncle Harry and the terrible situation that ruined Madaline's youth.

At five thirty Paul called it quits and walked her back to the theater.

The next morning, while Madaline was toweling herself dry, she heard the familiar knock that she was getting to resent.

"Isn't it a bit early to start the grueling session," she bitterly asked Paul.

"Believe me. Do you think I wanted to leave my bed early this morning? I'm as tired as you. The only reason I'm being persistent is because I want this job finished as much as you do."

Feeling like a total bitch she apologized and asked him to come in. I know you're doing this for my well-being and just ignore me when I get like this, okay."

She then told Paul about her aunts and relatives and went into detail about her stay at Aunt Mabels farmhouse. I never got to hear the Midwife's name. My mother called to inform me that Aunt Mabel died, God bless her soul. I know she thought that she was helping me and my parents through a hard situation and for that I'll forever be grateful. It hurts me when I think of the birth of my baby and how they wouldn't let me see or hold it, even for a few seconds. I still think that was cruel."

Paul interrupted Madaline at this time. Let's get back to your baby. You told me that they put it up for adoption, if I heard you correctly."

Yes, I definitely remember them saying that to me. They thought they would be helping out some young couple who couldn't have children of their own."

"Often times that's the case, but there are times when people do have children of their own and think they're doing a favor by taking in an infant that they think no one wants. Do you remember or does your mother remember if your aunt kept the baby around the South Dakota area where she could keep an eye on the little one as it matured? Now don't get your hopes up. She could have also put the newborn up for adoption and then it could have gone anywhere in the U. S."

"I was in such a state that if they told me, I put it out of my mind and honestly don't remember what transpired."

"You'll have to give me a date of the birth. That might help if the child was put up for adoption. Years ago you wouldn't have had a chance to find any information pertaining to the baby. With new laws the children and the real parents or parent can find out where the infant was placed, with who, and all sorts of things. Remember, nowadays, with all the medical problems and history, it's vital for the offspring to know their biological history."

"That's one date that I'll remember for the rest of my life. August 17, 1990. I got pregnant when I just turned 14 yrs. old. Can you believe how young that is? I delivered the baby when I was only 14. I know you're going to ask me my age and I never, ever, divulge that information. But, I realize how important this time line is so I'll tell you all that I can. I was born in 1966. Okay, okay, I'm 44 years young and if you breathe a word of this to anyone, I swear I'll follow you to the end of the world, if I have to, and kill you with my bare hands. You know I never thought about how old this child is before all this insane problem came up. My baby is now 20 years old. Now that really makes me feel mature. But I'll tell you another secret that you have to swear on your life you'll never divulge to a soul." Paul promised that he would die before he let out the secret she was about to reveal. "Suzanne is older than I am." Putting her hand over her mouth Paul could barely hear her when she softly said, "there's 2 years difference in our ages. I'm not going to tell you her age but she had her first child when she was only 20 and you can figure the rest out for yourself. Don't forget that her children are older than Kyle."

Putting his hands in the air he laughingly uttered and swore that he wouldn't tell a soul. "Cross my heart and hope to die, if I divulge your secret. Personally, I don't see anything wrong with being 44 or for that matter Suzanne's age. I crossed that line a few years ago myself and as long as I have confidence, still act young, keep myself in good shape and look youthful, who the hell cares how old I am," admitted paul. "It's how you feel that counts. Personally I feel as if I'm in my early 30's, so there. Now that's my thoughts on the subject on age and I won't mention it again." Shaking hands, that subject was closed to them both.

"Paul, I haven't asked you before today, but how do we go about the task at hand?"

"That's what you're paying me for. Try to get that off your mind for now, I know you're excited about this revelation, but we have to continue. The smallest detail can be crucial."

Madaline continued with her life as it started on Kellum Avenue and Ann Browning. She remembered Mrs. McCallum with admiration and most of the boarders that shared the boarding house with them. She continued on with Sheila and that miserable gossip columnist and the people, who she could remember that were cast members of the movies she made.

"I never realized how many people that I had contact with. My God, we filled up three complete secretarial notebooks and used up all these pens."

We're still not finished. Now we have to concentrate on Kyle and his friends. After that we have to list and find those husbands of yours, that are still alive."

"Those worthless husbands, in my opinion would either be dead from drug abuse or living life in the fast lane, if you know what I mean. But we'll see how many of those characters you can find. Looking back on my life I often ask myself how I could have married those no good for nothing losers. Oh well, you live and learn."

Madaline continued, "But it sure was fun with some of them, while it lasted that is." With a dreamy look in her eyes she went back and reminisced about their sexual experiences. With a wave of her hand she dismissed her dream like state and said, "Wait a second, will you. I don't know about you, but I'm famished. Let's go downstairs and get something to eat. My brain needs nourishment, as I'm sure yours does."

Teasing Madaline, Paul asked if all she thought about was food and filling her stomach. "You're not funny and yes, I love to eat. Does that bother you?"

“Hell, no. I’m just jiving you. I have to admit you made a very wise decision. I am getting a bit of a headache and I think this will clear it up.”

Paul brought all the necessary papers and pencils and decided that they’d continue with the time line while eating.

“That’s fine with me.” Madaline agreed. As they were going down the elevator Paul shook his head and asked Madaline if she realized how much food they’ve already consumed today. ”Who cares, I’m nervous and when I’m nervous I eat. Lucky I don’t weigh over 300 lbs.”

“In a way I like reminiscing about the past. Even though there are people who don’t like me and vice versa, there are so many people I’ve met and have loving and fond memories of. Let’s go back to when I first came to Hollywood. I was just a youngster, just 15 years old. The love of my life was Brad Mason. It was funny how we actually met and because of some stupid people, who I wanted to get even with, I accepted a date with him. No one knew my age. Everyone thought that I was older and I never disputed it. We couldn’t marry for a long time, I think almost 5 years and I became pregnant with Kyle a year later. We had to wait because of his jealous and hateful wife, Sheila. You would think I was a real bitch if you read and heard the gossip about the two evil people who were living in sin.”

“In those years, even though everything went on, no one spoke of the horrible stories and the many homosexuals that had to keep their secrets. People in the business never brought up the subject and left the actors alone to do his or her own thing. Some of those poor guys and some gals would have to get married to keep up the pretense that they were strait. Poor Rock had to and many more. It was the gossip columnists and the media who tried to destroy whatever headway or happiness that was bestowed us. I got pregnant again at age 21 with Kyle. Brad and I couldn’t get married until a year later. His divorce took a long time because Sheila kept postponing and tried everything in her power to have the process be a miserable one.”

“Wait a second,” interrupted Paul. If my math is correct, you’re telling me that Kyle is really only 23 yrs. old.” Shaking his head in disbelief he was truly, only for a moment, at a loss for words. ”You realize with all this bad publicity everything is going to come out. How can it be that this famous photographer is 23 years old? By the way I’ll call Kyle and ask him about his friends. There might be some people you have no idea of who he hangs out with.”

“That makes sense,” agreed Madaline.

Trying to defend her only son Madaline told Paul the true story. ”Kyle was always interested in camera’s and taking pictures of everything around him. As he got into his teens Brad and I could see how talented he was. By this time a lot of his works were displayed in galleries throughout California and then in other cities around the country. His name got around. He knew that people wouldn’t take him seriously if they found out that he was only 16 yrs. old at the time. He always looked older for his age and he told everyone he was 20. To this day, I can’t believe how people took him at his word. It didn’t take long for his name to get around and people and critics alike spoke highly of this new young man who was making a name for himself. When he met Carol she was a few years older but she didn't know their age difference. Anyway, I hope that when the truth does come out that people won't care. By this time he's proven himself a true artist that has so much imagination, especially with models of all types. As a matter of fact, he just got a chance to go to foreign countries with the National Graphic magazine. This will broaden his career tremendously." Madaline exclaimed like any proud mother would of her son.

While they were eating, a few people in the restaurant recognized Madaline and came over to ask for autographs. Of course she was delighted to do so, even if it killed her to be nice to people she didn't know. She had to remember that these were her fans and if it weren't for them she wouldn't be the star she was today. During coffee they talked about the reality of the list of people she had given him that would be likely candidates for the person who was trying to either kill or scare the hell out of her.

"The funny thing about this type of work is you never can dismiss anyone. People are crazy for a variety of reasons. A stupid thing that may have occurred years ago, they may think about over and over again. They continually think of that particular occurrence, sometimes adding things that never happened, but they truly believe it's the truth. Who knows what the reason is, except in their own mind and for years have been thinking of ways to harm you. You wouldn't think about those that are psychopathically deranged. Mental illness is a horrible disease. You would never realize that the person we're looking for looks like anyone else walking down the street. It's that there are manic depressive, insanity, psychosis, split personalities and many other types of psychogenic personalities, you might not believe what I just said but I've seen some bizarre incidents throughout my career. You have to trust me and we'll get to the bottom of this situation before they do you bodily harm. I promise. There are times when a fan is the insane one. Any reason will do for them to get agitated. There are too many actors and actresses that have been killed by some lunatic fan, or permanently scarred for life. I'm sure you know who they are. We can't dismiss this possibility."

"I'm going to keep you at your promise Mr. Winston, oh I mean Paul, then we'll be able to laugh over this entire sequence of events. I'll even take you out to your favorite restaurant and foot the bill."

"That will give me more of a reason to hurry up the process of elimination," laughed Paul, as he escorted her out of the restaurant and up to her suite.

It took another 5 hours to finish all the names and people that were involved in her and Kyle's life. "I think I have to call it a day. I'm really exhausted from all this unnerving memorabilia," feigned Madaline.

"If it will help to ease your mind, I'll get on it as early as tomorrow morning. We'll have a lot of answers by tomorrow evening. . Thanks for all the cooperation." Seeing himself out the door Paul couldn't wait to get into his bed as well.

It took all morning to find where Madaline's sisters and brothers lived. Like Madaline said, they stayed in the immediate area. Her mom and dad were still alive and living well at the same farm. It took him relentless hours to extract from her brothers and sisters their feelings for their sister, who many felt abandoned them, while others were proud of their famous sibling. There were some who found out what their mother did for her and resented the idea of giving Madaline the money, that they felt was rightfully theirs, to attend college and get away from the farm and all it represented. After many phone calls and asking favors from people on the force who owed him favors, he was able to reach many people. The one person he sought was Billy Martin. He was a computer analyst plus keeping the family farm. He was doing very well for himself. With Billy's help he was able to get in touch with other people who attended the same school that Madaline and Billy had gone to. Paul had a good feeling about Billy and could understand why Madaline and Billy were good friends when they were younger. 'Who knows,' he thought, 'this might reunite the two companions once again.'

Paul did a lot of investigation of the siblings who resented what their mother did for Madaline. After many grueling hours it turned up nothing of importance. Many a lead came to a dead end when the person he was looking for was either deceased or moved far away and people didn't know or hear from them again. He wanted to leave the biggest source of his insight for last. He hoped his intuition, for once, didn't pan out.

Meanwhile Madaline was going crazy with worry. She became paranoid of every unusual noise. She didn't want to look at people she didn't know. She wanted to leave the production and fly to Kyle and stay in California until Paul could find out who the culprit or culprits were. She appreciated all the help that Suzanne, Nancy and Justin were doing but realized that they couldn't spend more time trying to solve the mystery of Curtis Jones. Paul had all he could do to persuade Madaline to stay put and continue her regular routine.

The next step in Paul's assignment was calling up adoption agencies in and around the South Dakota area. He hoped that the particular agency he wanted to find wasn't out of business. If that didn't pan out, he intended to go to the various city halls and find out the names of the children born on Madaline's delivery date and the year. He found most of the agencies wanting to help him in his search but didn't have the information that he needed. After exhausting all the companies he then had to make the rounds of the various town halls in every city and county near their vicinity. In his quest he hoped that the child was placed around their area and not farmed out to a different state. It was difficult because he didn't know the sex of the child.

He was amazed at all the children born on that particular date. He wrote down all their names and the families who they lived with. Paul couldn't leave out lawyers who personally took money for the adoption of babies. These were private adoptions that sometimes occurred when people who couldn't go through the regular route of adoption for a variety of reasons. Sometimes the parents were too old or religion was another factor to consider. He toured the vast area and after three days visited all the various city halls and wrote down a compilation of children and their parents first and last names with the birth date that coincided with Madaline's baby. He didn't know if they were the birth parents or had adopted that particular child.

In the evening he didn't care what kind of mattress the motel supplied. He wanted to lay down and fall fast asleep. By the end of a week he was getting tired of fast food joints and lumpy mattresses. He made sure to call Madaline every evening with a report of his progress.

Madaline looked forward to receiving his phone call and even if the day wasn't as fruitful as anticipated she had hopes that they would prevail and find the child she so desperately wanted to meet and finally see for herself how he or she turned out. On the sixth evening, she was truly exhausted from the tedious and hard schedule of the ongoing play. Either from fatigue or not paying attention to detail, she found herself sprawled on the stage on her way to the hotel after the evening's performance. She wasn't sure if someone had tripped her, but there didn't seem to be anyone in sight. She also thought she was just clumsy and stumbled on something so small that the object couldn't be seen. Upon getting up she made sure that the injury that had just healed was not reinjured in the mishap. Grateful that all was well and she was intact she brushed herself off and continued to the stage door. Suddenly, without any noise whatsoever, she saw one of the large wooden barrels used in the play, quickly heading towards her. She was glad that she was in good shape and moved to the side, avoiding being hit by the runaway prop. Her heart was beating abnormally fast. She couldn't wait to get to her suite, lock the door, take a hot bath and go to sleep. She debated whether to call Paul and disturb him at this un-Godly hour and decided that when she spoke to him the following day she would mention what happened.

When Paul found out about the 'accident' he was determined, more than ever, to find the adopted child who was now an adult. If he was right, and his sixth sense usually was, then the person who was doing all this mayhem was most likely the same youngster that Madaline had given up for adoption. He hoped that he was wrong. This character had no knowledge that Madaline was also an unwilling individual who had no say in the way things turned out. If they knew that Madaline would have moved heaven and earth to keep the infant, then this entire situation would be moot. It took Paul another week to visit the parent or parents who were still living in the area to find out if their child, who's birthday was the same day and year as Madaline's delivery date, was their own offspring or had they adopted the infant. Most of the folks were personable and willing to divulge the information. There were a few individuals who were downright nasty and didn't want to see Paul or give any facts whatsoever. Unfortunately, those were the people he had to focus on. It was a difficult task and one that took time and visiting local police stations hoping that they would assist him in his responsibility to his client. When the local police found out who he was working for, he felt he had to divulge Madaline's name, they were happy to help him with his assignment. There turned out to be approximately 15 people who could possibly be the couple who had adopted the baby. It would have been a private adoption and most likely the parents never divulged their secret of the adoption to the child. He was fortunate that with all the hippa laws, because of Madaline's reputation, the regulations were not taken into consideration. He was grateful that the law enforcers looked the other way.

Paul did a lot of research on the subject and found out that in most cases the couple told their child about the adoption and wanted them to know how special he or she was. Half the children didn't want any information on who their birth parents were. They figured that they only knew them as their parents and were the mother and father who sacrificed and cared for them throughout their lifetime. The other half wanted to know for various reasons, that they alone knew, why they wanted the knowledge of their birth parent. Paul figured it was for medical reasons or just a curiosity factor to find out why they gave them up.

Some of these children, who were now adults had moved away and were pursuing careers of their own. Paul found out that a few of these adults were living in the New England area. About ten people decided to go into the acting profession, which Paul thought was interesting. These individuals were a mixture of men and women who had migrated from various states in the pursuit of a career in the arts. Paul had to find out, if by chance, any of these people were now working and where they were employed. He finalized the list down to five people who seemed like perspective prospects.

He returned the rental car and boarded the plane back to Boston. Before he left he thanked the various departments that had assisted him in his search. Without their help he could never have made the progress that he had. He made a note that when he returned to Boston he would send the various departments of the town halls fruit baskets to show his appreciation for their help.

When he landed at Logan he felt he was home at last. He couldn't wait to see Madaline and work with her on the list that he dwindled down to a few. Madaline was performing her role in the play, unaware that Paul was in the audience. At the end of the performance a dozen beautiful assortment of roses was waiting for her in her dressing room. A wide smile crossed her face as she turned around and saw Paul standing with his arms outstretched. She hurried into his massive arms burying her head into his expansive chest.

"You have no idea how happy I am to see you. The roses are gorgeous and I can't thank you enough for all the work you're doing," said an indebted Madaline.

"If you'd like, I'd love to walk you to your suite and then tell you what I've found out and let's see what other things might happen."

"Before we head out I think you'd better know what happened a while ago. I was going to call you the morning after it took place but figured you were busy enough. Madaline related the story of the run-a-way barrel and tried to make light of it. She put a finger on Paul's lips as he was about to speak. "I don't want to discuss the issue any further. It's passed and no harm came of it. So if you don't mind, let's get out of here," Madaline suggested. With a wide smile she took his hand and led him across the street. While Paul was away Madaline found herself thinking and missing him. She couldn't wait until his return. Now he was home and she was delighted, to say the least.

Madaline listened intently as Paul told her of his adventures and ultimate findings

He wanted her to help in the quest of trying to find the right individual who might be her long, lost child. She found herself joyful and at the same time apprehensive at the thought of what this now adult would think of her, knowing that she gave it up for adoption. Madaline didn't want to think that this child might be the person responsible for all the unfortunate accidents occurring. She couldn't let these wicked thoughts spoil her hopeful dreams.

As much as Suzanne wanted to stay in California and finish the project that she started she couldn't justify staying away from her loved ones and the spa any longer. Detective Colangelo and Nancy had a definite attraction for one another. Suzanne was sure that Nancy would be hearing from him shortly. He'd make excuses to inform Nancy on the investigation and then they'd see what would happen from there. Suzanne knew that she had to help Hope with her wedding plans and tried to act excited but deep in her heart she dreaded the upcoming event. After the wedding was over she knew that she'd return to San Diego and was sure that Nancy would come with her. After all, it would give Nancy an excuse to see Rich Colangelo once again.

When they left to come home it looked like a lot of progress was being made and likely the culprit or people who arranged for Mr. Jones murder would be found. When Nancy and Suzanne gave detective Colangelo all the data and material that they found at Curtis Jones' apartment, all categorized and filed, the police were able to put all the pieces of the puzzle together. It seemed like only a matter of time that justice would be served.

CHAPTER TWENTY EIGHT

Rich informed Nancy that through his on the street informants the police department apprehended the culprits that killed the store clerk. It turned out that they were juveniles that were high on cocaine and heroin and needed money to buy more. He was glad that the case was solved so he could put all of his attention on the Jones murder.

Suzanne couldn't wait to see Stephen again and arranged to meet with him the week before Hope's wedding. Although it seemed ages since they'd been together, talking on the telephone helped them discuss about their situation at length. Suzanne opened up to him about her concerns and disappointments in their relationship and hoped that it would spark Stephen to finally do something about their arrangement.

Meanwhile Nancy and Suzanne had to make plans to fly, once again, to Japan and straighten out some glitches in the operation. Sometimes Suzanne wondered if they made the right choice in opening this salon.

Time seemed to fly when Suzanne returned home to the Boston area after returning from their Japan spa. Words couldn't explain the disappointment she felt as she resumed her day to day schedule. She felt she'd let down her dear and close friends and couldn't put it out of her mind. She often found herself calling Justin to find out if any of his friend's leads had panned out.

"Suzanne my dear, I can only tell you that there is some headway being made. It seems that Mr. Jones had stolen quite a bit of valuable paintings and artifacts that were being sold at the gallery. Poor Mr. Weintraub hadn't a clue. But from these pieces the rightful owners were found and they were able to get their valuables back. Of course the people who had bought the stolen items were beside themselves. Some took it to the courts and the lawyers had a field day. There are still some artifacts and paintings that are in limbo until a decision from the court is finally made."

"Justin, I'm glad I called you. You've eased my mind considerably. Tell me, do they have any more information on who might have killed Curtis?"

"I'm afraid you'll have to get that information from detective Colangelo. The last time I spoke to him he was optimistic that between the records from the gallery and the bank statements and the stolen art and artifacts, they were narrowing the list considerably. The lists coincided with the deposits and thankfully Mr. Jones was a very meticulous person and had all his records in order. It seems that Kyle was right when he thought he heard and saw an oriental gentleman arguing with Curtis. There's one name that keeps coming up in Mr. Jones' file. This same gentleman would also by art from the gallery as well. The name he used was obviously falsified, but with their knowledge I believe they'll find the culprit very shortly. I know that they couldn't have gone as far as they have without our help. They are grateful that we were able to assist them."

"By any chance did Mr. Weintraub's gallery have a surveillance camera on the premises?" Suzanne inquired.

"As a matter of fact he did. Unfortunately, it seems that the particular tapes that would have shown the gentleman that Curtis met for the illegal transactions was somehow lost. Now isn't that a coincidence?"

"He was such a fool. In the long run, by his being overly cautious, he ultimately hurt himself by eliminating the one person who could have been part of his demise," Suzanne unhappily verbalized.

"After speaking to you and finding out all the headway the California police are making, I don't feel as bad as I did before," admitted Suzanne. "I feel much better getting back to my schedule and then following up and finding out from Madaline what is going to happen with Kyle. Make sure and call me and we can go out for lunch sometime soon. I don't want any excuses, do you understand."

"I promise, cross my heart, that within the next few weeks I'll definitely make a date for us to get together. I have so much catching up to do. Although Alan is a great young man, and he has great potential, a lot of material has to be dealt with. It wasn't his fault that I didn't write down, in detail, some of the essential items that had to be categorized and sent to various places. So all in all this seems to be the perfect time that we decided to come home," Justin admitted.

The wedding plans that were supposed to be pleasurable created depression and silent bitterness. To the outside world and acquaintances, they had no idea of the turmoil that Suzanne kept hidden in her heart. Only in the silence of her darkened bedroom did she allow her grievous thoughts to surface. Hope had no idea why her mother didn't share her enthusiasm of the upcoming nuptials and wedding plans.

Nancy felt Suzanne's pain, but couldn't extract her dear friend's inner feelings. Trying to alleviate the heavy, self-inflicted, burden of her friend, Nancy tried diverting Suzanne with amusing and witty stories of her new world in the single life and how it was going." As much as I hate dating and this single scene is for the birds, I have to admit I'm meeting some very interesting and nice men. Of course I come across some real jerks and try to extract myself from the date early, but then once in a while someone appealing comes along and I find myself having a good time. Sometimes I think I'm getting too old for this scene, especially when every married person wants to fix me up. I swear they want everyone to be mated," Nancy blurted as they dined at the local restaurant one evening after work.

"Of course Rich and I talk to each other often. I'm attracted to him and hopefully we'll be able to get together shortly." Suzanne found herself laughing at her friend's escapades and forgetting her own self-induced pain. Suzanne asked, "So when are you taking me away from here and back to Japan? I thought we'd be there by now. You had me thinking we were leaving as soon as we returned from California and Boston."

"I'm glad you brought the subject up. You're right. We do have to leave shortly. How about next week? Will that give you enough time to finish up your business here in Boston and some of the other spas in the states? By the way how are the wedding plans coming and what can I do to help?"

"Nothing really. Hope has most of the plans made, except she wants me to help her with the seating arrangements. That's the most complicated part in planning a wedding. Other than that all I have to do is pay for this large affair and attend. Getting back to the business, thank God, as of now, everything is fine at all the spas. Once we're back in Japan we'll get things straightened out. With what

I've seen and heard on all the reports it's just a matter of time and understanding the American way of doing things that has the estheticians miffed. The girls just need a bit more training and I'll incorporate their way of doing things with ours. Everything will work out fine." Looking at her friend and ordering a cup of Earl Grey tea she continued. "I think this trip is just what the doctor ordered. By the way, I'm glad to hear that you and Detective Colangelo are still communicating. Hey, you never know what might happen."

"As a matter of fact I spoke to him last evening. It seems that when he calls it's not always about the murder. I really enjoy our conversations. Hopefully, we'll be able to get together in the very near future. I want to take it slow. Can you understand?"

"Of course I do. You had such a bad experience the first time; you have every reason to be cautious. Though I have to tell you that when I see the two of you together, you look great. But as we both know, looking good together is not the only thing that makes a relationship work. I give you credit on not being rash. Now not too slow, mind you, you don't want to scare him away by making him think that you're not interested. Listen to me, I sound like the maven of love. My own situation is such a mess and it seems that I have solutions for everyone else except my own."

As Suzanne laid in bed, exhausted from a long day at work, the telephones ringing couldn't be ignored. Larry was on the line and a smile, she didn't expect, appeared on her face. They talked for a while and she told him what she was doing and opened up to him about her misgivings about Hope's plans.

"First of all, I understand how you feel about your daughter's conversion. I do have a lot of Jewish friends that live around here, Larry verbosely insisted. They've lived in the area for years and I've known them all my life. Some of them have gone through the same experience that you're going through. It took a toll on them. Others took their children's marriages in stride and didn't let the intermarriage bother them. They believed that love cured everything. Who knows what's right or wrong. Only you have to determine for yourself how to handle the situation. I'm here for you whenever you need someone to vent your feelings to, remember that."

"Thanks Larry, you have no idea how I appreciate your understanding."

Larry was very interested in the art thefts and then told her about some of his friends that had their own collections taken. "I can't thank you enough for your helpful input on both situations. I've been in such turmoil and haven't been able to verbalize my thoughts to many people without them thinking that I'm over-reacting. Another thing is you don't think I was foolish to fly to California to help my friends in their time of need."

"Suzanne, we've know each other for years now and I would never tell you something that I didn't really think was right. I probably would have done the same thing that you did. So go back to sleep, have a peaceful night and only good dreams. And, don't let the bed bugs bite."

She had to laugh at his last comment and again thanked him for his call. He re-assured her that she did the right thing by going to California.

She asked herself why it was so easy to talk to Larry when she found it difficult to talk to Stephen about her feelings. Maybe when they saw each other again, they'd be able to connect and then Suzanne can open up and tell him everything that she told Larry.

Suzanne was surprised how relaxed she was as the Jet took off and made their ascent. Looking over the paper work on the Japan Metamorphosis spa Suzanne was able to ascertain the problem as far as the written report went. The actual hands on evaluation needed to be reckoned with. It seemed that when they went to sleep, they woke up and were landing at the airport.

The limo was waiting and the efficient driver had their luggage and paraphernalia loaded in record time. "I can't wait to see how the salon is doing. It's so different and yet we're doing remarkably well. I have my theory but tell me what your thoughts are once we get there," Suzanne stated. Nancy stretched her legs and after some consideration let out a sigh. "Well, it doesn't hurt that the Japanese like anything that smacks of Americanism. Even though our spa is geared to the Japanese person it has enough of our regular treatments mixed in with theirs that they like it," Nancy admitted. "Yet, I do like the idea you had when you suggested bringing a few of our girls out here to train. They'll learn a lot from the Japanese estheticians and vice versa. Yes, Suzanne affirmed, I think we hit a definite gold mine with this spa."

"Don't be overconfident. We still have to fix a few glitches that seem to be wrong," confessed Nancy.

"Nancy, with every new spa there'll always be problems that crop up. That's why we're here, remember." Looking at her friend in a funny way Suzanne quipped, or did you just tell me there were problems so I would ride with you on our plane for that long distance just to prove me wrong about my mishigas about flying?"

"Now would I do something that stupid and contrived just to prove a point?" Nancy responded with an innocent look of her face.

Without any warning Suzanne reached over and tousled Nancy's mane of red hair. Their laughter was a pleasant surprise to the very serious driver who tried to overlook such blatant behavior from two adult American women.

Even though Suzanne rested on the plane trip the time difference took its toll. After settling into their suite Suzanne declined Nancy's invitation to dinner and wanted to rest. "I really want to be alert and at my best for tomorrow. Please call one of your friends for dinner tonight. I promise this will be the last time I'll beg off. I'll make it up to you okay?"

"Yeah, yeah, I knew your age would catch up to you sooner or later," Nancy teased as she threw a magazine on the bed where Suzanne was resting. "I might stay over my friend's house and if I do I'll see you in the morning, bright and early."

The wakeup call from the front desk woke Suzanne from her deep sleep. Realizing she didn't have much time before Nancy picked her up, she quickly showered and dressed. The salon came out better than Suzanne had envisioned when she was let into it by a beautiful Japanese woman who cordially greeted her. "That's a nice touch," she whispered to Nancy as the woman took their jackets from them. "Don't forget Suzanne, that the Japanese people are very formal and adhere to tradition." The Japanese woman became embarrassed when she realized who the two women were. Hiding her beautiful smile and concealing her laughter behind her petite hand, she apologized profusely, until the two owners made her see the humor of it all. It took Nancy and Suzanne approximately three long days and evenings to straighten any problem that the estheticians saw as possible obstacles or difficulties melding the two cultures. On the fourth evening as the two women were enjoying the evening's dinner Nancy told Suzanne she'd like to take her on a trip to Beppu. "I hear it's absolutely breathtaking and the mineral salts will take away anything that ails you. Now before you dismiss my idea, I know something is eating at you, and even though you haven't told me what your problem is, maybe this little diversion will do you some good. By the way, it doesn't have anything to do with Stephen does it? "Taking Nancy's hand into her own, she gently squeezed her dear friend and confidant's hand. "You are such a wonderful friend. I don't know what I'd do without you. Thank you for your concern, and thankfully Stephen and I are great. You know me too well. Yes, I do have a few situations that are bothering me, and I know they're all in my head, my craziness. Now tell me all about this place you have planned for us."

Suzanne found Beppo as enchanting as Nancy had described this beautiful village to be. The homes were beautiful and the people seemed more relaxed than the people on the mainland in Tokyo. It was a real resort with all the amenities. Before going to the artists' colony they wanted to walk around the area and get a feel for the area. "I can't get over how lovely these homes are. They don't seem as crowded as they are in Tokyo or some of the other Islands," exclaimed Nancy. "The homes look like any other resort area back in the States," Suzanne stated. "I hear it also gets some snow in the mountains and is a great resort for skiing. Maybe one of these days when we're visiting our salon we should take a vacation and I'll teach you how to ski."

"Thanks Nancy but no. If God wanted me to ski he would have made me with skis for feet." They both laughed as they walked a bit and then headed for the artist's colony.

There was a whole section devoted to artists and as Suzanne and Nancy were admiring the art work and crafts Nancy poked Suzanne. "You're not going to believe this, but isn't that Mr. Makino walking down the street."

"Who is Mr. Makino?" Suzanne asked as she put down a beautiful ceramic dish done in vibrant colors. "Remember, he's the Japanese gentleman I told you about that sent me my beautiful briefcase when I admired his. I sat next to him on the airplane coming home from Japan when I had my first visit to the country. I also saw him at the lobby of the Beverly Hills Hotel. "Yes, I vaguely remember you mentioning him."

"I'll be right back. I'm just going to say hi. Better yet come with me and I'll introduce you to him. He seems like a nice guy."

"Okay, but if someone buys this dish I won't forgive you."

"Come on, this won't take long."

Yoshy was taken by surprise as Nancy lightly tapped him on his shoulder as he scrutinized a lovely porcelain figurine. Bowing, he greeted his acquaintance and was genuinely pleased that Nancy recognized him. Normally Yoshy would never invite them to his retreat, but being alone, waiting for Robin to meet him the following day, he felt lucky to be in the company of such delightful women. 'This will give me a little diversion' he thought as he waited for Suzanne to purchase her treasured dish. "You must come back to my modest cottage and see for yourself the beauty of this wonderful land."

Suzanne couldn't get over the difference between the crowd and masses she encountered when she walked along the streets of Tokeo and the peacefulness and leisurely life style in this beautiful Island of Kyushu. "Mr. Makeno, this island is beautiful and so serene," voiced Suzanne as she admired the beautiful Japanese gardens and scenic views as they drove up the vast hills to get to Yoshy's modest bungalow. "I guess this is the same type of variance in our country when a foreign visitor encounters the hustle and bustle of some large cities and then visits the more remote parts of our nation, "Suzanne exclaimed as they came to a stop in front of Yoshy's beautiful manor. "Yes, that's why I originally purchased this piece of property. It affords me my private time and lets me have some tranquility."

"I can understand your falling in love with this beautiful island," chimed in Nancy as Yoshy gave them a tour of his Japanese garden. She was surprised as Nancy was, that one of the hot springs they heard about was located in his backyard.

It felt good when Suzanne removed her shoes at the entrance and changed into the slippers that were supplied. "I often wished we had this custom in our country. I would have saved many arguments with my children when I asked them to remove their shoes when they were younger. They tracked everything onto my floors and my knees would certainly be in better shape today if I didn't have to constantly be on them when I used to wash the floors. Thankfully, they are all out of the house, living on their own, that's one aspect of children growing up that I don't miss." 'They don't look bad to me,' thought Yoshy, as he stole a glance at his guests exposed legs. "Let me show you through my humble place." After Yoshy fixed them a pot of tea, he then led them onto the deck where the beginning of his private hot spring was located. It seemed as if they had just arrived, but in reality hours had passed, when Yoshy offered to drive them back to the hotel where they were staying. "Mr. Makino, I'd love to reciprocate your hospitality. On behalf of Suzanne and myself we'd like to thank you for this delightful afternoon. Your home is truly beautiful and we'd like you be our guest this evening for dinner?"

"Normally, I would love to join you, but unfortunately, I have some unfinished business that has to be attended to. I have a business colleague that will be arriving tomorrow morning."

"We'll have to schedule a special time that will be convenient for you. I hope you'll be our guest when we're back in the States and in California." Nancy proclaimed as she bowed saying goodbye.

Lying on the soft bed in the hotel room Suzanne thought of Yoshy and what a fine gentleman he seemed to be. "I think we're lucky, I imagine not many visitors are privy to see what the inside of a Japanese home looks like." Rolling over on her side Suzanne continued. "He's really reserved and doesn't speak of his family. Did he mention anything about his family when you were on the plane for that long time?"

"Come to think of it he didn't. I think he's married, but I don't know for sure because I didn't see any ring on his finger," Nancy answered as she lazily looked through the packet of restaurants that was in the envelope in the hotel room. "Suzanne they have 40 restaurant brochures. Everything from Asian, Continental, Japanese, a Steakhouse, Sushi and listen to this, they even have a pizza place."

"No sir," exclaimed Suzanne. After they giggled, like two school girls, for a few minutes Nancy got serious. "Have you decided which dining room will have the honor of serving us tonight?" Nancy asked as she forced herself off the bed. "No, you choose for a change."

"Okay, let's go for Sushi tonight."

"Um, can we go anyplace other than Sushi? I don't like to eat raw fish or any smoked fish either. Of course lux is entirely different and don't ask me why except that I grew up eating it."

"Mmm, let's see, I'll be original and go for Continental, does that make you happy?"

"Thanks Nancy, I feel better already. Before we go, I'd better call Mrs. Walsh and make sure everything is fine back home before we leave." Before Suzanne picked up the phone Nancy stopped her. "Do you realize that there is a thirteen hour time difference between the two countries?" Suzanne seemed confused. "You realize that I'm not that good at math or figuring out things like that. I'll call and if Mrs. Walsh is sleeping I'll leave a message telling her that we're fine and having a great time."

"Suzanne, you say you're not good at math, but you sure know how to make money and which store is making a profit."

"All I can say is that it's in my blood." They went out the door of their room after Suzanne left a message for Mrs. Walsh.

"Speaking of back home, you've kept awfully quiet about Stephen. Is everything ok?"

"Oh sure. I have so many feelings bottled up and whenever I think about our situation I get a little sad, that's all."

"You know you can always talk to me about anything, don't you." "Thanks, but for now I have a lot of thinking to do. I'm going to take a bath and I'll meet you down in the lobby in about an hour and a half if that's okay with you?"

"Sure, see you then." Nancy spoke softly as she let herself out of Suzanne's room.

Soaking in the tub, Suzanne couldn't help but think about her state of affairs after Nancy brought up Stephen's name. 'Stephen and I promised one another that what we have together is not just an affair. We're so lucky to have been given this second chance at happiness,' she thought as tears fell from her eyes and mixed into the hot water. For over two years now Suzanne suppressed her fears and frustrations over her deep love for her wonderful friend and lover. She wouldn't berate herself again, as she often did, thinking about the young girl who managed to mess up her life as well as Stephens. If only she'd have had more self confidence in herself she would have seen how much Stephen had loved her. She should have waited for him to get his life in order after his dad died. But no, because of her impatience and immaturity she managed to ruin both their lives.

After Stephen reminded her about their last meeting when they were teenagers, sitting in his car, with tears streaming down her face, as he held her in his arms, she told him not to try getting her back. She then remembered telling him that he would find a wonderful girl, marry, have children and not miss her. His life would go on, and it certainly did, as hers had. But what if's were impossible to realize. She couldn't take back all the years of their being apart. She couldn't take away the pain of his unhappy marriage and of all the years of hell in her own fatal wedded bliss. But now she found herself wanting and needing him more than ever and knew quite well that he was not hers alone. The thought of Lou Anne brought a shiver to her as she tried suppressing these emotions once again. She lifted herself out of the tub and briskly rubbed herself dry.

Hiro paced the floor of his small apartment and thought of his next two assignments. When Nobuaki called him into his private quarter Hiro had no idea what his job would be. He knew Nobuaki was upset at Yoshy, but he also knew that Yoshy and Nobuaki were old friends, their friendship spanning decades. He realized the inner turmoil his boss must have gone through to make this final deadly decision. He didn't get into the reason for this declaration of doom but knew that Yoshy must have done something very bad for Nobuaki to react as he did. And to make matters worse, he didn't like the idea of killing a woman. This Robin Sinclair, was absolutely beautiful he remembered from the one time he saw her in Yoshy's company. To argue and refuse an order would be inexcusable and surely guarantee his own death sentence.

No, he had no choice but to get this job done quickly and efficiently, he thought as he continued pacing his cramped living quarters. Nobuaki always left the method and timing up to the enforcer, this way in his own sick mind, he would rationalize that he didn't commit the actual crime. 'He certainly has all the bases covered,' he thought as he finally sat down to write a plan of action. Knowing Nobuaki as he did, Hiro was aware of the procedures to be followed. The first being never discussing the actual plan with his master. He had to admit that he enjoyed outlining, plotting a course of action and then following through. It gave him a sense of accomplishment when his job went smoothly and in some sick way he enjoyed baffling the authorities when they came out clueless.

He fixed himself a strong drink and gulped it down. The hot liquid burned his throat. He quickly downed another and this time the heat felt good. As much as he tried erasing the thought of eliminating Miss Sinclair, he couldn't. After much contemplation he resigned himself to the fact that he had no choice but to do his task, and not cause himself anymore grief. He knew what he was getting into when he joined the Yakuza years ago. He pledged his loyalty and in essence his life for the organization, realizing his life was not his own. He was a pawn for others to do what they wanted of him. His hands enclosing his arms tightly, he gently rocked back and forth hoping the motion would lull him and put his feelings at bay.

Mitsuko opened the door trying to conceal the happiness she felt when she saw it was Hiro at the entrance to her master's domain. She knew it was fruitless dreaming the dreams she did of this fine and wonderful man, whom she had grown to love, even from afar. Yes, he was not good looking, and he was a bit on the heavy side, but that didn't matter, all she saw was the love in his eyes whenever he addressed her. She led Hiro to the office of her employer.

Motioning Hiro to sit, Nobuaki wasted little time. "I found out Yoshy's schedule and I find it befitting he and his little pale girlfriend are on vacation this week in Beppu. When they return I think, no I want, this pale woman eliminated. It will take a while but everything has to be done with efficiency. No screw ups. If it's the last thing done, I want it done right. I don't care if it takes months to a year, it will happen. "With that said Nobuaki walked Hiro to his office door.

Nancy and Suzanne felt both exhilarated and content after working with the girls at their Tokyo salon. They couldn't get over how the estheticians learned quickly and liked the American way of doing the facials and were able to incorporate the knowledge with their own technique. "Well what do you think?" Nancy asked Suzanne while they were sipping their after dinner drinks at the restaurant located near the spa. "Is it time to go home or do you want them to do more training?"

"You know I can't wait to go home, but now I'd like to visit a few more islands and maybe we can go back to Beppu and stay at a small hotel or inn for a few days' rest. What do you think?"

Stirring her sombrero, contemplating only a few seconds she acknowledged her delight over Suzanne's spontaneity. "Boy have you changed. You'd never be this impulsive a few years ago. I love your new spirit. What's causing you to have this transformation?" Giving the question some serious thought Suzanne responded. "I hate to admit that I've changed, but I guess my whole attitudes been altered and I can't say one thing has caused it. Maybe it's because seeing people my age or younger die and not being able to enjoy a nice retirement of fulfilling their dreams that they worked so hard for. It could also be not being able to see their children or grandchildren grow up. I guess I want to live as if this is the last day of my life."

"I've always tried treating people as I'd want people to treat me, but I don't know, emotions and life's ever changing happenings have made me take a new stance on the way I want to live for the rest of my life."

"Now don't go getting maudlin on me. I just asked a simple question," Nancy remarked. Taking Suzanne's hand into her own she continued, "Seriously Suzanne, something heavy has been on your mind for some time now and I hope you feel that you can confide anything to me."

"I know honey, and I do appreciate your concern. But there are a few issues that I have to sort out in my mind before I express them to you. Please don't think that I'm shutting you out, but I have to come to terms with a few concerns that only I can sort out. Come on, let's make arrangements for finishing up with the salon within the next few days and then make plans for our extended vacation. I know that when we get home there'll be no letup for a long time."

By the time they arrived at the inn in Beppu they were exhilarated and ready for the rest that they fully deserved. "Let's rent a car and travel along the roads that are rarely seen, and then we can go to a few of those artists and crafts places that we loved. How does that sound?"

"Great," agreed Suzanne, "But before we start traveling again, let's go to one of the hot springs and indulge ourselves with a few mineral baths."

CHAPTER TWENTY NINE

Suzanne and Nancy were on their plane going back to the States. Looking across from Nancy, Suzanne couldn't help but expound her emotions about the vacation they had experienced. "This trip was more than I imagined. Our little get away to Beppu was beyond expectation. The people were terrific and went out of their way to be cordial and inviting. If I hadn't seen it for myself, I couldn't have imagined all the hot springs that are located on this Island. Who'd have thought that this city, which is located on the south island of Kyushu, is such a beautiful treasure. What a surprise when you brought me to Hamawaki resort. I couldn't believe my eyes when I saw the hot water rising and come out from under the sand on the beach. I do feel better since I took advantage of the various natural water slides and pools. I had ailments or minor defects that seem to be cured," professed a calm and refreshed Suzanne." People wouldn't believe all the natural springs unless they see these pictures for themselves." Nancy beamed at Suzanne's excitement.

"Take it easy girl. Let's hope you still feel this tranquil once you face the realities back home."

"I'm not going to let that corrupt remark break the way I feel," Suzanne professed to Nancy. After a few minutes of closing her eyes, enjoying the peaceful feelings within her, she suddenly opened her eyes. Out of nowhere she articulated, "It was an extra bonus that you spotted Mr. Makino. Wasn't it nice that he invited us into his cottage? If that's a cottage I'd hate to see what he considers a home. Getting back to my business mode, the spa was as beautiful, elegant and elaborate as I expected. All the girls working for us are go getters, willing to experiment and incorporate the American way that we do facials along with their methods. I think we've hit a gold mine in the Japanese market!"

With a slight grin Nancy was thrilled that Suzanne seemed to have enjoyed herself aside from the inner conflicts she seemed to be keeping to herself. Nancy thought that for a while, Suzanne was at peace with herself, feeling good inside her body and soul. "It pleases me that you had a good a time. I knew you would," Nancy verbalized.

Summoning the attendant, Nancy ordered wine glasses with a bottle of Suzanne's favorite Zinfandel. After the stewardess filled their glasses, they toasted to the success of the Metamorphosis spa in Japan.

"That was thoughtful of you to have my Zinfandel aboard our plane. It sounds so funny saying our plane. You know, I have to give you credit where credit is due. I enjoy flying in our aircraft and you were right with your decision to buy it. I often don't admit when I'm wrong, so take this as a compliment," Suzanne bowed, as a Japanese businessman would do, to her friend and partner.

Still smiling and gloating of her success, Nancy admitted to herself, 'at first I had reservations on how Suzanne would like the trip.' Thinking to herself, 'I'm thrilled that Suzanne seems truly content. I'm glad that I was able to divert her attention and unhappiness, if only for a while. I hope that by experiencing this gratification, her mindset might change.'

Afraid to bring any negativity into the conversation, especially about home, for she thought that was behind all of Suzanne's anxiety, she mentioned her happiness in finding Rich Colangelo. "I hope that when our business is finally finished in San Diego, that we'll continue our budding relationship and we'll see what happens from there."

"I have good vibes about the two of you and have a feeling that distance won't matter. You'll see, it will work out. I don't know how, but it will be accomplished, just wait and see."

"As you would say Suzanne, from your lips to God's ears."

The two women talked about past experiences, laughed and the time went by quickly. Before they knew it their plane was landing. As they were getting off the craft Suzanne turned around to Nancy. Hugging her friend she said, "I'm glad we're partners."

Returning home didn't seem like the usual hassle Suzanne thought. At first the cats ignored her to show how mad they were that she left them for the duration of time that she was away. Putting their tails up in the air, heads held high, they casually passed her and went upstairs without their usual joyful rubbing against her legs. Catherine greeted her with a big hug and smile. She then pushed her away, turned her around, examining her, and commented on how well and rested Suzanne looked after the long and tedious flight. "I hope, and it seems it has, the trip improved your disposition. I haven't seen you this relaxed in a long time. Come in the kitchen and while we're drinking our tea I want to hear everything that happened and don't leave anything out."

It didn't take long to verbalize all the experiences and sights that they had seen and done.

Catherine was excited listening to every word that Suzanne uttered and kept bobbing her head up and down. She looked like one of those novelty dolls, a bobble head. Suzanne held back laughter every time Suzanne looked at her. "I can't believe with all that you did, you look more carefree now then when you began this trip!"

"I think you're right. Let's see how I sleep tonight and I'll have a better idea on how positive this expedition was. I hate to be a stick in the mud, but I'm really tired and if you don't mind, I'll go upstairs and go to sleep."

"That sounds like a wonderful idea," Mrs. Walsh agreed. "If anyone calls, take messages and tell them I'll return their call sometime tomorrow."

"Looking directly at Catherine, Suzanne exclaimed, "As usual, you are truly my guardian angel. Thanks, and I'll see you at breakfast. By the way, when I finish unpacking, I'll bring down a little something I picked up for you on one of our expeditions."

"You shouldn't have, but I can't wait to see what my present will be."

Going up the stairs Suzanne smiled to herself. She thought of the surprised look on their faces when she would tell Mrs. Walsh and her parents their present. She wanted to thank them for all they've done for her through the years. 'I can see it now; all of us seated at the dining room table. Mrs. Walsh with her mouth opened wide, Dorothy and Morris shaking their heads in disbelief, when I announce my plans to take them to the beautiful island of Kyushu and then on to the city of Beppu for a vacation of a life time. I know, at their ages, they're ailing from one thing or another. Hopefully this unique gift will be a healing experience for them all. When they emerge themselves into the various hot springs and tubs it will prove beneficial in all ways. They have no idea how wonderful they'll feel,'

When Suzanne first entered her bedroom, Simka and Boston were laying on the bed, looking like the queen and king that they thought of themselves to be. When Suzanne put her belongings away from the suitcase, instead of jumping in and out of the satchels, as they usually did, they ran off the bed and went into another room. Suzanne knew that as soon as she was in bed, under the covers, that they'd resume their ongoing rituals like always. Sure enough, it didn't take them more than five minutes that they jumped on her bed, nestled beside her, purring as loud as always, when she scratched behind both their ears. All was forgiven.

When she closed her eyes, she willed all her negative thoughts away and made up her mind that whatever will be will be. 'Kay sira sira. I can't change people or events, (as much as I want to.) I have to realize that I can't always be in control of every situation.' With those thoughts she calmly rolled onto her side and slept peacefully.

Nancy got home in record time and came into the house that seemed quiet and empty. She was used to the quiet and it didn't disturb her as it once did. When Peter first left she'd walk through the house, tears running down her face, not liking what occurred. Eventually she got used to the peace and tranquility and rather enjoyed being alone. She wasn't as tired as she thought she'd be. Instead of heading upstairs to empty her cases, she picked up the telephone to listen and write down any important messages she felt had to be answered.

The usual amount of soliciting calls she received were immediately voided. She smiled as she listened to Rich's voice and attentively paid attention to his communication that only he did so well. He wanted her to call him, whenever she got home, and would look forward to hear her melodious voice once again. As thoughtful as she was, figuring out the time difference, she went ahead and made the requested summons. He was wide awake, and hoped that she had listened to her messages. He was optimistic that she would answer his plea.

"I couldn't wait till I'd hear your voice again," Nancy quickly replied. Rich responded, "Before I relate some happenings that I think you'll be pleased to know about, I want you to tell me all about the trip." Rich was sitting on pins and needles waiting for Nancy to finish her dissertation. It wasn't that he didn't want to hear her excitement about the trip, but knew she would be pleased at what he had to tell her. After, what appeared to Rich to take forever she finally finished her commentary. "Honey, I truly am happy that you and Suzanne's plans turned out better than you anticipated. To your question of us visiting the hot springs my answer will be, of course. It will be an unusual one, but one that I'm sure we'll never forget. Even though you had a great time with Suzanne, I'm sure that Suzanne couldn't fullfill some of your desires and wants that only I can do for you."

"Oh Rich, you really are a chauvinist. Seeing is believing," Nancy retorted back as she laughed. "Now what is your good news?" she asked Rich.

"We were able to figure out all of Curtis' bank accounts. We also matched the names of the individuals who requested the pieces of art that had been stolen and from where. The people or stores that bought these pieces, however, were not so pleased. Some sort of compensation will have to be made to the museums or individuals that were victimized. I can see a lot of lawyers rubbing their hands together, happy as pigs in shit, thinking of the money that'll be made through the legal system. They'll drag it on for quite some time, billing these people for as many hours as possible."

"Seriously, we could never have done it without you and Suzanne taking time to organize the receipts, bank accounts and all the other papers and list of art pieces that were stolen, where they were stolen from, and who eventually received these pieces of art. Of course your friend Justin was essential in introducing us to experts like Edward Murrey, the managing editor of Trace, to the people from the International Foundation for Art Research. Without their knowledge about the art theft organization, it would have been difficult to have tracked all of these pieces as quickly as we did."

"They were all helpful and delightful to work with. Someday I'll have to have a conversation, over lunch, and find out what got them interested in devoting their adult life and time to this cause. This is dedication to its fullest."

"I got off my train of thought, I'll try to continue. Thankfully, even though Curtis seemed to have been a piece of shit, at least he was an organized one." He laughed at his own sense of humor as he continued his dialogue. "We were able to have one of our artists draw Kyle's rendition of the man he saw arguing with Curtis. From what Kyle can see, it looks like the man that had the confrontation with Curtis. I think Kyle's interpretation off the Asian gentleman will be helpful. We'll be distributing the sketches to every precinct and hopefully to stores through-out the area. We don't want to scare this person away because we don't know for sure if it was him that actually committed the crime. Although I'm positive he had something to do with the death of Mr. Jones."

"There should be someone out there that will recognize this man and give us some information. I know it sounds great but there are so many variables that can take place. We have to keep a positive attitude that we'll get a call exposing this individual. Now that I've dominated the conversation I want to hear about the business part of the trip and everything that you encountered. Don't leave anything out."

"I can see this is going to be a very long conversation. Are you sure you're up to listening to me relate every little detail?"

"I love hearing your voice and if it takes hours I don't care. I envision your beautiful face as you're talking and it makes me happy. I'm ready. I've put a few cans of beer in front of me, have a blanket and pillow on the sofa for comfort, so go," Rich proclaimed.

They ended their conversation after a few hours. His speech was getting sluggish with the comments he made. It was getting harder for her to understand his words. They both had a hard time saying goodbye. After hanging up the receiver she went upstairs with a smile on her face and had a peaceful nights sleep. Nancy knew that she'd be dreaming of Detective Rich Colangelo when she closed her eyes.

It didn't take long for the two women to come down from their high and face the realities of life. Suzanne experienced the same bullshit that happened day after day when she returned to work. The only time she had to relax was when she called Madaline and went to her suite to get away from it all. She heard everything that Paul Winston was doing. Suzanne wasn't quite sure if Madaline was leaving an important part of the information deliberately out, but didn't care. She knew that when Madaline was ready to tell her certain details, she would. Suzanne was happy to hear about Kyle's fate and knew that the police would soon apprehend the real criminals that were responsible for his friend's death.

Even though Suzanne thought that Curtis Jones must have been a fraud and jerk, she didn't feel sorry that his life ended the way it did. She hoped God would forgive her for thinking these terrible thoughts. Suzanne couldn't help think of all the blessings that were happening around her. She was happy that Nancy was cheerful once again and hoped that her romantic feelings for Detective Colangelo was reciprocal. It was nice to see her friend and almost sister not haunted by all the terrible circumstances that happened to her.

Suzanne still waited while Madaline changed into her lounging p. j's. and made herself a drink, while she ordered tea to be brought up for Suzanne. Suzanne almost dozed while sitting on the comfortable sofa and had more time to reflect. With conflicting emotions, she wanted to hear and see Stephen once again. She needed, for her own sanity, to resolve all her misgivings and finally give him the ultimatum to choose her desire to finally make their love for each other legal. Otherwise she would have to make a decision that would break her heart. She could never love another man the way she loved Stephen. The feelings she had were special and she knew that she had to be strong for once, force him to make the choice of his life. Their happiness would depend on the decision he would choose. It will be the hardest statement for her to deliver. She knew it had to be done and deep down was afraid of what his answer would be.

As far as Hope was concerned, Suzanne had to let go. If Hope made a mistake then it was her decision and she had to live with whatever consequence came out of the marriage and her life. She honestly wished Hope and Spencer well. Suzanne wanted them to be truly happy. She'd tried not to be judgmental.

She left Madaline's suite after a while and slowly drove home. The weariness that she felt was overwhelming. She purposely rejected Madaline's offer to stay over, for she wanted to sleep in her own bed.

Suzanne was scratching the cats in back of their ears when the phone interrupted her tranquil state. When she heard Larry's voice at the other end of her phone, she immediately perked up. He told her of his family's trip to Russia and many of the Baltic countries. "I'm glad I took your advice to enjoy my children while they're still young and vivacious. The many pictures I took will fill a scrap book. I'll send some to you through the computer. "She noticed how gleeful he sounded and felt wonderful that, as a parent, he was finally getting to know the children better. The children also gained the intimacy and knowledge of what their father was really about. Other than seeing him pre-occupied as a business man, owning multiple business' they finally saw him as a compassionate parent. Suzanne was thrilled to hear that he made the effort to enjoy them and would cherish the vacation forever.

To Suzanne, it sounded as if he and his children were finally getting the fulfillment they all deserved. She related the trip that she and Nancy took and the experiences that they enjoyed. She thought of him as a good friend and confidentially told him of what she was going to ask Stephen to do. She thought she heard something different in his tone but put it out of her mind. After speaking for nearly 45 minutes they realized that Suzanne had to get some rest if she were to be efficient at her business in the morning.

When the receiver was gently put down, Lawrence put his hands under his head and Suzanne's beautiful face would not disappear before him. His thoughts were conflicting and although he wanted Suzanne to be happy, in his heart he hoped that Stephen would make the biggest mistake of his life. He realized that Suzanne would be broken hearted but he wanted to be the one to pick up the pieces. Knowing that Suzanne had him on the list for the upcoming nuptials, he was looking forward to seeing her once again.

During their conversation she told him that she'd be seeing Stephen a week before the wedding was to take place. He would know immediately if she had asked Stephen for a decision. He wondered if Stephen would be at the affair. He felt impatient while waiting for the event to take place. If he had a chance to make Suzanne his and his alone, this was the time.

Suzanne was waiting for Nancy to meet her at the spa. They were going out for their monthly dinner meeting. Usually Bev and Madaline joined them but for different reasons they each bowed out.

Suzanne and Nancy were seated at the restaurant when Suzanne said, "Please don't interrupt what I'm about to say."

"When I first met you I was in awe. Before knowing all the misfortunes that happened in your young life, you had everything that I wanted or dreamed of having. When you've grown up like I did, people who were rich seemed like snobs to me. I mean I was brought up in Dorchester, in a tenement house, living on the third floor in a five room apartment. We were five people living in this small apartment. My bedroom was in the back of the apartment, the railroad tracks behind the house. I hope I'm not boring you with my prattle?"

"No, no, please go on. I love to hear the way you were brought up and your perspective on the way you remember things being. Suzanne, please continue," a mesmerized Nancy pleaded.

"Okay, if I'm not boring you. Even though the apartment was small, it didn't stop many relatives coming, without invitations, to visit, kibbitz and have a great time reminiscing about the old days, where they came from and all sorts of things. In those days most relatives were called aunt and uncle, even though they weren't. On one of the visits, from cousins who lived out of state, they brought with them a wooden table and chair set from the furniture store they owned. I played for hours having tea parties with my dolls on that maple set. I can go on and on but I'll leave more stories for another time."

Suzanne was on a roll. "These days you're lucky if a relative comes over for a visit. People are so involved in keeping their children busy that the entire family has to schlepp the kids to all the sporting events that they take part in. Parents feel they always have to keep the youngsters occupied. God forbid the family should sit down at the dinner table and discuss what happened to each individual during the day."

"It's a shame that relatives don't get to know one another, make an effort to see each other, let the cousins play and get to know them. "Taking a large sip from her water glass Suzanne continued. "You see, communities change with time. As many Jewish families prospered they moved away from Dorchester or Mattapan and went to more affluent sections of the city, Roxbury, was another part of the Boston area that had many Jewish families living there. The homes were beautiful and kept up with flowers on what little land they had. Many moved to Newton, Brookline, Sharon, Stoughton, Randolph and places that other Jewish families had re-located to. People of the same ethnic faith always felt better when they had more people like themselves living in the same areas. If you look all the way back in time, the same behavioral habits keep repeating themselves. I don't know what got me on this soap box but I don't want to forget my heritage but at the same time I want to go on with my life as it is."

"Suzanne you have to promise me that you'll continue reminiscing about your childhood and the way you were brought up. I think it's fascinating," Nancy verbalized. "I love hearing your stories and I'll be disappointed if you don't finish them at another time."

"I dominated the conversation. We didn't have much time to talk about business."

"That'll give us an excuse to dine out again," Nancy said as they paid the bill.

SAN DIEGO, CALIFORNIA

Detective Rich Colangelo was just getting through his shift when Tom Curran caught his attention. "I think you should take this call. I think it's a possible lead in the Jones' case."

"Detective Colangelo speaking. Who's calling?"

"Detective Colangelo, I might have some information that you will find interesting. It's about the Curtis Jones murder."

"Who am I speaking to?"

"I don't think it's important at this time. I'll meet you, in say an hour, at the Owl Diner, three blocks from the Hong Kong Restaurant in China Town. I'll be sitting in the last booth. Do you know the place?"

"Sure do. I wouldn't be disappointed if we met at the Hong Kong, but for now I'll meet you at the Owl. They have a great menu. How will I know it's you?"

"You'll know." A loud click disconnected the call.

Rich walked over to where Tom was sitting. "Well, well, well," Rich expressed himself to his old partner. "It seems that we may have a lead after all. It's been how long since those posters went out?"

"I'd say about a month ago. Maybe three and a half weeks, the earliest. It certainly took a long time for this bozo to get in touch with us. Do you think this guy is jiving us or do you think he's legit?"

"One never knows. I'll go along and see what he has to say. I'll know in a few minutes if we have something worthwhile."

"I certainly hope so," Tom happily expressed his opinion. "If this guy knows anything, make sure you include me in whatever comes down. I hate being out of the mix. I've been a detective too many years to be sitting at this desk. I know, I know, the wife will have a bird if she finds out that I'm helping you. Hell, she'd have a bird if she even thought that I was thinking of helping you. Between you and me, what she doesn't know won't hurt her."

Rich smiled from ear to ear. "It'll be just between you and me."

"I realize you might have to tell Stu. The more I get to know him he seems to be a pretty nice guy. I think he'll be cool under the circumstance."

"Let's take it a day at a time for now. Let's see if this guy knows what he's talking about. How much longer are you on at the desk? My shift ends in about three and a half hours. Why?"

"Does Helen know what time you'll be home?"

"If you're asking me if she has me by the knuckers, no, she doesn't. I've been towing the line and once in a while it won't hurt if I went out with the guys after work. I'll call and tell her this little white lie. She won't know a thing cause I haven't given her anything to worry about. So far, that is. "He smacked Rich on the ass as Rich walked out of the precinct.

Rich wished he'd taken the corvette this morning but didn't want the rain to ruin the wax job that his neighbor's kid did for him two days ago. He gave the kid twenty five bucks and the kid was happy as a pig in shit. It wasn't often that Kenny, Rich always called him the kid, got to get close to the car he admired. Rich knew that Kenny loved his old vintage convertible and was happy to give the kid some extra bucks to do whatever he wanted with the extra money. When the time was right, he wanted to take the kid for a ride in the car. Hell, one day when the kid got his license, he might even let him take the car around the block for a kick.

Instead, Rich got into the Merc that, by now, he'd gotten used to. He had to admit it wasn't such a bad car, and the Captain had a special motor installed under the hood, for high speed chases. The Captain didn't want the rest of the guys to think he played favoritism and asked Rich to keep quiet about the heavy duty motor. He often wanted Stu to take the wheel but was paranoid that Stu would know the difference in the way the Mercury handled, compared to the other cars on the force. 'I guess life's a bitch, then you die,' he said to himself as he pulled away from his assigned parking spot in back of the precinct.

After taking three times circling the busy and long blocks to find a parking spot on the street, he spied a car leaving the curb. The rain was coming down hard as he pulled up the collar on his raincoat. As soon as he walked into the diner he spotted the guy in the last red vinyl booth. Rich slid into the seat opposite the, hope to be, informant. Rich took off his wet London Fog. He introduced himself to the guy who he saw was nervous. He could tell by the guy's actions that he'd rather be anyplace in the world other than sitting across from him.

"I understand you have information that I might find helpful. First of all, I'd like to know your name. I hate to talk to someone that I don't know, make sense to you?"

Rich could tell that the guy was scared shitless by the way he was looking all around and out the dirty windows. "What's your problem, you think I'm going to bite you?"

"No. I just don't want anyone to know that I'm snitching on someone that might make my life not worth living. My name is Sam and that's all you have to know for now, okay?"

"Sure Sam, I respect your wishes. Now tell me why you think you know whose picture is on the poster that's been around town for about a month." Rich could see the sweat visibly running down the guy's neck and the perspiration marks under each armpit.

CHAPTER THIRTY

“I understand there’s a reward for this information, right?”

“You’re correct. A reward will be coming to the person who gives us the information we’re looking for. It’s coming from a rich family who wants to find out who really killed an individual. I don’t know for sure how much money there will be, but it shouldn’t be less than $25,000. Do you honestly think you know the name of the individual whose picture is plastered all over the city?”

“Okay, I’m going to tell you a story that you might or might not believe. I assure you, I’m telling the truth. I work for this important firm that has offices all over the world. Last month I was working out of our New York office and didn’t get back till four days ago. I’m one of the head engineers for this well-known company. My position in this corporation is of great importance. The gentleman that I will tell you about is a well-recognized man in this influential industry. The reason that I’m telling you this, is for you to know the imperatively dangerous situation I’ll be putting myself in. I have a family that means a lot to me. I don’t want anything to happen to them or myself for that matter. You have no idea how powerful and harmful this man can be. He has contacts in the Japanese underworld that he can contact and by his giving them an order, they will execute without any hesitation.”

“I know all about the Japanese Mafia or as you people say ‘Yakuza.’ Go ahead, I’m all ears.”

Rich and Sam ordered from the menu and as they ate Rich listened intently to the information given to him.

“You have to promise me that you’ll protect me and my family. If they ever find out that I was the one that gave the police the name of the man they are looking for...”

Rich tried to explain to Sam that he would do all he could in keeping the data confidential. ”I can’t guarantee that word might not leak out, but I’ll do everything in my power to make sure it doesn’t. We’ll have to meet at another place and time when I verify that the report you give me pans out. Give me a number that I can reach you. It should be a number that only you can answer and I’ll make our conversation short and sweat. Here’s my card with all the phone numbers that you’ll need to get me.” Rich paid the bill and told Sam that he’d contact him within a few days. ”Now don’t sweat it Sam. Everything will be all right. Stay calm and pretend this night never happened. Don’t act nervous. Just be yourself and no one will know what’s just transpired between us, okay?”

“I’m taking you at your word Detective Colangelo. My life and that of my families are now in your hands.”

As Rich got into his car he shook his head. ‘Great, that’s all I need. Now I’m going to be responsible for this guy and his whole clan, wonderful!’

Rich called Tom from his cell phone and told him to come to his house when his shift ended. ”I’ll grab a pizza and I have lots of beer in the fridge. I know what you like on your pizza so don’t worry, lots of pepperoni.”

Tom sat on Rich’s sofa waiting for his buddy to tell him the information obtained from this guy. ”Do you think this info will pan out? There’s been so many false leads, I’m getting a little skeptical.”

"You know Tom, I really think we have something here. He mentioned something about the Yakuza. Our people have infiltrated this secret organization. It's dangerous for anyone who has joined the Yakuza. So far we've been lucky to keep these people under cover and they need this confidential security. I don't know who these guys are so it'll be hard for anyone to find out anything about these operatives. You have to realize that, like the mafia, there are various societies of Yakuza. There are new groups with different scruples making a name for themselves. I know that these undercover agents have been able to spy upon some important leaders of this mafia type organization. As soon as the court gives the okay we'll have these guys start wiretapping. We now have men in apartments that can literally see into some of the leader's windows. Sometime soon some of these spy's will be putting in devises so their conversations can be heard. It won't take too long as these operatives have been in the secret gang for quite some time now."

"They have won the respect and are considered good members who will give their life for the 'oyabun.' They have laws of their own, God forbid anyone betrays them. That's why it's imperative that no one knows who these men are. Christ, these guys even got the body art tattoo. It must have hurt like a bitch. When these guys are 'naked,' a fully tattooed yakuza looks like he's wearing long underwear. I understand that every member of the Yakuza is required to have tattooed their entire torso, front and back, as well the arms to below the elbow and the legs to mid-calf. There are different gang insignias and abstract designs that are typical images used for Yakuza body art. They have dragons, flowers, mountainous landscapes, turbulent seascapes, gang insignias and abstract designs. It can take hundreds of hours for the applications to be completed. The process is considered a test of a man's mettle. These guys look like the 1950's rat pack. They wear shiny tight-fitting suits, pointy-toed shoes and longish pomaded hair. They drive around in expensive automobiles and don't worry about fitting in with the crowd. Obviously they don't keep low profiles. These new gang members are altogether different. They're cocky son of a bitches that don't' dress up, still have all the tattoos, but drive scooters and motor cycles."

"I don't think I'd want an undercover assignment, even if it were the Italian mafia, like part of the Bonanno family. No, I don't think so. Between you and me I bet there are spies who work for the government and police agents that are on the take. There are a few guys I, personally, don't trust and have my suspicions about. " "I've heard about these double agents and as far as I know I wouldn't even spit on them. As far as I'm concerned they are the scum of the earth. They're getting paid by both sides. Their all nuts," Tom stated.

"I think I'll have another beer after hearing all this espionage stuff that's going on. For Christ's sake, you can't trust your own family with the things continuing to dissipate." Tom got another piece of pizza and washed it down with his second beer. "Another thing, we can't tell anyone, even the Captain about this guy. It's not that I don't trust the Cap. We don't know if any spys could be around the Captain or have his office bugged and then this guy and his family can be eliminated," Rich explained his position to his very best friend. "So, after hearing all this info, you still want in?"

"As long as I don't need no fucking tattoos. Hey we've been partners for over 20 years and we know we can trust each other. Hell, yes. It'll feel good to be on the inside again and help catch these guys, especially the head man and his family along with the guy who actually murdered this Curtis guy. So, tell me what I have to do. I'm there for you."

"I'll be calling this man 'Sam' in a few days to arrange another meeting. I think a good place to meet with him is the San Diego Zoo. There's so many people milling about. I think it'll provide a good cover."

"Hey, the exotic bird aviary would be a great place to meet. If the guy is ever followed, with all the noise the birds make, it'll be hard for anyone to hear your conversation, even if they are able to put a mike on him, without his knowledge," Tom suggested.

"I knew I could use you. You still haven't lost it buddy. Great idea. If the guy can find out more info on this person, whose picture has been plastered all over the place, we'll teach him a few tricks to make it safe for him, or as safe as we can. Who knows, this is becoming more interesting as time marches on."

"You know Rich, most cases, if not solved within a few weeks are considered cold cases. In this situation, it looks as if, even though many weeks have gone by, we might actually be able to solve this crime."

"No shit, Dick Tracy." Rich sarcastically said. "Rich, for being such a nice guy, you really are a prick."

"Thanks Tom, I've missed our bantering."

That evening Rich called Nancy. He was excited to tell her the good news about the progress and headway that might be coming down shortly. Nancy then tried prying some information about the case. "After all, you know how much Suzanne and I worked this investigation and took time getting the material that helped you in clearing up some of the missing pieces."

"Honey, as much as I want to tell you everything, I'm sworn to secrecy. Besides, we have to check out the story that this guy will be giving us. Hold tight. When this mess is cleared up, we'll be able to openly discuss everything pertaining to the case. Just bear with me and have faith in my judgment, okay?"

It was hard for Nancy to contain her curiosity. She tried with all her might to keep the conversation light, and not be her usual self, a curious and impatient Nelly. "Rich, I can't thank you enough for keeping us in the flow. I do understand the reason for all this espionage and secrecy. I'm trying with all my might not to bug you by being abrasive and nagging you to death. I'll be praying for your safety and of course all the people who are working the case. I'll be waiting with baited breath to hear from you."

"You don't have to worry about that. You won't be able to get rid of me that easy. I'll be calling you practically every evening, unless we're diligently scouting and working around the clock. Who knows where this will take us."

"With all the insane happenings in this world, I might have to be doing a lot of traveling. One never knows what this involves. Take care my love, and I'll be speaking to you real soon," Rich kissed Nancy over the phone and told her he loved her as he hung up. She wasn't sure she heard him and had mixed emotions about her hearing his declaration of love.

Nancy appreciated his loyalty to his men but on the other hand was frustrated that he couldn't tell her specific information so she could relate these facts to Suzanne.

BOSTON, MASSACHUSETTS

Paul left Madaline promising that he'd be returning shortly. He had a few more leads to follow up on and he was sure that he'd find her first born. "Now I don't want you to worry or think that your child is the person behind all of the bad things happening to you. . It's only a hunch. I'll get to the bottom of this assignment before you know it."

Madaline was getting anxious waiting for Paul to bring her information on their search for her missing child. While he was away gathering more information, she spoke to him every night after he finished investigating the mission at hand

"I think I've made some headway. Most of the people I'm speaking to are helpful and co-operative and are willing to divulge personal information to help us in our search. Somehow I have a feeling that one of these leads will pan out. I have a few more states to cover and then I'll be coming back to the East Coast."

"I hope your instincts are on the mark. Besides being curious on meeting the child that I had to give up, I'm waiting with baited breath to finally get to the bottom of this mystery on who is stalking me and trying to either kill me or do me harm. You can't believe how nervous I am, every day and night, that this insane person will attempt another stunt to hurt me. I'm listening for every little noise and am getting paranoid when I feel that someone is watching me. The hairs on the back of my neck actually stand up. You know, Paul, I don't think I'm imagining these occurrences."

"Keep cool and I'll be home shortly. If you're really worried about someone doing bodily harm to you, you might want to ask one of your friends to stay with you, especially before and after the show. I'm sure that they'll work something out to make arrangements to keep an eye out for you."

"As much as I'd love to take your advice, Suzanne and Nancy have already gone above their duty to help me out by taking so much time in California. I'd feel guilty asking them for any other favors. Thanks for the suggestion, but I'll have to be a big girl and fend for myself. I know that you'll be home shortly and with that knowledge I'll try to stay calm and collected."

"Okay, you know that you can call me at any time and don't forget that the police are always helpful. 911 is easy to call. Keep your cell phone with you at all times, understand?"

Laughing, Madaline responded, "Yes boss, I will obey."

"Very funny. Be careful and don't take any chances. I can't wait to see you. Till then, keep your chin up and for God sake, take something to calm your nerves. You'll feel a lot better once you feel relaxed," Paul told Madaline.

Paul got off the phone and sat on the soft bed in the Motel. He was traveling all over the Mid-West and was making some headway. In his heart he still thought that the person he was looking for was located in New England. He'd fly home tomorrow and surprise her. It was up to him to track down the people who he thought were in the acting profession and in the immediate area.

He was afraid to broach the subject about the investigation with Madaline but knew it couldn't be avoided. Paul hoped that the material he was gathering, for once, would be inconsequential and wrong. He was afraid that the one person who Madaline wanted to find in this whole world is a person who she comes in contact with every day. 'Deep down I'm hoping it isn't her that's the stalker.'

He poured himself a small glass of Wild Turkey and stared at the amber liquid. The warmth of the drink felt good as it smoothly went down his throat. He didn't want Madaline to know that he'd be landing in the east coast tomorrow. Paul was afraid that all hell will break loose when he had to tell her his findings. He didn't want this meeting to get out of hand. All he could do was try his best and do the diligent job that was asked of him. With those thoughts it didn't take him long to fall into a deep sleep. He woke to a dreary, cloud covered sky, looking like the ominous thoughts that were going through his mind. Paul rarely had headaches but this morning, no matter how much Advil he took, the sick feeling in the pit of his stomach and the pain that felt like a migraine, would not go away. It was a doozy. He realized that with the tension and knowledge he possessed, his mind was going a mile a minute. He understood that the evidence achieved could not be disputed.

Knowing Madaline as he did, Paul anticipated the verbal quarrel that would take place. Without knowing the complete facts, Madaline would try to convince him that a mistake was somehow made. He shook his head and was not looking forward to the next few days. It was tedious work substantiating and going over every paper and the many affidavits he had gathered. The only prayer he asked of God was whatever was going to happen or whoever was doing these awful and spiteful acts will hold up on any further actions, at least until he returned to Boston. He was sure that as long as he was protecting Madaline, that she would be safe.

When Hope asked Suzanne to help her finish some of the wedding preparations she was surprised that Suzanne was willing and happy to oblige. Hope didn't have any expectation, with all the arguments the two had. Her mother seemed to have made a 100% turnaround and was glad to co-operate with any assistance asked her. She knew that anything pertaining to the church service, Hope would not bother her mother with. She was sure that Spencer's parents wanted to take care of that detail. Anything pertaining to the impending reception, her mother would be delighted to give her valued opinion. She respected the knowledge that her mother had in design. Whenever Suzanne was in charge of any function, she would organize the affair to perfection. Every detail would not be missed.

Once Hope knew that she could count on her mother for that important assignment, she didn't have to worry about a thing. She was aware how her mother felt about explicit items, making sure that nothing would be forgotten. From the fresh flowers and a separate basket in the ladies room filled with hair spray, combs, extra panty hose, in all different sizes, tissues and various perfumes will be filled to the top of the basket. One thing Hope had to admit was that her mom was thoughtful and this touch would be noticed by all the women attending. She wanted to finalize the menu and Spencer said that he would leave everything pertaining to the reception to her. She valued her mother's knowledge about these things, from the smallest item to very important matters that guests would be aware of. The seating of the guests was an essential part of the wedding as well.

Suzanne knew that she'd have to get in touch with Spencer's parents about their list of guests and what their opinion was on who should be seated with who. She also realized that it was time to invite Spencer and his parents over the house for dinner. It was customary that this be done so the in-laws could mingle. She really wasn't looking forward to this meeting. Suzanne had a lovely home, it was the same house that the girls were raised in. Granted she updated the kitchen and bathrooms and the décor was beautiful. But she still felt like that little child who didn't like rich people and thought they'd pick her and her home apart. It was silly for her to feel this way and tried not to. She'd leave the entire meal to Mrs. Walsh's discernment, maybe she'd give an opinion or two, she thought as she went into her next client.

Suzanne went with Hope and the wedding attendants to the bridal store. Hope had gone ahead of time and picked out the gown of her choice. She brought Suzanne for support to see if she thought her bridal gown looked good on her. When Suzanne saw Hope in the white silk chiffon gown with a long train, with lace applique throughout the bodice and train with mother of pearls accents, Suzanne's heart skipped a beat. Hope's thin waist was accentuated and the beautiful neckline was perfect for Suzanne's pearls and earing set that would complement the gown to perfection. She tried to contain her tears. It suddenly occurred to Suzanne that she should ask if Hope would want to wear her wedding gown. It was specifically preserved and she had kept it in the back of her closet all these years. Before a deposit was put down she would ask Hope the question about the gown. All Suzanne could think of was holding Hope in her arms when she delivered her special bundle of joy. 'Where did all the years go?' she asked herself. She remembered her wedding day and it brought back good and sad memories.

In a few weeks she knew that Stephen would be coming to Boston and they were going to see one another. She wanted to have a great time and was looking forward to seeing him again after this long separation. She missed him terribly and was sure the feeling was mutual. She had to put the big question and ultimatum that had to be discussed, away for now. It was necessary not to bring the subject up at the beginning of their reunion, ultimately not wanting to make their time together miserable. She wanted to concentrate on their being together and of course their love making. She realized how horney she was and could almost imagine how sensual Stephen would be when they would finally get together.

When she arrived home she discovered the house unusually quiet. She figured Mrs. Walsh was out shopping, doing a few errands. Sitting on the floor of the den, she put slow music on the c. d. player; she wanted to reminisce. Opening the pages of the many photo books she saved, one by one, she remembered taking many of these pictures. The kids loved going to the zoo. There was a picture of the three young girls atop an elephant and later laughing at the chimpanzees.

She would never describe herself as maudlin, but for some reason she couldn't stop being emotional. She was glad that she was alone, that no one could see her sobbing uncontrollably. Suzanne kept going over and over the albums trying to remember the babies they were, now grown girls, who had become young women. She thought to herself how fast time went by.

'At least Hope won't realize how painful the wedding will be for me and my parents. Dorothy and Morris cried many a tear when they heard about Hopes' conversion. Let her enjoy her wedding, she doesn't need any aggravation on her special day.' Suzanne begged her parents and thankfully they would come to terms with their daughter's wishes. Suzanne hoped that none of her children had to endure the pain, agony and hardship that one gets when a divorce breaks up a family.

SAN DIEGO CALIFORNIA

Nobuaki again called Hirohito and asked him to come over. He needed to see him at once. Even though Nobuaki was eating his dinner, he pushed it away and hoped he would have time to finish it later. It was unusual to be summoned in the evening by Nobuaki. The only good thing he could think of was, he would once again see Mitsuko. She got more beautiful with every passing year. He remembered when Nobuaki first brought her home. She was working at one of the Love Clubs that his oyabun owned. Hirohito never thought that Nobuaki had a romantic relationship with the "little one," a nickname he had given her.

Mitsuko answered the door and greeted Hiro. He climbed the steps to Nobuaki's second floor office. He thought to himself: 'I could look at Misuko forever and never get tired of watching her.' When Nobuaki invited him to sit down he knew serious business was going to be discussed. Nobuaki called for Mitsuko to bring two glasses of saké upstairs to his office. When Mitsuko left he told Hirohito to drink and prepared him for his next task. I know you didn't do exactly what I asked of you the last time I wanted you to get rid of someone. This time, I shouldn't have to worry that I won't be disobeyed. This job will be completed by you. Hirohito nodded his head and told his leader that he learned his lesson and never again would he have to inflict pain to himself. Nobuaki nodded and knew exactly what Hirohito was talking about.

"Do you remember that I told you that one of my friends has a white ghost girlfriend? I told you what I wanted done. It's a definite that she has to be eliminated. As I told you before, there's no pressure as to time. Did you get her picture and study it? Make sure you keep following her. One of my Kyodai will put a device in her phone and in a few rooms, most likely in the chandeliers. This brother does not think she'll be aware of these transmitters in her home. Be discreet when you take more pictures of the young lady throughout the months to come. Be sure you keep track of her schedule. It's important to figure out her usual daily schedule, what she likes to do when not at home. I don't want this murder to be committed in her home. It has to look like an accident. Am I making myself perfectly clear, my friend? There are to be no slip ups. Do you have any questions?" "No great leader. You've made the assignment perfectly clear," voiced Hirohito. "I'll get in touch with you when I get the material you'll need. It's nice seeing you once again, my good friend, and you'll be hearing from me shortly." Hirohito bowed proficiently when leaving the room. 'Not to be disrespectful, but Nobuaki already went over most of these details. I hope he isn't losing his mind,' Hirohito thought as he smiled while he bowed to the woman he wanted to someday call his wife.

Sam called Rich. They set up a time and date to meet. Meanwhile, the FBI agents rented the house across the street from Nobuaki and started their surveillance keeping one man on for four hours at a time. The phone was bugged and they wrote every name and number that either he called or received. They also took pictures of the various people going to his house. The group hated these long periods of waiting and didn't know how much time they'd be assigned to this operation. The only good thing about this job was they got to eat on a regular basis, with the chief picking up the tab. They didn't have to live on deli or fast food. As soon as they got all the information they knew, the take down had to be fast. There was no room for dilly-dallying once the chief told them to move. It had taken years for the spies to get Nobuaki's confidence. He'd take a shit when he found out who the informants were. The only thing they'd have to worry about was retaliation from the leader to his trusted men. They would have to watch their backs for quite a while. Meanwhile, diligence had to take precedent. The Captain and a few high government officials were the only people who knew their real names. They hoped that the officials weren't corrupt and these men could be trusted, otherwise their work will have been in vain. They hoped that an unfortunate accident didn't befall them.

Rich and Tom walked through the zoo like any tourist would. They watched, took pictures of the animals in what seemed their natural habitat. While walking they remarked how beautiful the area was and eventually made it to the bird Aviary. Sam was also making his way to the sanctuary; their timing was exact. If Sam were followed, it would be difficult for the Japanese Yakuza to realize that Sam was meeting with the two operatives.

There were many people walking through the Aviary admiring Hawaii's native birds. There were many birds from different countries with vibrant colors that one had to stop and take pictures because their friends wouldn't believe what they saw.

"Sam, did you make sure that no one followed you? Asked a concerned Detective Colangelo. "I've been looking and tracking my movements and it doesn't seem that I'm under surveillance." He looked at Tom with suspicion. "Please, excuse my unmindful introduction. Sam this is my former partner Tom. We were together for many years and he's an extension of me. Tom, meet Sam, who I think will be instrumental in getting to the bottom of this case. Sam, you might also meet another partner of mine who'll be helpful in assisting us with the information you provide. We'll walk through the bird sanctuary and I don't think anyone will know the three of us are together. When we speak, we'll look and point at the other birds, except the conversation will be about your boss, who you think is one of the participants in this crime."

Rich asked, "Did any employer at the office ask you why you were leaving at an unusual time?" "First of all, with my experience and being one of the head engineers, I have pretty much free reign of the place. There are some employees that have more seniority than I, with some executives higher up the chain. But, in my position, little is asked on my whereabouts. I did some checking on my own and have been able to get my hands on a few pictures of Mr. Makino, who I believe is the person you have on the posters with a drawing of his head. He's the founder and president of the company and I can't understand why you would want to know aspects about him that obviously are of a criminal intent."

"Sam, I don't want to scare you, but we'll be needing your help in this situation. If Mr. Makino is the man we're looking for we hope you'll be able to assist us getting information that we might need. You have the option to refuse and we'll understand you're not being part of our investigation. It's not easy for a lay person to suddenly be thrown into something that you have no idea what we're going to ask of you. Sam, take your time and think about the matter carefully. I understand that you're worried not only for yourself but also your family as well. We really appreciate the pictures you have for us. That alone, with knowing who we're dealing with is tremendous. To have a name and his position in the company will be valuable. By the way, even if you don't lend a hand any more, you'll still be getting the reward money that you were promised. If you do decide to come on our team, we'll obviously teach you many aspects of our work that will be mind boggling. I hope we do hear from you, cause we know that you'll be instrumental in our investigation." They were coming out of the Aviary. "I hope to hear from you one way or another about your decision. Whichever way you decide, I can't thank you enough for all you've done."

When the three men left their meeting, Rich discreetly mentioned that they couldn't shake his hand. "Remember, we don't know you from a hole in the wall. We can't be obvious in our conversation. Sam, don't take a long time in making up your mind." Rich and Tom took a right turn heading for the lion's den and Sam walking out of the zoo, continually taking pictures as he did while he was inside, admiring the different species.

"What do you think his answer will be?" asked a concerned Tom. "It's a crap shoot. I have a feeling we'll be hearing from Sam shortly," Rich responded. "Now as much as I like seeing the zoo, let's get the hell out of here."

CHAPTER THIRTY ONE

BOSTON, MASSACHUSETTS

Paul's plane landed at Logan ahead of schedule. He hadn't eaten, and was hungry as hell. Thinking to himself he smacked his forehead, with the palm of his hand. He regretted not accepting Suzanne and Nancy's generosity, inviting him to take advantage of the use of their private airplane home. 'At least I would have been comfortable, instead of sitting next to a very heavy gentleman, who when not snoring while he slept, couldn't stop talking about how he enjoyed the trip to see his grandkids. He then proceeded by bringing out his photo album and showed me pictures that I didn't give a hoot about.' Paul heard the rumble his stomach was making and again berated himself for declining their thoughtful offer. Many times he heard Suzanne and Nancy talking about the meals served to them on their jet and was getting madder by the minute as his hunger pains increased.

He picked up his car at the airport. All he wanted to do was go home and rest before seeing Madaline again. He knew the confrontation ahead of him and didn't look forward to the battle. His car automatically turned into a Burger King. 'The hell with a diet' he told himself as he ordered a takeout of two double, bacon, cheese burgers with all the fixings, big bag of French fries, and a large, chocolate shake. He kept stuffing his mouth as if this meal was a prime rib smothered with aujūs, a twice baked potato smothered with sour cream, chives and bacon with a side order of asparagus sprinkled with seasoning. Unfortunately it was not, but to him this collation couldn't have tasted better. He let out a large belch as he finished the shake. Paul felt better and his mood changed considerably. He debated whether going to Madaline's performance and ultimately back to her suite. The unsettled problem kept going through his mind. As much as he wanted to go home and sleep for a while, he'd feel guilty not presenting her with the material she wanted to see. She then would be able to see for herself the progress report, that he worked hard obtaining.

Paul imagined her irritation if he didn't immediately bring over all the material he gathered with documentation showing his findings. Knowing it was critical for her to see, for herself, the substance of the information and go over the report and discuss the various parables with him.

When he got to the theater the performance was almost over. He was overjoyed that he didn't have to sit through it again. As much as he derived pleasure in seeing Madaline perform, he was exhausted, and eventually, when this ordeal was through, he wanted, nothing better than to go back to his apartment and sleep for a week. Besides, he hoped that after this assignment was finished, their relationship would continue. The connection between them was explosive at times. He'd have to see what would happen once their work was completed. As far as he was concerned, he hoped her feeling towards him increased. Being an idealist, he thought a romantic involvement would or could ensue. He took a deep breath as he entered her dressing room.

Madaline was thrilled to see Paul sitting and waiting for her while she changed. He raised his weary body slowly from the comfortable couch and was surprised that she ran into his outstretched arms, hugging him with all her strength. Madaline couldn't contain the honest happiness she exhibited when seeing him once again. Paul suggested going over to the Ritz to discuss the matters at hand.

Once seated on one of the many yellow chintz upholstered sofas, Madaline suggested a drink for them both. While sipping their beverages, Madaline wanted to see and hear about all the details that he obtained. Even though they communicated regularly while he was away, she wanted to see and hear for herself what his findings were. She hoped he was able to accomplish what he set out to do. Madaline couldn't wait to get his final assessment.

Paul didn't know where to start. He gathered his courage and told her about his experiences with all the people he met during his investigation. "First of all, I had a long conversation with Brian Martin. I found him to be a great guy and very accommodating."

"Madaline interrupted Paul. "Tell me how he looks, is he married, any children, and does he seem happy?"

"First I went to his ranch. Yes, I met his wife. Although she's not as beautiful as you, she's pretty, in her own way, and definitely a nice person. I wasn't there to access her, so I didn't observe what color eyes she had, or other attributes. I noticed that her eyes sparkled, and when she smiled her entire face lit up. She has long brown hair that she wore in a ponytail. There were toys in most of the rooms; I assume they belong to their children. I now know why your family thought the two of you would ultimately marry."

Ignoring his last remark Madaline continued. "I'm happy for him. He deserves someone wonderful to bring love and happiness to his life. Brian is special to me. He's truly a nice person. I'm happy that he's content and satisfied with his life. At least from you're observation it looks that he's achieved those goals."

"After I told him about you and your situation, explained my purpose and what I was there for, he went out of his way to accommodate me. He also asked about you. He told me he's kept abreast of your career and was proud that you got what you wanted and was content with your life. I found out that when the two of you were young, you always talked about famous movie stars and wanted, someday, to become one yourself. He was happy to hear that you're happy. When walking with his oldest child he tells him about a famous actress that he knows, showing him the tree the two of you sat under. I observed, without his looking, all the hearts, arrows, and initials that are still imbedded in its' trunk."

Madaline had a large smile. Tears were running down her face and heart-felt sobs emitted from her chest. Paul was surprised at her over-emotional sentiment.

Trying not to embarrass her, he continued with his dialogue. "Brian was kind enough to introduce me to your family. Your mother is very nice and your father is very different. Let me say he was standoffish. I realized that he's a cautious man. It takes him awhile to adjust to a situation, but when he thinks he knows you, he'll accept and consider you a friend. He provided me with information that he knew I needed. I was lucky that Brian came with me and acquainted us. If Brian didn't go out of his way to see your folks, I doubt your dad would have given me the time of day. I doubt your family would have been as nice to me either." Madaline laughed at Paul's description of her family.

"It seems that your siblings really weren't aware of what happened to you and why you left as abruptly as you did. Your parents are very conservative and never mentioned why you went away. They were hurt and upset that you went to your aunt's house in Kansas, without saying good bye to them. Even though there were rumors and speculation from other kids at school, your brothers and sisters disputed their theories and at times had to resort to physical violence to protect your name. It's a shame your parents hid all of the details of what transpired and never talked about what you went through."

"Do you think that's a normal way to handle such a meaningful and difficult situation? Personally I think I was brought up in a dysfunctional family. They would never discuss anything unpleasant that didn't fit in with their way of thinking. They preferred to sweep matters under the rug and pretend that all was fine and good. Anything that wasn't up to their standards was not discussed openly amongst the family. As a result, we were left in the dark, without understanding what happened in our community. Of course the kids and I always heard rumors but when we brought them to our parent's attention, they'd dispute them saying it was no one's business. We should all have gone for counseling, but in those days, who would have thought of an idea like that? It wasn't heard of that simple folks like us, who were poor and proud, would let anyone know of our troubles."

"Let me get back to my findings, okay? I understand why your brothers and sisters have so much bitterness toward you. The main reason for their hostility is they found out your mother gave you all her savings to go away. As far as they're concerned, this one act ruined their chances of getting college educations and be in a position to better themselves. Instead, they felt they had to stay with the rest of the family, never being able to leave the family farm. You and I both know that if a person wants to better him or herself, then nothing will stop that individual from doing what has to be done to make one's life better. It's easy to blame someone else for their lack of imagination or ambition."

"After a while, your parents sat down with the entire family, including Brian and me. At first your parents were afraid to broach the subject. I explained to your parents that they had to be open with the rest of the family. After telling your siblings about the terrible ordeal you had gone through, your mother covered her face with her hands and began to cry. They then realized the reason for your mother's action. Their feelings about you and your mom changed when they found out why your mother gave you all of her hard earned savings. They realized that she had no other choice, but did what she felt she had to do. After your mom explained how she hid the money from their father, he felt upset and embarrassed. He didn't want them to know that he was unaware of the money she had hoarded away. The feeling of bitterness somehow changed and was alleviated about 'the famous Madaline Mason.' The clan understood the predicament your parents were in. Your mom and dad had no other choice, but your siblings felt better knowing the truth. Brian and I were happy that your folks did the right thing by telling them the entire story. The truth always prevails."

"A little too late I'm afraid. What happened to dear 'Uncle Harry' the son of a bitch, bastard?"

"Months later your dad, finally, realized that you were telling the truth, only after speaking to Brian and your aunt. His life didn't turn out to be as harmonious as you'd think. Your family's attitude towards him changed drastically. Harry was no longer welcomed at your house. Your dad never spoke to him again. Sometime later, your father almost beat him to death when he saw Harry at a local bar. Their long, long, history and friendship was forever ended. He was lost without your father's companionship. He always felt your parent's family was like his own. He felt deprived and envious of what your father had. He would never be able to experience a family bonding from having a large and wonderful family.

After his exclusion from your dad and the fight that almost killed him, he was never the same. He believed he was an outcast from everyone in the area. Your folks never told a soul what happened. Harry ultimately became a recluse and an alcoholic. I spoke to him at his sister's house. Apparently, he has nowhere else to live. He's a habitual drunkard. I think with all his drinking his brain and liver is badly affected by all the booze he consumed throughout the years. I personally think he doesn't have long to live."

Paul had never seen a look of hatred that came over Madaline's face. "As far as 'Uncle Harry' is concerned, I don't feel sorry for the bastard. Regarding what happened, I feel he got what was coming to him. You reap what you sow. He should rot in hell. He ruined my life and that of an innocent child that shouldn't have anyone else bring her or him up, except the natural mother. I realize that I was very young, but you know what, I'd have been able to manage. I know for a fact I would have. He's the only person I wished death on." Moving her eyes a bit she continued, "I guess there's a few other's but that's for another time and story. You might have a different opinion, but everyone doesn't have to think alike. I'm sorry for interrupting. Please go on. Would you like some crackers and cheese to go along with your drink?"

"Thanks, maybe a beer would be nice." Taking a large swallow Paul continued. "Before I left, your father took me aside and we had a heart to heart talk. He asked me if you could ever find it in your heart to forgive him for not believing you. One by one, each of your siblings also came to me and told me to tell you that they think of you often. They don't hate you, they never did. They didn't understand why you went away and they were hurt that you never confided in them. They also wanted to have the entire family come to the farm and get together for an old fashioned family reunion. Your siblings, in my estimation, are very nice. They want you to think their offer over. They told me to tell you to take your time and think about it. They also wanted me to remind you that blood is thicker than water and you can never replace your true family."

"Thanks for giving me their offer of reconciliation. I'll think about it. Who knows, I might call each and every one of them, at different times, of course, just to get their goat. Let them stew a while longer. I will always respect and love my mother till the day I die or she goes to heaven. She is truly a saint, for her belief in me. As far as my father is concerned, that's going to take time, patience, forgiveness and understanding. I hope I can do it before too long. I realize that all of us are not getting younger and before I let more time go by, I'm sure that I'll find it in my heart to go there and have the kind of reunion that I'd like to have. Hell, Kyle will finally see his aunts, uncles, cousins and most of all, his grandparents that he always wanted to have. Like my brothers and sisters reminded me, 'blood is thicker than water.' There will come a day that this event will occur."

"Let's continue," Madaline stated, she wanted to hear more of Paul's escapades. "I did a lot of traveling, visiting orphanages, and I think I told you before, about the many lawyers who specialize in private adoptions, and many towns and city halls. I got to know the record people on a first-name bases. To make matters worse, a lot of parents that had adopted children were not co-operative. Thankfully, some were, and it was these people who helped me find out about some of the potential children, who are now grownups. Who knows, one of them might be the person you're looking for."

"Some of the younger lawyers, who took over the practices from the ones who either died or retired, were also helpful. If these lawyers had the records, they gave them to me. It was imperative that they coincided with the correct births and States where the adoptive babies came from. When I got in touch with the adoptive parents they told me where their children were and all about them. Many are now married with children of their own. Others still live at home while some of them left the State and have careers. Some are still going to college for advance degrees."

"I'm dismissing the people, who relocated elsewhere not near the Northeast. Deep down I think these young people are stable and have accepted and like themselves. They wouldn't change a thing. The ones I'm concentrating on are the young people who live in or around the Northeast, that have either jobs or going to school near the Boston area."

. "What kind of jobs do they have, what kind of careers, are they professionals, do they have a vocation or obligations? I found out if they are committed to a girlfriend or boyfriend. I did this by phone and I made them aware that this was for a private matter and that the person not be made aware of the questions asked about them. Most of these people were very co-operative and helpful. I also went to professors if they were attending colleges or universities nearby. I got a list of the times of their classes and asked if they had an idea if and when they missed any."

"I made a judgment call who I think are likely candidates. I found out their work schedules and time of their classes. Absences made it a little easier to eliminate them or to be suspects. BUT, and this is a big one, the kids who have boyfriends or girlfriends, who could help them do these awful, hateful, things to you, I kept on the list. I've pretty much eliminated those who I think are not likely candidates."

"How many of these, so called, potential individuals are on the list?" Madaline asked. She was curious and had many questions that she wanted Paul to answer.

"Before I get to your question I have to tell you what I did. I talked to them about their feelings about being an adopted child. Were they curious about whom their natural parents were? Many wanted to know about their natural parents, if only to know medical information, that wasn't available to them years ago. To make a long story short, I have a list of people that I found interesting and I'd like to go over the list with you. Do you think we should do this at another time when you're not so tired and we'll be able to talk and think with clearer heads?" Asked a cautious Paul.

Madaline proclaimed, "I'm too pent up with curiosity that I doubt if I could get any sleep. If you don't mind can we discuss, even a partial list, and then finish it tomorrow?"

"Okay, if you think you're up to it, I'll go along with whatever you want. You're the person footing the bill." Paul opened a notebook that contained many papers. The red, vinyl covered, three-ring-binder book was filled to capacity. "By the way, there are two more books like this one, only in different colors. I'll give you a condensed version and we'll be able to discuss this information with sensibility and, please, try to have your emotions under control."

"It'll be hard for me to do, but I realize that it has to be done in that manner. I promise to hold back questions until you're through. If I feel I have to ask you an important matter pertaining to a certain person, I hope you'll let me interrupt."

"That's seems fair enough," agreed Paul. "Come over here and sit closer so we can look at this book together. Let's start at the beginning and go from there. When I got to Kansas I found out that your aunt passed away a few years ago. I, unfortunately, couldn't get the name of the midwife that assisted in delivering the baby. I tried going to the many hospitals in the area that knew mid-wives who assisted pregnant women. A lot of the people who worked at these hospitals and were knowledgeable about the mid-wives were either deceased, moved away, or are in nursing homes. Many have lost their memories or are sickly and can't be spoken to or answer questions asked them without any rationality. That part of my venture was fruitless. Going to the closest town hall near where your aunt lived helped tremendously. I actually was able to get birth records. Although they were sealed for the adoptive parent's sake, never the less, I was able to pry out of these women, who worked at the town halls, information that normally wouldn't be given out."

"Boy, did I luck out. I then went to the lawyer's offices that were known to handle private adoptions during that time period. Again it was frustrating because many of them were no longer in practice, either by retiring or death. No one knew where the records were. I was able to find some lawyers who had taken over the practices of the older practitioners and was fortunate to obtain these records that were in cellars very dark and dim. I had to personally go through all these boxes, taking and looking at them one at a time. Besides killing my back, my eyesight is no longer 20/20."

"When I give you your final check I think that'll compensate for all the misery you had to endure and maybe you'll be able to go to a chiropractor to help with the alignment of your poor back. Yes, get your eyes checked also," Madaline laughed as she urged him to continue.

"Madaline, I don't think levity is a good suggestion at this time."

"Okay, I'm sorry. I hope you forgive me. I had to say something that would be funny. After all; it's rather depressing listening to you relate all that you had to go through. I have to admit this is fascinating. Please continue," a curious Madaline requested.

Taking in a deep breath, Paul continued his dissertation." I was able to gather the remaining names and wrote down the people who live in the Northeast. I think it's this list that we should concentrate on. Do you agree with me?"

"Absolutely! What professions have these people entered into and do they live anywhere near the Boston area?"

"There are some that live in New York and California, but are in this area for different reasons. The prevailing list includes professions that have them traveling, for different reasons, throughout the Northeast and some even in the Boston area."

With fingers on her jaw line she proceeded to say, "Mmm, interesting. Do you have the names of these individuals who we can find out more information about?"

Now Paul was getting nervous at what Madaline's reaction was going to be, once she found out that the main person, that he was interested in, was none other than Betty, her understudy. "Well, I do have a couple of names but the one that stands out is a person that you know and know very well."

"You've got to be shitting me. All this time the person who you think is my child is a person that I personally know. How can that be?"

"Get yourself another drink and don't dilute it as much this time. I want you to try to stay calm. You're going to hear this name and all I can say is, we can't make rash decisions on emotions alone. Will you do that for me?"

"Yes, yes, I promise to behave. I'm already on pins and needles. Please, Paul, don't drag this out. Just tell me who this person is. I realize you might be wrong and we'll have to look some more until we find the right individual. Am I correct in that assumption?" Madaline was now getting nervous. She didn't want to hear the response. She wanted this knowledge since she gave birth. Suddenly she was scared at what the answer would be. Madaline was biting the inside of her cheek, purely from nerves. "Come on. I'm ready for whatever or whoever you name. I just have to put this problematic discovery to a vigorous test and find out if your intuition is right. Okay, spill the beans." Madaline could taste the small amount of blood from biting the inside of her cheek.

With a heavy heart, Paul pulled out a picture of a very beautiful young lady. "You've got to be kidding. This is a picture of Betty, my understudy. It can't be!" a scornful and cynical Madaline protested. I've known this young lady for quite a while, maybe for more than a year now. We've rehearsed together, ate meals at the same table, and kibitzed for a while. I know I didn't treat her as nice as I should have, at times, that is, but I never treated her with distain. Paul, are you sure you haven't made a mistake? You're kidding me?" A nervous Madaline proclaimed.

Shoulders up to his head, palms up, he said with a regretful look, "I'm afraid not. Before you go ballistic, I have an idea you might go along with. Make a time, and place, with privacy, when the three of us can sit down and talk. Be sure she thinks it's spontaneous and purposeless. We have to make sure that the conversation is light and casual. We don't want to put her on the defensive. We'll try to find out all that we can about her. We'll have to do it in a way that she's unaware that we'll be prying into her private and personal life. Don't forget she doesn't know that we're aware who she is. Madaline, you have to be careful not to let on that you think she might be the daughter that you gave up, at least not for now. Are you willing to try my idea first and then see what ensues?"

"I don't know whether to laugh or cry. We have no choice. We have to find out if Betty is the child I delivered in that dreadful room that my aunt furnished and prepared it to become a delivery room. God love her, she thought she was helping my parents and me to overcome our misery. But you see, being pregnant, even though the baby was conceived in a dreadful manner, was not misery, but something that I looked forward to having. To deliver a normal and healthy baby that I could call my own."

CHAPTER THIRTY TWO

Madaline went on to explain, "At first I felt the little butterfly feeling or a scratch that one feels at the beginning of the pregnancy. I would wait, with anticipation for the little kicks; the legs or arms made while he or she was readjusting. I also saw my belly expand and could actually see the different positions the baby took by looking at my belly and seeing it move. It was a miracle that I had a life in my body. Of course, towards the end of the ninth month, I couldn't get comfortable if my life depended on it. It even felt uncomfortable sitting on a sofa, with pillows propped behind my back. If your judgment is right, she could very well be the person who has been stalking me. I'm at a loss for words."

A skeptical Paul said, "I find it hard to believe that the great Madaline Mason has ever been at a loss for words."

"It's true. For one of the first times in my life I'm scared. Of course when Brad died I was a basket case, but that's understandable. Even when Kyle was accused of murder, I knew that he was innocent. People who truly know the real Kyle, possessed the knowledge that he's a gentle soul who couldn't kill a bug if near him. I don't know how this young lady was raised and brought up. She must have thought of me as a horrible non-caring person and in her heart thinks or she knows that I'm her mother. We have to find out why she'd want to harm me. Could it be anger, jealously, greed or who knows what? Does she have an accomplice that's helping her? I'm sure if she does that it won't come up in this particular conversation."

"Honey, easier said than done. Please, I'm begging you, try not to think about it tonight. Try to get a good night's sleep. Tomorrow is going to be a critical day in your life. Even if we have to have this conversation, more like a confrontation, at another time because of conflicting schedules, don't get depressed. You're going to need all the strength you possess. It's imperative for you to be at your best. During this conversation, I'm depending on you to keep calm and let the dialogue flow. You have to promise me that for once, keep your mouth shut, even if you have to bite your tongue. If you have to lie to her, do so. Tell her it's about the play and you have some pointers she might find helpful if and when she becomes a leading actress. Now comes the hard part."

Madaline looked at Paul quizzically.

As if talking to himself, he held himself erect. "I didn't want to say this to you when this must be one of the hardest times in your life. But, I can't keep my mouth shut or my emotions at bay any longer. Many times I've wanted to tell you how I admire, respect and that I honestly love you. Not for the Madaline every one perceives as the actress or a person of distinction. I love you for who you are, without any pretension, a heart that is filled with goodness and a positive outlook on life. You've had to overcome adversity and you keep going, like the bunny in the Ever Ready commercial. No matter what, I love you, Madaline, with all my heart and soul. I don't want you to react in any way by the things I'm telling you. Think about what I declared and think hard. Whatever happens, will happen. I don't want you to lie to me because you don't want to hurt my feelings, that would be worse. No matter what the answer is, I'm prepared for it. I've kept my feelings pent up for so long that I had to get them out. You're not mad at me for blurting out my sentiments?"

Madaline was stunned. She literally felt as if she were tongue tied. With all the information processing in her mind she was bewildered. Stammering, "No, no, of course not, your emotions took me by surprise, that's all. Between the information you gave me about Betty and now your declaration of love, I'm truly at a loss for words."

Paul was kicking himself for blurting out his feelings and causing Madaline more confusion than before. Swallowing a deep gulp he continued, "Now I'm going to change the subject and return to Betty. The good thing about dialogue is, hopefully, the truth comes out. I think she knows that you're her natural parent. We have to find out why she feels the way she does about you and what made her carry out the actions that could dreadfully harm you. What would possess a young woman, who happens to be beautiful, like her natural mother, want to hurt you both emotionally and physically? These are important issues that have to be addressed. When you hear her side of the story, then it's up to you to tell her the truth about what happened to you. Don't leave out any grim details. You have to tell her how devastated you were when you were forced to give her up. It's important that she finds out how you really feel."

"This is essential for both of you. After you find out the entire story, it will be up to you to forgive her, if you can. She probably wants to injure you for all the hurt she has, not knowing the complete and real story. Then the ultimate test is to find out if she believes what you tell her. I have a feeling that you should hide all the tissues you're going to bring with you. You'll both be using them and more."

When Paul left the apartment, Madaline was stunned. 'I can't believe that with all that's on my plate, he tells me he loves me. Does he have any brains or feelings about what I'm going through?' Madaline asked herself. 'I always thought of him as smart and intelligent but he must not be the sharpest knife in the draw. How can he expect me to give his declaration of love any thought now? All my life I hoped and dreamed of finding my child and now it's about to happen. I'm going to take some Valium and Tylenol pm to calm, relax, and put me to sleep. This entire situation is getting out of hand. It's too much to handle.' With those thoughts whirling through her head, like objects being thrown about in a tornado, she didn't bother showering.

She put on her nightgown, picked up a J. D. Robb book, one of her favorite authors, and tried concentrating on Detective Eve, and her handsome hunk of a husband, Roarke. She knew, ahead of time, she would soon get tired, partly from the drugs she took and knew that reading put her to sleep. She laughed to herself thinking about the time she read Dean Koontz's, Relentless. She couldn't put it down and finally finished the entire book at five o'clock in the morning. That day was horrible. She couldn't concentrate because of not getting enough sleep. But, she had to admit, she enjoyed reading the book immensely, it was worth the discomfort. When reading a new script for a movie or play, she didn't get bored and enjoyed going through the text from top to bottom, unless it lacked imagination and was awful. Tonight she put the book down gently beside her and closed her eyes. Madaline was oblivious to the world of reality. She was asleep within 8 minutes. When she woke up in the morning her jaw hurt. She realized that she was grinding her teeth while she slept.

SAN DIEGO CALIFORNIA

Rich drove Tom back to the precinct after their 'boy's night out.' They discussed what information they got from Sam. "I know the guy is scared shitless and weighing his options. One way or another, he and the entire company will be screwed. If this Mr. Mikino is the president of the company, the corporation will either be dissolved or someone, maybe if there's a chain of command in this organization, that person can take over running this large firm. Sam is scared that he'll no longer have this prestigious association as being one of the head engineers. He's thinking all sorts of things. Plus he's frightened that if they find out that he was the one that betrayed the company's president and founder, all hell will break loose."

Rich agreed. He was quiet for a few minutes. He carefully contemplated his next sentence. "You know I think we have to bring Stu into the mix. Once we fill him in with what's happening we'll get all his cooperation. Not many bad cops are out there, we know he's a good cop, can't be bought off. He knows when to keep his mouth shut and he's efficient as hell. Stu will be a good source of knowledge and we'll have another cop we can trust."

"I'm sure the Captain knows about this case in more ways than one. He probably knows that the head of the Yakuza is being watched and spied upon this very minute. What they want to find out is who the people are that are involved in every aspect of the organization. They're hoping to find the higher ups in this awful structure. From the extortionists who threaten poor business people, who try to make an honest living, to the men who supply the drugs and how they get the drugs to the sellers. I'm sure the FBI and Interpol knows who's involved from the users to the suppliers."

"It also came to my mind that these people are probably in the business of child pornography, capturing young children, both boys and girls, to hire out for prostitution. I think all the law agencies are in on this mission. It's important that none of us, including the Captain, find out who these secret operatives are. They've probably been on this case for years now, working for the FBI, getting the mobs confidence in them. Hell, if word got into the wrong hands, they'd be dead meat," Rich verbalized.

"Our next step is to wait for Sam's answer. I hope it's the answer we want to hear."

Rich, Stu and Tom were on pins and needles waiting for their man, Sam, to contact them with his answer. One day they were positive that he'd help them, the next day they were down in the dumps, thinking negative thoughts about the entire scheme. Just when they were positive they wouldn't hear from Sam, the private phone line that Rich told him rang. Rich picked the phone up after 2 rings. Rich hoped, beyond hope, that Sam was willing to take a chance to help them in the termination of the awful Yakuza. He realized that the entire structure of the Yakuza couldn't be eliminated, but even if one cell could be demolished, that would be a coo. Sam's answer was positive when the phone call was over, the three men high fived each another.

In a low voice, Sam told Rich he'd meet him and his partners in Balboa Park in front of the ages of man exhibit. The time and day was imperative for him because his boss was going away, again, and it would be easier for him to leave the office without being noticed. If he wasn't there, his staff would think he's out for lunch. They arranged the day and time and everyone was looking forward to the meeting.

Sam showed up exactly on time and tried not to be obvious that he was talking to the gentlemen beside him. Addressing the three plain clothes detectives, "I'll be honest with you, I'm nervous as a jackrabbit in Farmer McGregger's garden." Tom tried to stifle his laughter, but had a hard time suppressing it. Sam was showing his anger at Tom's reaction to his nervous behavior. "Hey, I'm sorry if I pissed you off, but I think it's funny that you know that story."

"I do have little ones who I read stories to. We teach them to read and speak Japanese but feel it's important for them to know the ways of the American culture. Is this story not part of the American culture?"

Stu, who had young nieces and nephews, was impressed by Sam's initiative." Hey, there's nothing wrong with what you said. The answer is yes, almost every child knows about Mr. Mc Gregger's garden."

Trying to get to the reason of the meeting, Rich asked Sam if he was aware the part he was to play in this operation?

Sam hadn't a clue, but was willing to go along with anything they wanted him to do. "I received my American Citizenship papers and vowed my allegiance to the United States of America. I don't want people to think bad thoughts of the Japanese people. It's bad enough that the war between our countries brought distrust of my people. If I can help salvage our reputation in any way, I'm game."

"The Yakuza has an awful name, both here in America and in Japan. People are very scared of them. They are as bad or maybe even more wicked and sinful than the other types of mafia's over the world. I know the reputation of the Italian organizations and their activities, but I assure you gentlemen, they can't come close to the treachery of the Japanese Yakuza."

Rich was impressed by Sam's dedication and was proud of his feelings toward the American way. "It's like this Sam; we have to play it by ear for a while. We want you to act the way you always do, be as normal as possible. Meanwhile we'll teach you how to wire yourself without being caught. There are instruments that don't look like cameras to take pictures of the people you want. Being in the type of business that you are in, I'm sure you know of these devices. Anyway, there's a good chance that some people working with Mr. Makino or people that are gang related might be caught on your camera. Who knows, there might be no one in your work environment that is involved with Mr. Makino's shenanigans. But, we have to be prepared."

"Hey, even if he held a regular camera, people wouldn't know the difference, you always see Japanese people taking pictures wherever they go." Tom laughed as he thought it was the funniest humor he could have delivered.

Sam was offended by his ignorance but tried not to show his annoyance with the chubby man's insensitivity. His inexperience dealing with Japanese people was apparent, he thought, as he ignored his statement. "I'm willing to do anything you want me to do. You'll soon find out that I catch on fast and learn quickly, even though I say so myself. Where should we meet and when will you teach me how to use this equipment you're telling me about? If you don't mind, I'd like to do it as soon as possible, not knowing Mr. Makino's plans. He sometimes leaves abruptly and no one knows when he might show up at the office again."

"The faster we teach you, you'll have more confidence in your ability to use the equipment. Let's say tomorrow evening, at my house. I'll have everything you'll need there. We can't take the chance of you coming to the station house. I know your nervous and I'd be to if I were you. Before I give you more instructions I want to give you another thought. I don't know if you have the confidence to try to follow Mr. Makino to other places other than at work. In any event, we'll have undercover agents all around and they'll also be following him. Don't sweat it if you don't feel comfortable doing this add on."

"Meanwhile, never take the same route going to the office or coming home. When shopping, do the same thing. Always mind your back and be aware of cars that are behind you or as much as 4 cars behind you. Take a lot of side streets. That will let you know if the car you suspect is tailing you. I doubt if you have anything to worry about. Christ, you've been the model of a worker and efficient as hell. I don't think they'd think of you as a spy. But then again you never know," Rich remarked as he walked away. Before he did, he looked around and was sure that no one would think the men were talking amongst themselves. He had all he could do not to slap Sam on the ass and wish him good luck.

Yoshy called Robin just before she was ready to leave for the gym. "I'm glad I caught you before you left for your exercise class. Do you think you can pack and be ready to leave within 1 and ½ hours? I need a vacation and would like to take my favorite girl with me. It might be an extended holiday, so don't be afraid to fill your suitcase. Does that sound good to you?" Yoshy wanted Robin to accompany him on one of their many vacations together. "I'd like to surprise you and not tell you where we're going this time. Knowing you as I do, it's one of your favorite islands." They had traveled the world from Brazil, Australia, Hawaii, and many more exotic islands. 'As long as she's unaware of the real reason I'm taking her, she'll be okay. That nut, Nobuaki, thinks she's somehow involved in all of this nonsense. He doesn't know Robin as I do. If he did, he would know how preposterous his reasoning is.'

Since Nobuaki heard that Yoshy had taken Robin to his Island Paradise in Beppu, Nobuaki didn't trust Yoshy's white ghost girlfriend. He remembered Yoshy mentioning that Robin had seen his valuable paintings that he commissioned to be stolen from many museums and famous European castles. Nobuaki had known Yoshy since childhood. In numerous ways they chose different directions in life. Nobuaki had quickly moved up in the chain of command in the organization many people knew about and feared. He was now the leader of one of the Japanese Yakusa organizations. Yoshy was now fearful that Nobuaki had put Robin on his hit list. Nobuaki didn't want anyone or anything to compromise his position as the head of the organization. Nobuaki didn't know anything about Robin and was distrustful of anyone, especially white people.

If Yoshy remembered correctly, in one of their many conversations, he mentioned that Robin had seen his vast collection of paintings that he was proud of. With Curtis Jones murder still not solved, he didn't want anyone thinking that the Yakusa was responsible, in any way, for Curtis' untimely demise. Nobuaki was smart enough to know that people associated Yoshy with Nobuaki, as long time friends.

Yoshy felt ill thinking that Nobuaki was aware of the place that Yoshy kept all of his treasures. He wanted to protect Robin from any harm. He was sure that Nobuaki wanted her dead, only to assure that nobody could link Mr. Jones homicide to the Yakusa.

Yasuhito, Yoshy's limo driver, was outside Robins' house waiting for her to give him her suitcases for the trip. Yoshy was in the car anticipating their getaway. "I'm glad you packed lightly," he sarcastically remarked. "I can't believe you're actually on time. I'm impressed! Our plane leaves in about 2 hours. We'll make it just in time."

Robin, with an engaging smile, kissed Yoshy on the lips. "I can't wait to find out where you're taking me. Anyway, where ever it is, I'm sure I'll love it. By the way Yoshy, do you know how long we'll be traveling for? I want to be able to call the newspaper and mail and let them know when we'll be returning."

"Robin, let's play it by ear. I honestly don't know the length of the trip but it will be for at least a month or it can be up to four months." A sinister smile appeared on his face. "Yoshy, you're serious aren't you? I really don't care how long the trip is for as long as we're together. I'll tell the paper and the post office we'll be gone indefinitely."

"I'm sure you'll be happy with my choice. Most of the time you won't need clothes, with what I'm going to do to you. You'll have to wait and see." Yoshy tried to be enthusiastic and happy, but deep inside he had an ominous feeling that wouldn't go away. It was a distraction he didn't like. If he could leave everything behind and be with Robin alone, like a butterfly still in its chrysalis, not being bothered by anyone, living by themselves, with no interruptions, would be an ideal situation. Unfortunately, he knew it wasn't possible. He had too many obligations that couldn't be ignored. He wanted this vacation to last forever.

He hoped, beyond hope, that Nobuaki would overlook the wrong impression that Yoshy conveyed in a moment of reckless, passive bragging. He'd try to stay as long as possible, until he was needed back at the corporation. He was thankful that most of his business dealings could be done through the computer and communication wouldn't be a problem.

STONEY BROOK, MASSACHUSETTS

There were still a few weeks left till Hope's big day. Suzanne couldn't put off the invitation to Spenser's parents any longer. Suzanne picked up the phone, dreading the conversation she was about to have.

Suzanne had confidence in herself but still feared the idea of inviting these people to her house, probably by their standards, a modest home. A butler, she was sure, answered the telephone and asked Suzanne to please wait. A few minutes went by when Mrs. Johnson picked up the receiver. Suzanne, the evening before, tried rehearsing how she would speak and invite Spencer's parents over for a 'family' get-together. The telephone felt clammy in her hand as she introduced herself to Mrs. Johnson.

"I'm so glad you called Mrs. Morse. By the way, can I call you Suzanne? When Spencer mentions you, it's always favorable, he calls you by your given name. I'd like it if you call me Irene. My husband's given name is William. Believe it or not, he doesn't like it when people call him Bill. He always is called William. I'm telling you this so you'll be prepared ahead of time."

So far, Suzanne thought, Mrs. Johnson sounded very nice. "The reason for my call is to invite you for dinner next Saturday evening. I was thinking about 6:30, if that's a good time for you?"

"That sounds fine. William and I look forward to meeting you. If Hope is anything like you, we'll get along fine. She's a dear girl. We're looking forward to having her join our family. We'll get the directions from Spenser. Till then, ove-wa,"

Suzanne got off the phone and took in a deep breath. Thinking to herself, she thought the call went well. 'I hope her husband is as nice as she is. In a way I'm looking forward to meeting them.' "Mrs. Walsh, I invited Spencer's parents over for next Saturday evening and want to make this a special event. What do you suggest we serve? The appetizer should be something that everyone will enjoy. In a way I'm afraid to start with Shrimp cocktail. One of them might have allergies. For the main course I'd love to have something exceptional. For dessert, I might make my famous bee-hive and maybe a crème broulé. That way it will give them a choice. Of course I'll have nuts, cheese and crackers, and if we don't serve the shrimp cocktail as an appetizer, I'll also have that on my coffee table." Are Spencer and Hope going to join you?"

"With all that's going on I forgot to ask them. I hope they haven't made other plans. Of course I'd want them to be here. After all, it's a momentous affair."

"First of all, you're a great cook yourself. I'll definitely help you with the preparations, but I have confidence that whatever you decide will be up to your usual standards. That's not saying that I won't go over the menu with you. Then we'll discuss the dishes you choose and I'll give you my honest opinion. Is that okay with you?" Mrs. Walsh genuinely asked.

"I think that's a great idea. But before I get carried away let me tell you my idea. I'm thinking that I'd love to make my noodle pudding. That goes over so well, as one of the side dishes. In a way it will give them a little introduction to a Jewish dish, but it won't be a heavy handed reminder that Hope does come from a Jewish back-round. If they comment on it, I'll tell them it's an old Jewish recipe handed down from my grandmother and generations before her. I just thought of another dish that I'm sure they'll love. My mother's famous chopped liver with crackers on the side. Obviously, I'll also put out cheese, crackers and nuts."

"I love that idea. You might want to make some potato latkes as one of the appetizers, serve it with applesauce on the side. You make them so good. The children used to beg you to make them during Chanukah."

"That's a good possibility. The only thing I have to be careful of is that when I use the old fashioned grater, my fingers usually get scraped and bloody."

"Don't you tell me that the blood makes the latkes taste better?" Mrs. Walsh laughed, when Suzanne agreed.

"Thankfully I don't have aids or some other communicable disease. That means I'll have to prepare them while the guest are here. You can't serve them unless their hot and the edges are crispy."

"I don't want you to worry, so why don't you give me the honor and I'll make them for you? After all, you taught me how to make them the correct way by not using a blender, like many of the younger generation does. This way you can still entertain your guest and be able to converse with them. I'll even act as a servant. I'll pass the latkes, and the other hors d'oeuvre's you decide to have." That's a great idea. The only thing I don't like is that you're not my servant. I'd feel foolish passing you off as one. I'll introduce you as my surrogate mother, who, without you, I would never have been able to achieve my goals. I'll tell them that you were and still are, instrumental in bringing up the girls. I think that's a better introduction than you being my servant. After all, you are part of the family," Suzanne stubbornly explained.

"I'll go along with that. But that won't stop me from preparing the latkes and passing around the appetizers."

"Have it your way. I have to admit it'll make it a lot easier on me. I'll be nervous enough entertaining my, I don't know the English word to describe my relationship for my daughters, in-laws. I guess I have to depict them that way. It's so much easier to use the Yiddish word, muchatenistas. I remember that was how my parents and grandparents introduced them that way."

"You know what Suzanne, explain to them just what you told me and I'm sure they'll understand. Hell, they might want to learn that word when introducing you to their friends. It'll be between you and they might get a kick out of it. You never know!" With that as a final remark, Mrs. Walsh headed upstairs for her daily repose. Half way up the stairs, with raised voice, she asked Suzanne, "By the way, when do you expect Stephen to visit you? I hope it's not during that time frame."

"No, he'll be coming 2 weeks after, a week before the wedding. I'm looking forward to seeing him again. I know there are issues that we have to discuss, but for now I'm going to concentrate on the positive aspects of our get together. It's been a long time since we've actually been together. I'm sure he's as excited as I am for this reunion."

"I'll leave you alone so you can write down your menu for the entire dinner. I know how much you like to entertain. You'll have everything under control and as usual you'll have from soup to nuts. As Suzanne was listening to Mrs. Walsh,

Suzanne put up her finger and announced: "I know what I'm going to serve for the main meal."

"Don't keep me in suspense," voiced Mrs. Walsh. "My stuffed beef brisket, every time I make it I get rave comments. It's all in the special sauce and cooking it slow and for many hours. Yes, that's what I'll have. It's not traditional and that's why I like it."

"What a great idea," agreed Mrs. Walsh. "Though please, when writing down your list, don't leave anything out. Think what type of bread you'll be serving and for God sakes, when heating it, don't forget to take it out of the oven. I'm not going to mention how many times you forget to serve it. You know how there's something that you always forget to serve." Mrs. Walsh laughed as she went up the stairs.

Suzanne yelled up the stairs to Mrs. Walsh. I'll have a list and check everything off so I won't overlook anything, smarty pants."

SAN DIEGO, CALIFORNIA

Yoshy felt joyous as Robin slid beside him in the limo. He was happy that Robin was feeling relaxed and exhilarated at the same time. Besides taking her away from possible danger, he wanted to protect her as much as possible. "You'll enjoy where I'm taking you. I can't wait to see the expression on your face when you realize our final destination." He knew it would be a series of long flights but realized that it would be worth it. Yoshy also wanted to forget his obligations to his family, his business and all the other commitments he had on his busy agenda.

Last week Yoshy gave quite a bit of money to certain people that would be able to obtain illegal documents for both Robin and himself. Robin had not a clue what was going on. He didn't want to frighten her about the problem he was experiencing with the Yakuza regarding her safety. He managed to get a series of different names for both of them that would match their new U. S. licenses, U. S. passports, and new birth certificates and so on. These people had no contact with the Yakuza thus Yoshy felt comfortable getting the new documents from these American sources. When they entered the airport at LAX he then told her of his plan.

Again he told her not to ask any questions and go along with what he would tell her to do. 'As a matter of fact, Yasuhito hasn't a clue about my plan. The fewer people that know what we're doing and where we're going, the better. When Yasuhito drops us off at the airport I didn't care what airlines he leaves us at. I'm the only person who knows the terminal that we'll be boarding from.' "About an hour before we get our tickets, I'll hand you your new name, passport, etc. and I want you to memorize every detail about the papers. Please don't ask any questions and just do as I say, okay?"

"Yoshy, when you plan a vacation it really is exciting. I can't imagine what's on your mind, but whatever you say, you know I'll do anything you want me to. I promise not to ask any questions, on my girl scouts honor." Yoshy started laughing. "I didn't know that you were a girl scout. What other things are you keeping from me?" Smiling, he poked her side with his finger and they laughed together. ”There are a few things that you don’t know about me, but believe me, they’re no big deal. You never ask about my family for instance, or where I was brought up and any of the schools that I attended. You don’t even know if I have any siblings.”

CHAPTER THIRTY THREE

Getting serious, Yoshy felt terrible not knowing any of the important facts that Robin just mentioned. "Gee, I'm truly sorry that I never asked you about anything that was important to you. What a fool I am. We're going to have many hours on the plane and getting off at different countries. I want you to tell me everything that's important to you that you want me to know. Are you okay with that? Again, Robin, I'm sorry and I was in my own world. Will you forgive me for being so self-indulgent and not thinking of what's important to you?"

"Yoshy, I know how busy you are and you wouldn't think of these things. I understand you more than you think I do. You don't give me enough credit for many things, but again, I know what you're about and all I care is that we love one another and that's all that matters." He couldn't believe how lucky he was that he had such a wonderful woman who he both loved and adored. Of course he also loved his Toshiko, but in very different ways. Yes, he loved her, but wasn't sure if he was in love with her. He had deep respect and admiration for his wife but knew that wasn't all that was needed to make him happy.

Yoshy hoped that by his deception with different names and locations they'd be traveling under, Nobuaki will eventually give up on getting revenge on his Robin. Yoshy expected that Nobuaki would never find out his traveling plans. Nobuaki's idea's about Robin was completely wrong. Yoshy was sure that she would never tell anyone about him or reveal to someone, no matter what, about his private life. He would bet his life on it.

Holding hands, they walked to the first class section of the airplane and snuggled. While the rest of the passengers walked down the narrow isle, the two love birds couldn't take their eyes off each other. They were given a glass of Champagne and toasted each other before the rest of the meal was served. Yoshy told Robin that the flight would be different. "I'd like you not to ask any questions and leave everything to me. I want you to realize we are going to various destinations and the flights will be very long. I suggest that you walk around a bit during the air plane rides. I don't want anything to happen to the circulation in your legs. It will ruin our get away if that should happen." Robin complied with Yoshy's suggestion and made sure she went up and down the aisles as much as possible. Half way through the trip, Robin's head was on Yoshy's shoulder, while she slept, a peaceful look was upon her face.

She didn't have a clue of the perilous harm that might befall her after their vacation was over, when she arrived at their final destination or at home. He would do everything in his power to make sure she wasn't injured in any way. He didn't care if he had to fight the Yakuza with everything in his power to insure her safety. Since he met Robin his entire perspective on life changed. He couldn't stand to see anything bad happen to her. Even though his feeling towards his wife and son were beautiful, his feeling for this young, vibrant, beautiful woman was altogether different. For the first time in his life he felt truly happy and exhilarated. He couldn't imagine life without her.

Their flight finally over, they disembarked in Caracas, Venezuela, and Robin was speechless. "What a gorgeous location. This hotel is fabulous and remote.

How did you ever come up with an idea like this? I never thought that South America was so beautiful."

"There are many great sights that I want to take you to and see the wonders of the world. We'll stay for a few weeks and then I have another surprise for you." The two weeks flew by and she was disappointed when they were leaving. Again, another long flight was ahead for them. This time Robin was prepared for the flight but was still unaware of their destination. The flight was long and when they landed at Pestarini International airport she was aghast. "I can't believe I'm in Buenos Airis, Argentina. My God Yoshy, you certainly amaze me. This has to be a dream, pinch me, it has to be a dream. If it is, I don't want to wake up."

Yoshy squeezed her tightly at her comment. "We'll stay three weeks at this location and see all of the various cities and interesting sights around us. Wait until you see our little hide away." Robin wasn't disappointed when Yoshy brought her to their grand hotel. She jumped up and down like a little child, seeing Santa for the very first time. Again she took many pictures with the new camera he presented to her before their first flight. "I can't wait till I can have these pictures developed and I'll make both of us an album you will always cherish. I hope you know that I'll do it." Yoshy didn't know what to say. Unfortunately, the three weeks went by all too fast.

When they entered the next plane Robin was full of excitement. She didn't have a clue to their destination but if it was anything like the other places Yoshy had taken her to she knew she'd love it. For eight weeks they visited Brazil. Yoshy knew that it was divided into five regions and was an extremely large country. He wanted Robin to see it all and appreciate the beautiful country and it's people. They first visited the North Region and stayed in and around Manaus the largest city with many interesting sites. They took a large river boat tour that brought them six miles out of Manaus and saw the most incredible displays of nature's majesty. The Meeting of the waters, where two distinct bodies of water meet, but don't mix. Yoshy couldn't help but laugh when he saw how Robins' eyes were open wide and she stared at the two separate waters that ran side by side but didn't mix together.

They found out that the Rio Negro is darker, slower, and is a much heavier body of water that the Rio Solimoes. The temperate, density, velocity differences keep these two bodies of water separate for more than 6 miles before they join to form the great Amazon. On one of the tours Robin held a Sloth and went on a night cruise that brought them to see the anacondas, a small crocodile, and the piranhas that live in the same body of water. They walked the city for miles, enjoying the open market and finally ending at the famous Manaus Opera House. Robin was in awe when she found out that rubber merchants brought material from Europe by boat to build the famous structure. Even the "brick" walkway, where carriages used to leave off the guest, was made of rubber, so if these patrons were late, the carriages' wheels wouldn't distract the audience listening to the singer's performance. Robin and Yoshy had a hard time leaving this amazing country. "Yoshy, I can't thank you enough and especially when you surprised me by taking me to the Amazon Jungle. The rain forest was incredible and I'll never forget it for as long as I live."

"Now this last flight will take longer than any of them. We will have a few lay over's, but I'm sure you won't mind. Don't forget; make sure you walk up and down the isles."

"I'm sure you'll love our final destination." When they finally departed from their long journey and got off the plane, Robin recognized the beautiful island of Beppu. "Yoshy, this is truly a dream come true. You know how much I love this island. On your many excursions from San Diego, I've done some research about the attractions and I'd love if you'd take me to some of them. Of course I hope we stay at your beautiful house and I can, once again, admire your different and beautiful collection of art and antiques that you have."

"That sounds doable. I'm going to have you make our agenda and we'll go to as many places in the amount of time that we have. I'm hoping this will be an extended get away. I don't want this vacation to be hurried and short."

"That's fine with me. I'm always willing and able to be at your beckon call."

After arriving at Yoshy's palatial home, they unpacked and relaxed from their long, tiring and weary trip. Yoshy told Robin he felt fatigued and stretched out on his comfortable bed. He patted the bed, knowing that Robin would place her beautiful body beside his. With a shit eating grin he declared, "you know suddenly I'm not as tired as I thought I was." He took off his shirt and pants, leaving his underwear on. He slowly removed her outer garments, leaving her underwear exposed. He seductively rubbed her back, knowing how much she enjoyed this pleasure. She felt totally relaxed. As she closed her eyes, she was delighted with the pleasure she was receiving. Turning her onto her back he kissed her full lips, at first lightly and then put more pressure, feeling her response. He thrust his tongue and she enjoyed sucking and entwining it with hers. He could feel his penis expand, bulging under his jockey shorts. He expertly removed them, exposing his throbbing instrument of delight. He slipped her panties off and also undid her matching bra. Every time he saw her naked body, he couldn't get over how toned her long torso and legs were. He softly, caressed her back once more, then slowly moved to the front, to her smooth belly and lifting his hands further up, felt her large, full, upright breasts.

He could feel and see her reaction to his soft hands as he pinched her extended nipples. He took her breast into his hot mouth and sucked expertly on them, moving and biting, his tongue softly pinching the tip of her nipples. She moaned with delight as she felt her body responding to his touch. The wetness between her legs was apparent as she felt her womanly uterus twinging under his expert lovemaking. She wanted to reciprocate to see and feel his pleasure. With her eyes closed, she lovingly caressed his chest, twisting the little hair he had, into her flexible fingers. She moved her head down and sucked his nipples as he had done to hers. She then moved her hands slowly to his stomach and then expertly stroked his enlarged manhood with her smooth and soft hands. Their fast, rhythmic, thrusting movements were beyond anything either of them had experienced since they had been together. When they were finished making love they lay next to each other totally exhausted, yet at the same time exhilarated.

When they finally woke a beautiful full moon could be seen through the large window in his bedroom.

"It's a little late to take advantage of any of your suggestions. Why don't we go back to sleep for a while longer. In the morning, after a large and delicious breakfast, you can be my guide and tell me where we are to start our excursion," Yoshy softly spoke as he fell into a deep sleep.

Robin was delighted with his suggestion and more thrilled that he was letting her set the agenda for the entire trip. "Yoshy, I'm delighted that you're letting me act as your guide. I promise that, even though you're familiar with the area, this will be the first time that I'll be able to see all the delightful recreational places that this beautiful Island of Kyushu has. I also promise you that last night's lovemaking will not be the last during this trip. I believe we'll be enjoying the pleasure of your bed, on any bed, for that matter, every evening, if that's all right with you?"

Yoshy's smile couldn't be contained. As he poured the coffee for both of them, he sat down at the table and let her tell him the trip she was taking him on this glorious day.

"I suggest we go to the western part of Japan where Mts. Tsurue and Yufu would act as a backdrop that would face Beppu Bay. It'll take about one and a half hours from Tokyo. Maybe then you can show me some of the sights in Tokyo." Unable to tell her why, he sternly told Robin that they must avoid Toyko. Robin was disappointed about her suggestion but realized that Yoshy must know why he wanted to avoid the area. "Tomorrow we'll rest by going to one of the many hot springs throughout Kyushu Island and I'd love to enjoy the eclectic, blue, boiling mud pools. Then we can go to the milky, white colored spring of Monster hell. The next day I have planned for us to go to the most striking in Chinoike Jigoku. I heard they call it the blood pond where there are bright ponds of red, scalding waters."

"If I might make a suggestion, while we're at Monster Hell, we'll be able to see the crocodiles that are bred there."

"Yoshy, that's a great idea. Thanks for mentioning it."

"I thought on the third day we can rest and enjoy the hot spring right by your house for a little relaxation. I think we'll need it." Robin was exhibiting a big smile. "You know I've never been on an African Safari which is on Ajimie Plateau. I hear there are thirteen hundred animals that include bears, lions, giraffes, elephants, and Zebras. We'll be able to ride in protected vehicles and we can study animal ecology and actually feed them. I hear it's the largest Safari in Asia."

"I guess you have studied Beppu and some of the natural wonders that surround us. I'm proud of you."

"I'm sure that you heard about and read up on the 8 hells. They are one of the natural wonders of the world. Make sure you bring your camera to capture all that you're going to see. One of the largest is Boiling Hell. It's in Umil the Sea of Jigoku, which is an Azure color, in the North at the foot of Mt. Takasaki. It is 200 M. in depth and the temperature is 98 c. Have you been reading about the gurgling holes in Jigoku Meguri? It ejects mud and minerals."

Looking smug Robin explained that she had, indeed, seen everything he talked about while looking through the internet. You'd be surprised at all the wonderful ideas one gets from browsing and then printing out the pages you're interested in."

"Well, well, aren't you the internet queen." He laughed as he hugged her tightly. "I'm very proud that you investigated Beppu, which is on Kyushu Island; without knowing I was taking you here."

"I thought one of these days you would take me back and I wanted to be prepared for when you did. I didn't realize I'd be using my knowledge this quickly. But, I have to say, I'm very happy you brought me here. I can't wait to see some of the sights and then relax for the evening, retiring to the bedroom and have a repeat performance like last night."

"I think that can be arranged," as Yoshy got up from his seat and hugged her again.

STONEY BROOK, MASSACHUSETTS

Suzanne took the Saturday off for the 'big event.' She was nervous as she kept biting her bottom lip thinking of Mr. and Mrs. Johnson. She realized her jitters would subside when she had everything under control. Mrs. Walsh's help was invaluable and she knew she couldn't have accomplished what she did without her. She went upstairs to get dressed and pondered what appropriate clothes she should wear. Finally picking out an outfit that was not too casual and yet not dressy, she looked at herself in the mirror and approved of what she was wearing. When the doorbell rang, Mrs. Walsh greeted Hope and Spencer. She led them into the living room where Suzanne was waiting. "My folks will be here within 15 minutes, Spencer informed her. Hope and I are looking forward for the three of you meeting. We're sure you'll get along fabulously.

"I know we will. I'm also looking forward to meeting them. Hope has raved about them for quite a while. I trust that they like the food that Mrs. Walsh and I have prepared. It took a lot of thought on what should be served."

"You shouldn't have gone through all this trouble," Spenser thought out loud. "But I do appreciate it. I'm sure they'll like everything. They're really not hard to please." Looking at the chopped liver and smelled the potato pancakes in the fry pan he realized that ethnic food would be served. Trying to alleviate any misgivings on Hope's or Suzanne's part he mentioned, "When going out to a restaurant they usually order something unusual. They like to try different items. When they're home, which isn't often, they usually have the cook make simple dishes. I guess they think that it will keep their weight down. Who knows what they think. I certainly don't," Spencer calmly spoke. They were interrupted by the doorbell. After Mrs. Walsh brought them to the living room, Hope and Spencer made the introductions. Suzanne, although not deliberately, assessed Irene's skin and could tell that she pampered herself. Her skin looked very good, for a woman her age. She was rather tall and very slim. She looked at Spencer's father and could tell by his mannerisms that he was stuck on himself. Every hair was in place and he looked very fit. Suzanne thought he must be a tennis player and analyzing his skin, he was definitely an outdoorsman. Apparently, Irene didn't share her husband's affinity for his outdoor activities. Her skin, although beautiful, wasn't damaged by sun like other women who were the 'natural' gardener, skier, or boat person. He seemed cooler than Irene, who appeared a much warmer type of person. She knew that she'd like her very much.

Suzanne was dying to call William, Bill, but was warned ahead of time that he detested the nickname. After the formal introductions were made, they sat in the living room where the appetizers were readily at hand. Suzanne then asked them what they'd like for a drink, hoping that she had what they asked for. She could have smacked herself for not thinking to ask either Spencer or Hope what their preference in liquor would be. With bated breath she went to the mini bar and was delighted to see that the drinks they requested were on hand. Mrs. Walsh then came out of the kitchen, serving the hot potato latkes with applesauce on the side. Suzanne could tell that they never had this appetizer before. No one saw the look that Hope gave Suzanne. 'Good,' Suzanne thought, 'let them see for themselves what a Jewish household prepares before a meal.' Irene was curious and asked all sorts of questions about the latkes. Suzanne saw Hope rolling her eyes and knew that her daughter wanted to bury herself in the ground. She then told them what they were called and that they were served, especially during the Chanukah holidays. "Well, to be honest with you, Suzanne, I never tasted these latkes before, admitted William, but I hope to have them again sometime soon. They're delicious!!" With that remark she saw Hope relax a bit.

After eating and talking for 45 minutes they adjourned to the dining room. Place cards were displayed in front of the individual's seat. "I must admit I love the touch of these unusual place cards. Suzanne, you'll have to tell me where you purchased them" Irene remarked. Wine was served and a beautiful toast was delivered by William. 'Blah, blah, blah,' thought Suzanne at the usual, customary, boring delivery. 'Couldn't he think of an original speech, after all, this is a special occasion. His personality certainly shows through.' Suzanne smiled graciously, trying to find out about their life style and what they enjoyed doing most. Of course, William took over with his attributes on playing tennis, golf and sailing.

Suzanne thought, 'isn't that what every wealthy man does in his spare time.' She tried prying out of him his profession and found out that he was in banking, investments, and buying into start-up companies, a venture capitalist. 'Apparently he must have been good at his profession, they seem loaded and I don't think his wife works. Maybe she keeps herself busy by volunteering her time for needy causes but I doubt it.' Even though she liked Irene, she didn't seem the type to do this type of activity. She seemed more like the bridge club player and going shopping a lot. 'I hope I'm wrong about her, because she seems so nice. 'Wouldn't it be great to learn that William is charitable and has special causes that he donates a lot of his money to,' Suzanne thought as she smiled at them both.

They then got into Suzanne, her profession and her passion. She had to be careful not to let on that she and Nancy were amateur sleuths. She told them about her art and how involved she was with her best friend and partner Nancy. 'I hope they don't think we're a gay couple,' she thought, as she had to suppress her laugh. They were impressed that she was very friendly with the star,

Madaline Mason and also knew about the famous art studio of Justin Ferris. Thankfully, Brian's name or companies were not mentioned.

When the dinner was served, they loved the tender beef brisket and commented about the delicious sauce, which is what Suzanne usually makes when she wants to impress her guests. They loved the side dishes and exclaimed how tasty her noodle pudding was. Thankfully, Suzanne thought, they enjoyed the ethnic dish. When asked about it, Suzanne explained what she had to do to prepare it and Irene asked if she could have the recipe. "The only way I'll give it to you is if you and I do it together at one of our houses. You see in our type of cooking, regular measurements aren't spoken about. It's either a spoonful of this or a pinch of that. So if you are really serious, before you leave we'll make a definite day and time for me to show you how to make it."

Suzanne could see out of the corner or her eye, Hope rolling her eyes again, wanting to kill her mother. Suzanne had to smile at herself in getting Hope agitated. 'Shame on her for not respecting the wonderful way 'her people' prepared very delicious dishes.' The rest of the evening went well and the time seemed to fly by. Irene and Suzanne made plans for after the wedding to get together and try making the noodle pudding. When Suzanne closed the door after they left, she let out a large sigh. She was glad that Simka behaved herself and didn't try to grab an ankle, scaring her guests half to death. Of course Boston, his usual self, had to greet them at the door, lying on his back, legs up, waiting to be rubbed.

Mrs. Walsh came into the vestibule and shook Suzanne's hand. Suzanne grabbed Catherine and hugged her tightly. "I can't thank you enough for all your help. I don't think I'd have been able to entertain as well as I did without you."

"I thank you for the compliment, but you don't give yourself the credit you deserve. I know you would have done as good a job without my help. You have to have the confidence in yourself that you sometimes lack," Catherine expounded as she helped Suzanne clean up the dishes.

SAN DIEGO, CALIFORNIA

Nobuaki was sitting at his desk waiting for Hirohito to come into his office and tell him of the progress he was making on following Robin. Hirohito reluctantly knocked on his "Oyabun's" door and waited for Nobuaki to allow him to come in. "Well my friend, I gave you Yoshy's girlfriends picture and her address. What have you found out so far?"

"I don't think you're going to like what I'm about to tell you. After I received her picture that you gave me and where she lives I kept a close watch. I made sure that I wasn't noticed by anyone, not even Yoshy. I followed her throughout the day and getting her routine down pat. I trailed her for a good two weeks and her routine was the same old, same old. Nothing deviated. Then suddenly, something changed. Yesterday I saw Yoshy's limo pick up his girlfriend. I think Yoshy was also in the limosean. I followed, cautiously, again being mindful not to make a spectacle of myself, and saw them enter the airport. I saw luggage being taken out of the vehicle and being taken away by the outside attendant. Then I went inside and looked for them. It wasn't more than 3 minutes that went by, I swear. I then went to the terminal that they entered to find out the destinations of the planes and times of their takeoffs. I went to an agent and asked if a Mr. Makino has registered yet and his companion. She looked up on the computer and couldn't find a Makino registered for any destination. I called you as soon as this happened."

Nobuaki squinted his eyes, obviously thinking. "Well, Yoshy is a very smart man. He has a feeling that this Robin is not safe and he's taking her away, thinking that I'll have second thoughts about eliminating her. Little does he know, once I get something in my mind, I don't let it go until I accomplish my mission. It's obvious that he got a different passport for them both and made sure that he took her away for a long time. He might even stop at another destination, to throw us off guard. I think his limo driver might have some knowledge of his whereabouts. I'd like you to go see him and find out what he knows. He's been a faithful servant of Yoshy's for many years. I won't mind if you have to use tactics that, how would the American policemen describe, as rather heavy handed. I don't have to tell you your business. I'll trust you with whatever you have to do to get the information from him."

"I understand and it will be done. I think he's living in Yoshy's guest house as always. He won't expect a thing. Even though both houses have cameras and a good security system, that can easily be taken care of. Don't worry, I'll find out everything I can from Yasuhito." Bowing profusely, he silently went down the stairs, not even looking for the love of his life.

CHAPTER THIRTY FOUR

Yasuhito was relaxed. His boss was on an extended vacation. Mr. Makino worked long and hard hours, it was a well-deserved holiday, especially taking Miss Robin with him, he thought. 'It's nice to have the house to myself and not be at Mr. Makino's beckon call. Yes, he pays me well, and provides me with my own living quarters in a small bungalow near the garage. Unfortunately, Mr. Makino often forgets that I also have a life of my own.' Yasuhito went to the local Chinese restaurant, knowing that the people at the restaurant knew him well, preparing the food the way that he liked it. He, predictably, ordered chicken lo mein, fried rice with vegetables, beef in oyster sauce, with wantons, leaving them in the oyster sauce, so they were soggy. They made sure that besides packing the fortune cookies they put in the cubed pineapples for dessert.

Putting his feet on the sofa table, he ate the food right out of the cartons. Yasuhito was mad at himself for not ordering the scallion pancakes as an appetizer. He always enjoyed that and thinking to himself that he was getting old. 'I hope I don't get dementia in my old age; that's all I need.' He was listening to the news of the day, enjoying the food as always. He sipped wine out of the longed stemmed glass he took from behind the bar. After the news was over, he looked forward to a restful night's sleep. He left the living area and before doing anything else, made sure that the alarms in both houses were on. With everything in order and the cameras working properly he could have a peaceful, uneventful slumber. As he walked down the hallway of his small apartment, he couldn't wait for his nightly rituals to be done, looking forward to get into his comfortable bed.

Yasuhito took a long hot shower and got into his pajamas, knowing he'd have an undisturbed sleep. Before going to bed Yasuhito enjoyed the idea that he could sleep as late as he wanted. Smiling to himself, he realized that he wouldn't be called upon to get the limo, any time, day or night, and drive Mr. Makino to wherever he wanted to go. For once he had the pleasure to do whatever pleased his fancy, an indulgence he often didn't get. He'd been in Mr. Makino's service for many years and felt loyal to his employer. Whenever Mr. Makino went back home to Japan was the only time that Yasuhito had his own vacation. The only problem being is he didn't have any family or friends that he could visit while he had this free time. Mr. Makino made a slight reference that this vacation would be an extended one. 'Oh well, I'll find something to do that will occupy my time. Maybe this is a good sign that I make new acquaintances.' Settling under the covers he was grateful that Mr. Makino kept to himself and was a private person. Not knowing the personal business of his boss made it easier for him not to get involved.

The only thing he was cognizant of was that Mr. Makino owned a very prestigious business, having offices over the entire world. He also was aware that he had a wife and son in Japan, often feeling sorry for them. It didn't seem that Mr. Makino got to go home often, be it that he was busy with his business, or he didn't want to. Yasuhito recognized Mr. Makino's feelings for Miss Robin. He couldn't blame him. He had to admit, she was truly beautiful, as well as being a nice person, while having a great personality. Mr. Yasuhito understood why Mr.

Makino, although maintaining his own house with Mr. Yasuhito's separate quarters in the back, stayed over Ms. Robins' house most of the time. Even though the pictures of his wife were lovely, they couldn't compare to Miss Robins.' With those thoughts he fell into a deep sleep.

He woke up suddenly to an unusual sound. The alarm system was surely working, for he set it himself. He didn't think that anyone knew that Mr. Makino was away. He stayed still for a while, trying not to breathe. The noise, he thought he heard, must have been his imagination. Usually not an alarmist, the rattle seemed to have gone away. Trying not to think about his fear, hoped his dramatization, was just that, he once again tried to sleep.

Hirohito, put on the rubber gloves pulling them out from his back pocket. He was able to disable the intricate alarm system, acquired from being a studious apprentice under the guidance from a master of such devises. He then put paper over the cameras that were obviously displayed throughout the area. Although the doors were securely locked, there didn't seem to be a dead bolt on them. He put a credit card between the metal and door jam, patiently maneuvering his implement until he felt the lock disengage. Adjusting his plastic booties over his shoes, he lightly tiptoed through the backdoor entrance, seeing he was in the kitchen area of the house.

Hirohito slowly turned the corner, quietly passing the living room, observing empty cartons spread along a coffee table. He saw the one bedroom off the hallway. He knew that this was obviously Yasuhito's living quarters, apart from the main house. Thankfully there was a nightlight in the hallway, near the bathroom. He didn't want to kill Yasuhito until he was able to extract from him the whereabouts of Yoshy and his mistress and the estimated time of their arrival back home. As he slowly ascended the hall, from one of the floor boards, he heard a small creak, as he walked lightly down the hallway.

Yasuhito couldn't sleep well after he thought his imagination was playing tricks. If he heard another unusual sound, he might call 911, even though he would look foolish if there was nothing to be alarmed about. Suddenly he heard a slight squeak, even though it was imponderable. He carefully picked up the telephone on the night table beside the bed and was about to dial 911 when suddenly someone appeared in the doorway.

Yasuhito's head was spinning and he wasn't sure if his fingers actually dialed 911 when the intruder ran quickly to the bed, pushing a needle into the side of his neck. The telephone receiver dropped from his hand and he fell back onto the bed, like a limp piece of lettuce. Hirohito put the receiver back on its telephone and waited patiently for Yasuhito to wake up from the drug that he expertly administered. Yasuhito felt lightheaded and weak when he started to come out of the sedated state he was in.

He felt something funny on the back of his hand and turned to see an IV drip. He tried to say something but found it hard to clear his head from what appeared to be cob webs intruding his brain.

"Who are you, and what do you want from me? I'm just a limo driver and don't have anything of value. You can take anything you see. Please don't hurt me." Yasuhito didn't know if he actually spoke out loud to this ugly looking beast or if it was a figment of his imagination.

Hirohito laughed out loud. "I'm not a common burglar you fool." Lifting Yasuhito up by the neck of his pajama shirt he threw him forcefully back onto the bed, making sure that he didn't dislodge the IV he so painfully administered. Hirohito then lifted the slight built man from the bed onto the floor. He kicked him in the ribs and Yasuhito cringed as he felt a rib or two break. Every time he coughed the pain was excruciating. "Now listen to me real good, all I want from you is information about your boss, Mr. Makino. If I feel you're telling me the truth and all that you know, I might feel benevolent and let you go. But if I don't think you're being honest with me, I feel real sorry for you. Understand?" All Yasuhito could do was shake his head. He was scared and couldn't help shivering, like being in an ice storm, outside, without any protection from the atmospheric conditions.

Hirohito knew that most of the time the truth serum worked. He lifted Yasuhito off the floor and threw him back on the bed. Hirohito started slowly administrating the sodium amytal drip slowly until the bag of serum was empty.

"Stay still and look me straight in my eyes." Hirohito didn't know if Yasuhito's eyes would be closed or not. This was the first time he had used this particular drug and got it from a reputable source telling him that this would definitely work on an individual of Mr. Yasuhito's size and weight. At this point Yasuhito would do whatever this stranger asked of him. Hirohito saw that Yasuhito's eyes were closed and didn't know if he could hear any of the questions that he was going to ask. 'oh well, time will tell,' he told himself. "You work for Mr. Yoshy Makino as his limo driver, correct?" Yasuhito shook his head up and down and quietly answered yes. For no reason, whatsoever, Hirohito slapped his face hard, leaving a red welt on his right cheek. "Three days ago, you drove him and his girlfriend, Robin, to the LAX airport in Los Angeles and left them off at the Continental terminal, right?"

"Yes, yes, sir, I did." He felt as if his words were slurring but didn't know for sure. He thought he could feel his perspiration dripping down the inside of his arms. His ribs hurt badly every time he breathed or moved.

"I want you to tell me of Mr. Makino's plans for his vacation and whereabouts. Did Miss Robbin go with him for the entire trip?"

"Yes, that's right," a frightened Yasuhito agreed. "How long are they on vacation for and where did they go?"

"Do you have any idea of their plans?"

"I don't know," stammered Yasuhito. Yasuhito wanted to tell this barbarian that Mr. Makino never tells him his plans but couldn't seem to get the words out. "He just calls me to pick him up." Thinking to himself while at the same time wanting to go to sleep he thought, 'He wants me to be at his beckon call so he won't have to wait.' His head felt heavy as if it would fall off of his shoulders.

"You think I'm stupid? I know you're aware of his plans. My boss thinks he's got a different passport and papers. You know anything about that? Didn't you drive him downtown to pick up his illegal papers?" Hirohito didn't know much about the drug he administered. He didn't know if his captive would tell him what he wanted to know. So far when answering, the words were slurred. Stuttering, shaking his head, "No sir, I didn't. I don't know of any illegal papers, or for that matter, I didn't drive him downtown. It would be unusual for me not to drive him to any of his destinations, so I don't know what you're talking about." With every word he uttered, his head throbbed and with each breath his body was racked in pain.

Hirohito grabbed Yasuhito by his hair, pulling it hard, a few pieces were left in his hand. "You son of a bitch, I know you're lying. I don't have patience for a liar. If you don't come clean and tell me what I want to know, I'll break one arm at a time, until you tell me what I want to hear. If you still don't come up with anything, I'll then go to your legs and break them. Do you want to know what I'll do next, you asshole?" Yasuhito was scared to death. He didn't know what to say to make this goon realize that he was telling him the truth. He could feel pee dribbling down his legs. "I'm going to ask you one more time, where were they going, their destination, you asshole, and when will they be back?"

Yasuhito didn't possess any knowledge or retort to this brutes questions. He couldn't think of any way out of this horrible situation. He realized his life depended on his resourcefulness. He was all alone. He didn't have many friends, especially those who visited him, his schedule was very erratic. Before he had a chance to think, Hirohito cuffed him with the handle of the gun across his cheek. Yasuhito felt his cheek bone cave in, break, and his skin cut open. Yelling, Hirohito proclaimed, putting his head to the side and cuffing his own ear, "I don't hear you!!!"

Blood was gushing from the deep wound on Yasuhito's cheek, dripping profusely down his face, onto the bedroom floor. Hirohito kept asking questions and each time Yasuhito didn't know the answer or shook his head no, Hirohito punched him and kicked him over his entire body. No words were spoken by Mr. Yasuhito. He realized that after breaking all of Yasuhito's limbs and nearly beating him to death that the poor bastard was telling the truth. He believed Yasuhito didn't know anything that his boss was doing and was, for real, only a limo driver. Hirohito debated whether to continue with his torture and after due consideration, decided to be lenient. 'This guy is a real jerk. Who would tolerate this arrangement and not be bitter. If I was him I'd go sneaking around Yoshy's house to find any information I could get my hands on. He's his boss, but who cares, no one's home. This poor bastard is totally in the dark. He doesn't know anything concerning his boss or his girlfriend.' Instead of making a soprano out of him he decided not to castrate him and leave him be. He realized that already beaten to a pulp, Yasuhito was lucky if he lived through the night.

Hirohito saw the blood splatter on the walls and carpeting and laughed as he saw the poor bastard lying in all the goo.

Hirohito didn't want to be considered a wuss. Instead of putting a bullet through his head and leave his brain matter splattered on the walls, he kicked him viciously a few more times, with his steel toed boot, to his head and body. Hirohito yanked the IV and took that and the serum with him. He would dispose of it later. He hoped he didn't leave any evidence. Either for evidence to show his boss or for a memento he picked up a few teeth, that had flown out of his mouth onto the floor when he broke his jaw. As he carefully left the house he saw Yasuhito lying motionless on the floor. Hirohito could barely hear Yasuhito's soft moans. He carefully closed the door, walked to his car that was parked down the street and drove off. He was glad that Nobuaki left it up to him whether to let him live or die. Hirohito left it up to the Gods to decide Yasuhito's fate.

While at work Sam got a phone call from Mr. Makino's secretary asking him to set up a meeting with her at the end of the day. He wondered what the conference was about and speculated if any other workers would be in attendance. Sam called Rich as soon as Mr. Makino's private secretary made the arrangement for the encounter. Rich realized that Sam was fearing the worst and was thinking all sorts of evil thoughts.

Rich tried calming a nervous Sam down. "Hey Buddy, don't worry. Let's find out what's on the agenda and take it from there, okay? Do you want to meet us before hand and we can wire you? Just say the word and we'll arrange for us to get together."

Sam thought it over and thanked Rich for his consideration but realized that he might be over-reacting. He asked Rich, "Do you want to hear something funny? Last Christmas, as a gag gift, my wife bought me a spy pen that can record pictures and has the ability to tape record as well. It's amazing what products they sell at Brookstone." He heard Rich laughing and after his chuckling subsided Rich told him to call him back after he found out what she wanted. "By the way, make sure you bring a pad of paper with you so you can write down anything she wants to tell you with 'your special pen.'" With that said they hung up their phones.

Sam entered Miss Karoky's office and waited nervously to see if any of his colleagues would be at the meeting. When Miss Karoky called Sam into her private office he realized that he was the only employee present. "Sit down Sam and have a seat." He tried to act nonchalant, and crossed his legs, with pad and pen in hand. Miss Karoky started talking, "I don't know if you realized that Mr. Makino has been away for quite some time, and it intends to be a lengthy visit. I've been asked by him, if you'd mind being in charge while he's away. Of course he'll be able to communicate with you through the computer. At this time, telephone calls won't be necessary. We don't know how long his absence will be, so it's going to be on an ongoing basis."

"He realizes that you've been one of our longest employees, having knowledge of every department and what people's assignments are. Mr. Makino thinks this is his way of thanking you for your loyalty to the company. Do you think you can handle this corporation for a while? We realize it's going to be very demanding, with many more hours than you're working now. Of course, we will make sure you're generously compensated for the extra work that you'll have to handle. You don't have to give an answer right away. I want you to go home and discuss this with your family, only if you want to, and get back to me within a few days. I hope this gives you ample time to think about our proposition?"

"I'm truly flattered by your proposal. I will definitely discuss this with my wife and I'm sure you'll get a positive answer." Bowing deeply, he walked out of her office, a large smile on his face. He called Rich as soon as he entered his office with his cell phone. He didn't discuss the offer with his wife until he spoke to Rich.

After speaking with Sam, Rich was delighted with the news. "Let's get together this evening, after you finish dinner. We can meet at the diner where we usually convene. I'll talk over what you told me with the other guys and then we'll come up with a plan. See you around eight tonight. Save some appetite for dessert."

Rich was sitting at the back booth when Sam walked through the glass doors. Sam felt more secure with his back facing the entrance to the diner. "Thanks for getting together tonight. Being a bachelor I usually hate to cook for myself. That's about the only thing I miss about being married. The food here is acceptable and sometimes it even tastes pretty good." He tried getting Sam to relax. "The guys and I talked your situation over. Now that we know that Mr. Makino is going to be away for an extended period of time, we're going to go to his house and do a little search and discover mission. You won't be involved so you don't have to worry."

"As long as we can easily get into his house, we might find out a few important details. We realize that without a search warrant anything we discover can't be used in a court of law, but we're willing to take that chance. When we're through with what we're there for; no one will be the wiser, if you get my drift. I'll fill you in on what we come up with. There might be a possible chance that when he uses a computer to dialogue with you we'll be able to find out his whereabouts and track him. We might need to meet you at your place of work, when nobody's around or any place you think will be a safe place to get together."

"Meanwhile, we'll try to get a copy of his files out of his home computer and hope that there's some incriminating evidence that we'll be able to use. We'll keep this to ourselves and maybe we'll be able to get away with what we're about to do. You never heard what I just said, okay? We're lucky that Stu is a computer genius and has a degree in computer science. Who'd know we'd be so fortunate. By the way, I realize that Mr. Makino has a private computer in his office. Is there any way you can get to it, without getting caught, and copying all his files there as well?"

"It'll be hard. Maybe I can get an extra set of keys to his office. I'll have to try after Miss Karoky goes home for the evening. With my new responsibility, no one will think it strange that I enter Mr. Makino's office, even if it's after hours. By the way, I also happen to be skilled when it comes to computers. I won't have any trouble getting into his files, and copy them. It will be harder if he uses passwords. I have to admit I'm pretty good at getting the passwords or get around the blocks and who knows, I might even be able to get through and into his documents. By the way, when I do communicate with Mr. Makino from where ever he is, there's a good possibility I can track his whereabouts. Will it be helpful to you?" Sam asked Rich.

"Are you kidding? That information will help us out immensely. I hope it's possible to do so. When will your new position be starting?"

"As far as his secretary knows as soon as I give her the word. I guess I'm the new person in charge of Mr. Makino's empire. "With a broad grin on his face he finished his apple pie a la mode and shook Rich's hand. I hope I can live up to the expectations you think I'm capable of handling."

"We have all the confidence in the world of your ability Sam. Kick ass my boy." With that said Rich left the booth first and Sam waited for fifteen minutes before leaving.

They parked their vehicle a couple of blocks away. Wearing dark clothing, they pretended to jog through the neighborhood, trying not to make themselves obvious. They got to Yoshy's house and saw that all the lights were out. "You'd think that for someone going on an extended vacation, he'd have enough smarts to not make the house look vacant. Even if he has an expensive alarm system, burglars are quite sophisticated these days. Maybe not the young punks but the professional thieves. I guess he's not as smart as he thinks he is. I don't care if he owns the friggin Taj Mahal, he's not thinking with a clear head." Stu said.

Tom crudely said, "From what I hear, he uses a different head when he's with Miss Robin. By the way, does anyone know what her last name is?"

Rich smacked Tom on the back of his head. "Is that all that's on your sick mind? For the other question, no we don't know her last name. I'm sure after tonight we'll be able to find out."

They went around the entire house, making sure that they disabled the alarm system. They then demobilized the camera's they spotted around the entire property. As they walked from the walkway to the back door Stu noticed a blank piece of white paper under one of the cameras on the walkway. "That's strange he mentioned out loud. He put on his glove and put the piece of paper into an empty envelope that he carried with him. "Hey, there's another small house around the corner, near the garage. Let's take a look in there after we get everything done in the main house," suggested Tom. "Sounds good to me," agreed Rich.

"Guy's, we don't know if he's friendly with any of his neighbors. The houses are far apart, but you never know. Let's be sure and use our flashlights, using as little light as possible without missing anything important," suggested Stu, as they quietly opened the back door, using their specialized equipment.

Rich cautiously went up the spiral staircase to the second level. He moved quickly aside of each room, gun extended. Going into every cubicle, sweeping the entire area, making sure no one was in the rooms he entered. Stu and Tom searched the complete first floor. When they realized there was no one except them in the house, they were able to feel more comfortable. Stu yelled up to Rich to see if there might be an office on the second floor and possibly a safe hidden in any of the bedrooms or floorboards. There was an office on the first floor and Stu got to work on the computer that was sitting on the beautiful cherry wood, large desk.

He was lucky that Yoshy didn't have a special password on his home, personal computer. Once Stu opened and accessed all the files he found, it didn't take as long as he thought it would to copy all of them and put the disks safely in his sweat suits front pockets. Rich was excited when he found the two wall safes.

One was hidden in the wall in back of a picture. Rich thought he saw the picture that was in one of the museums he visited long ago. He speculated that it was a great reproduction. Another safe was tucked in the back wall of his walk-in closet. Unfortunately, he couldn't gain access from either of the steel vaults because of the numbered locks. He'd have to call one of the men who were trained to gain entry into these burglar-proof boxes. Rich hoped that the special agent he had in mind would be available before Mr. Makino returned from his trip. He hoped that once the safes were opened they'd find important papers that would give them information on some extracurricular activities that Mr. Makino had going for him.

After a second sweep of the entire house they made sure that nothing looked as if anything was out of place. Just before they were to walk back to the automobile, Tom remembered the second apartment that looked abandoned. "Hey guys, let's not forget the other small house located in back of the garage. You interested or should we leave?"

"I think it's Mr. Makino's chauffeur's place. But let's try to see if there's anything of value. Who knows maybe this guy is part of Yoshy's operation," Rich said.

Rich was grateful that Tom remembered about the second building. "You never know what we might find."

"Let's go," Rich spoke with authority. They crept silently around the entire garage, trying to look inside. They were unable to enter the garage without the garage, battery powered opener. The men peeked through the windows of the small, one level house. Nothing seemed out of place. "Hey, maybe we should take a looksee and make sure Mr. Makino doesn't have anything worthwhile, hidden there," proclaimed Stu as he tried the knobs of the front and back doors. Looks like they're locked and secured."

Tom expertly opened the front door. Rich moving cautiously inside, crouched down low, scanning the entire entrance way, which was part of the living room. He then moved into the back where the kitchen was located. Again, securing the area, they went from there into the bathroom. He quickly moved the curtain aside from the shower enclosure, making sure that the window was secure and closed. Stu looked for another computer in the living room and found none. Before entering the one bedroom, Rich was cognizant of an odor familiar to him. He expertly entered the room and with his flashlight saw the spatter of blood on the walls and floors. He then spotted the form lying on the floor.

"Holly Shit" Rich yelled over to Stu. He swiftly moved towards the still body and expertly picked up the broken wrist, listening intently for a pulse. He heard a faint one and called out to his partners to dial 911 and get an ambulance here, a.s.a.p. He was afraid to move the man, if indeed the disfigured person was a man. A soft moan expelled from the mouth of the body as they waited for the ambulance to arrive. "This poor bastard looks in real bad shape. I hope that he lives to tell us what the hell happened." They counted the minutes till the ambulance arrived. The EMT's expertly lifted the shattered body onto the hard gurney, aware of the multiple breaks and injury's the person sustained. They performed the necessary steps, opening his airway to give him ample air. They found blood was clogging his windpipe and performed a tracheotomy and put an IV into his arm while speeding to the ER.

As soon as they saw the medics bring in the man that was on the stretcher, the doctors yelled to each other to get him into the OR, STAT. The nurses and doctors carefully transferred him onto a large black gurney and ran quickly to the elevators to bring him immediately into surgery.

Yasuhito laid like a corpse, broken limbs in casts with his broken legs in traction, bandages wrapped around his head and face while in the ICU of the U C San Diego Medical Center. He was in a self-induced coma because of all the brain swelling. The only visible opening you could see where two eyes peering out from the white bandages encompassing his head and face. There was a cast on his nose and his jaw was wired. An IV through his cast, giving him the medications that were necessary to keep him alive, were his only companion. The doctors weren't sure if he would make it. They told Rich that he had extensive cerebral bleeding and only God, Yasuhito's will to live and good surgeons would be able to help him.

Rich stayed with this man that he didn't know. There was something about him that Rich felt sorry for. He stayed by his bed and his partners tried coaxing him away, if only to eat. Rich didn't know why he felt obligated to be by his side but he did. After work he made sure that he visited the man who he knew little of. Every evening Rich stayed by his side and kept talking to him, knowing that it would take time for a response, if he got any at all.

Nancy received the call late in the evening from Rich informing her of what happened to Yasuhito. He told her he'd be staying at the hospital and give the poor guy moral support. "There doesn't seem to be anyone or family around and it seems I'm the only person who really cares. I'm sure the police do but that's for a different reason. I hope they find the bastard or bastards that did this to him. Nancy asked Rich if he wanted her to join him. He told her it wasn't necessary.

"I'll call you often and keep you informed. I love you and thanks for listening to me jabber."

One evening while he was talking about nothing he thought he saw an eye open. Rich called the nurse in charge and she in turn left word for the doctor on call to come into Yasuhito's room. "It's a good sign and if he shows any other improvement or movement he might have a chance for recovery, only time will tell." Rich was grinning as if he won the lottery. Rich kept asking the doctor all sorts of questions but the doctor wouldn't give him any definite answers. No matter what was said, Rich prayed and asked God to help this man that he had no knowledge about. He just felt a kind of attachment that he hadn't felt in many years. Maybe it was the fact that he lost both parents, at an early age, in a terrible automobile accident and he wasn't there when they needed him the most. At least in his mind he thought so.

The doctors took Yasuhito out of the self-induced coma when they felt the swelling in his brain was subsiding. In the next few days Yasuhito became more and more aware of his surroundings. He became conscious of the multiple casts and metal contraptions and devices deftly holding his limbs still and in place. He had plastic tubing going down his throat and up his nostrils, enabling him to breathe. He still couldn't talk or communicate with anyone, not even Rich. His eyes were black and blue and still swollen. At times he thought he was hallucinating as he was going in and out of consciousness. Yosuhito could barely hear the monitors beeping. He could hardly open his eyes that were like slits, in a cut piece of paper, so when asked questions he was unable to blink. He didn't know where he was. The doctors made their rounds every morning and as they told the detectives, they were surprised he made it out of surgery and came out of the coma. The nurses were constantly keeping an eye on him. Rich didn't know who could have rendered such a horrible beating but didn't want to take any chances of more harm done to him. Knowing who he was he wasn't sure if his beating was related to Yoshy and the people who wanted to do him harm. He asked and received a guard outside Yasuhito's room. Yasuhito was still in ICU but Rich wanted a guard posted anyway.

Rich felt like Yasuhito was 'his patient.' He talked to the surgeons daily who operated and saved Yasuhito's life, if you could call it living. Because of his authority as a Detective, the doctors could discuss their patient's progress and the multiple operations that Yosuhito still needed. It also didn't help the police that Yosuhito had no relatives or close friends to contact in case of an emergency. They couldn't find where his boss, Mr. Makino, was vacationing. It seemed that he vanished without a trace of evidence. They realized that his boss, of many years, would want to be informed. No one except the police man, who was a diligent visitor, was the only person the hospital administration felt was close enough to be considered 'family.' Normally, without written consent from the patient or a family member, thanks to the fairly new Hippa law, Rich wouldn't be able to talk or act in his defense. He tried to find anything of relevance relating to this patient. Rich took personal attention to this man, who he had never before seen in his life. Rich felt sorry for the man who had to have his spleen removed and found out that the ribs that were broken, had to heal by themselves.

Another operation had to be performed to save at least one of his collapsed lungs. He had to have oxygen administered constantly, while checking his oxygen level to make sure that the one saved lung could work properly. He was hooked up to a ventilator giving him extra precaution for his lung. One of his kidneys was in bad shape because of the multiple, hard blows to that area. The doctors and surgeons were closely watching his liver function as well. When Rich first saw him after the multi operations that had been performed to save his life, Det. Colangelo could only think that the man looked like a mummy, mummified with bandages holding him together. In a way Rich was glad that Mr. Yosuhito was in and out of consciousness because if he knew the extent of his injuries he probably wouldn't want to live.

Rich sat outside Yasuhito's hospital room, remembering how they found the human form sprawled on the floor. In all his professional career, he never saw a human so disfigured and lived to see the dawn of day. Yasuhito's eyes, lips and face were swollen beyond recognition. Ace bandages were on top of the stitches holding his flesh together. The bandages had to be changed daily to avoid further infection. The wires attached to what was once his face were holding his jaws in place, hoping for them to heal correctly. Rich took a deep breath while sitting next to his 'new friend' and tears were freely flowing down his cheeks.

Rich reflected back to that terrible afternoon. After hearing the news of where Yasuhito was sent to, only then could Rich and his colleagues feel free to search, while they carefully looked into the bureau drawers and closets hoping to find identification. They were lucky that all his papers were neatly stacked inside one of his dresser draws, enabling them to find out who this person was. They hoped that the papers belonged to this individual, whose life was hanging on by a thread. Rich and his partners were especially careful not to disturb any evidence at this location, which was now considered a 'crime scene.' They felt fortunate that Molly, the chief Medical Examiner, had not been needed.

The Captain of the division never asked his detectives how they came about finding Yasuhito in his house. He knew he didn't want to hear their unscrupulous activities, enabling them entry into this victims home. He was only happy that they were able to find him and save his life. After a week went by, Rich knocked on the Captains door. "Come in" shouted Captain Morgan. Jack Morgan acknowledged Rich and told him to sit down. Putting his hand up, "I don't want to know how you found this Yasuhito character. I'm sure he'll be grateful, when he's finally able to recognize the fact that you and your partners, somehow, saved his life. Lowering his arm, I'm going to ask you a question and I want a straight answer. Has this anything to do with the case we're working on. I mean the Japanese Mafia, the Yakuza?"

"Captain, I think, I take it back, I know, it's somehow related to it. Yasuhito happens to be the limo driver of the man, known to be the suspect in the Curtis Jones case. We finally were able to get information that enabled us to identify the suspect whose picture was distributed throughout the entire State. It was a fluke that this gentleman saw the picture and finally called us. We're afraid to divulge the source of our information. Not that we can't tell you, sir, but somehow information gets into the wrong hands. If you know what I mean." Captain Morgan sadly shook his head in agreement. "I, unfortunately, understand what you're talking about. I recognize, for a fact, that we have bad cops in our division. Hell, I'm sure some of the high ups are involved as well. Now a day's you'd never suspect the corrupt individuals that run our government. We can't seem to get the goods on them. I agree with you that we have to keep all of our resources under lock and key. Sometimes, that isn't good enough. I won't ask you about your informant, but I want you to keep me abreast of all the things you find out. As for now, I never spoke to you and I have no idea how this Yasuhito was found. I hope we can get this murder cleared up real fast. Every day that goes by, we have less of a chance of solving this case. As far as the public is concerned, the killer or killers are still at large. This Kyle Mason is, in the public's mind, the man responsible for Curtis Jones' murder. You know where I'm coming from? The commissioner is getting a lot of heat from important members of the community and he, in turn, is on my ass. I realize I'm putting a lot of pressure on you and your men, but Christ, we've got to move faster on this than we are. I know you and your men are doing the best they can," Captain Morgan said as he got up from his chair behind the desk and dismissed his trusted friend.

"Yes, Captain, I understand where you're coming from. Just try to keep the influential people at bay, and we'll get this case cleared up ASAP. I promise, we're doing our very best. After all, I want you to be proud of me and my men." Rich quietly closed the door. He let out a deep breath and called the hospital again, trying to find out when Yasuhito can finally communicate some information to him. He realized that because of the condition the patient was in, they'd have to wait a very long time for him to be able to divulge any facts to help them identify the person or persons who did this horrible, intentional act.

CHAPTER THIRTY FIVE

BOSTON, MASSACHUSETTS

Madaline and the cast didn't have or need many rehearsals during the final month of the production. After their afternoon performance Madaline softly grabbed Betty's arm. Betty was startled at first, then composed herself and looked Madaline in the eyes and waited for Madaline to converse with her. She realized that Madaline had something on her mind and she wanted her to talk so she could finish errands before this evening's performance. "Betty, I was wondering if you have some time tomorrow afternoon to sit down and talk about your career?" Betty was taken off guard flabbergasted by Madaline's proposal. "I'll have to look at my schedule and if you give me your cell number, I'll call you as soon as I get to my apartment. If not, I'll catch you at tonight's performance, Thanks."

Paul was waiting for Madaline back at her hotel suite. Opening the door, Paul was anxious to find out what happened when Madaline confronted Betty. "I've been waiting on pins and needles," a nervous Paul said. "So far, so good. I think she was taken aback when I asked her for a meeting to 'discuss' her career. I didn't act high-strung or excited. You'd been proud of me. Of course it's easy to play out act I. Now let's see what happens when we sit down and actually have a conversation and how she'll behave once she finds out I'm on to her. I'm beginning to become a little apprehensive when the meeting evolves." Madaline walked over to the bar and instead of making herself a drink, poured club soda into her tall glass. "How rude of me. Paul, can I get you something to drink?"

"No, I don't think so. I can't believe your acting so nonchalant," Paul quickly responded.

"Paul, what's done is done. Now I have to be practical and not act like my usual emotional self. Let's see her reaction to our conversation. All different thoughts are going through my mind and the inside of my stomach is quivering. I can't wait till she either calls or I'll see her after the show. One way or another, we'll be having this meeting, I can guarantee it will happen." Madaline took a large gulp from her glass and went to the bedroom to lie down. "Is that all you can say?" Paul asked as he followed her into her personal territory.

Putting the covers to her chin she snuggled happily, closing her eyes and wanting to close her mind from thinking. "Oh, yes, what were you saying before I climbed into bed? "

"I was going to tell you that you're not the only person that has a lot on your mind. I've spent a lot of time and your money on this investigation. I hope you appreciate what I'm doing."

"Paul, I'm sorry if I offended you, of course I know how hard you're working." Patting the bed she asked him to sit down. "Where do you suggest we have this private meeting?" Paul answered, "I want to make sure this encounter is secluded and yet open at the same time. I don't want to frighten her by thinking she has no option to leave if the area is too remote. With what you have to say and ask, I don't want anyone around to distract either of you. Madaline, I have to have you by my side. I don't think you can handle this entire situation without my support. I realize I'm making you out to be like some kind of weak person who needs to have someone always with her. In a way, with all that's happened, I have to admit you probably are unstrung." Madaline softly spoke, "You're the glue that holds me together." She propped herself up on the bed and hugged him with all her strength.

Paul could feel her large breasts against his chest and he had all he could do not to grab and kiss her. He wanted to push her down and make love to her like never before. He had to calm himself down, before he couldn't control his emotions or bodies reaction. "You can count on me to be right by your side. For now, I think I'll let you get some rest before tonight's show and I'll meet you afterwards. Meanwhile if you hear from Betty before this evening, call me. I'm dying to find out when she contacts you. I'm sure, as we speak, she's speculating what this meeting has in store for her." He kissed her lightly on those gorgeous lips that he adored and walked slowly out of the bedroom, not looking back. He closed the door. 'God, I hope she didn't see my hard on when I got up from sitting next to her. I'd better keep my emotions under control,' Paul thought to himself as he waited for the elevator to take him to the lobby.

As usual, the performance went well. The audience loved it and Madaline and the cast got an outstanding and excellent standing ovation. Madaline was in her dressing room changing out of her costume when she heard a soft knock on her closed door. If the radio was on she was sure the tapping would not be heard. If she didn't know better, she would have thought it was either excess air in a hot water pipe or a faucet dripping. Madaline knew better and yelled for the person on the other side to come in. Betty meekly entered and waited for Madaline to ask her to sit down. She observed Betty's unnatural, nervous behavior. She avoided eye contact with Madaline. They decided to meet tomorrow afternoon, on a bench in the Boston Common. There were many benches near the concrete swimming pool and Madaline agreed. When Betty left, Madaline was glad they would be getting together in neutral territory. She immediately saw Paul, waiting in the front row, to accompany her to the hotel. "So tell me when and where is the summit?"

"I was hoping for an impartial place and sure enough we're to get together on one of the benches near the Commons' swimming pool. I would have preferred a place more comfortable with a table between us. When we get there, I probably will suggest a place not so open to the public. I know it's a lame excuse but we have to think of somewhere better. Paul do you have any suggestions?"

Thinking out loud, he eliminated many places and finally came up with a perfect answer. "When you meet at the designated area, suggest you'll get me to take my car, for more privacy and take a drive to Nantasket Beach. It won't take us long to get there, and sit near the pavilion or under it if we have inclement weather. It will afford you privacy, especially this time of year. Outside of the pavilion they have benches, if the MDC hasn't taken them away for the season. She might be apprehensive getting into my car. I'll assure her I don't bite. I'll even buy us a lunch at the Red Parrot and bring it back for the two of you. Though, I don't know if either of you will have much of an appetite. I suggest that the beginning of the meeting should be casual. You could gradually lead up to the real reason for the encounter and, for God's sake, be honest with her. I hope she'll be the same with you. I'll discreetly be off to the other side; she won't see me hanging around. I'll be cautious and use my discretion. I promise."

Madaline had a restless night's sleep. Her dreams reflected her past experiences as a young girl and the stalking experience as of late. When Madaline woke she found herself drenched in sweat. She showered quickly and dressed accordingly. The time seemed to be creeping by. After breakfast she took the elevator up to her suite and waited impatiently for Paul's knock on the door. She paced back and forth in the living room. If the carpeting were made of inferior material, a definite path would have shown and be ultimately worn-out.

"Here's to the best performance of my life," Madaline proclaimed as she handed a glass of water to Paul and clinked the two glasses. The silence in the car was oppressive. Paul was lucky as he drove around the area twice. Spotting a car leaving the curbside, he grabbed the space before anyone else. "Just stick with me baby, I'm here to bring you the luck of the Irish." Madaline, looking at him sideways, ridiculing Paul, "You're not even Irish." Offended, Paul silently shook his head back and forth, as a mime, silently simulating her proclamation.

After a few minutes of easy chit-chat between the two women, Madaline made the suggestion, just before lunch, that they should go somewhere that was more comfortable, yet still neutral territory. The look on Betty's face showed concern. Paul interrupted the conversation, pretending impassive concern and recommended the Nantasket Beach section he had in mind. Both women looked at him, then at each other and nodded their heads in agreement. While Paul drove to the designated destination, the women were quiet. They both had many thoughts going through their mind. It didn't take them long to arrive at the beach. Paul excused himself and went to the Red Parrot, a noted eatery in the area. Paul and the owner of the restaurant had been friends for years. She would do anything for Paul. A couple of years ago, he helped her with a matter. Since then they remained the best of friends. He delivered the meals from the Red Parrot and saw both women devour the lunch faster than Jack Rabbit snatching a carrot from a farmer's garden. Paul decided to leave the two women alone. He took off his shoes and took a slow walk along the edge of the beach's' water.

Although Betty came from various areas throughout her life, her main residence was New York. Once in a great while she went to the shore, always fascinated by the waves of the tides constant motion. Betty's eyes stayed glued to the steady action of the water. Madaline had spent over half her life in California and knew the mesmerizing affects also. Both women were quiet, waiting for the other to start the conversation.

Madaline cleared her throat, gaining Betty's attention away from the beautiful, blue water with it's large waves diminishing to small uneven rolls heading to the sand. "I'm sorry for my fascination regarding the sea," Betty proclaimed, as she wiped her mouth on the napkin provided and pushed the plastic container away from her. "I understand what you mean. When I was very young I was brought up on a farm in Iowa. Not many people know what I'm about to tell you. I'm taking a chance revealing to you certain things about my life and hope that you'll take me at my word. All I ask from you is to listen carefully.

Please don't ask any questions until I'm through with my story," a very serious Madaline exclaimed.

Feigning boredom, Betty nodded her head for Madaline to continue. In reality, Betty was listening intently, trying to gain perspective on the icon people respected, adored or hated with jealousy. "As I was saying, I grew up on a large farm in Fairfield, Iowa. I had many siblings, and we all adored each other. There was never any rivalry between us, only love and devotion to each other. Our parents were wonderful in most ways. They were devoted members of a church and a Sunday wouldn't go by without our entire clan attending services. I thought I was the luckiest girl in the world." She told Betty about all the animals on the farm and the chores that everyone had to do. Betty was starting to get bored, especially when she heard the next words out of Madaline's mouth.

"I had a horse that I loved to ride and take care of. I named him Trigger. You're too young to remember Roy Roger's other than the name on some of his restaurants. I adored the small, half Indian cowboy who millions watched on weekly TV. That's who I named my horse after. Mr. Roger's horse's name. Anyway, I would spend hours cleaning his pen and grooming him after we'd ride through the level land, enjoying the beautiful weather. One day a horrible incident occurred that changed my life forever." That got Betty's attention.

Betty could see the change in Madaline as she continued her story. She related exactly what happened to her that terrible afternoon and the way she and her parents reacted differently to the situation. Visible tears came to her eyes as she expertly wiped them away. "As I was saying, I never forgave them for what they did to me. At the time, they thought they were doing the right thing, but in reality a terrible injustice happened that changed my life forever." Betty was sitting on the edge of the bench, eyes wide open, and intensely listened to this woman, who apparently was a very private person. Betty couldn't stop the words that escaped her mouth. "Please continue!"

"To make a long, dramatic story short, I'll continue." Betty could visually see how upset Madaline was. "My parents sent me away to my Aunt Mabel's house in Kansas." Madaline curiously asked Betty, "have you ever been in Kansas?"

"Let's leave that question when I start talking, if that's all right with you?" Betty didn't want to start relating her story to Miss Mason, but realized that was the reason Madaline asked her for this meeting.

"With tears now streaming down her cheeks, Madaline half-heartedly, wiped them off with the back of her arm. Her nose started dripping as she continued. Madaline again wiped her nose with the back of her hand. "I'm sorry that I'm so emotional," apologized Madaline. Betty could see that Madaline was visually upset, 'either that or she really is the greatest actress alive.'

"Where was I? Oh, ye, anyway, I was to stay there until my pregnancy was over. Aunt Mabel thought that she was helping me and got a mid-wife to assist during the delivery of my baby. You see, or you might not understand, but I really wanted to keep my child. Even though the baby was not conceived the way I would have wanted it to be, I still loved it. I realized that I was young but that didn't matter to me. I begged my parents to let me keep my baby, pleaded with them and my aunt. No one understood that I would have done anything in my power to raise that child. I'm sure that once my parents saw and held the baby, they would have fallen in love and let the little angel be part of our lives. I was never given the chance. It was a hard delivery and I was exhausted by the end of it all. I can still remember the mid-wife telling me to push, with all my might, then breath heavily through my mouth, like panting. I was so young at the time."

"I was angry at everyone, God, my parents, siblings, my aunt, the mid-wife, and most of all Uncle Harry. They didn't even let me hold it when the baby came out. I can remember my aunt taking the baby away after the mid-wife slapped it and I heard the cry. I was hysterical, begging them to tell me what I had, a baby girl or boy. I pleaded for them to let me hold it, cradle it in my arms and love it. Unfortunately my words fell on deaf ears. I stayed at Aunt Mabel's house for another few months. I can tell you I was so depressed, my aunt, parents and even the minister were seriously thinking of sending me to a mental institution. All I did, all day long, was look out the window, not seeing a thing. I would hold myself with my arms tightly surrounding my body. When I sat down, I rocked constantly. I didn't want to live. My aunt, God bless her, didn't know what to do. She had never married and didn't have experience with raising children, let alone a young unwed child, pregnant, unhappy and suicidal. Do you know that every year on the date of my baby's birthday I cry myself to sleep? All I think about is what sex my baby was, was it healthy, happy, and have wonderful, loving parents who would take this child as their own and be good to it."

"You have to understand in those days there were a few ways to adopt a child. One way was for the parents to go through an accredited adoption agency. The parent that gave the child away, signed all papers, to make the transaction legal. I could not have signed those papers, but by then, I was emotionally unstable and didn't care about anything. Another way was a private adoption, through a lawyer's office. Both ways it cost the parents tons of money to adopt a new born baby. The ones that went through a private lawyer, the parents were usually a little older and didn't have a chance with going through a regular adoption agency. A lot of Jewish couples had to take this route because of the religious background. In those days it was important that the adoptive parents be of the same religious background as the baby's parents were. Also, all the records were closed to both the person who gave the baby away, the parents who adopted the baby and to the baby itself."

"After years and many protests from parents, children who were adopted and for medical history reasons, the records became open to the public. It took many years for legislation for that bill to pass. It was also important that after a few years went by, the adopted parents had to have the papers made legal by having the judge sign off on the case. If the natural parents went to the court and wanted the child back, those parents who had become attached and considered the baby theirs, would be devastated if the courts took 'their baby." These procedures could be a few months, but in some cases years would go by before hearing from the court. Many adoptive parents, fearful of the outcome, went so far as moving to a different State where entanglements such as these didn't happen, taking the baby, and changing their entire identity."

"The same matter had to be completed when the adoptive parents had gone through a private lawyer as well." By this time, Madaline was exhausted. Her hands were shaking and her body was drenched in sweat. She couldn't believe that Betty, although listening intently, didn't show one sign of emotion. "There's so much more to tell. I'd love to hear your life story and I only have about another half hour of my tale to continue. I think we'll have plenty of time for you to talk about yourself and still get back to Boston in time for our play. Does that sound all right to you?"

Betty's arms were folded, as if defensively holding herself away from Madaline. Madaline didn't know anything else to say except what happened to her after she left the farm. She explained to Betty that her mother gave her entire savings to her. She knew how unhappy her oldest daughter was and would do anything in her power to make amends for all the terrible experiences I had to endure. "With the small pittance my mother gave me, I then took my chances and went to Hollywood. You know the famous story about Lana Turner being discovered sitting on a stool at the soda fountain in a drug store. I think every girl who read magazines about the stars or True Romance, had a fantasy of becoming a movie star, like Lana Turner." Madaline laughed to herself, relating the old story to Betty. She was sure Betty had not a clue what Madaline was referring to. She then went on to describe how she met Ann Browning and how their friendship grew. She told her about Mrs. McCallum, the rooming house on Kellum Avenue, meeting Brad, the love of her life, and finally her son Kyle, who she adored. She wanted to see Betty's reaction and had a hard time doing so. After searching her pocketbook Madaline finally found some tissues and an old picture of Brad and Kyle.

Madaline was spent and exhausted when she finally finished confiding all her pent up emotions to Betty. She looked at Betty as she took a deep breath, trying to gain composure. When she looked at the young woman, who might be her long, lost daughter, she waited for some kind of reaction. Madaline was shocked and surprised that Betty couldn't be read or what was going through her mind.

After listening to Madaline, many conflicting emotions and thoughts were going through Betty's mind. 'If what Madaline told me is true, then my entire life of shame, hate and revenge has been in vain. "Madaline, I'm sorry that your life was changed when you were a young girl. I now realize the feelings of humiliation, hate, anger, that your parents, peer group, the church's opinion and everything else you had to endure made your life a living hell. The only thing your siblings were guilty of was not being more forceful in finding out from your parents and insisting on being informed on what really happened to you. They were truly out of the loop. I have my own thoughts about your Uncle Harry. He should only go to hell, and I believe he will. It's an awful feeling to feel so alone. I know from experience what that's all about. Are you ready to hear my story? Before I start, I have to tell you that part of me wants to believe you but another side is skeptical. I know what a terrific actress you are. I hope, with all my heart, you're words and the situations you described are true. What I'm about to reveal to you must also be kept in strict confidence. Unlike you, I do know where to begin." Taking a deep breath, Betty began her tale.

"You were right about me being born in Kansas. I was raised by adoring parents who would do anything for me and my younger sister. My parents were an older couple when they had me. When they brought my younger sister home from the hospital, I felt love. I never was jealous of her, as many siblings are of each other. My contemporary's mothers also had babies. I wondered why my mother didn't have the big belly that their mothers did. I didn't understand, but didn't want to embarrass her with my questions. I kept my thoughts at bay. I guess my parents, when they thought we were old enough to be told the truth, thought that they'd sit down with my sister and me, and explain very important matters. They truly were wonderful, caring, doting, and especially loving parents. Anything we wanted we would be sure to get, on occasions that is."

"They weren't rich people by any standards, but rich in other ways that money can't buy. Like your parents they were simple people and devoted to their young family. They worked hard to provide for us. They took care of my sister and me through sickness. When either of us became ill they were there to comfort us and if necessary bring us to the doctor's office. They would help us with our homework, testing us, and taking time out of their lives to be, in my opinion, the best parents in the world. They read to us every evening, made sure we said our prayers, and cuddled and calmed us until our bad dreams went away. One day when I was 12 and my sister 10 my parents wanted to have a family conference. It was then that they informed my sister and me that we were adopted. "I didn't know what the word adoption meant. They went on to explain what adoption stood for and how they were so lucky. They told us that we were special, like angels delivered us to them from God. We told them, that as far as we were concerned, we considered them our true parents. We didn't want to know or care about the people that gave us away. I can remember telling my parents that I felt sorry for those people because they gave up two wonderful children. Years later the laws changed and I could actually get my birth records if I wanted to. The only reason that I wanted to find my records was for the medical information that I may need in the future. Unfortunately, a terrible occurrence happened that would change my life altogether."

Madaline could see the emotions that Betty tried holding back. "It was during a Christmas Holiday that we all went to visit some of our relatives to bring them their presents. Coming from the same area all his life, my dad knew the roads like the back of his hands. I remember it being cold and windy that particular day. Suddenly a whiteout happened that blinded drivers. They couldn't see a foot in front of them. Dad tried calming us down and assured us that we'd be fine. I remember the wind sounding like wolves howling to each other. Even though my father kept his windshield wipers on high, the visibility was terrible. There wasn't any room for us to pull over and wait out the storm. Each of us were saying the Lord's prayer to ourselves. My father, although driving intensely, told my mother to keep us entertained by singing songs and playing word games."

"Suddenly out of the blue we could see something coming at us. We couldn't figure out what it was. Before we knew what happened the driver of a 16 wheeler lost control of his truck. He was turning a corner and plowed into us, demolishing the car and killing my parents and sister instantly. Other cars were also in the pileup and many more lives were lost in this freak accident. I don't know why God spared me, but he did. I stayed in the hospital for many months. Operation, after operation, then going through rehabilitation."

"I felt so alone. One of my cousins wanted to take me in and make me part of her family. That was nice of her. Psychologically, after many months I couldn't take it. I was very young at the time. The social workers couldn't let me stay alone. I went from one relative's house to another. I caused trouble. I hated God and was very bitter about life in general. I despised life and everything and everyone around me. When all the relatives were used up the social workers had a few options left. I would either go into an orphanage or a home for wayward children. Now remember, after the accident I was rebellious and got into a lot of trouble. Instead of an orphanage, where I could get out on my own at age 18, I was brought to a home for unwanted and troubled teens, in a cell with other children like myself."

"I learned a lot from those kids. Some of the girls were tough and I went through the normal initiation rituals. Thankfully I survived them. After a few months I was one of them. School work was available to us and luckily, I took advantage of that program. When I was younger I liked school and always did well, getting A's and B's. I have to admit, I was one of the smartest kids in the facility." Betty took a deep breath and Madaline could visibly see her eyes tearing. She also saw a hardness in her that frightened her.

"After good behavior and getting my GED they let me out at age 18. I was on my own and didn't have any place to go. Many nights I laid crying on my bunk, thinking back to the old days when I experienced happiness. I still carry my parents and sisters pictures everywhere I go. When I go to sleep, their faces appear in front of me and many nights I have terrible nightmares."

Well, Madaline found out what happened to her daughter. She was inconsolable and wanted to hug her offspring and tell her how sorry she was that life turned upside down for her. She knew in her heart that Betty would never accept her heartfelt sorrow. Tears were again flowing, like a hose, watering flowers in a garden. She hated her sentimentality. How could she handle this situation? She had no idea, but was determined to do something about Betty.

"Hey, I thought that this meeting was going to be about my career and how you could help me. What happened to that portion of our conversation?"

Madaline was dumbfounded. 'Here two horrible stories were told and Betty took it in stride.' How could Madaline tell her that she now thinks or knows that Betty is the daughter that she gave up? 'What will Betty's reaction be?' she asked herself.

'How can I confront Betty on the issue of stalking and trying to kill me? Does Betty know that I'm her mother? I changed my name and maybe she just assumes that I'm her biological mother. How can she be sure? Is she trying to get back at me if she thinks I'm her mom? Is she blaming me for all her unhappiness and how she had to endure the terrible life she went through after the unexpected accident that took the lives of her family?' All these questions were too much to handle in one day, Madaline thought.

"You know Betty, in many ways our history is almost the same. Not entirely, but we can see the unhappiness that the both of us had to go through. I think it's getting late and we'd better get going if we want to make the play in time. With the leading lady and the understudy not there, I don't think the patrons will be happy. I think I see Paul heading our way." Waving to him, he saw her and hurried to join them and drive back to Boston.

In the automobile driving home, Madaline asked Betty if they could continue their conversation in the next couple of days. Betty was hesitant and told Madaline that she'd have to think about it. It would probably be an affirmative answer and she'd get back to Madaline within a few days.

After the performance Madaline and Paul went back to her hotel room. Paul could see all through the ride home and during the play that Madaline wasn't acting her usual self. He had to restrain himself till they were alone and she could relate the story to him.

SAN DIEGO, CALIFORNIA

Nancy couldn't wait to call up Rich and find out how the case was coming. She knew he'd be honest with her and was looking forward to his telling her all about the investigation and his new friend who was still very sick. After she spoke to Rich she called Suzanne. "So, I know you had Spencer's parents over. How did it go? You have to tell me everything, and don't leave anything out."

Suzanne related how they enjoyed the dinner. She went into detail on what she and Mrs. Walsh prepared and served. She told Nancy that she enjoyed Irene's company very much. "Personally, I don't particularly like her husband. He seems to me to be a pompous ass."

"Oh Suzanne, only you can describe your future in law that way," stated Nancy. Then Suzanne told Nancy that she started liking Spencer more. The extended time she spent with Hope and Spencer she had gotten to know him and liked him. The more she became aware of his attributes, his sensibility. She now knows how and why Hope fell in love with him.

"Of course the issue of religion is a factor and I'm trying with all my might to overlook my feelings. After all, as long as we believe in God, we're all his children. Do you really believe me? Don't answer that question," Suzanne ordered. "Oh yes, I made plans with Irene, about a month after the wedding for me to go to her house. I'm going to teach her some of the Jewish recipes that she enjoyed. I explained to her that we don't have accurate measurements and I'd have to show her how I make the various dishes. At least I will get her to, maybe, keep part of the tradition by serving them during the holiday seasons. Both my grandmothers taught me how to prepare, cook and bake the old way of Jewish cooking. Unfortunately, my mom never got into it and my other grandmother had 4 sons. Their daughter-in-laws learned from their mothers. It gave my paternal mama satisfaction when I showed interest and wanted her to teach me the way she cooked as well. They were both great cooks and bakers and I feel fortunate that I now have the knowledge to prepare these foods. Of course if looks could kill, I wouldn't be talking to you now. Hope gave me such a look of hate when Irene and I talked about the Jewish dishes and how I'd go to her house and show her how to make them. I think if there was a hole in the floor Hope wanted to go into it." Suzanne laughed as she related this last part of the story to Nancy.

"Getting on to another subject," Nancy interrupted, "I spoke to Rich when I got home and he said he'd call me back shortly. He was busy working on a case that he said we'd be interested in. I can't wait to find out what it is. I'll call you as soon as he tells me what he has on his mind. Who knows, he might have more information on the case and discovered information that will also help us."

"I'll be waiting to hear from you. Meanwhile, I'm busy helping Hope with her wedding plans. I'm lucky to find time for myself and all the work it takes running the many spas. I know that Stephen will be arriving shortly and expects a positive reaction when we see each other again. I'm a little hesitant and hope that I can hide my resentment about our situation. I'm sure we'll have a great time." Nancy said out loud, "Just stay calm, think before you speak and enjoy being in each other's company while he's here."

"Thanks for the encouragement. I'll let you know what happens."

Rich called Nancy as promised and told her about Sam. "He's been very helpful and I think we're turning a corner in the investigation." He told her about Mr. Yasuhito and what happened to him. "He's getting better and before long will be able to tell us a little more about the case. Where he's Mr. Makino's chauffeur, I'm almost positive this is all part of our investigation."

Nancy was upset that Yasuhito was very ill because of his innocent job to a man who obviously is involved in either the murder or thefts that have occurred." 'As soon as Suzanne's daughter, Hope's, wedding is over, life will get back to normal, I hope.' "We'll probably take another trip to Japan and see how the spa is coming along. Although we speak on a regular basis with our spa in Japan, it's not the same thing as being hands on and finding out for ourselves what's happening." Rich interjected, "I want you to know that I'm interested in your spas but I have to tell you what's on my mind."

"Go ahead, I'm listening. "I think Sam's involvement with Mr. Makino's company will help us immensely. I also hope that you'll make a stop in San Diego to see me. I'm not pushing or anything, but it's a suggestion."

Laughing, Nancy teased him. "Oh yes, I almost forgot that California is a good spot to land before heading for Japan. No, silly, do you think I'd miss a chance to see you and find out if Suzanne and I can be of any help to you and your men with the case." Rich acknowledged that she and Suzanne are legit. "If I hadn't talked to Tim and Kevin myself I wouldn't believe either of you. Thankfully, they had only wonderful things to say about the two of you. It doesn't hurt that your connections with Interpol and the FBI will be a tremendous help. The only problem so far is Mr. Makino has vanished along with his girlfriend, Robin. We've tried everything in our power and we've come up with nada. Who knows, you and Suzanne might be the luck we need."

"Even though he communicates with Sam directly by computer, our experts can't seem to pin him down to one spot or country. He's illusive, if not anything else."

"I still can't believe that Mr. Makino is the gentleman that I sat next to on my first trip back from Japan. He seemed so nice. I also ran into him on two other occasions and again he was hospitable, I don't know, he seemed like a truly fine person."

"Oh boy, can I sell you a bridge in Brooklyn? Nancy because you're nice you automatically think everyone else is. Hate to burst your bubble, but that isn't how it is in the real world."

"Thanks," Nancy said. Then she sullenly asked, "Don't you think I'm realistic? I've ran into and known every type of person there is in the world. I'm not as naïve as you think I am. In my short life I've been through plenty and let me tell you, I usually can spot a fraud and miserable people when I first meet them. I have to admit that once in a while someone slips through my intuition and I suppose Mr. Makino is one of them. So put me in front of a firing squad and shoot me."

"My, my, are we getting a little testy? All I'm saying is that he's a sly character that we have to be careful with."

"On our next visit to Japan, after I stop on the way to San Diego, tell me again why I'm making a pit stop there?" she teasingly asked Rich. "I'll ignore that question, thank you."

"Okay, okay, Suzanne and I will make a stop and then we'll go on to Beppu. It's a beautiful place to visit and the scenery is magnificent. We happen to know where he lives in Beppu and we might see if he and Robin are there. You never know," replied Nancy.

"You and Suzanne have to be careful. We're dealing with a desperate man who'll do anything to get away with fraud and murder. I think, if I can talk the Captain to give me a leave or have it as part of the investigation, me and a few of the guys might meet you there." Nancy interrupted, "If you can talk the captain into letting you go outside of the US, then maybe you can fly with us. It'll certainly cost a lot less money for your department if you don't have to pay." "I'll have to speak to the captain. I don't know if he can put a requisition in for it, it's a bit unusual, but one never knows until one is asked, right?" Nancy continued, "While we're there, you'll get to see the spa and who knows, maybe a few Geisha girls will be glad to help your friends find some interesting places to visit. Don't even go there. I know how your sick mind works. No, I will be your personal Geisha and show you what the real Japan is like." Rich was laughing so hard his belly ached. "You are incredible woman! Since my divorce I swore off woman forever, but I might have second thoughts. Not that I'm rushing into any kind of relationship but keep it in mind. Getting back to our adventure, I'll speak to the Captain ASAP and hopefully he'll give us the go-ahead to try and find this character." Teasing he said, "I don't have an Italian nose for nothing. I'm like a blood hound; I can smell bad people out."

"You're truly a nut, but I like you anyway," Nancy admitted. Rich told Nancy that he'd call her as soon as he heard the plan of action that would be taking place. "If I don't hear quickly I'll call you anyway. I like hearing your voice," Rich said as he hung up the phone.

Nancy was elated when they ended their conversation. She dialed Suzanne's cell phone and when she picked up a smile crossed her face. "I'm glad I didn't get your voice-mail." Nancy related everything that was said during Rich and her conversation. "I had to tell someone how I feel. Like weightless clouds, slowly moving in the sky."

"I can honestly say this is one phone call I love to hear. Remember, we can't leave until a few days after the wedding. After all the preparation that I'm doing I'll be exhausted. I'll need those couple of days to get my energy back and put my nose to the grindstone. Stephen is coming into town in 10 days and I'm a bit nervous. I'm tough and while I'm sure we'll have fun during this visit, I'm not going to forget my ultimatum. I haven't had sex in so long. I hope I can wipe away the cob webs."

"You're such a jerk Suzanne. Everyone knows that you never forget how to make love. It's like riding a bike, you go back on and never forget how to." Suzanne was amused by Nancy's comparison and laughed as she hung up the phone. She ran up the stairs to continue doing laundry.

CHAPTER THIRTY SIX

BOSTON, MASSACHUSETTS

Paul met Madaline after the play and walked back to the Ritz. He could tell by her actions that, although the play went well, something was bothering her. He escorted her in silence until they closed the door to her suite. "Okay, I left the two of you alone to talk. Tell me what happened. It was so quiet in that automobile that I could have dropped a pin and heard it on the carpet of the car."

"Well you did your job well. I think she's my daughter. She never came out with the statement, but from all that was said between us, I don't think that we can ignore the evidence. It was obvious, like a tornado's whirlwind, twirling to its next building." Madaline was pacing the floor. It was recognizable that she was nervous. He could see that she was holding back tears she wanted to shed. Paul wanted to go over to her, take her into his arms, and envelope her. He cleared his mind of that thought, and went to the bar and poured some Dewar's over ice, handing it to her.

"Thanks. Why don't you join me and pour what you'd prefer for yourself. It's apparent you know what I like."

"We're going to meet again within a few days. I think she needs to ponder what was said and resolve in her mind and weigh the options she has. Personally, I don't think she can refuse to realize the undeniable facts. I mean it's plain as the nose on one's face. She's not as innocent as she appears to be. It's clearly obvious that she can't deny the conclusive evidence."

"It was hard for me to hear what she went through during the critical time in her young life. Teen years are difficult enough, without having the added burden of what she had to endure because of the accident.. I felt guilty when she related her story to me. Paul, I don't know what I can say to her. Do I declare that I'm sorry for the way both our lives were affected by this horrible circumstance? If I could go back in time, I'd erase all that happened, and re-arrange life's turmoil. I want her to believe me when I say if I could, I'd change the way people determined our lives for us. Another problem is how can I accuse her of stalking and trying to kill me. That's an awful accusation to lay on someone. She must really hate me. I think she blames me for all the bad situations that went wrong in her young life." As she talked out loud, as if talking to herself, Madaline pondered what would occur next. "And, I also feel guilty for not keeping abreast of Kyle's situation. What kind of mother am I? All I could think about was my own problems and how to deal with them."

"He must feel I don't care. I'm concerned what's going to happen between Carol and him. I love her like a daughter and can feel the pain that she must be going through. How humiliating to find out that your marriage was a sham and now everyone knows that, although he loves her, in his own way, he was in love with someone else. The saddest being he's gay and was in love with another man. She must be inconsolable. Thankfully most of her work is in Europe and Europeans don't get that upset when this kind of thing happens to them. As far as Kyle is concerned, he knows that I love him, no matter what. That's what mothers do. I don't think his work has been affected by the adverse publicity.

Most people realize that he's been out of jail and not considered a suspect any longer. Anyway, most people in the arts are gay. Isn't that an awful thing to say? I have many male and female friends that swing both ways. I love them for who they are. It doesn't matter to me what they do in their private life. Listen to me. I'm talking for the sake of talking. I can't stop rambling on. Paul, I thought I was devastated when Kyle was accused of murder. But this situation with Betty is going to drive me crazy. I don't know what to do next."

"I think you've got to relax. I know it's easier said than done. Honestly, take up yoga or something and think good thoughts. I don't know what I'm saying. Madaline, you're a grown woman and I'm sure you'll figure out what you have to do. You've never been one to procrastinate and I doubt you'll change now. Just remember, I'll always be with you, watching every move you make. I doubt if Betty will still try to harm you after she heard the truth from you. That's if she thinks you're sincere," Paul told an extremely upset Madeline.

"She already made a reference that she knows I'm a great actress and has misgivings about my story," Madaline said.

"That's her problem isn't it? She's a bright girl. She has to believe the frankness with which you spoke. She'd be a fool not to. I guess it's her move now. I hope for both your sakes the situation will be resolved shortly."

"You're right. I should take it one day at a time and think positive thoughts. For now I think I'll call Kyle. The time difference won't matter that much, and let him know I'm thinking of him. I hope he'll tell me some news about his personal life, but you're cognizant that men are more close to the vest and don't say much about what's happening to them. I feel like it's pulling teeth every time I ask him questions that affect his emotional well-being. He should understand that as a mother I want to know what's going on. With all these things on my plate, I'm lucky I know the play by heart. It's funny that I haven't heard from either Suzanne or Nancy for some time. I hope they're okay. I appreciate all they've done for Kyle when he was a suspect for murder, but they should be over their work now. I should also give them a call to find out what's going on."

"Let's get through one crisis at a time. If they wanted to talk I'm sure they would have found a way to communicate with you. Let them be and do their own thing. When the time is right, I know that they'll contact you."

"Okay." Madaline conceded, I won't be such a worry wart." Looking back at Paul she said, "I hope and pray that Betty follows through and gets in touch with me soon."

BOSTON, MASSACHUSETTS

Suzanne was busy finishing up the small details that had to be attended to before the wedding. Hope was nervous but at the same time grateful that she could rely on her mother for supervising the small specialized items that had to be dealt with. She realized that her mother and grandparents weren't happy with her converting to Catholism, but under the circumstances, they were handling the entire situation well. She understood that her mother had other things on her mind. It seemed that Hope couldn't find the words or show her mother how much she appreciated her. Maybe on their honeymoon she'd bring something back, especially nice, as a thank you for all the valuable help she did in making her special day come about.

Suzanne was coming out of the chocolate emporium, picking up the candied almonds and dipped nuts. These platters would be put on each table. She was about to head out to the florist to finalize the details when her cell phone rang. She was perplexed on whether to let it go to voice mail or pick it up. Deciding to pick up the phone, she put her packages onto the back seat and exasperated, answered the cell.

"That's a nice greeting for someone you haven't seen in a while," chided Stephen. "Oh, Stephen, I didn't look at the caller ID. You caught me in the middle of finishing up last minute details for Hope. How are you and when should I expect to see you?"

"You certainly are one busy lady. I hope you won't let me interrupt your agenda, but you will be seeing me at your house in about 45 minutes to an hour. I'm at Logan and waiting for my suitcase to come down the turnstile. Will it be an inconvenience if I come over now?"

"Of course not silly. I wasn't expecting to see you for another week, but I will be waiting with baited breath. I should be home at about the same time you arrive. I'll call Mrs. Walsh and make sure she prepares dinner for the three of us. I'm sure she'll be delighted to see you. Do you have any preferences?"

"Well, to be honest with you, I thought I'd take you out for dinner and then we can go back to your place. I can stay in the guest room, or we can go to the hotel that I made reservations for."

Suzanne was perplexed. Of course she'd rather Stephen stay at her house, but under the circumstance......."Let's play it by ear, if that's all right with you?"

`"Hey, I'm easy. Anything you say will be fine with me. I realize this is going to be a busy time for you. I shouldn't have imposed. I'll keep my plans to stay at the hotel. I'll be able to help you with anything you need. I'm your servant, and at your beckon call."

"If you put it that way, I think it will be best for you to be at the hotel. This week will be hectic and especially with last minute details. You understand, don't you?"

"Of course I do. As long as we're together and you'll come up to my suite. Then we'll have the privacy we need. I'll be as happy as a clam, lying in the bottom of the ocean. Who knows, I might come in handy. What restaurant would you like me to take you to this evening?"

After all the running around, Suzanne would enjoy relaxing and putting her feet up and just veg out. Of course she couldn't tell him what she really wanted and offend him. "Let's think about it when you get here. Was your flight good and how did you manage to get here a week earlier than expected?"

"To be honest with you, I couldn't put off seeing you any longer. Everyone at the plant knows their duties and I got the nurses to take extra shifts. The flight was fine, no turbulence what-so-ever. While I was on the plane I closed my eyes and imagined you in my arms. Your full lips against mine and the intimacy was, well let's put it this way, I had to hide my feelings with a pillow, hoping that we wouldn't land quickly."

Suzanne couldn't contain her laughter. "You're awful. I love it. See you soon." With all of Suzanne's mixed emotions regarding Stephen, she couldn't help but love him. Since she was a young girl, she couldn't get him out of her mind. She kept her date data book in her closet, hidden beneath her work out clothes. She would take it out and look at the book occasionally, remembering all the good times they had when they were young and carefree. As a matter of fact she often wondered why she still kept the book hidden. 'When it comes time for me to meet my maker, the kids will probably laugh at all my thoughts and most likely throw it, along with other items I treasured, away, not thinking what they meant to me.' She knew she couldn't let her emotions get in her way when the serious conversation with Stephen came to be. She'd have to quell her feelings and think rational. She prayed to God she'd have the strength to be mature and forceful.

She arrived home before Stephen and let Mrs. Walsh know what was happening. She avoided the look that Mrs. Walsh gave her and went upstairs to change. After-all, she couldn't let him see her in the sweaty clothes that she was wearing when running around doing the necessary errands that needed to be taken care of.

Nancy called Suzanne, not aware that Stephen arrived a week early. "Nancy, I know that you want to talk, but to be honest with you, Stephen will be here any minute. I have to get into the shower and put fresh clothes on. It's pretty bad when I can smell myself. Seriously, if you have to talk to me this minute and what you have to say is urgent, then by all means, tell me."

"No, I forgot to mention something trivial, it's not important. We'll talk later when you have more time. Tell Stephen I say hello. Have a great time, and Suzanne, be strong. I don't want to hear any excuses why you couldn't have that conversation with him. Until I hear from you soon, enjoy yourself."

Nancy hung up the phone and considered how to tell Suzanne her thoughts about helping Rich with the investigation. She hoped that Suzanne would go along with her idea about going back to Japan. She realized it wasn't long ago that they were away, but the importance of this new information was vital. They had to find out everything there was to get the goods on this phony who has everyone fooled thinking he's a nice guy. With what Rich told her about him, 'he is really a chameleon in disguise,' she thought to herself as she gazed out her large window overlooking the water.

When Suzanne got off the phone she stood at the desk for a while, contemplating Nancy's sound advice. For now she'd put all her worries behind her and would enjoy Stephen's company. After all, it wasn't often that they'd been able to physically be in each other's company. Berating herself for being the one that was responsible for the rift in their relationship this time, she shook her head, hoping these negative thoughts wouldn't interfere with their union. She hurried up the steps and ran the shower. While toweling herself dry, she was mad that, once again, she acted like an abused woman and put all the blame that was wrong with their relationship on herself. She knew she shouldn't think that way. She applied her makeup, fixed her hair, admiring herself in the mirror. Suzanne was looking forward to his arrival. She felt butterflies in her stomach and knew that whatever happened, she would always love him, no matter what.

The bell rang and Suzanne hurried down the stairs to greet him. He took her in his arms and kissed her. He always took her breath away. Boy how she had missed his passion. He carried in the suitcases and left them in the hallway. "I know that you wanted to take me out for dinner this evening but Mrs. Walsh insisted that she cook a good meal for the two of us. I hope you don't mind that I gave in to her request."

"No, that's fine with me." 'Sure, she always does what someone else asks of her but me. She knows how much I wanted the two of us to be alone, especially when we haven't seen each other for such a long time. I won't let her see my disappointment and try to act nice and civilized. I'll try to have a good time.' Suzanne took his hand and led him into the kitchen to greet Mrs. Walsh. When they settled down, she took Stephen into the living room and, excitedly, gave him a rundown on all the details she was doing for the wedding. She realized that he could never share her enthusiasm over this once in a lifetime occasion. If they had children together his interest would be different. Suzanne didn't want to, but couldn't contain telling him the plans that she worked hard on.

After looking at the baskets that Suzanne made up for the ladies room, and the many fastidious colors of cloths and favors for the guests an hour and a half went by. She realized that Stephen was hungry and abruptly started putting the items away. He was grateful for the reprieve but tried not to show his impatience.

"I'm going into the kitchen and see how Mrs. Walsh is coming along with dinner. Let me get you a drink and I'll be right back." After handing him his favorite glass of merlot, she quickly went into the kitchen, quietly closing the door. Mrs. Walsh lifted her right eyebrow knowing that Suzanne would know what that signified. "Okay, okay, I recognize that you're busy. You have everything under control? Suzanne laughed out loud, that's a foolish question. You won't tell me what's being served."

"Let it be a surprise for the both of you." Shooing Suzanne out of her domain, she finished putting the last minute garnishes on the platter and called the two lovebirds in. Stephen, always a gentleman, pulled out the chairs for both women. With appreciation of Mrs. Walsh's hard work, poured wine into the waiting glasses and proposed a toast to the very talented and beautiful Mrs. Walsh. "Oh, don't be lavishing praises to me. My head might get so big, that I'll ask for more money." She smiled, her blue eyes still twinkled as they did when she was younger. She sipped her wine and finally relaxed for the evening.

Stephen wouldn't let Mrs. Walsh clear the dishes when the meal was through. He and Suzanne washed the crystal and put away the left overs. "You really lucked out when you found Mrs. Walsh," Stephen declared as he licked his fingers after removing the excess frosting from the plate that the delicious chocolate cake was served from. "I don't know how you manage to stay as slim as you do with Mrs. Walsh preparing these dishes for you."

"If you want to know the truth, normally I don't have time to eat during the day. By the time I get home I'm exhausted and only have a light dinner. I hope you realize that I also prepare some of the meals for us." Pushing his chest with her finger she asked, "Do you forget that I was a housewife at one time before becoming an entrepreneur?"

Stephen couldn't help laughing as he grabbed her finger and gently kissed it while shaking his head in admission. At that point Suzanne realized how foolish she looked and admittedly joined him in laughter. "Come on, it's a beautiful night. Let's take a walk around the block and try to relax and keep things in perspective." Without letting her respond, he led her out the door and started walking. Suzanne knew that Stephen was right and actually enjoyed walking through the neighborhood, admiring the changes that the new owners did to the older homes. She remembered when the development was first built and the young couples took pride in planting the young seedlings that were now full grown trees. Many of the residents kept the same garden islands, adding their own touch of flowers for people to see and enjoy while, like them, wandering the streets with appreciation.

After making plans to see each other tomorrow, Suzanne closed the front door and let out a deep breath. When they said good evening it was as if they were young teenagers again, standing in her parent's vestibule, kissing until their lips were raw. While lying in bed she couldn't help think of Nancy and wondered what was on her mind. She knew she'd be waking her friend but acutely aware how Nancy was, realized that she wouldn't get mad at her intrusion.

"Okay, Stephen left and I can't contain my excitement about what you want to tell me. So let me hear what's on your mind and forget about all the chores that I'm doing."

"Before I begin my dialogue, what do you mean Stephen's left. This is your first night that the two of you have seen each other in a while and you're not with him. What's wrong with you? I'd be bouncing his bones if I were in the same situation. I mean it. How could you let him leave, especially on this first day?"

"You're right. I should have insisted I'd go to his hotel room this evening. After our phone call I'll surprise him and make him a happy camper. Now, you know how I'd let my mind wander unless I hear from you. What did you call me for?"

"Suzanne, I can't believe you. You're something else. How'd you know that I made a casual phone call, with nothing particular in mind?"

"My dear, how long have we known each other? You never call anyone unless there's something on your mind. So come on, you know you're dying to tell me, let's hear it."

"When you put it that way, okay. I spoke to Rich and he told me about his informant and they now know or have a handle on one of the men that they've been looking for in the murder of Curtis Jones. I really respect this spy, who's taking a big risk for himself and his family by helping the police with the investigation. Rich reminded me that we can't let on we know who this man is because you never know who could be working against us." Laughing, Nancy declared, "Hell, he never told me who this guy is. I was thinking we'd go back to California, once the wedding is over, and we can clear the business at hand. With Rich's guidance and from the help of the FBI and Interpol, we might be able to finally get to the bottom of this case. What is your input with regards to what I just told you?"

"Wow, this is getting very complicated, isn't it? You realize that I can never start something without finishing it. So you can count me in on anything we have to do to get the people responsible for the art thefts. Who knows how many other murders they're liable for. Let me get a little breather after the wedding and I'm sure it won't take a long time to finish up the business at Metamorphosis. By the way, when we go back to California, are we, just by coincidence, taking a trip back to Japan?"

"I'll keep you guessing. Make sure when we do travel, take lots of clothes. You never know where our next adventure will take us. You realize that in a couple of years you'll be old enough to retire and then think of all the fun trips we'll be able to go on." Nancy laughed as she was about to hang up the phone. "By the way, have a good night tonight." Suzanne retaliated by quickly stating that she had many years before she was of retirement age. Besides, who needs to be retired to go away and have fun." She quickly hung up the telephone.

Suzanne knocked on Stephen's hotel door. He was both surprised and delighted that the love of his life surprised him with this unexpected visit. He stood looking at her as an aberration before him. "Excuse my lack of grateful greeting, come in, come in. What a delightful surprise. He took her in his strong arms and held her tight. He pulled away, and then the magnetism between them couldn't be quelled any further. Their lips touched and the passion that they felt for each other showed, as their lips parted and their tongues intertwined. They stood standing in the entry way for about five minutes, their kisses becoming more intense. Finally they gently parted and he led her to the couch in the suite. "I can't believe you came here tonight. I know how busy you are with all the preparation you're doing for the wedding. Not that I'm delighted, more like flabbergasted that you're in front of me. You will stay the night, won't you?" asked a concerned Stephen.

"Of course, silly. I don't know why I let you leave by yourself in the first place. My head must be full of thoughts. It didn't occur to me that the right thing would be for me to be with you, especially on our first night of not seeing each other for a while."

"I don't have to tell you how delighted I am that you're here. I'm literally in shock. But a nice astonishment. Let me take your coat and while I'm getting us drinks get comfortable." Stephen's face reddened as soon as the words left his mouth. "I mean take off your shoes and relax." They talked for, what seemed, hours. Subjects that couldn't be spoken in front of Mrs. Walsh were verbalized freely, without any misgivings. Finally Stephen recommended that they retire for the evening and asked her if she wanted to take a shower first. He hoped she would tell him that he should join her, but that was not said. The radio was turned down low and under the covers they snuggled like they'd never been separated. He felt her beautiful, smooth body beneath his fingers and couldn't contain his manly feelings any longer. When they finished making love they were exhausted and happy that they were compatible as ever.

They fell asleep in each other's arms, all excuses, inhibitions and their problems were left for another time and place.

Stephen saw Suzanne off early the next morning after consuming a large breakfast in the hotel's restaurant. "What time do you want to meet or should I come to your house and pick you up?"

"Let's meet at my spa and we can figure out what we'll do in the late afternoon. I know that I have a few clients before 1:00 and I'll be free after that."

Suzanne shut off her Marvin Gaye CD after one of her clients and called Madaline. She knew that Madaline was experiencing difficulty with whatever predicament she was having. Suzanne wanted to help her if she could. "Hey it's me. I know you've been busy and have a lot on your mind, but don't forget that I'm your friend. If you need me for anything, all you have to do is ask."

"You are a dear. Unfortunately, I don't think you or anyone else can help me out in this particular situation. After this horrible mess is over I'll tell you everything that's happened and it should be resolved shortly. Thanks anyway. I'll call you in a few. Remember, I love you and I can never repay you for all that you, Nancy and Justin did for me and Kyle. By the way I spoke to Nancy last evening and she told me that Stephen came in earlier than expected." Madaline said, "I hope that you and he had a wonderful time when you were with each other."

"Let's say that, "Love Is A Many Splendid Thing," Suzanne said as she hung up the phone. Suzanne tried putting all worries and anxieties out of her mind when she saw Stephen waiting in her office.

A big smile appeared on his face when she entered her inner sanctum. She could feel the butterflies in her stomach when she saw his handsome face. Suzanne gave him an obligatory hug and tried to hold back her real feelings. 'I could jump his bones right here in the office if I could get away with it,' she thought. She told him where she had to go to finish the last of the wedding responsibilities and then the rest of the day and night would be devoted to him.

He took her to the Bay Tower Room for a beautiful, romantic dinner and taking her hand in his, kissed her fingers, lingering as long as he could. He didn't want to cause Suzanne unnecessary embarrassment. Suzanne felt her face and neck turn red. She hoped no one, especially Stephen saw her reaction. "I can't begin to tell you how happy I am that we're finally connecting," Stephen uttered as he finished his meal. "If you'd like dessert, I'll be glad to order one for you, but truthfully, I'd love to have it back at my hotel room."

Suzanne knew exactly what he meant but played dumb. "Sure, that's fine with me. Thanks for the delicious meal. I'm sure that room service will have some dessert equally as good as here."

On the way to the hotel Suzanne remembered the last time she dined at the Bay Tower Room and felt guilty when Larry came to mind. "A penny for your thoughts," Stephen asked Suzanne as he caught the look on her face.

Suzanne didn't like lying, but knew she couldn't tell him what was on her mind. "It's nothing, really. Just thought of the wedding and I wanted my mind to be free of all thoughts except you and I together. Like you said before, it's been too long since we've been intimate." Her smile melted his heart as he held her hand while getting to their final destination.

Stephen nodded to the woman behind the reception desk and told her quietly that he didn't want to be disturbed for the rest of the evening. As they ascended the elevator Suzanne was giddy with anticipation. She felt like a young girl in love for the first time. Stephen unlocked the door and quietly put the do not disturb sign on the outside of the door. As soon as he closed the door he captivated Suzanne, holding her against the wall he bent over and kissed her passionately. She could feel her knees weaken. His tongue automatically caressed her lips and she returned the stimulating sensation. She nibbled his lower lip with her teeth and felt the heat in his body reacting to their exchange of kisses. Suzanne had to catch her breath. Stephen's hands slowly went under her blouse and he caressed her midriff, gradually going around to her back.

He loved the smoothness of her skin. They didn't move from their position as he lightly scratched her back and with one swift movement undid her bra. He leisurely unbuttoned her blouse, letting it fall to the floor. He moved his thumbs over her beautiful, small, but hard buds of her breasts, the smoothness driving him insane. She in turn unbuttoned his shirt and quickly unbuckled his belt. She deftly unhooked and unzipped his pants. She felt his hard erection. He expertly lifted his legs and kicked his underwear aside. She was glad that she bought matching bra and panties at Victoria Secret before their long awaited reunion. Although she was sure that they would go unnoticed. He skillfully slid her panties down and they both were naked as their bodies meshed together against the cool outside wall. Without missing a beat, he continued kissing her as he led her to the bed. Not bothering to unmake the bedding, he pushed her gently onto her back. He was an expert lover and held himself in abeyance making sure that he satisfied his mate and then let himself have pleasure as well.

They held on to each other, their perspiration having a cooling effect on both of them. After showering together, they laid next to each other, her spooning against his chest and stomach. His legs were wrapped around hers.

In the middle of the night they awoke. As he was caressing her hair, taking and lifting her blond tresses off her face, he noticed tears teetering on the edge of her bottom lid. He lightly wiped them off her cheek and didn't say a word. He loved this woman, who should have rightfully been his wife. He couldn't understand why she was betraying her emotions as she was. Afraid to bring up a negative response he didn't say a word. He kissed her tears and lovingly patted her hair. They fell back asleep in each other's arms.

The next morning Suzanne felt exhausted but happy. She realized how much she missed being with and seeing him. He dropped her off at work and made plans for the evening. Suzanne realized it would be their last weekend together before the wedding. 'I can't stop loving him. As much as I try to tell myself all the reasons why I shouldn't stay with him, he'll always be in my heart and soul'

Madaline was waiting on pins and needles until Betty got in touch with her again. After the evening performance she was getting into her street clothes when she heard a knock on her door. Hoping it was Betty she quickly opened the entrance. 'It's about time,' she thought. 'It's been three long days since we last spoke. I wonder why she waited so long to finally give me an answer to meet again?' With a smile on her face she greeted her understudy and quite likely, her daughter. "Come in, I've been waiting for your response."

Betty awkwardly found herself entering this vain woman's dressing room. 'Look at that smile. It's as phony as a two dollar bill.' Acting nonchalant she sat down on the comfortable side chair, crossing her legs, waiting for Madaline to start the conversation. When Madaline saw she was waiting for her to start the dialogue she cleared her throat and began chattering. After a couple of minutes Madaline regained her composure and wanted an answer when they were to meet again for their important talk.

"I've been thinking these last past days and let's meet in your suite. It'll be private and we can clear the air that seems to be heavy between the two of us. Is that agreeable to you?" Betty asked, while she still seemed unapproachable.

"I think that's a great idea. Let's make it after tomorrow's afternoon performance." Without waiting for a response Madaline continued, "I'll have lunch brought up and we can talk while eating."

Getting up out of the chair, Betty walked to the door and announced, "see you then."

Madaline couldn't believe how distant that girl could be. 'She's really a grown woman. I have to stop thinking of her as a child.' She called Paul and related the plans. "I don't think she wants anyone else to be in the suite. I hope you don't mind if the two of us are alone."

Paul was worried but tried not to let her hear it in his voice. "I'll go along with that, but we have to devise a method if you should experience any trouble. I'd like to put a small microphone somewhere that will be hidden."

"Paul, you're saying you want to bug my suite?"

"If you put it that way, ya, I do. Even though you think you know her, we really don't. She could be up to something that could harm you. I know you think I'm going overboard but there's nothing wrong about being cautious. Or, I can be in the other room, not making a sound and come to your rescue, if need be. You let me know which you'd prefer once I get to the hotel, humor me, okay?"

"I feel like an agent for the CIA. I normally wouldn't go through this charade but in this case I bow to your professional training. I'm so nervous I can't think straight." Pacing back and forth she retrieved a cigarette from her purse and took a deep drag. Paul heard her intake of breath. "I thought you gave up smoking?"

"I did for the most part. Suzanne told me how bad smoking was for my skin. But now, screw it. When I get nervous I have a cigarette. Sue me."

"You're really a wise-guy, but hey, do what you have to do. I'll be at the hotel within an hour. See you then." With a mischievous grin Paul walked out of his house, shaking his head.

Madaline couldn't contain her nervousness when she finished the matinee. The two women met and walked silently to the hotel. The stillness was enough to cut with a knife. Madaline walked through the door of her suite and looked at Betty across the dark rosewood table. "I didn't want to take it upon myself to order for you. Look over the menu and I'll call room service."

"Sounds good to me," acknowledged Betty. Waiting for the food to arrive, the mother and daughter chattered uneasily. Betty was fidgeting with her hair while

Madeline took another cigarette and lit it. "I hope the smoke doesn't bother you, but for now I really need it." Betty started laughing. "If I had taken up the disgusting habit I'd probably be joining you." A small smile appeared on Betty's mouth.

'Maybe she does have some compassion. We'll have to wait and see,' Madaline thought to herself. The food arrived and the two women ate in silence. Madaline hoped that Paul could hear what was going on. When they finished their meal Madaline led the way to the couch. 'She can sit beside me or take the chair opposite the sofa. That will be an indication on how the conversation will go,' Madaline thought to herself as she crossed her legs and turning her palm up, indicated Betty to begin. Betty's nervousness was obvious. Betty sat on the chair opposite Madaline. Her arms rested on the wide, soft blue armchair, knowing if she didn't, her fingers would be constantly fidgeting.

"I've been thinking about this meeting ever since we last saw each other at Nantasket Beach. I couldn't sleep well since then. I'm not lying. This is the hardest situation that I've had to talk about since God knows when." Her hands were noticeably shaking as she took a deep breath and began her dialogue. "I don't know where to begin but I'll try to convey my thoughts and feelings the only way that I can. I believe what you said and it makes me feel better that you feel terrible and awful about what happened to you and your infant. I can only imagine what you went through for all these years. I have compassion for your sorrows and hope what I'm about to say will help your mental stability. Not that your not stable, but you know what I mean." Madaline nodded her head and let Betty continue while she put her cigarette out in the ashtray and fought herself not to light up another one. "First of all, you were right when you thought it might be me who was stalking you. It was a little easier for me to find out information about my adoption and medical history because of the new laws that are in effect. I believed and now almost positive that you are my birth mother."

"Before you get excited let me tell you how I felt while I was growing up. Please don't say anything until I'm through talking.... . When I was a youngster, and found out that I and my sister were adopted, I would go to bed and wonder why or how you could give up a beautiful baby. I was very resentful at first, but that dissipated with time and maturity. I saw many baby pictures that my parents took. I treasure the albums I have and look at them many times. Yes, it's sounds maudlin, but it keeps me remembering the people that I love and brings back terrific memories. Before I heard your part of the ordeal, I honestly hated you. I blamed you for all the bad things that happened to me. I wanted you to feel pain as I had experienced it. My boyfriend Dick, who knows everything about me, helped in my scheme to scare the hell out of you. You have to remember, that was before I heard your part of the story," An uncomfortable Betty continued.

With regret, she lowered her eyes and told her how sorry she was." I feel awful scaring you. In a way I wanted you to feel upset, not knowing if this stalker wanted you dead. In a way I did, but that seems years ago. I hope that you can forgive me and Dick. Yes, I was lucky to have two great parents who would give me the world if they could. I consider them my parents. They endured my awful teen years and I can go on and on about how lucky I was to have them. I was brought up as an only child until my younger sister came into our home. They spoiled me but not so much that I was a spoiled brat. I felt loved from both my parents and my baby sister. By the way, her name was Emily." She pulled out a wallet and showed Madaline their pictures. "You heard the story the first time we met. I'm again going to tell you that after my family was tragically taken from me I felt I had nothing to live for." By now tears were flowing freely down her cheeks.

Madaline desperately wanted to go over to her daughter, hug her, kiss the tears away, and tell her that everything will be okay. Letting go of her composure, she went to Betty, kneeling on her knees and put her head onto her lap. Visibly upset and crying, Madaline rocked back and forth, words were left unspoken. Finally, Madaline stood, took Betty's hands and led her to the sofa. Once seated, she held her tightly. She smoothed her hair and kept saying over and over again how sorry she was. Madaline knew that Betty realized that her birth mother had no choice in her decision to give her up for adoption. Both women were now crying openly for what seemed forever. Betty couldn't catch her breath and the deep sobs went uncontrolled. The woman said they were sorry simultaneously. She slightly squeezed her daughter's hand and with a quiver announced, "I think we have a lot of years to make up for."

CHAPTER THIRTY SEVEN

After Madaline sent for tea the two women talked and talked. Finally Madaline told Betty: "You do realize that you have a half-brother named Kyle. In many ways you look alike. When you're ready I'd like the two of you to meet. I don't know if you've read the papers and all the gossip Kyle has had to go through. I'm grateful that he's innocent and can pick up his life before all this bad publicity came out. But let's not talk about Kyle. You'll meet each other soon enough. Let's get back to our situation. I realize that I can never replace the people that you consider your parents, and you shouldn't. Someday I hope that we'll be able to create a special bond and you'll be able to love me, in your own way. I'm glad you realize and understand the lament I have and hope that one day we'll have a special relationship that we'll both cherish. I already feel a big weight lifting from my heart and soul. I can't talk for you, but hope that you can find it in your heart to someday have a special kind of love and realize that our relationship will be meaningful." She hugged Betty harder and found it difficult letting go of the daughter she gave birth to.

Betty up righted herself and looked into Madaline's eyes. "Do you realize that my eyes are the same color as yours? After finding out about you, I'd look at all the pictures that I could get a hold of and tried to find some of your features that I also possessed. I'm glad that I look more like you than that miserable bastard that fathered me. I never saw his picture but from all you told me I can only picture the devil, wearing all red. Of course he had a mustache and a hooked nose. He should only rot in hell." After a few minutes of silence Betty started laughing and Madaline joined her.

"Isn't that awful the way I characterized him. But if it wasn't for him, I wouldn't be here talking to you. So although deep in my heart, I really hate him, especially after hearing how your life turned to hell and back because of that miserable bastard, it doesn't stop me for being grateful that I'm alive and well. Can you understand these feelings of conflict?"

"Of course I can," Madaline voiced sincerely. Acutely aware of her tiredness, Madaline tried not to show her dull headache. Yawning, Betty told Madaline that she should go back to her room to rest before their performance this evening. "We both should take a break. A rest will do us good. Much emotion has been brought out and we both have a lot of thinking to do. We've learned so much about each other and it's going to take a lot of time to comprehend it all. Please have patience and if possible, can we try to start anew?" Madaline asked her daughter, who she thought she'd never see.

Betty leaned over to her birth mother and tightly held her in her arms for a long time, not wanting to let her go. She then realized how small Madaline was. She could feel her bones through her clothes. Emotions she hadn't thought about, she tried to bury within herself. She realized she had a lot to sort out and, hopefully, she'd be able to separate the first part of her life and the new one she found. They kissed each other's cheek and without saying a word Madaline walked Betty to the door. Madaline closed the door, her back to it, started crying uncontrollably and without thinking, went onto her bed. Covering herself with the blankets she tried to control her shivering.

Paul called on her phone and although she wanted to talk to him, begged off and told him she'd see him before the show. "I would like it if you'd come here and walk with me to the theater. I have many things to think about and sort over, but for now I'd feel better being left alone. I hope you can understand."

"After hearing your conversation with Betty, of course I understand how you feel. Try to rest. It's important that you do. I'm glad your meeting went as well as it did. Before the first words were spoken I had trepidation on what the meeting would be like. Get some sleep and I'll be over in a few hours." 'Sleep well my love,' he whispered to himself as he hung up the receiver.

The day of the wedding came before Suzanne realized it was here. The entire family was excited and at the same time Hope was nervous. Melanie went with Hope to the spa and with the other attendants in tow, had their hair and makeup done by the experts. They knew they were in capable hands and couldn't wait till they looked in the mirror to see how beautiful they were. After getting dressed in the home they grew up in, they were ready for the pictures to be taken. It was a bonding experience for the sisters that they hadn't had in years. Hope felt lucky that she had siblings who she adored and realized what a lucky young woman she was. Hope's expectations were that they would always be close, as families should be. A thought of dread took over and she prayed that nothing went wrong at the wedding and with great expectation led the bridesmaids into the waiting limo.

Suzanne was both nervous and excited when she woke that morning. She had faith in the girls and knew that the entire experience would go on without a glitch. She and her parents took their time getting dressed with Suzanne tending to her mother's hair and make-up. Of course Mrs. Walsh didn't want Suzanne to fuss over her and in her room did everything she needed to do for herself. In reality she wanted Suzanne and her parents to be alone to express their thoughts to each other. Nancy, Beverly with Louis and Madaline were to meet them at the church. Even thinking of that word made Suzanne sick to her stomach. She knew she had to get over her feelings of guilt and unhappiness. She had to enjoy the entire event and be happy for her first born. Suzanne tried cutting down the list of guests but in the end three hundred people would be in attendance. Even Kyle flew in for the evening to attend the wedding. Madaline had made a reservation for Kyle at the Ritz and was looking forward to seeing him as much as attending the wedding of her best friend's first born. Suzanne was happy that she put herself at the same table with her loyal pals. She knew her parents would like their brothers and sisters at their table. Their friends would be seated at the next table. She tried appeasing the guests and made sure that certain people who were not speaking to each other, for one reason or another would be seated apart. In the end, she was looking forward to the event.

The music that Hope and Spencer picked out for the church service was beautiful, with a great singer accompanied by the organist. The nearest and dearest were seated in the front pews and it was funny to see the brides and grooms family seated on opposite sides of the aisle. Stephen was seated next to Suzanne during the ceremony. They held hands throughout the entire service. How she wished she could finally become Stephen's wife instead of his lover and friend. She closed her eyes trying to forget the serious talk that the two of them had only a few days ago. Stephen at last realized how deep Suzanne's convictions were about their relationship. It was an important revelation that Suzanne finally expressed what was in her heart, and soul about their relationship. No matter whatever happened, she could never feel the same way with any other man. Knowing him as well as she did, she knew, in her heart, that he'd come up with valid excuses, but not valid enough for Suzanne to accept. After that evening, Suzanne cried herself to sleep and realized that Stephen was Stephen, and she couldn't change him.

The part of his sentimentality was one of the characteristics that she loved about him. His minds ability to never get rid of anything, whether, people or objects, were one of his flaws. Although she loved him more than anyone else in the world she asked herself if she could live with him on his conditions alone. Yes, he adored her and would do anything for her. She realized his fragibility in loving himself more than anyone else. Sometimes she felt that she was like one of his objects; he loved her and felt she was a possession of his that he couldn't let go. They talked for hours that evening and with all his emotions and arguing with what he thought was truly right; his words could not satisfy her demands. She didn't need his money. All she wanted was to make their commitment legal in the eyes of God. Suzanne didn't think that was too much to ask for. The music started playing and you could hear a pin drop as everyone viewed the attendants as they walked down the aisle. Suzanne closed her eyes and tried, for everyone concerned, not to let this special day be ruined. She opened her eyes, took a deep breath, put a smile on her face, and knew in her heart what had to be done. If anyone saw Suzanne and Stephen they would never surmise what Suzanne had in the back of her mind. A hush went through the church as Hope walked slowly down the aisle, waiting to take Spencer's hand. Suzanne couldn't get over how much Hope reminded her of herself when she saw the beautiful bride walk to meet her husband to be. Hope wanted to wear Suzanne's gown and with a few alterations, it was accomplished.

Suzanne prayed that her daughter's marriage would be happier than her own was. For superstitious reasons Suzanne didn't want Hope to wear the gown. She finally relented through Hope's continuous nagging. Expertly, she dabbed the tears in her eyes as she watched her first daughter walk down the aisle to be met by the man she loved and promise before God and to Spencer her undying love and devotion through sickness and health. Suzanne knew that there would be many heartaches throughout the years and their marriage. She hoped that their love for each other could overcome the ups and downs of life. She wouldn't sob out loud and embarrass herself or hope. Suzanne tried thinking of something mundane to squelch her emotions.

More pictures were taken after the ceremony. Suzanne was grateful that she had plenty of hors d'oeuvres, appetizers and wine on hand for the guests to enjoy while waiting for the festivities to begin. Suzanne, with her family, looked like the total picture of elegance. After the family and pictures of the attendants were over, Suzanne went to the bar and wanted a large glass of wine. She wanted to get wasted but knew better. The Zinfandel felt good as it went down her throat smoothly, certain that this glass of wine wouldn't be her last for the evening.

Suzanne scanned the guests and tried to keep her memories at bay. Berating herself, she realized this was not the time to get depressed. She couldn't help thinking and missing the relatives that were no longer alive to see another happy occasion. There were too many sad times when the relatives got together. She wanted everyone here to have a good time and enjoy themselves. She went into the ladies room to freshen her makeup. She was mad at herself for the sentimentality she was feeling. She didn't want to think of Stephen at this time; only to be content and feel good.

Most of the people were seated at their seats and tables waiting for the happy couple to make their entrance. The MC did his usual introductions and waited for the applause to die down before bringing in the next members of the wedding party. Suzanne waited patiently behind the double doors with her parents.

All her dear friends were seated at Suzanne's table with the exception of one person. Lawrence was seated next to Beverly and Louis and with baited breath waited for Suzanne to make her appearance. He didn't know if Stephen was going to come out from the closed door with Suzanne in hand and waited patiently for her to emerge. He looked at Louis and Beverly. They knew what Lawrence was thinking. After all these years what he hoped for might finally come true. Every one of her friends seated at the table knew of Suzanne's' ultimatum and waited nervously to see who won the debate. When Suzanne emerged alone Lawrence nudged Louis and a smile appeared on his face. Suzanne sat down at the table, not acknowledging the absence of Stephen.

Everyone rose as the newlyweds entered the hall. They toasted the couple with full glasses of champagne and Suzanne heard the spoons hitting the glasses, wanting the happy couple to kiss.

Suzanne and every invited guest enjoyed the evening. Lawrence asked Suzanne to dance to a slow song and held her close as he guided her across the dance floor. He felt her head against his chest and could enjoy the fragrant perfume she wore. They both danced with their eyes closed, their thoughts kept to themselves. He wanted the dance to last forever. Throughout the evening he saw Suzanne glance at the empty seat that no one spoke of. Only Suzanne knew what it signified. He noticed that Suzanne, not a heavy drinker, was enjoying her Zinfandel more than usual.

Before the evening was over, Nancy cornered Suzanne in the rest room. "Okay, what's going on. How come Stephen was at the church but he's not seated at our table. I'm dying of curiosity and promise not to say a word to anyone."

"Nancy, you're my dearest and closest friend, and as much as I'd love to spill my heart out to you, I can't do it at this time. I hope you understand and trust me on this one. I'll tell you all that's happened when the time is right, till then, let's go back to the festivities and have a good time. After the event I have to settle the bills and unlike years ago, I now have the money to pay everyone." Taking Nancy's hand they walked back to the table without anyone knowing what was said between the two best friends.

Suzanne was exhausted, everyone had left; she was sitting alone in her living room listening to sentimental, light, jazz music. Suzanne kept the Sarah Vaughn album on as she heard and sang the words of every song. She then put the The Flamingo's CD on and couldn't help sobbing as she took every word to those beautiful melodies to heart. She didn't want to stop the eruption of tears and sobs of her sentimentality. Mrs. Walsh had long ago retired for the evening. Before she went upstairs she expounded on the wonderful time she had at the wedding.

Suzanne finally went upstairs to bed, she patted Simka and Boston. The constant motion was relaxing to her. Their purrs were like music to her ears. She kept all thoughts of Stephen out of her mind and hoped her dreams wouldn't reflect the sadness in her heart.

Two weeks after the wedding she still hadn't heard from Stephen. She'd be damned if she'd pick up the phone and call him. 'He has fingers also,' she thought, as she continued her daily routine. Her heart was aching but tried not to let anyone see how depressed she was. Only a few of her dearest friends knew about the ultimatum that she had given Stephen. She had hoped that the answer to her demand would be one that she wanted to hear, but alas, it wasn't. The more she thought about his reaction to her final request the madder she became. 'After all the years they had been with each other, how could he have been so stubborn and not think about her feelings?' She kept her emotions to herself for many years and realized she could no longer live the life of lies. She knew in her heart that she couldn't change him. If she didn't make this clean break she would regret the lie she would be living. 'No,' she thought to herself, 'she made the right choice. Now it was a matter of learning to live with the decision she made.'

Suzanne noticed that Madaline was acting much happier when she saw her. She wouldn't pry and knew that when Madaline was ready to talk, she would tell Suzanne what changed her attitude. She realized that with Kyle's release from jail and no longer a suspect in the Curtis Jones murder, that alone, would make her happy. Kyle's recent trip to the wedding also had a positive effect on Madaline.

Nancy regularly came into the spa. When she saw Suzanne she purposely never mentioned Stephen or Lawrence. If Suzanne wanted to bring up the subject, she knew her friend would. "Suzanne, now that things are getting back to normal, what do you think about making arrangements with the estheticians to take over for you and come to San Diego with me?" Suzanne contemplated the suggestion and, on a whim, agreed to go on the, so called, vacation.

Packing her luggage, Suzanne left instructions for the girls at work and information for Mrs. Walsh, her daughters and parents of her agenda, or what she thought would be her plans. Thinking to herself that with all the intrigue she didn't know where Nancy and she would wind up. Hope and Spencer were taking an extended honeymoon and Suzanne couldn't wait to hear about it. Once on the airplane, Suzanne was finally able to relax. For two and a half weeks her nerves had taken a toll on her. She felt as if her body was like a pin cushion, with pins sticking over her entire body. She was fried, like an egg waiting to be eaten up by a hungry being. She hadn't told anyone of her talk with Stephen, not even her dear friends. She didn't know what he was thinking or going to do. As far as she was concerned, there was only one answer and if it wasn't what she wanted to hear, then her life would certainly change.

Their plane landed and they were greeted by Rich. Nancy and Rich made a great looking couple she thought, when she saw Rich hugging Nancy. He then, perfunctory, gave Suzanne a routine kiss on her cheek. "I'm glad you had a good and safe flight. They're predicting a major storm in the next few days. It's good that you beat it. Come into my car and I'll drive you to your hotel." Once situated in their room, Rich went over the case and what happened since they last talked. "I want you to meet Sam. He's the gentleman that's been helping us out. Very few people know about him for obvious reasons."

"We can't take a chance getting him exposed to any harm. Obviously, we trust the two of you and know that you're working along with us, not against our effort to solve this case. I'll leave the two of you to get some unpacking done and the needed rest. I'll pick you up in, let's say, four hours, and we'll have dinner with Sam. Is that okay with the two of you?"

Speaking for the two of them, Suzanne agreed on the time. "If you don't mind, let's go somewhere casual. I feel grungy. Even after we've showered I really don't want to get dressed up. I'd love to put on jeans and relax while we go over our tactics for the entire trip. Is that okay with you?"

"Sure, take it easy and I'll see you in about four hours." Rich walked over to Nancy as she was folding clothes and putting them into the bureau. He turned her around and kissed her tenderly on the mouth. Nancy walked him to the door. He put his tongue over his lips as he was leaving, "Tastes very good," he remarked as he closed the entrance.

Nancy, not embarrassed with this outward display of affection, looked back at Suzanne and shrugged her head. "What can I say? I think I'm in love."

Suzanne rolled one of her tops into a ball and threw it at Nancy. She ducked and started laughing. "It's good to see you happy. It's been too long since I've seen you this way," Suzanne said. "I'm going into the shower and then take a nap. See you when I wake up." Nancy finished putting away her clothes and couldn't wait to emulate Suzanne.

As they were waiting for Rich to pick them up outside of the hotel, they couldn't help notice the various people walking by. They both loved to people watch. While not making fun of some of the passersby they couldn't help smile as they saw all types of people, from polished, accessorized to the max, with groomed dogs to young girls, half their bodies showing out from their skimpy clothing.

Some of the girls and boys showed their visible tattoos off in areas that should not have been exposed. Suzanne whispered to Nancy, "I wonder where else on their body they have tattoos and piercings? Believe it or not I've seen some rings in the most awful and I believe, painful places to adorn themselves. Yuk!!" The girls would tell me stories about some of their, so called friends, leaving their house with decent clothing and then changing in the girls room before school started. I'm telling you, it's a different world. I don't think it's for the best, but only time will tell."

"Amen, sister," Nancy declared as they saw Rich's Mustang approaching, one of his many "toys," and climbed in.

Suzanne felt squished in the back seat but took it in stride. She couldn't wait till they got to their destination. The restaurant he chose was on the water-front with tables outside on the patio. Suzanne was awed by the beautiful boats in the marina or taking off for an expedition. Never an envious person, she wished that she could be on one of the larger yachts, sailing to an unknown destination and enjoying the wind and sun on her face. "Suzanne, I hate to break into your fantasy, but I think the gentleman walking towards us is the person Rich wants us to meet."

Rich got up from his seat and warmly greeted Sam. The introductions were made and the two woman liked him immediately. While they were enjoying their meal and drinks they talked about the business at hand. Suzanne was a bit skeptical about the assignment given to them but tried not to show her nervousness. She'd be sure to get the details from Rich when they were ready to embark on the chore assigned to them. She could see the excitement yet apprehension on Nancy's face and demeanor as well. As long as she'd known Nancy this was a different dimension of her friend that she was unaware of.

When Nancy and Suzanne entered his car he turned to both of these ladies who he felt an attachment to. He had a different affection towards Nancy and knew that she felt the same. He broached the subject that had been on his mind for a while now. "I don't know where to begin so let me talk and please don't interrupt." The two friends quizzically looked at each other.

"I know that you've worked for the FBI for a while and you've helped them and our department out immensely. With your assistance the authorities have been able to apprehend individuals who have gone against the law and in instances harmed innocent people. I realize that this is going to sound over the top to the two of you but here goes.... Have either or both of you ever discussed actually joining the FBI? I know people who are top ranking officials and I've spoken to them about the two of you. I want you to think seriously about this offer. There are people who are legitimate undercover agents who are certified FBI representatives. It's called the civilian Stasi force. Of course you'd have to complete and pass tests that are required to become one of them. It would necessitate you to go to Quantico and stay there for a while, learning procedures that are given to trainees. The FBI will expect you to follow through with these obligations until you pass the examination. They teach you counter-terrorism and counter-intelligence activities. They train you in the use of all types of firearms: 357 Magnum Smith and Wesson revolver; Glock model 22; MP-5 10mm; the U. S. military standard. 223 M4 carbine; Block Model 23; Glock Model 27; and the 12 gauge Remington shotgun, plus the preservation of physical evidence along with drug enforcement. You've already been cleared for security clearance. From what I've learned from the guys in the Boston FBI you've also been trained in B & E. Think about what I've said. Neither of you are under pressure but seriously understand what this will call for."

Suzanne looked at Nancy and whispered, "I feel if we go through with this I'll be calling myself Annie Oakley." Nancy jabbed Suzanne in the ribs, trying to avoid any reaction to her friend's comment.

With that said Rich and Nancy dropped Suzanne off at the hotel and took a ride around the area, wanting to exclude themselves from others. "I meant what I said. Don't talk to me about my suggestion. You and Suzanne have to discuss this amongst yourselves. Please let's just have a nice evening without any undue pressure."

He debated taking her to his house, but thought better of it. Rich didn't want to rush Nancy and make her feel uncomfortable. He settled on taking her up the hills and stopped at an overlook to view the lighted city below. Nancy enjoyed seeing the ocean with the illumination making the yachts even more beautiful. Slowly dipping side to side in the now dark waters, the large vessels appeared an aberration, darting back and forth among the many uninhabited boats, teetering from flank to flank. When looking and appreciating them she thought she heard, but realized it was her imagination playing tricks on her, the creaking and faint noises like the settling of an old house. Nancy couldn't help think that if she were so lucky to be on one of the many beautiful yachts, she'd be able to sleep soundly. The gentle rocking would be like being a baby, cuddled in the arms of its mother, hearing the low sound of the songs the mommy would lovingly sing to her baby. This would be a dream, Nancy knew, because her real mother was not the cuddling type of person. Yet, dreaming couldn't hurt, she thought, as she cuddled in Rich's arms.

He bent over her, his hands gliding through her thick red hair, caressing her back, his hands going slowly up her sweater and gently rubbing her body. With his other hand he lifted her face and softly kissed her beautiful lips. She responded by returning his lovingly endearment, feeling like a dainty butterfly, swaying in the light breeze.

Suzanne couldn't wait until Nancy's return. She sat up in the comfortable bed, reading one of the many novels she traveled with. When she heard the door opening she couldn't wait to hear what happened between the two of them. Suzanne waited for her friend to start the conversation. "I think I'm in love, she declared, as she sat down on the side of Suzanne's bed. Suzanne could tell by Nancy's actions that she was like a young teenager in love for the first time. "We'd better get a good night's sleep because from the conversation we had at lunch, were going to be like Laurel and Hardy again." "You mean 'thanks a lot, Olly, well, you did it again' as the comedians bantered back and forth. "I hope we're lucky and don't get into any dangerous situations this time."

"Suzanne, only time will tell. We'd better make sure we get our directions straight and talk to some of the intelligence agents and talk to the guys we know from the FBI. We also have to get in touch with Interpol agents and IFAR."

"Nancy, what the hell is IFAR?"

"It's a publication that documents global events. Especially in art thefts and art fraud. I think they might have renamed it. Something like Stolen Art Alert. We'll have to call Justin and find out more about it. It might have changed names again, but I'm sure Justin will know."

Suzanne was getting tired and told Nancy to get a good night's sleep. Shutting off the lights, Suzanne groggily brought up the conversation that Rich had presented to them about Quantico. "Suzanne, I don't think this is the right time to discuss the FBI. We're both exhausted and have a lot on our minds. Maybe when we get up tomorrow we can talk about it and find out more information."

"Good night Nancy." Suzanne pulled the blankets up and within five minutes, was in the arms of Morpheus.

BOSTON, MASSACHUSETTS

The play went well and as usual Madaline got a standing ovation. Going back to her dressing room she started changing into her street clothes. She suddenly spied a beautiful vase of flowers on top of the table next to the sofa. Instead of the black roses that she received, not too long ago, a completely different arrangement was sitting there for her to admire. The vase consisted of three different shades of pink with 4 yellow roses in the middle. A beautiful red and yellow bow adorned the vase. Madeline sat down and read the card. It was simply written, "thank you for my life" Love, Betty. With tears streaming down her face, Madaline softly kissed the note. She wasn't, by any means, a horticulturist, and wrote a note for herself to find out the different meanings for the roses and what the colors meant. Madaline found herself in a mood of contentment and hoped it would last forever. Going to meet Paul off the stage she thought, 'now how do I address this situation to Kyle?'

SAN DIEGO, CALIFORNIA

Nobuaki was pacing his office, agitated on the news brought before him. Hirohito left his office not even ten minutes ago and he could feel his blood pressure rising like Mt. Vesuvius. He didn't like what Hirohito told him, it was unsettling news. Word was out that Yasuhito was getting better by the day and a Detective Colangelo was making it his personal assignment to catch the person or persons responsible for his beating. The more he thought about the sequence of events, after Yoshy asked him for a personal favor, he laughed out loud. Nobuaki couldn't help but ruminate and get angry whenever he thought how things were turning out. 'First that fiasco with Yasuhito and now it seemed that Yoshy and Miss Robin were nowhere to be found. How could two people appear to have apparently left the face of this earth?' If he didn't know better, he would have thought they went to the moon and weren't coming back.

Nobuaki knew it was preposterous to think such an idiotic notion. By hook line and sinker, he would find the son of bitches and make mincemeat out of them both. A smile crossed his face at the thought of what will happen to them once his men uncovered their secret hiding place. 'How long could Yoshy keep away from his corporation without anyone getting suspicious? There had to be a way for them to communicate with their president.' Nobuaki knew the answer to his problem. Somehow he had to get someone inside the company to find out how the heads of the different departments were communicating with Yoshy. With that decided he left his office and went into his bedroom to try to get a peaceful nights rest. Before sleep overtook him he thought, 'pay backs a bitch and then you die.' Tomorrow he would start the ball rolling.

TEXAS

Stephen sat on his couch, a glass of wild turkey in his hand. He kept staring at the amber liquid debating whether to finish the bottle, it was his fourth glass. The tumbler sat next to the bottle as he sat on the sofa, his mind going a mile a minute. It was almost three weeks since he had seen or spoken to Suzanne. Hope's wedding ceremony was very beautiful and touching. While walking down the aisle he couldn't help but visualize how Suzanne looked when, as a young girl, he saw her wearing the same gown on her wedding day. He remembered vividly how he hid in the hall and watched as she walked down the aisle. Unfortunately, it wasn't him that was waiting for her at the bottom of the Beema, under the Chupah. Hope was the spitting image of Suzanne. Stephen shook his head, trying to rid that memory from his mind.

Without thinking he automatically reached for the bottle and swallowed the liquid in one gulp. For the past three weeks he couldn't come to a final conclusion on what he should do regarding Suzanne's demand. He loved Suzanne. There was no question about it. There was a big "but." How could he leave Lou Anne? Would he be remorseful for the rest of his life, to knowingly leave her? It was certain that he didn't love her. He made a vow before God that she was his wife through sickness and health. Whatever reasons in his mind, could it justify his desire to leave? Would his conscience allow him to live with his decision with her dependency on him? He would gladly pay for someone to attend to her daily needs. In his heart he possibly will never forgive her for taking his beloved son's away.

He conceded, years ago, that the accident was completely her fault. Many times, he weighed his options, even before Suzanne came back into his life. With a heavy heart he didn't know what to do. He realized that with each passing day, Suzanne was waiting for an answer. 'How long could she keep hoping and languish for his final decision? He couldn't blame her for wanting to make their love a permanent, legal relationship and ultimately, marriage.'

He questioned his manhood. He hated himself for his inability to make that final decision. Once and for all he had to make a choice. He got off the sofa and walked up the stairs to his bedroom. In doing so, he felt as if he were over a hundred years old. With his head lowered, back stooped, he slowly got into his bed. Times like this, he thought, he never wanted to wake up. While sleeping, his dreams were ubiquitous. Sometimes he could envision himself walking down the aisle to a waiting Suzanne. Other times he could see himself standing over Lou Anne, a knife in hand, blood dripping from the large gash he inflicted in her heart. At other times he saw himself handing Lou Anne a glass of poisoned lemonade, watching her eyes bulge, doubling over in pain and finally falling out of her wheelchair, gasping for breath, gagging, suffocating, and drowning in her own liquid throw-up, blood dribbling out the side of her slacken mouth. He woke, all wet, perspiration drenched his entire body, pajamas and bed sheets.

Completely exhausted, he didn't want to get out of bed. It was times like this he wished his own death.

SAN DIEGO, CALIFORNIA

They called Justin in Boston and got his answering machine. Disappointed, the two woman went down to breakfast. "We'll try to reach Justin in a bit. I'm sure he'll give us the answers to the questions we have, a determined Suzanne told Nancy. Have no fear, Mighty Mouse is Here." Nancy tried to conceal her laughter but it was impossible. "Suzanne I always thought you were a little crazy, but now I'm certain you're a mashugana." They both chuckled as they finished their morning liquids.

Opening her purse, Suzanne redialed Justin's number and was pleased that he answered on the third ring. They talked awhile and were assured that he'd get back to her with the answers to her questions. The two women went back to their room waiting for Rich's plans and directives. The orders were plain and basic. They listened intently as he told them what he wanted done and enlightened their education on how to get the assignment finished. He again assured them that he'd been in touch with the various policing agencies that were necessary to help them. It was now up to them to deliver the information to him and his team.

After hearing back from Justin with the answers to their inquiries they sat down. With the information given to them from all parties concerned, they made their own plans on how to implement the work that had to be done. They had their pilot make a flight plan and made reservations at hotels in the areas that they would be visiting. Nancy and Suzanne sat on their beds and looked at each other, not saying a word, lost in their own thoughts. After a while Suzanne rose and walked over to Nancy and high fived her. With a smile they started packing.

While filling her suitcase Suzanne's mind wondered back to Stephen and her demands of him. She was perplexed and broken hearted that she hadn't heard from him. She tried getting these thoughts out of her mind, knowing she and Nancy had an important assignment ahead of them.

Nancy spoke as they both were packing. "I personally think, in a way, we're doing it for ourselves. Let's not kid one another. We get a thrill doing what we do. Yes, we get in situations that are dangerous, but we also get satisfaction when we get to the truth and apprehend the criminals. It's what makes life interesting and worth-while. Like we said long ago, most people let the wicked keep doing what they do. We on the other hand, want to make the world a better place, eliminate evil, so people can live their lives in peace, not having to worry that corruption and wrong doing might befall them."

"Sometimes I feel like Mighty Mouse, come to save the day," answered Suzanne as she shut the suitcase and pounded it so it would close properly.

With a big sigh Nancy shrugged her shoulders and told Suzanne, " You're right, I hope, this time, everyone concerned will get justice." They left the hotel, driving the rented car back to the airport. They had one of the crew members pick them up. Once settled in their plane, they sat across from one another, bringing out papers to read to help them resolve and make a plan for the work ahead of them.

CHAPTER THIRTY EIGHT

The two women were in a world of their own. Suzanne tried concentrating on the work in front of her but found it difficult to do. Nancy kept reading the same material over and over again. The plane ride was smooth and both of them felt relaxed. They put down their papers and stared at each other. "Okay, you say what's on your mind first," Suzanne told Nancy. "Ever since Rich brought up the subject of us becoming undercover FBI agents I've thought of nothing else. One part of me thinks it's absurd, and then I imagine myself like Wonder Woman – an incredible Amazon woman from the mystical Island of Therayscira with great strength, ageless, agility and intelligence. Linda Carter has nothing on me."

"I can't believe my ears. If your idea wasn't so preposterous I'd think you're serious. I might be able to get some money if I bring you to a mental institution," threatened Suzanne. "You're aging yourself darling. They don't do those things anymore." A contrite Nancy persisted. "Okay wise guy, what are your feelings about the subject?"

"Part of me is excited and wants to go ahead with his idea. The practical part thinks it's a ridiculous thought. I mean, we're older, in the sense that we're not 20 years old anymore. Yes, we're in good shape. We've kept up with exercise and if I admit to myself I'm inclined, because of flattery, that we could conceivably be likely candidates. On the other hand, I think it's an illogical proposal. I mean, Nancy, we're business women who don't have enough hours in the day to do what we want to do. I'm inclined to dismiss this scheme."

Suzanne continued, "Let's be honest with ourselves; we do act like we're part of the FBI and eventually get the bad guys. We'd have to be away from the salons for a good amount of time and then what will happen to our company? Yes, I'm training my daughters to take over for me when I eventually want to retire. Do I think they're ready for this assignment? I'm not sure.... Like you, I have conflicting ideas. It's also crossed my mind, unlike you with Wonder Woman, Mata Hari comes to my mind. I know you're not old enough to have read about her but she was believed to be a spy. Not an ordinary spy but a double agent. She was, supposedly, a French spy in Belgium when it was occupied by German forces. They say she was a Dutch exotic dancer and a prostitute who was killed by the French when they thought she told the German's secret information. Of course she insisted that she gave the German's old information but the French killed her anyway on October 15, l917. I always wanted to be an exotic dancer. Though not a prostitute." Suzanne and Nancy laughed when they looked at each other and shrugged their shoulders. "For your information I do know about and read the entire story of Mata Hari," Nancy informed Suzanne.

"Well, I think we should think about it when we have more time. I have to admit that I looked into Quantico and there are men and woman who are unlikely candidates for espionage. They have many programs. One is a Citizens' Academy and they go through all the basic training as a regular FBI candidate. If we pass the exam we would be deemed an FBI agent. The training lasts for 20 weeks. We'll have a lot of thinking to do before we make that type of commitment," Nancy re-enforced Suzanne's thoughts. "I think that's the training that Rich was talking about," Nancy said as she got out the paper work she knew that they'd need for their work at the Tokyo spa.

Suzanne and Nancy finished the speculative work and decisions that had to be done before they arrived at the spa. They knew that once finished with dealing with Metamorphosis in Tokyo then the real work of espionage would begin. They realized that dealing with Rich was also transacting with the people involved in international art theft and murder. Both women were quiet as they each contemplated the various scenarios that could take place. With the papers put away they sat back and slept, all the while their dreams entwined with their inner thoughts, plotting the danger that might befall them. They felt the wheels of the plane land on solid ground in Tokyo. Suzanne's entire body shivered as she tried eliminating her encompassed dreams. As Suzanne stretched she remarked, "I wish Rich gave us more specific plans. They seemed rather vague, don't you think?"

"I agree with you Suzanne. Don't forget, by our own admission, we're going to plan our visit by ear. I think when we get closer and know exactly what we want to do. Rich will expect us to get in touch with him. I suppose he'll be the contact person to keep the other law enforcement agencies advised and from there we'll speak to the people who'll help us."

"I see your point. First and foremost we have to visit our salon. From there we'll make a plan to contact Rich with our agenda. I have every confidence that the right agencies will get in touch with us, hopefully help us, and tell us what we have to do. I mean, they wouldn't let us fend for ourselves and leave us ill prepared, do you agree?"

"Suzanne, you're such a worry wart. Come, let's relax and freshen up before we arrive at the salon. I'm dying to see it. I hope all our preparations were followed and everyone is doing their best."

"Nancy, now look who's the worry wart? I have all the confidence that the spa is working to perfection. Believe it or not I've been in contact with the manager of the salon practically every day. I'm aware of everything. I mean everything that goes on there. Thank God for computers because I get a complete printout of the appointments and all the moneys taken in. So far, it looks like everything is on the up and up."

"I think within or a little after a year we should see a profit. It was very expensive having the build out done to our specifications. It was especially hard when we had to rely on contractors we didn't personally know. We were very lucky when we hired Tom Donovan for all of our Eastern properties back in the States. He was nice enough to help us with some of the spa's in other parts of the U. S. as well. When all of the figures come in for the products, the equipment and build out, then we'll get a better feel when we'll see some real money. Until then, the other spas are still doing well and will offset the losses from our Japanese salon until we can operate it at even 92%. Let's hope my predictions are right. In this economy, I think we're pretty lucky to do as well as we're doing."

"I see where you're coming from and your assessment sounds good to me. Personally, I can go for a nice shower and relax a while before we see one of our dreams, or should I be more accurate and say your dream come true." With that said, Nancy high fived Suzanne and headed for the shower.

They wanted to surprise the workers at the spa. When they walked in the only people that recognized them were the women who they initially hired. They in turn made the choices to hire estheticians, beauticians, massage therapists, the nail techs and other areas of the spa that had to be taken care of. The phone calls didn't cease until the department heads told Suzanne and Nancy who they liked and their credentials. Only with their owner's approval could they hire the women of their choices.

The department heads were in awe when Suzanne and Nancy walked in. The bows didn't stop. They then Americanized their welcome by hugging the two owners. Suzanne and Nancy were introduced to the employees. They sat down with each new worker. They asked questions, had them show their techniques and a multitude of questions that came to their mind. All in all, the two women were happy with the choices that the managers of the departments made and felt good when they left the salon.

"Okay, now that this part of our journey is over, I'm exhausted," declared Nancy. "Before you suggest our next plan of action I think we should go back to the hotel and get some well-deserved sleep. I know that we rested and slept on the plane, but honestly, I'm worn out. I realized that this part of our assignment was going to take us a long time, but we spent practically the entire day and most of the evening with these women. I don't know how they managed to get to their clients and squeeze their services in while at the same time obliging us." "Are we getting a little old? I thought you were the youngster of our partnership and I would rely on you for encouragement when my energy was depleted," teased Suzanne as they walked the main streets with the multitude of population crowding the sidewalks. Nancy lightly hit Suzanne's shoulder in retaliation to Suzanne's ribbing. "Ow, that hurt." Suzanne winced as she again provoked Nancy.

"I'm not ignoring your request of what is going to happen next, and admittedly both of us need some tranquility. I do confess that we need plenty of rest before our next adventure begins," Suzanne announced. "Let my mind clear a bit, get some sleep and then I'll be able to give you my initial thought about what our next move should be. I hope that's okay?"

"Of course it is. I have ants in my pants and want to settle the matter as quickly as possible."

"I understand your concern. Let's walk a bit and when we get back to the hotel, I might come up with some ideas of my own, once we get the required rest we need. I still can't get over that the streets don't have names or signs identifying them. This is hard to get used to," Suzanne exclaimed, as she window shopped and saw some beautiful clothing that she wouldn't mind purchasing for herself. She had to rationalize why that would be impulsive buying and tried, with all her might, not to enter the doors of the boutiques with the unusual clothing.

Once back in their hotel room the two women plopped down on their beds and were drained yet satisfied from all they accomplished at the salon. They didn't realize how exhausted they were until they gradually woke up, still in the clothes that they wore the day before. "I'm glad we put the do not disturb sign on the outside of our door," announced Suzanne as she stretched, suddenly realizing they got the required sleep they needed. "I think it's time we call Richard and get an aggressive plan of action. I have some ideas of my own that we might be able to incorporate into his scheme."

"Suzanne, you said out loud what I was thinking. Sometime today, barring the time difference, we'll make our call."

SAN DIEGO, CALIFORNIA

Nobuaki had a hard time sleeping. For over two weeks he hadn't had a decent nights rest. He attributed his restlessness to the lack of finalizing his current situation. He tried not to blame his trusted friend Hiro for not killing Curtis himself. He then thought of his other friend Yoshy. After all these years their friendship had never been tested. Now Nobuaki was angry for this favor he bestowed upon him. Usually it wouldn't be any trouble for him to comply with a request from a friend, such as Yoshy has been. With all the aggravation and recriminations evolving around the entire fiasco he found no other choice but to eliminate Yoshy as well as Robin. Now it seemed that Yoshy and his whore were nowhere to be found. He wouldn't rest until they were discovered and eliminated, once and for all. The more he thought of it, the angrier he became. Getting up from bed, pacing once again, he said aloud, 'yes, 'I'll get the bastards and even if I have to do it myself, the job will be done right.' 'With that idea finalized, he returned to his bed and for the first time in weeks slept like a baby.

BOSTON, MASSACHUSETTS

Madaline was getting tired of the walk to and from the hotel to the theater every day. Luckily the weather wasn't bad and there seemed to be less rain than usual. Now that most of her worries were solved she couldn't wait to get to their next location and continue the play. She went into Harry Winston's Flower Shop on Newbury Street and asked about the various colors of roses and what they meant. Obviously she knew what black meant, ultimately death, but wanted to know information about the rest of the colors. When she walked out of the florist's establishment she was pleased with the assessment of the various roses. Light and regular pink was for admiration, happiness and joy, dark pink meant appreciation, gratitude and thank you. The single yellow rose in the middle was for joy, friendship and especially, promise of a new beginning. Madaline couldn't stop smiling until she finally got into her suite. Now that the dark past was finally revealed she felt she had to tell Kyle the entire story. She hoped that he would understand and be willing to accept his new 'half-sister' and that they could become a happy family. She then thought about some of her friends, even Suzanne, and wondered if there was such a thing as a happy family. 'Well, time will tell,' she thought as she got ready for this evenings performance.

When Paul knocked on her door Madaline greeted him warmly. Kissing both sides of his face she held his face in her hands and simply said, "thank you for all you've done. You're faithfulness, encouragement and loyalty, but above all, the love I know you feel for me. Hopefully, I'll be able to reciprocate your feelings."

With that he kissed her passionately and found it hard to stop his wanton desires. He curbed his longing and put his practicality in front of his inclination to devour Madaline. Pushing her gently back, with the sexiest voice he could muster, he promised her they would continue where they left off after the performance and were back in her hotel suite. With that in mind, she held his hand and walked to the elevator, anticipating the entire evening that was ahead for them.

As she walked backstage she saw Betty and thanked her profusely for the beautiful flowers delivered to her in the dressing room. Betty turned bright red and demurely looked down. Madaline lifted her daughters chin and kissed the top of her hair. They both hugged. laughed and cried at the same time. When the play was finished Madaline asked Betty to join her in the dressing room. Sitting Betty down, "I think we have to address the situation with Kyle. I honestly think he'll be shocked but once the emotion and confusion is dealt with, he'll be fine. We'll be able to have a family that we all desired for a long time. What are your feelings?"

Betty was astonished by what Madaline was proposing. It was one thing to realize and admit that Madaline, who was world renowned, was her biological mother, but it was another matter to face Kyle and realize that they both had a sibling that neither of them knew about. With that in mind, Betty nodded agreement and sat down on the couch. "It seems impossible that you didn't tell your son about the situation you kept hidden for years?" Betty spoke in disbelief. "It's not the type of circumstance that I would readily talk about, especially with my son. Kyle thinks that I can do no wrong and I didn't have the heart to tell him something that would be devastating. Let me mull it over for a while and I'm sure that within the next two weeks we'll fly to San Diego to pay Kyle a visit. Of course, I'll see him first. The shock will be distressing, but once he calms down I'll call you up from the lobby." Paul knocked on the dressing room door. He didn't want to interrupt their conversation but Madaline assured him all was well and they were done for the evening. As Betty left through the back entrance she felt like a little child, eating candy for the first time.

"Now do you think, Miss Mason, we can continue where we left off before you went to the theater?" Madaline put her head on his shoulder and looked up at this man, who she never thought she'd have the feelings she had. He was not the type of man that she was usually attracted to. She winked at him and they went up the elevator, anticipating the night ahead of them.

Hope called Suzanne at her hotel and told her mother, in detail, about their extended honeymoon. "Honey, I know you're exuberant, but I don't want to know all about your sex life. I might be a little old fashioned, but I don't want you to tell me everything."

"I'm sorry if I embarrassed you mom." Suzanne tried not smiling like a Cheshire cat and told Hope to continue. Again Hope announced how happy she was and that Spencer was the best thing that ever happened in her life. Suzanne got off the phone and sat on the bed. A big smile illuminated her face and for the first time was happy that Spencer was her son-in-law. 'Now,' she thought, hopefully this feeling of joyousness will never leave.'

Before retiring for the evening she called her parents for her perfunctory telephone conversation. Leaving the rest of her plans unsaid she asked them how they were and again assured them that her vacation was excellent and couldn't put a specific time for her return home. As she was ready to hang up, Dorothy told Suzanne to wait a moment. Dorothy went into another room and told Suzanne what was really happening. "I don't want to spoil your vacation dear, but I must be honest. Your father seems to be getting worse. Not all the time, mind you, but his episodes are becoming more frequent. So far, I can handle everything that is happening and when you come home we'll have to have a serious discussion on the reality of the situation. Now I don't want this to ruin your time away. Have fun and I'll see you when you return. I love you."

Suzanne sat on her bed in shock. Sure she realized that her dad was getting dementia, but didn't want to face the reality of how fast it would progress. Thankfully Nancy was still in the bathroom. Thinking to herself, 'well mother, you most certainly did put a blemish on my vacation, but I'll never let you know that you did. It was right of you to inform me but couldn't you have waited until I got home?' Half laughing and crying at the same time she remained on the bed, staring into nothingness. She felt void, drained of all emotions. Suzanne didn't want to burden Nancy with her troubles. Shutting out her bed light, she cried herself to sleep. When she woke the next morning, Nancy could feel the tension that her friend was experiencing. "Suzanne, are you all right?" a concerned Nancy asked. "I'm just nervous about the next part of our assignment. I think everything will go right, but I can't get this feeling of doom out of my system."

She didn't want to explain to Nancy that the feeling of disaster wasn't necessarily about their assignment. Knowing that Nancy loved Dorothy and Morris as if they were her own parents, she didn't want to burden Nancy with her inner thoughts about Morris and how she felt it was more than dementia that he was experiencing. "Suzanne, you always get worried before we go into battle. With the help of all the authorities, I know the situation will get resolved and one day, soon, we'll be laughing about the circumstances involved." Suzanne tried to be upbeat but thoughts of her dad kept re-entering her mind. She tried ignoring the pessimistic worry about her parents and tried, not to burden Nancy with her problem.

"I hope you're right, my red headed friend. It's our asses out there and I hope we land on them without incurring any type of catastrophe." Without telling Nancy of her conversation with her mother she related her discussion with Hope.

SAN DIEGO, CALIFORNIA

The more Nobuaki thought the idea over he realized he had to take Hirohito with him. 'After all, he is one of the best consigliere in his family. As a captain I should be able to depend on him. Hirohito always showed unquestioning loyalty and obedience.' Shaking his head he couldn't get over how his organization has changed. Sitting in his office he realized that he had to lower his standards for those individuals wanting to join the yakuza. 'Instead of choosing recruits like the traditional bakuto (gambler) and tekiye (peddler) classes I now have to resolve to rebel spirits who are willing to commit crime for an oyabun and that's all it takes to join the yakuza rank. These street punks (bosozuku, speed tribes,) certainly love their motorcycles. After all, who are the police to adopt the term boryokudan (the violent crimes) for the yakuza, and have the audacity lumping them with other crime groups.' Making a fist he pounded his hand on his desk and said out loud, 'it's an insult and degrades our beloved ancestral samurai. 'I learned long ago that we keep our friends close and our enemies closer. To me this is war, I will destroy Yoshy for all the aggravation and undo pressure he put upon the Yakuza. '

He rang the bell on his desk and called for Mitsuko for some hot tea, hoping the soothing liquid would calm him. He was afraid that if he asked for his usual chilled junmai, (High quality sake) he would not be content to have just one glass and he wanted his mind clear to make plans for his friends demise. He lifted his telephone and called Hirohito and told him to immediately come to his home. They would finalize their plans.

Meanwhile Rich had more discreet meetings with Sam to find out how Yoshy's business empire was working without the president of the company present. Unfortunately Sam told Rich that the operations were being handled with competence. His employees weren't showing signs of worry that Mr. Makino was on an extended vacation. Rich didn't like what he was hearing and with his captains authorization decided to call the FBI. They intern would probably call Interpol to find out the procedure that they had to do, in order to make the arrest or arrests stick. He didn't want an error to get Yoshy and whoever was an accomplice, off any of the charges made. He didn't want to worry about red tape.

At one of the meetings that Sam and Rich had, Sam told Rich that he was seeing a few new people working in the building. Using discretion he went down to human resources to find out about the newcomers. It seems that they mysteriously appeared and there was no record of their existence. "My gut reaction is that they're in the building to spy on me, or whoever is in charge and try to find the whereabouts of Mr. Makino. They walk the corridors like ghosts, cause no trouble, but there's no reason for their employment." Rich sat across from Sam and listened intently. After contemplating what was told to him he came to a conclusion. "I think the best thing to do is to do nothing. Make sure that when you do communicate with Mr. Makino there's no way that these 'men of treason' can get their hands on any evidence of where Yoshy is. It's another story for our subversion, it's helping the good guys, but if my feelings are the same as yours, we better cover our asses."

"Don't worry Rich, I know my job well, and there's no way in hell that they'll find anything out."

Meanwhile Justin called Suzanne and told her about the IFAR (International Foundation for Art Research). This was the publication he mentioned to her a few months ago. He would mail her the journal and fax over the art thefts and authentication of paintings and other artifacts such as pieces of art that were not paintings. Some were made of marble, alabaster, gold and ivory from locations all over the world. Some of these pieces were centuries old. There are religious candlesticks, animal-shaped vessels, and many pieces of jewelry included, as well as original books that are one of a kind. I'm not sure how to get the information to you. Let me think about it and you'll be receiving the material in an easy to handle form."

"I have to give you credit, you know your field well. I have complete confidence in your knowledge of the corrupt, illegal pieces in your area of expertise. I can't wait to tell Nancy and Rich what invaluable help this will be to us." Suzanne went on the explain Rich's plan and what the next step in the operation will be. "But won't there be difficulty in getting all these papers and books delivered in a reasonable amount of time?" My dear Suzanne, taking in a deep breath, trying to keep a tone of annoyance out of his voice, which was unlike Justin, he went on to explain, "How do you get communication from your salons on time? Don't answer because I'll tell you, I'm not going to send the actual books, I'll have them copied and then e-mail the list to an e-mail address that you tell me you can use."

Suzanne hit her forehead with the palm of her hand. "I'm such a dummy, of course that's the way to do it." She laughed at herself and had to admit to Justin that her head has been up her ass since before Hope's wedding. "It's not that I'm making excuses, but with all that's on my mind I didn't think over what you told me. Of course you're right. On another note; I'm sure that the authorities will involve the Japanese government and their police. Unfortunately, I don't think that the governing agency of Japan's police and their divisions are in accord with one another. From what I understand the policies are different for various areas of the country. I guess we'll have to wait and see what we find out. I can't wait to get the facts from you and of course Rich."

"Suzanne," Justin talked with encouragement, "No more berating. Take care of yourself and Nancy. I'm sure that the legal authorities won't let the two of you encumber difficulties. They'll be watching your back and help you. Be yourself and do the good job that you always do. Have confidence in the agencies."

"I know you're right. I guess it's just jitters. I suppose it's normal to have them. It's getting late and if I'm going to do my best, I'd better get some sleep. Thanks again for all your help and encouragement. I'll keep you informed about what happens." Nancy let herself into their suite and saw that Suzanne was out like a light. She shook her head knowing how her partner's mind worked. 'She'll be fine once we start the actual operation. It's the waiting that gets her all wound up.' With those thoughts she took her nightly shower and got into her own bed. She had a hard time getting to sleep. Thoughts of Rich kept entering her mind and she couldn't wait to hear from him again.

Nobuaki and Hirohito sat in the first class section of Japan Airlines. Besides enjoying the amenities bestowed upon them, they couldn't wait to land at Narita airport. Nobuaki knew that a limo would be driving them to the Hilton Tokyo Narita Airport Hotel. Nobuaki wanted to stay in Tokyo for a while to enjoy the flavor of his country. Although he'd left Japan when a young teenager, he still felt as if this were his real country. He made reservations for the Guest Room that had all the amenities he wanted.

Although exhausted, he wanted to take advantage of the sauna and enjoy a few laps in the indoor swimming pool. Looking at Hirohito he laughed to himself.

His Captain had become lazy over the years and he could tell that Hirohito didn't do much exercising. 'I think the only exercise he does is to bring the food from the plate to his mouth.'

"Hirohito, come and join me in the sauna. You'll feel better after you utilize some of the courtesy benefits that we can use. While I'm doing some laps in the pool you can utilize the workout room." Hirohito looked at his boss with astonishment. "Not to be disrespectful, but what would I want with any of those, flashing his hands in the air, things. All I want to do is to take off my clothes, put on the Yukata and slippers. I'll most likely lay on this comfortable bed, and put on the HDL flat panel TV. That'll put me asleep and I'll be ready to go tomorrow morning. Of course you intend for us to indulge in a lavish breakfast, I hope."

Nobuaki nodded his head in amazement. He didn't believe what his Captain told him of his plans for the evening. "You mean you don't want to take advantage of my hospitality and in a few hours join me in the Ginza. I might be a little, what people might call a middle aged gentleman, but I'm not dead. Don't be a lazy thing. When I come back from my exercising I'd like to see you dressed to accompany me to the ichi-ryu. I promise you'll thank me at the end of the night."

Reluctantly Hirohito gave in and told his leader he'll be ready when he comes back from his training session. "My friend," laughing out loud "You have no idea what a real work out is when we go into the love clubs and get all the drinks we want."

Hirohito put on the television for a while, called downstairs to the reception desk and asked for a wakeup call in two hours. He knew his leader would take that amount of time to complete his work out.

The next morning the two men woke up later than usual. Nobuaki, usually a light sleeper, never slept or stayed in bed after 6:30 a. m. Today was an exception. After the events of last evening Hirohito shook his head in amazement. He laughed to himself as he watched his boss sleeping, out like a light and oblivious to the world. His snoring acknowledging the state of his boss' shenanigans. He had to admit that he also had a good time. Thinking back to last evening he shook his head, never seeing Nobuaki let loose. Hirohito felt no reason to get up and closing his eyes, fell back into a sound sleep once again. The events of last evening kept re-occurring in his dreams.

Nobuaki took Hirohito to the Ginza. Although quieter and more sophisticated than other clubs, it had everything that Nobuaki was looking for. The bar and hostess clubs were ichi-ryu and he didn't have to put up with the usual tourists. After the Ginza, Nobuaki took Hirohito to the Hostess Club. After finishing two bottles of whiskey at $200 a bottle, the two then spoke for quite a time to the mama-san. The two men were feeling happy, foot-loose and fancy free. Nobuaki almost peed in his pants when Hirohito took it upon himself to go to the Karaoke machine. He sang and got people to get up with him to sing to their hearts content.

Nobuaki didn't remember how they got home, but obviously they made it to the hotel safely. When he finally got out of bed the entire room was spinning. He had to hold onto the walls in order to make it safely to the shower. Nobuaki felt better once out of the hot water. He shook Hirohito to wake him. Hiro was out like a light. Thinking to himself: 'I guess Hirohito is either too out of shape to handle all the excitement of last night, or he's so inebriated he could be hit over the head and not feel it. What am I laughing at, I didn't hear his loud snoring and that's quite loud. It could wake the dead. '

"Okay, okay, what are you doing?" Hirohito asked of his leader, in a daze, when he felt the heavy handed shakes being done to his body. "It's time to start our business. Do you think I'd let you sleep the entire day away? But you have to admit you enjoyed yourself once you let go." A big smile crossed the big man's face as he admitted it was fun. "We should do it again." Getting serious Nobuaki shook his head. "Lie, sumi masen. Now it's time to get down to business. We came here for a reason and we'll complete our task." Hiro knew that Nobuaki was serious when he heard his leader speak both Japanese and English in the same sentence. "I'll make arrangements with the airlines to get tickets to Kyushu. From there we'll take the efficient and high speed rail network to Beppu. First we'll go to Kokura Station and then we take two direct express limited trains to Beppu. I've never been to the Island of Kyushu but I understand it's Japan's pride and over a billion visitors go there regularly. They're noted for the largest bath range types. I wouldn't mind taking a mud bath. I understand all of the impurities in your body will be taken out. We'll have a great stay and while we're waiting for the bastard, we might as well enjoy ourselves. After all, we might have to wait a long time for him to come back to his little hide away. Won't he be surprised when we give him a visit? I think I'll make an itinerary of our trips to the various spas and hot springs. We might as well enjoy ourselves while hanging around."

CHAPTER THIRTY NINE

Hiro was dumbfounded. He didn't realize he'd be away from his home in San Diego for this length of time. He hoped that Yoshy would emerge soon so they're job will be done. "Our first assignment for the day is to find Yoshy. I have a feeling he can't keep going indefinitely, traveling from place to place. He has to eventually come to reality and settle down. Ultimately he has to go to his hide-a-way in Beppu. Won't he be surprised when he thinks all is forgotten and no one will be looking for him and his whore? He'll then realize he will also be eliminated." Hirohito shook his head in agreement. He walked slowly to the shower, hoping his inebriated body would respond to the level of task given to him.

Suzanne and Nancy tried calling Rich but for some reason he didn't pick up his phone. Nancy called him on his private line and that too was also unavailable. "I don't want to even think about it. BUT, how come we can't reach him. He assured us that he was only a phone call away," a worried Suzanne spoke out loud. Nancy tried not to show her own worry and assured Suzanne that nothing was wrong. "It must be he either forgot to put on his cell, or misplaced it. Don't worry. I'm sure we'll hear from him shortly. Meanwhile, let's go down for breakfast after we shower and get dressed. I don't know about you, but I'm starved."

"Okay Miss optimistic, I'll be ready in about 45 minutes. I'll dress casually and be comfortable. Whatever happens, I know I'll be ready for anything that comes our way. I already know that you'll be fine. If and when you're ready, I agree, we'll go downstairs and gorge ourselves with food. I'm hungry like a bear coming out of hibernation," Suzanne closed her eyes as the flavor of the food fulfilled her cravings. Suzanne enjoyed the Japanese tea after her satisfying meal.

While the two women were eating, content that their hunger pains had been abated, they leisurely enjoyed their hot drinks. Meanwhile, unbeknown to the two American women leisurely enjoying their liquid refreshments, an airplane was landing at Narita Airport. Rich checked into the Hilton Hotel at the Airport and told the receptionist behind the desk he was uncertain on how many days he would be staying. "If there's room for a few nights sleep over, I'd be pleased to extend my stay. I have to see how my plans turn out. "With complete compliancy the lovely receptionist shook her head. "I understand your dilemma. Don't worry, we're here to please. Just come down to the desk and let us know of your plans every day or night and we'll make arrangements for you."

"By the way, is it possible to find out if two of my friends are registered at this hotel?" Putting up his hands he announced, "I know it's illegal to give out a room number, I'm not asking or compromising your situation," with insistence he assured her, they were there. "I'll tell them to meet me at the lounge".

After searching the registration on her computer, Rich was relieved that they weren't staying at the same facility. He softly let out a sigh of relief. Rich liked the way the Japanese people were friendly and went out of their way to make a person feel comfortable.

Rich didn't want Nancy or Suzanne to know that he was in Japan, just yet. He wanted to get to the offices of the intelligence division/field intelligence group that the FBI agents at home recommended he see. They told him that they would be helpful with any criminal investigation and knowledge he had of information and theories that would be helpful to the local FBI Investigation. He made that a priority.

He took his one piece of luggage and threw it on the luggage rack in the closet and plopped on the bed. He didn't know how the two women could make this exhausting trip and not complain about it. He then remembered that they traveled in their own jet and realized that it was far more comfortable than a regular commercial flight. 'I'm glad that I'm falling in love with a sensual, intelligent and smart woman. I hope she feels the same about me. Someday I might be privileged enough to travel on her plane with her.' He called Nancy on his cell, not caring about the carrying charge. He had a hard time getting through to her cell but after a while they were connected and talked as usual, not letting on that he was located in the same city that they were in.

She then told him how difficult it was for them to get through to him as well and hoped that the situation would be taken care of. "I hope so because unless we have walkie-talkies, it's going to be difficult to find out your every move. Do you want us to put wires on you?"

"I don't think that'll be necessary for now, but it's a consideration for some time soon," Nancy acknowledged as she said goodbye.

After taking a hot shower he got dressed for his meeting at the Japanese headquarters of the FBI in Tokyo. In the States he got the name of a Mr. Wittman, who was a former FBI agent in art theft from Justin. He was happy that Justin was able to find Mr. Wittman's private telephone number. He spoke to this gentleman before he made this journey; at least he knew a little of what to expect when talking to people who were familiar with these types of crimes.

He went to the concierge and asked directions to the FBI offices in Tokeo. The concierge was very obliging, showing him a map of the city and how to get there. He recommended taking a taxi to the Ohasi Hospital and from there walk the rest of the way. He would be able to see some of the city as well and acquaint himself with Japan. He hailed a taxi and was taken aback when he saw all the cars, making the streets impossible to negotiate, 'Especially safely,' he thought, as he found himself nervous as the taxi took side streets, oblivious to the many people walking and some at a good clip to get to their appointments or destinations. He was glad when he got out of the vehicle and that it delivered him in one piece. He stopped passing individuals, asking the best way to get to the FBI offices. They either feigned that they didn't understand English or rudely ignored him, walking by, with no acknowledgement of his question.

Finally, a young girl, he guessed one that attended a university, stopped and gave him the directions. Thanking her, he started his quest. He was amazed at the throngs of people that were rushing by. Originally, coming from New York City, he was able to regain his memory of why he left the city for a more sedate life. Oh shit, he thought, who am I kidding? A cops life can never be uncomplicated. He'd seen it all. He'd never been able to forget the many killings he viewed, the children, so young and vulnerable, taken away, never to know what a good life was all about. The throngs of hookers, pimps, druggies, dealers, thieves, and every kind of vermin let out to deprive the world and manipulate the good people out of their inalienable rights to have a safe environment to live and learn.

Too many times he saw law abiding citizens quelled by these vermin. The policeman's personal life often suffered as well. Many spouses couldn't take the strain of this kind of life, putting undo pressure on a marriage that had other complications as well. His own included, with the ultimate tragedy of divorce. He didn't know why these thoughts entered his mind, but they did. He surmised it was the masses of people, going to different places, hurrying, like mice in a cage, climbing the round multi stepped wheel, ignoring people who they bump into, in their process of going to their various destinations.

Riches' feet were killing him. He'd no idea how long it had taken him to finally see the building he was to enter. Before taking his first step, he dialed Nancy's cell, waiting for her to pick up his call. With a twinkle in his eyes he made up a story to quell her anxiety of when he would arrive in Japan. With a handful of excuses he knowingly warded off her inquiries. He promised to talk to her soon. After finding out certain details that they needed to apprehend the criminals they were after, he'd be on the next plane to help them. When he closed the cell, he was certain that he reduced her anxieties. He headed up the steps, with apprehension, opened the revolving, partitioned, glass doors, and took a deep breath.

Rich was impressed by the enormity of the building. The branch was comprised of many floors and offices in this particular structure. After asking the security guard, located on the first floor, where he could find the offices of the Japanese FBI, he was directed to the seventh floor. After waiting for 15 minutes he was greeted by Mr. Tamamurō who asked Rich to follow him into his office. After the customary introductions Rich got down to business. Mr. Tamamurō interrupted Rich before he got too far in the dialogue. "I take it you understand that I am part of the growing FBI international Art Crime Team. This particular field is a growing international problem. Do you mind if I turn on my tape recorder and then if I miss anything of importance while writing, I can go back to the recording?"

"Of course not, be my guest."

Rich went back to the beginning of the complicated case. He explained every detail involved in the situation. Mr. Tamamurō listened attentively not interrupting, but instead, writing diligently on a large pad of yellow, legal size paper. As Rich was explaining the case and predicament involved in this particular circumstance, he tried reading Mr. Tamamurō. He was a tall, thin gentleman, who seemed knowledgeable about this type of occurrence. Rich couldn't guess what Mr. Tamamurō was thinking. After what seemed hours, but in reality, an hour and a half of continuous monologue, Rich was drained. Mr. Tamamurō put down his pen and after taking a deep breath, looked directly into Richs' eyes. "I don't know if you realize that all levels of law enforcement are involved with this problem. We have specialists from the Washington field office, with their art theft problem. We have agencies worldwide that include Interpol as well. We also have the international stolen art file. It's a computerized data base of stolen art and cultural property."

He was silent for a moment, wanting Rich to comprehend what information was given to him. After a while Mr. Tamamurō asked, "Would you like my secretary to bring us some light refreshment and something to quell your obvious dehydrated mouth?" Rich, feeling as if he was like Moses, walking endlessly through the dessert, desperately accepted Mr. Tamamurō's offer. While Mr. Tamamurō was looking at his notes Rich looked around the small office. The awareness of the sparse office overwhelmed him. How could this man of the law have so few articles in his working environment? Mr. Tamamurō, without looking up from his pad, as if reading Richs' mind, said out loud, "Most of the books and items that we need are downstairs in the library." Rich was taken aback by this gentleman's perception "I see," Rich weakly responded. Just then his secretary appeared with a cart on which food and beverages were displayed. "I think we deserve this respite, wouldn't you agree, Detective Colangelo?"

"I think we both can use a break."

After their intermission Mr. Tamamurō told Rich to please call him Mr. T. Putting up his hand, dissuading any argument, "I'm serious. If we're to be working closely I don't want the customary formality that you expect from us. I know that's what you think we're about. Let me assure you, yes we are formal people, but once you're a part of our intimate lives, as I'm sure you will be, I want us to also be friends. Someday I'll try to explain the variations of what you call a surname and how and what it derived from. The same thing goes for our given name. It's difficult for the people in the Western world to comprehend the various factors involved."

"It's a deal, Mr. T." Rich replied with a smile appearing on his rugged but handsome face. As they were heading for the elevator Mr. T. looked back at Rich and said, "By the way, please don't compare me to that wrestler, I receive many jokes about Mr. T. As you can see, I don't wear those noticeable, gaudy, gold necklaces and my hair is cut quite different."

Rich was taken aback by that comment but chose to ignore it. "Let's go downstairs and I'll introduce you to my cohorts. I'm sure you're going to like them and we'll be working together as one body, if you know what I mean. After our initial briefing, I'll call Interpol and get them involved as well. We really work very well together." Rich nodded, appreciating Mr. T's enthusiasm. After the introductions were made, Rich started to relax. It was hard remembering the names of the individual men, but realized he would eventually figure it out. Some of the men had the look of competence while others looked more like rookies. Even though it was hard to tell one man apart from the other, he knew that by associating certain distinguishing features, he'd get their names straight.

. He was escorted to another, larger, meeting room. Rich listened to Mr. Tomomurō explain the situation in detail and from there the men kept nodding their heads in agreement while the discussions didn't stop. They went over all the details that Rich had described and then put forth a plan of action. Rich interrupted them and told them that at this time they'd better get Suzanne and Nancy to their next meeting. The women would be beyond agitation if not being part of the procedure. The team had to work the two women into the scheme when they were to find and put down the men responsible for this operation of corruption, deceit, art robbery, and priceless artifacts too numerous in number to account for. Of course murder had to be dealt with also.

Rich re-emphasized, “Without these two women, if they didn’t come forth with their knowledge of the circumstances and all the factors that they found, we wouldn’t be as far along in this case.” Quietly looking at one another, the entire team shook their heads in agreement. ‘Now the hard part;’ Rich thought. He had to inform Suzanne and Nancy about the meeting he called for without their knowledge.

Rich was back in his room, hands behind his head, letting all the data he obtained from the conference with the FBI and the Interpol gentleman, remain fresh in his mind. He tried to absorb all the facts he gathered, wondering how to relate his secret meeting to the two women. He realized when he told them about the forum it would not set well with his two accòmplices. He didn’t like being deceptive but he understood that he had to tell them everything. His being in Japan without their knowledge was bad enough but his discussion with everyone concerned would really tick them off. Taking a deep breath he picked up the phone, dialing the hotel.

Nancy picked up the phone and was happy to hear Rich’s voice at the other end. ”Hey, I’m here in Japan and I’d love to come over to where you’re staying and talk awhile. Sound good to you?” Nancy was on cloud nine, knowing that she would see Rich again. ”Suzanne’s in the shower, but I’m sure she’d love to see you, as well as myself. How long will you be here?” Avoiding the obvious, he backtracked and told Nancy, “pretty soon.”

“Tell me the hotel that you’re staying at and the taxi will take me there.”

“Good luck. I think you’d be better off with a rickshaw. Seriously, we’re staying at the Four Seasons Hotel Tokyo at Marunouchi. It’s quite delightful. You’ll see when you get here. We’re in room 1021. Wait till you see it, you’ll be impressed as we were.” “I’ll see you soon, baby.” Nancy got into the shower as Suzanne got out. On her way in she told Suzanne that Rich was coming over. ”This is going to be the fastest shower ever taken. I’ll put on a beautiful outfit and my make-up will be done to perfection.” Suzanne looked at her friend. ”First of all, you’re beautiful without any, but if you feel you want to put some on, be my guest. Do what you want,” clearing her throat, “a professional to apply it?” Nancy, as if talking to herself informed Suzanne: “From all the times at the salon, and seeing it done, I think I can put on my own make-up. Thanks any way.” Suzanne shrugged her shoulders and contemplated which outfit to put on.

With their appearances in order, they waited for Rich’s presence. While passing the time Suzanne decided to put on the beautiful fireplace that encompassed almost one entire wall of the beautiful, spacious room. Getting a glass from the fully equipped bar, Suzanne poured herself a white Zinfandel. Nancy was surprised to see Suzanne drinking earlier than usual and asked, “Since when did you start drinking before going down to the dining room?” ”If you want to know, I’ll tell you, once in a while a drink calms me down. At this point in my life, with all this espionage going on, I'm frazzled. Not to mention my quandary about Stephen and what's going to happen to our relationship."

"I didn't want to bring up the subject, but since you did, Suzanne, what are you going to do if Stephen still won't be decisive?"

"I honestly don't know. I do realize that I love him with all my heart, and believe we're true soul mates. I hope he recognizes the fact that I'm serious about his making a commitment to me, to finally get divorced and make me his wife. I don't know if he's taking my threat seriously? I can assure you, I'm not playing games. If I'm disappointed about the decision he makes than I'll have no other choice to do what I have to do. When I make up my mind, nothing will dissuade me."

Suzanne lifted her glass, looked at her friend and made a toast. "To life and all its wonders." Nancy didn't know what to say. She was dumbfounded. She knew that Suzanne was unhappy with the way her relationship with Stephen was going. She never realized that Suzanne would make good on her promise to give him up if she didn't get her way. "Only time will tell," Nancy declared and went behind the bar, took a glass, filled it with scotch and water, and clinked Suzanne's glass. "To hopes, wishes, and Gods will, that whatever will be, will be." After their drinks were finished, the two partners, arm in arm walked to the sofa and sat down waiting for Rich to join them.

Looking at the fire, it's red, yellow and orange flames crackling in the pit, Suzanne thought it was like her heart, crackling and not knowing what life had in store for her.

Rich knocked on the door. Nancy got up and greeted him with a large kiss and hug. "I was waiting for this display of affection and thinking of your lips on mine throughout the entire plane ride. It was worth the wait." Taking Rich's hand they sat on the sofa opposite Suzanne. Rich looked over the large room and couldn't get over the gorgeous, luxurious furniture and the accessories that added warmth to it. "If you think this is beautiful, let me show you the rest of the suite. It's to die for." Rich was amazed at the rich ornamentations in every room. Sitting back down on the sofa all he could say was "WOW."

Nancy told Rich, "It's overwhelming when you first come in. I couldn't get used to the many beautiful appointments on the furniture. When you see beauty such as this, you become accustomed to it."

Suzanne gave her opinion, "You take it for granted, like two people who are married and forget what love and passion is all about. People take things and their loved ones for granted all the time."

"Don't be so pessimistic, Suzanne. God has a plan for everyone and HE knows what He's doing. I'm a fatalist." Rich had no clue what the two women were talking about, kept his mouth shut, until he could bring up the subject that he originally came to their hotel suite for.

Clearing his throat, he finally got their full attention. "Ladies, I've made contact with the local police force, the FBI and Interpol. We'll meet with them at 9:00 sharp and then we'll discuss our plan of action." Rich waited for the women's reaction in relating his private encounter with Japan's law enforcement agency. He couldn't believe that they didn't respond as he thought they would.

"Do you mean a. m. or p. m." Nancy retorted. "9:00 a. m. of course." With a groan the two women looked over to one another and shrugged. "I guess we've been lucky that we've lived a life of luxury and pampering so far. I could take this type of living forever, if I had my way," Rich said. "Well ladies, your time is up. Welcome to the real world once again." They both moaned, "seriously?" Suzanne broke into the conversation, "We're ready for action, aren't we Nancy." Dubiously, Nancy had no other choice than to agree.

"I'll pick you up at around 8:00. The three of us will go to the building that houses the men that are needed for our operation to succeed." "Okay, now down to real business, where shall we dine?" a very hungry Nancy asked. "We've only eaten at the fine dining room once since we arrived. We usually eat at the bar and grill which is situated in the lobby. I suggest, since Nancy and I are dressed for a fancy occasion, I favor the fine dining room."

"Sounds good to me," agreed Nancy, "Is it okay with you Rich?"

"Let's go, I'm famished. I'll follow my two beautiful women to the ends of the earth if I have to."

"There's no need of that, following us is enough thank you," retorted Suzanne.

After their first rounds of drinks were finished they ordered the main course, taking the waiter's suggestion for the best entrée of the evening. "I can't wait any longer," blurted Nancy. "Tell us what you found out, all about the people that will be helping and what our role in this investigation involves."

"Let Rich relax for a moment or two then when he's ready, he'll tell us," Suzanne advised Nancy. Rich laughed out loud. "I see the two of you haven't changed one bit. You're still bickering, as usual. "The two woman looked at each other, shrugged their shoulder and spoke at the same time. "What on earth are you talking about?" Suzanne, put out by his outlandish view, adamantly denied his verbal comment. "We don't argue or bicker about anything. We always get along, don't we Nancy?"

"Of course we do," Nancy agreed as she looked at Rich as if he was hallucinating. Rich put up his hands, as if surrendering. "Hey, I'm sorry that I offended you. It'll never happen again, okay?" They ignored his apology and when they were finished with their meal they asked for the dessert tray to be brought over. After agonizing, for what seemed a long time, the two women didn't want anything. Rich wasn't watching his weight and ordered an opulent dessert asking the waiter to bring 3 dishes and forks.

With a smug look on his face he told them; "I know that the two of you are always watching your weight, as most women do, but in case you change your mind, you can share some of mine." When the waiter brought out the large, chocolate, mousse, cake, that was delicious looking, Rich greedily put his arms around the plate. Looking at both women who were salivating with envy, "Too bad you didn't want to partake in any indulgence." Smugly, he put the plate in the middle of the table. "Grab your forks ladies and dig in." When every bit was consumed, a look of disgust appeared on Suzanne and Nancy's faces. Looking at Nancy, Suzanne admitted, "You know whatever goes into your mouth, is one more inch on the hips."

"Yes, I agree, but Suzanne you have to admit it was delicious."

"Okay, you and Rich win, I admit it was worth it. What the hell, live it up, you only exist in this world once." Suzanne looked at him, eyes squinted and announced, "You might think that thought but as for me, I'm coming back until I get life right. As a matter of fact I'll be back as a dancing plastic surgeon." The couple looked at Suzanne as if she were crazy. "I'll be in great shape from dancing and if I need a little tuck here and there, I'm sure one of my colleagues will make me beautiful once again." Changing the subject she addressed Rich, "you realize that you just made Nancy and I do an extra hour of exercising early this coming morning." With a smirk, Rich remarked, "Personally, looking at Nancy, I wouldn't want to hold a skinny, skeletal woman when I make love." Nancy turned bright red and tried to ignore his remark as they entered the elevator, bringing them back to the women's' suite.

When they were seated Nancy looked at Rich and asked, "Do you think that you can tell us everything you've learned?"

"Of course, I'm all ears," admitted Suzanne. "The floor is yours." Rich again related the people he met and gave more detail about the events discussed during his meeting. "They'll be diligently working with us." He didn't mention his early arrival and it was never brought up. "Tomorrow I'll come over here and then we'll go to the center of operations. With all the traffic we'll encounter it will take at least an hour to get to headquarters on time." Groaning, Suzanne admitted that they'd have to get up at 5 a. m. to be able to exercise, shower and make themselves presentable for their meeting."

"I didn't force you to help me with the dessert. Suck it up and I'll be here bright and early and expect the two of you to be ready." Nancy got up from the sofa. With a salute, "yes sir, your wishes are our command." Suzanne excused herself now that she had all the information she needed. "See you two love birds in the morning." She went into her bedroom and closed the door.

Suzanne tried going to sleep, but had a hard time doing so. Not being able to concentrate on the latest novel she was reading, she put the book aside. Putting her hands in back of her head, the same thoughts kept reoccurring. She couldn't stop thinking about Stephen's response after she gave him the ultimatum that weighed heavily on her mind. 'For years I've been asking Stephen to get divorced from Lou Anne and make me his legal wife. He professes I'm the love of his life. Even if he was in turmoil, I can't believe that he didn't put his thoughts aside and show up to the reception. Not only did he disgrace me but his lack of courtesy to Hope, who he's known since she was a young girl, was a bad move on his part. Did he realize that his absence wouldn't be noticed by many of the guests. I was humiliated but tried to put up a good front. My best friends could surmise how disappointed I was.' She remembered how when he was a boy he was controlling and only thought of himself. 'He would rationalize his actions, blaming others for their not understanding and always thought that he was right. I used to get frustrated when he always had to have the last word. '

She resisted calling him, even though it killed her not to hear his voice. She knew the answer she wanted to hear but deep in her heart she was familiar to what his response would be. Suzanne realized, all too late, that he must be a sick man in many ways and couldn't give anything up. She remembered when they were youngsters he could never throw out games or toys. Realizing all too late that his obsessive behavior was a flaw that would ultimately destroy his life. 'I guess that he feels that I'm one of his compulsive objects that he wants to keep forever. All the memories of the past he kept buried in his mind and never let go of his feelings of his possessions, myself included.' His act of refusing to give up his marriage was the straw that broke the camel's back. He will always be this way. 'I realized, too late that he will never change and we'll both have to live with the decision of his actions. Too bad he didn't go for therapy and counseling years ago when he was a youngster.' Disappointment did not allude her. The love she once had for him will never leave her heart. She truly believed they were and would always be soul mates. Anger now was starting to shadow the love. After tossing and turning she finally was able to allow herself to calm down, relax and fall into the arms of Morpheus.

As promised, Rich was right on time. The women got into his rented, small car and were ready for the assignment to be given them. When the women and Rich were in Mr. T's small, compact room, they shook hands. Rich introduced Mr. T. by his formal name and if Mr. T. wanted to have them use his formal surname it would be up to him to acknowledge it or ask for the abbreviated version. Suzanne assessed him without taking her eyes off him. He was not the type of man she envisioned. Instead of him being short and stocky, he was tall and thin. His features seemed to be of mixed heritage.

The people involved moved to a larger room. Mr. Tamamurō was articulate and stated the situation as he assumed it to be. After asking everyone in the conference room, Suzanne and Nancy included, their feelings about the matter at hand, he nodded to each of them as they told him their impression. They also voiced their concern and gut reaction with what might occur. The other gentlemen on the team gave Suzanne and Nancy a feeling of comfort knowing that they were there to help and watch their backs.

The six Interpol, CIS, and FBI officers, who arrived a little later, impressed both Suzanne and Nancy immensely. When Suzanne and Nancy entered another room the men were standing and bowing, introducing themselves by their entire name. There was agent number one, whose name was Sato Akira, the second agents name was Tanaka Kenji and the third, Ito Masso. He was shorter than the rest, but as well as having a broad smile, he obviously worked out on a regular basis. The women could see his powerfully built body and muscles under his jacket. His well-toned physique made up for his lack in stature.

Suzanne and Nancy gave up on the other agent's names, finding it too confusing to remember them all. They were sure the names would automatically be ingrained in their minds over time. While on break Both Sam and Mr. Tee explained to Suzanne and Nancy how the surname is always first and the given name is after the surname. Suzanne and Nancy looked at each other and tried to act as if they understood.

CHAPTER FORTY

After listening to the men talk on the subject at hand, Suzanne realized that they had a good feeling for the entire situation. They had confidence in the men and thought that they knew what they were talking about and what had to be done. Of course Mr. Makino was still eluding them. The task team thought, but figured, that he was the person of most importance in this case. Even though they had their men situated at different locations throughout Japan and the other Islands, he seemed to have fallen off the earth's hemisphere. They wanted Suzanne and Nancy to hang around Beppu. Rich then explained that through their source at Yoshy's main headquarters, they were able to track his whereabouts. They thought that once he was through running and figured it was safe, he would feel that he was no longer in jeopardy and return to his haven. It was up to Suzanne and Nancy to inform them of his return and wait until orders were given them as what to do. The head of the FBI in Japan, Mr. Tamomurō, was in agreement with all the men of law enforcement working the case. He didn't want the women to activate any confrontations that could result in serious repercussions to them. Suzanne agreed but secretly knew that she and Nancy could never be bystanders. She nodded earnestly, without being obvious. On the way home Nancy mentioned to Suzanne that maybe they should think twice about getting wired. "It wouldn't hurt and I'd feel better about the situation." Nancy reiterated her concern to Suzanne. "If you'd feel safer with the device on us then by all means speak to Rich about it. I'm sure it'd be nothing for them to put it on us," Suzanne replied.

The women checked out of their elegant hotel. After great discussion they decided to fly by a commercial airline and took a smaller plane, other than their own jet, to the Island of Kyushu. It took 2 hours for the plane to land on this beautiful Island. From there they'd find transportation to Beppu, which they previously found ranked as the hot springs capital of Japan. Beppu was the leader of the other hot spring areas. Once the women landed they talked amongst themselves and realized how lucky they were to have purchased their own plane. They were no longer used to riding in a money making company aircraft. "I don't want to seem snobbish but even though we didn't encounter any difficulties, it made me appreciate our vehicle more," Suzanne told Nancy.

"Hey, just listen to me and I'll always steer you in the right direction."

"Oh God, she's doing it again," Suzanne uttered out loud. Frustrated that her friend would never pass up the opportunity to send forth the message that she was the person responsible for that decision.

After landing, Nancy and Suzanne decided to go right to the Suginoi Hotel, located on the side of a hill. They were told that you see Mt. Yufu and Mt. Tsurunidake from their location. In the morning they would visit Mt. Tsurunidake. Various breed's and numerous monkeys were there and they could walk through the natural gardens.

Nancy announced, "You know Suzanne, as they were almost at the top of the mountain, I never mentioned that I am petrified of monkeys."

"Oh great, now you tell me. Well there's nothing I can do about it. From what I've read just don't make quick moves and be quiet," Suzanne tried reassuring her partner. Nancy retaliated, "I also heard some awful stories about monkeys that attacked humans and terrible tragedies have happened throughout the years by these dreadful beasts. The main reason, at least for me, is to walk amongst the beautiful, natural gardens."

Sarcastically Suzanne pointed out, "I could have saved us a trip and taken you to the Boston Public. Gardens and then we wouldn't have encountered any monkeys." Suzanne laughed and shook her head. Suzanne lightly pushed Nancy, "Come on slow poke the faster we finish this tour the faster we can go back to our hotel. I understand that they don't have a workout room but it does have a nice swimming pool. I guess I'll have to take quite a few lapses to make up for not working out." Nancy was still speechless as she wondered through the mountain, trying to avoid the many monkeys aimlessly walking and swinging from the few trees.

Once back at the hotel Nancy seemed to relax and felt relieved that she didn't have to encounter any more primates, scattering about. Suzanne stated, "While we're here I'd like to visit some of the mineral baths. I might even emerge into one of them, if only to feel cleansed and healed of any bad ailments that not knowing, might be lurking in my system."

"You're crazy. You know that, don't you? I'll go along with you. I might join you in going into a few, just to keep you company, that is." They both smiled as they readied themselves for bed. "Oh, by the way," stated Nancy, "remember we saw some nice artists' colonies throughout the island? I'd like to visit them again. I didn't buy a few pieces that I admired. This time I'll buy them."

"Since when didn't you buy something you liked, on the spot?" asked Suzanne." I don't know, I just didn't."

Suzanne and Nancy woke early and headed for a few of the mineral baths that were recommended to them by the people at the hotel. At the last one on their tour they decided to plunge in and take advantage of this enjoyable experience. They realized how lucky they were. No other place in the world could boast about the many hot springs and mineral baths that existed in their Country or States.

The next day, while walking amongst the various venders, Suzanne mentioned, while watching Nancy bickering with the owner over the price of a very beautiful bracelet, that the next time they spoke to Rich they should mention the hidden microphones for them. Next to Nancy was a lovely looking blond, who seemed interested in some of the items also on display. Suzanne couldn't help but notice how exquisite this person was. She seemed rather shy and Suzanne knew that the pretty blond would not be dickering like Nancy automatically did. While the blond was waiting patiently for the obvious owner to finish the sale with Nancy, Suzanne tried starting a conversation, sensing that the woman was an American. The young lady seemed introverted and wouldn't look directly at Suzanne, which she perceived a little odd. She answered the questions reluctantly and gave one word answers. "The hell with her," Suzanne thought as she went back to Nancy's quest for a good buy.

Finishing her purchase, Nancy was admiring her new piece of jewelry as they walked along the many and various stores along the way in this particular section of town. When it was getting dark Nancy suggested that they head back to the hotel. "You know Nancy, tomorrow, why don't we meander to where Mr. Makino's house is and see what's happening there. I'm sure nothing, but one never knows when he could show up."

"That's a good idea. You're right, we might spot him walking or going to one of the springs near his house."

As the two women were making their arrangements so were Nobuaki and Hiro planning strategies of their own. "Well, we've spent a good part of three weeks hold up in this hotel. I think it's about time that we head to Yoshy's secluded home and see what's happening."

"Good idea boss. Nobuaki justified his actions." He's been gone so long that he probably figures that the people who are looking for him have given up and gone on to other things," Hiro agreed as he started to pack his clothes.

Suzanne didn't rush getting out of her comfortable bed. Thinking they didn't have an urgent meeting or had to hurry off to an appointment she enjoyed the peace and quiet of staying in. Suzanne put certain issues aside and concentrated on her parent's dilemma.

She was definitely a daddy's girl. She loved her mother with all her heart but there was a special bond between the two of them. She refused to get maudlin and tried remembering the good times that they had and enjoyed together. He took her to the first movie she saw. Of course it was a cowboy, one starring Buck Jones. Her poor father couldn't enjoy the movie because every second she kept asking him, "What's going to happen next, daddy?" He was the first man that she loved. He took the day off to teach her to ride a bike. There were so many memories she never wanted to forget. Once she found out about his condition she didn't tell a soul. Not Nancy, Beverly, Madaline or Mrs. Walsh. In time her dear friends would have to be told and her children of course. But for now the tears she shed would be hers and hers alone.

Suzanne couldn't understand why, after all these years, she found herself thrashing and her body drenched in sweat in the middle of the night. When she realized that episodes of Brian's violent behavior towards her were reappearing in dreams she was mortified. After all these years she was surprised that they would continue to upset her, even now, when her life had made a 100% turnaround. She tried putting her unpleasant dreams away and willed herself to think of the good attributes in front of anything else. But as hard as she tried, her anguished mental activity wouldn't stop.

Suzanne was worried sick about what lay in the future for her parents and ultimately with the way she would have to deal with the decisions to be made. She remembered vividly the phone call his doctor made to her. Dr. Hess was an old family friend and felt he could talk to Suzanne before he told Morris and Dorothy. He called one afternoon before their trip and informed Suzanne that her father has prostate cancer. It was too far gone and unfortunately the cancer was now in his bones. He hadn't told her parents yet and was wondering if the dire news would be better if Suzanne delivered it to them or if she wanted to accompany them to his office. She told him about her trip and he assured her that the disclosure could wait until her return. "So far Morris knows he has prostate cancer and God willing, we can hold off telling him about the bone cancer if he doesn't have any bad incidents." Suzanne agreed with his decision. She realized that Dorothy thought that Morris was only dealing with dementia. Dorothy thought that the prostate cancer was slow growing. 'This new aspect about his health will really have an effect on both of them.'

As far as Brian was concerned, thoughts of him should have been buried, with his body, a long time ago. She was heartsick knowing what lie ahead for Morris. As these thoughts entered her mind, she felt the tears of sorrow slowly descending down her cheeks. She and Dorothy had to be strong for the ultimate outcome of his untimely illness. She brought herself to sit at the side of the bed, her legs soundly on the soft carpet, and tried to rid her mind of these horrible thoughts.

"Hey sleepyhead, it's about time you got up. I've been waiting for you for over an hour. I was about to shake you awake when I saw you sitting up." Looking at her friend she was suddenly aware of how fatigued Suzanne looked. Forestalling any headstrong opposition, she warily walked over to Suzanne. Nancy compared her to a sullen, hurt deer, her eyes dull and glazed, as she saw her beloved doe, lying on the ground, never to take another breath. "Are you all right?" Nancy asked hesitantly, afraid to hear a negative response.

Trying to camouflage her true worries, Suzanne responded cheerfully," of course, silly, why would you think otherwise?" Nancy hesitated, "I don't know, you don't seem like yourself, that's all."

"I'm fine, just thinking crazy thoughts. I'll take a shower and cleanse all my bad emotions away, they'll go down the drain."

"Okay, okay, if you say so," Nancy cautiously responded. "I'll see you when you're dressed and ready to go out and we'll have a good day."

"You said what I was thinking," lied Suzanne, as she quickly lifted herself from the side of the bed and headed for the shower.

When Nancy heard the shower running at full capacity, she gently opened her cell phone and called Rich. She told him her feelings and how she perceived Suzanne this morning. Hoping he'd have some answers, she was disappointed that his response was not what she was eager to hear. Nancy then told him the plans for the day. "I think after we have our breakfast, we'll go for a ride around town and wind up near Mr. Makino's house. I'm sure we won't find anything outstanding or sight him, but hey, you never know," Nancy said. "By the way, Suzanne and I discussed a matter that was brought up at one of the meeting. You mentioned that it wouldn't hurt if we had a device so that you and your officers can hear us. Not that we'd get ourselves into trouble, but you never know."

"Okay, I'll be at headquarters and I'll make sure that we get you and Suzanne hooked up a.s.a.p. You, obviously know my cell number. I'm not sure if you can reach me on it while we're in Japan. Wait a second and I'll get you Mr. T's cell number. Even if you don't find anything of interest, call us anyway. After a few minutes he made sure she had all the numbers she needed. I have a conference with the men from Interpol and I'm sure it'll be interesting. I'll fill you in on the details of the meeting when I see you next; which should be within the next day or two. We'll meet and make sure to put the microphones on the two of you, okay?" She closed her cell phone and waited for Suzanne to get dressed to go downstairs for breakfast.

"I don't know about you, but this hit the spot," Suzanne declared as she moved her chair back from the table. Now satisfied, a look of complete pleasure showed on her face. "A cup of hot tea and I'll be ready to fight the world;" Suzanne verbalized as she gently picked up her cup, trying not to shake the cup while drinking the hot liquid. 'She'll think I'm coming down from a binge if she sees my hands shaking. I have to control my emotions,' Suzanne thought to herself as her beautiful smile erupted on her face, looking directly at her best friend.

They both went back upstairs and put on lightweight jackets. They were disappointed that the weather was not as hot as they expected it to be. They waited at the bus stop instead of taking their rental car. Nancy wanted to see how the citizens of the area lived. It would be easier to take public transportation, not having to think and worry of any complications occurring if reading directions from the map incorrectly. They took their seats, silently listening to the conversations around them. They, miraculously, got off at the right bus stop and slowly walked to the various shops in the area that Mr. Makino's hidden retreat was located. "You know Nancy, it's times like this that I wish we had some hidden devise that would let Rich know where we are."

"Yha, I know what you mean. I spoke to Rich about it and he and his buddies will be here to put it on us. See I was thoughtful before you had to mention it to me again," Nancy smugly told Suzanne. "But we don't, so until we do, let's act like regular tourists and go about our business, barely visible to the people in the village or any of the sightseers."

Taking their time, meandering through the streets, admiring the beauty of the area and enjoying the various quaint shops around, they appreciated the articles each saw. "Come, let's go over there," pointed Suzanne, as she spotted an unusual outfit hanging in the window of a boutique. Stepping up to the store, Suzanne couldn't help be in awe of the lovely outfits hanging on the racks. Not able to resist her impulsivity, she removed some items and asked the saleswoman to please put them in a dressing room so she could try them on. "I hope that you don't buy them all, we didn't bring enough suitcases to put them into if you purchase these garments."

"Don't worry, if I have to, I'll buy another valise to put these items into," declared Suzanne as she finally went into the fitting room to try the clothes on. "Besides, I don't have to pay any extra money with having an excess of weight for my baggage. That's one of the perks of owning our own plane." Nancy tapped Suzanne on the shoulder as they were leaving the shop. "Did you forget that we flew commercial this time?" Suzanne's arms, full of new purchases, shrugged her shoulders, "whatever." She enjoyed walking amongst other tourists, and enjoyed the slight breeze, making the weather comfortable. "You know if we didn't buy these clothes, we would have had to carry our jackets all day long. Aren't we lucky that I now have some bags to put them into?"

"Yes," Nancy agreed. "Suzanne I know you're enjoying yourself, be happy with your purchases and as you taught me to say through the years, use, enjoy and wear them in the best of health." With a smile on her face she answered sincerely, "thank you Nancy, for your thoughtfulness." They walked the streets with not a care in the world.

Poking Nancy discreetly, she whispered, "Don't look now until I tell you to turn around. I think I see that rich snob who snubbed me like I didn't exist when you were buying your jewelry. Is she following us, or is it a coincidence that she seems to be shopping in the same areas that we go to?"

"Suzanne, I'm sure it's a coincidence. Why would she be tailing us. As far as anyone knows, we're tourists like anyone else. I think you're being paranoid."

"Now, look, look, that's her, over there."

"I see she's as beautiful as you said she is. I really don't think we have anything to worry about. She's probably shy and doesn't seem to have anyone with her. Obviously it's her prerogative or she's lonely, with no one to share her pleasure of shopping."

"Get her out of your thoughts, mind your own business. I'm sure she doesn't have a care in the world and is happy being by herself. Maybe she has a husband or whoever, and he's in a business meeting and she's not able to join him. I bet she's shopping like we are, that's all. Try not to be suspicious of everyone you see."

"I can't help it, you and I are on an assignment and we can't be cautious enough." With a sigh, Nancy stated, "I don't believe you, take a chill pill and get over it. Leave it alone. The poor dear is enjoying this beautiful day as we are. Let it go."

"Okay boss, I will." Reluctantly, Suzanne kept up with Nancy as she walked through the bizzare and other shops admiring the many items but still keeping a unobtrusive eye on the fair-haired woman.

Once finished shopping, they meandered near Mr. Makino's house, which was obviously bought because of its hidden location. "Look at that beautiful hot spring, practically in back of his retreat," motioned Suzanne. "It looks delightful," declared Nancy as she enviously looked at the body of hot, steamy, water waiting to be enjoyed by whoever submerged themselves into it. "Now that's a vacation retreat that anyone would enjoy," stated Suzanne. "Maybe, now that I have a rich son-in-law, he could purchase a hot tub to put into my back yard."

"It's not the same as a mineral bath and you know it."

"Well, I can put mud from the Israel sea on the bottom and sprinkle some essential oils about and then I can call it my own de-cleansing and purifying hot tub."

"You are truly losing it, you know you are, don't you?" Nancy said jokingly.

At headquarters Rich was pacing back and forth. Verbalizing his frustration to the men in the unit, he told them that he was upset he hadn't heard from Nancy and Suzanne. This isn't like them. They know to touch base with us. As the hours prolonged, the more tense and upset Rich became. Mr. T., realizing Rich's agitation told him to sit down. Paging his secretary he asked her to bring up tea for the men. "You know Rich, to make you feel better, I'll ring Nancy and you'll be relieved when you find out that everything's all right.

As they sauntered by slowly, trying not to be obvious, Suzanne suddenly poked Nancy. "Don't look now, but that same 'lonely woman' has come from the back door of Mr. Makino's cottage, if you can call it that, and is going to submerge herself in the mineral bath in back of his house."

"Personally, I can't wait till she takes off her robe and is bare naked as she goes into it."

"Are you some kind of pervert? Since when do you take pleasure in seeing another woman naked?"

"I don't, but one never tires of viewing a picture of beauty, does one?"

"Are you sure deep down you're not a lesbian?" Suzanne asked. "You did go to an all-girls school when you were younger."

"You are a sick person, Suzanne."

"Obviously I'm kidding," Suzanne said. Nancy stated, "I'll tell Rich about her when we call him. Oh my God, I can't find my cell phone." Nancy rummaged through her pocketbook but to no avail, she couldn't find it. "I must have lost or left it at one of the many stores we were in," a worried Nancy pronounced.

Suzanne tried to calm Nancy. "Don't be such a worry wart. We'll call him from the hotel's phone when we get back to our room."

"On the plane I was positive that Mr. Makino told me that he was married to a lovely Japanese woman and had a son who was going to the university this year," announced Nancy. "I wouldn't be so trusting if I were you. That's all I'm saying. A man thinks with his other head, and don't you ever forget it," Suzanne declared, as she too watched in silence, as the woman descended into the large pool of hot, steamy water, shedding her outer robe.

Unnoticed, the two men saw the same woman as Nancy and Suzanne. They were discreetly observing her as they sat outside one of the tea houses, situated near Yoshy's retreat. "I knew he couldn't keep away for a longer period of time. We timed this trip just right," Nobuaki declared as he sipped his tea and took a bite of his pastry, putting it selfishly into his mouth. "You're always right, boss," Hiro declared as he also enjoyed his tea. He couldn't take his eyes off of the beautiful blonde as she submerged herself into the hot spring water.

"Well, well, well, it seems that whore Robin is enjoying herself. Won't she be surprised when we unexpectedly pay them a visit," Nobuaki laughed as he put down his finished cup of tea.

Meanwhile, back at the Tokyo Police Headquarters Rich and the people from Interpol were strategizing their plan of action. "Do you think that we should have left your two women friends by themselves to see if this Yoshy character is home by now?"

"I've been thinking about that myself. I honestly don't know. I do recognize that they have common sense and wouldn't do anything foolish without contacting us first."

"I hope that you're right because from what we've learned he and his friends are not nice people, especially when they feel threatened or cornered."

"Let's give them awhile. They're probably on their way to the hotel as we speak now."

"I hope so, or we'd better move fast if they don't show up."

"Well, Miss Nancy, since you're sort of Mr. Yoshy's friend, would it be inappropriate for you to knock on his door? I mean, you just happened to be in the area."

"I honestly, don't know what to do. Maybe I should call Rich and tell him that by deduction, I think he's probably home. Wouldn't that make sense since his girlfriend is here?"

"I hate to disillusion you, but aren't you the woman who lost her cell phone? Unfortunately, I purposely left mine back in the hotel, knowing you were bringing yours." declared Suzanne, as she studiously observed his girlfriend enjoying the spring. "But on the other hand," Nancy said aloud, "it wouldn't hurt anyone if we discreetly watch the house and see what happens."

"Truthfully, I'm on the same page as you."

When Nobaki noticed Robin emerge from the mineral bath he got up from his chair and ordered Hiro to come with him.

"Let's make a call to his house, and see if anyone answers. "Nobaki pulled out his cell and dialed the number. He was lucky he saved the telephone # and Yoshy's cell # as he walked around the café waiting for someone to pick up at least one of the phones. After letting both phone's ring he walked over to Hiro. "I don't know what the fuck is going on but something strange is happening."

"Boss, maybe after her little dip in the spring, Yoshy decided to dip his stick into her."

"That's a possibility. Let's wait for an hour and try again. If I still get an answering machine, I think some decisive action should be taken. Let's play it by ear. Did you pick up the guns, ammunition and all the tools we need from our friend in Tokeo?"

"Yes boss, that was easy. He had everything we asked for waiting for me to retrieve it. I have everything we need in my satchel."

"Good, let's walk around a bit and kill an hour or so till I think we should be ready to knock on his door."

"Come, let's window shop to kill some time. If I see something that I think Mitsuko would like I'll bring a little present home for her. She's a good girl and she's a help around the house and really takes care of everything I need." After looking some merchandise over Nobaki asked Hiro what he thought of a particular piece of jewelry. Nobaki stated, "She's such a delicate girl, I don't think a large piece of jewelry would look good on her. She doesn't go anywhere outside of the house. Maybe someday she will and then she'll have some nice jewelry to wear with an outfit of her choice. What do you think, you like it?"

"Doesn't someone give a woman a piece of jewelry if they have something going on between the two of them?" Hiro asked Nobaki, waiting for an answer that he hoped he didn't wanted to hear. Nobaki laughed, slapped Hiro on the back and asked, "Do you think I'm an idiot? She's merely a child to me. A servant, that's all. I want to bring something nice back from our trip to show my appreciation for her loyalty. As a matter of fact I intend to also buy something for my wife."

"When I'm through with Yoshy, nobody will recognize him and no one will be able to find him either. As for that whore, Robin, she's going to be dealt with as well. Hey boss, if you want to have fun with her before I finish her off, why don't you please yourself. For a white ghost, she's awfully pretty. Not to mention how large her chest is."

"Good idea, my friend. I'd love nothing more than get off doing anything I want to her. And seeing you are the one to polish her off, why don't you take her after I finish my pleasures with the bitch."

"I just might." Hiro said as he rubbed his hands together not wanting to put off the inevitable.

"Time's wasting. Let's pay the two unsuspecting hosts a visit and give Yoshy another asshole. I'd like nothing more than to gut him like a fish. First he'll watch us do everything possible to his whore," announced Nobuaki. "Great idea, I'm looking forward to start and finish this assignment."

"Let's go and knock on his door," a confident Nobuaki ordered as he crossed the street and walked to the secluded house.

Standing in front of the door the 2 men rapped loudly. No one answered as Nobuaki expected. "Okay, Hiro, get the implements needed and we'll pay them an unforeseen visit." Hiro opened his valise and found the devices to be used. "You know boss, I'm surprised that being such a geek and computer genius nerd, his house doesn't have a complex alarm system. I don't see anything around like that at all."

"I was thinking the same. There are two things on my mind. First, he thinks he's very clever, and superior to the people living in this village. His house looks modest from the outside, except secluded. Second, there might be something of value other than in the main part of the house. My guess is that's where we'll find the alarm system. They're in the house somewhere, and before we're through, we'll find them," Nobuaki said with conviction.

Yoshy was delighted when Robin came into the house with only a robe covering her body. Completely clean from her bath he wanted to make love to the woman who he adored and loved. He pushed her onto the master bed and commanded her to take off the robe. He then started kissing her from her long neck, down to her toes. She was going crazy with anticipation. Suckling on one breast at a time, deftly feeling her heavy breast with his other hand he alternated each bosom. His fingers pinched her large pink nipples until the hard large bud was blossoming with electricity. "Oh, Oh, Yoshy, you have me so hot." Both completely sated, Robin laid her body over his. As their breathing labored they clung to each other, like two people clinging on a raft, not wanting to get eaten alive by the alligators in the swampy water.

While stroking her long, silky, blonde hair, caressing her back, he suddenly heard a strange noise coming from the front of the house. He pushed her off, and made a motion to be still and quiet. 'Yes,' he thought, 'I'm not imagining that sound. It's definitely something out of the ordinary.' Motioning for Robin to put on the robe he grabbed for his own. He took her hand and quietly, not wanting to further announce where they were, rushed them both into the basement. He deftly pushed numbers from a pad hidden on the back wall of the bookcase that were covered with many books. After he lifted a lever that was concealed under a cement block that was undistinguishable from the rest of the unit, he pulled her into the hidden room and then let out a deep breath. "Yoshy, what's this about?"

"Don't worry my pet, nothing to be alarmed over. I think some very nasty people, that want to harm you and possibly me, found my little hide away."

"Remember when I took you on the extended trip that you enjoyed?"

"Yes", she replied, suddenly afraid of what he was going to say next. "I took you away from some people that I thought might do you harm." With a look of surprise, she put her hand to her heart and while shaking her head in denial, Robin was sobbing. His heart was breaking watching her emotions and seeing her crumble before him. "Now, now, my pet, don't worry, they'll never find us here. It's my secret hideaway from the world. The best part is that it's sound proof as well. Remember I once took you down here and showed you my personal treasures?"

"Yes, Yoshy I do. But why would anyone want to hurt me? I've never offended anyone in my life."

"There are strange people in this world, my dear, who are envious and have devious thoughts. They don't care who or how they harm individuals, they enjoy hurting and killing people for their own pleasure."

"Yoshy, I'm scared!! Tell me they won't find or do what they want with us."

"Now, now, let me dry your eyes. Sit down on this comfortable lounging chair and take some deep breaths. I assure you, I won't let anything happen to my little doll." With gratitude and love, Robin took Yoshy's hands into her own and then brought them to her mouth, kissing them.

Nobuaki and Hiro went through each room thoroughly. With pistols drawn, they searched high and low and couldn't find the two people. They went into the master suite and saw the tell-tale signs that two people had left suddenly. The sheets were still warm and wet with sweat and liquid pleasures. "Where the fuck could they have gone?" Hiro asked his boss. Pushing Hiro, Nobuaki sarcastically remarked, "into the great blue yonder."

"Huh" Hiro stupidly remarked. "Never mind. Come, let's go downstairs to the basement. The door is ajar and they probably ran there, not realizing that they left the door open. Feeling for the switch to get light, Nobuaki found it and quicker than Hiro ever saw his boss move, followed him down the stairs, gun drawn, looking for their quest. The two men looked in every nook and cranny but didn't find the people they were looking for. "I know they're here. Where, is the question," Nobuaki remarked as he kicked the cement wall in frustration.

Meanwhile Suzanne and Nancy walked casually to Yoshy's front door, unaware of the drama being played out within the walls of this beautiful, secluded house that was hidden from the public. Suzanne whispered to Nancy, "I think you should knock and when they answer tell them that you came back to our salon and while in Japan wanted to stop by and say hello."

"That sounds good to me," agreed Nancy. Just as Nancy was about to tap on the door, she realized that it was ajar and motioned for Suzanne to take note." That's strange. A man like Mr. Yoshirhero wouldn't leave his front door open like this. Let's go inside Suzanne."

Nancy declared, "Are you crazy?" "If he's home with that girlfriend of his, it's the perfect opportunity to announce you're here and let them know that you found the front door open. I think that makes sense, don't you?"

"Weeell," with hesitation, Nancy didn't want to let this occasion go by the wayside. "I guess you're right. But if we find that they're not here, we're not going to wait for them to return. We'll come back at another time, after we call Rich and the guys. Agree to that and then I'll comply with your suggestion."

"You're such a dork sometimes. Yeh, yeh," as she pushed Nancy into the small but elegant foyer and then walked into the living room.

CHAPTER FORTY ONE

"Geez, Suzanne, this gives me the creeps."

"Stop being such a wimp. Call Mr. Makino's name and see if he answers. It's easy. Go on, just call out his name." Against her gut feeling she called for him. They both found nothing but quiet and an eerie element languishing throughout the cottage.

As the two women walked quietly through the rooms, they were astounded that no one was home. "This is very strange," Suzanne voiced her opinion. "See this bed here, it looks like there was a lot of action going on," Suzanne said as she lifted her eyebrows. "Feel, the bed is still warm and it looks like a good time was had by all!!" Waving her hand at her accomplice; "Oh Suzanne, all you ever think about is sex. There's more important things than that."

"Well, aren't you the prude. Who is it that whenever she comes in the company of a certain Detective, I can hear her heart go pitter patter and the redness on your face matches your hair."

"You know Suzanne, you can be such a jerk, sometimes."

"Face it, you love me," Suzanne spoke aloud, tousling Nancy's hair. "Okay, now I feel like Goldilocks, going into the three bear's cottage!!!!" Suzanne verbalized as they were about to leave the master suite.

Nobuaki thought he heard footsteps above and put a hand out to stop Hiro in his tracks. "Do you hear a noise upstairs, or is it my imagination?" Hiro listened intently and motioned with his head, bobbing up and down, that he heard the same sound as his boss. Pushing Hiro slightly, "Let's see if there's a way out of this basement, go around front and let's see who's upstairs."

"I'll shut the lights. Remember where the bulkhead is because it's dark in here." The cellar was large but they finally saw the partition a few feet away. Quietly, Hiro lifted the steel doors, the light from outside now illuminating the darkened cellar. He climbed the cement steps and waited for his boss to emerge. Leaving the doors open for fear of making further noise, he softly followed Nobuaki to the front of the house.

With guns held skillfully in hand, the two men quietly made their way through the house until they saw the two women conversing in the master bedroom suite. Motioning for Hiro to move aside he spied the women and pulled back, his body against the wall, knowing that he was unobserved. He whispered to Hiro, "That's the woman I met with Yoshy in the lobby of The Beverly Hills Hotel in Hollywood. I wonder what she's doing at Yoshy's house?"

"If you ask me boss, no good, that's why she's here. I don't like what I'm feeling." Shaking his head in frustration, Nobuaki motioned for Hiro to go into the room and if necessary, use force to find out who they are and what they're doing.

While conversing, Nancy and Suzanne didn't see Hiro enter the bedroom. Suddenly without warning, Nancy found an arm around her neck and a gun pressed against her back. It happened so fast that Suzanne was dumbfounded. "You," motioning to Suzanne, "Go against the wall, face it, hands up and shut your trap, understand Blondie?" Suzanne had all she could do not to start yelling at the humongous beast. Suzanne with all her effort closed her mouth, resigned to keep still and quiet. Her insides were quivering, and her head felt as if it were spinning out of control. Nancy was petrified.

"Who the hell are you and what the fuck do you think you're doing?" Nancy got up the courage to ask this ugly, fat man. "Shut the fuck up lady, if you know what's good for you." Suzanne never heard Nancy utter a swear and besides being taken by surprise by this maniac, she was more astonished by Nancy's foul language. Thinking to herself, 'being brought up in Dorchester, a long way from here, that word was always spoken, but to hear it come out of innocent Nancy's mouth, I can't believe it,' other ideas went through her mind. 'What's happening and how the hell are we going to get out of this mess?' Suzanne tried to assess the situation to herself as she held her hands up high, her sweaty palms pressed against the wall.

Suddenly another man emerged and Nancy recognized him. "Aren't you the man that Mr. Makino was with when I ran into him in the lobby of that hotel?"

"Shut up broad. I'll ask the questions." With a gun pointing at her, Nancy did as she was told. "Who the hell are you and your pal? Why are you in my friend's house?" Nobuaki asked as he pulled her by her long red hair. Nancy felt as if her neck would break and all her hair would come out of her scalp. Suzanne, seeing what this jerk was doing to her friend wanted to run into him with all her might. Like a full back, crush him and his friend to smithereens, stand over him, heel of shoe to his stomach after karate chopping them and see their guns skittering across the floor.

With this thought going through her mind, a giggle of apprehension and nerves emerged from her. She was mad at herself for not having the will power not to laugh when she was nervous. She heard the smaller man come over to her and punch her, with all his might, in the kidney. "Shit," she said out loud as the obvious leader told her to keep still, turn her head around to keep facing the wall or he'd permanently shut her up. Suzanne's kidney was throbbing and hurt so bad that red spots were forming in front of her eyes. She knew she had to stay in this position but wanted to crumble to the floor. "If you know what's good for you, you better shut up while the red head tells us why you're here or we'll re-arrange that pretty face of yours that no one will recognize it."

Nobuaki turned around to Hirohito and Nancy. Mr. Nobuaki told Hiro to close the door in case Yoshy returned. We don't want him to know that anyone is in his domain. While the drama started enfolding Suzanne couldn't help but think of the years of abuse Brian had afflicted upon her. 'Crap,' she thought, 'I've lived through more than this during my past experiences, I hope I'll be strong enough for both Nancy and me,' Her kidney and insides were burning like hell. The pain was excruciating. She wanted to lie on the ground but knowing if she did, the maniac might do more harm to both of them.

"I'm going to count to 20 and if you don't start telling me answers to my questions, there's going to be hell to pay. As a matter of fact, you'd wish you were in hell by the time I finish with the two of you." Nancy was scared as she never was in her entire life. She saw her life flash before her. As Hiro was slowly counting, Nancy tried to gather her thoughts. She had to say something that would appease them and yet she knew she couldn't tell them the truth. She deliberated whether to act like an innocent bystander, coming to visit Mr. Makino, because her business in Japan had finished earlier than expected.

She and Suzanne thought that they'd surprise him. 'Yes, that's how I'm going to play it. I can't tell them the truth. They're probably mixed up with the bad guys, hell, these are some of the bad guys and we'll be killed for sure.' Stuttering, Nancy gave them the rendition of her story. Luckily Suzanne was in the same room. She knew that Suzanne would collaborate whatever story she told them. For the first time in her life, she put her acting skills to work. She tried acting like Lucille Ball and become a ditz and a half. Performing that way, they couldn't think of her as a serious player and hopefully let them go.

Unfortunately for Nancy and Suzanne the two men weren't buying Nancy's story. Nobuaki motioned for Hiro. Hiro shoved Nancy and went to his leaders side. Making sure neither women heard their conversation he whispered in Hiro's ear. "Let's see how strong they are when they see each other get beaten up. Then they'll tell us the truth or if they keep their story in tack, I might let them go." With a deep bow, "Oyabun," Hiro asked, "We're really not going to let them off easy? They'll go running to the cops as fast as a jackrabbit. We have no other choice but to whack them and gut them like fish and throw them out to sea." "I agree, Hiro, but first we'll play with them like a cat with a mouse."

"Which one do you want to do first?" Hiro looked at both women and decided that he'd continue with the redhead. Hiro thought,' assuming I can't get any information out of her, I'll break her body into little pieces. Once the blonde sees her friend beaten she'd better tell me what I want to hear, or she'll be my next victim.' He took the gun from Nancy's back and redirected it to the side of her throat, cocking the gun. She thought, for sure that he'd kill her. "Please don't kill me," Begged Nancy, "I honestly don't know a thing that you want me to tell you. I'm too young to die."

"No such luck sweety, I have other plans for you." With that said, he hit her squarely in the stomach and Nancy doubled over with pain.

He then went higher on her body, with all his might, punched her diaphragm. Nancy could feel and hear her ribs breaking. "Now sweetie pie, tell uncle Hiro what you're really doing here. If you don't, your nose, oh such a pretty one, will be re-arranged across your face." With that said he slapped her hard with the handgun on the side of the face. She felt her cheek bone shatter. 'Oh my God', she thought, as she saw the blood pouring down her face and onto the floor. "I don't care if you kill me. I can't tell you anything else because what I told you is the truth. You have to believe me." He slapped her hard across the face then punched her mouth, some teeth flying onto the floor. She heard herself talking and knew that as she spoke blood was spurting out from her split lips. She wanted to faint and get it over with. Nancy felt as if she were in a nightmare; a living hell, with no return in sight.

Nancy didn't know if he could understand her mumbling; she barely recognized her voice or what she tried to say. "Kill me you fat pig. I'm telling you the truth. I can't help it if you don't believe me. Come on, finish up your job and get it over with." Nancy screamed or thought she did, but realized because of the terrible beating, her words sounded like gibberish. Nancy's words weren't coming out as coherently as she wanted them to. She sought to curl up and die. She saw a knife emerge from his inside pocket and realized that this goon wasn't going to make it easy for her. Nancy, in all her pain, thought she'd end up like a turkey at Thanksgiving. The last thing she remembered was darkness surrounding her. Torture was his intent. Suzanne, was in shock. She couldn't believe what was happening to Nancy. 'Oh my dear and pretty Nancy,' 'hang in there,' she kept yelling,' but nothing came out.

"Hey, blondie, you'll be up next and have your turn. What's happening to your friend will happen to you, maybe even worse so shut your fuckin mouth." Suzanne wanted to faint but mustered all her strength to somehow think of a way to stop these goons from killing her best friend and her. 'Why didn't we tell Rich our plans?By now he would have come to a conclusion and already be here with troops ready to help.' Hiro looked at his sharp knife. For some unknown reason, as he was about to put a deep incision underneath her cheek, towards her mouth, he stopped.

Nancy came to after fainting and found the pain excruciating. She started to dry heave, then actually throw up what little food she had in her system onto her clothes and floor. 'Oh God, oh God, let this nightmare be over she begged to herself and God.' Not one of tremendous religious beliefs, she found herself putting her prayers, spirit and body in God's hands, wisdom, charity and strength. After more questions from Hiro she stuck to her story and wouldn't let the bastard find out the truth. Hiro threw her to the side, like tossing away a rag doll. He then pulled Suzanne from the wall and looked her over, up and down, as if assessing a piece of meat. "So blondie, or why don't you tell me your name." Suzanne spit into Hiro's face and let the spiddle slowly creep down his face. "That wasn't a wise thing to do, you cunt. For that stupid move you'll want to die real fast. You know what, I won't let you. You'll go slow, torturous, then beg me to finish you off, you piece of shit."

Suzanne's ribs and kidneys were killing like a bitch, after he again punched her with all his might. She wouldn't let him know how frightened and in pain she was. 'For all the years I took Brian's abuse, I can hold on and make him work real hard to put me down,' Suzanne thought as he punched her, like a fighter punching a heavy punching bag with her stomach. She emitted a loud cough as the wind was knocked out of her, she felt as though she'd break in two. To herself she kept thinking, 'you think you're so tough, I've had the shit kicked out of me more times than you can imagine, I still lived to talk about it. '"Come on," she tried to talk, but mumbling was all she heard. Her breath labored, "Keep hurting two defenseless women who are telling you the truth."

"Don't you think after all I've seen and the way you beat Nancy and myself up," she whispered, not able to talk louder," we would have told you why we're here, and anything you want to know." Nobuaki motioned for Hiro to come over to him." I think they're telling us the truth. Let's tie them up individually like hogs, and let them die a natural death from the beatings and starvation. No one will find them, and when we're finished with Yoshy and his whore, the authorities will think that Yoshy murdered them."

"Good idea oyabun." Hiro tried propping them up. It was difficult because both women we no longer conscious. They were like two limp, wet rags. While tying them up he made sure to break each of their arms and kicked each one for good measure on their legs, making sure that they couldn't walk, even if they tried. He heard the bones shattering each time his boot came in contact with their legs.

By now, Rich was frantic. He gave the girls the specific task to call him. 'Where the hell are they?' he asked himself, the look of concern showing on his face. He called for a meeting with the other men working the case. "Gentlemen, I'm not going to beat around the bush. I'm frightened for my friends. They were to get in touch with me a while ago and I haven't heard from either of them. I'd like to go to the Island of Kyushu and then on to the city of Beppu. Tell me, how long will it will take for me to get there by air and then take transportation to Beppu?"

"First of all Rich, we'd never let you go there alone. Especially with the concern you have for your two women friends and accomplices.

We'll go in our own airplane and not have to wait for a commercial flight to take off. Once on the island it won't take us long to drive to Beppo. All in all about two, maybe two and a half hours, if we push it." Talking to everyone in the small, cramped office Mr T. told the officers to take as much ammunition as possible, and bring extra cartridges. "Let's get the hell out of here and make it fast. Oh yes, wear your riot gear as well. We don't know what we'll find once we get there." In Japanese Mr. T. spoke and waved his hands to the swat team to rush them out, literally motioning with his hands as he yelled, "Isoga Seru, Hayaku Shite, hurry hurry up!"

Mr. T. pulled Rich aside and assured him that the Tokūshū Kyūshū Butai are the primary counter terrorism unit under the Japanese police agency. "Rich it's like you have in the States, your swat team." Rich was beside himself with grief and urgency. In his mind he was worried sick about Nancy and Suzanne, one becoming his lover; he had plans to one day, soon, ask her to marry him. 'Why didn't they call me?' he kept asking himself. He was mad that he didn't act faster when they didn't get in touch with him or the authorities. He asked Mr. T. if he could put on one of the uniforms that the Tokūshū Kyūshū Butai were wearing. "I want to be there, right in the action, you know how I feel, don't you?" "Of course I do. I'm going to bend the rules. You can definitely wear one and be with us when we enter the house."

"Thanks"

All sorts of bad thoughts entered his mind as he sat beside his friend and companion, the head of Interpol, Mr. Sato Akura. Mr. Sato was quiet for a long time, after a while tapped Riche's knee cap, "Trust us, we won't let anything bad happen to your friends. We're well prepared and nothing will get in our way. We know our business." Rich felt a bit relieved when Mr. Sato spoke those words but thought to himself, 'Seeing is believing.' The other Interpol agents sat together, Tanaka Kenji and Ito Norio. They were talking low amongst themselves as they strategized their moves once they confronted Mr. Yoshirhiro. The other FBI agents sat quietly, internalizing their thoughts and then speaking quickly to each other. The men of the Tokūshū Kyūshū Butai were sitting by themselves, not a word spoken. After what seemed hours, the plane landed. They headed for the cars that were waiting for them in front of the hanger.

As Hiro was about to work Suzanne over again, Yoshy shook his shoulder. Wait, I think I hear the door opening. Put a gag into their mouths. Anything, go to a draw and grab something that will shut the two of them up. This is going to be fun when we get Yoshy and his whore. "Boss, the two women seem to be completely out cold. Still want me to gag them?"

"Yes, you imbecile, they're not going to be out forever. We'll dispose of them later or let them die here. Let's surprise Yoshy. I'm sure he'll be delighted at our unexpected visit." After gagging the two unconscious woman, Hiro joined Nobuaki with guns extended.

They waited patiently for Yoshy and Robin to enter the living room and make themselves comfortable. Yoshy was sitting on the sofa, his arm around Robin's shoulder, not noticing anything unusual. "I'm glad that we took precautions and went downstairs. No one would have been able to find us there. I think that whoever was at the door gave up and left." Robin looked into Yoshy's eyes and nodded her head in agreement. Nobuaki spoke softly in Hiro's ear. "Glad that I told you to close the door. They didn't even notice that anything is amiss." Hiro nodded his head.

Nobuaki, motioned for Hiro to follow him and walking silently, entered from behind the couch and slipped in front of his friend. With his gun extended a large smile crossed Nobuaki's face. Yoshy couldn't believe his eyes. The last person in the world he expected or wanted to see was this man of menace. With a surprised look upon his face, he addressed his old and longtime friend. Robin didn't know what to make of it all.

Yoshy was frightened when he saw his friend jump in front of him. "What are you doing here, and why the handgun pointed at us? I thought we are friends? Friends don't greet one another with a weapon in hand." Trying to make light of the situation Yoshy was talking nonsensical. He told Nobuaki: "Put down the handgun. I think you know of Robin, she'll go into the kitchen and get us all a cup of tea."

"That won't be necessary my friend." Addressing Robin while at the same time appeasing her, he told them both to stay put.

Taking the seat across from them, Nobuaki crossed his legs, the gun now lowered to the floor. Hiro remained standing with his gun aimed at the two people who his 'father' wanted eliminated. "So tell me, you were away for quite some time. I take it the two of you had a good vacation?" Yoshy didn't want to respond but knew if he didn't there would be hell to pay. "Yes my friend, we went on an extended holiday. I felt tired and need of a rest. You know my business is quite an enterprise and sometimes I get overwhelmed. Even though I have many people over-seeing the workers, it's ultimately up to me to make the final decisions on all matters." Yoshy didn't want to say as much, but out of nervous energy he rambled on about their vacation and at the same time of his business. Nobuaki sat still, smiling at Yoshy as Yoshy kept jibbering. Yoshy's hands were starting to sweat and he removed his arm from Robin's shoulder and wiped his palms on his trousers.

As the dialogue continued in the living area Suzanne was slowly coming out of her unconsciousness. She felt the piece of cloth, she presumed some sort of underwear, from the feel and size, pressed into her mouth. She was grateful that her eyes weren't covered because she would become panicky. As it was, she found it hard to breath. Her hands were tied in back of her. She looked over to where Nancy lay.

She didn't know if her dear friend and partner were dead or alive. Every bone in Suzanne's body ached and as she tried to wiggle herself to get free the pain was unbearable and found it impossible to do so. She struggled to untie her ropes. She wanted to go over to where Nancy was. After a fruitless effort she realized that her legs hurt like hell. She knew from previous experiences that her legs were broken. She found she couldn't undo the heavily knotted rope. Her arms, felt like knives with pain stabbing them every time she tried moving. She realized that they were limp and broken also. Suzanne saw that Nancy remained comatose. As much as she knew Nancy couldn't hear her, she kept saying softly, "don't worry honey, Rich will come here to save us." In her heart she wanted her words to reach God and come true but realistically thought that it was impossible.

As she was squirming, she realized there was more to her injuries than she first thought. It was agony. The excruciating injuries wouldn't stop her. The fear for Nancy made her more determined. Adrenaline kicked in after what seemed eternity. Ignoring the severe pain, she somehow managed to free the rope that was binding her. It seemed to take forever to get to her friend. She tried to quell her hurting body and fear, but found it impossible. Suzanne felt bile entering her esophagus, suddenly it spewed from her mouth.

She painstakingly reached her friend, slowly moving inch by inch. She gently patted Nancy's blood soaked hair. The tears were falling, like a river flowing over the large rocks, onto her face. She quietly and gently called out Nancy's name. She looked for any motion or breathing. She barely got to Nancy's wrist and tried feeling for a pulse. At first she felt nothing, but then she realized a faint throbbing under her fingers.

"Hold on honey, we'll get out of this mess, just hold on and I'll get you out of here." Suzanne voiced her optimism and prayed that it would come true. She realized that she was physically unable to remove Nancy from where they were. All she could hope for was a miracle. She closed her eyes, the while still affectionately stroking Nancy's red, wet, sticky hair with her own broken arm and hands. After what seemed hours, she heard a groan emit from Nancy. A smile crossed Suzanne's weary face.

"Honey, don't exert yourself, nod your head so I'll know you're conscious, okay?" She didn't know if Nancy heard her or not. After a while, she noticed Nancy trying to lift her head, but without any energy left in her withered body, she found she couldn't do so.

"It's going to be okay, honey," whispered Suzanne. She kept repeating the same sentence over and over again, wanting to believe what she was saying.

While Suzanne maintained her restrain from yelling for help, she tried listening for any voices in the other room.

Nobuaki was laughing inwardly at his friend's uneasy demeanor. He let Yoshy keep talking, all the while looking Robin over from her blonde hair, down to her beautiful, long, shapely legs. After listening to Yoshy's rambling he softly told him to be quiet. Yoshy barely heard his request. Nobuaki, more forcefully, told him once again to shut up. He looked over to Hiro and motioned for him to be by his side. Hiro obediently did so. Sweat was now pouring down Yoshy's back.

"I think I'm tired of listening to his gibberish and nonsense." As he addressed Hiro he commanded Yoshy to stand up. Yoshy obediently complied. His legs felt wobbly as he stood there, not knowing what Nobuaki had on his mind. A menacing grin adorned Nobuaki's mouth. "What you speak is nonsense. Shut your mouth or I'll have Hiro shut it for you." Nobuaki was getting impatient. "Hiro, bring this coward over to me." Hiro grabbed Yoshy's arm and pulled him to his boss. Nobuaki looked Yoshy over, knowing that he made Yoshy feel uncomfortable and awkward.

"You made me loose face. Do you realize how that appears to the people who look up to and respect me. You, you are a laugh. You're not a man, but a sickening imbecile. I don't like morons. You took advantage of our friendship, not caring about the consequence that might occur to me or my organization. I don't like to be made fun of. Do you understand?" Yoshy tried to dispute his intentions. Nobuaki slapped his face hard and saw Yoshy's spittle fly from his mouth. "Shut up, when I want you to say something, I'll tell you."

"Hiro, get his whore and bring her to me." Commanded Nobuaki. Addresssing Yoshy he mockingly told him what he intended to do to Robin. "I don't like you, I once did, but you benefited from my generosity. I'm sure you don't grasp the hurt that you bestowed upon me. I will not be taken advantage from no one. I'm going to have you watch my trusted saiko-komon, I think you know Hiro. But before Hiro does what he wants to do, I'm going to take your precious Robin and do with her whatever I want to, then if she lives Hiro will have his way with her. I'll be pleasured and you can feel the pain I'm inflicting on her. Feel shame, for you deserve it. We won't allow you to turn your head. You watch our pleasure and her pain. After he takes care of her, before I kill you, I'll make sure you Yubizume, (take off your finger). Although I'm supposed to accept your apology, after you give me your finger, I won't."

Nobuaki stood up and spit in Yoshy's face. "Anger has been building up in me for some time now. I feel like a giant pressure is going to explode in my body. Do you have any understanding about what I'm saying?" Yoshy stood still as he felt Nobuaki's spittle slide down the side of his face. "Leave Robin alone. She didn't have anything to do with our agreement. She did nothing. You can do with me as you want, but I plead with you, leave her alone."

Nobuaki laughed." I have no use for a woman, you should know that. They have big mouths and gossip all the time. If she were younger I'd take her and put her into one of my date clubs. Unfortunately, she's too old. Of course I might have made a lot of money showing my customers a white woman and a blonde to boot. What of your loyal wife. Does she know of your infidelity? She waits for you and keeps your home clean, brought your son up and is still a dutiful wife."

"That's what a real wife is, not a whore that you buy presents and keep her happy while she waits for you to take her out and then fuck her whenever you want to. No, my friend, you'll wish yourself death after you view what Hiro and I are going to do to your whore. When you see what happens to her, then you'll present me with your finger and I'll throw it away like I will dispose of you and your white ghost when the time comes."

Yoshy knew that whatever he said to this maniac, who is the oyabun of one of the largest yakuza organizations in all of Japan and The States, was of no consequence. It was a moot point. He didn't care what Hiro would, eventually, do to him. His concern was for Robin. 'Poor, innocent Robin, all she knew was to be loved by her savior and nothing else.' He wanted to die for her. He knew, realistically, that Nobuaki didn't have any feelings and would relish in the delight of their deaths.

Rich was moving about restlessly in his seat. He kept looking at his watch, anticipating their final arrival to Beppu. He realized that they'd have to drive like hell to get to Yoshy's hide-a-way before anything bad happened to Nancy and Suzanne. 'If something awful hasn't already happened,' he thought to himself. Mr. Tamamurō, sat silently beside Rich.

Richs' thoughts were being internalized and he didn't realize who or what was happening. Suddenly he felt a hand on his arm. "I know you're worrying my friend. There's nothing we can do until we get to Yoshy's house. Have faith Rich, we'll get there on time." Mr. T's gentle touch soothed Rich a bit. Although his mind was going all over the place, he had to rely on this group of prominent police men to save the women from the dire predictions that kept going through his mind.

Nobuaki nodded to Hiro to step aside. Suddenly Nobuaki grabbed Robin by her hair, bringing her in front of him. He quickly ripped off her top and then pushed her to expose her backside to him. He unhooked her bra and then turned her around again. Like a piece of meat, he inspected her from head to toe. He touched her lightly, as he moved his fingers up and down her body, stopping at her large, firm, uplifted breasts. He began to squeeze them harder and harder. He didn't say a word while he was manipulating his fingers on her breasts.

Robin tried to stifle her cries of despair but her body was shaking like a leaf in a rapid breeze. His hands were coarse, with stubby fingers that squeezed her breasts, as he sucked each nipple until they hardened and then bit them off. The blood spouting from her body. The damage was insurmountable. It hurt more than a mammogram vise in an ex-ray machine when she got her yearly breast exam. She tried stifling a cry but couldn't maintain her composure. She bit her lower lip till she could taste the blood oozing down her chin. When Nobuaki was through with her breasts he then took out his sharp bladed knife. Robin was petrified thinking what he would do to her with the cruel instrument. She turned her head towards Yoshy, the pleading in her eyes made him sick. He knew that he was rendered useless while being held at gun point by Hiro. With a wicked, merciless laugh, Nobuaki slightly put his knife in between her breasts. Pressing lightly, he punctured her skin letting the blood start oozing down her body and drop onto the floor.

Robin was mortified but didn't know what she could do in order to flee this psychopathic maniac. She tried wrenching free from his strong arms holding her right upper limb. It was to no avail. He only laughed his cruel merriment as his knife zigzagged down the length of her entire arm, stopping at her wrists. She couldn't contain her anger any longer and started yelling at this lunatic. "Stop this insanity. If you want to kill me just go ahead. But I promise, I'll haunt you day and night and you'll never have another peaceful moment in your life," sobbed Robin. She then spit directly into his eye. Blinded for a second, Nobuaki rubbed his eye and slapped her hard across her face. "No one does that to me, bitch."

"That was a fatal mistake. For that stupid move let Yoshy see what else I can do to you. He pushed her to the floor and mounted her. He pulled her stiff, closed legs apart and entered his extended penis into her. He rocked back and forth and forced himself not to climax. He then turned her over onto her stomach, and ordered her to go onto her knees. He then put his extended organ into her anus and could feel her ripping inside. He rocked harder and faster until he could feel the pent up liquid shoot into her. As he removed his organ he saw the blood from her anus along with his white semen. Blood from the other parts of her body were now forming in puddles onto the white rug.

CHAPTER FORTY TWO

He looked over at Yoshy who had tightly closed his eyes. He went to him and ordered him to open them. "Now I know why you enjoyed her company. She's built like a brick shit house. It felt good exploding in her. You must have felt the same way. No wonder you kept her as your whore." Yoshy cried out in despair, "I love her, kill me, but don't do any more harm to her. She's innocent of any wrong doing, I swear."

Hiro only laughed in his face as he told Yoshy his next intentions. "I'll make sure to press harder on her skin until her blood seeps faster and you can watch your loved one being cut up, piece by piece." With that comment, He called for Hiro. "Hold her right arm tightly. He pressed harder as the knife zigzagged downward. The blood seemed to spiral faster onto the floor. At that point Robin couldn't help herself but throw up onto herself and saw her own blood take on her vomit, like sawdust, seizing the blood from the butchered chickens. Suddenly, Robin looking at her own blood, felt her head spinning and all she felt was black enveloping her. She fell to the ground.

Yoshy kept yelling at the two men to stop torturing the love of his life. It went onto deaf ears. The tears were flowing from his face and his body was racked with pain at the sight of what was happening. His crying compulsively wracked his body with misery. "Kill me, you bastards, leave Robin alone. She had nothing to do with any of this. She's innocent of all the terrible crimes that I ordered." In her darkness, Robin didn't understand what Yoshy was talking about. Nobuaki and Hiro felt they were through with Yoshy's 'Robin'. Laughing to himself, Nobuaki looked down at her and said aloud to Yoshy, "Now she really looks like a dead Robin Red Breast." His laugh was that of an inhuman soul, the devil in disguise.

Suzanne could hear the yelling emanating from the other room. She felt sick to her stomach as she heard the sobbing and cries of the beautiful blond young woman. She remembered standing next to her at one of the stalls and could imagine or believe what was happening to this youthful, pretty maiden. Suzanne could feel her head spinning; all the while talking calmly and low to her friend. She prayed silently that Nancy come to and waited with bated breath until she could feel her best friend's pulse beat harder. Suddenly, a soft moan escaped from Nancy. She tried getting up, but to no avail. "Keep still honey, I'm with you. We've been hurt badly, but at least we're alive."

"The maniacs who did this to us are in the next room so I beg you not to make another sound, okay. If you can hear me, nod your head." Suzanne waited anxiously to see Nancy's head bob in recognition to her plea, but didn't see any movement. Her eyes didn't leave Nancy as she remained looking for a stir of some kind. She then went back to patting Nancy's head and talking soothingly to alleviate more fear than necessary. Suzanne, although in dire pain, didn't want to think of herself at that moment. She hoped that Rich and his police re-enforcements would get to them quickly. She didn't know the status of Rich's knowledge, but felt that if he didn't hear from his two accomplices he would think something was amiss.

Yoshy was going out of his mind. He couldn't stand seeing Robin in excruciating pain, crying out loud at every cut inflicted upon her. He didn't know if Robin had fainted or was dead. Looking at his beautiful Robin, knowing that his greed did this to her, his cries were like wolfs, howling, cutting through the night like a wounded animal or a call for his mate. Nobuaki had his gun pointed directly in line of Yoshy's head. He knew that his old friend would not hesitate to pull the trigger, ending his life. Yoshy realized that Nobuaki really thought that he betrayed him. Yoshy also struggled with the thought that if he didn't kill him immediately, he was in for the worst nightmare of his life. What he saw Robin go through would only be a fraction for what was ahead for him. Yoshy didn't care what happened, his life was now worthless.

Robin was young; had a whole life ahead of her. He saw her lay immobile, traumatized or dead. She had gone through hurt, humiliation, and despair. The life of her draining out of her body. Yoshy turned his head and closed his eyes, unable to bear to see the blood draining out from her body. He wanted to die himself realizing the pain that was rendered to his sweat, innocent little butterfly.

Yoshy's cries could be heard throughout the cabin. His pleading to Nobuaki to end his life was heartfelt and real.

Suzanne heard a crying and realized that it was Yoshy who was making this inhuman, merciless cry of despair. With that mission completed Hiro stood in front of Yoshy. As he was about to pull him up from his seat, Nobuaki put out his hand to stop him. "Hiro, go into the room where we left the two airheads. I thought I heard something coming from there. "He dropped Yoshy's shirt and threw him back onto the chair. Suzanne heard Hiro's footsteps coming towards their soon to be debacle. She quickly put her head onto the floor, feigning unconsciousness. Hiro quickly looked into the room and saw the two women still unmoving. He went back to report to his boss. "It looks like they won't be up for quite a while. They're out like a light."

"Okay, now let's get to our friend here."

Moving his hands and palms back and forth in acknowledgment of enjoyment, Hiro pulled Yoshy up by his shirt. Looking at Yoshy, Nobuaki ordered him to open his eyes and observe Robin. His heartfelt sobs and outward crying fell on deaf ears. Nobuaki's unfeeling and unconcerned emotions couldn't be penetrated. "Now, my friend, you are going to know what pain really feels like. You saw what your whore went through. You'll be experiencing 100 times more anguish than you ever thought possible."

"Do with me what you want. Don't you ever call me your friend. I'm already dead. You killed the one person who I ever cared for and loved. Without her I have no life. "Nobuaki laughed out loud and with defiance, nodded his head for Hiro to commence his torture.

When Suzanne realized that Hiro was no longer in view, she raised her head. She was thankful that the large, unmerciful, inhuman, brute could not observe her defiance. She again, quietly, coaxed Nancy to show some kind of consciousness. Without as much as a groan, Nancy tried lifting her head. "Good honey, I'm proud of you. I want you to put your head back down and continue to act unconscious. I'm here with you. We're both badly injured but we'll get out of here shortly." Thinking to herself she kept praying for Rich and his associates to get to them as quickly as possible. 'Meanwhile, what the hell am I going to do if he doesn't get here soon? Nancy and I are immobile. If only I could pull myself out. But where the hell do I go? There's no way out, but through the front door from where we are. '

Rich was seated beside Mr. T. Rich couldn't read what Mr. T. was thinking because the look on his face was impassive. Rich looked around at the other gentlemen in the same car, also with stoical expressions. He couldn't get a feeling on their thoughts. Rich wasn't about to interrupt them. He tried calming himself, but to no avail. He quelled his desire to yell at them, talk to him and tell him the speculation of their mission.

He told himself to breathe deeply. 'Inhale, exhale, keep doing this.' He constantly chanted, to himself, the serenity prayer, hoping that this would calm his anxiety of what was to come. Rich constantly looked at his watch, wishing the hands would move quicker. "We're almost there, only another ten minutes or so," said Mr. Kenji. "Make sure your guns are ready and loaded," Sato told the men in his lead vehicle. The other three vehicles were behind them with the local police and the rest of the men from the F. B. I. and Swat Team. 'Please, get there on time, I can't let anything happen to Nancy or Suzanne.' He bit his bottom lip till he tasted the blood ooze ever so slightly from it. His nerves were shot to hell.

"Hiro, I want to first see Yoshy cut off every finger, one at a time. Make sure that the gun is against his head. If he tries anything to hurt you in the process feel free to either kill him or beat him, slowly to death."

With that said, Hiro gave Yoshy an extremely dull knife. He saw Yoshy quiver as he tried sawing each finger. Yoshy had a hard time because the knife was very dull. Hiro got impatient and after looking at him unsuccessfully maim himself, Hiro asked his boss, "Could you look after him while I get something to make this operation go faster? "Hiro got a large ax that he saw in the kitchen. "Be fast about it. I don't want to waste unnecessary time with this piece of shit," he commanded his head man. 'So, how does it feel to be the victim? Not nice."

"I thought I could trust you, but like others, you disobeyed my command. Now you'll know what pain is all about." Yoshy's entire body was shaking. Addressing Nobuaki, "How could you do such inhuman acts? Robin did nothing. You wouldn't listen to any explanation." As Yoshy talked to Nobuaki he could feel the pain in the joints of his fingers. The blood was slowly coming out from where he tried, unsuccessfully, to dismember his finger.

They heard Hiro return and saw the implement in his hands. The ax was very sharp and when Yoshy saw it he wanted to crawl into a hole, never to be seen again. His imagination went rampant. He closed his eyes. "Open your eyes, you coward." Hiro commanded. Yoshy kept his eyes shut, knowing that even if he opened them it wouldn't matter. Hiro was on a mission. His life was over. Hiro put the ax on the floor and punched Yoshy squarely in the stomach. Yoshy lost his breath and the pain was excruciating. Then Hiro went onto punching his ribs and felt them break upon the deftly hard placed punches. He then jabbed him and hit both kidneys with a terrible force.

Yoshy felt faint and wanted to fall to the floor, put himself into a fetal position and die. Hiro wouldn't let Yoshy do as he wanted. Pulling Yoshy up he kept punching him all over, like a fighter using a punching bag. This time the punching bag was Yoshy's body. Without as much as a blink of the eye, Hiro deftly picked up the sharp ax and at the same time, with one hand, lifted Yoshy from the ground. Suzanne and Nancy heard Yoshy scream, as if he were seeing the devil himself. His screams were so loud that both Hiro and Nobuaki almost blocked their ears from the pain that was invading their ear drums.

Hiro chopped off, in one swing, the fingers on Yoshy's left hand. The blood came pouring out. Then within a second later, he deftly swung the ax again, dismembering the fingers on the right hand. "I'm not through yet, you asshole," Hiro yelled. He was getting angrier by the minute. Hiro kept thinking of the disloyalty Yoshy rendered to his leader and the unnecessary work that he had to do to eradicate the wrongful act that Yoshy displayed. With those thoughts in mind, he took the left arm and bent it back until the snap of the bone could be heard within the room. A screeching, like Suzannne never heard, emerged from what seemed the depths of his soul. It fell on deaf ears as Hiro mirrored his act to his right arm. Yoshy thought that he'd faint from the pain he was experiencing.

He was coughing up blood and knew that his internal injuries were serious. He knew he would meet his maker shortly. He yelled out the numbers 5508 and said out loud, "Akuma." Nobuaki and Hiro looked at each other when they heard Yoshy's constant chant. They were aware of the name Akuma and the mystic number it represented. Realizing that Yoshy was prepared for death, didn't serve to satisfy their lust for increasing Yoshy's torment. Akuma was the mythology of demons with flaming heads, fiery eyes and swords. They assumed that their enemy, Yoshy, knew that he was heading to the land where Akuma was the demon. He was ready to face Akuma. "Kill me now you cowards, I'm ready. I will see you there also, you pieces of shit."

Again closing his eyes he waited for the gun fire, knife, or strangulation that would end his life. The mystic Akuma was visualized in front of him. "One last thing I want to do, if it's okay with you, my oyabun?"

"Do whatever you want to this piece of garbage." With that heard Hiro lifted his ax and dismembered the shriveled penis before him. "Now he is truly not a man." Before leaving, Hero turned around, lifted his gun and shot Yoshy through the head. Brain matter splattered everywhere. "Very good Hiro, let's get out of here. Our work is done for the day."

Mr. T. had his driver call the local police to have them ready. The men in the cars were all set to put their riot gear on as soon as the cars stopped. They were prepared for any battle that they envisioned may occur. Rich could tell that the driver was coming to a stop and without hesitation jumped out of the immobile car. He felt a hand on his shoulder. Ito Masso was nodding his head back and forth to Rich.

"First you put on this gear. We don't know what lies ahead my friend. The good people of Japan don't want anything to happen to you. This situation might be worse than we anticipated. On the other hand, hopefully, we won't have a struggle with many enemies in the house." Rich obeyed. Talking quietly to the men, who were now in gear for any given situation, they all assumed their pre-instructed positions.

"Wait, I want to go in there with the first team," Rich spoke as soft as possible to Mr. T.. Mr. T. looked at the Interpol men and the head man, Mr. Akira, nodded his head in assent. Mr. Akira then walked over to Rich and put his hands on Rich's shoulders. "May the god of fortunate warriors and guards be with you. Bishamonten will be with you to punish the criminals you seek. I will pray for all of us."

"Shechi Fuku. Jin." Mr. Tamamorō whispered in Rich's ear before he headed for the elaborate wooden door. One of the Interpol men, accompaning Rich spoke softly and pointed, "I'll take this side, you take the other side of the door. We won't bother to ring or knock. You think you can kick the door down. If not, I'll get Ito to do it for us."

"Are you kidding. This door is solid. There's no way in hell I can do it. I'm good, but I'm used to doors that are not built as solid as this one."

The head of Interpol, Mr. Akira motioned for Ito Masso to come forth and with hand gestures told him what he wanted done. "No problem." Mr. T. explained to Rich that Ito Masso was a known world champion in Japan for the art of Taekwondo. "He's excellent in his naranhi sogi, a front snap kick or a neutral stance from where a variety of kicks are done."

"I'll have to take some lessons from Ito when this operation is finished. Let's hope Ito can break this heavy wooden door down. To me it looks like it belongs as the front door to a wooden English castle," Rich told his friend and confidant. Mr. T. smiled and gave a gesture for Rich to watch Ito Masso perform his brilliance.

Ito Masso, with one quick kick the door was chopped, split in two and knocked down from its solid brass hinges. Rich didn't know what his partner was saying. It was foreign language to him. All he heard was Japanese words, yelling and then the fire of guns were being exchanged.

When Nobuaki saw the front door fall in, he and Hiro ran and took cover in back of the seating arrangements in the living room. They knew the circumstances that lay ahead.

Suzanne and Nancy heard the gunfire and knew that there was serious trouble out in the main living quarter of the house. Suzanne dragged her broken body to Nancy and tried pulling Nancy under the high bed. The pain that both women were experiencing was unbearable but necessary. Suzanne wanted them to be out of harm's way. Suzanne could see the bloody path, but at that point, she didn't care.

Rich and his cohorts crouched down and aimed at the two men who were hiding behind the furniture. Rich saw one local policeman fall down. He saw blood coming from his shoulder and was thankful that an organ wasn't hit. Suddenly, the crashing of windows was heard and two more groups of men came barging into the battle ground.

Nobuaki didn't want to die this disgraceful way. He knew that there were too many men for him to fight off. He could try to run to the bedroom and use the two women as hostages. 'If I can run quick enough I have a chance to make it,' he thought to himself. Leaving Hiro to fend for himself, he crouched down and ran as fast as he could into the bedroom, avoiding the barrage of bullets coming at him. The Japanese police force, along with the FBI and Interpol were shouting for Hiro to come out from hiding or they would shoot him dead. "Not before some of you, would be heroes, will die from my gun." Without warning Rich saw the barrel of the gun from behind the chair. Hiro was firing as fast as he could at anyone moving toward him.

With all his bullets, none of them penetrated his enemy's heavy armored suits. Hiro's head was swimming with thoughts, none of which made sense. He knew he didn't want to be caught, indicted, and sent to prison. If that did happen, he realized when it was time to be released from prison. He would be looked upon as a hero amongst his peers. He came to the realization that when interrogated by the police he would say nothing. They could torture him to their hearts content, but he remembered the oath he took and would abide by it. They'd never get any information from his lips.

Without warning he threw his gun in front of the chair and slowly got up, his hands in the air. He was speaking in Japanese, a language unknown to Rich. Apparently the other enforcement agents were conversing with this massive man. Two men ran towards Hiro, grabbed him by his jacket and pulled him outside, all the while speaking rapidly. When handcuffed and pushed into the back of the patrol car he then realized that they couldn't accuse him for the murder of Yoshy and Robbin. His Oyabun would most certainly be felled and probably killed. The authorities had no idea who caused the demise of the man and woman lying sprawled on the bloody floor, not a heartbeat between them. If anything, he would be convicted of an accessory to murder which wasn't as bad as first degree murder.

Rich was still worried about Nancy and Suzanne. After stepping over the two people lying on the floor, he only wanted to save his two dear friends, one he hoped to become his future wife.

He saw the other man run into the bedroom. All negative thoughts were in his mind as he slowly got up and approached the door leading to the room. His back was against the hallway wall, he slowly peeked around the door frame watching the man holding a gun that was aimed under the bed. Rich automatically assumed that's where the two women were. He didn't know how many men were in the room and was waiting until he cleared his mind on what he would do.

Without warning he saw the window above the side of the bed being blown in by powerful shotgun blasts. He yelled but couldn't be heard amongst the commotion. He knew that his two friends were in there. He saw Mr. T. emerge from the basement; with an affirmative nod that no one was downstairs. Rich explained that the two women were in this room, didn't know their condition and certainly didn't want any more harm done to them. Mr. T. ran to the side of the house yelling for the rest of the troops to cease their fire

Nobuaki moved his gun and told them to get out from under the bed. It took them awhile to emerge from their refuge. Both women were experiencing immense pain which made their every movement unbearable. "Hurry up,"

Yelling incessantly for the woman to hasten their departure from where they felt safe. "Come on, come on, I'll put a bullet through you this very minute if you don't make it fast."

The woman, through their physical agony, tried moving quicker. They couldn't help but moan out loud with every inch they took. When they finally emerged Nobuaki realized that they couldn't stand in a prone position. He lowered himself to their level and yelled to the enforcement officers to stop their barrage of gunfire. "I've got your two women with me. My gun is pointing at their foreheads. If you don't get out of here and allow me to leave I'll blow their brains out. Do you hear me?" Rich was beside himself with worry.

He looked at the officers, who he considered his friends, and whispered, "What are we going to do?" The man in charge answered, "We've no choice if you want your accomplices to stay alive. I don't know who's threatening them. We're not sure if it's Mr. Makino or someone else."

"That's just great," exclaimed Rich. Sato Akura spoke to the other gentlemen and gave them precise orders to back off. "I want a few men to remain with me, the rest of you are to leave so he thinks we took his deal. In a low voice he told Kato Satoshi, the head of the Special Forces division of the local police department, to get his men ready.

"Make sure that you have your best man, with skills in sniper and long range firing, to get ready in camouflage and be ready to fire at my command."

"Yes, Mr. Akura, it is done." He then spoke to his men, telling them exactly what the plans were.

Nobuaki crouched closer to Nancy and Suzanne and warned them not to utter a sound. They heard his threat and knew he meant business. "All my men are leaving. What do you want from us? You assured me that the two women would be unharmed. I presume you are a man of your word," Detective Akura yelled to the man in the other room. Nobuaki's mind was quickly turning. He realized that he couldn't take two hostages out in their condition. While wondering which one to take, Suzanne spoke to him as calmly as she could.

"Mr. whoever you are, I heard your demands to the police. You know you don't have a chance in hell."

"Shut the fuck up you bitch." Suddenly, Nobuaki knew what he had to do. "Bitch, I'm going to hold you up and take you with me for my protection. If you make any move to get away from me, you can consider yourself dead. I won't hesitate to put a bullet through your heart. Understand what I'm saying?" Trying to buy some time, Suzanne struggled to keep him in conversation. "My name is Suzanne, not bitch. If you take me, at least tell me who you are."

"Shut the fuck up. I'm the one in control. You know nothing. You're a useless bitch and when I'm through with what I need from you, you can consider yourself dead meat. Understand?" Suzanne was trembling with concern and worry. Her complete life past through her mind as she prepared to do as he said. The tears were flowing freely as she thought of her parents, her children, the grandchildren she'd never know, Mrs. Walsh and of course her many friends that she'd hadn't said goodbye to and told them how much they meant to her.

Suddenly, she thought of Stephen and realized that before this moment she hadn't thought of him, once. 'That must be a sign of some sort,' she realized as she knew she had to be the one to surrender to this madman. If anyone were to die, she wanted to be the one. 'Nancy is young and has a long life ahead of her,' she thought as she pronounced, "Let's get this over with you asshole." She tried to lift herself up, but her broken legs wouldn't hold her. Nobuaki, lifted her up and kept the gun trained on her all the while. "I'm going to lift you in my arms, and if you try anything to get away, I won't hesitate to use this gun on you."

"Hey, Mr. Policeman, or whoever you are. I want a helicopter brought to me. I want the pilot not to be armed or you can say goodbye to both this blondie and the pilot. How long will it take to get the chopper here?" Nobuaki yelled out as he asked Head Detective Akura. Nobuaki had no knowledge that the man he was negotiating with was the head of Interpol operations. "I'll call ahead and find out what you want to know. Don't harm these women and the pilot will be unarmed. We will adhere to your demands. Just don't do anything foolish." With those words spoken, Sato Akura spoke into the portable phone with the exact directions demanded of him. "I just spoke to the pilot of the chopper. It won't be more than fifteen minutes. Let me speak to the two women. I have to know that you haven't already killed them and I have to have your assurance that they won't be harmed by you in any way."

Nobuaki was thinking only of himself, then suddenly thought of Hiro." One more question. What happened to my partner?" he asked.

"We have him in our custody. He's unharmed, I assure you."

Nobuaki knew that Hiro wouldn't talk about the Yakuza or give them any information. Hiro wasn't a fool. He realized the connections and what would be done to him if he ratted on his family in any way. "Okay, I want to be assured that he's not harmed, understand me? You pig."

"Yes, yes, now let me talk to the women."

Nobuaki waved the gun in front of Suzanne and Nancy. "You heard him. Tell him you're here and declare that you're fine. Red, you speak first," he demanded of Nancy. She yelled out that she was fine and will be okay. She was talking as loud as possible under the circumstance of the pain she was experiencing. "Now you, blondie, do the same."

Suzanne knew she had no choice and did as she was asked. All the while she kept praying to God and asked Him that the madman wouldn't kill her when this was all said and done. Suzanne prayed, 'Please, please, let us live through this horrible nightmare, dear God.' Suzanne kept her eyes closed and tried not to think of the terrible acts that this man could do to them.

The head of the Swat team was in the tree. He hoped the branch he was on would sustain his weight. From his position he could easily fire his gun and have the bullet enter this man's hand and the gun would fly out of harm's way. He waited patiently for his boss to give him the go ahead to perform what he does best.

Rich heard the helicopter approaching and was thinking of Nancy and Suzanne and the torment they were experiencing. He knew that they were brave but wondered to himself if they realized how courageous they had to be. As a police officer and detective, he vowed his oath to protect the people of the community. These women were doing this act of heroics only for their own debt to society. He couldn't get over how wonderful they were to do this for their own piece of mind, to help people in time of need. They were truly do-gooders. He knew their philosophy of doing unto others as you'd want them to do to you. They took this idealism to an extreme, he thought, as he heard and saw the chopper land in front of the palatial cabin.

The marksman was camouflaged well. He was ready and able to do whatever necessary to bring down this mad man. He knew he had only this one shot to obtain his goal. He didn't want any harm or, God forbid, any deaths to occur to the hostages. Patiently he waited for the signal to fire. Finally he saw the man emerge from the cabin, holding a woman in his arms. He realized he couldn't take a chance in aiming any other place than this man's head. The bully's hands were under the blonde woman. He didn't want to take any chances of wounding the hostage.

Of course, there was always a chance of botching the assignment, but prayed to Hachiman-shin to protect the injured hostage and for himself to have courage to be on target. Accuracy had to be on his side. Looking through the telescopic view finder he waited patiently until the man was about to get into the open door of the chopper. He had complete concentration and was focused on the enemy. Suddenly there was a flapping of wings above his head. He tried ignoring the sound but quickly looked up. A dove was soaring over his head, consistently circling above. A big smile emerged on his face realizing that Hachiman-shin had sent his messenger to tell him that he was looking over him. He again concentrated on his job.

Realizing that at that point the man had no other choice but to hand the woman to either the pilot or put her on the floor and step over her. This was his only chance to kill the bastard. He took a deep breath and waited patiently until he was assured that the target could be felled with one bullet.

Suzanne felt faint. She knew that she was going to die one way or the other. The pain was excruciating, nothing like she had ever felt. 'Well, I certainly got myself in one hell of a mess,' Suzanne thought to herself. Suddenly a loud noise occurred, at the exact moment as the man that held her in his arms dropped her onto the floor of the helicopter. The only indication that something terrible had happened was she saw something fly by her, landing on the inside wall of the whirlybird. Another bullet passed her and she saw a red blood stain in the middle of his forehead.

She felt a spray of blood on her body and realized that the man holding her had fallen next to her. The last thing she saw was a large hole in the man's head. His brain matter was oozing out. There was a loud commotion as she tried to understand what was happening. The next thing Suzanne could see was blackness encircling her entire being. She didn't feel a thing and thought that she was at heaven's door.

CHAPTER FORTY THREE

His mind a blur, he followed the ambulance to the Kyushu University Hospital at Beppu. Rich was walking back and forth in the hospital's waiting room. The carpet was showing an indication of a path that was worn into the fibers of the rug, from him and all the other people, who had been waiting for the results of their loved ones. The surgeons and God were the only ones who held the lives of the people that they cherish, in their hands.

At the same time that Rich' life was on hold, his mind only being for the concern of Nancy and her best friend, a complete investigation was going on at the elaborate cabin in Beppu.

Sato Akura headed the investigation. He instructed his men to go through the house with a fine tooth comb. "I don't want anything overlooked. This refuge, most likely, is the place where Mr. Makino felt was safe to store the stolen art and artifacts. That is unless he had another place that he felt was safer than here. The bodies, as you know, Mr. Makino and the unidentified woman, are in the morgue. When the police are finished with the interrogation of the large, heavy set man, we'll find out the name of the man who was killed in the chopper and as much information as possible."

"Mr. Makino's wife and son have been notified and I expect them to come to the hospital and identify the body within the day. I doubt if she knows anything about his secret life, but one never knows. We can hope that she will be able to help us find out more information. Only time will tell," he told the other agents, Tanaka Kenjo and Ito Norio, who were in charge of the other men. They had the job of finding where the objects were being hidden. Sato Akura told the others that Mr. Makino might have had another location where he hid more stolen objects and paintings. The authorities were to do a thorough investigation here and all over Japan. They were to look through all records and his computers to find if he had holding companies that he used to purchase other properties in other corporate names.

Mr. Tamamurō, head of the FBI in Japan wanted his men to help in the search. He instructed them to listen to the men from Interpol and be of any assistance as needed. Mr. Tamamurō left his men and went to the hospital to be with his friend, Rich Colangelo. He considered Rich a friend, more than an acquaintance, and realized that Rich needed him for support in the ordeal he was facing at the moment.

The FBI and Interpol were not leaving a stone unturned. They took one room at a time and examined everything, from objects that could be moved to stationary walls, bookcases, and floors that looked, as far as the naked eye could tell, fixed and part of the building of the original construction. After the initial rooms were assessed and deemed useless, they then went into the basement to do the same microscopic examination.

One if the Interpol men asked Mr. Kenji to look at a piece of concrete that didn't look the same as the rest of the basement's floor. "I had the men pull up the carpet and on our hands and knees inspected every inch of concrete that covered the basement. The piece in question is lighter than the rest and it seems that a person can lift it up. Let's get a crow bar, and see what we find."

"Good observation, let's begin the work."

It took all of five minutes to remove the cement. They found a staircase leading down to another level under the basement floor. When the men went down the staircase they noticed another entrance as well. Their mouths were agape, like seeing an aberration before them. The room was furnished with a beautiful, large rosewood desk, matching leather and rosewood armed chair and a modern large television attached to the wall. Surround speakers were installed throughout the ceiling. There was another door and upon opening it they saw the most remarkable collection of paintings and period pieces, one would find in museums from around the world.

After many hours of surgery the surgeon finally emerged from the swinging door. Rich and Mr. T. couldn't read his face for the outcome of the surgeries on the two women. Rich hadn't called Suzanne's relatives as yet, wanting to notify them of what the prognosis would be. Looking around the room, at the various family members of other patients, he hesitantly approached Rich. "Excuse me, are you Detective Colango and Mr. Tamamurō from the FBI and the San Diego homicide division?" Both men nodded their heads in unison. "Please sit down."

At this point the both men didn't know what the surgeon would inform them. It was like an expectant mother, not knowing the outcome of the child after carrying the baby for nine months. Extending his hand he shook theirs and introduced himself. "I'm Dr. Yamada, head of surgery in the hospital. Your two woman accomplices, I take it, are two lucky women." Rich's smile was beaming. "Don't be so happy, just yet. We finished most of the surgeries, but they have to go through more to finish the job correctly. They were in very bad shape when they were brought into the O. R. It was touch and go for a while."

"The women are fortunate that some very special doctors from America and other parts of the world, are visiting. We always have symposiums, doctors from all over the world come to our hospital and in turn we go to theirs to learn and co-operate with the latest techniques in medicine and surgery. We happened to have some special orthopedic doctors from the States and an eminent plastic surgeon with us. Our own doctors were able to operate on the internal injuries that the two women sustained. Needless to say, they aren't through yet or out of the woods."

"There are a few more operations that they have to undergo to make them whole again." Rich had all sorts of questions that he wanted answered but realized, from what the doctor was telling him, that he had to wait until the doctor finished his speech or couldn't answer questions that weren't answerable. "They're in I.C.U. and will be monitored closely. I'm going to give them a chance to recover from their exceptionally long operations and then, when we feel they're stronger and ready, we will bring them back for more surgeries."

"We don't know how many times they'll have to go into the operating rooms for more procedures. We hope that these operations will be soon. We had plastic surgeons, orthopedic men and I'm a general surgeon that specializes in internal injuries. Right now they're heavily sedated, and it will be hours before they can see anyone. If you give me your numbers, I'll call you when they're ready and awake to see you."

Rich cleared his throat. "Doctor, I know that they're out of it now, but is there any chance that I can view them from outside their rooms. You see, they're my partners, I feel responsible for what happened to them." He wanted to beg, but knew it would be useless, unless the doctor had any sensitivity in his body. After thinking the question over in his mind, he told Rich and Mr. Tamamurō to follow him.

Looking back at the gentlemen walking behind him, he turned around and said, "This is an unusual circumstance. I think you can see them for a few minutes. But only for a few." Dr. Yamada was about to leave I. C. U. , after writing down in the patients charts, instructions for the nurses. "Now remember, don't abuse my consent. I'll call you when they come out of the anesthesia." Rich closed his eyes and thanked God that they came out of the operations and lived to see another sunset. He realized they weren't out of the woods and still had to undergo more operations, with many months of rehabilitation necessary for them to get back to their original selves.

When he and Mr. T. went into the women's rooms they didn't recognize the two patients that lay in their hospital beds. Mr. T. put his arm around Rich, as a father would his son when comforting him. "Don't be shocked Rich, this is normal for the type of injuries that they sustained. The bandages and the breathing tubes are normal procedures." "But I can't tell under all the gauze what their faces look like. They seem so swollen and deformed, I can't envision them looking like the same people that I know. They look like disfigured mummies." Rich was not ashamed to cry on Mr. T's shoulder.

"We're lucky that they're alive. You'll see, they'll be back to normal in a while. Just have patience and all will work out." Their arms and legs are in traction with heavy casts." A lonely tear ran down his cheek. "Let's go my friend. They need their rest. The doctor will call you when they wake. But when you go to see them, don't have an expression of horror on your face, okay?"

"I wouldn't do that. They're hurting enough. Don't worry, I'll be optimistic and they won't know how bad they really look. I assure you, I could have been an actor, if I wanted to." Mr. Tomamorō smiled and slapped Rich on the back." Come on Rambo, I'll bring you for a cup of tea. It will make you feel better."

"I think I need more than a cup of tea. Something like a shot of whiskey will do."

"Whatever."

It took a while for Suzanne to wake up from the anesthesia. She felt like hell. She saw her arms and legs in contraptions and felt like a piece of meat going to be slaughtered. She tried to move a bit but was too weak to do so. When she managed to move she felt as if a truck was sitting on top of her. The nurse came in and Suzanne tried, but found it difficult to speak. In what sounded like garbled language she attempted to ask the nurse in charge questions about Nancy.

"Young lady, I think you'd better worry about yourself. Yes, your friend is in the next room and she's doing as well as can be expected." Suzanne couldn't understand her that well, but surmised what she was saying. "What does that mean?"

"It means that the two of you are lucky to be alive and talking to me. You need your rest and that will help tremendously."

"Do me a favor Suzanne, try not to talk because your jaw is wired and you have breathing tubes. Get rest and shortly communication with the outside world will be a heck of a lot easier than it is now." She smiled as she left the room and told her patient that she'd be checking on her constantly. "Your room is behind our desk so we can monitor you and Nancy all the time."

"I'll be coming in with a shot to put you at ease and very soon you'll be asleep. If you're wondering what those tubes are going from your arms to your body, they're antibiotics and fluids. You won't be able to eat regular food, so until you do, the liquids have to suffice for a while. Unfortunately, you don't have a choice in the matter." With that statement the nurse left the room. Suzanne waited anxiously for her to return and administer the necessary drugs that would put her in la la land.

Rich waited patiently for the doctor to call. He debated if he should call Suzanne's relatives and decided, with the time difference, he'd wait until it was morning in the States. He pondered how he would tell them about their daughter and mother. If he remembered correctly, Suzanne hadn't revealed her undercover mission to any of her family. He didn't know how to explain it. He hoped Suzanne would be awake enough to tell him what to say.

While Rich was contemplating on what he would say to Suzanne's relatives there was a knock on his hotel room door. He saw Mr. Tamamurō thru the peep hole and let him in. Mr. T. bowed as did Rich and then shook hands. "Have a seat." Rich motioned for his friend so sit down on the comfortable oversized chair. "I wanted to personally come over and tell you what's been going on at our end. We found out who everyone was. It seems that Mr. Makino didn't survive the beatings and enormous disfigurements rendered him. He died, apparently, immediately."

"If he had lived I know we would have found out the illogical acts that caused all these needless killings. Oh yes, one of the men found a hidden staircase that led to a complete other area in the basement. It was overwhelming. The paintings and artifacts were hidden treasures that left us speechless."

"That's crazy," announced Rich. "I know a gentleman who can help us determine what and where some of these pieces come from,"

Mr. T. interjected. "Men from the FBI have a special Art Crime Team. I think it began in 2003. Anyway, we were aware that the theft of individual works of art, also from Museums, was a growing international crime problem. People and gangs were illegally exporting objects and pillaging archaeological sites. We had cooperation at all levels of law enforcement. The FBI's Art Theft Program assists law enforcement agencies worldwide. It's supported by the National Stolen Art File, it's a computerized database of stolen art and cultural property that's reported to the FBI by U. S. and international law enforcement officials."

Rich knew that Art theft was a big international business but never thought it was as extensive as Mr. T. was telling him. "Well, then, I guess I won't have to get in touch with Justin. He's the gentleman that I know who could have helped us.

By what you're telling me, you guys have a good handle on the situation." Rich got up from the sofa and slapped Mr. T. gently on his shoulder.

"Seriously, I don't know what I and the girls could have done without you and your men's cooperation. When this horrific situation is finally at its end, we'll go out and celebrate. My treat of course." Mr. Tomamurō smiled broadly, and nodded his head. Laughing he said, "I can't wait till that day comes, my friend." Rich nodded his head in agreement and said, "Come, let's go to the hospital and see how the girls are doing."

Back in the States, Hope, Melanie, and Taylor were beside themselves with worry. As soon as they received the call from Rich they immediately called Dorothy and Morris. The girls went over to their grandparent's house and discussed the situation at length. They all wanted to go and see Suzanne and Nancy but realized the impracticality of it. Even if they utilized the private corporate jet, they needed people who could run the many offices throughout the States and foreign countries.

When all was said and done, Dorothy made the proclamation that she would be the one to attend to her daughter and Nancy, who she figured was like a daughter to her as well. "I'm not going to hear any arguments from any of you. Mrs. Walsh and I are going and that's all there is to it. "Mrs. Walsh was speechless. She hadn't said a word throughout the entire dialogue and listened intently on what was said.

Never in a million years did she expect to be included in Dorothy's plan. "Well, well, of course Dorothy. You know how I feel as if I'm part of the family. I'm just overwhelmed emotionally. It's an awful way to realize how much you think of me, but in the same way, what a terrible circumstance this entire ordeal has become. If I knew the danger that these girls were going to be in, I would have done my darndest to stop them."

"That's a great statement, Mrs. Walsh, but you and the rest of us know that once mummy gets an idea into her head, nothing we say or do will stop her. She's as stubborn as a mule," proclaimed Hope. The rest of the girls nodded in agreement.

"Well, that's settled. I'll call the pilot, you do know how to get in touch with whoever we need to, to get the necessary arrangements for Mrs. Walsh and I to use the corporate airplane?," Dorothy asked Hope. "Of course. It's all written down in mummy's office. Don't worry about anything. Go and get packed and by tomorrow the two of you will be on your way to Japan." When Melanie dropped Mrs. Walsh off at the house the tears, from her beloved Mrs. Walsh, were flowing like buckets of water from a spout.

"Now, now, Mrs. Walsh," Melanie held her dear surrogate mother in her arms. I know, I know. I know how you love mummy and all of us. My gosh, you've known us for most of our lives. Everything will work out fine. Mom and Nancy will be so happy to see you and nana. Come, I'll walk you into the house and make sure everything's okay." Catching her breath, Mrs. Walsh felt a bit embarrassed. "You don't have to go out of your way, honey. I'm fine, believe me."

"I know you are, but humor me and let me get you upstairs and tucked in."

"Melanie, I used to do that to you. I'm not some invalid who needs assistance. I'm still capable to do what I have to."

"I'm honestly not worried about you, but I'd feel better if I know that you'll be ready when the limousine comes to pick you up tomorrow. Come on, I'll help you pack." Knowing it was fruitless to argue with Melanie, she consented, and, deep down, was grateful for her help.

Meanwhile, unbeknownst to Madaline about the entire situation in Beppu, she wanted her entire family to finally be together. She contemplated on how to broach the subject with Kyle. She wasn't worried about Betty. She was thrilled that she had a sibling, even if he was a half-brother.

She worried if he would accept her as she was ready to accept him. She couldn't wait until Madaline spoke or made arrangement to see Kyle and tell him the entire state of affairs. She hoped that with Madaline's gift of persuasiveness, Kyle would be understanding and forgive her for the terrible actions she rendered to 'their' mother. She couldn't get over the fact that she actually had a blood brother. She hoped he was as nice as Madaline told her he was.

When Madaline received the phone call from Hope she sat down. She was stunned and found it hard to believe what she was hearing. After getting the call, she kept going through her mind and hoped that what happened to her two good friends had nothing to do with Kyle's predicament and their attempt to help him and her out in their time of need.

Madaline convinced herself that it wasn't her or Kyle that caused her dear friends to put themselves in harm's way. Shaking that thought from her mind, she called her son and after telling him about Suzanne and Nancy's ordeal asked him when a good time would be for her to come and pay him a visit. "Don't you think that you should fly to Japan and see your two friends? They're like the only family we have." A distressed Kyle confronted his mother.

"Honey, I know Suzanne and Nancy all too well. Believe me. They'd kill me if they were to see me looking at them when they're trying to recover and who knows what else they need done."

"All I'm saying is they'd appreciate knowing that you're there for them."

"I think I know my friends a little better than you do." Madaline was getting angrier by the minute. "When they come home I'll be there to give them all the support that I can. Until then, let's talk about other pleasantries."

"Now that you're formally cleared of any wrong doing for the dreadful murder of that Curtis Jones, I think it's about time that I paid you a long overdue visit."

"Mom, why all the formality? You know anytime is a good time for you to come over. It's you who usually has a schedule that I have to work around." Madaline was insistent, "now is as good a time as ever. I'm sure we'll have a great visit. It's been too long since we've actually been with each other. We'll catch up on all the happenings and then some. "Tell me when you're coming and I'll be waiting with open arms," Kyle said.

Tears of joy were brimming from Madaline's eyes when she closed the cell phone. With a deep sigh she sat down on the sofa after pacing back and forth, too nervous to sit down while talking to Kyle. She then called Betty and relayed the conversation that she had with her son. Betty was beside herself with anxiety. On one hand she hoped he would accept her and on the other hand was pessimistic that with all that happened, he would be upset and not want to have anything to do with her. She prayed that her optimism would win over any negativity she was experiencing.

Madaline made the meeting with Kyle in a week and a half. She arranged for Betty to act in her place as her understudy. She was proud that her daughter would be a great actress in time. After all, she thought, it's in her genes. She asked Paul to accompany her on the trip and wanted him to meet Kyle. "We might as well kill two birds with one stone," she announced as a big smile showed her beautiful dimples. Whenever Paul looked at her gorgeous face he couldn't believe how lucky he was that she reciprocated the same feeling of love towards him as he felt for her. He thanked his lucky stars and knew that God was looking over him to be blessed with such love.

The limousine picked Dorothy and Mrs. Walsh up and was driving the two nervous women to the private hanger. They held hands, not saying much, their individual thoughts took precedence over any conversation that they wanted to discuss with each other. When they finally got situated and made comfortable they were able to take deep breaths and Mrs. Walsh let Dorothy say her piece. Clearing her throat, Suzanne's mother began, "when we debark and are at the hospital I think we can't let our emotions get in the way of our reactions to seeing them."

"From what I was told they're both in very bad shape and pretty banged up. It's imperative that they don't know how awful they really look. Now I realize that it's not going to be that way forever. The swelling and more plastic surgery will eliminate any deformities or broken bones in their faces. Oh God, I'm so nervous. Especially these two women, who are very concerned about their personal appearance. But I'm going to say it again, we can't let our facial expressions show any kind of horror, if we see what they look like." Mrs. Walsh affirmed Dorothy's sentiments.

"We have to be bright and say all positive things to make them feel that very shortly they'll be good as new." With these statements and thoughts said aloud, knowing how their attitude had to be, they were ready for the drinks and appetizers that were served to them.

"You know Catherine, I'm usually not a drinking woman but I think I'd like a strong pick me up at this time."

"Well, I usually think that a glass of something won't hurt and in this case it will let us unwind to accomplish the task at hand." When the stewardess came with their drinks they toasted to Suzanne and Nancy's health and a speedy recovery.

"I don't know if Suzanne has mentioned about the difficulty Morris is experiencing. I'm not going to get into it now but I want you to know that I hired a nurse to be at the house. We'll have a few LPNS and RNS all the time, 24/7. That way while I'm with Suzanne and Nancy I'll know that Morris is well taken care of. "Mrs. Walsh's mouth was open with bewilderment. Suzanne hadn't mentioned anything was wrong with Morris. 'That might be one of the reasons that she's been upset lately,' Catherine thought as she nodded her head in agreement with Dorothy.

Rich and Mr. T. were constantly monitoring the progress of their two friends. They took the bitching and complaining in stride and saw the progress that they were making. Rich couldn't wait till Dorothy and Mrs. Walsh would arrive and hoped that they would not display any negativity that they obviously would have. He thought to himself that he had to speak to them before they saw the two women and make sure they would see them as they've never seen them before. With these thoughts he put on a smile and walked into Nancy's room.

Suzanne and Nancy had come through the many operations they needed with flying colors. It was touch and go for a while but they eventually pulled through like the pro's they were. They still didn't have mirrors in their rooms to see what they looked like. Rich realized that because of the plastic surgeons that were at their disposal, minimal damage would be recognized. He knew that in their profession it couldn't be any other way. They were now in regular rooms, no longer needing the ICU. Their apparatus was still heavy and awkward but they knew that it wouldn't be long before they'd be up and about. Rich was in constant contact with Justin and because of his friendship with the art connoisseurs, Justin was kept abreast of all the art pieces that was found.

The rehab would take a while and they were prepared for that process. It was going to be a while until they could start rehab. As soon as the casts were removed then they could transfer to the United States and begin their therapy back home. Suzanne wanted to know all about the art that was found and every detail that Rich could remember. Mr. T. was instrumental in filling in the gaps that Rich either forgot or didn't have. The knowledge that Mr. T. possessed on the subjects was easy for him to relate all the details that were asked of him. Rich's cell phone rang. The call he was expecting from Dorothy and Mrs. Walsh telling him that they arrived was made. He wanted to see how their feelings were and if they were mentally prepared for the sight that they would see.

After Mrs. Walsh and Dorothy came to the hospital Rich excused himself and made an important phone call he'd been meaning to make. He finally got through to Mr. Yasuhito's room at the rehabilitation center and a nurse answered the phone beside his bed. Rich asked many questions and was assured that his friend was progressing nicely. Rich didn't want to give up the friendship he had developed for this fine gentleman who seemed to have no one else to look after him. As far as Rich was concerned, Mr. Yasuhito had no say in the matter. Rich would take care of him forever, if he had to. He was sure that once Nancy recovered she would be of the same mind set.

CHAPTER FORTY FOUR

Dorothy and Mrs. Walsh decided to settle into the hotel room before visiting the two women. They didn't say much while putting away their clothes, their thoughts ruminating within their own minds.

While Catherine was fixing her hair she told Dorothy, "I've prepared myself for the worst. Hopefully our thoughts are an overreaction to the story that was told to us."

"I'm in agreement with you, Dorothy said. If there's nothing else we have to do, I'm ready. Let's tell our driver to take us to the hospital, before I chicken out." The two women left, holding each other's arms and were ready for any impending disasters that lie ahead of them.

Toshiko, Yoshy's devoted wife, was in her home in Japan, preparing dinner for her son, Kazuhiko, who was finishing his last year of college. He was getting ready for his exams and knew how important it was for him to get good grades. He had his entire life mapped out for him by his parents. Since Kazuhiko was a youngster his father told him that he'd semi-retire and have Kazuhiko take over the day to day operations of the large corporation. During the summers off from the university he'd take his annual trip to the States. His father groomed him to take part in and observe the day to day labor and see how the business worked.

Kazuhiko worked throughout the years starting in the mail room and working himself up. He was able to sit in and listen, taking part in the electrical and mechanical engineering groups, to the actual production team putting together the various components that made the company one of the most prestigious and largest manufacturing businesses in the world for the varied products produced by this famous conglomerate. There was a knock on the door and Toshiko asked Kazuhiko to please see who was there. A tall gentleman in a business suit introduced himself as Sasaki Yasuo. He was the second man in charge of the FBI in Japan. "May I come in?"

"How rude of me, of course, come in and I'll introduce you to my mother. My father is away now, I suppose doing business for his company. Please sit down. Can I get you some tea and sandwiches?"

"I'm afraid that I can't, but thank you anyway." With the Makino's in front of him Mr. Yasuo began. "The reason why I'm here is to inform you that an unfortunate accident has happened." Toshiko, sat down, eyes cast down, knowing in her heart that the news had to do with Yoshy. She tried preparing herself for the worst and was worried that Kazuhiko would be devastated if anything bad happened to his father. For years, Toshiko new that Yoshy was not the same person who she had married many years ago.

His change was apparent and though she saw it, tried ignoring the signs and acted as if life was the same as it always was. Kazuhiko, on the other hand, adored his father. The world rose and he worshiped him. In his eyes, his father could do no wrong. She tentatively walked to her son, put her hands on his shoulders and waited patiently for the agent to tell her the news that she knew was in her heart.

Sasaki hated these assignments and knew that the news delivered to the family would, most times, destroy them. "Um, mam, I'm sorry to tell you that, nodding his head to Toshiko, your husband, and then doing the same to Kazuhiko, your father, had a very bad accident and unfortunately, did not survive."

Kazuhiko couldn't help but cry, not letting his emotions be controlled. Toshiko, on the other hand was only worried of her son's reaction. For years she held her emotions at bay for her husband, who was no longer the young man that she married and loved. He had become a stranger to her.

As much as she wanted to feel sadness, her altered love made it impossible to do so. Kazuhiko saw his mother's reaction and took it as a sign of her courage not to make him feel worse than he was already feeling. Kazuhiko had many questions for Sasaki, although Sasaki tried avoiding them as much as possible. He didn't want him to know, that in reality, his father was a thief and collector of stolen art and delicate wares stolen from all over the world.

The news would come soon enough. His intention wasn't to be the one to destroy the image of his father. "We have the body in the hospital and if you could be so kind to make the trip to Kyushu Island, in the city of Beppu, you can identify the body. I will not rush you, for I know this extremely bad news comes as a surprise to you. If you'd like me to leave and come back, I will be glad to do so."

"No, it won't take us long to get ready and if you don't mind waiting we'll be able to accompany you shorty," Toshiko said as she walked up the stairs to her room with a heavy heart. Kazuhiko had many questions that he wanted answered. What was his father doing in Kyushu Island and why was he in the hospital in Beppu? Sasaki, didn't know how to answer the questions asked of him and told him that all he was informed of was that's where the body was located.

Kazuhiko, for the first time, saw that his mother was a woman of courage no matter what extreme pressure was presented to her. He always had respect and admiration for her, but at this time, she showed more strength than what he expected and now thought she was a hero when adversity struck. He wanted to be the person who took control. Now he saw that the table had turned and she would be there for him. "I'll call my professors and tell them the circumstances and I'm sure that they'll allow me to make up my exams at another time."

"If you'll excuse me officer, I'll go upstairs and get ready for the trip." He walked up the stairs, as if lead were in his shoes. He could feel the tears flowing down his cheeks and he was literally nauseous. Not one to have headaches he felt one coming on. His hands were shaking, his body shivering, it seemed, as hard as he tried, he couldn't control these reactions.

When Toshiko came down she saw that Sasaki was sitting, waiting patiently for them. "Are you sure you don't need more time. I can come back later if you wish." Toshiko, looking behind her to make sure that Kazuhiko was still in his room, spoke to Mr. Sasaki, making sure her conversation would not be heard by her son. In a soft voice, "Mr. Sasaki, I'm not a young girl. I've lived a long and fruitful life. In the years I've learned many of life's experiences. I know that you're trying to have as much discretion as possible, but I'd like you to be honest with me. This conversation will be between the two of us. I realize how important it is for my son to continue to think highly of his father. I on the other hand, realized long ago, that my husband was a man of many faces. To the outside world he was admired and loved for his brilliance and innovative imagination. These qualities will always be remembered."

"Between you and I, there was another side to my husband that most of society had no knowledge of." Lifting her hand to stop the officer from speaking, she continued. "I realize that there are protocols to be respected and I wouldn't want you to disobey your orders. I'm not here to cause you or anyone else trouble. All I'm asking of you is to be discreet as possible and save my son humiliation on what his father's other side was. I don't know for sure many of the acts that he did, but I'm sure, there were many that were not, how they say, on the up and up."

Before Sasaki had time to answer Toshiko's questions and request, Kazuhiko was slowly descending the steps. "We will continue this conversation at a later time, officer Sasaki, if it's all right with you?" Sasaki was speechless. He then realized how smart a woman Toshiko was and admired her immensely. "Yes, Mrs. Makino, I and my superiors will be glad to answer any questions you may have. I understand it will be in the strictest confidence. You have my word on that. I can't guarantee that this story won't leak out to the press. After all, your husband was a prominent figure in today's world economy."

"We'll try our best to honor your request and try to minimize any bad press that might occur. That's all that I and my department can do. You know how the television and newspapers can take one's name and discredit any good that was done and turn the story around to make the general public want to buy their side of an article. I only hope for you and your son that the people reporting will take your feelings into consideration."

"That's all that I can ask for," replied Toshiko. "I see you're ready to go, my son. I'm prepared also."

"This kind gentleman and officer will take us in his car to wherever we have to go to identify your father. Have strength, and we'll get through this ordeal. I'll always be here for you, Kazuhiko, you can rely on that," Toshiko pronounced as she went to the bottom of the stairs and hugged her only son.

Toshiko and Kazuhiko were quiet on the long journey to the Island of Kyushu then to the city of Beppu. FBI agent Sasaki had them fill out forms at the hospital and then escorted them to the morgue where Yoshy's body lies in wait for them to identify his remains. Sasaki hated this part of his job. He knew it was necessary but he couldn't help feel sorry for the relatives that had the responsibility to identify their loved one. After identifying the body, both mother and son sat beside Yoshy, lying on the cold metal slab, their opinions kept inside their hearts. Mother and son had different thoughts that were going through their minds. One of pure sorrow, the other mixed emotions that couldn't be put into words. They then stepped outside the morgue, lost in their own reflections.

Finally, Toshiko took hold of her son's hand and with a squeeze told him of the funeral arrangements that had to be made. "The death certificate is being issued and as you know, you're the eldest and only son. It's up to you to have the responsibility to contact the temple and schedule the funeral. Since you've been a young boy you learned, from going to temple, how we must prepare for the funeral arrangements. You'll talk to the holy leader and he'll tell you what must be done. The hospital knows to wash the body and the openings are stuffed with cotton. Your father and I discussed, years ago, when it was our time to leave this earth what we wanted."

"I know which suit your father wants to be dressed in. From there I know where he wanted the wake to be held. It will be made easy for you because of your fathers and my wishes. Your father picked out the alter, and the type of casket he wants to be buried in. We'll stay with the body until it's time for the service. We have the money to put in the casket, as a symbol, to pay for the toll across the River of the 3 Hells. I'll make sure that a table is set up at the entrance of the hall. We'll have a special holder for the Koden."

"These special envelopes have a thin black and white ribbon wrapped around the envelope. Your father chose the gifts that are to be given to those who come to the service. We are fortunate that your father wrote down all the arrangements that he wanted done for his internment. It will make our mourning a lot easier. Come, let's go and finalize all the plans." With this said the mother and son walked out of the hospital and were greeted by FBI agent Sasaki who would escort them back to their home in Tokyo.

Rich and his colleagues were stupefied at all the inventory that was found in Yoshy's secret hiding place. People from various museums who specialized in stolen objects were flown in, busy categorizing and writing down the items that were discovered. When Rich felt he was getting in the way he went back to the hospital to see Nancy and Suzanne. He was sure that Mrs. Walsh and Suzanne's mother would be there by now. He was ready to leave the house, letting Mr. T. know where he was going. "If you need me for any reason, call and I'll come back."

"I hope that this frenzy of people will subside. This group, they are like vultures. The cameras, reporters and all the other media will make it hard for me to get the hell out of here."

"Don't worry my friend. I've taken care of your departure. Come with me and I'll show you a secret path that was detected only yesterday. We'll fool them all," Mr. Tamamurō winked at Rich as he led him out the private chamber.

Dorothy and Mrs. Walsh walked with trepidation to the room that the two women were in. At the closed door the senior females made a pact that no matter what shape they saw their loved ones in, to be optimistic and not let their emotions show on their faces. With that said they knocked on the wooden door. Suzanne didn't know who their guest was. She thought it was either one of the nurses or Rich coming for his daily visit. "Come in," Suzanne spoke, trying to gain enough strength to make herself heard. She felt like crap but didn't want to display to anyone her true feelings. When she saw it was Dorothy and Mrs. Walsh a large smile appeared on her face. Realizing that the bandages that were covering the stitches were inhibiting her from a larger smile she motioned, as best she could, for them to come in.

"Don't get nervous seeing us hung up in these contraptions. It's only for a little while longer. They'll help the bones that were broken mend easier. I don't want to wake Nancy, since she had a restless sleep last evening. The nurses gave her a shot to put her out for a while. When she wakes, I'm sure she'll be happy to see you. You really didn't have to come all this way. We'll be back to normal very shortly."

"First of all, it wasn't anything for us to get here. With the use of your corporate jet it was delightful. We weren't packed in like a sardine in its oily packaging and we could relax and actually fall asleep. Besides that, how in the world could the two of us not come and see our two favorite daughters? You know that we think of Nancy as one of us."

"Thanks mom and Catherine. When Nancy comes to, she'll appreciate you coming over and you know how grateful I am at your visit. Tell me, how are the girls and dad doing? Is everything going as well as can be expected?"

"I know that Hope has called and kept you up to date on the business end. All I can say is that, speaking for Catherine, we're relieved to see you and Nancy doing so well."

"Mom and Catherine, you don't know how much this visit means to me or I should say, us. Do you know how long you'll be staying for?" Dorothy, looking at Catherine, verbalized, "do you believe it, we just walked into the room and already she wants to know when where leaving."

"Dorothy, I don't think Suzanne meant what it sounded like, did you my dear?" Thank you Mrs. Walsh, no, I'm sorry to have offended you, but I really didn't mean it the way you interpreted it."

Going over to Suzanne, Dorothy tried to hug her but felt uncomfortable, not knowing, the way she was bandaged and all, if she would hurt Suzanne. "Don't worry mom, pretty soon when we're out of these contraptions and the gauze taken off our faces, there will be plenty of hugs to go around." A large smile appeared on Dorothy's face. An hour into their visit they saw Nancy stirring and waited for her to fully wake up. When she opened her eyes, Nancy was surprised, yet happy, at the two women in their room. "I don't believe it. You're like an apparition before my eyes."

Tears were welling up in Nancy, flowing onto bandaged cheeks, she was speechless. Finally she got her voice back and suddenly everyone in the room heard Nancy sobbing. That's all the others needed to hear because all at once Suzanne, Dorothy and Mrs. Walsh joined Nancy with their own weeping. Realizing that the two patients couldn't wipe their own eyes, each woman went to them, with tissues in hand, drying the tears that were falling upon their bandaged cheeks. The room was quiet for a while and then the nurse came in to dispense their medications for the afternoon. The visitors were reluctant to leave and decided to stay for at least another hour or so.

They realized that Suzanne and Nancy needed as much rest as possible. Before they left they heard another knock on the door and saw that Rich was entering the room. He was happy to see that the two older women were well and seemed to be taking the sight of their loved ones in good stride. After a while Dorothy and Mrs. Walsh decided to depart and told the girls that they would be back tomorrow. They told everyone in the room, "as long as we came all the way to Japan, we might as well see some of the sights," Dorothy announced after kissing both women on the cheek. She took Mrs. Walsh's arm and headed out the door.

Rich waited a few minutes before relating the amount of items being classified and matched to what places they were stolen from. Although Suzanne and Nancy were still in pain, they were happy to hear that everything was turning out for the best. "I feel sorry for the relatives of Mr. Yoshihiro's family. It must have come as quite a surprise for them to find out what he was really like. It was as if he were living a double life."

"You're right Suzanne. You want to hear something that I haven't told a soul?" Not waiting for an answer Nancy verbalized what was on her mind. "The person who I really feel sorry for is the innocent young woman who was Yoshy's lover back in the States. I'm sure she realized that he had a family back home but maybe they really did love or care for one another deeply. I wonder if we'll be able to find out if she has any family that we can get in touch with? If she does, they have to be informed of her death."

"We'll try to get her address from Yoshy's limo driver and once in her home I'm sure we'll find papers that will tell us of any close relatives," answered Rich. "Speaking of limo driver, how is Mr. Yashuhito doing?" A curious Nancy asked. "He's coming along as well as can be expected." Rich then went into detail on his recuperation. "Within a few weeks he should be able to start rehabilitation. He got beaten up as bad as the two of you. Both of you are lucky that you have family that cares for you. As far as I can tell, Mr. Yashuhito doesn't have a soul in the world that's family. His only family was Yoshy and I'm sure Robin had special feelings for him as well."

Both women were quiet as Rich related his story of Mr. Yashuhito. Nancy, a large lump formed in her throat, was the first to speak. "I know how Mr. Yashuhito must feel. In a way he's a lot like I was. I didn't have any family either, until I was lucky enough to meet up with Suzanne and her clan. When I get home, we'll see what we can do for this man who was loyal to his employer to the end." No one spoke. A pin could be heard if dropped on the floor. Silence enveloped all.

Just then there was a knock on the door. Suzanne had a hard time clearing her throat. "Boy, I feel I'm at Grand Central Station," Suzanne said aloud as she told the person to come in.

"I've come to deliver this beautiful arrangement to Miss Suzanne Morse." The delivery man was hesitant for their placement. "I'm here. Why don't you put them on the ledge so everyone can admire them? Can I please see who sent them?"

The messenger handed the card to Suzanne and left the room. Suzanne was expecting the flowers to be from Stephen or the children but was pleasantly surprised to see a beautiful note. It was signed from Lawrence. "Wasn't that caring and nice. Lawrence heard about our plight and wanted me to know that he was thinking of me and hope that the two of us get better quickly." Nancy and Rich looked at each other and without saying a word knew that Suzanne was a little disappointed that she hadn't received anything, not even a card, from Stephen.

They were positive that Suzanne's daughters had called him to tell him of Suzanne's serious injuries. Rich and Nancy couldn't stop talking about how beautiful and thoughtful the flowers were. Suzanne agreed and then she said she was tired after the unexpected visitors and wanted to get some rest. Rich divided the two beds by the curtain to give each of them some privacy.

Nancy spoke quietly, as not to disturb Suzanne. "Well, what do you think of that?" Rich was speechless. He lifted his shoulders and went to Nancy's side. He kissed her gently on the lips and softly announced, "When you get better, there's going to be a lot more of that, plus other things I won't mention. Get out of here soon so you can find out what I have in store for you." Nancy could feel herself blushing. For once she was speechless and smiled at the man she knew would someday be her husband.

Suzanne was glad that the partition was closed. She didn't want her friends to see the tears flowing from her eyes. She was disappointed that Stephen hadn't sent her a note, called or sent her flowers once he heard of her horrifying ordeal. When speaking to her daughters they informed her that they called Stephen and other close friends immediately to let them know of her and Nancy's terrifying experience. 'It's been six weeks since we've been here, not even a card from him. I guess the question I've had on my mind has been answered,.' Suzanne thought to herself and she closed her eyes.

MASSACHUSETTS

Meanwhile, Madaline made plans with Kyle for a visit within the week. She knew that Betty would fill in and do a beautiful job replacing her. She kept thinking how to broach the subject of Kyle's step sister. She kept wavering different ways to inform him and wasn't sure until she actually saw him how she would explain what happened. 'I suppose I have to be honest with him and tell him the truth. There's no other way to handle the situation. The only thing I'm worried about is how Kyle will take the news.' When Paul came into her suite that evening before their flight she told him of her misgivings and listened intently to his input.

"I'll drive to the airport and I know that everything will turn out fine. When this is over, you'll smile and I want you to think of me. I feel as if I'm the luckiest man in the world. After all, who can boast that the woman they love is the one and only Madaline Mason, not only that, but she feels the same way about me." With those words spoken, Madaline went over to Paul and kissed him passionately on the lips.

"Let's not waste any time, honey, we'll be missing each other while you're away. I have to give you a going away present." They held hands as they gently closed the bedroom door of the suite and like two people in love, undressed and soaped each other in the shower that they took together. While drying off Madaline again thanked Paul for his understanding her need to tell Kyle, by herself, the real story of her life. "I promise that you and I will see Kyle together and tell him how happy we are." Reiterating again, Madaline continued her conversation. "I don't know what his reaction will be with the news I present to him."

"I don't want other things to get in the way, if you know what I mean."

"Of course I do sweetheart. Let's hope that he takes the news well. We'll have plenty of time to meet each other and I'll tell your son about our feelings."

"Thanks again, for your understanding. You don't know how much I appreciate your help throughout this entire ordeal. I always knew that you were smart, now I realize your intelligence and how much empathy and discernment you showed throughout this unbelievable situation. I'll never be able to thank you enough." Leading her to the massive bed he kissed her gently. "I'll let you show me how much you really appreciate my cooperation." With that said they both laughed and let the mood take over.

Suzanne couldn't get comfortable with the way her body was held in casts and multi contraptions. All she wanted to do was curl up in a ball and like a hermit crab, never let anyone see her again. She knew in her heart that she and Stephen were finished. 'Even if he pleads with me until eternity I can never forgive him for all the pain and misery he has put me through. Especially now, when I need him for both moral and mental support, he couldn't have the decency to acknowledge my pain with a lousy arrangement of flowers.' She knew that with all they had been through that she would never forgive him for his lack of thoughtfulness. 'It's been over six weeks that we've been here, not a word from Stephen. We'll be home shortly; I'll fill my time with something useful to do. To heck with him.' With those thoughts she fell into a drug induced sleep.

After Dorothy and Mrs. Walsh left after their second visit Nancy and Suzanne were in need of a good rest. The doctors made their customary visit and informed them of their next and probably last, operation that had to be performed. After the nurse administered the pain medications another nurse came into the room. "Suzanne I have a phone call for you. Would you like me to hold the phone for you while you're still up and can talk?"

Suzanne had no idea who would be calling and presumed it was one of her daughters. "Sure, that would be nice of you." Within minutes the call was forwarded to their room. The nurse put the receiver to Suzanne's ear and let her converse with the caller. "Suzanne? Suzanne, can you hear me?" She knew that voice. "Of course, Larry, how nice of you to call. By the way, thank you for the beautiful arrangement of flowers. Whenever I see them I think of you. It was unnecessary but I'm glad you sent them."

"I don't have to ask you how you're feeling. I've heard from the grapevine that you've been in better shape. I know in no time you'll be up and around and be back to your old, I mean young, adorable self." Suzanne laughed out loud and felt as if she were in someone else's body. The hardy laughter made her stitches feel drawn, hurting her face. The doctors assured her that after every operation her appearance would be back to normal as possible. The personal at the hospital weren't permitted to have a mirror of any sort in their room.

The drugs were starting to have an effect on her. "Larry, I can't thank you enough. You can't possibly know how much I appreciate your thoughtfulness and caring."

"You don't have to thank me. You know how I feel about you. As a matter of fact, I might be on my way to see you now. You'll never know until I'm there."

"I wouldn't want you to do that Larry. You're such a busy man and with all your responsibilities I'd understand if you'd visit me when I'm out of here and home again."

"We'll see. For now, go to sleep and get well soon. Think of me in your dreams and maybe they'll come true. Sleep tight baby and don't say a word, but I love you." Suzanne couldn't believe what she heard Larry say. She wasn't sure what she heard and thought it might have been the drugs giving her hallucinations. Starting to slur her words she said, "Thank's again Larry. I love you too." When the nurse put the receiver back on the phone Suzanne fell sound asleep.

The nurses came into the room and transferred the women on to gurney's to bring them down for their last operation. With trepidation the two women were quiet on the way to the operating rooms. They were left in a room waiting to be prepped. Nancy and Suzanne looked at each other and couldn't say a word. Their own thoughts were milling through their heads. Suddenly Nancy looked over and said to Suzanne, "Well, you did it again Olly. Thanks a lot. I should have known better than listen to you." With that said, the two women laughed and waited for the doctors to administer the necessary drugs to put them in never, never land.

SAN DIEGO, CALIFORNIA

Madaline was used to flying and couldn't wait till the plane landed and she could, once again, see her one and only son. She kept wavering back and forth on his reaction to her news but knew there was nothing she could do except pray to God that he'd be understanding and want to meet Betty. The flight was perfect and Kyle was there to greet her at the gate.

A big smile crossed her face when she saw her handsome son waiting for her. After hugging, Kyle took her luggage and put it into the trunk of his car. "You packed lightly this time. I was prepared to have to rent a U-Haul for all of your luggage." Madaline laughed and informed him, "I don't think I can stay for an extended visit, but couldn't put off seeing you any longer. Grabbing his arm she let him open the front door for her and was anxious to head to his spacious apartment.

Once back in his residence Madaline walked over to the window looking at the beautiful view. "You really know how to pick them. I don't think I'd ever leave this glass. The panorama scene is spectacular." Walking to his mother he took her from behind and hugged her. "Mom, I can't thank you enough for all your help and support when I was going through my ordeal. Now, with this new complication with Carol I'm beside myself. Yes, I knew it was only a matter of time before she found out the truth about me, but I thought we could be civil and talk things out like two sensible human beings. She's being a real bitch. I guess I can't blame her, but I don't know. It still stinks."

"I know honey. That's one of the reasons why I came out here to be with you." 'Little does he know half of it.' While Madaline was peering out the window, enjoying the exquisite view, the expanse of water seemed to go on forever. Thoughts of the first time she landed in California crossed her mind. 'I've come a long way from Ketchum Ave and Mrs. McCallum's rooming house,' she thought as she turned around and returned Kyle's hug. "By the way, I've talked to Ann and she's doing great. There are a few new scripts she's looking into and might be interested in one of them. I really should keep in contact with her more. You remember Ann, don't you?"

"Of course I do. How can I forget the first friend you met in California? Wasn't she the girl that was with you when you met my father?"

"Yes, if it wasn't for Ann, we'd had never met. I guess it was fate."

"Well, whatever it was, look at the wonderful product that the two of you produced."

A large smile crossed her face and taking her son's hand led him to the couch. "Can I get you something to drink or give you lunch? I forgot about how hungry you must be from the plane ride."

"No honey, maybe after we talk we'll eat. Right now I have some things that are on my mind." With a quizzical look, Kyle viewed his mother. "Now don't get yourself in a dither. What I'm going to tell you has been on my mind for many years and I feel this is the right time to get it off my chest and be honest with you. After all you finally were honest with me. I want to be straightforward and candid with you."

"You're not going to tell me that my father isn't really my dad?"

"No silly, it's nothing like that. When I've finished you can ask any questions you'd like, fair?"

"Mom, as far as I know, you've always been honest and told me straight out about all your thoughts and dreams. Whatever it is, I'm up for it." Madaline was contemplative and after a while took a deep breath and began the story of her sad past. Madaline found some fringe on one of the pillows that was adorning his couch. While relating the narrative she kept twisting the fringe around her finger. She realized that she was doing this act from pure nerves and when Kyle saw her action she abruptly stopped. Kyle sat on the couch in bewilderment. After hearing most of the story he was numb. He couldn't fathom how she could have kept this kind of secret hidden for so many years.

It was as if he was in a state of shock. "Should I keep going on with this sordid tale or do you want me to stop and continue this dialogue a little later?"

"No Mom, you can't keep me in suspense any longer. I have to hear the rest of it," a solemn Kyle replied. When Madaline was coming to the end of her saga she hoped that Kyle would be receptive to the idea of her finding Betty and now realizing that instead of being an only child, he now had a half-sister to contend with.

Kyle sat beside his mother in stunned silence. He was taken by surprise by this terrible ordeal that his mother had lived with since a young girl. He was speechless for a while, not knowing what to say or do. Madaline sat waiting for Kyle's thoughts and remarks, like a writer waiting for a review of his latest book. Clearing his throat he got up, went to the kitchen and poured himself a stiff drink. He actually went there for water, but felt a drink would be more appropriate. Yelling from the galley he asked Madaline if she'd like him to pour her one. "I'd usually say no in the middle of the day, but yes, I'd love one."

Bringing the glasses back into the living room he placed hers on the coffee table. Lifting his glass he made a toast. "Here's to honesty and new beginnings."

"I'll drink to that," replied Madaline as their glasses were lifted and clinked together. "I'm at a loss for words, mom." Putting his hand up for her not to speak he continued. "There are many emotions I'm feeling at this point. First of all, how you could have lived with this horrific situation for years, kept hidden from everyone you loved and go on with your life, I'm, I'm stupefied. At this point, I'm angry at grandma and grandpa for not believing in you. How could your brothers and sisters have let them treat you as a leper?"

"Honey in those days, everything was so different than it is today. It was shameful for a young girl to become pregnant. The only part I'm disappointed in is that they didn't believe or stand by me. Instead, they sent me away to bear my agony by myself. For that it's difficult to forgive them. But as time goes by your views change and forgiveness is part of what the Lord would expect one to do. It's hard at times but I'm starting to have a relationship with my parents and in time I'll heal, as they will. They still feel guilty about the way they scorned and sent me away to fend for myself."

"Thank God for Aunt Mabel. She was my rock. Without her tenderness and love I wanted to die. When she wouldn't let me hold my newborn I did want to end my life. She talked to me for endless hours and days trying to justify her actions and my parents' wishes. The hatred in my soul was overwhelming. But time does heal and with time I learned to live with my sorrow. I never told anyone. Your father and Ann didn't even know. It was time for me to tell you all about my ordeal and let you know that your sister wants to meet you. She respects your wishes and won't get in touch with you if you choose not to see her." Madaline looked into Kyle's eyes and while holding her breath was not sure what his answer would be.

"Mom, this is overwhelming. I don't know what to say. When you started telling me your story, a part of me didn't want to hear you tell me anything negative about your life. Sure, I knew about the hard times you had growing up on the farm, coming to Hollywood and making yourself a worldwide figure to be loved and admired by all. But in reality you were tormented by your past. I understand why you didn't want to tell anyone about what went on in your youth. I feel honored that you bared your soul to me. You ask me if I want to meet my sister. At first I would have said no, absolutely not. I don't want to share you. I guess you'd call me a spoiled brat."

"No you're not," interrupted Madaline.

"You were loved and I remember disciplining you many a time. I wouldn't allow you to become like so many other children of famous people. Now they were really spoiled brats." They both laughed and took a large drink from their glasses." I feel like getting drunk, admitted Kyle, as he polished off his glass of Cutty Sark. Going back to the kitchen he returned with another full glass of liquor. After being quiet for a while, Kyle admitted to Madaline that he would like to meet his half-sister. If she's anything like you, I know I'll like her."

"I have to give her a chance. It wasn't her fault the way she was conceived. Yes, I'd love for you to arrange a meeting for the two of us to get together. Of course, it's obvious that you're included in this gathering." He lifted his glass and with another cheer, they began to drink to their hearts content. Lunch and dinner was forgotten and only glasses of alcohol were their mainstay. After giggling they wobbled to their bedrooms and without getting undressed, fell onto their beds, falling fast asleep on top of the covers.

The next morning Madaline thought her head would split in half. When she took a hot shower, it seemed as if the entire enclosure was spinning. She didn't know how she walked out of the steamy shower. She toweled herself dry and had a hard time putting on her clothes. When entering the kitchen she looked at her handsome son and knew he was also feeling the effects of yesterday's drinking. They both looked at each other and broke out in laughter. "Come on mom, I'll show you how I've learned to make the best omelet you've ever tasted."

"I'm not about to stop you. I don't think I have the energy to argue."

"Well, you know what some people say. When you wake up with a hangover the best thing to do is to take another drink. Would you like a Bloody Mary?"

"I don't think so. That's all I need. Too many of my friends like their nips a little too much, if you know what I mean." Madaline laughed as she got up and set the table. "I don't know about you, but I'm famished. Mom, would you put the bagels in the toaster and bring out the cream cheese? This will be better than any restaurant we could have gone to. You still like your coffee black?"

"You know me too well. I'm sweet enough. I don't need any sugar or milk to make me happy."

"While we're being honest with one another there's another detail that I have to tell you."

"Oh no, I don't know if I'm up to any more of your 'true stories,' admitted Kyle. "This revelation will make you happy as a pig in shit, I think."

"Okay, let's hear it," Kyle said as he sat down waiting for her next admission. "This isn't about Betty. It's about me and how, not expected, I've fallen in love. He's a wonderful man and I know once you meet him, you'll know what a fine man he is. If it's okay with you, I'd like to take him along when Betty and I return on the trip for your meeting. Of course he'll be back at the hotel room when you and Betty finally meet."

"He and I realize that this is a very special meeting and we don't want anything else to get in the way. When you tell me it's okay to meet Paul, that's his name by the way, I'll tell him to come over. As a matter of fact, it was Paul that helped me find Betty. Without going into details, it was quite an ordeal. Paul knows all about the situation and only when you're ready will he come and meet you."

"Too many things are happening at once," Kyle admitted, as he shook his head and sat down. "Is there anything else you want to reveal to me?"

"No," Madaline said, as she went over to Kyle and hugged him. "After all, there has to be some good news along with everything else that I've told you, wouldn't you agree?"

"Yes, I guess so," admitted her son as he got up. "Are you ready for the best breakfast you've ever had?"

"You know Kyle. At this point, anything will taste good. Knowing you the way I do, I'm sure your cooking will live up to your bragging and to my expectation." Mother and son finally sat down and ate to their hearts content. After everything was consumed they sat around the table sipping their coffee and smiling at each other. Words weren't necessary at this point.

JAPAN – HOSPITAL ROOM

This time Rich wasn't alone, his friends from the FBI were there also. He was glad that Dorothy and Catherine were also waiting for the two women to come out from the operating room. They tried busying themselves as best they could, not wanting to think what was happening to their loved ones. They knew the risks of any operation, especially under anesthesia. The hours seemed to go by slowly and after going down to the cafeteria, they again went into the family waiting area. Suddenly the door opened and Dr. Yamada emerged with a grim look on his face.

He immediately went to the two older women and told them about the operations that he and his fellow doctors performed on Suzanne and Nancy. When he left, Rich went to Dorothy and Catherine. "So, what did he tell you?"

"All in all, it was a good report" replied Dorothy. "You'd never know it from the look on his face," Rich answered. "It seems that even though it was a long operation, they accomplished the necessary procedures. The swelling in their limbs went down considerably, thanks to the tractions, they were able to put regular casts on their limbs. Of course some pins were required but that's minor compared to what might have had to be done."

"They took MRI's and even though their spleen was removed from each of them, the contusions that they incurred are healing up fine. The kidneys are coming along, thankfully, not one had to be removed. The ribs will need time to mend but nothing but rest will restore their health. Thankfully the best plastic surgeons were visiting the hospital at the time of the mishap. Minimal damage seems to be obvious to the eye. The average person will never know the damage they conveyed. Of course they'll need a long time for physical therapy, but that can be done back home."

"One other thing for your information. The doctor or I should say the plastic surgeon that performed the operation on the actress Ann Margaret, when she fell off the stage and broke practically every bone in her face, was the same surgeon that was one of the visiting physicians. The women have no idea how lucky they are that they had such a great doctor that tended to their awful wounds and broken bones on their beautiful faces. Dr. Yamada thinks that within the week they'll be ready to travel."

"Doesn't that guy ever smile? My heart sank when I saw him enter the family room. I thought when he came out we'd be hearing bleak news," Rich verbalized." I think it's just the way he is," answered Dorothy.

All the while Mrs. Walsh was wringing her hands, tears flowing down her tired looking face. "Now, now, Catherine, everything will be fine. We know you'll take good care of Suzanne while she's recovering. I even gave you my homemade chicken soup recipe. Nothing like chicken soup to put a person on the mend. I'll come over to help and you'll see, all will be better," Dorothy said as she put her arm around Mrs. Walsh.

"I'll take a leave of absence for a while and tend to Nancy at her house. Even though I know she'll protest, I'm going to go against her wishes. At least for a few weeks. By then I'm sure she'll hire a regular nurse to take care of her and drive her to the therapy sessions, informed Rich. With their plans resolved they left the hospital and let the women sleep in the recovery room.

CHAPTER FORTY FIVE

Not knowing what was happening, Lawrence had his private jet fly him to the hospital that Suzanne was in. He entered her room to find it empty. A feeling of deja vu came over him as he remembered the awful torture he endured during his wife's desperate fight for life. Since that time he hated hospitals but made this exception for Suzanne. He hoped nothing bad happened and went to the nurses' station.

He was told of their last operation and a sigh of relief emitted from him. He was told approximately how long they'd be in recovery and to come back in about four hours where they'd be in ICU. Lawrence felt better knowing that their last operation had taken place and would wait as long as he had to to see the woman he loved. He hoped that she would soon be able to reciprocate the feelings he had for her. With that thought he walked out of the hospital and went to register at a hotel not far from the facility.

The women were groggy and felt out of it when they started waking up from the anesthesia. They looked for each other and when they saw that the other was doing okay a big relief was felt by both of them. They were finally wheeled back to their room in ICU. Suzanne tried fighting off the sleepy feeling she had but to no avail. Within minutes, she succumbed to slumber. In the evening Lawrence knocked softly on the door. He finally heard the head nurse inform him that the women were probably asleep. He asked her permission to go into the room and be there when they woke up. "It's against the rules, sir, we cannot let a non-member of the family to wait beyond visiting hours."

"You don't understand. I'm Ms. Morse's fiancé and I know she'd want me to be at her side when she wakes."

"Oh, I'm sorry, sir. I didn't realize that Ms. Morse was engaged."

"I was out of the country on business when I heard of the mishap."

"In that case, I'll make an exception. There's a comfortable chair in the room and I'm sure she'll like seeing you when she wakes."

"I can't thank you enough," a delighted Lawrence replied as he opened the door and took the seat near Suzanne. Usually not one to embellish the truth he figured one little lie wouldn't hurt.

Nancy was the first to wake. She slowly took in the room and was surprised when she saw Lawrence sleeping soundly in the chair next to Suzanne's bed. She didn't want to disturb him so she rang for the nurse and when the nurse came into the room put her finger to her mouth, as telling her to be quiet.

Whispering, the nurse explained the reason why she let the gentleman into their room. Nancy laughed at his ingenuity. Lawrence was slowly waking, disoriented at first. Nancy waved to him and gave him a thumbs up. Fifteen minutes later Lawrence saw Suzanne stirring and when she seemed less sleepy kissed her gently on the cheek. A smile lighted up her face when she saw Lawrence. 'Did she imagine that he kissed her cheek?' "How did you get into the room? Only family members are allowed during non-visiting hours." Lawrence raised his shoulders and put his palms up.

"I don't know, they just did."

"Anyway, when Justin called and told me that you and Nancy were going through your last operation I dropped everything I had on my agenda and had my pilot take me to see you. I couldn't let you wonder if I had heard of your plight. Anyway, I'm not going to pry into how this awful ordeal happened. I'm just grateful that you and Nancy pulled through and both of you are on your way to a full recovery."

Suzanne laughed to herself knowing that he had not a clue on what they had to do to make their full recovery happen. "Larry, I can't thank you enough for your concern. You're such a busy man. I'm flattered that you took the time out of your schedule to visit us." A little embarrassed, Lawrence said to Suzanne, "you know how important you are to me. I couldn't wait around and wonder what was happening. I had to see for myself and again tell you that I love and adore you. I realize that the feelings aren't reciprocated, but hoping that someday you'll realize how important I am to you and that you really love me as well."

Suzanne was thankful that most of her face was still bandaged so he couldn't see the blush on her face. She ignored his remark and again thanked him. "Come closer, will you?" When he did, Suzanne kissed the part of his face that was closest to her. At first he thought that he had imagined the reciprocal kiss but realized that she too had kissed him back. He didn't know how to react and smiled from ear to ear. Having a hard time pronouncing her words, she asked him how he got into their room.

"Let's say I told a little white lie, for now that is." Suzanne didn't know what he meant by that, but decided to drop the question. "Do you know when they'll release you from here so you can get back to the States and finish your rehabilitation there?"

"I'm not sure. I'll have a conversation with the head doctor in charge and go from there. I couldn't imagine staying here much longer." In her heart she hoped that they'd send her and Nancy home very soon. She knew that the facilities back home would give her the ability to recuperate faster than the doctors here thought and told the two women how long the process of recovery would probably be.

CALIFORNIA

Betty was nervous sitting beside Madaline in the airplane heading to California. Even though she'd been to California before, it was for business. This time she would be meeting her half-brother and didn't know what the reactions would be to each other. "Are you sure he's happy to be meeting me?" asked an anxious Betty. With a calm pat on her daughter's hand, Madaline laughed. "I'm not laughing at your reaction to meeting Kyle honey, but I've assured you over a dozen times that everything your imagining is all unnecessary."

Paul sat a few rows in back of Madaline and Betty. He didn't want to disturb their conversation. When Kyle picked them up at the airport he would rent a car and go to the hotel where his reservation was waiting. He was happy that this small family would finally be together and hoped that Kyle would accept him as well.

"I can't wait till we land and Kyle will pick us up."

"You didn't tell me that he's the person picking us up," a worried Betty voiced her concern. "Well, you have to eventually meet and I think the sooner the better. Don't be scared, he's a doll. I really did raise him to be a wonderful human being, don't have any negative thoughts. I assure you, this episode will turn out right for the both of you."

The plane landed and after picking up their luggage from the carousel they waited outside the terminal for Kyle's car to appear. Madaline waived to Paul as he got on the bus to pick up his rented auto. From nerves Betty was lifting one leg and then the other. Suddenly Kyle's auto appeared and was in front of them, Betty wanted to faint. She thought to herself, 'he's absolutely handsome and this car must have cost a small fortune. She became more sure of herself when she saw the smile on her baby brother's face. He went over to Betty and before putting their suitcases in the trunk gave her a big bear hug.

Betty automatically felt more relaxed when they got into his vehicle and were going to his apartment. Once inside his massive and beautifully appointed space Betty was in awe. He told them where to put their luggage and started making coffee and tea for his mother and step sister. As nervous as Betty was, Kyle was unusually apprehensive, but didn't want to show Betty how anxious he really was. He couldn't wait until they sat down and started talking to each other.

On the coffee table in front of the sofa he displayed some crackers, cheese and a plate of pastries. From the other side of the room, behind the tall mirrored bar, he asked them what they'd like to drink. Both women declined but Kyle poured himself a stiff large whiskey on ice and stirred it vigorously from nerves that he was experiencing. Taking a deep breath he brought himself and his drink over and sat on the large chair facing his mother and Betty. Putting his right leg over his left knee he tried calming himself down. When they were finally settled, Kyle took in a deep breath and started the conversation.

"Mom told me what happened to her and the way the incident occurred. But you know what Betty? I look at it from a different perspective. From hurt, anger and betrayal came a wonderful human being that I can honestly say I want to get to know and eventually, we'll become part of each other's lives. I don't know how you feel about this situation, but I've always wanted a sibling. Instead of having to listen to you cry, like all babies do, I'm lucky that you've gone through your awkward stages and here you are."

Betty started laughing and before they knew what was happening the three people talked and talked until the wee hours of the night. They kissed each other good night and as Betty settled down in her guest room she silently thanked God that everything she hoped for had come true. In the room next to Betty's, Madaline was talking to Paul and told him everything that had taken place. She told him how proud she was of Kyle's reaction to Betty. "The next meeting I'll set up is for you and Kyle to meet one another. I've told him a little about the two of us but I'd rather tell him all about our relationship when the three of us are together."

"Honey, I think your idea is great. I can't wait to actually meet your son and hope the reception he gave Betty will be in the same vein."

When they put down the telephone receivers, Madaline had a peaceful and dreamless sleep. It was the best sleep that Madaline had since this terrible incident came to be. In the master bedroom Kyle went about his normal routine but his mind wouldn't shut down. All sorts of thoughts kept going through his head. After taking a long hot shower, he toweled himself off and thoughts of Curtis, once again, entered his mind. Like so many times before, he couldn't get rid of the mental activity that permeated in his head. He took two Lorazepams and washed them down with the sink water. He tried imagining how his step sister, Betty, had grown up these years knowing that there was a biological family waiting for her to appear. Hoping his negative thoughts would disappear he looked forward to dreaming about Betty and how their new life as step siblings would change their perspective on life.

BEPPO, JAPAN

When Rich left the police station he immediately took a cab to the hospital. He couldn't wait to see Nancy and find out the latest happening after her last of many, successful operations. When Nancy almost lost her life, he realized how much she'd meant to him. He vowed he'd never let her get away and wanted to be part of her existence forever. He even went to a jewelry store and purchased a promise ring for her to wear. Once the casts came off of her hands and arms he wanted to give the ring to her. When the time was right he knew the speech she would receive from him. With an enthusiastic gate in his step he walked into the hospital and went up the elevator to her floor where her room was located.

Lawrence understood that Suzanne was going through a tough time, both physically and mentally. He was conscious that patience was required of him when dealing with her. He would wait forever if he had to. He found out, through Justin, that Stephen was out of the picture, for now he thought. 'Sure', Suzanne will have many thoughts of my arch enemy in the war of love, but I know, in my heart that I will win her over with my devotion and love.'

Both Rich and Lawrence came up the same elevator and exchanged pleasantries. Lawrence remembered Rich from Hope's wedding and they discussed, what they hoped, would be a speedy recovery for both woman. When the girls saw who their visitors were, smiles appeared on their battered faces. Lawrence automatically went to Suzanne's side. He was afraid to touch any part of her body with all the contraptions and casts, adorning her.

All he could do was look at her lovingly and tell her how glad he was that she would heal and soon be back to her old self. "I hope you're right Larry, but I'm not so sure I want to keep this Suzy Sleuth part of my life. It's getting more dangerous than I ever anticipated."

"Knowing you, you'll soon forget this ordeal ever happened. Unfortunately too many people realize that now that this type of undercover work has gotten in your system, it's going to be hard to stop."

"Well, we'll see," Suzanne acknowledged Larry's wisdom. "I can't thank you enough for the flowers you've sent. I mean every day is a little much. Not that I don't appreciate them. But as you can see, the room is sort of small."

"If you don't mind, I sent some of the arrangements up to the children's ward. I also had some of the nurses buy stuffed toys to disperse among the young patients," Suzanne informed Lawrence. "That's so thoughtful of you. But, I'd expect that you'd do something like that. I wish I could hug you, but I'm afraid to touch any part of your body. You look soo uncomfortable."

"It's not as bad as it looks, believe me. Once these pain in the ass casts are finally off Nancy and I will feel a lot better. Come over here, you big sweetheart. Have I told you how much you're concern has helped me both mentally and physically. I won't go into anything complicated now but believe me when I tell you that I can't thank you enough for your involvement."

It meant a lot to Lawrence hearing those words coming from Suzanne. He knew how hard it must be to try to remove Stephen from her heart and soul. He didn't want these thoughts to enter his mind as he gently kissed some flesh on her face that wasn't covered with gauze. "Suzanne, believe me when I tell you I'd do anything in the world for you. I've been in love with you for years. Unfortunately, I realized it wasn't reciprocated, but hopefully that won't be for long."

"Larry, you know how I respect and adore you, yes, my feelings are changing, but for now, can we take it one day at a time?" Even with that said, Lawrence felt as if he were is seventh heaven. "Of course Suzanne, you've been through so much, I understand all the emotions that are going through that beautiful head of yours. Take as long as you want to get your feelings under control."

"Everything good comes with time and patience. Meanwhile, what can I do for you to make you more comfortable?" Not knowing if Nancy heard their conversation she yelled to her partner who looked like a star struck maiden, "Nancy, Larry wants to know if he can get us anything to get us to feel better." Nancy thought a bit and suppressing a laugh she asked for Brad Pitt but she'd understand if he couldn't deliver the goods. BUT, maybe if you can come back with a couple of ice cream Sundays we wouldn't turn them down."

"Hey, what's with Brad Pitt anyway. I thought you liked my look instead."

"Only kidding honey, you know I wouldn't trade you for anything or anyone else in this world." With that said Rich motioned for Larry to join him on the excursion to find a couple of ice cream Sundays. On the way out of the hospital Rich remarked, with all the other food chains in Japan I certainly hope that Ben and Jerry's is one of them. "They both smiled in unison as they walked along the crowded streets.

"Suzanne," Nancy spoke a little louder than usually to gain her attention, "How come you wanted me to get the men out of the room?" "To be honest with you, Lawrence's conversation was getting a little heavy and I didn't want to continue in the same vain. Do you mind?"

"Of course not, I hope he gets me pistachio or orange pineapple. They forgot to ask what flavors we'd like."

"I think Rich would know what your favorite flavor is by now. I know Lawrence does, and we've only been on a few dates before this fiasco occurred."

"We'll just have to wait and see," Nancy said as she changed channels. "I don't know why I bother with the TV. Most of the stations are in Japanese and I don't understand a word they're saying. "Suzanne agreed and closed her eyes hoping to get a few minutes reprieve from any other people who would be visiting them.

While out on the excursion for the ice cream Sundays Rich heard his cell phone ring. Reaching in his pocket he saw that Mr. T. was calling. "Hey, what's happening? Anything I should be aware of?"

"That's the reason I'm calling. The people from the FBI dedicated Art Crime Team are sending a couple of their 13 agents to the scene. They have a stolen arts file with a computerized printed index of reported stolen art and cultural properties. Some men from Interpol Stolen Works of Art will also be accompanying them. Between the two organizations and bringing with them the Art lost register, we might be able to return most of the articles to the rightful museums and also to the personal individuals that have had their art stolen through the years."

"It might be a bit difficult. I read that only 5 % of all stolen art is recovered, but it seems we're on the right track. After they come and examine the pieces I'll have a better understanding and can report their findings to you. From what I understand from their conversations on the phone, most cultural objects are from 2 countries. Mostly from France and Italy. "Rich then stated, "I believe what you're telling me, but it seems that a lot of museums from all over the world have been affected as well. Look at America alone. From the Isabella Stewart Gardner Museum, The Huntington Museum and God only knows how many more that we don't know about. I guess that a lot of private art has been stolen from homes throughout the States as well. Also from private castles in England, France, Belgium, Montreal and Spain with many more Spanish, Dutch and Flemish art among the list. I guess we were lucky to have come across these works of art. At least some of the missing paintings and objects can now go back to their rightful owners and places where they belong." Mr. T. responded, "That reminds me of all the work that the Nazi's stole and to this day we still haven't been able to recover most of the pieces."

"When put that way Rich, you're right. From all the awful atrocities we found and your friend's horrendous beatings, we were lucky that everything is working out well. When the men come in I'll be sure to call you so you can meet them."

"That will be fine with me. I'd love to speak to them and learn more about this wide world of art theft. These guys must be some characters. The thieves who do this type of burglary for a living are crazy people. I guess from all I've read that there's no single profile that fits the individual. They can be men who do it for their own impulsive wants and desires to small-time crooks to sophisticated thieves who methodically plot their crimes and wait for years to unload the goods."

"Yes, my friend,"Mr. T. continued, "it seems there's no single profile that fits. We're lucky that, like the characters they chase, art theft investigators come in a variety of sizes and colors. They all have different strengths, background and experiences. We're lucky that we have men such as these." Rich went on to say, "I read that upward of eight billion dollars in losses are incurred and is a growing problem. Some of the cases can drag on for years." Mr. T said, "With that said, I'll call you when the men arrive. Till then, take care of your lady and hope all goes well."

"Thank you my friend. Thanks for calling and I'll be waiting for your next call."

"That was a long conversation," Lawrence remarked to Rich. "I couldn't help but hear your part of the dialogue. You don't have to tell me anything I shouldn't be privy to, but I'm glad that it seems you've got more than you bargained for." Rich retorted, "You might say that. Come. Let's find that fucking ice cream before we get hit over our heads with their casts." They both laughed as their search continued.

"What on earth is taking Rich and Lawrence so long to get a simple ice cream Sunday?" remarked Nancy. "Now don't become a CAP on me now."

"What do you mean by that?"

"Well, you've heard about Jewish American Princess's, well, there are just as many Christian American Princess's as well. Believe me, I've worked on many." Suzanne chided her best friend." I realize you came from money honey, but you usually aren't that demanding. What gives?"

"Oh Suzanne, I'm so torn. I guess I'm taking my frustration out on everyone. I'm sorry."

"Tell, Mama Suzanne what's bothering you, maybe I can help?" With a deep sigh Nancy tried shaking her head. "I don't know if anyone can figure out what's bothering me. Maybe I have to go back to my shrink. On one hand I think, no, I know I love Rich. On the other hand I don't know or I'm unsure of his feelings for me. Does that make sense Suzanne?"

"I can see where you're coming from honey. All I can tell you is to relax and take one day at a time. From my observation I think Rich is crazy for you. I can see it by the way he looks at you. You have to have more confidence in yourself."

"Go with the flow, I'm sure he'll make his intentions known to you very shortly. Just think how good those ice cream Sundays will taste."

"Yea, if they get them and they're not melted by the time we get to eat those delicious Sunday's."

"Now there you go again with your negativity. See the glass half full, or in this case, ice cream that's hard, creamy and delicious." With that said, Nancy tried smiling as she waited patiently for the men to return.

"It's about time," the two women stated as Rich and Lawrence entered the room." No complaining ladies. If you knew what we had to go through to find an ice cream store, you'd be forever grateful," exclaimed Rich. "Never mind that, I have such a stitch on my side from running all the way back here to make sure that the ice cream didn't melt," Lawrence interjected. Both women tried to squelch their insensitive amusement as the two men spooned the ice creams in their mouth. Both Suzanne and Nancy had all they could do not to choke or spurt out the delicious parfait as they stifled their laughter. Both the gentlemen glared at their women as they spoon fed the dessert. Larry and Rich used restraint not to shove the ice cream in another orifice if it was more available for them to reach.

When it came time for the nurses to bring in their dinners the two women looked at them and couldn't touch a morsel. "Why don't you guys have the dinners? It's a shame to have them go to waste," expressed Nancy. "As much as we love you and would want to help you any way we can, I think that Rich and I will go to a restaurant and indulge ourselves in some local gourmet delight. That's if you don't mind," teased Lawrence. Both women insisted they leave and to enjoy their meal. "After all, we enjoyed the delicious Sundays you labored to bring us," Suzanne conceded as she closed her eyes and tried falling asleep. When they heard the door close both women couldn't help but smile as they tried to let slumber take over.

The next morning Mrs. Walsh and Dorothy made their appearance. "My, my," exclaimed Dorothy, "the two of you look like you're recovering nicely. Has the doctor come in this morning with any more information on when you might depart this hospital?"

"As a matter of fact he made his rounds early and at 7:15 he examined us and told us in about 2 days we could head home," a jubilant Suzanne remarked.

"Do you think you can call the pilot and tell him of the plans?" asked Nancy. "Of course my dear," exclaimed Mrs. Walsh. "We expect that the two of you will accompany us home, right?"

"Now Suzanne, when have Mrs. Walsh and I ever disappointed you? Of course, that's what we expected."

"One more thing mom, can you please call home, tell the girls of our plans and line up therapists and appointments for us. We'll have to see the orthopedic and other specialists before that can occur, I'd think."

"Yes Suzanne that was our intention without you having to tell us. By the way, we'd want Nancy to come home with you so we can keep an eye out for the two of you."

"Does that meet with your approval, Nancy?" interjected Mrs. Walsh. After giving Nancy the eye, Nancy had no other recourse but to relent to their wishes. After they left, Nancy and Suzanne looked at each other and at the same time said, "Do you think we can stand being with each other for another month or so?," the two friends asked each other as they made their mental lists of what had to be done. "As much as I'd love to accompany you home on our return, I think Rich has another idea. He's going to hire a nurse for me and he's taking the time off to be with me. Isn't that thoughtful Suzanne?"

"You know I think he has the right idea. As much as we love each other we've been with each other so long it seems as if we're Siamese Twins. Seriously Nancy, I think that's the best idea Rich has come up with in a long time."

RETURNING TO BOSTON

When the plane landed, Suzanne was grateful that no one was there to greet them. Although they were getting better, the plane ride took a lot of physical and mental strength out of them. They both got into ambulances for their return to Stoney Brook and Ipswich. "I told my mother that it wasn't necessary to have this type of transportation back home. Do you think she'd listen to me? No, she does as she pleases."

"Well Suzanne, the apple doesn't fall far from the tree," retorted Nancy, as she was hoisted into the waiting vehicle.

The drivers opened the door to Suzanne's house and the two women were greeted by Suzanne's daughters and most of the staff from the spas. 'Oh great,' thought Suzanne, and who the hell is minding the spas' if everyone and their brother is here for this party, which I really don't want.' Everyone started talking at once and suddenly Hope stepped up to the front of the group. "Welcome home. You have no idea how worried everyone was and we all missed you. Speaking for everyone we're glad you're back and know that you'll be back to work in no time at all. We won't stay because we realize that you're tired but we wanted you to know how happy we are that you're on the mend."

"Needless to say," Taylor remarked, "we know you'll be back to your old selves when you start barking orders to us, right girls?" Everyone agreed in unison. When left alone Suzanne and Nancy hugged each other as best they could and Suzanne had a tear or two when she saw her friend and Rich heading back home to Ipswich.

It seemed like forever when the different specialists gave Suzanne and Nancy the go ahead to start physical therapy. Suzanne felt tons lighter when all the casts were finally removed as did Nancy. Rich was glad that he was the person taking Nancy back home and be there for her. He didn't know how long he would be able to take off for a leave of absence but knew that all these details could be worked out. He also thought that he'd have to make a decision on whether to stay in San Diego or move to the Boston area.

Nancy was thrilled that Rich would be going home with her. She also had a feeling that there was more to Richs' plans than he let on.

When Suzanne finally snuggled under her warm, white, blanket she felt protected from all the bad elements. Simka and Boston were sound asleep within minutes. Their purring was a comfort to Suzanne as she tried to sleep. She found the physical therapy to be exhausting at times and knew that was the reason she required the sleep she wanted and needed. She remembered her grandmother Pessa telling her that sleep was the best medicine. Suzanne realized that there was something to the old way of thinking.

As much as Suzanne craved a night of tranquility she found herself unable to do so. The same dream kept reoccurring. She would be in the house in Beppo and the grotesque episodes she heard and had happen to her and Nancy would constantly replay in her mind. She saw herself trying to protect the two of them and saw herself run away from those maniacs. Other times she would see Stephen's face before her and she could feel herself thrashing from side to side. Why couldn't she get him out of her system? Suzanne kept asking herself when she woke up in a cold sweat.

When Rich and Nancy finally stepped foot in her small castle after one of her physical therapy sessions Nancy sighed heavily." My, my, that was quite a breath. I'm sure you're glad to finally be home." Leaning against Rich, Nancy turned and put both arms around him. She looked into his gorgeous eyes and gave him a passionate kiss. "I don't know if I properly thanked you for everything you did for us. I don't know if I can ever repay you, but I owe you one."

"Nancy, I did what I did because I love you, and besides, it's part of my job." He laughed as he said the last part of the sentence. "Seriously Nancy, isn't it apparent how I feel about you? As a matter of fact I've asked my captain if there's a way that I can transfer from my headquarters in San Diego to Boston. It may take a while for an opening to occur but Cap told me he'd do everything in his power to expedite matters."

Nancy was pleased with that information and a large smile appeared on her beautiful face." Come upstairs and I want to properly thank you in a way that I think you'll like." As they ascended the stairway, Rich asked, "Nancy, do you feel up to it?" "My Rich, what a filthy mind you have. What on earth are you thinking of?" Nancy shook her head as she headed up the steps. Rich could only shake his head and realized that was Nancy. He couldn't thank the stars for bringing this dynamo of sunshine and loveliness into his life. Lying next to each other, spent and happy, lying under the warm covers, Rich and Nancy looked into each other's eyes. "Have I told you how happy I am since I've met you?" Rich asked a sleepy Nancy.

Nancy snuggled closer and emanated the same. Nancy felt elated as she hadn't felt in years. Only a small concern came to mind but she tried ignoring it. She couldn't get it off of her mind and try as she might, the thought kept to cogitate, not allowing her to fully relax. "You look awfully serious my love. What's bothering you?" Rich asked. "It's really nothing."

"Come on, spill it out. I think I know you well enough to realize that something is bothering you."

After being quiet for a while, snuggling deeper into Rich's chest she suddenly looked at him. "It's really nothing that concerns you, honey. I was thinking that I've been alone for a few years now, as you've been, and wondering how we will be able to acclimate to each other."

"Are you kidding? I've been wanting a woman like you for years. Sure, we'll be taking a chance but I feel we'll be considerate of each other and think of the other person first, we'll conquer all that comes our way. All couples need is trust, respect, like the same things and want to satisfy their mate and especially have love and devotion for each other. I know you will always come first in my life and I'll always consider you my best friend. What else is there than those things to make a couple happy and content?" Rich asked of Nancy. Nancy contemplated what he said and a smile appeared on her face.

"You know Rich, those are the same ideals that I have. I know this next question might be premature but how do you feel about children? Not to bring negativity to the subject but as I once told you, Peter completely changed his mind on the idea of the two of us having a family. This time I don't want any surprises." Rich grinned. "Nancy honey, don't forget I come from a large Italian family. My siblings and I have a great relationship and I don't know how we could have grown up without each other's support."

"Of course I want us to have children. What would life be without them?" With that said, Nancy was finally relieved. "Honey, I was so worried. Now I can relax and everything I ever dreamed of will come true." With a hint of mischief in her eyes she started caressing and arousing Rich once again. "With the way your reaction was to my answer it looks like we'll be having lots of kids filling up this house. Lucky it's large enough that we won't have any problems with lack of space." Nancy said, "Let's practice a bit, you know practice makes perfect."

Rich quickly got off of the bed and hurried to the closet. "I forgot something." He retrieved the promise ring and with great ceremony put it on her finger. "I've had this for a while and I want you to know that pretty soon we'll take a trip to the Jeweler's building in Boston for an official engagement ring."

"I hate to disappoint you honey, but before you get nervous, my answer is yes, yes, yes, with a big but. We don't have to go to Boston. Lawrence owns diamond mines throughout Africa and other countries as well. I'm sure he'll make sure we get a gorgeous diamond for you to place on my finger. Now before you jumped out of bed, I think we both had something on our minds."

"Nancy, you are a vixen!!!"

Suzanne came home from physical therapy truly exhausted. All she wanted to do was go into the great room and lie down on the comfortable sofa. She knew she should call her office and check up on how the various salons were doing. She kept putting off the inevitable but realized she had to bite the bullet and get it done. She asked Mrs. Walsh if she could make her a cup of steaming hot Vanilla Almond tea and relax her muscles from the strenuous session she just came back from.

While enjoying her tea and biscuits Suzanne was ready to finally make her required call. She was about to pick up the receiver when the phone's ringing interrupted her train of thought. "Hi," Larry announced. "Thought I'd give you a ring and see if you were up for some company?" With baited breath he waited and hoped for the answer he was looking for. "I'm always up to seeing you, you know that. What brings you back to the States?"

"You of course. No I had some business that I had to attend to and stayed a little longer hoping to see you."

"Well, I'm not in shape to go dancing as yet, but do come over. I'd love to see you. It seems the only place I go to is my therapy sessions."

"I'll be over shortly. Can I bring you something? "Thank's, but no. Just bring yourself. See you soon."

Mrs. Walsh looked at Suzanne and without speaking looked at her as if asking, and who was that? Addressing Mrs. Walsh Suzanne answered, "Don't look at me that way. Larry happens to be in town and wants to come over and see me. Does that meet with your approval?"

"My, aren't we grouchy, get up on the wrong side of the bed this morning?"

"No, I didn't. Why do you think I'm grouchy? You know I'm not a cantankerous person. I just don't want Larry to think there's more to our relationship than he wants to read into it."

"I do like him. As a matter of fact, I could really like him, if you get the gist. But I know it'll take me some time to get over Stephen. You know, Catherine, I thought that Stephen and I could never be apart from one another. I thought we'd always be a couple. Sure it upsets me when I think of all that we were to one another. That will never change. What's upsetting me is that we never had closure of our relationship. But I'm amazed that, in a way, I'm not sad as I thought I'd be. I guess for months I was so busy trying to get physically better that I put that aspect of my life in the back of my mind. Sure, maybe I have dreams of him and sometimes I find myself wondering what he's doing at that moment. For the most part, I don't feel the pressure of our relationship and I'm proud that I'm doing as well as I am." Mrs. Walsh came over to where Suzanne was seated and hugged her. "I knew it wouldn't take that long to get over him. You know, even though he was your first boyfriend, your parents and I didn't like him. There was something about him that bugged me. Maybe I saw you unhappy and crying over the situation but Dorothy confided to me that even as a youngster, there was something about him that your parents didn't like. Although, let's not kid ourselves, Brian was 100 times worse than Stephen could have been."

Suzanne looked amused at Mrs. Walsh's assessment of the situation and couldn't help but shake her head. Within minutes the doorbell rang and Mrs. Walsh hurried over to the door and opened it. With a large smile she ushered him into the house. Larry had brought another beautiful arrangement of flowers and a box of English teas and a large box of Belgium chocolates. "I thought you got used to all my flowers that I sent you so I didn't want you to miss them and me too much. On one of my trips to Belgium and Brussels I couldn't resist buying these chocolates for you. My mother sent the teas over with me. She knows how you enjoy your cup of tea."

"That's so thoughtful of both of you. Thanks. You can put the arrangement on the round end table by the sofa. Mrs. Walsh, would you put the teas in the cupboard with the others, thanks." When Mrs. Walsh departed Larry bent over Suzanne and gave her a light kiss on the lips. Suzanne was a bit surprised but said nothing. She patted the seat next to her and wanted him to sit beside her. Larry talked about his businesses and the world's situation, that seemed would never improve. Then his conversation took on a more personal note.

"I hope you re-cooperate soon. I can't wait to take you out for a date. Maybe dinner and dancing. Would you like that?" He wanted to call her sweetheart, but decided he didn't want to push her too fast. Taken aback by his determination, she told him that sounded like a lovely idea but didn't know if she was up to dancing yet. They talked awhile and Mrs. Walsh insisted he stay for dinner. After dessert, when Mrs. Walsh was clearing the table, he kissed Suzanne, a little more passionately than the first time. It took a lot of self-restraint not to stay when it seemed to be getting late, he didn't want to wear out his welcome. Lawrence thanked Mrs. Walsh for a delicious meal and after lingering a bit he left.

"Well, well, I'm keeping my mouth shut, but did I see what I think I saw?" Mrs. Walsh asked Suzanne, as she ducked when Suzanne threw a small pillow towards her. Later that evening, while the two cats were frolicking and then settled down next to Suzanne, she couldn't help but think of Larry. She tried putting Stephen out of her mind and concentrated on Larry. Mentally she made a list of the positive and negative aspects about him that she liked or disliked. After pondering for a while she got up and got writing paper to write everything down that was on her mind.

When she was finished Suzanne got back into bed and felt better that she actually put all her concerns and things she liked about Larry down on paper. With only good thoughts on her mind she fell into a deep sleep. Suzanne descended the stairs early in the morning and for once Mrs. Walsh remarked, "you look very well rested. I take it no nightmares to wake you up in the middle of the night? "Suzanne smiled and put the kettle on for a cup of tea. Sitting down at the kitchen table she again looked over the list. To herself she thought, 'time will tell. One can never know what's going to happen in life.' She started reading the paper and couldn't concentrate on the news of the day. Thoughts of Larry kept interrupting her train of thought. With a smile and a devilish look on her face she took out her cell phone and before calling Nancy up for their regular morning chat she automatically dialed Larry's cell. 'What will be, will be,' she thought as he answered on the third ring

Rich got a telephone call from Sam explaining that the international company was being taken over by Mr. Makino's son. He explained that he would keep him abreast of what was occurring within the company, but was sure that it was in capable and good hands. Immediately after, he received another call from Mr. T. Mr. Tamamuro explained what was happening in regards to the stolen pieces of art. He then told Rich that rumor had it that the Yakuza was now being taken over by Nobuaki's widow.

It seems that she was well respected in the underworld community. To avoid any internal wars amongst other Yakuza groups it was better that she take over the helm. The FBI wasn't sure about her but had people infiltrated in the organization that would keep them abreast of the happenings going on in the underworld of the Japanese mafia. Mr. T told Rich that after the death of the head of the Yakuza it would be up to the widow to find a suitable replacement as the head of the organization after she found the right person who would be capable to become the new leader without any resentment from the organization or other leaders of other Yakuza groups.

Rich closed the cell phone and walked to where Nancy was preparing dinner for the two of them. He crept in back of her and slipped his arms around her waist. He could feel her relax immediately. He nuzzled her neck and the two of them looked out the window as the bright lights in back of their house illuminated the water. He told her that after dinner that they should go upstairs and he'd tell her of the outcome of everything that he knew was happening after they got all the pictures, or most of them, back to their rightful owners." And then, we'll see what develops," he said, as he turned her around and kissed her passionately." "You know what?" Nancy spontaneously interjected. I think dinner can wait awhile." Taking his hand she led him to the stairs and shut off the lights downstairs. On the way upstairs Rich mentioned Mr. Yasuhito. It had been awhile that he had mentioned his new and faithful companion. "Nancy, I've been thinking, this house is awfully large, do you think we could use a person like a butler or housekeeper of some kind?" Nancy smiled, knowing and waiting for Rich to bring up the subject of Mr. Yasuhito. "Rich, you know what people say, that when two people think alike, there must be something that the God's are trying to tell them. Ya, this house does seem awfully big for just the two of us."

EPILOGUE - CHAPTER FORTY SIX

After a few months of grueling therapy Suzanne and Nancy felt well enough to resume going back to work. They knew enough to take it slowly and start off by going in a few hours at a time. The Plastic Surgeries were very successful and no one could tell that anything happened to the two beautiful women before them.

Rich was kept abreast of the progress of Mr. Yasuhito, Mr. Makino's limo driver from Mr. T. Whenever he thought of the savage beating that was rendered to this kindly old gentleman all Rich could do was shake his head in wonder. He often thought of this nice and loyal man and wanted in some way to see how he was doing after he was on his way to recovery. He didn't know if Mrs. Makino was even aware of Mr. Yasuhito. Thinking about how Mr. Makino was so very secretive he doubted if she knew that he existed. He often looked out of Nancy's large, expansive picture window in her kitchen, looking at the water as the waves went onto the shore and trickled into small, uneven lines on the water's edge. Rich had to find out if there was any compensation that was given to this kindly gentleman who was so faithful to his employer.

Once he knew that Mr. Yasuhito was all right, only then could Rich relax and finally let this uneasiness about the kindly gentleman, be put to rest. He went to the telephone and got Mr. T. on the phone. He explained what was bothering him and asked his friend, in a discerning way to find out about Mr. Yasuhito and get back to him as soon as he could. Rich and Nancy discussed what they'd like see come about once they knew what was happening with Mr. Yasuhito. The only thing stopping the two lovebirds was getting in touch with the kindly old gentleman and finding out his feelings about relocating to the Boston area. "Let's hope the old guy will like Ipswich," Rich and Nancy spoke out loud at the same time.

Beyond Murder had another week until the play ended its Boston run. From there they would go to Chicago and other cities until it hit Broadway in New York City. After one of her last performances Madaline sat in her dressing room on the sofa that she rested on these many months of performing the play. She decided to lie down on the comfy couch one more time and let her mind wonder. So many things and events had happened since she came to Boston that left her speechless at times. She found herself thinking of all that had happened in these past months.

'Who would have thought that I'd find my child, a daughter that I always prayed for, after giving up this helpless newborn so many years ago? It's a wonderful feeling knowing that Kyle and Betty hit it off so well. They'll always be in touch with one another, I know it. Paul, what can I say or think about him? He makes me happy. I know that we'll always be together and in time we'll see what happens. You never know, I might be another Elizabeth or Za Za. I'll have so many husbands on my list I'll probably forget the number of them as I age,' she laughed to herself. 'One of these days I'll have to call Ann, really when you think about it, she's the first person who I met when I landed in this crazy world of show business. She'll be surprised when I finally tell her what happened. Won't she be astonished when at last she'll hear my secret that I've kept hidden from her all these years?'

When Hope and Spencer got back from their honeymoon, like two normal, young newlyweds, they enjoyed buying furniture for their new house and couldn't wait to fill it up with children of their own. Of course, Spencer joined his father's firm and Hope still went to the many Metamorphosis' Spas hoping, one day to take over her mother's position. She realized that her mother was still young and thought of all the many crazy and wild things that have happened to her family in the past. She often asked herself how her mother and Nancy became involved in their secretive detective projects. She could only shake her head in bewilderment.

Melanie and Taylor were still young ladies that had agendas of their own. They enjoyed life and although one wasn't supposed to wish life away, couldn't wait to find out what would happen to them in years to come. They often felt fortunate to have a mother like Suzanne and blessed that besides their own family that they had other people in their lives that were extensions of their personal family.

Unfortunately, the police and other agencies never found Robin's family. Rich took it upon himself to have her buried in a beautiful cemetery near his own family's graves. Whenever he visited the memorial park he would take Nancy and they would put a beautiful bouquet of flowers in front of her headstone.

Mrs. Makino was a widow who many people admired and respected. She didn't feel alone because she realized that although she had been married to Yoshy for many years she really didn't know him at all. She spent her time between her own home and that of her son's and his new family. It was her pleasure to be with her new daughter-in-law, who she felt was like her own daughter. She enjoyed the pleasure of spoiling her grandchild who her son named after his beloved father. In Mrs. Makino's mind, heart and soul, she hoped that her grandchild would never grow up as its namesake. Mr. Makino's secretary told Kazuhiko about Sam's wonderful work and how he managed the company in his father's absence. As a reward for being such a loyal and good worker, Kazuhiko made Sam a vice president of the company with many responsibilities that Sam was glad to take on.

Suzanne's parents, Morris and Dorothy Pollack, went back to Florida after spending the summer with Suzanne and Mrs. Walsh. In Dorothy's heart she knew that something was wrong with Morris but kept her feelings to herself. There would be plenty of time to voice her concerns to her daughter.

Justin Ferris made Alan a partner in his art gallery and they went from the United States to Europe many times acquiring pieces of art and finding places to open their new art galleries.

Lawrence Van Der Hyde was kept busy with his many businesses' and trying to bring up his three growing children. Although he had help in his homes and the children went to private schools, he made sure that he was around when vacation times came for him to interact with his growing brood. He would often pay unexpected visits to each child at their boarding schools to spend time and special moments with them at their individual schools. He was grateful that

Suzanne made him realize that time went by quickly and to enjoy them and as Suzanne would say, kvel, in his offspring. As far as Suzanne was concerned he knew that he couldn't push her too far and had to take his time. She had to heal both mentally and physically. He would give her the time she needed to realize that he was the man for her.

Nancy was getting better a day at a time and loved the idea of having Rich in her life. When she felt healed she started participating in the running of the spa's and it gave her a purpose to feel good about herself. Of course the day would come that she and Rich would name the wedding date and that would be fun, with Suzanne's help, to plan this blessed event. She didn't know what her best friend, Suzanne, would have up her sleeve once she felt better. Nancy would shake her head in bewilderment just thinking of what Suzanne would find themselves involved in. Sometimes her heart would beat rapidly whenever she thought about the future and what it had in store for her. 'Only time will tell,' she reflected as she called down to Rich to remind him that it was time to go to her next physical therapy appointment.

The happy owners of most of the paintings, artifacts, ceramics, manuscripts and hand carved silver, jewelry and other famous objects that were found, relished in acquiring them back to enjoy. The museums were proud to, once again, put these precious paintings and articles back in their rightful places for all the patrons to see and take pleasure in admiring them.

Mrs. Walsh was busy helping Suzanne and trying to keep up with her surrogate daughters plans and new procedures that only Suzanne had up her sleeve. She realized that dealing with Suzanne and her many adventures took the meaning of diplomacy to a new level. She knew that she wasn't getting any younger and many times would find herself sitting down or take some pills to get the aches and pains out of her tired body.

The Yakuza continued as it always did. The dealings never changed. Mrs. Nobuaki mourned for her beloved husband but knew it was her duty to head up the organization until she found a person who she thought was worthy of becoming the leader of this prestigious organization. Mrs. Nobuaki kept Mitsuko on as her personal servant. Unfortunately Mrs. Nobuaki had not been able to have any children and as a result thought of Mitsuko as her child. Mitsuko heard the horrible news about her boss and his right hand man, Hirohito, and she was heartbroken. She continued working for Mrs. Nobuaki and felt she was like the mother that she didn't remember.

Carol Williams continued with her illustrious career as a super model, adorning the front covers of all the popular magazines. She couldn't keep up the pretense of being married to Kyle and they eventually got a divorce. It took her a long time to learn to trust any man again but in do time started dating and ultimately found the man of her dreams.

Peter finished his jail term and was released from prison. He didn't know what he wanted to do in life. In time, after wandering from State to State, Peter wound up in the State of Colorado. He was always athletic and now wanted to go on with his life. In time he found himself on the slopes and enjoyed his leisure time skiing with many people who he befriended. In due course he finally started doing hair once again and finally became the proud owner of a prestigious salon that all the "in" people went to. He became the hairdresser to the stars when they vacationed in this lovely resort town of Bolder.

One evening Rich and Nancy were sitting down enjoying the nightly news when Rich turned off the television. Turning to Nancy he held her hand and asked her to marry him. Without hesitation they both knew what the answer would be. After a while Rich brought up the subject of Mr. Yasuhito. He asked Nancy that when he officially transferred to the Boston division of the police, would she consider hiring Mr. Yasuhito." As we discussed before, we can use him as our butler or anything you deem necessary to give him some purpose for living. Do you think he'll come?"

"Hmm." She rolled her eyes for a moment, then with a smile on her face agreed with Rich that they probably could use someone of Mr. Yasuhito's experience around the house." I wonder how he is at putting on an infant's diaper?" They both laughed knowing that he would be a good person for them to enjoy and have him take care of the house and anything else that would come their way.

Suzanne was leisurely sitting on her couch, sipping a glass of Zinfandel listening to her favorite songs of the oldies. She was remembering all the times in her life, the good and the bad. With tears streaming down her face she poured herself another glass full of wine. She tried putting her mind at peace and putting events of the past in their perspective place in her mind. She could never change her feelings and only wanted the aching in her heart to dissipate. Wiping the tears from her face she slowly got up from the sofa. It still took her a little bit of time to get up but she was progressing very well from all the broken bones in her body that were rapidly mending. Steadying herself, she walked to the bottom of the stairs. Mrs. Walsh had retired to bed earlier. Suzanne was happy to be alone. As she ascended the stairs she berated herself for over indulging. 'Get yourself together, girl, you have a lot to live for and stop thinking of the past. You have a lot of time to enjoy your life and like the song goes, "If You Can't Be With The One You Love, Love The One You're With." '

CPSIA information can be obtained
at www.ICGtesting.com
Printed in the USA
BVHW04s1951080918
526932BV00020B/259/P